Treasure

Other books by the author

Blood Is Thicker Than Water
Love & Benjamins
Brethren: Raised By Wolves, Volume One
Matelots: Raised By Wolves, Volume Two

Treasure
Raised By Wolves
Volume Three

W.A. Hoffman

Aurora, Colorado

This book is a work of fiction written for the purposes of entertainment. Though some personages mentioned herein were actual people, their personification in this story is purely of the author's fabrication and not meant to reflect in any way upon the original individuals. Readers interested in separating relative truth from fiction in regard to the historical people, events, or social structures portrayed in this novel are invited to read the resource material listed in the bibliography and make their own determinations.

Treasure: Raised By Wolves, Volume Three
First Trade Edition - Published 2008
Printed in the United States and United Kingdom by Lightning Source

Published by:
Alien Perspective
4255 S. Buckley Rd., #127
Aurora, CO, 80013
www.alienperspective.com
info@alienperspective.com
1-866-GOALIEN

Text Copyright 2008 © W.A. Hoffman
Cover & Interior Design W.A. Hoffman

All rights reserved. No part of this book may be reproduced or transmitted in any form or by any means, electronic or mechanical, without the express permission of the copyright holder, except for brief excerpts used solely for the purposes of publicity or review.

ISBN10 - 0-9721098-4-6
ISBN13 - 978-0-9721098-4-0
Library of Congress Control Number: 2008903475

Dedication

This book and its brothers have been labors of love and faith, made possible by the following people. I dearly wish to thank:

My husband, John, for being my matelot through thick and thin, artistic despair and ecstasy, and for richer or poorer. Thank you for loving me. I could not do it without you.

Barb, my editor and bestest writing buddy ever, for her unflagging optimism and encouragement, loving critiques, and eagle eye. Thank you for helping me look good.

Wren, my favorite fangirl and friend, for assisting with my work at every step, from reading rough drafts to copyediting and beyond.

My mother, for teaching me how to dream and always reach for what I want. My brother, for being my biggest fan. My sister, for her love and support. My father, for teaching me to think and judge for myself. I am very grateful I was not raised by, or with, wolves or sheep.

And all the people who have read my work, either this piece or others, and offered their support and encouragement. Thank you all.

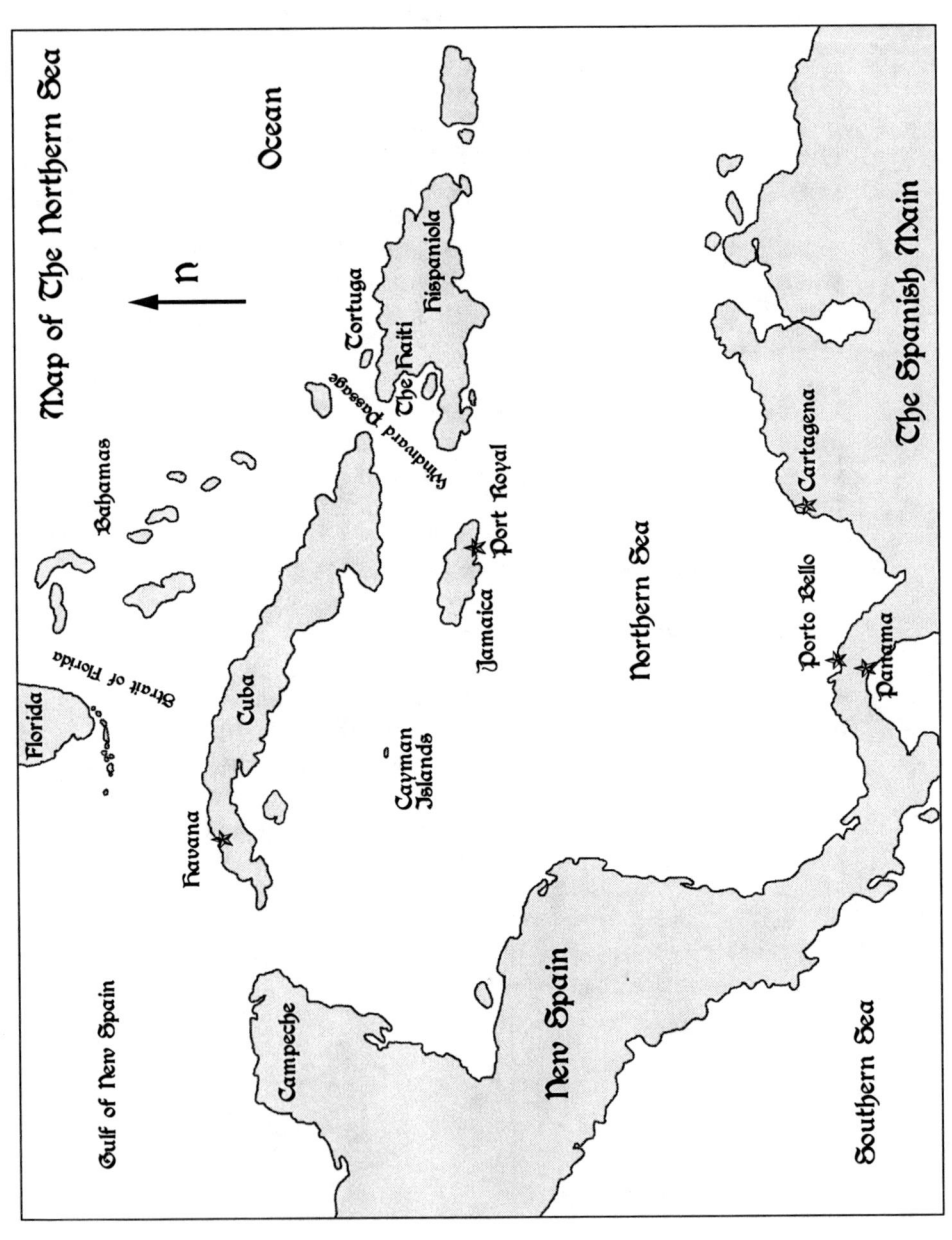

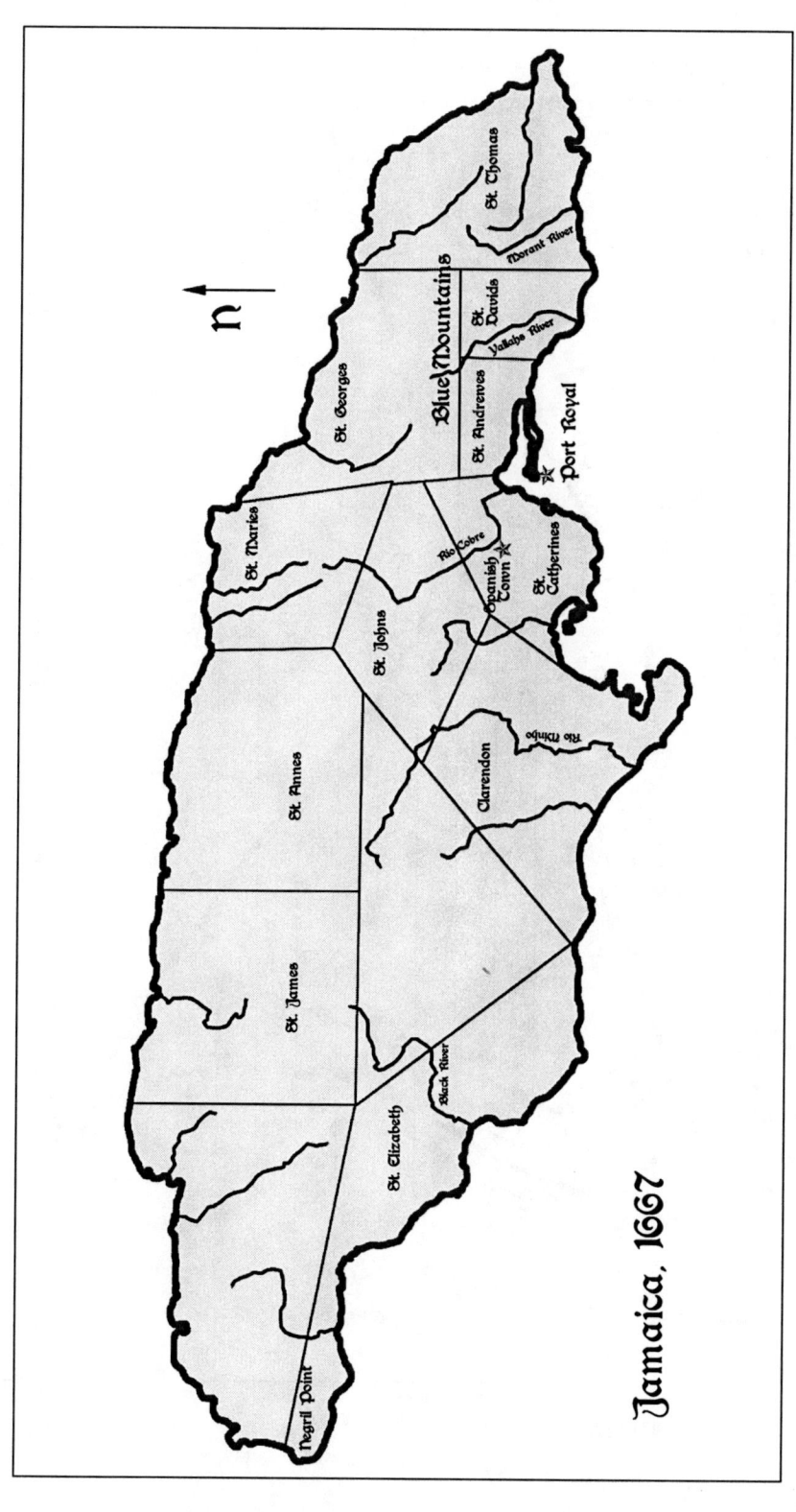

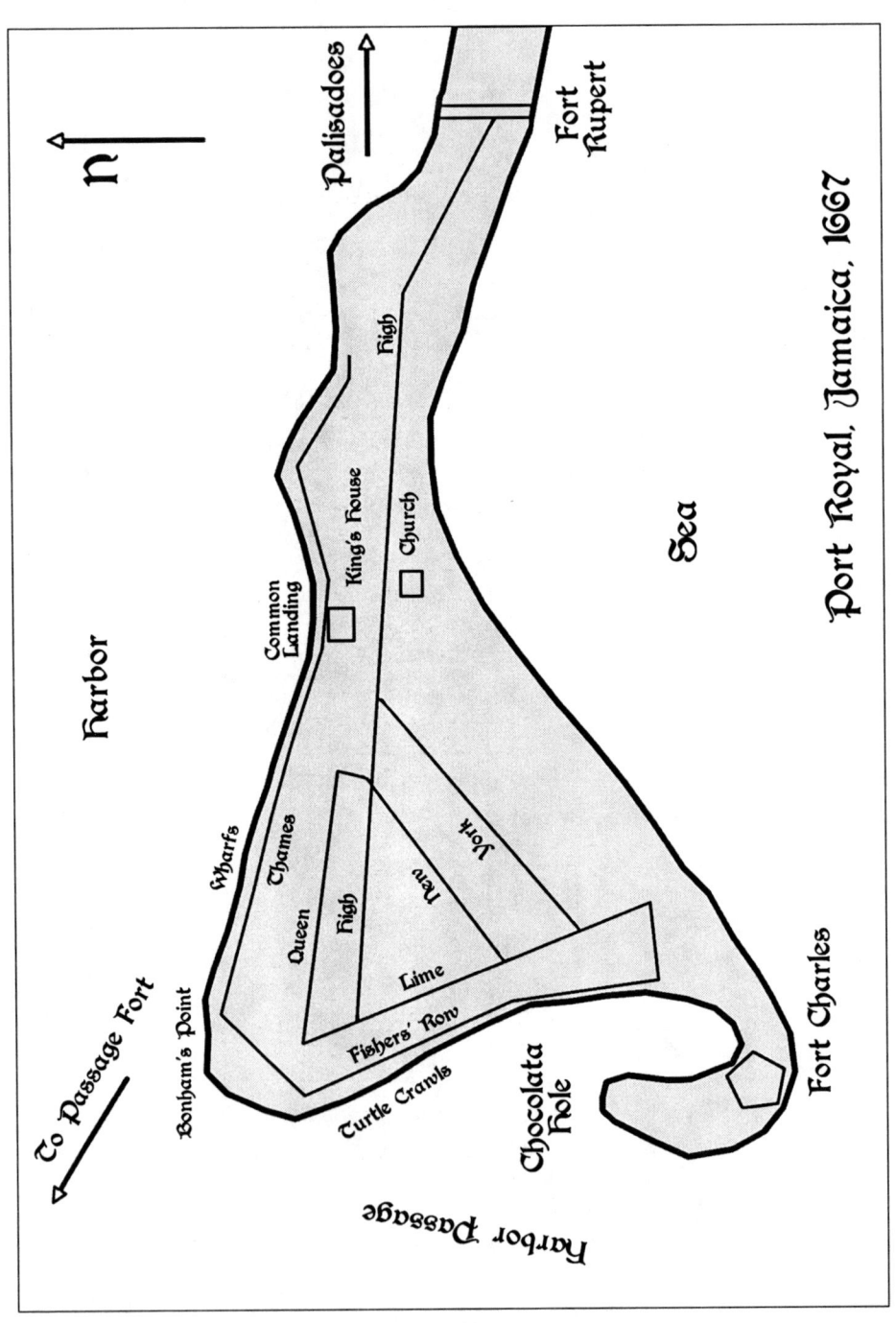

Table of Contents

I: Negril Point - November, 1668
Wherein a Wolf Comes Calling - 13
Wherein We Are Distracted - 29

II: Port Royal - November - December, 1668
Wherein We Return to Homes We Have Not Known - 51
Wherein We Face a Trail of Brambles - 69
Wherein We Float, Steeped in Irony - 89
Wherein We Contemplate Sacred Trusts - 107
Wherein We Run Wild On the Chessboard - 125
Wherein We Revisit Meals Left Uneaten - 141
Wherein Unwanted Things Are Born - 159
Wherein We Claim Jamaica - 179
Wherein We Provide Succor and Solace to Girls - 195
Wherein We Are Nearly Outmaneuvered - 213
Wherein We Are Considered Mad - 229
Wherein Motivations Are Exposed - 247
Wherein We Surrender the Field - 267
Wherein We Learn of Women - 283
Wherein We Choose To Play - 303
Wherein We Seek Peace - 329
Wherein We Are Reunited With Hope - 347
Wherein We Run Toward Ruin - 367
Wherein We Face Judgment - 389
Wherein We Stand In The Face of Madness - 405
Wherein We Say Farewell - 421

III: Roving - January - May, 1669
Wherein We Regard Ambition - 437
Wherein We Are Challenged - 455
Wherein We Suffer a Loss - 471
Wherein We Face Dreams and Fears - 487
Wherein We Confront Old Enemies - 505
Wherein We Are Ensnared - 525
Wherein We Must Escape - 541
Epilogue - 561

Negril Point

November 1668

I

Fifty-Three

Wherein a Wolf Comes Calling

    A muffled retort split the hazy afternoon air, carving a little notch in my hearing somewhere amongst the occasional pop of the fire, the distant crash of the waves upon the rocks below, the pecking of chickens, the cud-chewing of goats, and the omnipresent buzz of insects. I stilled my hand and cocked my head to listen, glancing at Bella to see if I heard phantoms or if it had been a thing a dog could corroborate. Her great brindle head was raised and her eyes peered north toward the beach. She did not seem alarmed, but as she was gravid with pups she longed to whelp, I felt it would take much to rouse her from the shade where she lounged and I worked.
    I was not alarmed, either: merely curious. We had very few neighbors this autumn: many of our cabal were off smuggling to the Spanish, and the rest had stayed in Port Royal. Of the men with whom we did share Negril Point, most were far inland, hunting, as there was little game to be had on the promontory itself. So it was likely – if it were truly a thing that had occurred – that the retort had issued from the beach below. It had become customary for our vessels to alert the denizens of the Point of their arrival, so we could join them on the beach and help them carry up anything they might have brought.
    "So you heard it too, Bella my girl," I said lightly, as I wiped the excess paint from my brush.
    She looked quickly my way, and opened and closed her mouth with a nearly silent huff of annoyance, before slowly rolling her bulk onto her legs so she could push herself erect.

"I concur," I said.

I set aside the chair I had been decorating, and carefully closed the lid on the jar of paint. I placed my tools on the high shelf made by the top of the rock wall of the house, and stuck my tongue out at the goat eyeing them hungrily. The damn animals had not managed to reach anything I placed under the eaves yet, but they were often upon the thatched roof seeking a means to do so. Sure enough, the matriarch of our little herd began to make her way to the hill that formed one side of our home. From the hill she could climb onto the roof with ease. I rather hoped she would fall through the thatch and we could dine on roast goat.

I followed Bella to the front of the house, but whereas she continued on to the edge of the promontory, I stopped by the cook fire, where Gaston was brewing medicinal concoctions. I found him staring into the distance in the same direction the dog now headed. He did not seem to be listening, though; just deep in thought.

I took time to drink in the sight of him, as it was seldom that he was in such repose and unaware of my gaze. As always, I marveled that my love would find such a fine form. I would have taken him even if his eyes were hooded, his jaw weak, or his nose beaked; but his features were truly finely wrought: handsome without prettiness; strong without crudeness. In the deep shade of the awning we had erected beside the fire, his eyes were the color of a pine forest at dusk, and his red hair was reduced in magnificence to the hue of dried blood. I could barely see the small gold hoops at his ears that marked him a buccaneer, or the scar upon his forehead that spoke of so many others. His lean muscular body – the physique of a man who ran two leagues and sparred for over an hour every morn – was folded beneath him in a way that seemed uncomfortable but was surely not, as he was not coiled or poised to move, but relaxed and at peace: like a cat who seems boneless and not prone to ever move again until it stands and stretches with the grace of a dancer.

He finally felt my gaze and squinted up at me curiously. I knew he sometimes watched me when I was not aware, and I wondered what he thought. He always said he found me handsome: but I am not like him, as I am somewhat more lanky than sculpted, in feature as well as physique. I feel I would not remind anyone of a cat, but rather a lean hound with an amiable boyish smile and hair the color of straw never to be spun into gold. By all accounts, I have remarkably blue eyes, though.

"I thought I heard a shot," I said, and scratched the wheat stubble of my jaw. We had not shaved in days.

He did not reply for a time, and then he turned to peer around our land with a slight frown and a slow nod. "Oui."

I looked about. We appeared to be alone atop Negril Point. To the south and east, nothing moved for as far as the haze allowed my gaze to travel, except the breeze upon the grass and bushes. And in the other directions, there was only the endless sea meeting an endless sky.

"Bella did too," I added. "I will investigate."

"I should stay with these," he said, and indicated the little pots he had boiling on the fire. Then he cursed quietly and looked about him with annoyance.

I smiled as I headed to the door to the house: neither of us had a weapon within reach. I fetched our sword belts, ammunition pouches, and a pistol for each of us.

"We have grown lax," he muttered as he accepted the pistol.

"We are living well, with not a care in the world," I chided as I loaded my piece. "But oui, you describe the other side of the coin quite well. Let us see how it has landed this day."

He sighed as he loaded his. "If it was a shot from the beach, do not go down without telling me."

"Of course not." I leaned down and kissed the scar upon his forehead.

He snorted with annoyance, and then his hand snaked around the back of my neck and he nearly pulled me to the ground as he brought my lips to his.

I left him with a jaunty grin upon both our faces.

Bella sat at the head of the path that led down to the strand of beach, which ran due north of us between the wide bay and the great bog. I did not see anyone upon the steep, winding trail, but I did see a flyboat landed upon the sand below. Three men were working about it: I could not truly ascertain their identities at such a distance, but as one wore a shirt and was in the process of doffing shoes and hose, and the other two were nearly-naked bronzed buccaneers, I thought it entirely possible Striker, Pete, and Theodore were paying us a visit. I saw nothing else upon the sea or sand.

I returned to our abode and told Gaston of what I surmised as to the identity of our guests.

"Do they have much that must be carried?" he asked with annoyance.

I shrugged. I could not recall seeing them unloading anything at all. "Nor goats to herd."

He snorted. We had viewed the arrival of the goats at their last visit as a mixed blessing.

"I will stay, then," he said. "If it pleases you," he added.

I shrugged again.

I called for Bella to remain with Gaston. I saw no reason for her to waddle down to the beach after me and back up again. I wished our big black male, Taro, were about so he could accompany me, but he appeared to be off hunting, or perhaps avoiding his grouchy mate.

This thought minded me that our dog was not the only one heavy with child this autumn; and I wondered if our visitors were here to avoid their own surely grumpy wife. Or perhaps it was later in the year than I suspected, and they came bearing news of new relations.

Our visitors were indeed Theodore, Pete, and Striker. My dear friend and barrister appeared as he always did, his dark eyes calm and serious, the hint of a smile playing about his thin lips. His somewhat stout body looked no wider or thinner than when last I saw him – in May, I believed, or was it April? Our favorite lion and wolf, one gold, the other dark, both bronzed to copper, appeared as scuffed and bruised as they ever did when they spent time in Port Royal amongst so many taverns and bored buccaneers. So their marriage to my sister had changed little in that regard. As always, my matelot not withstanding, they were two of the handsomest men I have ever beheld.

"What is the month?" I asked them when at last we were close enough to speak.

My inquiry was greeted by confused stares on the part of two of their number, and a chuckle from Pete, who then lifted me off my feet in an exuberant embrace.

"November," Striker said, as if I were daft. "You look well and it is good to hear you speaking again."

"It is good to speak again." To my ear, my voice still sounded a trifle rusty, after two months of having my jaw bound so it could heal; but I still sounded better than my poor matelot, whose voice was permanently husky and rough, having been broken such that it would never heal.

"*We* are well," I said, and embraced Theodore. "And how is everyone? And to what honor do we owe this visit?"

Theodore appeared caught between answering my question truthfully – a thing that seemed to pain him – and uttering the usual pleasantries.

"We?" Striker queried doggedly as I turned to him. He glanced past me and up toward the promontory with curious concern.

Annoyance flared in my heart. There was still much to be mended between us, though I understood his concern.

"Aye, we." I let the annoyance be heard in my tone, even as I embraced him. "Gaston is brewing some concoctions from the bark of various trees in the hope of producing a cure for malaria, since no one but the damn Spanish can yet locate quinine. The pots could not be left."

"The malaria? Are you both well?" Theodore asked with alarm.

"Nay, aye, we do not ail," I said quickly. "We lost so many returning from Porto Bello that the physician in his soul has become obsessed with finding another means to combat the damn malady, though. Some of our men only live because we did locate quinine in an apothecary in that damned cesspool of a port. Gaston knew of it because the Jesuit that Doucette often dealt with had it."

"Considering what the Spanish are said to sell the substance for in Christendom, if he does locate another cure, you would be very wealthy men," Theodore said thoughtfully.

I shrugged. "We are wealthy men, and I feel my matelot would simply give it away anyway. I would not feel right in turning such a thing to coin, either."

Theodore smiled indulgently. "Nay, because you are wealthier in virtue than in gold."

"Or perhaps common sense," I said with a grin. I turned back to Striker. "We are quite well, as we were when last you visited." I met his eyes with a strong gaze that he at last turned from with a sheepish mien.

"We worry," Striker said.

I glanced to Pete: his expression told me his matelot was the only one engaged in the activity.

"You are fond of worrying," I told Striker. "Now, what news have you? Or did you come to escape my sister? Or has she birthed yet?"

Pete and Striker looked to Theodore and frowned in unison.

"'EKnowsTheWhyO'It," Pete said with mock annoyance. "An"EWillNa' Speak."

Theodore was now the one appearing sheepish – and poised to speak. His gaze darted up the hill behind me: to where he could envision Gaston, I presumed.

I felt Theodore could be little but the herald of doom, so I sought to delay it.

"So you have news?" I said quickly. "How is Mistress Theodore? And your babe?"

He seemed relieved and amused by this change of topic. "Mistress Theodore is quite well indeed. And our child, Elizabeth, is also doing well by all accounts. She has taken to sleeping through the night, and I am greatly pleased."

His happy information was accompanied by a chorus of frustrated groans from the other two members of his audience.

I chuckled and turned on Striker. "And how is my sister, Sarah, your fine wife? Is she not due?"

"She is well!" he shouted with amusement. "She has begun her lying-in. She is quite miserable between the heat and the size of her."

Pete was indicating a truly gargantuan size indeed with his hands before his belly; but as my sister was such a small thing, I thought it likely she merely appeared far larger with child than an average-sized woman would.

"ItBeKickin'AnRollin'About," Pete said proudly, as if he alone were somehow responsible for this miracle.

"She's doing well," Striker reiterated softly, his regard for my sister showing in his dark eyes.

"I am pleased to hear it," I told him sincerely before turning back to Theodore. "And all others? Have the men returned from their smuggling ventures? And Agnes, is she well? And Mister Rucker, and my uncle?"

There were chuckles and sighs all about.

"Agnes, Rucker, and your uncle are well," Theodore assured me and began to say more.

"And we haven't heard from the Bard and Cudro, yet; but they've only been gone two months," Striker said before Theodore could say whatever had parted his lips.

"And I will bet you worry over that, too," I teased Striker.

Striker rolled his eyes. "You're damn right I worry!"

"Naw," Pete huffed with amusement that evolved into mock sorrow. "'EBeBoredAn'Angry'IsShipSailedWithout'Im. An'EBeStuckInTownWith Nuthin'TaDoButBallsAtTheGov'ners."

Striker swore. "Just one!"

I laughed.

"The new houses were completed this summer," Theodore said. "And the plantation, Ithaca, will be having their first harvest after the New Year. Your uncle has taken up the management of the endeavor; but true to his word to you, the men are being educated, even the Negroes. And they are growing some small amount of food there, though it is mainly for the Negroes."

"At least those poor souls shall be healthier," I sighed, remembering how gaunt Fletcher had been when last I saw him. He had suffered from malaria, contracted most probably because the plantation was well inland and away from the clean breezes of the coast. Fletcher's health had been further injured by his refusal to eat the native foods, though; and the ignorance responsible for that was not a thing one could cure with a tonic.

"And my Damn Wife, Lady Marsdale, does she yet live?" I asked. "Is she well? Is she still with child?"

The three of them shrugged.

"She lives. By all accounts she has begun her lying-in and should birth before the end of the year," Theodore said thoughtfully. "We have actually heard little of her of late. Since she moved into her home, she has behaved in a ladylike manner and deprived the gossips of further fodder." He frowned at me curiously. "Do you still truly intend to keep her if she bears a boy?"

I shook my head. Gaston and I had discussed it on occasion these last months. We had determined that we probably did not wish to keep – as it was not mine – any get she might produce. But if it were a boy, I could claim him as my heir and he could be the key to my inheriting the plantation and pleasing my father such that he might not wish to further meddle in our affairs. But, in that possible turn of events, could we be so uncaring – even to the get of her womb – as to send any child off to live with my father if he so demanded it? That was a fate best reserved for enemies: and the poor child, whatever its sex, had done nothing wrong.

"I know," I sighed. "I should seek an annulment no matter which she produces. But... What will become of her? I feel some sympathy for her in the matter. She did not wish for this. And now, due to her foolish indiscretion, she is truly ruined."

"You have more than adequate funds to set her up with a house somewhere in England," Theodore said.

I shook my head. "Send her off to England where she will spread tales of my perfidy with few about to tell of hers? That plays well into my father's hands."

"Then petition for annulment and ensconce her at Ithaca," Theodore said with a shrug.

"Perhaps." I nodded. I knew it was what must be done, but I had little taste for it.

"Speaking of wives, or rather those who are not," Striker said. "At the one damn ball I had to attend last month." He glared at his grinning matelot. "I saw that girl you wished to marry."

"Christine Vines?" I asked with true surprise.

"That be the one." Striker shrugged. "She asked of you. We couldn't speak much. She has a stepmother now, who doesn't let the poor girl out of her sight."

So Sir Christopher had married. And Christine had been caught and returned to him. As angry and distraught as he had been at her running away to Gods-knew-where after my proposal, I was not surprised he kept her under guard. I felt sorrow in that. I had rather fancied she had been traveling about Christendom all this time, dressed as a boy, practicing what little swordplay we had time to teach her.

"Is she married?" I asked them. "Betrothed?"

Theodore's eyebrow rose.

"Nay, nay," I quickly assured him. "I will not attempt to beat my way up that wind twice." Gaston would not stand for it.

"Not that I have heard," Theodore said.

I nodded. Perhaps she had dodged that thrust for a time, but it was a blade ever at her throat.

As this information had done much to diminish my mood, I thought perhaps I should hear Theodore's real reason for coming, as it could not now make me feel worse. "And what other news?" I asked him.

"Well," he said with a thoughtful mien. "The King has sent Modyford a man of war."

"Oh bloody Hell!" Striker yelled.

Pete groaned and laughed: and I did, too, as Theodore shot Striker a triumphant smile.

"Aye, aye," Striker said. "Our king sent our governor a man of war to guard the colony, the *Oxford*. She's a true warship, all right: thirty-four guns and two hundred aboard her."

He shook his head, and it was obvious there was something tempering his glee over this ship, which to my ear sounded like a boon for Jamaica. Then I remembered he had been raised as a pirate, and the presence of an English Naval vessel was likely not a thing he wished to countenance, even if most of his current pursuits were legitimate business ventures or encouraged by the Crown.

"The governor gave her over to Morgan," Striker said. "And now our admiral wishes to sail against Cartagena or Havana. Though the *Oxford* might be able to face the guns of their forts, she's still only one ship."

Now I truly understood his concern. I did not like the sounds of it either, and we well knew *Admiral* Morgan's ambitions. And then I could see other problems with the matter.

"Hold," I said. "Modyford passed the ship, an English Naval vessel, to Morgan? How does the captain of this fine ship feel on the matter?"

"His name's Collier, and he seems to accept it, for now," Striker said with a shrug. "He's the one they threw the ball for. And Morgan's hauled him off to his plantations, and every other damn fool of any import has been quick to kiss his arse. But that good and proper naval officer has not seen the rest of our fleet, or our crews. I think he's in for a bit of a surprise."

I doubted the composition of the English Navy and the buccaneers were dissimilar. Both contained all manner of men from bondsmen to nobles, from all the nations of Christendom: all rakehells and ne'er-do-wells of some fashion. But whereas the Brethren of the Coast were comprised of free men who had escaped some enslavement of the spirit or body – and free armed men at that – the English Navy was comprised of conscripted men well-accustomed to the lash. It was likely this good Captain Collier would not understand how such a rabble could be commanded. I found amusement in that, and wished I would be about to see his face when the concept of the Articles was explained to him.

"So the fleet will sail in the new year?" I asked, though I well knew the answer. The Brethren, whether French or English, had been sailing against the Spanish in some manner every winter for over thirty years.

"Morgan wishes to sail to Cow Island to provision this next month, but it will be the New Year before we can get the lot of us together," Striker said with a sigh.

We would be some of the laggards, as our ship, the *Virgin Queen*, was off on a smuggling expedition. Or rather, perhaps Pete and Striker and the rest of our cabal would be the laggards: I did not wish to sail. Gaston and I had been doing well enough alone here, so well we no longer kept a weapon in reach even in our sleep; and I liked living as we did now.

And then Striker's words struck me with amusement. "Morgan wishes to provision?" I asked.

Striker snorted. "The colony has agreed to provision the *Oxford*, so there's no need for it for that vessel. He wishes to gather as many men as possible, though; and that takes time, and those men must be fed."

"He has at last come to this conclusion?" I asked.

Striker snorted again. "After many a night drinking with us captains, aye, he's decided to humor us."

"NowEnuffO'ThisShite," Pete grumbled and turned on Theodore. "WhyBeWe'Ere?"

Theodore awarded him a patient smile and turned to me. "I am here to meet with Gaston and you."

"Concerning?" I asked, my stomach already constricting. Though I could not know what the matter was, I could imagine a great many things I would not wish to hear. And though we had already covered almost all the possible sources of news, there was one we had not. "News from my father?"

"Not unless he's French," Striker said.

"What?" I asked.

Theodore sighed and dug about in the satchel slung over his shoulder.

"A French frigate sailed into port a few days ago," Striker said. "And a couple gentlemen came ashore and asked about for Theodore."

Theodore handed me a thin missive. It was addressed to Gaston, or rather to Gabriel Denis Michel David de Sable, Gaston's christened name. I recognized the arms in the seal. The letter came from Gaston's father, or someone emboldened or empowered to speak for him.

"Gaston's father, the Marquis de Tervent, wishes to see his son," Theodore said.

I could not breathe for a time: the air did not enter my lungs.

"He is here?" I gasped at last.

"Aye, he commissioned a ship and sailed here," Theodore said.

"Hold," Striker said. "Gaston's father? Bloody Hell! Isn't he the one who…?"

"Aye," I muttered, and left them. I ran up the promontory. Fury gripped me. We had been doing so damn well. What kind of fool was I to think the Gods would let us be? Though never would I have envisioned this, even in my wildest nightmares. *My* father shattering our idyllic existence I could grasp readily enough, but this… this was not a thing I had ever expected.

Gaston found alarm in the rapidity of my approach, and stood to meet me, pistol in hand.

"Will?" he queried.

I could not breathe enough to speak. I thrust the letter at him. He read his name without taking it: his only movement was to touch the seal with a fingertip.

"From your father," I gasped foolishly.

He nodded, without derision that I should say a thing so obvious.

"Read it," he whispered, "and tell me of it."

Though, I was, of course, greatly curious, and I had thought he would make such a request, I still waited to compose myself somewhat before breaking the seal and perusing the contents of the single page. It was addressed to "My beloved son, Gabriel," and ended with a simple, "Your Father". However, the words between thankfully did not gush with such confusing sentiment. The Marquis' language was succinct, if not somewhat timorous. As there was not a single letter out of place, or wavering pen stroke, I thought it likely this was a much-rehearsed final draft, or else the Marquis was a very organized man. As for the actual gist of it, the Marquis had indeed sailed halfway round the world to meet with his son. He hoped that Gaston still felt the forgiveness he had expressed in his letter from a year ago, and that they could at last lay the events of the past to rest.

"He is on a ship anchored off Port Royal," I told Gaston, "and he wishes to meet with you and lay the past to rest – and he hopes, one could assume sincerely, that you still harbor forgiveness for him."

Gaston collapsed to sit heavily where he had been standing. All pretense of control disappeared along with the strength in his legs. "He is here?" he asked with amazement.

"Oui, Theodore said as much. I do not think he has seen him, though."

"He came here, he came here…" Gaston repeated dully while looking at the dirt and beginning to rock very slowly back and forth. He had retreated into the mask of the Child.

I cursed at the Gods and went to hold him. We had been doing so well.

"Hush, hush," I murmured in his ear. "He can never hurt you again. I will not let him."

But my words were a lie. The damn man was already hurting him.

"I will not let him hurt me," Gaston growled, and his shoulders tightened beneath my hands.

Resigned to the wild ride I knew would be my life until this matter was eventually behind us, I pulled back and regarded his face. He had not fully given the reins to his Horse: there was still some of the Man about his eyes.

"Do you wish to meet with him?" I asked calmly. Though I felt it was a thing he could not know with great certainty at this early juncture, I was curious as to his response.

My question brought the Child back to his eyes. "I am afraid," he whispered.

"Of what?"

"That he will still hate me."

I smoothed the letter, which I had crumpled in holding him, and held it up before his eyes. "I feel he is more afraid of you in that regard. And damn well he should be."

Gaston shook his head and looked away. He was chewing on his lip such that I thought he would draw blood.

I heard footsteps behind us. Theodore cleared his throat.

I did not turn to face them. "We need to be alone for a time," I said firmly. "Perhaps you could make use of one of the other homes. I am sorry for the…"

"Think nothing of it," Theodore said quickly. "We will await your decision as to what is to be done about the matter."

"Aye," Pete added. "WeBeFine. WeGotRum, An'NoWomenfolkAboutTa TellUsNa'TaDrinkIt."

Theodore chuckled appreciatively.

Striker said nothing as they walked away, but I could feel his gaze upon us. I wished I did not feel such anger towards him over the matter of his undying concern for us, but it was one of those feelings that come of our Horses and hearts and not our thinking minds. I turned my attention back to Gaston and his wrestling with his bucking and frightened animal.

    I did not know what to say to comfort him, or whether, indeed, he could be comforted. I tried to imagine the state I would be in if my cousin Shane, the one who had caused my scars, were to arrive here on Jamaica and express a wish to apologize. I could not envision it, though: if such a thing were to occur, it would surely be a ruse, and I would know it as such and not be lost and floundering in feelings of surprise or pain over the incongruity of his attempting to set things right. I looked at the letter I held. Was this, too, a ruse? Did the Marquis have some ulterior motive?

    Our fathers were among the wolves of the world: they countenanced any necessity if it enhanced their survival or stature. What motives would a Marquis have for sailing across the sea? He had not heard from Gaston since exiling him here to the West Indies twelve years ago. Just as my father had not heard from me in the ten years I spent roaming Christendom. The Marquis had known of Gaston, though – that Gaston lived – from Doucette. He had sent a great amount of money to see that Gaston was well cared for. He had sent letters expressing regret. My father had been concerned I would return, which is to say I believe he wished I would not; and when I did, he had not known what to do with me, as I had upset his plans. The Marquis had already disinherited Gaston, though: had him declared unsound of mind and delivered him into Doucette's legal custody. Gaston was no threat to him. But now... Now the Marquis had received word from his son that the arrangement with Doucette was no longer acceptable, and that his son had gone off with some English Lord. Perhaps the Marquis felt his plans were now in danger if his eldest son were not where he had left him and was now running about in the company of another wolf. Gaston had made it very clear in his letter to his father that we were lovers. Perhaps I was the threat the Marquis sailed around the world to face. Perhaps he was afraid I would urge Gaston to attempt to reclaim his title and inheritance.

    Gazing upon my distraught matelot, though, I did not feel I should voice this new suspicion. He had been sincere when he told his father he forgave him. He did not hate the man, despite what had occurred. He blamed himself as much as anyone. He wanted his father's forgiveness, and I daresay held hope of being loved by the damn man. I understood that well enough. I had journeyed here to Jamaica to gain favor with my damn father, on the mistaken notion that such a thing could be done at all. I had since learned otherwise, or at least I felt I had: much of my father's motivations remained a mystery. Yet, there was still some little part of my soul that wished to grant him the benefit of doubt: that harbored a tiny flickering hope that perhaps all the wolfish machinations we ascribed to him were products of our fancy.

    I let that hope cling to life, but I would not fan it to flame. I felt doing that would be foolishness of a high order, and I refused to be hurt yet again. Yet I let it remain, flickering there.

Would we be fools to assume Gaston's father meant what he said in his letter?

"What are you thinking?" Gaston asked with great worry.

I cursed myself for not schooling my face. I had not thought he still had his wits about him enough to be concerned with my frowning.

"I am puzzling why he is here," I said.

"You feel he lies?" Gaston asked with sudden ire.

"Non, non, I do not know. Hush. I am ascribing things to him as if he were my father, and perhaps that is not fair. Perhaps he is sincere in ways I feel my father could never be."

He calmed a little, but the Horse's words were hard. "My father is a good man."

He spoke such truths of his soul when he was thus, yet I felt compelled to voice my surprise. "You truly believe that?"

"Oui," he said firmly. "He was angry that night, very angry... and he had great cause," he added softly and looked away. He began fidgeting again.

"Oui," I sighed, "that night, but... My love, he sent you away, he kept you in schools all those years, he..."

"That was what is done!" His eyes were glittering emeralds again: sharp and hard. "It is not his fault I am mad!"

"Oui," I conceded and looked away. "You are correct." I sighed as I folded the letter. "But he hurt you, and I cannot forgive him for it. I am sorry."

He gave a sob and threw himself about me. "I am sorry. I love you. I love you. I am afraid. I am... Do you truly feel he is insincere?"

I rubbed his back and held him. "Non, non, my love. I do not know. I think it is my own fears speaking. I think, though, that we should at least be cautious."

"You must meet with him," he breathed against my cheek.

"With you?" Though I surely was not going to allow him to go alone.

"Non, first. Read him," he sighed, "and tell me of it."

I pulled away enough to see the small, sad smile on his lips.

"Whatever you wish, my love," I breathed.

"I wish for you to care for me and never leave me." He buried his face in my shoulder again.

I held him for a time, and then at last I roused us and we moved under the awning. The contents of most of his pots were quite boiled away, and in a few instances I felt a chisel would be necessary to chip out the remaining sludge. He set them aside without comment. I heated the chicken stew we had made the day before, and we carried a bowl of it to the rock on which we always sat to watch the sunset.

I sipped broth, and watched the golden rays upon him, and not the sea. His eyes glowed a pale green in that light, his skin shone like bronze, and as always, his unruly cropped hair looked as if flames licked his scalp. Unbidden, curiosity about his father's visage crept into my thoughts. How similar were they, or was there any similarity at all? Had all my matelot's madness truly come from his mother, or was there some in his father's blood as well?

"What else did they say?" Gaston asked quietly, his gaze still upon the sun. "Is there other news?"

He did not sound sincerely curious, and I wondered at his need to make conversation.

I sifted through what I could remember. "The king sent the governor a man of war, and the governor gave it over to Morgan. Of course, the idiot now wishes to sail against Cartagena or Havana. He has called for all to meet him at Cow Island this winter. Striker thinks Morgan a fool for wanting to attempt so much, but he chafes as he wishes to sail; yet their babe is unborn and our ship is out smuggling."

Gaston nodded thoughtfully. "How is Sarah?"

"Well enough, she is as big and uncomfortable as Bella from what they say."

He smiled at that, and then frowned. "We cannot leave here until Bella births."

I had not thought of that, but he was correct. I would not dream of abandoning our dog, though I thought it likely she needed us not at all for the endeavor. And I surely would not leave without Gaston having a chance to find some solace in the innocence of puppies. He found them very calming.

"Could we not take her with us?" I asked.

"Do you wish to sail?" he asked. His gaze met mine.

"To Port Royal to meet your father, or to Cow Island to raid against the Spanish?"

"To rove and raid," he said, his gaze still earnest. "The Devil with my father."

"I have been quite content here this autumn with you. We do not need the money it... might bring. I do not feel we need the trouble it always seems to bring, either. But..."

Last year we had sailed because of Gaston's madness, because he needed to unleash it on occasion against enemies.

"I do not wish to go," he said suddenly. "To Port Royal or elsewhere. But, I cannot have him here. And..."

He gave a ragged sigh and rubbed the heels of his hands upon his temples, as if he were trying to massage the dark thoughts away, or squeeze them into the back corners of his skull where he claimed they always lurked.

"Let us go to Port Royal," I said softly, "and tend to the business that must be tended to there, and then let us return here."

He took a deep breath and nodded. "What other business?"

"We must..." I sighed. "I must make some decision about the Damn Wife and act upon it. She is also soon to birth."

"Could we not live here forever?" he asked hopefully with a childish mien.

I smiled. "As long as the Gods will let us. We have more than enough money, and… I am sure we can find some suitable woman to bear children so that you might revel in them. I do not see where I need my inheritance. Even Theodore's concerns of… Well, I do not see where I must be my father's heir to accomplish anything else here. I feel many of those concerns shifted when Sarah arrived and married Striker. The plantation will be as it is and I do not feel I can rescue them as I once intended. I have not felt that I could in a long time. And we have the R&R Merchant Company to make us all honest men. I say the Devil with it all."

This seemed to please him.

It did not please me: I felt great unease, as if I had forgotten something, and I wondered at it until his kiss drove my dark thoughts away. Soon we were naked as babes and cuddled together in our wide hammock. We made love tenderly, seeking more reassurance than passion in our caresses and kisses. We eschewed the act of sodomy, choosing instead to hump against one another fitfully, belly to belly, until we at last found our pleasure. And as I drifted to sleep, I could not imagine anything better than spending the rest of my days at his side in our little corner of the world.

I woke to him hissing in my ear, "Will, I wish to ride."

It was dark, and at first the words seemed a distant thing, devoid of meaning. Then his mouth covered mine while his hands woke my flesh with increasing urgency. My cock swelled and, ears pricked and tail raised, my Horse pranced into the light to play with his. Our common need for such games was a thing born of the demons that haunted us, and not a thing we indulged often, but when we did play, I embraced it with fervor and gave myself over to it and him with abandon.

With nips and licks he traced a path of fire down my jaw and neck until he was somewhat below my ear, and then the nips became biting and he sucked and chewed until I mewled and rocked under him in an ecstatic mix of pleasure and pain. He guided my hands to the netting above my head, and with touch alone, bade me tangle myself there so that I was bound after a fashion. Then his torturous teeth moved away from my neck and down my chest. I writhed and uttered harsh cries and growls, more animal than human. He was silent except for the occasional rumble of mirth. To my gratification and amazement, he left little of me in peace, chewing upon my back, buttocks, thighs, and belly such that I feared for my manhood several times. At last I could run beneath him no more, and the ever-peculiar cessation of the pain came as it always did. I slumped beneath him, sated beyond sex alone, and drifting on a cloud that felt like laudanum, only so much better.

He covered my face in gentle kisses and moved us such that he could truly mount me. I smelled the almond of our favorite salve and then he was within me. I was run out, but he was far from finished. He rode me with hard thrusts that set the hammock creaking. I felt as if I were the rocks being pounded by the waves of the surf, and then I was the waves and he was the rocks, and then we were both the water, rushing in and out. When at last he came, it was as if he did it for both of us, and I cried out with the joy of it as I felt him spasm within me.

He withdrew almost before his cry had finished echoing off the stone walls of our tiny abode. He kissed me lightly on the lips and he was gone. He always did that after we played so. His reason returned in the aftermath, and with it, shame.

I did not wish to move, yet I knew if I did not, it would be that much worse when I did. Sleep would not be a balm for the aches I would suffer for the first day or two. I took my time in stretching and rolling out of the hammock.

I saw him standing by the cook fire, staring pensively at the glow on the eastern horizon. He was still naked. I went and relieved myself around the side of the hill. I ran curious fingers over the now-darkening marks he had left. Aye, I would be very sore this day.

When I returned, he winced at my appearance as I approached, and despite the dim light I could see him flush. I sidled up in front of him, to press the right of my chest to the right of his and rest my head atop his shoulder in a way horses sometimes stand together in a pasture. I cupped his balls playfully and he hissed with surprise.

"Why do you tolerate me?" he asked.

"Tolerate? Hmmm?" I chuckled. "I believe the question is why do I delight in you when you are thus? Non, tolerate is not the word. Trust, that is the word. I trust you. You are the only one I will ever allow to call the pieces of my soul I wish to keep hidden into the light."

He sighed and his arm stole about my waist. "I love you," he whispered.

"I know," I said succinctly. "And I love you, and I wish you were not so troubled over the matter."

He shook his head. "I am not troubled over that... If you are not. Which in that regard, you are truly as mad as I. Non, I am troubled that when things trouble me I... need to run so. I wish my damn father had not come."

"So do I," I sighed.

"I feel I will have to sail, Will. I am sorry. I feel seeing him will..."

"It will bring much into the light, my love, I know. But, perhaps, that is for the best. Because truly, would it not be best to lay that night, and your sister, and mother, and all else that lies between the two of you, to rest?"

He nodded. "Oui, it will. But it will be as if I undergo a complicated surgery. I will need much time to convalesce."

"I feel you are making light of it. If you feel you must sail, then you expect that this visit will open all those wounds and leave you draining noxious fluids upon the world for some time."

"Oui," he said softly. "I am afraid much will be drained upon you, and I cannot..."

I put fingers upon his lips and moved so that I could meet his tearful gaze.

"You will do what you must to heal, and I will assist you," I said firmly. "We can weather any storm as long as we hold to one another."

"It will be a very bad storm, Will," he said seriously, and then the words began to tumble out in an ever-faster torrent. "I have not had to be as I was before here, without you." He shook his head with frustration. "I have not had to wear a mask. I cannot imagine meeting him without… He has become tangled with Doucette in my mind, and I cannot… He must not see me as mad. I do not wish for him to see me as mad. Yet, I know I will not be able to help myself. I cannot hide it away any longer. I cannot wear the mask as I once did. He will see. He will see and he will hate me and… And that angers me. That he should judge me so. That he should be allowed to judge me so. It is not my fault! I cannot make it go away!"

I held him tightly with tears of fear and frustration in my eyes. He did not need to tell me how bad the storm was going to be. It was already upon us and I saw no end in sight. Only the Gods could know what shore we would eventually wash up on.

Fifty-Four

Wherein We Are Distracted

Gaston and I did our morning run down to the beach and up it for a good league or so. We knew we could not allow his daily routine of calisthenics to lapse now: it helped keep his Horse calm. At the end of this exercise, we did not feel like frolicking in the waves or sparring as we were usually wont to do; we chose instead to walk hand in hand in the surf in silence for a time, listening to the raucous morning call of gulls along the shore and other birds in the bog.

I felt acutely how much I would miss being alone with him. I, who had spent so much of my life craving constant social interaction with anyone who would spend time with me, no longer wished to engage in pointless conversation, drinking to numb my heart, and, of course, carnal pleasures without love. Gaston's presence had weaned me of those needs these past two and half years, such that I now viewed the life I once had as being lived by another.

Our silence this morning was not as companionable as either of us would have liked, though; and at last I felt compelled to speak.

"I will miss this, this life we have here," I said carefully, "but I feel we will be all the fonder of it when we are able to return."

He sighed and smiled wistfully before turning to look at me. "I pray that someday I will not be the cause of us having to leave it yet again."

"Who are you praying to?" I asked with amusement and curiosity.

He grinned briefly, but his words were somber. "To the Gods of old, as you do. I have told any divinity that cares to listen that I will not always have to rove to release the anger within me, that I will not always be possessed of such anger."

I smiled. "I am sure They have heard you, and I have great faith that such a thing will come to pass, either by our hand or Theirs."

He chuckled at that, and started walking again. "It is a wonder They tolerate you at all."

"Well, the Gods surely help those who help themselves," I said with mock defensiveness.

He took a long deep breath. "I also have prayed that I will face my father with dignity, no matter how he behaves."

"I am sure you will." And I was. I had great faith that the mask which he had so often worn while about others would slip easily into place when he was confronted by such a foe. It saddened me in part, in that we had worked so hard this last year toward his being in harmony with all parts of his being, but I thought it far more important he face his father from a position of perceived strength; and that mask, that tight control he could maintain on his madness for short periods of time, granted him a knight's armor in facing what he must.

"How does your Horse feel on the matter... this morning?" I asked. "Does it wish to fight him or flee him?"

Gaston shook his head. "It wishes for his respect and... love. I know you cannot understand..."

I stopped and pulled him to face me. "Non, non, it is not that I cannot; it is just that I have not reached that turn of the road as of yet. I will understand, just give me time."

His eyes were as grey-green as the sea in the hazy morning light, and seemingly as old. "I hate your father, too," he said softly, so that I had to strain to hear him above the surf.

"I will try to meet yours with a lack of prejudice," I said solemnly.

He smiled and nodded. "You honor me."

"Non, I love you, and we will endure and conquer, and come home again."

"Amen," he breathed.

With the grins of foxes, we ran up the winding path to our house.

Though the sun was fully in the sky and no longer hovering about the horizon, we still found ourselves alone. Gaston seemed relieved by this; and when I asked him of it, thinking he merely did not wish to confront their lingering gazes of concern, he fingered one of the marks he had made upon my chest. Feeling the fool that I had forgotten a thing so obvious, I went and found a tunic to don. Between that and my breeches, I hoped all he had done was now safely hidden. When I returned to him, I turned about and asked him to inspect me.

"The one upon your neck is quite visible," he sighed. This was followed by a feral and lusty grin such that it drew my mouth to quirk in mirror of it.

"What?" I asked huskily, and closed the distance between us.

"You are mine and you are beautiful," he whispered. He drew my hand to his turgid member.

"That much?" I teased as I stroked him. "Then let us..."

He pushed my hand and then me away playfully. "Non, I wish to ache with it."

I understood: there were times when the aching anticipation, billowed upon sound faith that it could always be sated, was better than the release. I let him be with only a swat of feigned annoyance.

As we prepared our morning repast of eggs mixed with minced boucan, I mused on how much I loved to see him as he was this morning: unmasked and mercurial of mood. Some would say it was his madness, but I no longer could define madness as I once would have. I saw the rigid mask he had worn when first we met as a larger symptom of his madness than the openness of soul he was imbued with now. Aye, his Horse's honesty of emotion was a danger when he became riled, and he had difficulty controlling it still, but I felt he fared far better at the matter of control when he was not constantly reining the animal in. Then, it felt compelled to bolt beneath him when it became troubled. It was far more tractable now that he let it have its head most days.

And thus, his wish to be masked and under such control about his father concerned me: that was precisely the time when his Horse should have been allowed to choose its own path through the thorny thicket of emotion the whole scenario presented. I hoped the matter of their supposed reconciliation could be quickly done with, and the Marquis would return to France and I could then spend several months assisting Gaston with healing his newly opened wounds: in becoming the man I knew and loved again.

We were still alone after we had eaten, and it was becoming a matter of amusement for us. I guessed the blame could be laid upon the demon of rum for their absence. And so, we donned our sword belts and kerchiefs, took up several bottles of water, and with the dogs excited that we were off for a romp, went in search of our guests. Taro took the vanguard and ranged all about us in the brush, while we kept our pace slow in honor of Bella's waddling. She quickly licked our hands when we patted her wide head.

"Do you truly feel we should take her to Port Royal?" I asked. "I suppose they will be lonely here if we do not, though."

Gaston gave me an admonishing look. "Will, we can leave the goats and chickens: they will be well enough as there is much for them to forage on. But if we leave the dogs, they will eat our goats and chickens, and our neighbors', and the nearest plantations'..."

I was chuckling as I looked over our canine behemoths. Neither of them weighed less than six stone, and we went hunting for cattle to feed them every fortnight. "Aye, we best take them and let Agnes feed them in town."

This set me thinking though. "Do you feel she still works for us?"

Gaston shrugged. "She loves the dogs."

I decided that truly did answer the question of where her loyalties lay.

We found our guests at Liam's. Our good Scots musketeer had

deemed his abode upon the Point to no longer be a home in which he could remain without his beloved and deceased matelot, Otter; and thus he had gone on the smuggling venture with the rest of our cabal. Gaston and I did not often visit what had been their house. I felt its haunted-seeming emptiness to be a dire warning of what befell all pairs of matelots who roved too long. This morn it was pleasant to hear snores as we approached it. The reverberations rolling across the hillside were affirmations of life and things being as they should.

Liam's house was a small two-room structure much like ours, with one wall constructed of the side of a hill and the rest of stacked and mortared stones. We found Theodore sleeping on the large table in the front room, and Striker and Pete entangled with one another and a hastily strung hammock in the back. They should well thank the Gods we were not Spanish marauders, as we had to kick them before they noticed us. I found great amusement in watching Pete scrambling about and managing to get a pistol aimed at me with his left hand, when all other limbs were trapped in some manner, either by netting or his matelot. I supposed I should be thankful he did not shoot me, especially while I was laughing.

Striker swore at us a great deal while they got themselves untangled. Pete stumbled across the room to embrace Gaston. Theodore appeared quite green as he lurched awake and hurried outside to relieve himself of all manner of fluids his body thought it should no longer contain.

"How many bottles did you daft buggers bring?" I asked once they were fairly coherent.

"One," Striker sighed as he stretched so that his back popped several times. "But we found more here."

"A tavern's worth," I teased.

"Go fuck yourself," he said with a grin.

I chuckled. "No need, I have a matelot."

"Aye, you do," he said seriously.

Our gazes met, and underneath the after effects of rum and the bleariness of waking, I saw grudging respect in his. It gladdened my heart. I smiled. And that seemed to gladden his, as he came to embrace me.

"I'll try very hard to stop… being an arse," he whispered.

"Thank you," I said solemnly. "But understand, I would not have you stop caring, I would just have you show more faith."

He nodded as he released me. "I'll try. Truly Will, it's not so…" He sighed.

I glanced about, and found that Theodore had returned and was eyeing us sheepishly. He was not the only one watching our exchange. Gaston stood tensely in the doorway, and Pete was sprawled in a chair gazing upon Striker with pride.

"Was this the topic of much discussion last night?" I asked.

Pete smirked.

Theodore sighed. "Aye, much drunken discussion."

I supposed there was little help for it. We discussed ourselves endlessly, why should others not? But, of course, we were centaurs, and philosophy was our way. I did not see where it was the way of wolves, or in Pete's case, lions, or in Theodore's case – and there I thought I should discuss with Gaston how to categorize Theodore in a world of wolves and sheep: as our good friend and barrister was surely neither, yet he did not strike me as a mythical creature, either. I smiled a smile only my matelot would understand once I explained it to him.

"Thank you for coming," Gaston said hesitantly. "For bearing the news."

"Will you be returning with us?" Theodore asked.

Gaston nodded.

"May I ask…?" Theodore began slowly. He sighed and rubbed his temples before gazing at Gaston again, this time with a more barrister-like mien. "May I ask what the letter contained?"

"He wishes to lay matters to rest between us," Gaston said.

Theodore nodded. "His men said he received a letter from you a year ago. It listed me as a person who might know your whereabouts or how to contact you. It apparently made mention of Will by his given name and title as well."

Gaston nodded tightly. "I wrote him. After the incident with Doucette."

"But not after you were granted English citizenship?" Theodore asked.

Gaston and I shook our heads.

Theodore nodded sagely and frowned. "I did not discuss that with them. As you can imagine, I was quite surprised when this man Vittese appeared in my office."

"Vittese?" Gaston snapped, his eyes hard.

"Who is he?" I asked.

"My father's trusted man," Gaston growled. "He was the one always sent to fetch me from the schools, and he was the one charged with bringing me to exile. He gave me over to Doucette."

"I got the distinct impression he is not fond of you, either," Theodore said. "In fact, I would hazard a guess he feels his Lord's business here is folly."

"You got the impression…?" I asked.

"There was little he said concerning your matelot that *you* would *not* take offense at," Theodore said with a sheepish shrug.

"I look forward to making his acquaintance," I said.

"Oh Lord," Theodore groaned. "I thought as much." Then he gave a frown and his gaze flicked from one of us to the other. "I feel it would be wise if Gaston remained on English soil, in the company of the Brethren at all times, until this matter is resolved."

"You feel they might abduct him?" I asked with alarm.

"I feel…" Theodore said carefully, "That they perceive him as being of limited mental capacity, and definitely not sane. They spoke of him as if he were a child."

Gaston shook his head, and I could see the tears he fought. "Did you speak with my father?" he asked Theodore.

"Nay," Theodore said kindly.

"I was a child when last they saw me," Gaston said sadly, and left us.

I asked Theodore, "If I must slaughter a large number of Frenchmen, will there be trouble with the governor or any other?"

Theodore fought a smile. "I put great thought into that matter as we sailed here; as I think, judging by their demeanor toward your matelot, and your demeanor toward any who disparage your matelot, the deaths of several of these Frenchmen will likely result from this matter. Our beloved Governor Modyford hates the French. I feel there would be no lasting repercussions as long as it occurs on English soil and it can be construed that they prompted the matter. And... as long as the Marquis is not harmed." His gaze met mine and he sobered considerably. "I must ask: does Gaston bear his father any ill-will?"

I took a deep breath and answered as truthfully as I could. "He does not feel so at this time. However, if the man does something foolish..."

"Like show him a whip," Striker said, and threw his hands wide in apology when I turned to him.

"Just so," I said. "Aye, if his father does something that magnificently stupid, then... well, then only the Gods can know. I will meet with the man first to determine his motives. I do not feel that Gaston should meet with him alone, if possibly at all, depending on the circumstances."

Theodore seemed relieved by this, but he quickly frowned and studied Striker speculatively before shifting his attention to me. "I feel there are pieces to this matter that..."

"The Marquis is responsible for Gaston's scars," I said. "Personally responsible. Gaston forgives him, as he feels he gave his father just cause."

"Good Lord," Theodore sighed.

I did not spare Pete and Striker a glance: they already knew that aspect of the matter. None knew why, of course, but that was not a thing I felt they ever need know.

"He must not kill the Marquis," Theodore said seriously. "And neither must you. Such a thing would cause a diplomatic incident beyond Modyford's ability to mitigate."

"I understand," I said solemnly, and I did. Killing a nobleman of any nation was not a thing to be done lightly.

"If such a thing is to occur, it would be best if you left Jamaica," Theodore added sadly.

"I do understand that," I assured him, and then I slipped outside.

I found Gaston sitting in the shade of a tree with the dogs. He was a good distance from the house, enough so that he would not have heard the end of the conversation there. He pawed angrily at the tears upon his cheeks as I approached.

"What is Theodore?" I asked as I sat before him. "He is neither wolf nor sheep."

At first he frowned with annoyance that I should pose such a question under the circumstances, and then he smiled with understanding.

I continued. "I do not feel he is a mythical being, born to be one thing and yet another. Nor do I feel he is a common docile form of livestock."

"He is a raven," Gaston said.

"How so?" I could not picture Theodore taking flight in any manner.

"He is intelligent, observant, and barristers feed off the dead and are the harbingers of doom," Gaston said, without any seeming insult in the last.

I smiled and nodded as I thought of Theodore the Raven. "As always, I feel you have seen the truth of the matter."

Gaston sighed and met my gaze. "I cannot remember how to don the mask, Will. I can recall what it felt like to wear it. How safe it was: that no one could see my thoughts, like painting my eyes with the Caribbe mask. But I cannot find that place in my heart where I need go."

"My love," I sighed. "I do not think the place you go to don the mask is in your heart. I feel it is alien to it."

He thought on this. "But, I am not without compassion when I tend the sick, and I wear a mask then, too."

"Oui, but it is a different one, I feel. You are at your finest then. Well, perhaps not, not for me anyway, as there is brusqueness and remove to your manner when you are healing and mending that I would not have aimed at my person in other situations. But, oui, you are in control then, and yet not so removed as you sometimes were when wearing the other mask. But, as we have discussed, it is because your Horse is... much engaged with the matter at hand. Or rather, it finds its concerns of the moment secondary to the needs of the man you are healing. But... As we have also discussed, we are centaurs, both Horse and Man, and we need to walk through this world as such. We cannot hide one half or the other in the cave: it does us little good, and it is not truth."

"But Will," he said earnestly, "Sane men do not cry. Grown men do not cry." He held his hand up to stop the refutation upon my lips. "I know that we are not like them. I know we are different and that we must measure ourselves by one another. But, they... My Father and his men will not measure us by that; and I wish for them to perceive me as sane, and grown, and not the child they knew, the beast they knew."

"Were you beastly to your father?" I asked.

"Non, non," he said quickly. "I was ever decorous about him. He was my father. I did not wish to battle him; I did not feel I could win if I did. But Vittese and the others," he growled. "I clawed and bit and spat on that bastard every chance he gave me. I hated him."

"Was he cruel to you?"

Gaston sighed and looked away to wipe more tears from his cheeks.

"Non, he would not hurt me more than necessary to restrain me. He is the man my father has ever sent to do things that require discretion. I was always one of those things. My father would never retrieve me from a school himself. So after whatever incident made them send me away, I would spend days or weeks, or one time, months, locked away until Vittese would arrive to take me to my next place of exile. And he always had this look about him, like I was a thing to be scorned and despised. I was an embarrassment. And… he was never my father. For years at a time, Vittese was all I saw of my father. I could only imagine how much my father hated me."

I embraced him. I was at a loss as to how to resolve our dilemma. The more I thought on it, the more I thought disaster loomed if Gaston tried to become the man he wished to present to them. All his old hurts and angers would seep out of the darkest recesses of his soul and make his Horse ever more difficult to control; and all the while he would be attempting to hold it still with an iron hand upon the reins. Eventually, it would explode beneath him – with righteous indignation if nothing else – and then someone would most likely die. Yet, I well understood his need to present himself as a grown man, a sane and grown man: we so wanted our fathers' respect.

"Perhaps if they ailed you could tend them, and thus show them the best you show anyone other than me," I said lightly. "I could wound them for you."

He stiffened in my arms, but then I felt the welcome rumble of amusement in his chest that finally bubbled a little to his lips in a half-hearted huff of laughter.

He pulled away to regard me. "I wish they could see me as you do, as our friends do, but they are not my friends, and I do not know if I can show them that face, either."

I frowned. "Perhaps you should simply show them you. You are a good man. You are loved. You have friends. Damn them to Hell and back if they cannot respect that. And I fear, as I know you do, that they will not. They will never see us as we are: they will only see phantoms of their own devising, and thus they will think what they will. And we have no part to truly play in the matter. So, in truth, if that is the way of it, if they are chained by their habits so that they only see the shadows upon the cave wall, then there is no harm in showing them the truth and in being as you are. If they know you to be mad, no amount of acting sane will change their minds, will it? Look at Striker, and he is our friend."

He thought for a time, his eyes holding mine with deep regard, and then he smiled slowly. "You are the one blessed to see the truth of things."

I knew not if my words were the truth of the matter, or merely a prayer. I prayed after my fashion anyway as we walked back to the others. I told the Gods that all I dearly wished to see in the resolution of the matter was that Gaston's father would leave us no worse than he found us: that his visitation should not result in harm coming to Gaston or myself or anyone we cared for.

Striker averred there should be enough moon to sail by that night, and so we spent the next hours preparing what we would leave behind to weather our absence, and packing all we wished to take. Gaston and I discussed whether we should dig up our small chest of gold or leave it hidden here. On the one hand, due to some unforeseen circumstance – a thing our lives were often plagued by – we might have need of the money, and it would be difficult to quickly return here and fetch it. But on the other, we knew not where we could safely hide such a princely sum in Port Royal if any were to become aware of it – and it was heavy. We at last decided to take it with us, but not in the chest with the Sable family crest upon it. We dug up that chest and placed the coins in the bottom of Gaston's medicine chest in neat layers that would not rattle. We would have to remove the gold, and either leave it in someone's keeping or hide it elsewhere, before we went roving.

Striker was not pleased that we wished to bring the dogs. Pete was elated. Striker grumbled a great deal. And thus we said goodbye to the goats and chickens, called the dogs to us, and made our way to the boat laden with all the weapons we owned, two bags of personal items, and Gaston's now extremely heavy medicine chest – not that it had ever been particularly light. We were under way with the evening breezes, sailing quickly about the Point and then east along the southern coast. The sun made its magnificent descent in our wake. I thought it poetically appropriate that we sailed into looming darkness.

While we had been engaged in packing, our visitors had left us alone and attempted to recover from their night's excesses. Now that we were all aboard the small flyboat, and there was little to do other than change the sail for each tack, an awkward silence settled over us with the deepening twilight. Striker and Theodore contemplated the sea, the deck, and the sails with frowns and sighs and avoided meeting my eye. I wearied of it quickly. I would have been concerned for its affect upon Gaston, if my matelot had not been deeply lost in his own thoughts, which appeared to be of a distressing nature, enough to cause him to fidget endlessly. This, of course, was not lost upon the others, and even Pete eyed him with concern. I did not think addressing any of their concerns would put anyone at ease; however, I did feel that perhaps addressing the matter from a different angle might be in order: there were things I was curious about. And so I sat before Gaston and took his hands in mine. He appeared both relieved and embarrassed by my attention.

"From what does your father's wealth derive?" I asked. In two and a half years, we had rarely discussed his father or his birthplace, and never in regards to matters mundane. "My father's wealth stems from tariffs he manages for the king, and rents on the family estate."

Gaston regarded me blankly for several moments and then frowned in troubled thought.

Striker spoke into the silence. "Just that? Your father's not some merchant? You always speak of your damn cousin being involved with his business."

I smiled. "Aye, but the business at hand is being a noble and all that entails. Noblemen, whether French or English, are not allowed to engage in anything so base as commerce or practice a trade. In France it is law. If they engage in business not in keeping with their heritage, they suffer *dérogeance* – they are stripped of their titles. That is why dallying about at court, and maintaining good relations, if not the favor of one's king or emperor, is important. Without being granted position by the king, or being in his favor to enhance their status and lands, nobles often become poor."

"So they can't work?" Striker asked incredulously. "Even if they want to."

"Even if they need to," I chuckled. "Aye, but if you feel that engaging in the politics of court is not exhausting, time-consuming, and fraught with peril, you are sadly mistaken."

"My father does none of that," Gaston spat. "He is a member of the parliament of Toulouse, but he begs no one for money and we are *noblesse ancienne*."

"You are from the County of Toulouse?" I asked, surprised. Then I teased. "I have heard much of that region but never visited it. It is said to be rife with heretics."

Gaston snorted. "I have heard the same: I was ever being insulted for being a provincial at the schools. But the Cathars were destroyed centuries ago, and the Hugenots are all in Languedoc. Toulouse is just old and proud and has seen many emperors come and go. They govern as if the fools in Paris will not always exist." He sighed. "To answer your question, our *seigneurie* has several mines and forges: that is where the money comes from."

"You mine gold?" Striker asked with a befuddled frown. "But..."

"Nay," Gaston said quickly. "Iron and coal, and my father does not own them, he is paid *banalités*, rents, by the men that do."

"Your father controls an iron mine and a forge? No wonder..." Theodore said thoughtfully.

"Aye," Gaston said with a shrug. "And our land is good for growing wheat. We are quite wealthy without the Emperor's favor."

I regarded my matelot with the bemusement I always felt when he spoke of either his father or his heritage with such pride, but I could understand some of it now: his father was truly a powerful nobleman, not some fool relying on the King's favor and the machinations of court as mine was. Gaston being disinherited was truly a great blow. He had once stood to gain far more than some farm fields and his father's name and reputation.

"I had not understood," I said quietly in French. "You have lost far more than I could ever hope to gain."

Gaston shrugged and sighed. "I have not wished to think about it. I was unfit. That is the way of it. He has his other sons." He frowned.

"They must be men now."

I moved so I could embrace him.

"I have come to resent losing my name and title most of all," he said sadly. "I do not care about the money."

"I know," I sighed. I found only confusion when thinking of my title. I had seen so many fools with titles over the years, and lived so long without the one I was born to, that I was tempted to say it held little meaning. But I found in my heart that the idea of being a lord held great meaning for me. Commoners were often sheep, and sheep were sheared and eaten. Though I did not wish to consider myself a wolf, having others consider me so was very useful and oft kept me alive.

We sat in thought for a time, the others not choosing to disturb us even if Gaston's revelations had given them cause to ask questions, until Pete suddenly remarked, "ThatStarThereBeAPlanet," and pointed at the sky. "WeSeenItThroughTheTellyScope."

I looked at the reddish dot in the sky with surprise and wonder. "Agnes' telescope arrived?"

"Aye. ItBeALittleThing." He indicated a tube the circumference of his hands and perhaps a foot beyond the width of his shoulders.

"If it weren't so damn fragile it would be damn useful at sea," Striker said. "During the day we could see to the Passage Fort from the roof: we could nearly see men's faces enough to tell if they were smiling or frowning. Rucker says this one cannot be jostled, though, lest the lens move and then it won't focus or some such thing."

Gaston nodded, his eyes still on the heavens. "Someone will solve that matter," he murmured.

"So what did that planet look like?" I asked Pete.

"LikeALittleOrangeBallWithLines. AgnesAn'RuckerSayTheLittleDots AboutItWereMoons. LookedLikeMoreStarsTaMe."

"That would be Jupiter. If they cross the disk of the planet they are moons," Gaston said.

I still sat holding his hands and marveling that the reddish dot could be resolved into a ball with lines. "What color are the lines? And which way did they run?"

Pete was delighted to tell me, and thus we spent several hours discussing the things they had seen with the telescope and the other lenses Agnes had received. Pete was apparently now quite convinced all water should be boiled. In addition to viewing the things only a lens could see in water, Agnes had taken to examining all manner of things, and Gaston was became quite distracted from his troubles while questioning Pete on what had been observed.

When at last Gaston and I curled together to sleep, he seemed relaxed and much more himself. I rubbed his back and wondered how we would keep him in this state.

In the darkest hours before dawn, Bella proved her loyalty – or perhaps that of the Gods – by beginning to give birth. Gaston happily immersed himself in ministering to Bella's needs as best he could – not that she needed much, as she was a dog and well versed at this activity. Nothing else existed for him. I thought even I was a phantom at the edge of his memory. When at last Bella had finished delivering six blind and mewling pups the size of my two fists held together, I crawled to her and kissed her nose in thanks.

The following morning, Gaston and Pete took great care and delight in fashioning a sling so one of them could carry the pups once we arrived in port.

"I suppose they can stay in the stable," Striker said as he watched them from the tiller.

"Stable?" I asked. "You have horses in town?"

He shook his head quickly. "Nay, it is more a shed. There is talk of buying a jackass or pony for a small cart, and to help with the water wheel."

At this, Gaston looked up from his work to regard Striker as quizzically as I.

Striker sighed and smiled. "Sarah had Fletcher come to town and construct a water wheel and buckets and troughs to lift water to a high cistern." He held up a hand to stave off the obvious question. "It's for the bathing room. I've not been to Bath, but Rucker claims he has, and that it is a thing similar to what the Romans had. Apparently they were as fond of bathing as the two of you. So there's a room with a great raised tub and tile all about. It can be filled from a pipe from the cistern that sits well above it, and heated by coals in a tray underneath, and emptied with a spigot."

Gaston and I exchanged a look of happy surprise and grinned like thieves.

"Sarah felt you would be pleased," Striker said with a grin of his own. "It's nice. Pete and I've made use of it, and Agnes and Rucker – though I felt he did it more to see what it was like than out of need or enjoyment – but alas, Sarah was too big with child by the time it was completed to get over the edge, and the midwife said bathing isn't healthy for a pregnant woman anyway."

Striker looked to Gaston for confirmation of that, and my matelot shrugged.

"I would think it would be a poor thing to do in dirty water," Gaston said thoughtfully. "But perhaps the midwife knows a thing I do not. My knowledge of the anatomy of women is lacking. I have never dissected one."

Theodore and I grimaced.

"TheyGotTheSameOrgans?" Pete asked.

Gaston snorted disparagingly, but awarded Pete an indulgent smile. "Aye, they are much the same as men in all respects save their sex, and that is the part I know little of. For instance, I do not know if they have muscles within their sex to keep themselves closed, such as a man's anus possesses."

Theodore colored a little at this, and Striker grimaced in thought.

I sighed. "They have muscles in their sex. A woman can close up around a man if she chooses, not like an arse can, but similarly. Whether it could keep water from entering her, I do not know."

"Truly?" Striker asked with interest. "Is it a thing they just do, or must they learn it?"

"I feel all of them have the ability, but the skill of pleasing a man with it is rather a thing they must be taught." Then I realized we discussed my sister. "So there is a bathing room, what other wonders does this house possess?"

Striker frowned at the change of topic, but Pete chuckled and Theodore appeared relieved. Gaston was frowning much as Striker was, but I thought his furrowed brow was on the matter of women and their sex and not specifically his sexual fulfillment, or my sister.

"It is a dwelling like no other in Port Royal, of that you can be assured," Theodore said.

"Aye," Striker said with a shrug. "It's much like Doucette's house on Tortuga. The whole of it's like a big horseshoe, with a courtyard in the center. The rooms downstairs all open into the yard. The sleeping rooms upstairs all open onto a balcony that looks down upon the yard. There are lots of windows upstairs for the breeze. Downstairs we kept the outer windows small. More secure that way. I didn't want windows a man could feel he could just climb in opening onto the alley or the street."

"That is wonderful," I said as I pictured it. "Was there much problem with the construction? I imagine the carpenters and brick masons were unfamiliar with the design."

Theodore snorted and sighed. "Oh aye, but your sister was quite stubborn on the matter, and when they found that Striker supported her on it and that she was willing to pay a little extra, it was built readily enough. She has established quite the name for herself, though. Mistress Theodore says she is talked about nearly as much as your wife."

I shrugged, and was pleased to see Striker express the same nonchalance on the matter.

"Rucker will be the first to tell you that meek women are recorded in the annals of history even less than meek men," I said.

"That is all very fine if one wishes to be remarked on in the pages of history," Theodore said with a smile.

"Having one's deeds recounted is the mark of a great man," I teased.

"Aye," Striker intoned. "Or the mark of a great pissing idiot."

I laughed. "Aye, men remember the great and the stupid with equal alacrity. Average men are the only ones spared."

"Well, pardon me for striving to be an average man," Theodore said.

"Well," I said. "Since many men strive to be great and fail, and then are renowned as fools, you are probably noteworthy for not engaging in the quest at all. I, for one, will say that I feel you have failed in the endeavor, though. I feel you are a great man."

"As long as you keep your opinion quiet, I will still succeed,"

Theodore said with a smile. "Because Lord knows, men take heed at your utterances."

"I wonder who that makes the fool of," I said.

My mood dimmed as I thought of all the times I had heard of other men thinking me a fool: most notably Cork, the man who led us to Porto Bello to rescue his matelot. He had thought me a lucky fool who accomplished what no one else could because I did not know I should not attempt it.

"You are not a fool," Gaston said quietly in French.

I looked up with surprise that my shift in emotion had been so transparent. I found our friends were still amused by the string of jests, only my matelot had seen enough to gaze at me with concern and regard. I was heartened in that. It meant that he was no longer suffering such from his madness that he could not pay heed to his surroundings; and that only he, who knew me so very well, could see through the mask I wished to show the world.

I went to sit beside him as Striker told a tale of some great pissing idiot he had known. I did not ask Gaston how he was: his kiss upon my cheek and the regard in his eyes spoke more than words. So I took his hand and we sat and listened to stories and the water beneath the hull and the mewling of puppies.

When we at last came in sight of Port Royal on the evening of the third day, Striker remarked how good it was to be home. I looked at the orderly rows of buildings crammed together on the cay at the end of the peninsula and tried to recall how it had appeared when first I arrived here two and a half years ago. There had surely been fewer buildings. I remembered standing on the deck of the *King's Hope* with Dickey, Harry, Tom, and Belfry, and wondering about this new town I was to call home. But I had never called it home. Thinking on it, and counting on my fingers, I judged that in all the months I spent in the West Indies, and on Jamaica herself, I had spent far less than a month of days in Port Royal. They had been days filled with turmoil and momentous decisions and actions, to be sure; but still, only about twenty days. I wondered how long I would be in the damn place this time. And once again, the stage was set for all manner of drama. All things considered, I doubted I would ever be willing to live in Port Royal: despite it being the place I met Gaston, most of my memories of the place were poor. It represented civilization and my father, things I wished to avoid.

There were no ships anchored about the cays and passage into the bay, but a number of masts could be seen near and beyond Port Royal's proper wharfs on the north side of town.

"What ship did the Marquis arrive on?" I asked as we entered the passage.

"A proper French merchantman, two hundred tons, sixteen guns. She's anchored yonder," Striker said, and gestured toward the bay. "The merchants were happy to see her, though she sold most of her cargo on Tortuga. When she leaves she'll be full of goods."

"So they stopped at Tortuga first?" I queried Theodore. "Did they make mention of Doucette?"

He shook his head and frowned, as if Striker's information were new to him.

I wondered if the Marquis had seen Doucette, or what was left of him. After corresponding with the man for ten years and sending him money for his son's upkeep, I thought it likely Gaston's father would want to meet him. And even if he had not spoken to Doucette, it was likely he had inquired as to what occurred to change the arrangement.

I glanced at Gaston: he was napping next to Bella, with the puppies between them. I thought I should wake him so he could prepare himself before we landed, but I also wished to allow him the peaceful bliss of slumber for as long as I could.

I was able to give him little time, though, as the winds were brisk and Striker soon had us maneuvering around two buccaneer sloops in the Chocolata Hole: the small shallow bay tucked into the western edge of the cay. It was crowded with men, with several small vessels upon the wide beach, canoes darting here and there, and clumps of buccaneers haggling with merchants or simply sitting about passing bottles. Men with whom we had sailed before called out greeting, and Striker was teased by one of the sloop's captains about missing his ship.

I shook Gaston gently as we approached the beach, leaving Pete to admonish Striker about not running us up onto it until the puppies could be situated so as not to alarm Bella when our craft listed.

"We have arrived," I whispered.

Gaston's face, initially happy to greet me, fell, and he took a long steadying breath.

"You have puppies to tend," I added.

He awarded me a knowing smile; and I kissed his cheek.

"It is good we brought the dogs," he whispered.

"Oui, oui, else I would have had to wound myself to see you so distracted," I said.

He grinned. "Though I would appreciate the sentiment, I would be quite vexed with you. You have a propensity for harming yourself as it is."

"Well, I will view it only as an option of last resort," I said with mock somberness.

Pete, in a moment of wisdom or charity, agreed to allow Gaston to carry the precious puppies, and they took great care in arranging them in the sling under Bella's anxious gaze. Only when they were secure did we push the boat ashore. While Pete and Striker secured our craft, Theodore and I gathered weapons and bags, and Gaston reassured Bella with calm words and kept Taro from running off to sniff this or that. Soon we had apportioned the weapons and baggage and begun to wend our way through the buccaneers, merchants, carts, and piles of cargo on our way to Lime Street.

A man stepped in front of us as we neared the street. He was stout, with wide shoulders and burly arms, and it was muscle and not fat that prevented his tight coat from closing. I studied his square face and small eyes and decided I had not met him before. Then I noticed he was eyeing Gaston intently.

"Excuse me," I said, and dropped my hand to the pommel of a pistol.

The stout man had no interest in me. "He is the one," he said in French. Then he addressed Gaston. "Gabriel, you are to come with us."

Pete hit the stout man with an uppercut that rocked the man back on his heels. Time seemed to still for a moment as we waited for the man to fall back. He did not. With a great defiance of the hold the Earth should have had upon him, he stayed upright and snapped forward, head lowered to glower up at Pete.

"YaNa'BeSpeakinTa'ImThatWay," Pete growled.

Though I was sure the language was lost upon the stout man, even if he had understood Pete's pronunciation, Pete's intent was not.

"Get them!" the stout man roared in French and lunged at Pete.

I sensed movement around us. It was too late for the stout man, though; I had already pulled my piece and fired.

My left hand was holding Gaston's medicine chest. My matelot's right hand was likewise occupied, and his left arm cradled the sling with the puppies across his chest. In the precious first moments of the battle, we essentially only had one free arm between us – thankfully it was my right. I pulled a second pistol. A man clutched at me, attempting to prevent me from bringing the pistol up. I saw something other than sand at the end of the barrel. I pulled the trigger. The man yowled and fell away. I pivoted so the chest and Gaston were behind me, and drew my rapier, but by then, it was over.

We stood in a circle of cursing, or quite still, prone men. Around that, there was a great circle of buccaneers with weapons aimed at the men on the ground. There was still a cacophony, much of which seemed to be the growling of dogs and Pete yelling at them.

I made a more careful perusal. Gaston was well, though he had no weapon drawn. He still held only the puppies and the medicine chest. He awarded me a taut smile. I grinned in return. Striker and Pete had thankfully not been laden with a medicine chest, or puppies. They had accounted for four of our seven assailants. Not all of those men appeared to be dead. I had shot two: the stout man was dead, and the other, the one who had clutched at my arm, was rolling about and yowling with blood gushing from his right thigh. Bella and her mate had seen to the seventh, and it appeared Pete's intervention was the only reason that bleeding man was yet able to crawl slowly backwards toward the legs of the men with pistols pointed at him.

"These Frenchies been standin' about lookin' fur someone fur near a week now," a man was telling Striker. "We been wunderin' what they be about."

I did not see Theodore. Gaston swore and began to set the chest down. I followed his lead and turned enough to see Theodore collapsed on the sand behind us.

Gaston quickly had his fingers at Theodore's throat, and then relieved at what he found there, felt down our friend's body, searching for injury. My heart pounded painfully as I dropped to kneel beside him. I sighed with relief when my matelot did.

"He has fainted," Gaston said quietly.

I chuckled.

Above me, Striker was swearing. "Jesus! How bad is he?"

I waved him off. "He is..." I thought it would be difficult for men to ever forget Theodore swooned. "He must have taken a clout on the head. He is not wounded, though."

Gaston and I pulled Theodore upright to lean against the chest as Striker and the others discussed what to do with our surviving assailants. There were apparently members of the militia present, and it was decided that the men should be taken to the gaol until the matter could be sorted through. I heard Gaston's name mentioned once. I thought it likely we had a long day of explanations ahead of us. I hoped I could spare Gaston most, if not all, of it.

Theodore came around quickly when Gaston put salts under his nose. He sputtered for a moment and patted his body with alarm.

"You are well," I said lightly.

Gaston gave me an admonishing look to say that he would be the judge of that.

"Do you feel well?" he asked Theodore. "Is there pain?"

"Only my pride I feel," Theodore whispered. "Did I... swoon?"

We nodded.

"I told all you took a blow to the head," I said kindly.

He appeared greatly relieved. "Are we...? Are they...?" He looked about.

"Dead or wounded," I assured him. "We are all well. The survivors are being taken to the gaol. I would imagine the dead will be too."

Gaston was frowning at the man I had shot in the leg.

Behind me, one of the wounded was protesting in French as men hauled him to his feet. "But he is French."

"We know ya be French!" one of the men holding him upright yelled in English.

I stood. "Nay, he is saying that my matelot is French, which is wrong. He is an English citizen now."

The men from the militia, not all of whom were buccaneers, turned to regard me.

"Is that Lord Marsdale?" their leader asked Striker, who nodded and shrugged.

"Would you know what this is about, my Lord?" the man asked me.

I sighed. "Aye, I feel I do, but I do not wish to discuss it here."

There was a great deal of grumbling in the crowd around us.

I addressed them. "It concerns my matelot, who is an English citizen now."

This seemed to assuage many of them, but others seemed more

hostile than curious. I suffered an odd moment of disorientation, as if I had seen all this before. I had. Though the facts were different, the gist of it all was much the same. Then I suffered the realization that it would always be thus with Gaston and me in relation to the rest of humanity. We would always be subjected to scrutiny, and judged wanting.

I turned away from them.

The puppies were now in Theodore's lap. He was cradling them carefully with Bella and Taro standing guard – over or of him, I could not be sure.

Gaston was digging about in his medicine chest. He found what he wished and went to the man with the leg wound, before the buccaneers who were taking him to the gaol could roll him onto a sheet of sailcloth to carry him.

"Hold him still," Gaston told two of the men.

One of them was a man we had sailed with, and he quickly complied and the other one followed his lead. While they pinned the wounded man down, Gaston shoved his fingers into the man's wound. He probed about inside the man's leg with great concentration, his lips between his teeth and his eyes on some distant thing so his vision did not distract from what he sought to feel. The man screamed and all other activity about us stopped.

"He be a surgeon," a buccaneer to my left told someone.

Gaston at last found what he sought, and pulled a thick red blood vessel from the hole in the man's thigh. He placed a clamp on it. The pulsing flow of blood from the wound stopped.

"There," Gaston said. "Now he will live long enough for someone to amputate the leg. He might even live beyond that."

As many were still quiet about us, the militia leader had apparently heard him.

"So we should find them a surgeon?" the man asked.

"If you wish them to live," I said.

"I care not," the man said quickly. "Do you want them to live?"

Gaston swore softly in French and studied the sand with angry eyes. I could see his need to act: either to fight or heal. His Horse had had quite enough with being still whilst a barn burnt around it. It now needed to run, either under his hand, or away from it.

"Aye," I said. "We wish them to live."

Gaston looked up at me with bitter amusement. "I will tend them," he muttered in French.

I nodded. I turned to the militia leader. "Gaston is a physician; he will see to them."

The man shrugged.

As it appeared the medicine chest must be moved, I went to help Theodore rise. He was trying to awkwardly position the sling over his shoulder.

"I'llTakeIt," Pete said, and carefully took the puppies from him. He positioned the sling across his shoulder and shushed and cooed the now-mewling and hungry puppies. Then he looked at Striker, Theodore, Gaston, and me. "ITake'EmHome. TellTheWomenWeLive. Y'allGetTaTheGaol. Don'tNeedMeNow."

Striker rolled his eyes. "How do you know that?"

Pete grinned. "AllThatBeLeftBeTheTalkin'." With that he walked off with the dogs at his heels.

I sincerely hoped he was correct, but with so many men about us now, I doubted even the stupidest of men would move against us. Still, I looked about as everything and everyone was gathered up for the move to the gaol.

A tall man at the edge of the crowd caught my gaze. He was watching Gaston with hard and speculative eyes, and disdain etched deep into his sharply-featured visage. I assessed his clothes and arms, and saw he made choices based upon quality and functionality: not only was he not fashionable, he seemed to care little for aesthetics, but his pistols and blade were finely wrought and well-used.

The thin man next to him was quite the opposite. His clothes and mannerisms said "courtier" more clearly than if he had a placard strapped to his chest saying the same. As I watched, he whispered almost continuously in the tall man's ear, in a manner that suggested he was repeating what he heard, or rather, translating.

One of the men carrying Gaston's medicine chest bumped into me accidentally, and I turned my attention back to the last of the chaos around me. Gaston was gazing down at the stout man. I went to stand next to him. I saw I had shot the stout man in the eye.

Gaston gave me a wry smile. "You are amazingly precise when startled."

"Are you implying my shooting lacks precision when I am calm?" I teased.

He snorted. "You are always precise."

"Do you recognize him, or any of them?" I asked.

He shook his head. "This bastard was staring at me as if he recognized me, but I cannot recall him."

"What of that tall man over there?" I gestured surreptitiously to where the disdainful man and the courtier still stood.

Gaston caught the meaning of my low hand movement, and casually glanced about, letting his gaze slowly travel to where I had indicated. He froze and quickly turned back to me.

"Vittese," he hissed.

"The tall stony-faced man with the fop beside him?" I asked.

He nodded tightly.

"Well, then..." I said.

"Will," Gaston said quickly. "He is competent."

I met his gaze and shrugged.

He shook his head with frustration, but I thought it more at his own thoughts and not me. "You are a thousand times better, but... do not think he is as foolish as these were."

"I understand," I said solemnly. "I wish to speak with him, though. Will you stay with me?"

He regarded his blood-stained hands and looked to where the wounded were already disappearing into the crowd on Lime Street. "I should not."

"All right then, is there anything you would have me tell him?" I asked.

He sighed, and a small smile graced his lips. "I am sure you will make him angry. You can tell me of it later."

I smiled and leaned close to whisper. "I am proud of you. You are doing well this day."

He met my gaze with startled eyes and then a rueful smile. "Am I?" He thought on it and nodded to himself before smiling at me. "I am loved."

"Oui," I breathed.

He seemed to have to work up to it with little rocking motions, but he grabbed me and kissed me deeply there on the beach of the Chocolata Hole, in front of dozens of people, and Vittese. He grinned triumphantly when he released me.

"I am loved," I said with a matching grin.

"More than I can ever express," my matelot said happily, and then he left, walking swiftly through the crowd without looking toward his former gaoler.

I did turn to look at Vittese. The man was glowering at Gaston's back.

The courtier had his kerchief over his mouth and amusement all about his eyes. I thought he might be blushing. He reminded me very much of Dickey when first we met.

Vittese moved to follow Gaston, the courtier at his heel.

I stepped into their path. "Vittese!"

The man's hand darted to his sword hilt. I grinned, and dropped one leg back in preparation of drawing. I awarded him a raised eyebrow. He let his hand drop away.

"I am the Viscount of Marsdale," I said in French.

Both the courtier's and his eyes widened, but Vittese's narrowed quickly, whilst the other man's mouth dropped open.

I let my grin widen. "Tell your *master* that we have done him a great favor by removing several imbeciles from his employ, and that we will be delighted to continue to perform this service for him."

Vittese did not reply, but Gaston was correct, I had succeeded in making him very angry.

"And," I continued, "tell him he will meet with me, alone, and I will judge whether or not he shall be granted audience with his son, at a place and time of our choosing."

"That will not be acceptable," Vittese rasped.

"Then your master has sailed very far for nothing."

With that, I left them and went to follow my matelot to the gaol. We would see who the Gods followed this day.

Port Royal

November–December 1668

II

Fifty-Five

Wherein We Return to Homes We Have Not Known

The gaol was a house one of Jamaica's worthy citizens, a Sir Thomas Lynch, had donated to the town. It had been built within the first years of the colony, and sat on the wharfs, and by all rights was prime warehouse property. The place was in the grips of chaos when I arrived, and I had to shoulder my way through the throng of curious onlookers to reach a member of the militia, then argue with him before I was granted entry. I hoped someone had been available to lead Gaston through it. Someone apparently had, as my matelot was inside and working on the man whose leg I had shot. I soon had a great deal of the poor fellow's blood upon me, as Gaston required my aid in performing the amputation. Thankfully, he had drugged the man with sufficient laudanum to keep him not only quiet but unconscious. From the state of intense concentration my matelot was in, I thought it possible I would be drugging him to calm him so that he might sleep before the day was out.

Once the amputation was complete and cauterized, we moved on to the others. The assailant Striker had shot died. One of the men Pete struck had a broken jaw – which I heartily sympathized with. Gaston cleaned and sewed the blade wounds Pete and Striker left in two of the others. Then we turned to the man Bella and Taro had mauled. He would be severely scarred for life. Dogs with heads the size of a man's, and jaws that can break marrow bones, will do that to a man. Both bones in the arm he had thrown up to defend himself were broken and all of the tendons torn. Gaston gave the man laudanum and had a calm discussion with him about whether he wished to keep the hand – which would be little more than a club – or have it removed, which was going to be a likely result of the matter anyway if any sort of putrefaction set in on the wound.

During this discussion, Theodore came to ask if I could join him in the doorway. I looked where he indicated and saw several well-dressed notables there, including our Governor Modyford and Sir Thomas Lynch. With a sigh, I wiped the blood from my hands, whispered to Gaston that I needed to play diplomat, and followed Theodore.

Modyford looked me over with some degree of confusion until at last he recognized me and smiled. "Lord Marsdale? It is you." He bowed. "Well, you do seem to take to the buccaneer life quite well."

I smiled in return. I had only seen the man a handful of times, and always while dressed like a proper English gentleman. "Aye, Governor Modyford. It is a pleasure to see you." I bowed in return. "I am sorry it is under such circumstances."

"Ah," he shrugged, "I was in town anyway. What is this about, my Lord? I understand you were assaulted by the French."

His gaze found its way repeatedly to my neck, and I wiped at the area his eyes seemed drawn to and discovered it as not errant blood that held his attention, but the mark Gaston had given me.

I snorted and shrugged. "I do not believe they intended such bloodshed, but aye."

Modyford pointed at the body of the stout man, which had been laid, uncovered, outside the door, as the room within was crowded. He spoke with amusement. "Was there not some other altercation involving you shooting a man in the eye? An escaped bondsman of yours, was it not?"

I was surprised he remembered, and then I remembered that was another burden of nobility: to be notable whether one was a great man or a great pissing idiot. "Aye, his name was Creek, and I still view the matter as unfortunate."

"Aye, bondsmen are expensive to replace," Modyford said with a shrug.

I suppressed a sigh. "Creek was a drunkard who had fallen in with some very foolish fellows. I did not wish to shoot him, but... the situation unfolded much as today's did. When we disembarked at the Chocolata Hole, we were approached by this man." I gestured at the dead man at our feet. "He was eyeing my matelot in a manner I did not like. He informed his fellows, in French, that Gaston was the man they were seeking, and then he rudely addressed him. Our good friend Pete struck the man and admonished him for his rudeness. At which point, the man ordered his fellows to attack us. Though in thinking on it now, I realize they did not draw weapons. I was not aware of that at the time, though, I merely saw that we were set upon. And Pete, Captain Striker, Gaston and myself did as any buccaneer would do in a like situation: we prevailed."

This brought appreciative chuckles from most of my listeners, but I was distracted from gauging their sidelong looks at one another by the eerie sound of my words being repeated in French. Vittese had apparently joined us, courtier at his heel. I looked toward the sound, and froze with surprise such that I doubt I kept it from my features.

Vittese was indeed there, and the courtier, but he was whispering in another man's ear. This man bore a great resemblance to my matelot, though not in coloring or build: as he had blue eyes and did not appear to be red-headed, though I could not be sure beneath his wig, but as he was not powdered, it was evident his eyebrows, and even his long lashes, were golden and not red. He was also slimmer than Gaston, and at first I thought it might be due to frailty of age or illness, as he leaned upon a cane and appeared many years older than my father. But then I saw that my perception of his age was misled by the great many lines upon his face. They were not the deep and trenchant etchings of a man in his dotage, but the fine feathery web about the mouth and eyes a middle-aged man receives for a life spent smiling and frowning, and simply expressing emotion with his face – a thing I think my father did everything in his power to avoid, and not because it would help him cling to the vestiges of youth. Even now this man was smiling, not seemingly maliciously at my surprise, but a fox's grin of perpetual amusement at the world. His smile danced in his eyes, though they were narrowed a little in speculation. I had only rarely seen Gaston with a similar expression, but so many details of their faces, in the little angles formed by muscles and the bones beneath, were the same that I could well imagine my matelot gazing at me as this man did now.

"I must apologize," he said strongly in French, with a fine voice that made me wonder what Gaston's would sound like if it had not been broken.

"These men were in my employ," he continued, the courtier repeating each phrase in proper English. "I gave them poor orders. I did not intend for an altercation to occur."

"And you are?" Modyford asked suspiciously.

"I am the Marquis de Tervent," the man said with a smile toward me.

Modyford glanced at me.

I smiled thinly. "As my matelot's father is the Marquis de Tervent, and this man bears a striking resemblance to my matelot, I would judge him to be who he says."

The Marquis smirked once he heard the translation.

Modyford frowned, but quickly rearranged his features into a genteel smile of diplomacy and bowed. "Greetings, my Lord, I am Governor Modyford, appointed by the King of England to govern this English colony."

The Marquis gave a slight bow and smiled. "As I said, I regret to make your acquaintance under these circumstances."

The governor nodded thoughtfully, and his gaze darted from the Marquis to me and back again to settle on the Marquis. "My Lord, I must ask, what this is about?"

"It should not have been a matter of your concern, Governor,"

Vittese stepped forward to say in French, earning him a short-lived glare of annoyance from the Marquis. "The matter involved a French citizen, and my Lord Tervent takes needless blame in the matter. I am the one responsible for the poorly given orders. We did not understand that the man we sought would be in the company of others."

"But..." Modyford began, while eyeing Theodore and me.

"The man you sought," Theodore said briskly, "is now an English citizen. Governor Modyford signed the petition himself."

This surprised both Vittese and the Marquis.

"We received notification from the Marquis that he was here and wished to meet with his son," I said smoothly. "Mister Theodore delivered it to us. We came, but before we could arrange any sort of meeting, or for that matter, even deposit our baggage in our house, we were accosted on the street."

Vittese took umbrage at that, but the Marquis seemed to feel guilt – and his glare at Vittese showed who he blamed for it.

"I am sorry," the Marquis said, to me, in French, and waved off the courtier's translation. The fox's grin was gone. "That was not my intent. The last thing I wished to do was cause more harm."

I bit back many words, not only because to my amazement I judged him sincere, but also because we were still surrounded by others who had no business in the matter.

"We must speak," I said in French.

He nodded resolutely.

I turned to the governor. "I need to speak with the Marquis in private. Is there anything else you need from either of us?"

"My Lord," Lynch said from beside the governor. "Do you wish for these men to be charged with a crime?"

"Nay," I said quickly, and then paused to think. "I feel they have paid for their hubris and indiscretion far more than they deserve. I would see nothing more come to them."

"Very good, my Lord," Lynch said. He turned to address the Marquis. "Then, my Lord, if you would be so kind as to arrange to have men from your ship remove these men from my gaol. Your son has already been kind enough to tend to their wounds."

This surprised the Marquis, but he gestured at Vittese. "My man will see to it." Then he looked to me.

"Your son is a fine physician and surgeon," I said. "Doucette trained him."

The Marquis nodded thoughtfully. "Shall we speak then?" He looked to Modyford and the others. "If you gentlemen will excuse us."

They nodded, and I nodded, and the Marquis and I began to stroll down the side of the building toward the wharf, with Vittese and the courtier.

I stopped. "As you already know, you will not need him." I pointed at the courtier and nodded politely. "And I will not countenance his being present." I looked at Vittese.

As expected, Vittese was not pleased, but he kept his eyes on the horizon and did not comment. I found it interesting he did not look at his lord for instruction, either.

The Marquis sighed. "Vittese, you have…" He licked his lips and considered his words and me with narrowed eyes before smiling again. "Go and get those men back on the ship."

"Non," I said quickly, and all eyes were immediately on me. "I will not have him near Gaston."

"You need not fear another attempted abduction," the Marquis said amiably.

"I do not," I said. "But I do fear another incident of violence. They hate one another."

"Lord Marsdale," Vittese said tightly. "Please do not presume to know how I feel. And I will not harm him."

"You sent men to collect him from the street like a wayward dog," I snapped. "I do not call that respect or fondness. And you will not harm him because I sincerely doubt you are capable of it. Non, I am concerned that you will provoke him such that he will harm you. And I care not if he tears you to pieces, I simply do not wish to have to explain the matter to the governor."

The Marquis was chuckling. He grabbed the front of Vittese's coat and looked the man in the eye, and then all amusement vanished from him and his voice held the command of a wolf. "Go to the ship and tell Deloise to send his man around to collect them. You have done enough this day."

Vittese winced at the rebuke, but he said nothing to defend himself. He nodded and left us smartly.

With a final nod and a "Good day, my Lord," to both of us, the courtier followed.

The Marquis cleared his throat and fidgeted with his cane, whilst a parade of emotions marched across his features. It was as if he displayed every thought he had, but none remained long enough for anyone witnessing them to know which would stay and govern what he did. The fox's smile at last returned, though, and stayed. I realized it was a mask. I knew I must watch him carefully if I wished to truly see anything of merit revealed.

"Gaston…" he said at last with a bemused little smile. "However did he gain that name?"

I shrugged. "He was ever quiet among the men he hunted with on the Haiti. They awarded it to him as a jest. He is now known as Gaston Sable. Amongst the Brethren he is known as Gaston the Ghoul."

"The Ghoul?" He seemed amused by this. "Because he is a surgeon?"

"Non, because in the aftermath of battles he would arrange bodies to honor them." It was not a thing I expected him to understand, nor one I wished to explain. And I knew I should not have said it, but my Horse was battling me for my tongue. Gaston felt his father had sent him away as a child because Gaston and his sister had arranged their mother's body to mimic a painting of the Madonna and Child after their mother died in childbirth.

The Marquis was frowning, but even that basic expression was tinged with a flow of regret, guilt, and anger.

He quickly collected himself, the grin returned, and he changed his tack. "In his letter, he mentioned you. He implied that you were... lovers." His eyes narrowed as he gauged my response.

I sighed. "We are not *merely* lovers. We are matelots, which among the Brethren is akin to marriage. We are partners in all things."

"I had not known he favored men..." he said with a moue and a sideways nod of his head, rather like a shrug, as if it were no matter to him, merely a thing to be noted. It was disingenuous, though.

"He does not favor men in general," I said coldly. "But he favors me in specific a great deal."

He seemed relieved: I could see some of the tension leave his grip on the cane and the set of his shoulders. "And why is that?" he asked with genuine curiosity.

I decided not to lie. I did not wish to give this man anything, but I wished for him to know the truth.

"Because I love him despite... everything," I said. "Because he has lived a life devoid of love."

It was true, but I found it caused my stomach to roil, as if I had just overturned a stone and discovered a dead thing beneath it. I wondered at that, but I could spare it no more than a glance. The truth in it had hurt the Marquis, and I pushed the unsettled feeling away with my satisfaction that I had scored some point upon him. Then I thought that foolishness: if he was truly hurt by my words and what they implied, maybe he was not as worthy of my hate as I wished him to be.

He turned away and gazed with feigned interest at the ship being unloaded on the nearest wharf. "Is he angry over today's incident?" he asked at last, turning back to me nonchalantly.

I gasped with incredulity as the anger bit deep. Damn my attempts to view this meeting without prejudice. Damn my attempts to award him the benefit of doubt. My father, his father, they were baffling figures I wished to smite again and again until I could break through their armor, their masks of social propriety, their wolfish miens that smiled only to bare their teeth. I wished to reveal some truth of their souls, to reveal that they even possessed souls.

"Well," I said with force. "We have not had a chance to truly discuss the matter, as he has been busy tending the wounded, some of whom have lost limbs, which I suppose is better than the fate of those who lost their lives, all because of some poorly given orders and a fundamental lack of respect..." I let that part of it go, lest I charge off in the wrong direction. "I believe *your son* is hurt to be treated so. For you to send your damn man to collect him as you ever did when he had to be moved from one horrid school to another throughout his childhood. He feels you hate him."

He recoiled as if I had struck him, and his mouth moved, forming the start of words he did not voice. Initially there was no anger, only regret and pain, and then the rage flashed deep in his eyes, as he reached for it in defense as most men do when cornered.

"He has ever been the cause of his being treated as he was," he snarled, sounding so very much like Gaston that it was eerie. "Do not lay all blame on Vittese; there were times when I wished to leave the boy wherever he was, but Vittese always volunteered to fetch him. And it was Vittese who suggested the monastery, which was the only damned place *my son* did not harm someone. I paid thousands of pounds to repair property and met with dozens of lords with wounded sons to make amends. And you can thank Vittese for his life. I wanted to beat him to death that night, but Vittese suggested I flog him, and then that I send him far away instead of locking him in an asylum as everyone with any sense said I should!"

It was far more than I expected, but it did not dampen my anger. "Non, I shall not blame Vittese if that is the case, and I will thank him heartily when next I see him. But you have explained a great deal. I thought you were merely some cold-hearted bastard capable of flogging your son near to death in the name of punishment. But non, I will give you credit for your mercy then, and Vittese too. But you are to blame for your loss of money and pride. You are the damn fool who sent a boy with no control over his emotions off to be harassed and provoked by others of his kind that are whelped and nursed on nothing but cruelty. And do not blame him for that night. That was his mad sister's doing. She summoned him home. She drugged him. She seduced him. She asked him to deliver her from pain by ending her life so that she would not suffer the sin of suicide. And I pray God is not so stupid that he did not judge her for it anyway. Then she left him there for your wrath. And then, you bastard, you did not kill him when he wished for death, when he had lost the only person he believed had ever cared for him. You cast him into Hell. But the final jest is on you. He became a man anyway. One who is loved. One who can love."

I could read nothing on his face or in his stance as I wiped the rage-born froth from my lips. He stood still, every thought hidden. I knew I had struck home, and I felt great satisfaction in it.

He turned and hurried away, nearly tripping on coiled ropes and colliding with barrels and crates.

I stood there, panting, the rage coursing through me, my fists clenched such that my nails dug into my palms. I was tempted to chase him down and strike him. I wished to punch him as I had my father.

Then I was moved to spew the bile in my stomach into the dirty waters of the wharf.

"Will?" Theodore queried softly from nearby as I straightened and wiped my mouth.

"That went poorly," I said quietly in English. "I am ever at the mercy of my temper." That was not true, but it was a sentiment he would expect.

My temper had not run away with me; I had let my Horse have the bit. My Horse had wished to run the man down in the name of countless injustices, many of which he had not committed. And my making such an outburst was not a thing common in my life: not until recently, when I had learned I must let my Horse run on occasion too, just as Gaston did. There was a time when I could have exchanged pleasant-sounding jabs with a man I wished to kill all day and into the night in the name of propriety, but those days had passed.

I hoped Gaston would understand, or at least not be terribly disappointed that I had driven the man away before he could say such things himself. But perhaps he would not have said such things; and that made me sadder still, that I had not spoken for him as I should, in that I had not honored his wishes, perhaps. But, it also concerned me that he might not ever say what truly needed to be said to the man. And thus, perhaps the entirety of it had not gone poorly at all. This thought did nothing to assuage my feeling troubled, though.

I followed Theodore back to the gaol. I looked about, truly aware of my surroundings for the first time since the encounter began: I had been so intent upon the Marquis I had not deigned to notice much else. Several men were looking at me from the deck of the ship, but as she was an English vessel, I took heart that they probably did not speak French, and thus were merely curious at the angry exchange and not now in possession of secrets of Gaston's past. The same was true of Theodore and the men from the militia who stood outside the gaol.

There were now a number of Frenchmen inside the gaol who might have understood the angry words, and not the ones we had wounded. These newcomers were busy helping the wounded who could walk to their feet and putting the man who lost his leg on a litter. Gaston was busy speaking with a man in French.

I waited outside until he finished; guilt and anger still roiling about in my belly. At last I was able to go inside and help him with his medicine chest. He appeared much calmer than before, and he immediately sensed my duress.

"What is wrong?" he asked urgently in French as we carried the box outside to where Theodore and Striker were waiting.

"I have met with your father," I whispered with guilt. "My Horse had a great deal to say."

He stopped walking and regarded me with neither amusement nor recrimination across the chest. "Is he dead?"

I gave a short bark of laughter. I supposed that would have been a far worse outcome. "Non, not when last I saw him. I did not strike him, but I hurled a great many words, such that he fled the battlefield. And then I found I was so overwrought I spewed my belly in the bay."

His gaze was sympathetic and filled with love. It made my heart ache and brought tears to my eyes.

"I am sorry," I whispered. "But I cannot unknot him from my father in my heart, or forgive him for how you have been treated."

He leaned across the chest and kissed me gently. "I forgive you. Let us find the puppies and see where we will sleep, and then you can tell me of it," he said calmly, and returned to walking toward our friends.

As Striker led us to the new house, I mused that all the love I felt for Gaston was truly warranted, and that I could do no wrong in defending it.

Theodore parted our company at New Street.

"Please thank Mistress Theodore for her patience and forbearance in doing without you these last days," I told him as we embraced in parting.

He snorted. "That will do little to calm her, but I appreciate the sentiment. And I was glad to be of such service to my friends. And... it is nice to get away on occasion." He grinned and began to leave us, only to pause and turn. "And thank you for the bump on my head."

I chuckled. "Well, it is often a thing that happens when a man is unused to combat. You do not know where to move or stand, thus you get struck by something."

He laughed and left us.

We continued down High Street until we came to York, and then walked down it until I saw a wide two-story building with a balcony that I was sure must be Sarah's: it did not resemble the white-washed frame structures surrounding it.

Striker stopped before the narrow and towering three-story house next to it, though. "This is your... wife's house."

I sighed. I had forgotten about her yet again. "I will pay her a visit on the morrow."

"I thought as much," Striker said with a grin.

I ignored the dwelling place of matters I did not wish to face, and studied Sarah's house as we walked up to the double doors set deep upon a low stoop. The walls were stone for the first floor, and the second floor wood. On the street side, the entire width of the second floor was fronted by a balcony, with tall louvered doors opening onto it from what must have been several rooms. It formed a nice shady overhang before the entranceway.

Striker opened the door, and light spilled out to greet us, making me realize how very late in the day it was.

We entered a tiled foyer with benches that opened into an atrium – or courtyard as Striker called it, though it was not technically one – containing awnings, wooden settees, tables, a pond, and many flower planters. Rooms ringed it on three sides, and the back was open to the cookhouse, stable, and other assorted outbuildings. I gasped with pleasure. She had indeed duplicated what I had described of Doucette's house in Cayonne. The rooms on the second story were even fronted by a balcony that ran all the way about the structure in a horseshoe shape, with stairs in the interior corners. All of the second floor rooms opened onto the balcony with louvered doors.

We were set upon by happy women before I could see much else. Sarah was every bit as large as Pete had described, such that I wondered if she carried more than one babe, but her pale blue eyes glowed with life and in all she looked happy and healthy. Agnes was thin and fidgety as usual, but she embraced Gaston and me with fervor.

Behind them I was happy to see Theodore's slave, Samuel. Though, since he was here, I thought it likely he was now Sarah's and not Theodore's. He smiled and bowed for us.

"What happened?" Sarah asked. "Pete said you were set upon by French fools, and that it has to do with Theodore and his message to you? What is amiss?"

I looked to Gaston and he shrugged.

"Gaston's father, the Marquis de Tervent, is in port," I told them. "He has come all this way to see Gaston. His method of inviting us to that meeting, or rather, Gaston, left a great deal to be desired, though. They apparently thought they could just collect Gaston upon the street and haul him before his father."

She embraced Gaston yet again. "I am sorry for you. Pete said they were rude."

"My father's men were as they have always been toward me," he sighed. "I feel they think me still a child."

"ThemThatWereThereDon'tNoMore," Pete said and handed me a bottle of wine. "SoWeBeMeetin'WithThisLord?"

"We?" I teased him, but I quickly sobered. "I have met with him. I do not know now..."

"Where are the puppies?" Gaston interjected.

Agnes waved for him to follow and led him to the stable.

"You met with him?" Striker asked quietly after Gaston was beyond hearing. "How did he seem?"

"Everything and nothing like I expected," I said and took a long pull of wine. "I do not know what will come of it. I told him many things I wished to say and he did not wish to hear."

"Good," Striker said, and Pete nodded agreement.

Sarah was studying all of us intently. "Does Gaston have a relationship with his father similar to the one we have with ours?"

"Aye and nay," I sighed. I was actually surprised Striker and Pete had not divulged more of what they knew. "Gaston's father exiled him here. He disinherited him due to his madness, and even went so far as to have him declared incompetent to manage his affairs and gave him over to Doucette as his ward."

Pete and Striker exchanged a look, and then they frowned at me.

"I will not tell you why the other occurred," I said.

"What other?" Sarah asked.

I took her shoulders and spoke quietly. "Gaston's father flogged him almost to death before sending him here. It is complicated, and I am not at liberty to speak of why."

"That is horrible," she said sympathetically. "And now you have seen this man. What does he want?"

"According to his letter, to make amends," I sighed, "but we did not speak of that this day."

"So what will...?" she began to ask.

I cut her off with a shake of my head. "No more tonight. I wish to see the rest of this fine house you have built. I am very pleased with what I have seen so far."

She smiled and looked about happily. "Thank you, and I have been waiting most anxiously for you to see it." She turned to me and sobered. "But there are other matters we should discuss, though I doubt you will wish to do so tonight."

"I know, I know," I sighed. "Was there word from our father before the storm season?"

She shrugged and then shook her head. "Aye and nay. Mister Theodore received a letter, which he shared with me, bless his heart, but it was very succinct and spoke little of me or you other than to inquire of Lady Marsdale, and I think that was primarily a bid to have Mister Theodore corroborate her continued existence and the marriage. He also sent a letter to Uncle Cedric, but it said nothing of import, or so our Uncle says."

"He would not let you read it?" I asked.

"Nay," she sighed and moved to sit. "And there was no missive for you or me."

"I hate them," I said.

"Who?" Striker asked as he sat next to his wife and put an arm about her shoulders.

"Fathers," I said.

"Aye," Pete said.

Sarah smiled with bemusement. "We would not exist without them."

"I was fond of mine," Striker said. "I wish I had known him when I was older, but from what I saw of him as a boy, and what my uncle and others said of him, he seemed a good sort, and he left me his name and what he could. Yours is a right bastard, though, and Pete's, whoever the devil he was, and Gaston's too."

"Poor fathers then, I hate poor fathers," I said.

"We shall not be poor fathers," Striker said with a grin at Pete as he placed his hand on Sarah's belly.

"Nay. WeBeRightGood," Pete agreed.

Sarah smiled at both of them with love, her hand moving to cover Striker's; and then the baby kicked, much to their amusement, and they cooed in harmony. It curdled what little bile remained in my stomach and I felt the winds of melancholy sweeping toward me. I would not be a good father, not to the babe that would soon be born with my name upon it, and that was only if I chose to claim the bastard. I was sure he or she would curse me to Hell and back just as I did my own father, and I felt helpless to do anything about the matter, even though it had not yet occurred.

I could imagine, at the very edges of my fancy, just such a scene with Gaston and I cooing over some impending child, but I could not see any woman beneath my hand: it was as if that part of the image were a hazy clouded thing and I placed my hand on a rounded piece of mist and smiled up at him while sitting next to nothing.

"I need to find Gaston, and our room," I told Sarah.

"It is the one at the end on that side." She indicated the right leg of the house's horseshoe.

"How many rooms are there?" I asked, wondering how much space would separate us from the others.

"There are three chambers along there," she said with a knowing smile. "The two between your room and our Uncle's room in the corner are empty, and he is rarely in residence." She then pointed over her shoulder at the left side of the upper floor. "My chamber is at the end here, and we have a second room next to it, then the nursery, and then Agnes' room in the front right corner. Mister Rucker has the room between Agnes' and Uncle's. Samuel has that room there." She pointed at a door at the end of the lower floor.

"You have built quite the house here, my dear," I said. "Why so many rooms?"

"We plan for a great number of children, and guests," she said with a smile.

"The more children we have, the less guests," Striker said with a grin.

"So in due time you will kick us all out on the street," I teased.

"Where you belong," he said.

I awarded him a rude gesture and went to find Gaston. I located my matelot and Agnes with Bella and the puppies in the stable. Sadly, as the structure had never been occupied by one of my favorite animals, there was no comforting horse smell about the place. Bales of straw had been delivered, though, and several of them had been broken open and spread about to form a nest for the dogs. Bella was chewing on a juicy bone, the puppies were nursing, and Gaston and Agnes were reclined in the straw on either side of the nest, speaking of telescopes and lenses and things seen both big and small. I shed my weapons and joined them, lying on my back with my head and shoulders on Gaston's hip, and listened to the contended sucking of puppies and Agnes complaining about the haze and how you could only see the stars tolerably well after a big storm.

All the bile fled my stomach and the winds blew the brooding clouds of melancholy away. I felt more contentment than I ever had upon the cay of Port Royal.

"Master Will?" Sam called from somewhere outside the stable.

Gaston and I sighed heavily and Agnes chuckled at us.

"In the stable," I called.

Sam's dark face appeared in the doorway. "Master Will, there be a gentleman ta see you and Master Gaston. He doesn't speak English. I put him in the sittin' room. And dinner be served. You want I should give the man some rum and let you eat?"

"Did he give a name?" I asked.

"With him not speaking English I don't know what he said, Master Will. I'm sorry. I heard your names." He frowned. "He's dressed nice, and he has a wig, and a cane."

Gaston was as tense as I, and I gave him a questioning look. He nodded tightly.

"We will see him before we dine," I told Sam. "Wait, is he alone?"

Sam nodded.

I donned my sword belt and shoved a pistol into it. Gaston considered his weapons where they lay heaped near the stable door. He at last shook his head and squared his shoulders.

"There will be nothing that you cannot defend us from," he whispered quietly in French.

As we crossed the atrium, Pete and Striker watched us from a doorway on the lower level. I waved them off. The entry foyer was now blocked from view by a latticed gate. Sam led us to a door to the right of it. I thanked him, and told him we hoped to be along shortly for dinner, and then I turned to Gaston. He was regarding his clothes – our usual attire of dark kerchief, tunic, and breeches, and nothing else – with dismay.

"We are as we are," I whispered kindly. "You are as you are. You are loved."

He met my gaze with a grateful nod and took a deep breath. "I am calm," he whispered. "See if it is him."

I kissed his cheek and opened the door. The room was a sitting room with settees and a table. There was another entry from the foyer, and that door was closed. The chamber's sole occupant was the Marquis de Tervent. He met my gaze levelly, no fox's smile. I could read nothing but resignation in the lines and shadows of his face in the lantern light.

I looked over my shoulder at Gaston and nodded. He radiated nothing but fear, but it was not the Child's fear, or the Horse's. I stepped inside the room and he followed me.

They regarded one another with trepidation, not like men prepared to fight, but ones dangling on the precipice of fleeing.

And then the emotions flowed across the Marquis' face and he opened his mouth to speak several times. "You have grown," he floundered at last. "You are a man... now. You do not look... You do not look like her anymore." He tilted his head and gave a self-deprecating snort. "There is a resemblance, to be sure, but... My God, you are..."

The sudden burst of energy seemed to leave him and he sagged onto a settee. "May we sit? I feel I must sit."

Gaston nodded mutely and cautiously lowered himself onto the front edge of a chair. I remained standing near the door, which I closed.

"What... Why do you need a cane?" Gaston asked with a shadow of his physician's mien. It was enough to compose his face, though, and not leave him looking so lost and fearful.

The Marquis nodded appreciatively at that raft of a topic, and swam to it. "I fell from a horse... five... was it five... about five years ago. I broke my hip. It healed well enough, I suppose, though it aches in the cold. It does not ache here." He smiled awkwardly and quickly abandoned it. "Though I can walk, it gives way on occasion. I cannot rely on it."

Gaston nodded. "So you are not ill."

"Non, non, not in body." The Marquis grimaced at that, and his eyes darted to the upper corner of the room as if he consulted the Gods. "In spirit, I ail," he told Gaston sincerely. "And that is why I am here." He glanced at me and gave a small sigh of resignation.

"Will stays," Gaston said.

"I realize that," the Marquis said with another glance at me: this one apologetic.

He sat the cane aside, and his hands, now free of that duty, moved in as mobile a fashion as his face.

"I have imagined this meeting so many times… and now here I am and I do not know…" He sighed and smiled at Gaston. The expression quickly left and wonder and sadness took hold of his face.

"I loved your mother," he said at last. "Beyond all reason. I defied my father to marry her. I ignored the warnings from her family, and the nuns and… Her family kept her at a convent. They thought her possessed. There was a war and the convent she lived in was due to be overrun and the nuns were moved and many stayed on our estate and I saw her. I was sixteen and she was an angel. She was so beautiful. She had the hair of a devil, yet she seemed to float in the grace of God. She… The Mother Superior told me she was not always so. That she was possessed and that they had twice tried exorcism to no avail."

He shook his head angrily and his gaze, which had retreated from the room to look upon his memories, came back to Gaston. "You do not believe your madness is a thing of the Devil, do you? God forbid you have been burdened with that foolishness."

"Non," Gaston said with wonder and surprise. "It is an ailment of the mind."

The Marquis was relieved. He settled back a little in his seat and considered his memories again, though his tone was still angry. "Your mother always believed that. That is what they told her. I could not… I thought I was rescuing her, and I suppose I was. There were no more exorcisms, and I never allowed some more enlightened fool, like that damn Doucette," he spat, "to attempt to cure her. I gave her the best life I could. But… I could never free her from the things she was taught as a child. She thought the Devil rode her soul. She thought…" He gazed at Gaston guiltily. "She thought all things carnal were the work of the Devil and that… children, her children, you and your sister, were things of evil. We had to keep her away from you. She once tried to strangle… you." He looked away, his eyes welling with tears.

Gaston took a long shuddering breath. His gaze was now on the floor and his hands gripped the chair arms tightly. I laid a reassuring hand on his shoulder.

"She could be so... loving... and... passionate," the Marquis said quietly to the carpet between his feet. "And then she would despise herself for it so the morning after. I had to... She once stabbed me." He shrugged. "Well, she tried several times, but she succeeded the morning after she discovered she was pregnant the second time. She was intent on gelding me so that it would not happen again. We had to keep her restrained for a week because we thought she might harm herself.

"I could not help her; by God I tried. There were days when she was... sane, or appeared so. She would be like any other. I lived for those days."

His words had been winding their way deep into my soul, and the last ones bit deep, such that I was compelled to give a gasping sob from the pain and surprise of it. Gaston looked up at me with guilty tear-filled eyes. "Non, non," I gasped anew, and dropped to kneel beside him and take his face in my hands. "You are not that bad," I whispered.

"I am sorry," the Marquis said, his voice as thick as mine. "I do not say this to hurt you, either of you."

I looked to him, our eyes met, and something passed between us, some deep knowing, a kinship of the soul. He nodded solemnly in recognition of it, as did I. Few walked where either of us had, and despite everything I could despise this man for, I found comfort that he was like me, because it meant I was not alone on this path.

I turned back to Gaston and found him pulling my hands away to regard his father. "Please," he whispered, his voice so low I was not sure if the Marquis could hear him. "I need to hear these things. I have wondered for so very long... about them. Please continue."

The Marquis nodded and looked away to wipe tears from his eyes. "I am sorry. I have..." He sighed and turned back to Gaston. "When she died I was angry... no, furious, beyond reason... with God, and myself. I blamed us for destroying her. I railed against the unfairness of it all. And... By the time she died it was obvious you and your sister were her children in every way." He shook his head with a sad and bitter smile. Though he cried openly now, his words were angry. "I could not bear the sight of you. I hated you. There were moments when I felt that perhaps all her mad superstitious fears were true and somehow the Devil had gripped her soul and delivered her with two of His get. So I sent you away. I would have sent your sister away as well, but... she was sickly. And I would not let the damn nuns have another child.

"I am sorry for that." He slid off the settee to kneel before it. "I beg your forgiveness. I wronged you. And now I have heard from your man that I wronged you worst of all... that night. I had not realized your sister was so like her... I had not..."

"Will!" Gaston gasped and collapsed on the floor, his hand held out in warding against his father, his other arm hugging his belly as if he were being disemboweled.

I pulled him to me and gave his father a warning shake of my head. The Marquis nodded and remained silent, slumping back against the settee to drown in his own tears.

I pulled Gaston's face up so that I could see his eyes: they were desperate and sad.

"I am falling," he hissed.

"I have you. I have the cart. Puppies?" I asked hopefully.

He nodded pitifully. "I cannot lose him... but..."

"I understand, trust me."

He nodded with more assurance.

I kissed his forehead and helped him stand and make his way out the door, praying none of our well-minded friends came between him and his objective. I need not have worried: once out of the room, he ran across the atrium to the stable.

I turned back to the Marquis and closed the door. He was still on the floor, sunk in on himself, and looked to be in as much need of comfort as my matelot, but I could not bring myself to go to him. Despite his contrition and my kinship with him, he was still a monster in our midst. I cast about and spied the sideboard and a bottle of something corked. There were glasses, and I poured us each a draught of what turned out to be rum. I drank mine quickly, savoring the burn, and then gingerly approached him to offer the other glass.

"It is rum," I said, as I tapped his shoulder. "Drink it slow or fast."

He chose fast, and grimaced at the taste, but it seemed to help him regain his composure. He pulled himself back up to sit on the settee and proffered his glass to be filled.

I sat on the closest chair and poured again for us. We drank the second round just as we had done the first, and regarded each other with our teeth bared in a grimace.

"He is overwhelmed," I said as I wiped my lips with the back of my hand.

"*He* is?" the Marquis asked and smiled wryly.

I gave a short bark of laughter and was not surprised when it was followed by another. The Marquis chuckled in kind. The dim room did not echo the sound of merry men.

"He does not wish for you to leave," I said. "He would know you better. I would... know you better as well. We... are all tangled in the past."

He nodded solemnly. "I have spent too many years tangled in it."

Though there was still some little part of me that did not trust him, I felt we were already laid bare to one another. "Gaston did not remember much of what occurred until... well, until right before the incident occurred with Doucette. He could not bear to remember that night."

The Marquis shook his head sadly. "I could not think of anything else for many years. I thought I had descended into madness. Or perhaps, I realized I had."

"I have had to change my definitions of madness since meeting Gaston. You should know, perhaps, that... I am not as sane as I appear." I sighed. "Not that I may have appeared sane to you this day."

He snorted with amusement and held out his glass again. "You have appeared to be a man who loves my son."

I nodded and filled our glasses again. "Beyond all reason."

He smiled and sipped the rum. "I heard he stabbed you."

"Oui, but it was an accident: I got between Doucette and him. Not that... he has not pulled a blade on me." I sighed. "Or I him."

"Perhaps it is easier that you are both men," he said thoughtfully.

I smiled. "Perhaps, or perhaps it is worse."

His amusement transmuted to guilt. "I have never understood men who loved other men, but I will try and view the matter without prejudice."

"I have hated you every time I see his scars," I said quietly, "but I will try and view you without prejudice."

He winced. "I understand."

The rum had seeped deep into my heart so that it was drowsy in the aftermath of so much emotion. I wanted to speak more with the enigma before me, but not this night.

"Will you remain in port?" I asked.

He nodded. "Until..." He smiled quickly and brightly. "My son and I can converse without tears, perhaps."

I chuckled, but my words were serious. "Give him time. He is... doing well, but this is a great deal for him to swallow in one sitting."

"I know. His mother..." He looked away. "She would not have survived any of the trials I put upon him."

Tired as I was, I could not let that lie. "Was that your intent?"

He shook his head and frowned as if he were mulling over the matter. "Not by any design I was aware of. But... I have questioned the workings of my soul these last years, and occasionally it surprises me with..." He met my gaze, his eyes sincere. "Things I am both ashamed and proud of."

Something rose from the depths of my soul, and I realized it was sadness. I could never speak to my father this way. I once thought we had come close to it, that Christmas morn when he told me he wished for me to go to Jamaica, but even then I had seen the clockworks of his wolfish mind behind his eyes. I saw none of that in the man before me, and I knew it was not because my vision was blurred by tears and rum.

"There is a great deal I would speak to you of," I said.

He was surprised. "There is a great deal more I have to say too, but not tonight, non?"

"Non, not tonight." I spied his cane, and how very dark the night was beyond the narrow, shuttered and barred window. "Did you come alone?"

He nodded and grinned with some satisfaction. "I escaped them."

I grinned in return. "Good for you, but this is a dangerous town at night for a Lord who dresses like one."

He nodded amiably. "So I have heard."

"Do you wish for an escort back to your ship, or... would you choose to remain here? I believe, though I have just come to this house this night, that there are rooms for guests."

He leaned forward and took the bottle from my hand. "I believe I would like to drink more of this rum and then pass into oblivion without laying eyes on another soul. I would be content to sleep on this settee."

I smiled. Could the damn man now do nothing that I disliked? "I think we can do better than that, and thus assure that you will not be woken at an early hour, and if all goes well you will only have to suffer the brief attentions of the housekeeper."

He grinned. "If you can arrange that, then I am pleased to be your guest."

I left him sipping rum and went to find Sam. He was surprised, but willing to show the Marquis to one of the guest rooms. I assured him the Marquis probably did not wish to eat, but that a good supply of fresh water should be left for him to find in the morning.

I found Striker, Pete, Sarah, Agnes and Rucker eating in a fine dining hall along the left side of the house. Rucker bounded to his feet at my appearance and rushed to greet me, but upon seeing my face, he paused. The others were frowning at me as well.

"I am well, now. And Gaston will be, in time," I assured them. "I will greet you properly on the morrow, my dear friend," I told Rucker. And then I informed my sister, "We have a guest. I hope you do not mind. I asked Sam to show him to a room."

"He's staying here?" Striker asked incredulously.

"Aye," I sighed. "He seems genuine in his wish to mend things."

"Some things can't be mended, Will," he said.

I walked the length of the table to cuff his head. "We will forgive who we want, when we want," I hissed in his ear.

Sarah and Pete laughed.

Striker appeared recalcitrant, even amused. "Aye, aye. It is your concern."

I took a thick hunk of beef from the platter and left them. I was not hungry, but I knew it would be best if I put something in my belly, and Gaston should too.

I found him curled on his side close to Bella and the puppies. His eyes were open, but he was oblivious to the world. He was not moving to stop Bella from cleaning his face.

I decided he would not eat, and after taking but a mouthful, I split the meat between the Bella and her mate. Then I doffed my weapons and went to lie behind Gaston. As I positioned a pistol within reach above our heads, he spoke.

"You do not like straw." It was the Child's voice.

"I feel it will not call forth any bad memories this night," I murmured as I curled around him.

He settled back against me. "You are loved," he whispered.

"As are you."

I brushed a kiss on his ear and wondered at this new place to which the Gods had led us.

Fifty-Six

Wherein We Face a Trail of Brambles

I woke to gentle fingers on my face tracing the outline of my eyes and mouth and the length of my nose. I heard Bella tending her young and a clatter from the cookhouse, and the world smelled of straw, puppies, bacon, and my matelot – who did not possess the finest odor at the moment, but at least it was familiar and comforting. I was stiff and ached: not in my bones, but once again, in the flesh beneath the marks he had left upon me. I stretched slowly and opened my eyes. The stable was cool and dim, but the light streaming through the doorway between the stall and the corner in which we lay and was disconcertingly bright, and I wondered how high the sun had risen and whether there was any water readily available.

Gaston was sitting by my head, with his back to the wall and his knees to his chest. His mien was soft and childlike, but I saw much of the Man in his eyes. I kissed his fingers, and he smiled down at me with such great regard that my aches faded before it.

"Did I dream... him?" he asked quietly.

"Non," I said with a smile.

"He was here," he stated, but his tone displayed a need for corroboration.

"Oui, he was here; and... to the best of my knowledge – unless he has risen and left this morn – he is still here, sleeping in one of the guest rooms upstairs."

Gaston tensed with alarm and his gaze shot to the open doorway and presumably what he could see of the house.

I stroked his leg reassuringly. "What do you remember? Or do you wish for me to relay what I can recall?"

He released his held breath in a long quiet sigh and spoke as if he did not wish to be heard by any other than me. "Did he truly fall to his knees and beg my forgiveness?"

"Oui."

He pulled his gaze from the door with obvious effort and looked down at me with his teeth worrying his lip. "You judged him sincere?"

I nodded solemnly.

"And my mother was far madder than I." He looked away again.

"Judging from what he said..." I considered my words carefully. "She was either madder than you, or she possessed far less control and they did not know how to... manage... her Horse, and, of course, she was apparently plagued by a misapprehension of the nature of her illness."

He sighed. "What days do you live for?" he asked timorously.

I had been afraid he would remember that. I pushed up to my knees so we were face to face, and locked my gaze with his. "Every day that I am with you, however you might be."

He closed his eyes and pressed his forehead to mine, but a subtle smile curved his lips. "Thank you," he breathed.

"I did... understand him, though," I said.

He nodded, rolling his forehead up and down on mine. "Did you speak after I left?"

"Oui, and shared some rum." I tried to recall what was said. All I could immediately remember was gazing into those blue eyes in the dim lantern light and seeing a reflection of myself.

I pushed the image away and recalled what I could. "I told him you were overwhelmed, but that we wished to know more of him. He said there was more he wished to say. We spoke of all of us being tangled in the past, and I told him you had not been able to remember that night for many years. He admitted to feeling as if he had become mad himself that night."

"He was," Gaston said distantly.

I was thankful for the interruption, as I was reluctant to mention his father's issues with sodomites.

"I drove him mad," Gaston added sadly. "He said he hated me, did he not?"

"Oui," I sighed, "but that was due to..."

He put his finger on my lips. "I know. He does not feel it now. He did then, though." He pulled his head back enough to gaze into my eyes. "Why do you feel he is here now? To mend things between us, oui; but why now?"

"I would imagine it is because you wrote him, in part; but also because he wishes to make peace with God and his soul perhaps. Older men sometimes..."

Gaston's eyes hardened with sudden ire as his Horse raised its head. "That belittles me," he hissed.

I did not recoil from the sudden change. "How so?" I asked.

"He should be here to make amends with me, not God," he growled, and stood to step around me and out of the stable.

Equally amused and bemused, I stood and followed him. I caught up with him as he entered the latrine at the back of the property. I ignored his scowl and joined him in the shed above a surprisingly large wooden cover. My sister must have decided she did not wish to have a new one dug anytime soon. Judging from the depth our piss fell, I thought she had bought herself many fine years with this pit. And she had hidden it all behind a great mass of flower trellises. Their heady blooms did not completely diminish the stench, but they did keep it from drifting toward the house. I decided that we must remember to empty the chamber pot out here, and not simply dump it out the window.

"Looks as if they dug a well," I noted as we stepped out. "And it sounds like they found water."

"Dig a hole on any cay and you will quickly find the sea," Gaston said irritably.

"I cannot speak for your father's reasons," I said amiably as we started to walk back to the house.

He sighed and turned to regard me. "I do not know what I want. I have dreamed of his apologizing to me for years: for all my life. And now..." He shook his head. "It does not make it all go away. It does not take the scars off my hide. Or my heart," he added sadly.

"Can you take any comfort in the reasons he gave: in that it was not you who caused it, but situations concerning your mother?" I asked gently.

He nodded slowly. "Oui, but that... just gives me more I must think on and wonder at."

I was interrupted from asking of those thoughts by Sam stepping into our path from the doorway to the cookhouse. "Masters, will you be eating? I made bacon and eggs."

"And water?" I queried as we nodded agreeably to the mention of food.

"Aye, Master, always boiled water for you, and tay," he said.

"Tay?" I asked.

He frowned. "Leaves from the Orient in water. The Mistresses be fond of it."

"Oh, that," I sighed. "I will take water without leaves."

At this, Agnes stepped into view and handed me an onion bottle. "It's really quite good, the tea, you know." She fidgeted with her long fingers. "Do you want to see my sketches?"

I took a long drink of water and looked at Gaston, whose Horse was still obviously prancing about, and sighed. "Not just yet," I told the girl. "Let us... perform our morning toilette, and eat. Our room is that one there?" Then I remembered a thing that made me smile. "And where is this bathing room?"

Agnes' wide mouth split her face asunder in a smile and she

squealed quietly with glee. "You have not seen it yet. Come! Come!" She scampered around the stable and over to a door on the main floor of the house, below our room.

I very nearly squealed with delight myself at the bathing room. It was as Striker had described it: a great iron tub supported by huge bricks over a stone bed for coals, with a brazier to heat the coals in the corner. Water was delivered to the tub by a pipe protruding through the wall. There was a handle and a weighted trap at the end of the pipe. I went out and looked around the corner of the building, and saw the covered wooden cistern sitting on brick stilts and posts so it stood even with the first floor ceiling. Its water was supplied from the main cistern next to the stable, by an ingenious contraption of small buckets on a cable. That apparatus was apparently driven by a capstan which either a person could push around or a donkey could pull. We had not seen any of it the night before, as the entirety of the works was hidden by a trellis of flowers and the side of the stable.

Gaston, now totally distracted from his earlier ire, was walking about the works and the room. "This is extraordinary," he told Agnes in passing.

"Aye," I added. "Striker told us of it, but the seeing of it is a wonder."

"Mister Rucker said it is somewhat like what the Romans had," she said with pride. "He has been to Bath, and seen mechanical drawings of similar rooms and devices. Mister Fletcher, the miller, came in from the plantation to design and build it."

Hearing that, I was reminded of Theodore's words about having to pay men extra to have this house built. I thought it likely the cost for Mister Fletcher's services had been paid in the coin of having to listen to Donoughy whine about Fletcher's absence from the plantation and then by having to listen to Fletcher's complain about a bathing room being an odd and unseemly thing to build. Yet, he was proud of his engineering marvels at the plantation, and so perhaps he had viewed this project as one of curiosity and worthy of his efforts and ingenuity.

"How did you find Mister Fletcher?" I asked.

The girl stiffened, and she regarded me as if I had suddenly bit her.

"Was he well?" I asked cautiously. "The last Gaston and I saw of him he was recovering from a fever."

She sighed with relief and shook her head. "He was fine. Thin perhaps, but hale enough, I suppose."

Gaston came to join us: he too had seen her reaction.

"What did you think I meant?" I asked quietly.

Her thin shoulders slumped a little and she looked about to see if anyone listened. "There are many who feel I should marry. Mister Fletcher feels he should marry. I feel I should not. We did not find one another agreeable."

I looked at her skinny figure and recalled Gaston's thoughts as to her future as the mother of our children once I put the Damn Wife out. She still appeared to be a gawky child, but I knew she was old enough to marry.

"You do not have to marry anyone," I told her. "Unless you wish, but do you not still favor women?"

"Aye," she said emphatically. "And I do not wish to marry any man, but..." She began to fidget, her long fingers twining in that mesmerizing manner they had.

"Speak," I said.

"I worry sometimes," she finally said, her eyes on the ground. "You have both been very kind to me. And Sarah says I shall always have a place in this household. But I worry about what will occur if you are not... alive, to... keep things as they are. I think sometimes that perhaps I should marry – as you suggested Christine do – a man who will allow me to have unusual freedoms. But... I am not sure that will solve anything, either, because what will I do if he dies?"

I cursed quietly and she looked up at me with surprise. I shook my head. "I am not angry at you. I am angry at myself for not remembering all those who might suffer in our absence."

"We should not have left you to worry," Gaston said. "You will be cared for."

"Aye," I said. "We will speak to Theodore and make arrangements. For one thing, we will see to it that there are proper papers making you a free woman and negating the bond contract made with your stepfather. And we will provide for you in our wills."

Her eyes were large and teary and she looked from one to the other of us. "Thank you," she whispered.

"And who the Devil, other than Fletcher, feels you should marry?" I asked.

She regarded me with a perplexed frown, as if she could not understand why I was daft, and then her words tumbled out in a frustrated rush. "All the women – with the exception of Sarah who knows my feelings on the matter – feel I should be betrothed at the very least. They say it is not natural for a girl my age not to be entertaining suitors unless I am betrothed. And we have not wished to tell them I am a bondswoman and thus it is your decision. Your Uncle often asks if I am married off yet, and he even suggested such a thing to Mister Donoughy and Mister Fletcher. And even if marriage is not on their minds... Captain Striker has asked if I am... enamored of someone. He is not mean-spirited about it, but every time I go out he teases me about meeting with some young man. And your uncle is ever telling Sarah I should be chaperoned more lest I be ruined. But in truth, I feel I would rather be chaperoned at times when I go about town with all the men eying me: men old enough to be my grandfather." She shuddered. "And I know that has ever been the way of it, but still... The only time I feel safe about the matter is when I am about Pete or the other buccaneers from your ship. There are days when I feel I will have to use this pistol." She pulled the small piece she wore on a lanyard about her neck and shoulder from a slit in her skirt. "Not to shoot a man attempting to attack me, but to shoot one who wishes to marry me honorably, because he will not take *nay* for an answer. I wear baggy dresses to hide myself, but still, I am tall, and they ask of me. Women are so scarce they do not care what my age is or how I appear. I thank God for the dogs, who at least growl at them to drive them away."

Gaston was looking righteously appalled, but I could no longer contain my humor. They glared at my chuckling.

"I am sorry, I am sorry," I said quickly. "But damn it, girl, it is funny. Not that they should pursue you so, but... your rendition of it holds great amusement."

My matelot awarded me another glare before taking her by the shoulders and addressing her earnestly. "Agnes, you are meant for... better things." He cast another look at me over her shoulder that implied he was not sure of the truth of that statement.

I snorted and rolled my eyes, but I told her, "Aye, Agnes, we will not see you marrying some damn fool who could not appreciate your talents. You will be cared for. I say it again; you need never marry if it is not your wish."

She nodded with relief. "You two have been a true blessing upon my life. Thank you." She began to walk away, but stopped and turned.

"We will be delighted to see your sketches after we bathe," I said.

She shook her head. "Did you know Christine is here, in town?"

"Aye," I said with a frown. "Striker made mention of it. He saw her at a ball or someplace. He said she is watched at all times now."

Agnes nodded sadly. "I have not been allowed to see her."

"Truly? Well, that is unfair," I said. "You could not besmirch her virtue..." I regretted my words. "Even if you were to..." I decided I should just shut my mouth.

She colored slightly. "True, but I am considered... troublesome. Her stepmother came here and spoke to Sarah and told her to keep me away."

I swore. "I am sorry."

She shrugged. "I thought perhaps you could see her... As you are married, and thus..." She frowned. "But perhaps not. I just want someone to see her and tell me that she is well. Sarah cannot since she is lying in."

"We will see what we can arrange," I assured her.

She left, and I turned to find Gaston glaring at me.

I raised an eyebrow. "What?"

"Why did you not tell me?" he asked.

"Oh, bloody Hell... I forgot! Striker made mention of it, but we were discussing numerous things, and then Theodore produced your father's letter. I have not thought of Christine since; not before Agnes' mention of her just now."

He massaged his temples. "I am sorry."

"I know." I said softly and rubbed his shoulder. "You have enough to think about; that is why I would not have mentioned her, even if I had remembered her."

"Why?" His question was more curiosity than suspicion.

"Because…" I sighed. "Apparently she was found and returned to her father, who is very likely quite concerned that she will bolt again – and probably with good reason. And her father is married now, and Striker said the stepmother would not let him speak to Christine for any amount of time. I feel sorry for the girl. I had hoped she was happily away somewhere, dressed as a boy and practicing her swordsmanship, but instead she is imprisoned here – not even allowed to see old friends."

"We should help her escape," he said seriously.

"Oui, that I am willing to do. I will not attempt to rescue her by marrying her again, though."

He sighed and smiled wryly. "Non, because your matelot is mad."

I grinned. "Non, because I love my matelot. Now let us see our room and make use of this lovely tub." I went to the stable and retrieved our things.

He did not follow me. When I returned he was standing where I had left him. I handed him his weapons and bag.

"Will you marry Agnes?" he asked quietly.

I shrugged. "If it is your wish, after we decide what to do about the Damn Wife. And I do not know what to do about that."

"You must either have it annulled or get a divorce," he said, not as if I were a fool, but as if he were curious that there could be another outcome.

"And then what do we do with her and the babe?" I asked without rancor. "At this moment, I feel I will be very lucky if she dies giving birth."

"The Gods should make it so easy," he snapped, but his ire was not directed at me.

"Not that I wish that on her or the child," I sighed. "In truth, I find I feel some sympathy for her."

"Go and speak to her. I am sure she will dispel it," he said.

I smirked as I thought of my prior encounters with the woman. "That is true."

He shook his head in apology. "I would not wish it on the child, either."

"I suppose we should see her today."

Gaston was incredulous. "We? That will not please her."

"We need not please her now," I scoffed and walked to the stairs. "And I would have her know I make no decision without you. If she wants to continue to have dealings with me, she will also deal with you."

I heard snoring when I reached the top of the stairs. I was minded that open windows and walls that provide ample access to the breeze also provide ample access to sound. We would not have as much privacy as I desired, though it would be more than we would have while roving. Thankfully, no one here spoke French except for Sarah, and she lived on the other side of the house; so essentially, we could discuss anything we wanted as long as we did not raise our voices.

And then I realized who was snoring in the room we were passing: the Marquis. I stopped, and found Gaston had not been so self-absorbed. He stood at the top of the stairs, regarding the guest room's louvered doors with trepidation. I wished to say something amusing and light, but I knew Gaston would be alarmed if I spoke at all. Instead, I motioned for him to follow. He did with careful quiet steps, as if he were tiptoeing past a sleeping monster. I did not tease him on the matter as we finished walking to our door.

It occurred to me that I have never heard my father snore. For that matter, I had never seen him take a piss. The only things of a bodily nature I had ever witnessed of him were eating, drinking, and smoking.

I opened the wide double doors to our room, and we stood like curious cats in the doorway, letting our eyes wander while our feet remained still. Our room, being on the end of this wing, was a large white-washed square blessed with two windows in addition to the louvered doors that opened onto the balcony. It was dominated by a large, ornately-worked, iron, posted and canopied bed set in the center of the floor. Instead of being hung with curtains to keep the heat in, as it would have been anywhere else in the world, the bed was hung all about with gauzy pieces of netting to keep the insects out. With its white linens and white netting wafting in the breeze from the two windows, it appeared like a cloud captured in a cage of black filigree.

I found amusement in the fact that it had been situated in the middle of the floor and not up against the interior wall; because, of course, that wall was shared with another room. Placing the bed away from a wall would serve to minimize any sound the bed might make when being used for something other than slumber. I wondered who had thought of that: my sister or the wolves.

My trunks from the old house, a tall chest of drawers, two small tables set near the bed, and two chairs completed the furnishings. They were all painted white, except for my trunks, and with the pale wood floor and ceiling, the room reminded me unpleasantly of the white rooms we had occupied at Theodore's and Doucette's. I ever felt dirty and unsuitable in comparison to them.

Gaston regarded it all, seemingly as I did, with a degree of dismay.

"I wish to paint the walls another color," I said. "Or perhaps dye the bed linens."

"Oui," he said tightly. "The netting is an excellent thing, but it is… disturbing."

I sat my things upon a trunk, and conscious of the footprints I left on the scrubbed floor, made my way to the bed. The mattress was of down, and I thought of the joy of sinking into it until I remembered the heat. Why could one not suspend a hammock from such a frame? The mattress was of a fine height, though, being just below my hips. I found more amusement in that as I thrust against it vigorously several times.

It did not squeak. I took hold of a post and shook the canopy. It was all quite solid.

I grinned at Gaston and found him flushing and looking at the floor.

"Do you think of anything but trysting?" he hissed.

"Non," I teased. "And you, truly, what did you think of just now?"

He shook his head with annoyance but at last whispered, "That I could bind you to it," as if the admission pained him greatly.

My cock stirred at the thought and I regarded the bed in a new light. "Oh, oui. It offers many possibilities." Then I looked back at him with concern. "What is wrong?"

He pointed in a commanding fashion, with his entire arm, toward the room with the snoring occupant, and regarded me as if I were daft.

I sighed. I had encountered this before with a young lover I had in Vienna. He had invited me to his family's estate for a fortnight, and I had gone, happy to be free of the city and expecting many lovely nights of trysting. The man's parents had been in residence, though, and he had refused to engage in any activity while sharing a roof with them. And that man had gotten along quite well with his parents.

Once more I bit my tongue to stop the light-hearted things I could say, such as observations about the need to keep me very quiet. We did not know how long his father would be about, and Gaston could not know how his feelings on the matter might progress. There was simply no point in arguing.

"Let us bathe," I said, and began to rummage through our things for a clean pair of breeches and a tunic.

"Do you have anything I can wear?" he asked. "Not like... Proper clothes."

I found almost as much dismay in that as in his concern over trysting – almost.

"My love," I said gently. "I have shirts and proper breeches, and I believe you have those soft leather boots, and I have my less than comfortable ones, but if you insist that we take to wearing wigs and coats or removing our earrings, I shall smack you."

He opened his mouth to protest, but closed it and awarded me a rueful smile.

The snoring stopped. We stood tense, our breath held, but the sound did not resume before I was forced to breath. Gaston hurriedly closed the door.

"Well," I said lightly but quietly, "if we wish to bathe and dress before seeing him, I suppose we can climb out." I looked out the window in the end wall: we could indeed climb onto the cistern and down. "And I believe we could return the same way," I noted with delight. "It will make it easier to sneak away if we have the need."

"I will not be fucking you on the Palisadoes when we have this fine bed," he hissed with the Horse's anger. He immediately shook his head and cursed silently. "I am sorry. I am..." He sighed bitterly.

"Running amuck," I whispered. "Oui, he has you spooked. But, my love, it is... to be expected, at least by me. I understand. And we have the cart of our love, and it is sturdy and can be dragged almost anywhere, and I am lashed in the traces to it and you, not to anything else we must strain against. I am with you. I will go wherever you go."

"Until I kick your legs out from under you again," he said with guilt.

I smiled and embraced him. "And then we will fall together and yet we will still have the cart. Our love will not roll away if we are both lying on the ground holding it still. We have proven that."

He relaxed in my arms. "Do you think me the fool for wishing to please him?"

"If I had not once sought to please my father, we would not have met."

He nodded, but he was deep in thought as I gathered the clothing he wished for us to wear and dropped it out the window. He followed me out the window and we made quick and easy work of dropping to the ground.

"WePutALadderUp," Pete said from the stable's door.

I chuckled. "Then let us do the same on this side."

Striker poked his head around the flower trellis. "There are Frenchies out front, and militia men watching them. The French arrived last night. One of them demanded to see the Marquis."

"And?" I asked.

Striker shrugged. "I told him his Lord was fine and would be spending the night as our honored guest, and then I put a pistol in his face and told him to piss off."

"Tall man with sharp features, very arrogant manner?" I asked.

"ThatBeTheOne," Pete said.

I sighed and eyed the Marquis' door. The snoring had still not resumed. Resigned, I marched upstairs.

There was no response to my polite knocking, so I pounded on the door frame and called out. "Lord Tervent! Tervent! It is Marsdale. Are you well?"

I at last heard movement and soon the door opened. He greeted me with bleary eyes and no wig. What remained of his short cropped hair was white, and I noted it had the same tendency as his son's to stand on end. I was more interested that he was not completely bald, however; perhaps Gaston would keep his hair well into his middle years.

"The sun is well risen," I said pleasantly. "You should drink the water, there. It is clean." I gestured at the onion bottles Sam had left inside the door. "I believe we have bacon and eggs to break the fast. Vittese is across the street. There are men from the militia watching him. Should we tell them anything?"

He looked slowly from me to the sky and then down at the bottles and sighed. "That I should not drink rum."

I smiled. "I do not believe that will assure him as to your well-being."

He snorted. "Have him... Bring my translator, Dupree, in, please. He can relay messages to Vittese. Dupree is unctuous, but at least... Well, let us say I have little good to say to Vittese this morning. And I will gladly accept your kind offer of food."

"All right, then," I said.

Pete joined me at the bottom of the stairs and followed me to the door. I was pleased in this, as I was not armed and Pete was. Vittese was halfway across the street when I opened the door. Apparently he had begun to move from the shady place his men occupied at the sound of our removing the bar. At the sight of me he stopped.

"Your Lord has risen," I said with my best wolf's tone of command, "along with the rest of our household. He wishes to see his translator, Dupree, and no one else."

Vittese eyed Pete, who leaned on the doorjamb, a pistol held loosely at his side, and then the men of the militia who had moved closer as he approached the house. I could see him cursing but heard none of it. He turned smartly and went to the shaded alley across the street. Dupree scurried from the shadows a moment later. The poor courtier appeared quite disheveled, and I wondered if Vittese had forced him remain in the alley all night.

"Good morning, Monsieur Dupree," I said pleasantly as he approached.

"Good morning, my Lord," he said, with apparent relief that I should smile upon him.

I ushered him through the door and Pete closed it firmly behind us. I told Dupree where to find the Marquis and then I went to find Gaston.

He was in the bathing room, filling the tub. There were already hot coals in the tray beneath it, and I supposed Sam had anticipated our need and lit the brazier some time ago.

"How is he?" Gaston asked quickly.

"Rum-bleary, but awake." I quickly relayed all his father had said.

"I am pleased he is angry with Vittese," Gaston said thoughtfully as he doffed his clothes.

I was, too; I felt the man was far too arrogant for his own good. But I also felt some pity for him: he was doing his job, and I remembered the Marquis' words on the dock.

"Your father, when we spoke outside the gaol," I said carefully, "said that we owe Vittese your life: that he would have beaten you to death that night, but Vittese suggested the whip, and later, Vittese suggested you be exiled rather than sent to an asylum."

Gaston stirred the water in the tub with a thoughtful mien. I watched the glide of muscle beneath the deep scars on his back. I could understand his father's anger on that night, and perhaps even before, especially when it was housed in a body and soul that were perhaps as volatile as my matelot's. I thought Gaston had not inherited madness from his mother alone. Yet, it still filled me with sorrow and rage to look upon him and know the whole of it could have been avoided.

"I do not feel Vittese ever did anything for me out of kindness," Gaston said softly.

"Non, I suppose not," I sighed and gazed upon the matter through the glass of wolfish cynicism. "He was probably doing much to mitigate the situation his Lord found himself in. Your sister was expected to die. Your death would have had to be explained in some fashion, though. But, of course, many already believed you mad, so saying you took your own life would probably have sufficed. And as for sending you here. Well, if you were in an asylum in France, your father's enemies could have located you. So, non, it was not for you most probably, but for your father. Still, a deed in your favor is a deed in your favor."

Gaston nodded. He turned to face me, and unbidden, my fingers traced the ragged scar across his chest that I had made, as they often did. I do not know why I was so compelled to touch it.

"I forgive you," he whispered. "Because I did much to earn this, and I forgive my father, because I did much to earn his wrath that night, though... I know not how I feel about the rest of what he said last night. But Vittese I do not forgive."

I shrugged. "Good, I do not wish to defend him. I hope your father lets him sleep in the street for the rest of his stay here."

I let my hand trace over the rest of his scarred chest, and brush lightly over his unscarred nipple. He grabbed my hand and held it fast.

"Do not," he whispered, his gaze beseeching. "Promise me you will not attempt to arouse me this day."

I sighed and nodded. "I will not. Yet... I would say that it is for your benefit: we have not followed our morning regimen and trysting often calms you when you are troubled. But that would be disingenuous. I actually seek reassurance. I am concerned that we will not do anything until your father leaves, and that troubles me, as it stirs my ghosts to life. I am sorry."

He smiled sadly. "I do not know if I can, and you know it is not you."

"Oui, I know. It is him, and that minds me of my father and then..." I sighed. I knew I surely could not tell him of his father's feelings about sodomites now.

He sighed and frowned. "I feel... I tell myself that he begged my forgiveness; that he gave the answers I have ever wondered at; that all is well; that... I am not evil; that his hatred of me had cause, the cause of his own angry heart; and that was caused by my mother's madness; and that there is cause for all of the evil done to me, and it is not me; but I do not feel any different, Will."

I caressed his cheek with the hand he did not hold. "How do you feel?"

He shook his head. "I do not know. Sad. Angry. Hurt. I wish for something, but I cannot name it. Proof of his sincerity, perhaps, or absolution. Something. Some end to it all, because I do not feel it is finished and done with and laid to rest."

"Then let us keep him here until you receive it," I said softly.

"Non," he said sadly. "I do not know if it is a thing he can give."

I nodded solemnly. "I understand, truly."

"I know." He smiled with resignation and kissed my cheek. "Let us bathe."

He gingerly climbed into the tub. He had only filled it partway, and the water was only as high as his lap. He could extend his legs somewhat ,though, and I thought we could both fit into it if we desired; though it would be cozy.

"How is it?" I asked.

He grimaced. "Rather like being in a stew pot. The metal beneath me is warm and the water is still tepid."

I was disappointed. "I feel more engineering will be necessary, then. We will have to determine how to heat the water before it is added to the tub. Perhaps some of the water could be diverted into a boiling pot that could then be emptied into the tub. We will likely have to summon Fletcher here again."

Gaston was frowning at the spigot above his head. He turned his gaze to me and smiled. "You know I love you."

"Very much." I grinned.

We bathed quickly, not because sitting in the tub was very much like sitting in a stewpot, but because we wished to avoid all eroticism we had come to associate with the act of bathing. Still, I could not help but see how very handsome he was in the clothes I had found for him. I think it was because I had seldom seen him attired in boots, or anything other than our buccaneer tunic and breeches. The ecru shirt he wore was not overly ornate or ruffled, but it was tight across his chest with long loose sleeves, and I had forgotten how such a thing could make a man appear wider in the shoulders and more muscular. The same was true for the light brown suede breeches he borrowed. He was a little thicker in the thigh and buttocks than I, and so the pants fit him in ways they did not fit me before tapering to blend with the soft dark brown boots he laced up his legs to the knee.

It was only by concentrating upon my own impending discomfort – as my boots were black, thigh high, and heavily cuffed, and surely contained the leather of an entire steer; and my grey shirt, though linen, seemed to weigh ten pounds and it scratched; and my coal breeches were wool, need I say more – that I did not fling myself upon him.

He regarded me with curiosity when I stood after jamming my foot into my last boot.

"What?" I asked, as I could see mischief begin to play about his eyes.

"You are not revolting," he said, fighting a smile. "And you do not look as you do when you dress for the part of Lord Marsdale," he added seriously.

"Thank the Gods for that," I sighed.

He stepped in close and kissed me, deeply. I savored it and fought the urge to touch him.

"You are mine," he whispered. "And not even my father will keep me from enjoying that this night."

My breath caught, and my cock stirred in a somewhat annoyed

manner that I should not have informed it before now that something was afoot. I wished to strangle my matelot, or rather, I wished to throttle another piece of his anatomy first until it bestowed its happy blessing upon me, and then strangle him.

Knowing me far too well, he quickly dodged out the door.

I was intent on telling him what a cock tease he was, but as I stepped out of the bathing room I saw that everyone was dining in the morning shade of the atrium, and while I think Pete and Striker, and possibly even Dupree, Rucker, and Agnes would have found amusement in my sentiment, I thought the Marquis, and my sister, who appeared somewhat green as pregnant women often do in the morning hours, would not.

Gaston squared his stance, and I knew he struggled to find the mask. I stepped up beside him and placed my arm across his shoulders, hoping he would accept the gesture as one of reassurance and not an unwanted display of affection. He thankfully relaxed beneath my arm.

"Good morning," I said cheerily to the assemblage.

I assumed all introductions had been made. They were arrayed casually about two small tables that sat somewhat askew to one another, so we were not forced to negotiate the potential confusion of a formal seating arrangement. Striker, Pete, Sarah, and the Marquis, with Dupree sitting in a chair nearby sipping tea, sat around one table, and Rucker and Agnes sat at the other. We quickly joined Agnes and Rucker with great relief, which I struggled to keep from my face. The positioning did leave us facing the Marquis, but Gaston did not care. He barely had time to give his father a polite nod before Agnes shoved a sketchbook in front of him.

Thus we began to eat and an exhaustive discussion of each sketch ensued while Sarah, Striker, and Pete remarked from the other table on ones they found particularly enlightening or disturbing, such as Agnes' rendering of globules in blood or of the number of little parts an insect possessed. The Marquis frowned with interest; and Dupree with consternation as he attempted to translate the English. At last they moved closer to the table. Gaston was too involved in what he was seeing to show concern at his father's change in proximity, but he did turn the sketchbook somewhat so his father might have a better view, and he began to discuss the various pieces in both French and English. I found amusement in the fact that my matelot did not do this so that he was speaking directly to his father, but such that he spoke to Dupree so that he might make a better translation.

I was, of course, quite interested in what the book held, but I knew I could see it again any time I wished and that we would probably be spending many an afternoon looking through the lenses ourselves. I was more interested in the Marquis. He was far less disheveled, with his hair combed and his clothes straightened, but he had eschewed his wig and coat. He spent as much time studying his son as he did the book, and was surely aware of my scrutiny though he made no remark of it, not even by a silent meeting of my gaze. And he was truly paying attention to what was being discussed and not merely observing his son: when the pages were turned to Agnes' sketches of the things she found in water, he looked down at his tea cup with alarm.

"They do not exist in boiled water, such as that used in the tea," I said quickly in French.

Agnes frowned at us, and Gaston quickly translated for her.

"Nay," she said. "They do still exist, they are just dead." She pointed to another page. "At least the larger things are. I boiled a very small sample of water and viewed it. I suppose one would not notice the dead ones in a large pot, as they sink to the bottom."

I thought it likely we would have to change our instructions to Sam concerning the boiling of water.

My sister proved my father sired no fools once again. "I have told Samuel to never use the dregs," she said.

"Would it not be something akin to soup?" the Marquis asked after Dupree translated for him.

Gaston frowned at this, and actually met his father's gaze. "Oui."

"Did you learn all this from Doucette?" the Marquis asked.

"Non," Gaston said and returned his gaze to the book. "I started learning of such things from the monks."

The Marguis gave a little head bob with a small moue of surprise. "I am impressed."

"Thank you," Gaston said. Then he regarded his father again and asked, "That the monks should know such things, or that I should learn it?"

His father raised one thin eyebrow and cocked his head. "Both. I did not realize the monks would be so interested in the natural world, I have always felt they are much like priests and nuns in that regard."

"Non," Gaston said. "The monks I lived with regarded the natural world as God's creation and a thing to be studied in order to gain a better understanding of God."

He continued to gaze at his father.

"And..." the Marquis sighed with a sheepish mien. "Your mother was never particularly intelligent, but perhaps it was because she was educated by nuns."

"So you have felt I was mentally deficient?" Gaston asked him with the beginnings of the Horse's usual tone.

His father shrugged. "I have lacked any evidence to the contrary until I arrived here and found you were considered a physician. I supposed your letter was written by another for you, and that Doucette had lied in all of his in order to gain favor with me, and prior to that, the only reports I received from any school's headmasters said nothing about your academic performance."

I lay a calming hand on Gaston's thigh and was rewarded by his returning his attention to the sketchbook and sighing heavily.

The courtyard was silent: even though only Sarah, Rucker, and

Dupree understood the exchange, they did not translate it for anyone, and thus all felt the tension but few understood the why of it. I was interested to note the Marquis had even changed his position in his chair, pulling back and away from Gaston in a seemingly casual fashion. It made me wonder how Gaston's mother's Horse had sounded, and what warning signs she had given.

"I can see where you may have come to such a supposition over the years," I said carefully, "if your mind was already prejudiced to that outcome, and, as you said, you had no information to contradict it."

"I meant no offense," the Marquis told Gaston. "I am pleased and relieved to see that I was very wrong."

Gaston's Horse was now very evident to me, to the degree I no longer cared how evident He was to anyone else. He seemed to take up the entire table, nostrils flaring, eyes intent, and flanks quivering with the need to charge or flee.

I tightened my grip on my matelot's thigh until he turned to me with glittering orbs of emerald rage.

I met his gaze calmly. "Perhaps..." I began.

Gaston's head cocked ever so slightly in warning, in the manner of a dog ready to bite or a bull to charge.

I darted my head closer, and whispered firm words in his ear. "It is unfair. But do not kill him. Say what you wish to say, or do what you wish to do, and be done with it. Or go and visit the puppies and calm yourself."

He gave a hissing inhalation. I sat back. His eyes were calmer: still angry, but not with madness.

He turned on his father, who was frowning at us intently. "I am not my mother," Gaston said levelly. "And you have destroyed my illusions of her and left me with... *you*." He spat the last word contemptuously.

Gaston stood and took stock of his surroundings: embarrassment gripped him. He gave Agnes an apologetic look and spoke in English. "Agnes, you are, as always, brilliant and talented. I will wish to see the lenses later." Then he looked at Sarah and nodded. "If you will excuse me." Then he left us, marching himself around the atrium and out to the stable.

Pete and Striker relaxed; Sarah appeared sympathetic; Rucker was curious, as was Dupree; and Agnes was close to tears, as she ever was when praised so.

Seemingly oblivious to everything but making his point, the Marquis leaned across the table and spoke earnestly to me in French. "I did not mean to offend him, but to compliment him."

Sarah heard him, and began speaking to Striker about some matter in English in a ploy of politeness. Dupree proved he was well-versed in the diplomacy of large households, and withdrew to pour himself another cup of the tea. Rucker, the only other French speaker at the tables, also realized he should not listen, and quickly excused himself. The Marquis and I were essentially left alone with our discussion in

French, though Agnes watched us with curiosity.

I awarded the Marquis a small smile. "Oui, but are men not ever at the mercy of others' interpretations of their actions, no matter what their intention might be?" I shook my head. "He loved his mother. I feel she has been an angel in his heart all these years, a Madonna who would have loved him if only she had been allowed; whereas, you have been a demon who must be placated."

He winced. "He knew she was mad," he beseeched.

Agnes decided we were indeed having a private conversation, and excused herself almost inaudibly.

"Oui, but he is mad, and he knows his madness, and I think he has thought hers quite similar in manifestation when perhaps it was not." I shrugged. "Without evidence to the contrary," I gave a pause to allow my choice of words to be noted, "she was the perfect mother, flawed only by her madness, which from his experience would not make her mean or hateful toward him. It is why he loved his sister so. He saw no duplicity, only love. And since it was such a damn rare thing in his life, he had nothing else to compare it to."

"He has thought me evil all these years?" he asked with a pained expression.

I tried to keep the incredulity from my face, and then I realized I was not doing as I should yet again. I was letting my Horse handle the matter and stir up my memories when it was not my Horse's problem.

"Non," I said softly. "He has thought he failed you all these years. He has thought you cast him aside because he was flawed and deficient in your eyes. And your attempt to lay the matter to rest by admitting this was indeed the case has brought no resolution in his heart. It will take time."

He sat back, the fingers of one hand pinching his lips, and studied the potted plant next to the table.

"How long can you stay?" I prompted after a time.

He shrugged. "Hopefully as long as necessary." His gaze returned to mine. "How do you control him so well?"

I shook my head. "I do not control him; I assist him in controlling himself. And it is more complex than that… and I do not feel I wish to discuss it this day."

"All right. Then can you answer some other questions?" he asked with another shrug that seemed to cast the whole matter aside.

"If they are brief. I should go to him."

He seemed somewhat surprised in that, and then apologetic. "Ah. I will be brief then. Who should I request the hospitality of if I wish to stay for some time?"

"My sister, and I will see to it," I said.

"Your sister?" he asked, and glanced at Sarah.

"Oui, Madame Striker," I said.

He raised an eyebrow at that, and I went to speak quietly with Sarah and Striker. Pete's golden head was quickly bowed into the circle.

"He wishes to stay for a time," I said. "It is acceptable to Gaston and me. I feel it is necessary. There is much they need to discuss and it will take time."

"Is he going to be setting Gaston off every time they talk?" Striker asked.

"Possibly," I said with a touch of annoyance. "And thus it is best done amongst friends in a place of safety rather than elsewhere."

Striker held up a placating hand. "I'm just curious how much Gaston wants to see him if they don't get on well. I'm thinking of him, not worried about what kind of ruckus they might cause."

"They need time to learn to get on well," Sarah chided him. "I wish we had such an opportunity with our father."

Her husband frowned at that, but he nodded. "That would piss me off to the ends of the Earth, watching you argue with him."

I was not sure whether I wished for such a thing to happen, but I supposed I did.

I left Sarah to tender their hospitality to the Marquis and went to find Gaston. I was momentarily alarmed when he was not with Bella, but then I found him behind the stable. He had bloodied his knuckles punching a beam, and now sagged with his head and hands against the wall.

"I should have left with you," I murmured as I pulled him into my arms.

"Why?" he asked, all Horse. "Did he say something to anger you?"

I sighed and held him tighter.

At last he relaxed and pulled back to regard me. "I knew they still thought me a child, but I did not think they thought me an imbecile. It makes me wonder how he truly treated my mother, despite his affirmations of love for her. Or was she truly what he describes?"

I sighed. "I do not know if we can ever know the truth, but... He is staying. You shall have ample time to discuss the matter with him as you are able."

"I do not know if I can," he said sadly.

"It is only the first day you have seen him in so many years," I said and kissed his cheek. "You will grow more accustomed to his presence, and perhaps it will become easier. And you are doing well."

He looked down at his bloodied hand and shook his head. "You are too kind."

"He even remarked upon it," I said, and then thought better of it, but it was too late. I told him all his father and I had said.

He snorted when I finished. "You shall speak for me. You will discuss it with him and relay it to me." He grinned.

"I do not know if... He is not my father," I said.

He regarded me with curiosity.

I shrugged and sighed. "They are deeply tangled in my heart, and my Horse is tripping trying to tread the proper path in dealing with yours. I find myself saying things that are from my heart and not necessarily your sentiments. I represent you poorly, as I cannot seem to do it selflessly."

He smiled and pulled me into his arms again. "I do not hold it against you. You speak truth, and whether it is my heart or yours, it does not matter. We are one."

Though my heart ached at his sentiment, it did matter to me. I told the Gods I would need guidance on this path They had set before us.

Fifty-Seven

Wherein We Float, Steeped in Irony

We sat for a time with Bella and the puppies. Though Gaston was far from truly calm, our silence was at least companionable and not burdened by things unsaid. He held my hand and finally lay down with his head upon my thigh. I played with his hair and let him think. I did not wish to think: I felt if I allowed my mind to wander it would find old trails that were best left dusty and unused. I did not feel those thorny paths would discover the proper words to tell Gaston's father how to make Gaston happy, or make mine do the same for me.

Sam poked his head in the doorway sometime later. "Masters? There's a messenger from the governor here, and Mister Theodore."

I told him we would be along shortly, and swore silently once he departed.

Gaston smiled as he pulled himself upright. "I hate Port Royal."

I sighed and grinned. "As we came into port, I was thinking the same, and how the only good thing about the place is that I met you here, and Theodore, and Striker and Pete, and... I suppose we must take the bad with the good."

He nodded thoughtfully. "I wish for a better definition of love."

I frowned.

He smiled apologetically. "I am sorry, I have been thinking. I wish to determine the true nature of love, so that I can measure people's declarations of love and find them either within the parameters of true love or outside of it. You once thought you loved, and you did not, truly. I have done the same."

"And now you question your father's definition?" I asked.

"Oui."

I grinned. "My love, far be it from me to disparage any endeavor of yours, but you are attempting to tread in the realm of poets, playwrights, and Gods. Men spend there entire lives there and produce nothing but sophistic verse."

He seemed to think on that, and then awarded me a fine grin. "I am already mad; what would it matter?"

I laughed; and thus in good humor we picked the straw from each other and went to discover what the Gods wanted of us now.

Sarah had apparently retreated upstairs, possibly with Striker or Pete, or both, as none of them were present. Rucker was also absent. Agnes was sitting at a table watching our guests with her sketchbook open and charcoal in hand, and I wondered what she had been drawing before the messenger arrived. The Marquis was sitting in a chair perusing a small folded piece of paper, with Dupree leaning over his shoulder to read and translate it while the governor's messenger stood waiting for their reply. I thought it likely it was an invitation. I suppressed a sigh.

Theodore greeted us warmly as always.

"What is this about?" I asked him quietly.

"The governor wishes to have a party in the Marquis' honor," he said.

Though I had not expected it, I now wondered why I should be surprised.

"How thoughtful of him," I murmured.

Gaston swore quietly and walked away to join Agnes.

At seeing me speaking with Theodore, the Marquis stood and approached. "I have been invited to attend a party given by your governor. Should I attend?" he asked me in French. "I feel it would be rude of me not to accept, as I am a guest here on this lovely island; but I am not privy to your politics, and I would not want to accept an invitation of this nature if it will cause... Gaston, or you, any difficulty."

I was surprised at his thoughtfulness. "I do not believe so; in truth it will probably put us in better favor with the governor. But hold a moment, and let me consult my advisor in such matters."

I relayed his question to Theodore, very quietly.

Theodore was quick to answer. "I did not come here to advise you not to attend, just the opposite. The governor was quite astounded a Marquis had slipped into port under his nose, as it were, and wishes to extend every hospitality. I do not feel it is solely to keep an eye on him. Modyford enjoys rubbing shoulders with the nobility, of any nation, and he does wish for pleasant relations with the French, or at least the appearance of it."

I turned back to the Marquis and switched to French. "You should attend, as should we. Apparently, the governor is very keen on it: he is an ambitious man."

The Marquis eyed Theodore speculatively.

"This is our good friend and barrister, Mister Jonathon Theodore," I told the Marquis in French. "He is not an ambitious man, but he is well-respected on Jamaica by those who are, and I value his counsel in dealing with them."

The Marquis grinned and awarded Theodore a nod of respect. Theodore bowed.

The messenger was quite pleased to hear the Marquis' acceptance. Upon receiving it, he opened his satchel and produced a small bundle of invitations. He quickly sorted through them and gave Theodore one, me two, and asked if he could leave two for Captain Striker. I accepted those as well. I waited until Sam had ushered the man out the door before I started laughing at who the sealed notes were addressed to.

Gaston was appalled when I handed him his, but he chuckled when I showed him Pete's.

"You have four days to prepare – well less, actually," Theodore said after reading his. "I trust you have attire," he told me. "But if anything must be made for Gaston, you should visit the tailor as soon as possible." He punctuated this last by looking up at the sky, where the sun was obviously close to being overhead.

I tried to give Gaston an apologetic look, but it was ruined by my amusement. "Well, at least we will get you some proper clothes."

My matelot rolled his eyes.

Agnes was examining Gaston's invitation.

"Do you wish to go?" I asked her.

"Nay," she said quickly and dropped the paper. "I might as well hang myself on display at the butcher's."

She was correct, but I could not resist teasing her. "But come now," I leaned close to whisper. "How else will you meet any pretty girls?"

Gaston smiled but patted Agnes' back reassuringly.

She flushed. "By standing about the butcher's. All the bondswomen come there."

I snorted, but her words reminded me of our earlier conversation. I turned to Theodore. "I need to make Agnes my ward, and we want to provide for her in our wills."

He nodded. "Before you sail again, I presume. Though if you intend to marry her off, she should begin attending the parties and balls before then."

Agnes buried her face in her hands.

"That is not our intent," I said with amusement. "Agnes is destined for better things than being some planter's wife."

Theodore frowned at me speculatively.

I shrugged.

He nodded and smiled. "I will keep that in mind."

With a final bow to all, he began to leave, only to pause at the foyer doorway. "You do know where the tailor is, do you not?"

"It is a small town and I believe we can read the signage," I assured him.

He left with a chuckle.

The Marquis was watching me with curiosity. When I met his gaze he glanced at Agnes. Dupree was at his elbow, and had likely translated all that he had heard.

I went to join them.

"Might I ask?" the Marquis began with a compressed smile. "Who is she? And…" He seemed to be carefully considering his next question.

"She is a very talented young lady we rescued from certain doom. Her well-bred mother passed away and left the girl at her common stepfather's command."

"Ah," he said with an appreciative nod. "Do you intend to marry her?"

"Possibly," I said. I was still not sure how much I wished to reveal to him: but there was no denying any truth he could discover by simply asking anyone in town. "Though the matter is currently complicated by my being married."

He regarded me with surprise.

"I am a Lord's son," I chided lightly. "My father sent a bride: a completely unsuitable woman. She is ever drunk and she engaged in an indiscreet affair when last I sailed. Now all on Jamaica, and possibly in England, know her as a drunkard and a whore, such that I must put her out even though I have no real interest in replacing her, even with a better example of ladylike decorum."

"You are lucky to be English," he said.

"Oui," I sighed. "I can divorce her without a Papal Bull."

He frowned for a time. "Is the girl of sufficient lineage to satisfy your father?"

I shrugged. "I think not, but if events progress in that direction, it will not matter."

His gaze was quite compelling, and as I thought on it, I decided there was no harm in his knowing this either. "It is very likely I will never become the Earl of Dorshire."

"Why?" he asked with more speculation than curiosity.

I sighed. "Because my father does not wish me to, and… I do not feel I shall ever return to England anyway."

"Because you are a sodomite?" he asked quietly. Then he gave the little moue and sideways nod that he seemed so fond of, as he did it often. "Though, if sodomy were a proscription against inheriting, half our kings could not have accepted their crowns."

I snorted. "My favoring men is but one reason of my father's. Non, the real reason is that he has another man who he wishes to leave his title to, my second cousin, who he feels is far more suitable as an heir than I." But the two matters were so much more complicated than that, and I could not foresee ever discussing that with this man.

The Marquis studied me. "But you married this woman anyway?"

That was a good question, one I wondered at with every passing month. "To appease him for a time. There are other matters at stake, or at least, there were."

He nodded thoughtfully. "You said you do not think you will ever return to England?" With this he seemed more curious than speculative. "Do you find this climate so very pleasant?"

I frowned. "Non, I cannot see how Gaston will ever do well in such civilization. We are happy here where we can avoid other men for long periods of time, or allow him to shower his anger against readily available enemies."

This surprised him. He studied Gaston with a frown.

"Did you think he would return with you?" I asked.

"I do not know what I thought," he said slowly.

He was lying: one of my fears upon reading his letter was correct; he had come here with the design of taking Gaston with him – thus the attempted abduction at the Chocolata Hole. Lead filled my belly.

He met my gaze and frowned at what he saw there. "I know I did not expect to find him so well… cared for."

"He is well-guarded too," I said quickly, guessing at his original choice of words.

He smiled apologetically, and held up a placating hand. "Having seen what I have now, I would not dream of attempting to take him from your side."

"I hope not," I said coldly. "For your sake. Gaston is my life. I have killed many men for things of far less value to me, including noblemen."

His smile departed, and I saw the wolf in his eyes. "I would not have us be enemies."

I spoke from my Horse. "Then do not cross me."

His eyes narrowed with seeming bemusement. "You are correct: you are perhaps as mad as he, and certainly as temperamental."

The words stung, and I left him and went to Gaston. "We should find the tailor's," I said, attempting to keep my tone light.

Gaston would have none of it; and he was on his feet, his gaze hard upon his father.

"I will explain outside," I said quietly. Shame at my hasty anger already threatened to color my cheeks. "Please," I hissed.

With a frown, he followed me out the door. The Marquis pretended not to watch us leave. I was thankful we were already armed with swords and a pistol apiece: I would have left the building without arms rather than stay long enough to fetch them from our room.

I acutely felt Vittese's gaze upon us as we walked down the street.

"What did he say?" Gaston hissed when we were beyond the hearing of Vittese or his men.

"I do not know if he is incredibly cunning or whether I am a fool," I growled.

Gaston's hand closed about my arm, and I knew I had best stop or deliver Vittese the spectacle of seeing my matelot pulling me off my feet. I turned to face Gaston.

"I feel he wished for you to return with him to France," I said.

Gaston's gaze hardened even more and he glanced angrily back at the house.

"Non," I said. "I do not know if he still wishes that. He professes that he would not dream of separating us now," I said sarcastically. "But I do not know if we should trust him. And so I lost my temper and threatened him. And... He made me feel the fool for it, quite deftly."

Gaston's face contorted from anger to concern and then sympathy. "What did he say?" he asked again.

So I told him all I could recall, and while I was not clear as to exactly what I had said concerning my wife or Agnes, the last words we exchanged were quite clear in my heart, and so I am sure I repeated them correctly.

"You are sure he was lying when he said he did not know what he expected?" Gaston asked thoughtfully.

"I felt it in my bones... but... perhaps..." I shook my head as melancholy rushed up to swamp me. "Perhaps it was my father talking, or rather me talking to my father. I just... I am sorry I am such a fool. You need me to be..."

He grasped my jaw and pulled my gaze to his. "I need you to love me, and you prove it with every word you say or deed you do."

The regard in his eyes choked any other refutation I could make. I nodded as much as his hand on my jaw would allow.

He released me. "You suspected this from the day we received the letter," he said.

I nodded sadly. "But... He might not have been lying when he said he would not dream of it now."

"He need not separate us to haul me off to France," Gaston said angrily. "He only need haul you with me."

I had not considered that. Gaston did not give me much time to consider it now. He pulled me back toward the house, and I went without protest though I knew not what he planned.

He found his father sitting and chatting – with the help of Dupree – with Agnes. The Marquis appeared surprised at our return, but the look he gave me was somewhat smug until Gaston spoke.

"Why did you come here?" Gaston asked.

"To make amends," the Marquis protested and shook his head.

Gaston stood with his arms crossed and his feet wide: appearing as immovable as the day I first saw him.

The Marquis was not so daft as to think he could navigate around him. "I wished to make amends and find out how you were living, and insure that you were being cared for. I did not know if the letter I received could be believed, or if it was even written by your hand."

"So you planned to make amends by taking me back to France by force?" Gaston demanded.

His father sighed and smiled grimly. "I did not think you would wish to see me, and I wished to meet with you to gauge your..."

"Sanity? Competence?" Gaston snapped. "While I was bound at your feet, or bludgeoned senseless by Vittese's men, or perhaps in a cage?"

"I had hoped it would not be like that, though we did prepare accordingly in case it was," the Marquis said sadly, with more grim amusement.

"You are no different than Doucette," Gaston spat. "Leave; you have said your peace. I hope God lets you sleep well now that you have confessed your sins."

The Marquis appeared stricken. "Non, non. You misunderstand…»

"I understand that you see me as incompetent and insane," Gaston growled. "I will never return to France. I cannot. You have named me such and made me less than human there. I will not spend my life locked in a cage so that you can feel you care for me or make amends with God or my mother's ghost."

His father shook his head. "You are…" He turned beseeching eyes to me. "Can you calm him?"

"Non! He is not mad at the moment," I scoffed. "He is angry, and with good cause."

Gaston was more than angry, though, he was furious; and I could see he was teetering on the precipice of allowing his Horse to run wild. I felt the Marquis deserved whatever came of it, but I knew I would serve Gaston poorly in allowing it.

I grasped Gaston's arm. "Let us go."

He shook me off, but he turned and walked away.

"Will?" Striker queried.

Pete stood beside him. Sarah stood in the doorway of a room to the left of the foyer – a room from which the wolves must have just emerged. Their proximity was such that I knew they must have heard all that was said, though only Sarah had understood it. She was regarding me with alarm.

I thought of the havoc that would be caused and the people possibly harmed if the Marquis did try to abduct us. We did not know how many men he had. We did not know anything. We had simply assumed he was a gentleman. The Marquis was a wolf, and we had been fools to trust him.

The image of Gaston beaten and bound filled my head such that I could see little else. The last time I had envisioned such horror with such clarity had been in the church at Puerto Principe. I had run, dragging Gaston with me, his madness thundering at our heels, and… it had been my madness, not his.

I took a deep breath and was surprised at how ragged it was. Striker's gaze was darting between the front door, which Gaston had just walked out, and me. Neither Pete nor he were going in pursuit of Gaston. They seemed far more concerned at my condition.

I had to go with Gaston. I needed Gaston. I was not well.

I went to Sarah and whispered, "I cannot make this decision. He is our father in my eyes and I am not able to… think clearly on the matter. Gaston cannot either. I fear he… the Marquis, not Gaston, will…"

"I heard," she said quickly, her face compassionate. "All of it. We will speak with him, and..." She shook her head. "You go. It is all right."

I ran into the street and collided with Gaston. He was still wild, but not so wild he did not sense my duress.

"Let us run," I said.

We ran. I thought we should go to the Palisadoes and run until our Horses calmed.

And then we realized Vittese and his men were pursuing us.

As we darted into an alley, I turned and fired. My ball narrowly missed the tall man. Perhaps I do possess better aim when startled, as opposed to mad.

My miss slowed the tall man down, though; but it made him extol his men to run faster. Gaston led us through alleys, and even buildings, at a pace that left me capable of little other than attempting to stay with him.

When at last we slowed as we neared Fort Rupert and the gate to the Palisadoes, I was dismayed to see that Vittese had been smart enough to send men ahead of us. Gaston was unfazed, though. He snatched my empty pistol and tossed it, along with his own, to a cluster of buccaneers who had just entered the gate, and implored them to drop them at the gunsmith's. Then he led me into the water. The men pursuing us could not swim, apparently, and they had not been told they might shoot us either. So there was little they could do but yell imprecations from the shore.

I stopped and turned – well out of musket range – and awarded Vittese my middle finger. There was a great deal of laughter from the buccaneers who had witnessed the chase. Our enemy did not see the gesture, though, as his men and he were now surrounded by the militia and the Brethren.

"We will kill him later," Gaston growled, and began to swim parallel to the shore.

I began to follow, and then wondered how I had managed to come as far as I had into the water, even with the threat of pursuit. My boots seemed to weigh as much as the damn steer they comprised the hide of. They surely held a barrel of water. I took a deep breath and, with much struggling beneath the surface, managed to get one foot and then the other free of the damn things. They promptly sank.

Gaston had thankfully discerned what I was about and waited for me. He was, of course, not hampered by the leather wrapped close about his calves.

We began to swim east along the Palisadoes again, angling a little closer to shore, but as there were still men to be seen, and Gaston wished to avoid them, we stayed in the deeper water well beyond the surf.

After more than a hundred yards, I could take no more. My chest felt tight, and a weariness that should have come after far more exertion had settled into my limbs.

"Stop," I sputtered.

I rolled onto my back and floated, eyes closed tightly against the brilliant sun. Gaston came to tread water beside me.

"I am run out," I gasped. "I know I should not be, yet, but..."

"Hush," he said.

"Are we in danger here?" I asked.

"Non," he said. "The current will take us in, not to sea."

I tried not to think of all the things that might be in the water beneath us. I tried not to think of all the things waiting for us ashore. And we had only blades, no guns. Our powder was soaked through and useless even if we had a piece.

I tried to trust the Gods. I found peace there; just as I found peace in trusting Gaston.

"I am sorry," I said at last. "My Horse bolted. I thought of you being harmed, and how foolish I had been to trust him, and..."

"Hush," he said again. He eased onto his back to float beside me, and took my hand.

I wondered what we looked like from above, floating there in the deep blue sea. The water was warm, and our gentle bobbing was relaxing.

"How are we?" I asked.

He snorted. "Well enough."

"Because I fell and you found your feet to guard over me as you always do?" I asked.

"Non," he said gently and squeezed my hand. "Because I no longer fear him. I do not care if he ever loves me. It is as if I have finally pulled his talons from my heart."

"That is good," I said. "I must learn how to extract my father's from mine."

He sighed. "I am sorry I asked you to appease him to preserve your title. That was foolishness. It was... me talking to my father. As long as I can remember, I was taught that a gentleman's title is of great importance."

"I understand," I said. "More than I wish to, perhaps."

"The Devil with it," he said. "Unless it is a thing you want in order to spite your damn cousin."

I shook my head, though I did not think he would see the gesture. "Non. I do wish to spite him; but non, I think I will spite him more by relinquishing gladly the thing he has ever coveted. And I do not blame you for the marriage. I will have it annulled, and marry Agnes, and give you sane puppies. Though by the Gods, I wonder at that last."

He did not reply immediately, and I wondered how he truly thought of me. Tension returned to my heart and limbs, and I felt vulnerable atop the waves. I forced myself to trust him, and the Gods, and the water yet again. I remembered once suggesting he learn to float upon his madness. Surely I could take my own advice.

When he spoke at last I knew my concerns had been madness-born and foolish.

"I wonder how insane I would be if I had been treated as you treat me now throughout my life," he said. "You surely would not suffer bouts of madness as you do if you had not been so misused. I would most probably still be mad, but..."

"Would you be mad?" I asked as the thought resonated deep in my soul. "Or would you merely be overly sensitive to sound and emotion and... perhaps your Horse would not be so very sovereign if he did not feel he must be in order to survive."

"Perhaps it was the same with my mother," he said softly.

"Perhaps," I said. "Surely being told one is possessed will not make one sane."

He snorted. "We are back where we began."

I shook my head. "Non, I feel we have come far."

"In relation to the beach," he said with amusement.

I turned my head and squinted across the glare upon the water. We were indeed even with Fort Rupert again. I sighed.

"Can you swim now?" he asked as he began to tread water again.

I nodded and flipped over. While I did not feel reinvigorated in the least, I felt confident of my ability to swim as far as the beach.

We were watched as we came ashore, but no one present made any remark. Vittese and his men and the militia, except for those left guarding the gate, were gone. I wondered what the outcome of it all would be.

I decided we should stop by Theodore's and apprise him of our latest escapade. His Negress, Hannah, answered the door. Her master was not home. The mistress of the house inquired who was calling, though, and at hearing our names came into view with a babe on her hip.

Our former Jewess housekeeper was a bit plumper than she had once been, but she looked happy and hale, and the little girl in her arms was round and jolly, with little wisps of fine black hair about her head and lovely brown eyes.

"Hello Mistress Theodore," I said. "And this must be Miss Elizabeth."

"Aye," Rachel said. She was gazing at Gaston with a quizzical look.

I turned to find him enthralled by the baby.

With a bemused smirk, Mistress Theodore handed him the child. Gaston accepted the girl awkwardly, and then he was lost in saying small stupid things to her in French and gazing at her with wonder while she stared at him curiously.

Mistress Theodore shook her head. "He likes children, I see."

"Aye, and puppies," I said.

She smiled. "I can't wait to see the big golden one with Mistress Striker's babe. I hope it's a girl. She'll have Pete eating out of her hand in no time."

I laughed. "Aye, she'll be doted upon to be sure."

"It's a shame you won't have one for Gaston to dote on," she said with a shrug.

I sighed. "We will see how fate and fortune smile upon us in the coming years."

She nodded. "Mister Theodore was called away… to your house, or rather the Striker's."

"Ah, so soon," I sighed.

"Would it have a thing to do with why you're dripping on my floor and getting my child sopping wet?" she asked.

"Aye, Madam, it would." I smiled. "And I am sorry we are ever such a bother, and that he must always be called upon to mitigate our troubled ways."

She shrugged. "He has ever spoken highly of you." She gave me an appraising look that said she might not agree with her husband's sentiments. "And he relishes it. You're far more exciting than the planters or even the other buccaneers."

I chuckled. "Well I am glad we perform some service."

Gaston was quite reluctant to relinquish the child, and I was reluctant to leave, but we at last did.

"We will find some means of providing you with children," I said with amusement and love once we were on the street again.

He smiled warmly. "Oui. I have not held one before. I think I would like them more when they are older and they can speak and learn things."

I snorted. "You could like one more?"

He gave a rueful smile. "I will like them when they are small, and I will be happy they are small and in my arms, because it will mean they cannot be abused such as we were if they are with us. And then they will grow into the people that we might have wished to be."

Though my heart swelled at the sentiment, I wondered once again how fine a father I was destined to be. I supposed with my matelot as an example, I would do far better than if tasked with the matter alone.

We ambled toward Sarah's house. I paused as we passed my wife's home.

Gaston shook his head. "Not today."

"I thought it might provide a further divertissement," I sighed. "Someone else to hate."

"Let us deal with what we must," he said.

"How are we?" I asked. "I am… calmer, and clearer of mind and spirit."

He nodded thoughtfully. "I am well enough. Did you say anything when you left?"

"I told Sarah I was incapable of making a determination as to what should be done about him."

"Let us see what they decided," he said. "Hopefully he is gone."

He did not sound sad; nor did he sound angry.

We were dismayed to find, not only the Marquis still in the house, but Vittese there as well, along with several men from the militia; though they were thankfully all members of the Brethren by the look of them. With Sarah, Striker, Pete, Agnes, Rucker, and, of course,

Theodore there too, the atrium was quite crowded. All eyes were on us, at least those of them that could see us from where they stood as we entered.

Our friends seemed quite relieved at our arrival.

I told Theodore, "I apologized to your lady for your having to muster again to our defense."

He smirked and chuckled.

"Elizabeth is very cute," Gaston said.

"Thank you," Theodore said sincerely, and the nod he gave me when Gaston glanced away from him appeared even more relieved than the one he had given at our arrival.

Apparently Sarah and Striker had not told him I was the one to be concerned about.

"Now," I said. "Why are they still here?"

There were heavy sighs all around, including from the Marquis.

"He says he did not send his man to chase you," Striker said tiredly, as if perhaps the point had been thoroughly argued. "That the man did it on his own and will be reprimanded for it."

I snorted and glared at Vittese.

"I was alarmed at the manner of your leaving," Vittese said in French. "Trustworthy men do not exit a dwelling in such haste and then run. I thought my lord had been harmed."

Dupree immediately translated loudly enough for all to hear.

I supposed what he said was true, but I saw a flaw in his reasoning; and with that realization, my confidence returned. "So you were so concerned about your lord that you immediately pursued two potential assailants down the street rather than entering the house to see if your lord had indeed been harmed?" I asked in French.

Dupree translated this as well, and Theodore, Pete, Striker and several others smirked.

I glanced at the Marquis. He was contemplating the air before him with little expression.

"One of them is lying," I said in English.

Pete and Striker chuckled.

Gaston grinned. "Let us find out," he said, also in English, and began to remove his belt and baldric.

"I was thinking of dueling him," I said.

Gaston snorted. "Nay, then he would die. I want him to suffer."

Vittese was frowning as he listened to Dupree's translation as Gaston approached. Then he understood, and his surprise transmuted to a look of cunning as Gaston came within reach. The tall man might have indeed been competent, but he was no match for Gaston. The first blow caught Vittese in the groin, the second broke his nose, the third sent him sprawling such that Agnes and Rucker were forced to abandon their table and scramble out of the way. My man did not stop there, he continued to strike: each blow a thing of precision delivered to break bone, damage organs, or wrench limbs. It was much as he had once beaten Cudro, but without the pauses between attacks to ask for the man's surrender. And Vittese never touched him.

"Enough!" the Marquis at last stood and roared. "For the love of God, someone make him stop!"

Gaston stopped kicking Vittese and turned to regard his father with the Horse's eyes.

"I gave order that you were not to be allowed to disappear," the Marquis said with exasperation.

My matelot gave no response. He walked back to me, and I handed him his belt and baldric.

"Why should you care?" Striker demanded of the Marquis after Dupree finished translating.

The Marquis did not look at Striker; his eyes were on Gaston. "He is my son."

Gaston stopped at the foot of the stairs. "I am your son no longer. You have seen to that," he said with a tired sigh.

"You are my only son," the Marquis growled. "Neither of us can change that."

Gaston paused, his foot on the second step. "I have two half-brothers. They are your sons. They are the ones you wanted."

The Marquis slammed his cane against the table. "They are dead!"

My matelot turned and looked at him. His face betrayed no emotion, and I saw the mask. He had managed to find it after all.

The Marquis swore under his breath and looked away. "Michael contracted the pox at court… and, Denis died in battle. He was a cavalry officer. Your half-sisters still live, but my wife can bear no more children, and I would not divorce her even if the Church allowed it."

The atrium was silent as an ashen-faced Dupree translated.

Gaston turned away and walked up the stairs.

I snorted contemptuously and told the Marquis, "You are as big a damn fool as my father. You could have spared us all pain if you had simply said that when you arrived."

He awarded me a glare that told me very plainly he knew that, but one such as I was not to question the reasoning of a lord.

I glanced at Vittese and shrugged. The Marquis winced.

I caught up with Gaston as he entered our room. I closed the door behind us. He stood, looking at nothing.

"Come, let us rinse the salt away and get dry," I said.

He nodded, and moved as I directed so that we could strip him. I filled the basin with water from the ewer and wiped the sticky salt away, then I applied unguents to the few cuts and bruises he had given himself by striking Vittese, especially on the hand he had injured this morn by punching a post.

When I finished, he crawled onto the bed to curl on his side. He was not in the same state of remove he had been last night, but he soon began to make little rocking movements. I let him be for a time, and occupied myself with cleaning the salt from my skin and rinsing and oiling our leather gear and blades. Only once all was seen to, and I was dressed in clean breeches and tunic, and had knives and several loaded pistols positioned about the bed, did I go to him.

He closed his eyes at my tentative touch on his shoulder.

"Make it all go away," he murmured.

With a grim smile at his sentimentality at such a time – that he should still ask for me to minister to him in that fashion – I went and fetched a bottle of oil. He was putty beneath my hands as I massaged his back and arms: there was no tension in his muscles.

He mumbled something after I pushed him onto his belly. I leaned closer and asked him to repeat it. "It is not about him anymore," he said.

I kissed his temple. "What do you want?"

"What is mine," he said as if it were a matter of wonder.

My Horse shied from thinking of what that might entail.

I was massaging his legs and buttocks when there was a knock on the door. It was Theodore and Striker. Gaston rolled onto his back and scooted up the bed to lean on the headboard with the sheet about his waist.

"First," Striker said as he entered the room. He kept his voice low but his words were fierce. "I will not have you bastards thinking any who love you are against you. If either of you think for one moment that we're siding with that son of a bitch while trying to untangle this mess, I swear I will go down there and shoot him now."

Gaston and I exchanged a look: my matelot smiled.

"Nay, we shall strive not to interpret the manner in that fashion," I assured Striker.

He appeared relieved, and threw himself down to sprawl in one corner of the foot of the bed. "I should probably shoot him anyway."

"Not yet," Theodore implored. He pulled one of the chairs to the side of the bed and sat. His grimace at the scars across Gaston's chest was very brief. He quickly fixed his eyes on my matelot's face and adopted his most barrister-like mien. "The Marquis has made offers to satisfy our lack of trust; however, I would know what you wish of the matter before we proceed."

Gaston was at his best and I was proud of him beyond measure. His eyes were bright with the Horse's fierceness, but all about him was the Man's control. Now there was no mask, and he appeared comfortable in his skin, scars and all. It was the way he had often been when we were alone these last months.

I found his words incredibly chilling, however; even though I knew how much it all meant to him.

"I want all that is due me as the firstborn son of the House of Sable," he said firmly.

Theodore nodded thoughtfully. "So your title as the Comte de Montren, and any lands or money due that title?"

Gaston sighed at that. "I care not for the money or lands, but I want the title, and I want my name cleared so that I am a man again under

French law."

"Do you wish to return to France?" Theodore asked.

"I do not wish to, but I will do what I must to claim what is mine by right," Gaston said, and then he looked to me with a frown.

I smiled at him, and did everything in my power to hide my concern. "I will go with you wherever you wish."

Either I did a poor job of masking my feelings, or we thought very much alike: I saw the trace of fear in his eyes for a moment, but he quickly dismissed it before turning back to Theodore.

"Sadly," Theodore said with a shrug, "I only know enough of French law to know how areas of it are similar to English law for the purposes of making contracts between the English and French merchants and Brethren. According to the documents your father sent Doucette, your name is impugned as you say, as your father has had some court judge you incompetent to handle your affairs and therefore you are to be assigned a guardian. I do not know how such a matter is undone. I feel that my ignorance is of such an extent on the matter that if your father presented us with a paper saying the matter was resolved I would not know if the document was valid. Thus, I shall contact a barrister I have dealt with on Tortuga, and have him engage a barrister in France to handle the matter on your behalf. I believe the matter can be taken care of without your father's consent. His assistance in the matter would ease it considerably, though. Still, with or without his assistance or objection, I feel that portion of this matter will take years to resolve, and that under no circumstances should you set foot on French soil or a French vessel until such time as it is resolved, no matter what promises anyone makes you."

"Thank you," Gaston said. "I understand."

"We will provide you with more money to handle such things," I said.

Theodore shrugged again. "I believe in the end your father will provide all the money any of us might seek."

"Truly?" Striker asked with amusement.

"Not you," Theodore said without looking at him. "Now, clearing your name and establishing your competence in the eyes of the French courts will surely be necessary for you to inherit your father's title. However, I know of no reason – but please remember my ignorance of French law – but I know of no reason why you cannot hold the title due his son, to wit, the title of the Comte de Montren. But I must ask; how is it that you do not hold it now? It is my understanding you are his oldest son by legal marriage and that there is no question of that. Is it your understanding that the title was lost when you were exiled here?"

Gaston frowned and shook his head sadly. "I signed a paper my father had drawn up, saying that I would relinquish the title and my inheritance in favor of my half-brothers."

"How old were you?" Theodore asked.

"Sixteen years," Gaston said. "I planned to become a monk. But... that was right before... that night." He shook his head irritably. "We all thought it would be better. I knew so little of myself then, and he... hated me."

"I do not know how binding such a document could be," Theodore said with a frown. "Of course, it is eclipsed by the determination of the court as to your competence. However, it could be said that if you are as incompetent as the other suggests, then you are, and were, incapable of executing an agreement of that nature. But that is all neither here nor there at the moment. Let us assume the other matter will be resolved, and in the meantime, the matter of your being the Comte de Montren, and all that that entails, is between you and your father alone. Once the matter of your competence is resolved, you could, of course, go to court and make suit against him over the matter, but until then, you do not have the legal standing to do so."

"Has he said he will return it to me?" Gaston asked sadly.

"Nay," Theodore sighed and gave him a kind smile. "But he is willing to go to great length to remain here and assuage your fears as to his intent, despite all the misunderstanding and trouble today. He has agreed to send the ship he arrived on away, to Petit Goave. It will be instructed to return in December. Until then, he wishes to remain in this house, or in some other dwelling from which he can visit with you as often as possible."

"He says if we see any of his men about town we can shoot them," Striker added. "And they took that bastard Vittese out on a litter. You well know he won't be a problem for a long time."

It was infuriating. I wished for Gaston's father's reasoning to be as enigmatic as my own father's: then we could muster ample reason to hate him. But Gaston's half-brothers must have died before the Marquis received the letter of last year from Gaston; and their deaths and his being without an heir must have prompted his great need to make amends with God and his son. And even though he professed not to believe his only surviving son had written the letter, he had still sailed halfway around the world on the hope that he had. I could see where he wished to come and claim whatever son he might have here, in whatever manner he had to, in order to make things right and recover what he could of the shambles his plans had fallen to. Of which much of it, if I were honest, was not his fault at all.

I shook my head and swore. They all turned to regard me and I sighed. I did not wish to admit to the real reason behind my anger.

"It appears the Marquis truly wishes to gauge Gaston's competence and madness," I said. "So what is Gaston to do to prove himself?"

"That has not been discussed," Theodore said, and quickly held up his hand to stave off any interruption I could make while he chose his next words. "I do feel that he has judged Gaston to be worthy of the effort. He is willing to leave himself stranded in a vulnerable and awkward situation in order to accomplish his professed aim of making amends with his son."

"I see that," I said.

"We're willing to let him stay, if it's what you want," Striker said.

"I do not wish to have to appease him." Gaston said angrily.

"Unfortunately," Theodore said gently but firmly, "that is the way of it with all sons who wish to inherit from their fathers." He gave me a pointed look.

"I do not wish to inherit," I said.

Theodore sighed tiredly.

"And," I added, "If Gaston is to inherit, then I cannot."

"True," Theodore said with resignation, "However, I still maintain that you will do yourself and those associated with you a great favor by continuing the illusion that you will inherit for as long as you can. And Gaston's inheritance will take years to resolve."

I wished to rage with childish petulance at the unfairness of that, but it would be to no avail and only serve to make me appear the fool. And Theodore was correct, despite all I might say about how there was little value in it when I did not plan to keep it, I knew well there was value in my being a lord. The incident at the Chocolata Hole yesterday proved that: any other than a lord would have been seriously questioned over such a matter, but as Modyford valued his ambition and that entailed bowing and scraping before nobility, I had been allowed to make whatever excuse I wished for the deaths of several men.

"So," Theodore was saying to Gaston. "Do you wish for your father to remain here, alone? Except for his translator. I feel it is in your best interests if you truly wish to claim what is due you. But, of course, you must feel comfortable with the arrangement and not be concerned for your security. If there is some aspect of the matter I have missed – that would lead to you not being safe – then please let me know." He smiled ruefully. "I am trained to see how men can harm one another with laws and papers, not with swords and pistols."

I smiled grimly. "As long as he does not have any men about, I do not see how he can do much by himself. Unless he goes to Modyford and demands his son."

Theodore sighed. "I did think of that. I believe your being a lord of his own country and obviously not being in favor of surrendering Gaston far outweighs any attempted claim the Marquis could make to grant favor to our governor."

I sighed and slumped with resignation and defeat.

"As for any trouble when the French return in December, our men will be back before his ship returns," Striker said thoughtfully. "At least they should be," he sighed.

"The arrangement will be acceptable," Gaston said at last.

Theodore nodded.

I looked to Striker. "Thank you, and my sister, for housing this mess until it is resolved."

Striker shrugged. "I think it'll be a bigger bloody mess if your father ever comes calling."

"I cannot see him finding us worth the effort," I said, as much to reassure myself as him.

They left us. I sat on the bed next to Gaston and took his hand.

"You will do this for me?" he asked quietly.

His confidence had apparently fled with our friends, and now I beheld a scared and befuddled boy, though there was none of the Child about him.

I met his beseeching and apologetic gaze and whispered, "Oui."

"I am sorry I did not…" he began.

I shook my head. "There has been no time to discuss it, and you have been in no state to do so."

"It is a thing I never thought I could have," he whispered, and began plucking at the bedding. "When he said they were dead… it was as if the Heavens smiled upon me. Now *he* needs *me*."

"I understand," I said. And I truly did.

I mustered as much cheer as I could. "Well, at least he is not my father, who we must ask the Gods for portents of concerning his intentions. He will be here and you can demand to know what he wants."

"I cannot prove I am sane," Gaston said sadly.

"Neither can he," I said. "Or, I, or any of us, truly. I feel he wants to know if you can control your madness, or be controlled."

"What if he wishes for me to marry and have children, as your father wishes of you?" he asked quietly and with great concern.

I sighed. "Then you shall marry Agnes and… As you said today, perhaps your children need not be as mad as you."

He considered this with a thoughtful frown. "That would not be so very bad."

Then he moved to sit astride my legs, his eyes boring into mine. "I want this, Will, but I will not surrender you for it."

Tears filled my eyes as I realized how very much I had needed to hear that. "I know, my love," I whispered.

He embraced me, and I held him, and wondered what the Devil the Gods wanted and what They were willing to sacrifice to gain it.

Fifty-Eight

Wherein We Contemplate Sacred Trusts

Pete arrived at our door to inform us that Sam had made supper, despite all the chaos. I discovered I was grateful for this news when my stomach grumbled at the thought of it. We left the doors open, and Gaston dressed hurriedly, not in his proper clothes, but in his usual maroon canvas breeches and tunic. I decided we would carry arms to dinner.

"WeBeEatin'InTheDinin'Room," Pete added as he watched us prepare.

"Is that why you are wearing a shirt?" I teased. "And that is a fine shirt."

"Nay, BeWearin'It'CauseWeGotGuests."

Pete leaned on the balcony railing and smoothed the shirt he wore with some pride. It was fine linen, and so blue it matched his eyes. It was not Striker's, as Pete's physique is more muscular than his matelot's, and anything tailored to fit Striker would have looked stretched and uncomfortable on Pete. I guessed Sarah had insisted he wear something other than breeches on occasion, and had had clothes made for him.

It reminded me that we now must truly do the same for Gaston. The tailor would be our first order of business on the morrow. Though perhaps sparring on the beach for a time in order to tire our Horses should come first, as it could be done before the shops opened – and most probably should be done before delivering Gaston on to those shops for hours of measuring and perusing fabrics and all the falderal a visit to a tailor's entails. And the Devil with his Horse, I would likely have to fortify mine with wine in order to tolerate the endeavor.

If I was not careful, I would be doing a great deal of drinking until the end of the year; and though it was how I had managed to drift through my prior life, I did not wish to ever again live in a manner that required my being drunk to sleep or even carry on pleasant conversations. But here we were, going to a very awkward supper, the first of many; and then there was the party on Saturday, and I prayed there would not be many more of those in the weeks before we were rid of the Marquis.

But that reminded me of yet another thing. "Did you see your invitation?" I asked Pete with glee, because misery so loves company.

"NotGoin'." He crossed his arms and awarded me a disappointed sigh that I should tease him.

"Would Sarah not be pleased to have you go and look after Striker?" I asked.

He snorted. "SarahAn'MeLikeTaHaveTheLoutOuttaTheHouseAtTimes."

I stopped adjusting my baldric and regarded him with a raised brow. "She is with child."

"YaDaftBugger," he said with another derisive snort. "WePlayChess. Canna"Ave'ImAroun'. 'EDoesna'UnderstandTheGame, An"E'sAlways Sayin'How'EWouldDoItAnAskin'WhatWeBeDoin'Next."

"I would like to play chess with you again," Gaston said with interest.

Pete grinned with feral glee. "Aye. WeNa'PlayedMuchSinceYaTaught Me. IBeBetterNow."

Gaston sighed as we followed Pete down the balcony. "I could barely beat him before," he muttered in French.

"Have your father play him," I said with amusement.

Gaston smiled. "That would serve him."

Everyone else was already gathered in the dining room. Gaston touched my arm as we crossed the atrium. He kissed me lightly when I turned to him. He appeared earnest and concerned.

"I do not know how I will face him," he said. "I do not wish to meet his gaze."

"You found your mask this afternoon."

He shook his head. "That is only because I was so angry. I cannot now."

"Well, not that I wish to advocate for the Devil, but if you feel uncomfortable, imagine how he must feel. He is not loved here, and you are."

"I am loved," he said softly and nodded. "And you are loved."

I smiled. I wished to say that that love was all I wanted in the world, but I thought that might sound as if I were prodding him to guilt over his desires. And thinking that, and realizing I could not voice either thought, made me very much want to drink, because I could see no path to the future that did not involve brambles. But if I drank, it would only be worse, because instead of following even the roughest path, I would simply brazen my way through the thick of them.

I affixed a presentable smile upon my face as we entered the room. Gaston simply chose to study the floor and the food. Striker sat at one end of the long table, with Sarah at the other and Pete at her right hand. Their chosen seats had little to do with decorum. The positioning allowed Striker to watch one door to the room, and Pete the other. With that in mind, Gaston and I walked around to the back side of the table where we could watch both doors. The Marquis had apparently never had to be mindful of who might enter a room behind him, so he sat on the outside of the table, with his back to the doors and Dupree on one side of him and Agnes and Rucker on the other. I chose to sit across from the Marquis, and Gaston settled in next to Pete and across from Agnes. All were uncomfortably silent.

Our supper was to consist of the spiced stew I had once had the pleasure of eating at the Theodores', and a thick cake or bread made of some type of yellow meal that proved to be surprisingly tasty with butter when I sampled it. There was wine, but even though the cake was rich, I did not gulp my glass dry, and when Sam asked what else we might need, I requested water and Gaston did likewise.

I finally glanced at the Marquis and found him regarding Gaston. My matelot was, of course, sitting at the table with excellent posture, and he had straightened his spoon and bowl several times while waiting for Sam to bring the tureen around.

"Pete and Gaston are considering a game of chess this night," I said pleasantly.

Striker sighed, but his wife chuckled.

"Well," Sarah said, "I am sure it will be entertaining, but I would rather not have Pete get any practice. I cannot win as it is."

"YarTooCautious," Pete said.

Dupree – who like all good translators would eat very little of his meal – had been translating all that was said, but at Pete's statement, he stopped, his head slightly cocked and his face contorted in concentration in a quite comical manner.

I tried very hard not to laugh at the poor fellow. "Pete's… accent requires time to master," I said lightly in French. "He said that my sister's game is too cautious."

"Thank you, my Lord," Dupree said quickly.

"He plays chess?" the Marquis asked quietly of Pete in French, with a gesture at Dupree to indicate his words should not be translated.

"Aye, Pete is one of the best chess players we have ever seen," I said loudly enough for all to hear in English. "Perhaps you would like a game with him. I see you as a man who likes to play games of strategy."

The Marquis waited patiently for Dupree's translation, and then he awarded me a small and cunning smile. "Whereas I do not see you as a man who favors games of strategy. Do you perhaps favor games of chance?" He did not wave off Dupree's translation this time.

I smiled. "I do, but it is because I consider games of chance, and dueling, to be matters of strategy. But, as I have aged, though my age is not as venerable as some, I have come to realize I would quite prefer to shoot a man rather than engage him in games of the mind, whether they are over a chess board, a hand of cards, or even stew."

Gaston spit a mouthful of stew back into his bowl. "I cannot take you anywhere," he said quietly in French with a grin.

Everyone else, except Agnes, Dupree and the Marquis, had smiled or chuckled at my words.

"At least I am consistent," I told my matelot gleefully.

"How many men do you think you have killed?" the Marquis asked.

He was not quite as challenging as Sarah had been when she asked me that question at my father's table. It amused me that she answered.

"I believe you said the count was at nineteen – that you were sure of their death and who were not merely wounded – before you came here," Sarah said. "I would not hazard a guess as to how many men my brother has killed in the West Indies," she told the Marquis.

"Well," I said with a shrug, "there has only been the one in the past two months, and that was yesterday."

"Is this a thing you are proud of?" the Marquis asked. It was a coy question.

I snorted, and met his gaze levelly. "Aye, I am proud it has only been the one of late. But, nay, I am not proud of them, not the Spanish, not the men I feel I have downed rightfully, and most especially, not the ones who I should not have had to kill due to a *misunderstanding,* such as the man I shot yesterday. I am proud that during my travels I have killed far fewer men than my father ever has by taxing the men who work his land to starvation or urging his associates in the House of Lords to do the same for all the country. With the exception of the military engagements I have been involved in here against the Spanish, I have had to look every man I have killed in the eye; and while I have not known all their names, I do remember their faces. I feel there is some honor in that."

His eyes had fallen from mine as I talked, and now he studied the table thoughtfully. "There is honor in that." He shook his head. "I have never killed a man."

I bit back many words. I was sure Vittese had killed men for him: that was why a lord had a man like Vittese in his employ.

"And the families that work my land live well," he continued. "I pay the salary of the physician, support an orphanage, and provide other relief for the poor as is needed. I feel it is the sacred duty of a nobleman to care for the land and the people upon it who are entrusted to him." This last was said with a note of rebuke.

"That is what I was taught was the duty of the nobility – by men other than my father," I said with amusement. "I believe my father views the sacred duty of the nobility to be guaranteeing the continuation of the nobility. The first Williams was named Earl of Dorshire for supporting Henry the Sixth in his battle for the throne."

The Marquis frowned, but there was little anger in it, only disappointment. "Kings come and go, but there has been a Sable guarding the land of Tervent for five hundred years. Our titles have changed on occasion with the politics of the nation, but we are Gentilhomme and take our duty seriously."

"That is a fine thing," I said carefully, "and I would like not to doubt you, but there is no one here who can corroborate the welfare of your peasants, and in ten years of wandering among the nobles of Christendom, you would be a rare lord indeed compared to all those I have met. And perhaps that is because they frequented the courts and politics, and did not stay on their land to husband it as they should. But to a man or woman, they have proven to my eyes to be wolves ever ready to feed off the sheep in their pastures."

The slyness and challenge left him in a prolonged sigh. "It is a sad testament to the state of the world that you, a nobleman's son, should have only been taught by experience so dim a view of the nobility."

Our companions at the table were quiet. Sarah stirred her stew with a thoughtful frown, and Pete and Striker were watching the Marquis and me with interest, as if they were curious what nobles spoke about while dining. Rucker, who had instilled in me as a child the ideals of which the Marquis spoke, was nodding. Agnes was frowning at Gaston, and Gaston had become very withdrawn.

"And what is your opinion, Gab... Gaston?" the Marquis asked.

Gaston gave a small smile and sat his spoon down. He did not look at his father, but he spoke in French. "I feel that I will be useless to you as an heir. Though I want very much to maintain the family tradition, and I do feel it is our sacred duty to care for the people, I am only recently able to care for myself enough that it need not be my sole concern, and so that I am able to use my training as a physician to care for others. Those gains are all due to Will."

The Marquis looked away with teary eyes.

My own eyes were thick, and I leaned over and kissed my matelot on the cheek.

Gaston looked down the table at Striker and spoke in English. "I wish to sail as a surgeon this time. Whether or not I can win the vote is of no concern. I wish to tender my services and have that as my primary duty."

Striker smiled and nodded with enthusiasm. "God knows you're the best we have. And many of the Brethren know it too," he added with a grin.

Gaston looked at his father as Dupree finished translating Striker's words. He spoke French again. "Will and I view the Brethren as our people, and we feel it is our duty to serve them as we can. It is a thing Doucette instilled in me as well, the need for a physician to serve mankind, regardless of war or politics, social station, or even religion."

The Marquis met his gaze earnestly. "My son, the more I learn of you, the more I learn how very foolish my fears were." He nodded, almost to himself, and stood. "Now, if you will excuse me. I am sorry I am ill-disposed to enjoy this lovely food. Ladies." He bowed and left, waving Dupree back to his seat.

Dupree sat again, timidly.

"Well, you will be able to eat now," I told the man kindly. "I always feel sorry for translators, but you perform a very necessary function. And what I hear of your translation is excellent."

"Thank you, Lord Marsdale." He dove into his food.

"Pete," Gaston said quietly. "I have no head for chess tonight."

The Golden One smiled and moved his chair so that he could throw an arm around Gaston's shoulders and give him a quick kiss on the head. "MaybeTomorraNothin'll'AppenTaRileThingsUp."

"If the Gods would only be so kind," I said and raised my water glass in toast.

The others smiled or chuckled.

I looked to Gaston and raised an eyebrow.

He nodded as if even that caused him great effort.

"We must retire," I said, and grabbed my remaining hunk of the meal cake as I stood.

"You can take your bowls with you," Sarah said.

I poured Gaston's into mine and cradled it in my hand. "Thank you, thank you all for being such fine friends."

"You make things exciting," Agnes said, as if it were an abstract thought.

I thought of Mistress Theodore's words about her husband finding his duties to us more interesting than dealing with planters. I grinned. "Well, at least we perform some useful service."

Striker was grinning. "We'll sail by year end, and then things'll calm down."

"They always do," I said over my shoulder as Gaston and I slipped out the door, but I was quite concerned that the maelstrom we now lived in would only worsen over the weeks before we could at last escape it.

We made our way quietly past the Marquis' door. Lantern light flickered from within between the louvers. I heard nothing, though I paused to listen. I wondered if he had indeed returned to his room or if he had left the house.

Once we were in our room, I closed the thin doors against the world and set our half-finished repast on a chair. Gaston embraced me fervently. I held him until our hearts, which were racing fast in our quiet bodies, slowed and formed a quiet rhythm that I found quite mesmerizing.

At last he stirred and kissed me chastely upon the lips.

"Do you wish to discuss it?" I asked. "Him?"

He pulled away from me gently and went to light a lamp. The flame showed him frowning, but the expression passed with a sigh when he turned to me.

"I wish to hear your thoughts," he said quietly, and doffed his weapons and tunic.

"He is not a saint you must emulate," I said as I shed my gear. "He may be a very fine lord indeed, but he still allowed those men to go to their deaths yesterday, and expressed no regret over it in any of the times the matter has been mentioned. Perhaps he did not like them." I sighed and removed my tunic. "And… I still feel I am a poor ally, because the Gods know I am not a saint."

He smirked, but his words were said sadly. "I feel you are a better man than my father."

"Thank you, but I am glad to hear that for reasons other than my pride."

Gaston nodded. "I do not know how my father truly treats his peasants. I am trying to remember all I can of how I have seen him interact with the servants. He was ever polite to them, but he seemed to treat them as servants. But… I was in the house and saw such things so seldom, and when I was, all was tinged with my being in awe of him, or mad with anger. And, if I was home, it meant something had gone wrong again, and so everything was not as calm as it should have been in the household. So except for when I was so young I cannot remember it clearly, I cannot bear witness to how he rules his house when all is as it should be.

"I had forgotten," he said with a wondering shake of his head. "Whenever I was brought before him he always lectured me on how it was a lord's duty to stand as an example, and in order to lead and shepherd those placed in his care, a lord must be strong. I remember one time I was furious with him, because I felt I had proven I was strong: I had defeated everyone the damn school had sent at me. He, of course, had been trying to impress upon me that I must be stronger than my madness or my emotions, but…" He shook his head again. "My father might have laid the foundation, or at least attempted to, but Doucette made me much of the man I am now in regards to how I feel others should be treated and how I define good and evil. There is much of the monks in here too, and a few others I have met along the way. It is no wonder my father finds me surprising; he does not know me at all. I am a thing he allowed to be shaped by others and now finds he must embrace."

His words resonated in my swollen heart. "My father seemed to feel much the same when he met me as a man," I said.

Gaston nodded and regarded me with a hopeful smile. "Perhaps we were not raised by wolves at all."

I grinned. "We were born of wolves and raised by other creatures, and taught to fear wolves, or at least know them for what they are. And in thinking on that, I feel Rucker is another crow."

"And then what is Doucette?" Gaston asked with amusement.

I shook my head. "Non, you knew him better, and you are far better at this game than I."

He snorted. "I feel I do not have the luxury of viewing him from a distance."

"What manner of creature is blind to the pain and ways of those closest to it; yet possesses great compassion for those at a distance, and great knowledge?" I asked.

"Perhaps an eagle," he said. "I would say a gryphon, because there was much of Pete's lion-heartedness about him, but Doucette does not fit within our definition of a mythical creature: he did not strive to be something other than what he was born to be. And from what I remember, he came from a family of scholars and engineers: eagles ever watching the horizon but blind to the things in their talons."

"You never cease to amaze me," I said softly.

Despite what I had told him this morning in refutation of his father's words, there were times when he was the man I lived to love – the days that I lived for – and this was one of them.

"You can be the lord that you wish to be," I added. "You are becoming stronger all the time, and we are learning better ways to handle your Horse so that it carries you where you wish. All that talk of Rucker's that I should become the Earl of Dorshire so I can do good in the world, well, perhaps the Fates have had you in mind all along, and I will do my good in the world by helping you do yours."

His eyes were wet, and he crossed the distance between us to hold me. His mouth covered mine, and we both nearly strangled on our tears and the kiss.

"I cannot do anything without you," he gasped when he relinquished my mouth.

"Nor I you," I whispered.

His mouth trailed down my throat to the mark he had made upon my neck the last time we made love – a seeming eternity of four days ago. He licked my martyred skin. I pulled us backwards, seeking support, until at last I found the doorframe. I leaned against it and locked my knees as he continued to bestow healing kisses upon my bruises. As he moved down my body, he turned me a little so that he could reach the mark on my right buttock. I savored the sensation of his tongue on the skin there. We seldom allowed our mouths to travel below our waists: tonight he licked every usually forbidden place he had bit, saving the bruises he had left upon my tender inner thighs for last.

I watched his progress with fascination and silent panting. I had once had a woman kneel between my legs and offer to lick far more than my thighs, but I had found the mere thought of her teeth closing about my member so appalling I had pushed her away before she could reach it. The sucking of cocks was a thing of lowly desperate whores who had no choice but to offer any and every service no matter how horrid, or highly-compensated courtesans who made damn sure their clients bathed before they offered such carnal delicacies. I had often felt a strange compulsion to kiss or lick Gaston's cock, flaccid or hard, but I had never dared. I decided I wanted to, and I would allow myself the opportunity as soon as I could get him on the bed.

And then he grinned up at me mischievously from just beyond the end of my turgid cock and I knew I would not be the first one to attempt such an experiment.

I held my breath as he gently pushed my foreskin away to expose my dome. I gasped at the first touch of his lips upon the tip, as much from surprise as the sensation. And then he extended his tongue to lick the slit and I lost my ability to breathe. His following licks and swirls about my head slowly sucked the air back into my lungs.

"Does it not taste horrible?" I gasped.

He stopped, and I regretted my words.

"Non, just salty," he said as if it were a curiosity.

"This is a first," I said.

"Truly?" he asked with wonder.

"No one," I managed.

Oddly, his huge grin at this information did not put me in fear of his teeth. Instead, I quivered with anticipation.

He fell upon me with relish. His lips and tongue and even his teeth explored the entirety of my shaft, skin, and balls. Each place he found to suck, nip, or probe was a new sensation to savor. And then his hand closed about my shaft to hold me still and he sucked the head into his mouth as far as he could. I fought the urge to thrust, or grasp his head and pull him closer. Then he moved his head to suck me in repeatedly and I could stand no more. As I felt my pending pleasure, I tried to push him away, but he held on and took me deeper and I could not contain myself: I pumped into his mouth.

He pulled back, my cum dripping from his lips, and smiled smugly.

"For God's sake, spit it out!" I hissed.

He swallowed and chuckled. "It is just salty." He stood and his mouth covered mine to share just how salty I tasted.

I did not find it bad. In truth, I found it quite tasty.

He was laughing as I pushed him back to the bed and upon it; thus he was little help in removing his breeches. His humor fled as I knelt between his knees, and he rose up on his elbows to watch me with great anticipation. I considered his prick, which, as always, had risen straight up to lie against the hard wall of his belly. I grasped the shaft and pulled him perpendicular to his body. I pushed his foreskin away with my lips, so that his head was like a huge peeled grape filling my mouth. I was surprised at how smooth he was under my tongue, and how a thing so hard could feel so soft. And he did taste salty; but also like he did elsewhere, only thick and rich almost to the point of sourness, like the dregs of a good flagon of wine.

He fell back on the bed and I rose to crouch over him like a feasting animal. I explored with my tongue, finding the precious places that made him gasp and claw at the bedding. Then I took to sucking rhythmically as he had, feeling great satisfaction in making him arch and strain until at last he exploded in my mouth. I decided I liked that sensation almost as much as feeling him throb in my arse.

I dove atop his chest, and shared his taste with him, and we laughed like children and licked one another's faces clean like kittens.

"We will have to add that to our regimen," I said when at last we sprawled side by side.

"Daily?" he asked with a grin.

"Non, I think we will save it for the days we bathe," I said with amusement.

"We must bathe often, then," he sighed.

"Damn good thing this house has a bathing room."

We were still chuckling with pleasure at one another when we placed our weapons, blew out the light, and drew the netting about the bed. We slept in a cloud of contentment and moonlit white linen, like angels.

We woke languorously to the sounds of the house's residents gathering in the atrium. I knew Gaston was awake: he squeezed my hand when I encountered his while stretching. Though I was piss hard, I felt no great urge to tryst, and Gaston's thoughts were apparently elsewhere.

"We should check on the puppies," he said.

I grunted. "We must go to the tailors."

"You should see your wife," he sighed.

"*We* should see my wife," I said, and rolled from bed to relieve myself in the chamber pot.

"I suppose we must speak with my father," he said with a feigned lack of concern.

"Well, he is downstairs," I teased.

"What shall we say?" he asked.

I studied him as I dressed in my buccaneer attire. He seemed pensive yet calm.

"How are we?" I asked.

He frowned. "Well enough, but..." He smiled at me. "Things are very easy to see in the cave, with you; but, when I consider walking out into the light of day it all becomes very confusing."

I nodded. "I do not want to dine again as we did last night."

He dressed as I did, as a buccaneer, and we armed ourselves to go about town. We could see that everyone was in the atrium as we traversed the balcony, and we received hearty greeting from most as we descended the stairs. The Marquis sat at a table with Dupree, somewhat apart from the others, and as I had not seen them arrive and choose their seats, I could not be sure who was avoiding who. I led Gaston to the Marquis' table and sat.

"Gaston, Marsdale, good morning," he said. His tone was light, but his features held a reserve I felt was unfamiliar to them, and his eyes seemed wary.

"Please call me Will," I said.

He nodded.

"Let us talk," I said. "In private, please."

He waved Dupree away.

I spoke quickly, and though I had not known precisely what I would say, it seemed to come with ease. "I fled my father's home when I was sixteen, and spent ten years traveling throughout Christendom living by my wits and skill with the blade and pistol, and languages." I shrugged. "I have spent too many days of my life... dueling, whether it be with words or swords. I do not wish to do it here. I do not wish for us to be enemies. I do not wish to tell you lies or hear them.

"We have a very fine life here. We are learning to... heal from our pasts. We work very hard at that. We have endless discussions on matters of the heart and mind that most men would label sophism. It has aided Gaston greatly in controlling his madness.

"We surround ourselves with people who love us. We try and avoid doing things that trouble us. And to continue this life, because I place very little value on being a nobleman, I am willing to leave my inheritance behind and spend the rest of my days with Gaston. I only maintain the pretense that I will one day inherit because it is useful in dealing with ambitious men, and I can use what little power it affords me to affect the lives of others for the good.

"Gaston places great value on being a nobleman, though. It is a thing he has thought long lost to him – along with the love of any he might call kin. He wants what should be his by birthright. He is willing to try to live up to the expectations of the title. He is willing to attempt to please you. He is willing to leave the life we have here to accept the duty of his name.

"Beyond that, he wants his name cleared of any question as to his competence in the eyes of French law.

"Now what do you want?" I asked.

Gaston was smiling and he slipped his hand in mine beneath the table and entwined our fingers.

His father was gazing upon me as if I were either daft or a saint and he could not decide which.

"I wish to know that all I have ever attempted in my life was not in vain," the Marquis said at last.

I smiled at him. I had truly not expected so honest an answer.

"I wish to know that I yet have an heir worthy of the title," he said, his gaze on Gaston.

My matelot nodded solemnly.

"I wish to know I have an heir who will carry on the family traditions and name," the Marquis said, this time his gaze was aimed at me.

My smile thinned considerably. "We know he would have to marry."

The Marquis held up a placating hand. "I see how you are a boon to my son's well-being and happiness. I am not... suggesting you be parted. I am merely concerned that the presence of someone to whom he is so very close would impede the formation of the loving bonds of marriage."

I was incredulous. "My Lord, you are indeed an idealistic man. Many would ask what love has to do with the production of heirs, but I suppose that could be viewed as yet another reason most of the nobility are as jaded and amoral as they are."

The Marquis awarded me a compressed smile of agreement.

I glanced at Gaston: he nodded.

"Gaston wishes for children," I said. "He is fond of them; and in dealing with the necessity of my marrying, we have discussed the matter at length. He has, of course, been concerned that any offspring he produced would be mad, but we believe there might be a way to mitigate that now."

"How?" the Marquis asked.

I suppressed a sigh: I did not wish to offend the man now by bringing into question all he had done for his wife. "We know how we deal with his madness, and we think it likely that if a child was raised learning to deal with any possible madness in that fashion, they could be taught to manage themselves far better than Gaston had the opportunity to."

He thought on that and at last nodded. "I, too, have been concerned that any children of that bloodline would be mad."

I continued quickly. "Prior to deciding that the madness might be mitigated in a child, we had thought I would father any children we would raise. That is the primary reason we have found the wife my father sent so unacceptable. She appears to have no qualities we wish to see in a child, and we fear any child she bears might somehow inherit her... hatefulness, and perhaps even her love of rum. So, we had been planning on... putting her out and procuring a more suitable mother for our children. If Gaston is now to marry, we would wish for him to marry a woman that would be a fine mother and have qualities that we wish to see in a child. We would want her to be accepting of our relationship as well, and hope that perhaps there could be respect, if not fondness, between all parties."

The Marquis frowned. "Would you intend to bed her too?" His tone was somewhat chiding.

I sighed. "Non, non, I would not."

He glanced toward the table where Sarah, Striker and Pete sat.

I sighed again. "My sister, and her husband, and his matelot, have a, while not unique, definitely a rare relationship, and I do not feel it is one that could easily be emulated, or perhaps should be emulated."

He nodded thoughtfully. "So she does bed both of them?"

"We are discussing my sister, sir," I said with a slight edge to my tone.

He winced apologetically. "I meant no offense."

"Do you already have alliances that you wished to make through the marriage of Gaston's half-brothers?" I asked.

He shook his head sadly. "That is all gone now. And with what is known of Gaston among many of my peers, I do not feel I could procure a match that would be as suitable as I would like."

I tried not to smile at that. It was very likely anyone the Marquis might wish to marry Gaston to was related to some school bully my matelot had struck or even maimed.

"I will wish for the girl to be of noble blood, though," he added. "Noble French blood."

I sighed. He was saying Agnes was unacceptable. I supposed I could still marry the girl and we could bring her along to France.

And then I was struck with the breadth and scope of what I was thinking of so casually. My heart skipped a beat. We were mad to pursue this. Things did not become very confusing in the light beyond the cave as Gaston had said; nay, they became very clear, and thus we could see them for the insanity they were. In the cave they were nice, safe shadows upon the wall.

"I am sure some suitable candidate can be found," the Marquis was saying. "As long as you will not impede the marriage."

Visions of all the horrors I had ever wished to avoid with a lover came to me, such as his having to sneak into my bed in order to hide our relationship from his wife.

I found myself saying, "I will do whatever is necessary to make Gaston happy." I would, and I did not feel it would lead to the horrors I imagined, because I did not feel living in that situation would make Gaston happy either, at least I prayed it would not.

The Marquis was studying Gaston, and my matelot met his gaze with level resignation.

"You appear to be... less mad than your mother," the Marquis said carefully.

"I cannot judge that," Gaston said.

The Marquis nodded and gave a little sigh and moue. "I do not know if I can judge that." He shrugged. "Your mother could not manage her own servants, much less a household. Yet, you are trusted by men to heal them and fight alongside them. You can take orders and maintain yourself such that those around you do not fear some outburst or action that would cause them trouble or harm. That is more than ever could have been said of your mother."

I kept my lips tightly sealed and watched Gaston. He was not wearing any mask, and he appeared regretful and somewhat guilty.

"That has not always been so," Gaston said. "And not all trust me now. But, I am far better now than I was three years ago."

I squeezed his fingers lightly. He glanced at me and smiled ruefully. My smile was as reassuring as I could make it. He would be as he was, and his father would accept him or not.

"Will gives me focus, and mitigates my interaction with others," Gaston said. "Without him..." He sighed and met his father's gaze again. "I used to spend several months a year sitting on a ship with other men, not talking to them or allowing them to talk to me. I was like a vicious dog they let lie until we reached the Spanish, then... I would attack the enemy until my rage was spent, and sometimes, I would not be able to calm myself and the men I roved with would truss me and lock me away for their safety until I became quiet and withdrawn again.

"When I felt particularly sane, I would visit Doucette and learn from him. I never showed him my madness. I could go for months sometimes hiding it from him before I at last needed to flee again. He is… was, incapable of seeing the signs of it for what they were.

"When I could stand the company of no man, I hid myself away on the Haiti and lived as a wild hermit. I cannot always remember what I did during those times, but I lived, and eventually I always emerged and took my place among men again. And that is how I spent the first ten years I lived in the West Indies.

"Then Will arrived, and for the first time I had someone to talk to about my madness, someone who will stand by me and speak for me when I am at my worst, someone I care enough for that even at my maddest I will attempt to control myself for his benefit.

"I have not gone raving in the wilderness for a year now, or needed to be chained in some dark place until I calmed." He frowned. "And I have the respect of friends, and I am able to use what I learned from Doucette for the good of others."

I suppressed a wince at the irony of his words. In Porto Bello, Striker, our dear friend, had chained him in a dark place when there had been no need: because I had gone mad, not Gaston.

"And I feel I will become stronger yet," Gaston continued. "But, the madness always looms, like a storm on the horizon. Your arrival cast me from the calm we lived in into a maelstrom. Yet, Will feels I am doing well, and you seem to think I am saner than my mother."

The Marquis' face had fallen with disappointment while Gaston talked. "So your sanity, such that it is…" He frowned. "Is a recent acquisition?"

I suppressed a sigh as I saw Gaston struggle with that answer, the resignation deepening its hold on his face. He would never be sane enough for his father. How many years must Gaston act sane before his father would be able to say he was capable? And what did it prove? That Gaston was able to act sane like other men? How sane were they?

I experienced an epiphany. It came blazing out of the light at the cave mouth, and then I realized I was not standing in the cave anymore, not even in the mouth. We stood in the light as we had often surmised. Centaurs stand in the light. There were trees and grass and flowers, and our cart stood there on a road leading to only the Gods knew where.

"Non," I said firmly, and they regarded me with surprise. "His sanity is as it has always been. He is no more sane or mad than he was as a child. And he has always possessed the ability to control his madness. He has merely spent most of his life in situations that did not warrant that control; situations in which he has been thrust: such as battle, or roving for months crowded together with other dangerous and sometimes inhospitable men – men no more sane than he because they were cast here like refuse just as he was – or in schools where he was badgered and beaten for being different, and he learned to fight in order to survive. His madness is what has allowed him to survive."

The Horse of his madness was the truth of his soul as we had long known: the cussedly stubborn part of him that just wanted to live; that was angered when he was told he could not be as he was born, that he was evil, that he must be punished.

The Marquis was frowning at me as if I had gone mad, and I almost laughed. Gaston was regarding me with wonder and rapt attention. I grinned at him.

"There is madness that is… surely mad," I told them and sighed as I realized I needed to explain much much more. "I once had a friend named Joseph. He saw and spoke to people others did not see. That… that is madness of an order…" And then I realized something of that matter. "But we all see people who are not real: we all see shadows on the wall of our memories and…" Joseph had just taken it far further than was comfortable.

I took a deep breath and tried again. "Are you familiar with Plato's allegory of the cave?" I asked the Marquis.

He began to nod and then shook his head. "Perhaps you should…"

"It is the allegory in which he speaks of a man being chained in a seat in a cave. All he sees of the world are shadows cast on the cave wall by the real images of things that exist in the light beyond the cave. He does not see truth, only the representation of truth."

The Marquis nodded and spoke with surety. "Oui, God is the light of truth, and unless we turn to see him we are ever chained in the dark."

I was momentarily appalled he had been taught it in that manner. I supposed that was one interpretation, but it was so… limiting. I struggled to find a way to convey my original intent, or perhaps use his thoughts to prove my own.

"What if I said we were speaking of something more profound than God?" I asked.

He stiffened, and leaned back in his chair with a foreboding frown.

"You would say I blasphemed, or that I was mad," I quickly interjected.

He nodded tightly.

"You would say that, because I do not perceive the same shadows on the wall, or make the same interpretations of them that you, or most men, do."

He became angry. "I have spent much of the last years learning to turn in that seat and see God and accept His light as I am able."

That explained a great deal, but I pushed it aside.

"So have we!" I said earnestly. "It is the same thing. It is… I say it is more profound than God, because we are not seeking God in the light as some rarified deity, but the answers to the mysteries of our souls that God gave us. We are seeking truth."

He shook his head and gave me a troubled frown.

"I am mad," I said.

His frown deepened, such that he looked very old and not at all wise.

"I am mad," I said, and nodded encouragingly.

He sighed. "You sound mad. I can see where it is merely different words for the same thing, but your words sound blasphemous."

I grinned. "All men are mad who do not perceive things, or speak of them, as others do," I said carefully. "But if one stands in the light, one sees that most men are still chained in those seats, seeing shadows on the wall, shadows that are not truth. And... It is very difficult to call that sanity, but since it is a lie shared by so many, the few are judged as being mad, and the many as being sane."

Gaston nearly toppled me from my chair in diving atop me. His mouth closed over mine and his kiss was short and sweet. He released me and I found green eyes glowing with happiness.

"We are centaurs," he whispered.

"We cannot hide in caves," I whispered with a grin. "Or watch shadows on the wall... anymore. It is a thing we have known, I have simply not seen it in this manner before. Much like the revelation you delivered to me by saying I was not a piss poor wolf, but something else entirely, a centaur."

He nodded enthusiastically and stood with elation. "We must think on it."

I looked back at his father, who seemed quite bemused.

"When Gaston is mad, he speaks or acts from the truth of his soul, and he has a very big and sensitive soul that hears and sees things clearly that other men find quiet or dim. The more he lives in harmony with that truth, the more control he exercises in his dealings with other men. But in truth..." I grinned. "He will always be perceived as being mad by you and others. Because to think and feel and act as others do, to accept their truths, he would have to sit in the cave again and be chained in his seat. And even by your interpretation, that is not what God wants, is it? And that way leads to true madness, in that the more he tries to be a thing he is not, the more the truth within him fights to be free."

I took a deep breath. I felt I was walking in the clouds hearing the chorus of angels, and it was with great difficulty I brought my thoughts back to earth.

I smiled at him. "You might decide that that renders him too mad to be your heir, to accept the sacred duty of being the Lord Tervent. That is your decision. There is nothing we can do for it. We are going to go now, to the tailor's, to have proper clothes made so that Gaston can attend the party."

Gaston was fairly bouncing with excitement. He seemed disappointed when I delayed being away from there even for the moment it took to stop by the other table to snatch a handful of bacon. I gave my sister, Striker, and Pete – who were obviously curious as to our agitation – each a kiss on the head, and hurried out the door.

Gaston pulled me into his arms and kissed me again with great relish. It was a thing of sanity of such an order I could no longer comprehend how anyone could say that two men kissing on the street because they were happy was madness.

"We are mad!" Gaston proclaimed, and we giggled like boys.

"But I feel we shall never be lords," I said when the wave of mirth passed.

This sobered him, but he did not lose his happy expression. "And rule over sane men?"

"More like shepherd over them." I sighed. "I became disillusioned with herding sheep with the men of the plantation. I do not now believe that sheep can be herded to any meaningful destination. The best one can hope to do is give them arms and thus make them dogs, who then behave like wolves."

He thought on this for a time as we began walking toward the shops of Lime Street. "Is not a shepherd's duty to merely keep them from being eaten by wolves or falling off cliffs?"

I grinned. "And keep them orderly when they are to be fleeced."

"Just so," he said with amusement. "I suppose I do not wish to be a shepherd."

"So we are once again at the question: what do centaurs do?"

"Practice sophism," Gaston said with a sly smile.

I laughed and reminded him, "It is only sophism if it serves no practical use." And then I sighed for comic effect. "Of course, we are sophists, and unless we are lords, we serve no practical use."

"I wish to be a physician," Gaston said. "And we should serve as guides for creatures other than sheep."

"So you said at dinner," I said. "I have always felt that is a wonderful thing you should pursue, you are ever at your best then. But what is a guide for other creatures? Or is that not the definition we decided on of a centaur: a mythical being that comes from the caves to dispense wisdom and healing?"

He grinned. "Just so. A madman."

This set us laughing again. I thought the Gods laughed with us in this: as They were beings of the light, They surely knew the difference between madness and sanity enough to laugh at it.

Fifty-Nine

Wherein We Run Wild On the Chessboard

We stopped at Massey's, the gunsmith's, on the way to the tailor's. We were somewhat surprised and quite pleased to find our pistols there waiting for us. We thanked him and gave him some coin for both his trouble, and to give to the men who had delivered our pieces.

That happy matter behind us, we forced ourselves into the tailor's. He was delighted to make our acquaintance, of course, but dismayed as to the amount of time we gave him. After much discussion of what I had available in clothing and what he had partially completed on hand, it was decided that he would make a coat for Gaston for the party, which my matelot would wear over one of my shirts and a pair of my breeches. And then at a more leisurely pace, he would make Gaston two suits of matching jackets and breeches.

We were pleased to note that, though his cloth selections ranged from wool to velvet, he did not make his coats with the full lining and padding a similar piece would require in England. At my inquiry, he assured me one of his apprentices would have time to remove much of the lining from the coat I would wear for the party. I was much relieved I would not be as hot as I had been at the prior formal functions I had attended here on Jamaica.

I was also relieved I would not need to strip to the waist in order to be measured and fitted; as I was still covered by livid bruises from our Horse play before we left Negril.

To my surprise, Gaston delighted in the choosing of fabrics. He had never visited a tailor and had clothes made for him. We chose a deep green velvet for Gaston's new coat: I liked the color; my matelot liked the feel of it.

At the man's question of what footgear we would have, I remembered I had left my boots in the sea. I had shoes, of course, but they required wearing hose, a thing I was loathe to do in the heat. Gaston had nothing other than his soft boots, so we decided he would wear those. The tailor was appalled when we described them, and even more so when I told him I would wear the same if we could but locate some.

Thus when the tailor finished measuring Gaston, we eschewed visiting our friend Belfry at the haberdashery next door, and went in search of a leatherworker who could make boots similar to Gaston's. The cobbler could not fathom why any man would want a boot without a hard sole, and at our description of Gaston's boots, denounced them as improper. So we went to Massey and inquired of members of the Brethren who might be leatherworkers. He suggested a man who made belts, baldrics, and ammunition pouches for many of his customers. We at last located that man in a tavern. He was quite drunk, but he assured us he could make anything. We asked the barkeep and found out he had not been sober for three days. We bought him another tankard and left him there. Then we went to the leather shop next to the apothecary, where once I had bought a whip when Gaston wished to become inured to one. The establishment carried a great many things for horses and men, but no footgear. Still, the owner said he could do much with leather, and if we would provide him of an example of what we sought, he would see what he could do. So we returned to the house to fetch the boots – and my coat that would be altered – and returned to the shop. After examining Gaston's boots, both on my matelot and off, the man agreed he could make them, provided we left the boots as a model. He then took many measurements of my foot, ankle, and calf before allowing us to leave.

The sun had passed its zenith when at last we dropped off the coat at the tailor's. Weary in ways hours of battle did not leave us, we decided we wished to do no more shopping this day. Belfry would have to wait: Gaston had no interest in viewing hats or any other gentlemanly accoutrement, and I did not wish to endure the surely odd looks we would receive from Mistress Belfry after all the trouble in their shop with Sarah and Striker.

We wandered into the market and bought boucan and a pineapple, and ate as we walked slowly back home.

"So, now what shall we do?" I asked as we approached the house. "Spend time with Bella and the puppies? Damn, we should have bought her something."

"Perhaps we should see to another item on our agenda," Gaston said glumly and regarded the house next door.

It took me a moment to remember why it held import, and then I cursed.

He awarded me a grim smile. "I have been thinking, we cannot resolve the matter with my father."

"We could shoot him," I said with a grin.

"That would not settle the matter of my inheriting or not," he said after frowning for a moment.

"You are correct, it would only complicate it immensely," I sighed.

"So," he said, "let us resolve the things that we can." He pointed at the house.

"I still do not know how this should be resolved," I sighed, "but I suppose you are correct. And, we should at least ask her what she wishes."

"Will we honor her wishes?" he asked with grim amusement.

"It will depend on what she wishes," I said.

I was disappointed when Coswold answered the door. If any man should die of the flux, it was he.

He glared down his nose at us. "What do you want?"

Thankfully for him, I saw no light of recognition in his eyes.

"I am Lord Marsdale, Coswold," I said with annoyance.

He winced. Whether it was because he had committed a grave error in not recognizing his rightful employer, or rather it was because he was now reminded of whom his rightful employer actually was, I do not know. I rather suspect it was the latter.

"Lady Marsdale is not expecting you," he said.

"Of course she is not," I said coldly. "I own this house. Get out of my way."

He stepped aside with a bow.

"Were that the door?" a woman's voice called out. It was not my wife.

I peered down the dim hallway past the foyer, and spied the plump housekeeper, Henrietta, scurrying toward us, squinting at what she could see of us in the light streaming through the door.

Coswold closed the door behind Gaston, and Henrietta stopped and truly saw us.

"Oh," she said, and then, "Oh!" She curtsied belatedly and scurried back down the hall and up a flight of stairs. "My Lady!"

We found a sitting room off the foyer. It was filled with fine furniture pieces. All had thin carved legs and ornately embroidered cushions; I thought it likely they were French, and I wondered where she had found them in Port Royal: she surely had not had time to have them shipped. Cursing wafted down through the ceiling as we sat on the settee. Coswold stood in the doorway like a statue. I thought of asking him for water or perhaps wine, but suspected he might spit in it.

There were slow steps on the stairs. Coswold finally moved, his nose held high as he walked down the hall toward the back of the house. And then she appeared.

She had become plump since last I saw her, and it was not the baby. Her belly was surely as huge as my sister's, but Sarah was still thin about the limbs and face. Though she was perhaps not truly fat, Vivian Williams looked as if she were carrying a little baby everywhere, and the loose pink dress she wore only served to make her look rounder. Her long honey-colored hair was plaited simply, and hung over her shoulder. As always, her hazel eyes would have been lovely if she were not scowling.

"I wondered when you would turn up," she said, and made her way to a chair to sit.

"We arrived in town two days ago. How are you?" I asked.

She snorted with wry amusement. "Pregnant."

"When are you due to birth?" Gaston asked.

She glared at him, and her answer was smug. "Within a month, or so the silly midwife says."

Gaston and I exchanged a glance. Sarah was due within a month. We knew when Sarah had conceived: likely her wedding night, if not two days earlier during her tryst with Striker in the back room of the haberdashery. I knew Vivian had not conceived on our wedding night the day before Striker's. When we returned in April, Sarah had mentioned that my wife was telling all she was with child, but also, that she appeared to have taken a lover. I had thought Vivian had taken her lover in March, perhaps, at the earliest; but if she were indeed as far along in her pregnancy as my sister, she had taken the lover sooner after I had sailed than we had realized. It made it possible for her to claim the child was mine.

If she had not been indiscreet – presumably because she was drunk on rum, as she had been every time I had seen her – no one would have known of her ruse; except me, who knew good and well where my cock had and had not gone.

She was glaring at me, now. "You proved to be able to do something right."

"It is said you took a lover," I said.

She glanced toward the doorway and frowned, and then leaned forward as much as her belly would allow to whisper, "What do you care? If I have a boy, we can be done with one another."

I leaned forward and whispered in return. "I thought that, too. But then I heard everyone on Jamaica knows of your infidelity. It is likely my father will not even believe the child is mine."

She snorted dismissively. "It could be yours; all you need do is claim it so."

"If I in any way thought it was mine, I might," I said. "And though it seems you moved far more quickly than I gave you credit for, I still feel the ruse will be discovered even if your lover has my coloring."

"I do not have a lover," she hissed. "And how do you know it is not yours? God could have smiled on our wedding union just as He did your sister's."

"Only if I am an angel," I said. "I did not put my prick in you that night. You were being such a bitch I wanted no part of you. So I broke your maidenhead with my dagger hilt."

She slapped me. I saw it coming but I did not flinch. Her eyes were filled with such cold fury she would have struck me down with lightning bolts had she the power.

She clambered to her feet and nearly ran to the door to look up and down the hall.

"Out!" she screamed at someone. "Go to the market! Do something useful, you damn bastard!"

"Lady, I do not listen to your conversations," Coswold said stiffly.

"If I am careful!" she snarled. "Now leave!"

She turned back to us and seemed to want to pace; but the effort, or perhaps the might of her rage, tired her and she returned to the chair to collapse into it ungracefully.

"I hate him," she snarled at me. "Almost as much as I hate you."

"Then dismiss him," I said.

"I have tried," she hissed. "He will not go. He says you are his employer, not I."

"That is easily mended," I said. I looked to Gaston. "How much coin do you have?"

He handed me all he carried and I considered the contents of my coin purse. The silver we carried was more than adequate to get the damn man back to England. I pulled the gold from my bag and his and gave it to Gaston. I combined the silver together in one pouch. Then I went in search of Coswold.

I found him donning a hat with ponderous dignity near the door to the yard. I handed him the silver coins. "You are dismissed. Pack your things and leave immediately. We are waiting."

"My Lord, surely you jest!" he cried.

"Nay, I do not," I said with a smile. "I have never liked you. I have ever found you disrespectful. And if she does not like you, either, then you are gone. Now pack, and do not give me reason to inspect your things before you leave."

"I would never," he hissed and turned away to stomp up the stairs.

"Is there anything you feel he might steal?" I asked as I returned to the drawing room.

Vivian was regarding me with guarded wonder. "Aye," she snapped and lurched to her feet again. She climbed the stairs and soon we heard more yelling.

Gaston came to join me in the hall. "Should we go up?" he asked.

I sighed and shrugged.

He began to ascend the stairs. I awarded him a raised eyebrow. He shrugged and kept walking.

I soon heard, "This is not your concern!" from Coswold. I did not hear Gaston's reply, but Vivian laughed.

There was a sound beside me and I turned to find Henrietta regarding me fearfully.

"You are not dismissed," I said kindly.

She sighed with relief.

"Was there not another girl, a maid?" I asked.

"Tess, my Lord," she said quickly. "She's gone."

"Did she become ill?"

Henrietta shook her head. "Nay, my Lord. She stole some of the Mistress' money and took a ship home. She had a man she wished to marry there, and she... Well, it were just best is all, my Lord."

"Do you wish to return to England?" I asked.

She shrugged her wide shoulders. "Nay, my Lord, got no kin left. An' I be just a maid there."

"Well, since you will now have to do all of the work, you can have Coswold's and Tess' salaries in addition to your own," I said.

Her jaw dropped. "Thank you, my Lord," she at last managed to say.

Coswold finally stomped down the stairs, with Gaston and Vivian in his wake. With one last look of concern at Gaston, the man hurried out the front door.

"Did you tell him what you did to the last arrogant servant we encountered?" I asked.

Gaston shrugged as he walked past me into the sitting room. "I told him he would not be missed if I slit his throat."

I grinned, and turned to find Vivian doing the same. She quickly sobered, as if I were not allowed to see her smile.

"Henrietta has told me about Tess," I said. "I have informed her that since she now must do the work of three, she can have all three salaries."

Vivian nodded slowly, and gave Henrietta an actual kind smile. "I agree to that. Henrietta has been with me since I left the nursery."

"Thank you, my Lady," Henrietta said with a warm smile of her own. "Would you like tay?"

"Nay," Vivian said, and made her way past me into the sitting room. I smelled an odor about her that I often had: pineapple, coconut, and rum. I was seized with the odd thought that her child would most likely smell like that, and not the innocent milk smell of puppies.

"So now what will you do?" she asked as she returned to the chair she had occupied before. Her rage seemed past, but I knew the reserve she now seemed to possess was due to rum and not fortitude.

I went to sit next to Gaston on the settee. "What do you wish?"

She smirked. "I have spent the last year wishing you would die, but that has not happened."

I smiled in kind. "I have spent the last eight months thinking how lucky I would be if you died while birthing."

She made great work of smoothing her skirt and snorted with amusement, her mouth contorted someplace between a smirk and a grimace. "So we are even on that account. Do you wish my child dead as well?" she asked with an edge to her voice, and I saw fear tighten her features for but a moment. Then she glanced at Gaston.

"You would be missed," my matelot said with a shrug.

She glared at him, and then quickly took to studying her skirt again.

"We do not wish for any harm to befall the child," I assured her. "No matter what the outcome is to be between you and me, I would see the child cared for."

She gave a short sigh of relief and nodded to herself. Then she adopted a hopeful air. "What if it is a boy? Would that not...?"

I shook my head quickly, but then I sighed. She was correct: if it were a boy, it would solve many problems with my father and allow me to stave off questions of my inheritance, and thus retain my title for the benefit of all, that much longer. I had not heard from anyone, including my father, as to whether he had heard of her indiscretion. I could claim a boy as mine, and even if it took my damn father years to decide if I had a legitimate heir, those would still be years in which I was the Viscount of Marsdale. But, I would be stuck with her, as I could not divorce her for adultery or annul the marriage for lack of consummation if I claimed the child. Nay, the sex of the babe did not matter: if I was to be rid of her, I needed to do it now. I had waited too long as it was.

"I do not wish to be married to you," I told her. "And I am reluctant to claim any issue of yours, male or not, because I feel he might inherit your poor judgment and meanness of spirit."

She recoiled and tears filled her eyes. "You bastard," she gasped.

"I will provide money for the child to be raised," I said. "Now, what do you wish? I will pursue whatever method I must to end this marriage, be it divorce or annulment, whichever will be the easiest and most convenient – for me. Where do you wish to live? Is there anyone who could take you in?"

"Nay," she breathed. "No one."

I sighed. "If necessary, I will find someplace to put you and the child, and provide for your support as well. I will even pay Henrietta's salary. But I will not set you up in a fine house in London. In truth, I will not support you if you return to England at all."

Her ire had returned in full force. "Why?" she demanded.

"I do not wish to have my name, such as it is, slandered in court," I sighed.

"Oh," she said with venom, "so you do not want anyone to know you are a pirate who lets that bastard fuck you up the arse every night?"

Gaston gave a quiet hiss of annoyance.

I smiled. "While that is actually a thing of which I am quite proud, nay, I do not wish to have the likes of you speaking of it."

"I can write letters," she snarled.

"And I can put you out on the street naked without a penny," I said. "I hear the brothels are always looking for more."

She winced. "I am not a whore."

"Nay, you are a drunkard," I said sadly.

"You would be, too," she said so quietly I almost did not hear her, and I had to spend several moments puzzling through the sounds I had heard to make sense of them.

"We all choose how we will survive the things life compels us to endure," I said carefully.

She glared at me, and then snorted and rolled her eyes. "Do not speak to me like a man of God."

I sighed and stood. "Think on whether you wish to raise the child or not. Think on how you wish to live. I am sure we can find you a house in town. Or you could live on the plantation."

"Why can I not remain here?" she asked. "This is my house."

"Nay, it is actually my father's house as I understand the finances of it. He supplied the money to have it built for my bride. I imagine he will expect me to ensconce my next wife in it."

"You fucking bastard," she said with new tears.

Gaston and I walked to the door.

"Wait!" she called as we began to leave. She came to lean in the sitting room doorway. "I can keep Henrietta, and I need not… work? And I can have a house of my own?"

I nodded.

She nodded, and pulled herself to stand with squared shoulders and an air of nonchalance. "That will be fine, then. Do what you must."

We left.

"She is scarred," Gaston said quietly, once we were safely on the street.

"Oui," I sighed. "I thought that on my wedding night. She is a scared and lonely little girl with many scars. Someone has given her great anger and sadness and she has learned to find solace in the bottle."

"I feel sympathy for her," he said with a rueful smile.

"You wish for me to stay married to her?" I asked.

His eyes hardened. "Non, I wish to have fine puppies." He frowned a little and looked at Sarah's house. "And we should see the ones we have."

As we did not wish to face anyone in the atrium, we went down the wide alley between Sarah's house and my wife's, and slipped in the back gate of Sarah's yard. We were immediately met by dogs, and it was a good thing they knew us. Sam's head emerged from the cookhouse to see what all the ado was about. He greeted us with a smile and silence, and we were left to pet the dogs and sneak into the stable without seeing another soul. The puppies were sleeping, and Bella was happy to see us, even though we had not brought her anything. We lay in the straw and inhaled innocence for a time.

"What is true madness?" Gaston asked.

I had been nearly asleep, and it took me several moments to recall why he would ask such a thing. A day spent attempting to have a simple pair of boots made, and then seeing the Damn Wife, had robbed me of the morning's philosophic bent.

He rolled onto his side to peer down at me. "Not all madness can be dismissed as a difference between those in the cave and those without. I have seen men who raved without any knowledge of their location or identity. I have occasionally been reduced to that state. That is not a truth," he said sadly.

"Non," I agreed. "I did not mean my revelation to be an answer, but merely an illustration of another view of the matter, perhaps. Maybe some men wander too far into the cave, where there is no light, or maybe some men stand in the full heat of the sun too long, and it boils their heads. But all allegory aside, I feel – as we have decided before – that not all those things or thoughts we call mad, are. And surely men who live their lives watching and acting out lies cannot see the truth."

Gaston nodded with a thoughtful frown. "There is comfort to be found in the shade – and common ground. When my Horse takes the bit and runs, I feel I stand too long in the light, and then my eyes cannot see into the darkness of the cave to know what other men perceive, and I know not how to speak with them."

I smiled. "Perhaps we need to live in the mouth of the cave."

"If we are to deal with other men," he said seriously.

And as if our words had called him, Sam appeared to tell us supper was being served.

All chose to seat themselves as they had the night before, and though the Marquis was eyeing Gaston and me curiously, there was far less tension in the room: faces were smiling, and people entered speaking of trivial things.

"I spoke to Lady Marsdale today," I told Sarah as we waited for Sam to finish serving roast chicken and soup.

"How is she?" Sarah asked with sincere curiosity.

"She seems much the same, though now she is obviously with child; and she is somewhat plumper," I said. "She claims she should birth within a month."

Sarah raised an eyebrow and spoke wryly. "Truly? Does she also claim it is a boy, and yours?"

I shrugged. "She wished to claim that, but I corrected her."

"You claim the child is not yours?" the Marquis asked with an amused frown.

"My Lord, I know the child is not mine," I said with a grin. "My seed was not sown on that field, or for that matter, anywhere near that property."

This set the men at the table chuckling and caused Agnes to flush.

"Why?" the Marquis asked with narrowed eyes. "Did you find her completely disagreeable?" His glance flicked to Gaston.

I sighed. "She is quite pretty, beautiful perhaps, and I would have been happy to do my duty as her husband if the damn woman had possessed any interest in performing her wifely duties. She came here, to this island, quite furious that she should be forced to leave England, to marry someone as disreputable as me, and to even be made to marry at all. I cannot speak for other men, but if a lady is unwilling to have me share her bed, I do not wish to do so."

"So the marriage is unconsummated?" Sarah asked. "Then you do not need a divorce. An annulment should be easy enough to arrange."

I awarded her an admonishing look. "And how will that be perceived? People will assume, as the Marquis did here, that I chose not to for other reasons; or that I am incapable. So I will address the matter with Theodore on the morrow. For now, she has been apprised that I will proceed to put her out as soon as possible, preferably before she births. As she might truly be as near to birthing as she claims, I may have waited too damn long as it is. Either way, though, I have told her I will see that she and the child are cared for. Tell me, who owns that house?"

Sarah sighed. "Father's instructions to Theodore were quite explicit: it is father's, as is the plantation, until such time as you shall produce an heir. It is for the use of Lady Marsdale, whoever she might be."

"Well, damn, that is as I thought," I sighed. "The current Lady Marsdale rather likes the place, and, as I have no other abode to ensconce her in, I rather hoped she could remain there. I suppose I will have to speak to Theodore about that as well. And about the change in servants," I added to myself.

"What about the servants?" she asked. "I suppose they told you about the maid."

"Aye, but now they have lost one more," I said. "I dismissed that arrogant arse, Coswold. All that is left is the housekeeper, Henrietta."

"Oh, well, that is not a matter for Theodore, but for me," Sarah said.

I raised an eyebrow.

She shrugged. "He does not have an entire bevy of clarks hidden away to see to these things, so I manage your lady's house account, along with ours and the business."

I was surprised; not that Sarah could do such a thing, but that Vivian would allow it. "Does she know this?" I asked.

Sarah shook her head. "She would not be pleased if she did."

"Is she costly to maintain?" I asked.

"Nay," Sarah said, as if she found the matter surprising. "We were fortunate to have several plantations being sold when we needed to acquire furniture and the like for her house and ours, so that was not unduly expensive, though we would still have paid less in England for the same. And since then, her primary expenses have been the servants and food. Though I have thought much of that was due to her being with child and not prone to entertaining or needing gowns for parties. But even in the matter of the food, Henrietta has proven to be an excellent cook, and they eat food grown here and not shipped from England. She is the one who taught Samuel to cook."

I smiled as I sipped more of the tasty soup. "That is good to hear, it means I made one good decision this day: I have promised Henrietta the salaries of the other two since she is now left with the work of three."

Sarah's eyebrows rose in surprise, but she nodded agreeably. "That is a bit of money: Coswold was overpaid, but Henrietta is well worth it. She might stay with that, though I feel she has stayed as long as she has because she is loyal to your wife."

The Marquis had been listening to Dupree's translation with amusement, and now he asked, "Is it difficult to retain servants here?"

Many of us regarded him as if he were daft.

"Lord Tervent," Sarah said with a smile, "it is difficult to obtain servants here. Women, of any variety, are scarce. So, if one imports maids or cooks from England, they are courted by men who earn as much as their masters. Bondswomen suitable for housework are often sold to men who wish to marry them. Negroes suitable for housework are very rare and very expensive. The plantations cannot get enough slaves as it is. And any young man one might employ in a house runs away to become a buccaneer, because they think they will get rich."

"Will they not?" the Marquis asked with a smile.

"Nay, my Lord," Striker said. "To be sure, in a good year they'll make more than most honest men are paid in England, but in a bad year, or if they drink overmuch, they find themselves sold to the plantations to cover their tavern bills. The smart ones put their money in land or other enterprises."

"And which have you done?" the Marquis asked him with more good humor.

Striker grinned. "We started a merchant company to import and export goods."

"Ah," the Marquis nodded appreciatively. "It seems that would be quite lucrative, especially if one imported slaves and servants."

Everyone stilled after his words were translated, and he immediately sensed the unease.

"What did I say?" he asked, and glanced with annoyance at Dupree.

"We won't deal in slaves," Striker said quickly. "Not all of us arrived here as free men."

"And some of us feel that no man should be owned," I added.

He looked about, as I did, and saw agreement all about the table. I was glad my uncle was not there to gainsay us.

"That is admirable," he said with a thoughtful nod. "But can you make money with such sentiments if, presumably, your competitors do not hold them?"

"Aye," Striker said, "if we ship everything the plantations need and produce."

The Marquis frowned at that. "From what I hear of plantations, their greatest need seems to be men, and so if you do not ship men, then you are only carrying cargo out," and he shrugged in seeming dismissal of the amounts of that, "and bringing nothing back."

"I thought of it that way, once," I said with a smile. "But we are speaking of plantations and Englishmen. We English, if we are anything, are steadfast in our traditions. We do not like to change our housing or dress to better match the local climes, and we do not eat the local food – this household excepted, of course. We do not even like to make a different style of boot." I sighed. "And sugar plantations, or even cocoa and indigo plantations, do not grow food. They also do not employ draft animals. All the work on a plantation is done by men, thus they require great numbers of men, who they cannot feed or clothe, thus all things for those men must be imported, as must all things be imported for their owners – even though we live here in a veritable Garden of Eden as regards the climate and fruit of the vine and field. Planters prefer to eat pickled herring and wormy apples rather than assign any of their precious slaves or cleared land to farming to support the rest. I have been told this all meets with sound fiscal policy as long as the plantation produces well, and that one should not view the entirety of it as a farm, but as a mine."

He nodded his understanding. "So you stand to benefit from the foolishness of others. Did I hear correctly that there is a plantation in your future?" he asked me.

I snorted and shrugged. "If I produce an heir, my father has promised to give me the plantation he sent me here to start. If, by some fluke of fate, I do manage to produce an heir and he keeps his word, that land will no longer be a sugar plantation."

The Marquis frowned.

"Sugar is a vile and useless crop," Gaston said.

His father was quite amused at this pronouncement. "But… is it lucrative?"

"It can be," Sarah said, "but the real money is made by the import taxes into England and the selling of it there. Our father is one of the men who stands to gain from that, and thus, he cares not whether this plantation does well at all, as long as all the rest produce."

The Marquis raised an eyebrow and regarded Sarah. "I mean no offense," he said carefully, "but you seem to possess a great deal of knowledge about business and finance, for a young lady."

Sarah sighed and awarded him a compressed smile. "I was the youngest and I possessed an interest and talent for such things, and so my father indulged me."

"Aye," I added, "truly, if any of my father's true offspring are to inherit, it should be Sarah. She possesses far more interest in the matter than I, and a better head for it; but women are not considered suitable heirs: pity that."

The Marquis nodded his thoughtful agreement. "I left the rearing of my daughters to my wife, and by all accounts, they appear to be fine wives."

"My half-sisters are married?" Gaston asked.

"Oui, one to the son of a Duke, and the other to a Comte," the Marquis said with pride.

"Do they have names?" I asked.

"The Comte de…" the Marquis began, but my look cut him off, and he sighed and gave a sheepish smile. "Marie and Josephine." He frowned thoughtfully at Gaston. "I suppose you never knew them."

Gaston shook his head. "Nor the boys."

"Your brothers were…" The Marquis sighed sadly. "Perhaps I did not raise them to be lords, either; well, perhaps the youngest; but, as he would not inherit and thus carry the family name in that manner, he chose the military, and it ended him."

"And neither was married with an heir?" I asked gently.

The Marquis shook his head sadly. I could see the effort he expended in not gazing upon Gaston. At last he apparently decided I was the better, or perhaps easier, target.

"Your father wishing for you to produce an heir seems to indicate his commitment to your inheriting," he said.

"So it would seem," I said. "Or that he is as committed as I to maintaining the pretense that I will inherit for as long as it is convenient."

"You hate him," the Marquis said. It was not a question, though there was some wonder in his tone.

"Oui," I said, and as I often did, felt the nagging guilt that perhaps I was wrong: that my father's intentions were not so nefarious; that perhaps this was all some great misunderstanding; but then many things sprang to mind and stirred my ire. "Non. I feel for him much as he feels for me. I always thought he hated me, but when last we met, he avowed he was merely displeased with me, that I was not the son he would have wished for. Well, I am displeased with him, as he is not the father I would have wished for. And... he has ever placed the welfare of another before mine, and he allowed – both me and my sister – to be driven from his home by this other individual: my second cousin."

The Marquis frowned slightly and glanced at my sister, whose face was as hard as mine. He gave a shallow nod of acknowledgment to our anger. Then his eyes returned to mine. "Well, all things considered, it is a wonder you have not shot me. You seem to have seen or learned of nothing but trouble and betrayal from noblemen and fathers."

Understanding passed between us, as it had the night he confessed his sins to Gaston and me. It once again robbed me of my anger and hatred. I took a deep breath and nodded.

I spoke French. "I do not hate you, but I do not trust you."

He nodded and smiled, and waved off Dupree's translation. "Perhaps you are not mad in that."

Everyone was silent; Gaston was tense beside me.

I grinned. "Let us proceed from this new understanding, then." I raised my glass in toast.

"Let us," he said, and clinked his glass with mine.

Though the others were curious, the rest of the meal proceeded without incident. Afterward, Gaston played Pete at chess while Sarah and Striker discussed the R&R Merchant Company's plans to acquire ships, and extolled the virtue of our one possession, the *Virgin Queen*. Rucker told me of the plantations he had visited with my uncle while we watched Agnes sketch Pete and Gaston.

When my matelot conceded the game, we bid everyone good evening and retreated to our room in good cheer. I felt we had accomplished much this day, though we had little to show for it that could be measured or remarked upon as resolved. Gaston proved to be of an amorous bent as soon as the doors were closed, and we set about seeing how much the bed would creak from various angles. His earnest listening to the iron frame while thrusting away at me brought me to laughter, and when he joined me in it, I was sure the others about the house heard it far more than they would ever hear the bed. This led to even more antics on both our parts to make the bed move, until at last we fell off the corner of the mattress to finish storming Heaven on the floor, with grins upon our faces and breathless gasps of pleasure at the world.

The next day, we remembered to go and exercise on the beach; and we happily climbed out the window and down the cistern, to give greeting to Bella and the puppies and then slip away through the back gate, before anyone else seemed to have risen. We ran, sparred, and frolicked like fools in the surf before sitting to eat a little boucan and fruit and discuss what we would do for the day.

Our clothes were still drying when we reached Theodore's.

"I have informed my wife of my intent to divorce her, or have the marriage annulled," I told him once we were seated in his office.

"And how did she receive this news?" he asked with thinly veiled amusement.

"Poorly," I said, and then I told him all that had transpired with my wife, and my thoughts on the matter.

"So truly, there is ground for annulment?" Theodore asked.

"Truly," I sighed.

He shoved papers from the leather blotter upon his huge desk, and leaned on his elbows on it, with his hands clasped and his frowning face resting upon them. "It would be much easier to arrange an annulment, but it should surely weaken your case with your father, as you have already surmised. It would be better for her in some ways," he added with a thoughtful nod.

"Sarah said you received a letter," I said.

Theodore nodded and went to the shelves to retrieve the satchel where he stored all mail from my father. He dug through it and handed a thin missive to me.

It was much as Sarah had said. After his daughter had shot the man he wished to adopt and leave as his heir, fled to Jamaica, and married a commoner, all he asked Theodore of was whether I had truly married Vivian Barclay, as I had told him I had, and whether or not she was with child, as my father had apparently heard from other sources. I wondered what he had heard rumored; if he had heard she was pregnant, he had surely heard it was likely not mine.

I snorted and handed the letter to Gaston.

"In my reply," Theodore said with a smile, "I told him you had indeed married Lady Marsdale, and that she was indeed pregnant. I made no other remark or indication as to the parentage of said child, or to her behavior."

"Has there been time to receive a response to that?" I asked.

Theodore shook his head and shrugged. "With the storm season, nay."

"He is an enigma," I sighed.

"It is a game," Gaston said thoughtfully, "like chess, but we do not know if he is planning moves well ahead of us, or merely reacting to unexpected moves we have made. We should ask Pete how to play it." He grinned.

I grinned in return. "As Pete is all Horse, he is as mad as we."

Theodore frowned and I waved it away.

"What would you do?" I asked my matelot. "As a centaur: what does your Horse wish to do?"

He took a deep breath and considered the window for a time. "Fight him, and win. I wish to see him grant you the title and then have you fling it in his face. And even if he will not grant it, I wish to see him have to force you out."

I listened to my Horse and found it fond of that idea as well. If I gave up now, it proved nothing. Well, it proved I could walk away; but my father expected me to, and it was what he wanted: I did not wish for him to receive anything he wanted.

"If that is to be your course," Theodore said with amusement, "then you should remain married to the woman, and claim the child as yours, and wait and see what move he makes."

I swore and slumped in my chair.

Gaston sighed likewise.

With surprise I realized my Horse did not view that as being completely odious. It cared not for marrying and having children whoever the dam might be, though it was not pleased that it must be saddled with a wife I hated and probably inferior children. The Man in me was the one who bridled the most, though. He heard what people saw and thought: the shadows on the wall through which they perceived the situation. But that was not truth, was it?

I looked to Gaston. "Do you truly feel you are willing to risk having children?" I asked quietly in French. "With or without your father's blessing of your choice of bride?"

He looked out the window again as he thought on it, and at last turned to me. "Do you truly feel we could mitigate their madness?"

I did not have to think before answering. "Oui. And even if they are as mad as you, I feel I would still love them. And you are not such a horror that we should not dare inflict another of you upon the world."

He smiled. "Thank you," he whispered. "Then I shall try and make our puppies, and you shall stay married to that bitch to fight your father, and we will see where the game leads."

I looked back to Theodore and sighed. "We will fight. I shall not put her out. We will see what she produces. We shall see what my father's next move is."

And I prayed the Gods would smile upon us, and if they did not grant us that which we thought we desired, that They would at least grant us happiness through some other turn of events.

Sixty

Wherein We Revisit Meals Left Uneaten

After all that had been said yesterday, I thought I would feel quite the fool if I were to go and tell Vivian of our new decision so soon, so I lead Gaston past her house and into Sarah's without so much as a hesitant step.

"When will you tell her?" he asked wryly, once we were within the comfortable shade of the atrium.

"I do not know," I sighed, "and we might change our mind, and I feel it will do no harm if she continues to think I am divorcing her."

"It might make her reflect upon her actions," he said with a shrug.

"We can only hope."

Agnes was about, and I felt some guilt in seeing her. It was foolish: she had never known our plans and probably would have been aghast if she had. Moreover, I could not know how the game would play out and what move we would be upon years from now – or even months from now, for that matter.

We spent the afternoon engrossed in viewing things through Agnes' lenses. I was both appalled and fascinated at how common things appeared when magnified, especially insects. They are the most vicious-appearing creatures I have ever beheld, and yet no one thinks of them as such, because they are so small we cannot readily see their wicked hooked claws and strange spiky mouths.

As all in the household had come to join in the activity of seeing the unseen over the course of the day, our discussion at supper held more talk of the same; the Marquis asked Gaston many questions – and thankfully expressed fascination and not dismay when my matelot told him he thought the medical theories of humors and the like to be foolishness, not a reasoned way of viewing the human body and how it behaved or the causes and treatment of illnesses.

After we ate, Agnes brought out the telescope, and we saw what we could. I was disappointed that stars looked much the same through it, only brighter and more colorful on occasion. Then Jupiter rose high enough for us to see, and I was stricken with awe at the wonder of it: to think that the striped, orange disk I beheld was another world like our own was a wondrous thing indeed.

Several of us, the Marquis included, chose to wait until the moon rose late in the night. Discussion turned as it once had while roving to how the denizens of other worlds might look or behave. Here again, the Marquis surprised me by not deeming the whole discussion blasphemy, and I was proud he showed such interest in the depth of Gaston's knowledge of things physiological.

Tired and contented, we slept like babes that night. The next day was very much like the last, only we did not need to go to Theodore's after frolicking on the beach; instead, we went to the leather shop and tailor's. My new boots were indeed wondrously comfortable, and the tailor was happy to see Gaston and make a final fitting for his new coat. Then we went to the haberdashery to pay our old friend Belfry a visit and buy any additional accoutrements we would need to appear as fine gentleman. Unfortunately, Mister Belfry was out, and we were left with Mistress Belfry, who although she still stood somewhat in awe of my being a lord, had apparently not forgotten whatever she had witnessed between my sister and Striker in her back room. We bought Gaston a fine hat and gloves to match his coat and left with haste.

The afternoon and evening were much like the day before, with the distinction of the supper conversation turning to talk of Jamaican politics and economy. Rucker delivered a wonderful lecture concerning his predictions for the future of our fair isle; and though they were sad, in that he saw the influence of the buccaneers waning due to their earnings decreasing considerably after an inevitable peace with Spain, I agreed with him.

Saturday came, and I realized with dread that we must attend the damn party. We ran several leagues of beach in the morning before picking up our clothes at the tailor's. Once home, Gaston attempted to distract himself by studying more with the lenses while I sorted clothes from my sea chests. Eventually I was forced to call him up to bathe and dress.

He stood with his arms crossed and his back to the wall and regarded the clothes laid out on the bed with trepidation. "Perhaps I should not attend."

We had not discussed the matter in days; we had simply gone about the business of acquiring his coat and the like as if he would attend. "Do you sense a storm?" I asked gently.

He shook his head. "Non, I sense… I am afraid I will make a fool of myself and disappoint my father… and you."

"Well, that is foolishness," I chided gently. "However could you disappoint me?"

He sighed with resignation. "Will, I have never attended a formal affair."

I grinned. "My love, this is Jamaica, not the Sun King's court. There is nothing and no one here that would be considered of merit by people who regularly attend formal affairs. And as for your father, you need not impress him."

"I feel I will say or do some stupid thing," Gaston said doggedly.

"I feel you will not. You ever comport yourself as a gentleman. In all the time I have known you, your social deportment when dealing with matters of status and decorum has proven to be as impeccable as your table manners."

"I am afraid that I will not be if my Horse becomes spooked about so many," he sighed.

"Do you feel you will experience the sudden urge to bite the governor?" I teased.

"Non." He snorted. "Nor do I fear striking him," he added with annoyance. "I fear I will become unsettled and be unable to speak as I should and I will wish to leave in a rude manner."

I nodded soberly. "That I can see occurring," I said gently. "If such a thing does occur, then you shall catch my eye, and then simply walk out the door, and I will make the necessary apologies."

"And excuses," he muttered.

"My love," I sighed. "You would be quite surprised at how many men and women suddenly take ill at parties."

He frowned. "Truly?"

"Truly. Parties, dinners, fêtes of all sorts, are battlegrounds of love and politics, and not everyone holds the field. In your case, they know little of you, and so no one will assume you lost the day. And sometimes, leaving is a form of victory or a battle feint."

He gave another resigned sigh. "I still know I will stand there as I do on ships when I know few, and not speak and…" He sighed yet again.

"You will be at my side," I said reassuringly and grinned. "You know I speak enough for any three men."

"Ten," he said with a small nod and a weak attempt at a smile.

I chuckled. "Well, there are probably some things you should avoid. Do not drink deeply if it even appears I will begin to spar with some fool. You have a tendency of spitting your food or drink when I say something particularly… witty, perhaps."

He smirked.

"I would not have you spitting on the governor, or Morgan, or… Well, there will likely be so many potential targets. Considering that, if you feel your Horse has the urge to take the bit and speak his mind, say you wish to smoke, and head out to the veranda."

Gaston rolled his eyes, but he finally uncrossed his arms. "I will not speak. I feel the Horse will like none of them."

"Then perhaps that is best," I teased. "You should also not drink. Not that you are so very prone to it as I have ever been. For that matter, do not let me indulge in that vice, lest I hand my Horse the reins and then you will be spitting what you sip upon all in attendance."

"What else must I not do?" he asked with a smile. "That you would do if your Horse had the reins."

I laughed. "Do not become flirtatious with the governor's wife, or his mistress."

He raised an eyebrow. "Modyford has a mistress?"

"I know not. Most men of his station do, but perhaps this island is too very small for such an indulgence. But on that matter, in all seriousness, there will be ladies present, and you will be with the guest of honor, and it is likely..." I grinned and I looked him over. "Non, it is inevitable, that someone, young or old, will choose to flirt with you. Be kind: smile and accept it with dignity."

He frowned and then quickly blushed. "I would not," he said indignantly.

"My love, you have seldom been around as many women... Damn, it is likely you will never have been around as many women showing décolletage as you will see this night. Even the matrons will have them stuffed above their stays up to here." I indicated two pomegranates beneath my chin. "A gentleman should not stare. Though when they are young, that is precisely what they wish. And," I sighed, remembering the first time he had seen a pretty and eligible young lady, "if you should become aroused, sit down if possible, or say you need to smoke and go to the veranda."

His arms were crossed again. "And then what do I do?"

"I will be along to see to you," I teased.

He rolled his eyes and then sobered. "I am sorry, Will. If it is as you say, I feel I will be staring at the ceiling a great deal."

I shrugged. "As I recall, the governor has many fine chandeliers. I can only see so many happy mounds before my cock, too, begins to wonder what will explode from beneath a dress. And I will not take offense as long as you are not inviting young ladies to the veranda to smoke with you. So let them flirt... Many will flirt just to see if you will regard their bosom. You can look if they are at that: just do not allow them to spook you."

Then I realized another aspect of the matter. "And, as you are with the guest of honor, there will be men who will flirt, too. They will be courting your attention just as much as the women, though for other reasons, of course."

He frowned. "So I should be polite and smile and nod to any who flirt with me and show their bosoms. What if it is the governor?"

As always, I marveled how he could jest so deftly with such a stony face. "In that instance, you may be as rude as you desire," I said with as little amusement as I could manage. "As all who understand the Ways of the Coast know us to be matelots, if Modyford is flirting with you and revealing his bosom, it will be as insult to me, and I can guarantee you I shall duel him. Then it will not matter how your rudeness is interpreted: we will have to leave the island anyway."

Gaston finally dissolved into laughter and came to embrace me.

"Do not leave me alone," he whispered in my ear.

"Never." I kissed him.

We climbed down the cistern and took turns bathing in the tub and then shaving one another's stubbly faces and shearing our hair to less than a finger's breadth. When we returned to our room, we eschewed wigs despite our shorn hair: I decided they would simply have to gaze upon our ear rings and appreciate the fine shape of our skulls when we doffed our hats. My azure brocade coat, sans lining, fit comfortably over a blue-grey shirt with fine white lace at the wrist and collar. My charcoal wool breeches were a bit more fashionable, and thus baggier, than I would have liked, but the best I had. My new suede boots were black, and fit as they should, all the way over my knee to the cuff of the breeches.

We had rinsed the salt from the fawn suede breeches Gaston had worn during our swimming escapade several days ago, and allowed them to dry in the shade since then. After such treatment, where they had been taut across his thighs and buttocks before, they were now remarkably so: to the extent that, with his high suede boots, he appeared to be clad in skin-tight brown leather from toe to waist. I found it quite fetching. I had chosen for him a snowy white linen shirt embroidered in gold thread with a very small pattern of entwining ivy vines. He took time to study the design before donning it, and pronounced it quite pleasing. His new forest green coat matched it all quite well, and hung so as to prevent me – or anyone else – from spending the evening staring at his arse. Knowing the leather-clad firmness of it was just beyond the loose velvet was enough to stir my cock.

I grinned as he donned his gloves and hat. "I feel I will be staring at the ceiling all night," I said.

He frowned, and then grinned as he saw my smile and hungry eyes. He looked me over appreciatively, but not lustfully. "I will stare at you," he said.

"And not need a walk to the veranda," I teased.

He came to me, and nuzzled my ear lobe while brushing his fingers over my crotch. "It is good your pants are so baggy," he hissed playfully. "Because you are ever on display. I can exercise control."

I cast all playfulness aside, and took his shoulders to push him to arm's length and regard the taut leather across his crotch with dismay. "You best do so, my love, or keep your eyes steadfastly on something chaste and innocuous, or everyone will surely know your thoughts. As much as I adore those breeches on you, perhaps…"

He moved quickly to smother my words with a deep kiss. I surrendered to it, and my great desire of the moment, and slipped my hands beneath his coat to caress and cup his arse. He ground against me slowly, only to stop a minute later and reach into his breeches to adjust his member in its close confines – much to my amusement.

"You best tend to me now, then," he growled huskily in a way I adored far more than the breeches.

"How?" I teased.

"I have bathed," he said with a mischievous grin.

"That you have," I sighed happily, and pushed him back to the bed where I knelt between his knees and nuzzled his suede-covered bulge. "I will wish to do this again: after you have worn these long enough for your skin to smell and taste like them."

He gave a happy gasp at the idea as I applied myself to the task. His cock proved eager for my tongue, and we made regrettably short work of the endeavor. Mine ached with need as he finished, but we heard Striker calling for us from the atrium.

"They can wait," Gaston murmured, and pulled me into his arms as we stood.

"Non," I said. "It is a pleasant thing, and well-disguised. I will savor it."

His only argument was to hold me in his arms a moment longer while gazing into my eyes with great regard, and then kissing me, such that I savored my aching member all the more.

We at last descended the stairs to meet the Marquis, Dupree, and Striker with happy smiles and good cheer. Sarah pronounced us pleasing, if a little rakish, as we buckled on our sword belts. Striker was dressed in an unadorned but nicely fitting dark brown coat and breeches, with high leather boots, much like the ones I had left to the sea. He looked handsome and like many of the other captains I had seen at the few gatherings I had attended. Gaston's father appeared every bit the lord, dressed in a finely worked pale blue satin ensemble of coat, breeches, and vest, with flounces of delicate lace at neck and cuff, and blue gems adorning his accoutrements, including the buckles of his blue suede shoes.

Agnes was regarding us all with a cocked head from the doorway to the foyer. When I met her curious gaze she remarked, "All your coats match your eyes."

I looked around and saw she was correct: even Dupree's elegantly tailored golden coat complemented his light brown eyes.

"How delightfully odd," I said.

She shrugged. "I thought all men wore black in England, or here, for parties and such."

"My dear," I said, as I patted her head on our way out the door, "that was during the Reformation. Only the Protestants despise color."

"And here the men merely seem to be sadly out of fashion," Dupree added earnestly.

"Wait," Agnes called after me. When I turned she quickly said, "Give my best to Christine if you see her."

"I will," I assured her. I hoped we would not see the girl: it would be a bit of awkwardness I wished to avoid.

We stepped out onto the street and encountered a carriage and Theodore. The vehicle's driver informed us he had been sent to take us to the ferry landing, and then another carriage would take us to the Governor's House after we crossed the Passage.

I looked to Gaston and sighed. Though we had made no arrangement to fetch our horses from the farm on which they whiled away their days, I had still expected to acquire mounts at the livery and enjoy a pleasant ride to Spanish Town. Though he did not voice it, he seemed to share my dismay.

His father was quite pleased at the governor's thoughtfulness, though; and so we all climbed aboard for the bumpy ride through Port Royal's rutted and uneven streets. Gaston and Striker took the outer seats of the front bench, leaving me to cram myself between them. Theodore, the Marquis and Dupree were similarly arranged on the other bench; but whereas I had been forced to take the middle, Lord Tervent had chosen it.

"You look like gentlemen," Theodore remarked loudly over the rumble of wheels.

"I should hope so," I said, as I tried to accustom myself to the unfamiliar sensation of riding in a carriage after so many years.

I glanced at my matelot, and found he seemed quite happy now that we were underway; and I supposed it was such a novelty for him he had no complaint, much as visiting the tailor's had been. I hoped he would view the party in much the same light.

Though the carriage rides in and of themselves were not pleasant, they were not odious either. Unfortunately, the rumble of so many hooves and wheels, and the proximity of driver and footman, as well as the other passengers on the ferry, robbed us of any chance for conversation to make the journey pass quickly or allay my matelot's addled thoughts. I was keenly aware that the Marquis would frown upon my taking Gaston's hand to reassure him, and that dark thing settled into my heart to brew into anger, such that I was gripped by a foul mood once we reached the Governor's. I kept a smile on my face, though.

They had apparently set watchmen with signal torches along our approach to the House itself, and once we pulled to a stop, we were greeted by musicians playing a regal-sounding march and a great deal of applause from the guests – seemingly all of Jamaica's notable planters, merchants, captains, and their wives – gathered on the steps and about the yard such that we were surrounded by well over a hundred people. I was surprised at Modyford's need for such pomp. The Marquis appeared to be quite pleased, and led the way out of the carriage with a gracious word and nod of approval for everyone his gaze met.

Gaston and I followed. I felt him reach for me as we began to walk through the throng of people to the doors. I stepped beyond his reach, making it seem as if I had stumbled a little, and laid a steadying hand on his arm. As he queried whether I was well, I leaned in to whisper, "I cannot hold your hand here," in French. Anger immediately lit his eyes, burning away all trace of his apprehension. Once it was done, I was not sure if that was the best route to take, but it had been the only path I had seen readily available. He, of course, could unfortunately not mask his ire with a false smile with any degree of credibility, though he did try. I kept myself somewhat between him and all others, greeting them first with kind words and a boyish smile before moving quickly on toward the yawning doors of the house.

The Marquis halted our process on the lower steps. He stood there, smiling nobly at all assembled, and Dupree waved for silence. The music stopped and the crowd settled down to hear.

"I thank you all very much for this gracious reception," he said with excellent projection so that all heard, but none could say he shouted. "As you might have heard..." He paused to grin. "I am the Marquis de Tervent. I am visiting your fair colony to see my son." At this, he extended a hand to Gaston.

I swore silently with a smile fixed upon my lips and laid a hand on my matelot's very stiff back and urged him forward as Dupree translated the words. "Smile and nod," I hissed. Gaston went reluctantly; his face wearing a grimace that vaguely resembled a smile, and took his father's hand.

"This is my son," the Marquis said, once Gaston stood beside him. "The Comte de Montren."

The words struck me like an unexpected blow to the stomach. I thought Gaston's knees would buckle as he regarded his father with wonder.

I clapped: a sudden sound that brought Gaston's startled eyes to me and prompted a round of applause that prevented the Marquis from saying anything else until I could join Gaston on the steps. And though those brief words had needed no translation for the discerning, Dupree was drowned out as well. Perhaps this would mitigate people wondering why the Marquis' introduction of him had made his son appear a daft cow.

I stepped to my matelot's side in the calm pool inside the surging ring of sound, and hissed, "Smile, it is much like taking a ship."

He regarded me with a startled frown and then a weak smile quirked his lips.

Then I awarded his father a murderous glare.

The damn man blinked with surprise and then truly looked at his son. "Oh," he said, and then turned to smile and wave for silence. A frown tightened his features as he chose his words, but then he was all teeth and good cheer as he spoke. "My son and I have been estranged for some years, and he has lived here among the buccaneers, where I understand he has made a name for himself."

I managed not to wince at the irony of that, and there were appreciative snorts and mutters from the clump of captains. Others were regarding us with curiosity and furrowed brows, though; and there was the sibilance of whispers from behind fans and hands.

I glanced to Gaston and found his gaze fixed upon me. His face was composed, though.

"He has not used his title in many years," the Marquis continued, "and my use of it tonight surprised him. I do not know if he wishes to be known as a nobleman among the Brethren, as I understand they are a very egalitarian lot, but I hope he will forgive the enthusiasm of an old man who is very proud to call him his own."

I was very impressed, and I thanked the Gods for the Marquis' quick wit and Rucker's lecture of the other night.

Gaston took a long breath, and I could see a thousand thoughts thundering behind his eyes. I gave him a nod of reassurance. He turned to smile at his father and embrace him as Dupree finished translating. The crowd was quite pleased with this outcome.

We at last were able to continue up the steps to the doors, the throng parting before us and surging in behind.

"You are very, very good," I told the Marquis in French as we walked close together with Gaston safely between us, my arm about his shoulders and his about my waist.

"I have been told I possess an excellent talent to respond well to my own mishaps," he said with a grin.

I grinned in return. "So have I."

Governor Modyford, of course, had to make his personal greeting and introduce the entire colony council, along with Admiral Morgan, Captain Collier of the *Oxford* – who proved to be a rather stiff figure in countenance and stance – and a blur of several notable planters, before we were at last able to get our backs to a wall and secure full wine goblets. During it, Striker had slipped away to be with the captains, and Theodore had been hauled away to meet with other guests.

Gaston had run the gauntlet very well: he said nothing and nodded, smiled, and bowed as was appropriate; though, I sensed he did all this by following our lead and could not have told one man or woman from another when all was done.

"I love you," I leaned to him and whispered nonchalantly, as I sipped wine and smiled at another approaching couple.

"He has truly claimed me, Will," Gaston whispered.

"Oui, that he has, and now you see what that has earned you," I said lightly in French, and kissed the hand of an elderly plump matron in stays laced such that she could have rested her wobbly chin upon her doughy breasts with little effort.

"This room has many fine chandeliers," Gaston said as he smiled pleasantly.

"Do we need to smoke?" I asked curiously, as most of what we had seen had not been a delight to gaze upon in the least.

"Non," he said quickly. "I am averting my gaze in order to avoid seeing things I do not wish to see, not things I might find pleasurable to see."

I laughed briefly and quickly sobered to accept the good wishes of Captain Norman of the *Lilly*. His wife was actually quite pretty, and very young. I made much of complimenting her dress, which delighted her and earned me a stern look from her husband. I frowned at him with bemusement and flicked my gaze to my matelot, and Norman appeared sheepish and sighed.

And then we were greeted by Sir Christopher Vines. He was as portly and perspiring as I had remembered him. A very tall, thin, sharp-faced, dark-haired woman was on his arm.

"My Lord Marsdale," Sir Christopher said, "might I introduce my wife, Lady Mary Vines. And my dear, this is Lord Marsdale."

The woman curtsied while studying me with narrowed eyes and a forced pleasant smile. "I have heard a great deal about you, my Lord," she said.

"It is a pleasure to meet you," I said. "This is Lord Tervent, and I believe you have met my... friend, the Comte de Montren, Gaston Sable."

"Ah, aye," Sir Christopher said to Gaston, "I did not recognize you, my Lord. And it is a great honor to meet you, Lord Tervent."

The Marquis nodded and bowed appropriately, as he had with all the guests.

Then I heard Gaston's sudden breath, and I turned to find the girl I had asked to marry: the girl who had run from us like a scared filly; the girl Gaston had deemed a formidable opponent; the girl who wished to lead nations and battles and we had taught to fence; the girl Agnes still adored; the girl Gaston had named the Brisket, after I had described her to him as a meal I would have gladly eaten if I were not full with him: Miss Christine Vines. She looked much as I had first seen her in this very room: lithe, long-limbed and lovely, her golden curls coiled atop her head with just a few strands accenting her swanlike neck, her décolletage displayed in a pretty embroidered blue gown that matched her eyes – such that I was sure Gaston would soon need to go to the veranda, as he had ever done when seeing her. I met her sardonic smirk with one of my own as I kissed her lazily-offered hand.

"It is good to see you again," I said honestly in French – surprising myself, as I had not thought I wished to see her.

"I wish... we could speak," she whispered ruefully in the same language and cast a glance at her parents, who were watching us quite anxiously. She smiled at Gaston – who was studying a chandelier – and spoke in a normal tone. "And it is good to see you, too, Lord Montren." Then she stepped before the Marquis and curtsied. "I am honored to make your acquaintance, Lord Tervent."

His eyebrows rose. "As I am charmed to make yours, I am sure. Your French is excellent, my dear."

"My mother was French, and I have spent many years in Geneva, as well as in France," Christine said.

"Why Geneva?" the Marquis asked.

"My aunt maintains a residence there. She is sister to the Duke of Verlain, as was my mother."

This last was obviously a gouge at her step-mother, but the Marquis could not have cared less: he was fascinated. I was surprised, and then I remembered there was a reason I had courted her – beyond the obvious. According to Theodore, she had a lineage that could have proven suitable to my father. I had not known her uncle was a French duke, though. I wondered why the Devil her mother would have ever married Vines. I recalled Theodore saying she had married beneath her station, but by the Gods, Vines must have been a charming and dashing young man, or someone owed him a great deal. There must be quite a tale behind it.

And then the cold claws of another realization gripped me: my father was not the only one who might view her as sufficiently noble to marry a Lord's son. I remembered that I had discovered her to be my formidable opponent, not Gaston's.

"I know the Duke of Verlain," the Marquis was saying, his eyes narrowed speculatively.

"Have you seen him of late, before you sailed here?" Christine asked, as if she had not noted his challenge – a thing I viewed with incredulity, as she had been trained by her aunt to negotiate a court. "In the last letter I received from my aunt, she spoke of him ailing."

"Non," the Marquis said. "I have heard he ails as well, though. I have not seen him in… five years, at least. I am not often at court, and when last I was, he had already taken ill. A matter of the heart, I am told."

"Oui," Christine said. "The physicians have said he suffers from an abundance of bile and it is affecting his heart."

Gaston swore under his breath and then spoke. "That is absurd. If it is his heart, then it is his heart that ails. Bile has nothing to do with it. Is he fat?"

"Non, quite thin," Christine said with a smirk. "It is said he often suffers from pains in his chest when he becomes angered or even climbs the stairs."

"Then it is possible he should be bled," Gaston said with annoyance. "Instead they are probably treating him with infusions or powders to reduce his bile."

The Marquis regarded his son with dismay.

I chuckled and told him quietly, "We know her."

This seemed to relieve him, and then he regarded me with curiosity.

"I asked her to marry me," I said quietly. "She did not wish to be married, to me or anyone; so do not smirk about it."

The Marquis did anyway, and with a snort of annoyance I turned to her parents.

"They are discussing her Uncle's health," I explained in English. "My…" I suppressed a curse and decided I would play that game no longer. "Matelot is a physician."

Sir Christopher nodded absently and led me a little further away from Gaston and his daughter. His wife followed and he turned to her with a large smile. "My dear, perhaps you could find us some wine."

"Of course, my dear," she said, but I could see she was not pleased with being dismissed.

Once she was gone, he turned to me. "Well, as you see, we recovered her, and she is safe."

"Aye," I said. "However did you find her?"

"Well, as your… as Lord Montren and Mister Theodore were kind enough to inform me what ship she had booked passage on, as a boy…" He sighed as if that still troubled him and mopped his brow. "I was able to send word on several other ships sailing to the northern colonies. By God's grace, one of them arrived at the Virginia colony before her vessel, and thus they were able to apprehend her when she arrived in port."

"Ah," I said, and imagined she had been quite angry: as she had not tipped her hand, but others had, namely us.

"You were correct," he said. "She was afraid of the speed at which the matter was handled: she was not fleeing you, but the circumstances. She deeply regrets that she did not accept your offer."

I nodded and kept the smile from my lips. I was sure she did regret it: we had offered her a great deal of freedom, and now she had none.

"But now… of course… you are married," he said with a shrug. His gaze was earnest and assessing. "We have heard… a great deal about your bride."

"I am sure everyone has," I said with a shrug.

I knew what he wished to ask, and I was not sure if I wished to give it to him.

"I know I should not ask this," he sighed at last, "but…"

"Will I put her out, and would I still consider your daughter?" I said for him.

"Oh, Lord," he sighed. "Aye, aye."

"In all honesty, Sir Christopher, I do not know. I am awaiting word from my father. He sent her, I married her to please him, and now…"

He looked away with a sad sigh and mopped his brow. "Aye, of course. You are a good son. It is just… I wish for her to be happy, and she has been so unhappy of late and… I do not see where I will find a good match for her now, not that she will likely accept any we find, and I will not have her marry against her will. I despair for her future. And, she does not like Mary, nor Mary her, and there is ever a silent war in my house, and it troubles me."

I was reminded that Sir Christopher was a good father in his way. "If… such a thing were to come to pass, I would still consider your fine daughter," I offered.

"Thank you, for that, my Lord," he said somberly.

I looked to where Gaston and Christine were still talking, with the Marquis watching them with interest. Stupid words welled into my mouth, and I had to bite my lip to keep from saying them; but swallowing them made me queasy, as I felt they should not have existed at all, and thus were not a thing I wished to contain in my heart and soul.

Lady Mary returned with three goblets, and I happily accepted one. The wine did not wash the bad taste from my mouth, though.

"Is…" Lady Mary began tentatively, "is your friend, the Comte, married?"

And there it was. Sir Christopher looked at my matelot and his daughter with new eyes.

"Nay, he is not," I said with a small smile. And then the stupid words rose again and I burped them forth like the bad air of a putrid meal. "And he is as fond of her as I. And his father might feel her lineage is sufficient."

Lady Mary seemed quite pleased with this, and left us to go and listen to the other conversation, though I was sure she spoke no French.

Sir Christopher gave me a guilty look, and then his eyes narrowed. "Would… you have difficulty with… such a thing?"

"Nay," I lied. "It could prove to be in the best interests of both parties."

"But…" he said with a deep frown. "He is your matelot, correct?"

"Aye."

He seemed on the verge of asking much more, but reconsidered it every time he began to open his mouth.

"The Comte de Montren favors women," I said at last with a tired sigh.

"Oh," he said with great relief.

Thankfully he left me. I drained my goblet. Gaston was still seemingly at ease talking to Christine. She was leaning her fan demurely across her chest: I supposed she had tired of his talking to the chandeliers. I went to find more wine. When I returned, Gaston and Christine were discussing Agnes' lenses. My matelot glanced at me and frowned. I was sure he was either angry with me for disappearing or wondering how much I was drinking.

I wondered how much I would drink this night. I wondered a great many things.

The Marquis came to stand beside me and I stifled a curse.

"So you asked for her hand?" he asked.

"I asked her," I said bitterly. "We knew my father was sending a bride, and I had met Miss Vines by chance when I arrived on Jamaica. I thought she would be a far more acceptable candidate than any my father might send. But she bolted: disguised herself as a boy and booked passage on a ship in an attempt to reach Christendom. She claimed she simply did not wish to marry."

"How do you feel she views the matter now?" he asked.

"How the Devil should I know?" I asked. "I have not seen her in nearly a year."

The Marquis regarded me with concern and speculation. "Would you allow him to marry her?"

Doucette's words rose from my memory. *If he were to meet a proper girl he would be attracted to, would you release him?*

"I will not stand in the way of his happiness," I said.

"That does not specifically answer my question," the Marquis said diffidently.

"*If* he wishes to marry her, and *if* it will appease you, and *if* it is a thing the girl desires, then I will do nothing to impede it," I growled.

He nodded thoughtfully. "Will you stay with him?"

I swore vehemently in English before returning to French. "I love him. I will stay with him until I die, unless *he* wishes otherwise."

"I do not mean..." the Marquis began with a frown of sincere concern.

"Then shut up," I said, and went to stand by Gaston.

My matelot quickly regarded me with concern. "Will?"

I met his green eyes and wondered what I could say. He was oblivious to what was occurring, and I felt I should not end his bliss while we were here.

When I did not answer, he took my arm, "We should..."

But then the musicians began to play and Christine was on my other arm.

"Come dance with me," she said.

"Perhaps the Comte wishes to dance, Christine," Lady Mary said.

"I doubt it," Christine told her sharply.

Gaston was appalled. "I do not dance."

"Well," Christine leaned to him to say conspiratorially, "Do you mind if I borrow Will for a round?"

He sighed and shrugged, but he tightened his grip on my arm before she could pull me away. "Are you well?" he hissed.

"Well enough," I sighed. "Do not worry."

He did not appear to wish to heed my advice as Christine towed me away.

"What did you speak to my father about?" Christine asked in French as soon as we took the first position for an allemande.

I was acutely aware of all the eyes upon us. I kept my voice pitched for her alone; though I doubted few of the other dancers could speak French, one could never be sure. "How you were captured and how he despairs of finding you a husband," I said pleasantly.

She grimaced, but quickly disguised it as a smile as we changed partners. When we returned, she whispered, "He has this insane notion that you will divorce your wife and marry me, despite..." She shook her head and the dance pulled us apart again.

"That will not happen," I told her as we closed once more. "And not because of you."

She appeared crestfallen, but quickly disguised that too as we spun apart.

"The question is now whether you will marry Gaston," I hissed as we came around.

She stumbled and missed her cue from her next partner and had to hurry to catch up.

She was silent when next we closed, and would not meet my eye.

Then we were around again and she asked with a searching gaze, "Is that a thing you would wish?"

I was minded of Gaston's jealous words that she had truly coveted me and resented him, and Agnes saying that Christine had indeed fancied herself enamored with me. I did not stumble or miss a step, but I did not speak.

"I wish for you to be happy," I whispered as we closed.

She shook her head regretfully as we passed.

"I cannot aid you in that now," I added. "But perhaps he can."

She nodded thoughtfully.

"They will want children," I added.

She sighed and rolled her eyes.

"I would not have to live at my father's?" she asked.

"Non, and you could travel someday as we once agreed."

"I will think on it," she said as the dance ended.

I took her arm and walked her back to her frowning parents and a curious Marquis, who had been joined by an equally curious Theodore. Gaston was standing apart, with his back to the wall and his arms crossed.

"I could have loved you," Christine whispered.

"And I you, but I met him first," I said.

She winced at that, but turned to give me a taut nod before going to her parents.

I went to Gaston. He was all Horse, coiled and ready to run or fight.

"What is happening?" he hissed.

I sighed. "Your father feels Christine might be a suitable bride. Sir Christopher feels you might be a suitable suitor. Christine wishes to escape her father's house yet again."

For a moment I thought he might strike me – not from anger at me, per se, but from the need to vent the sheer amount of fury boiling behind his eyes. I held still and told myself I would not cringe.

"We must leave," he said.

"Oui," I sighed with relief.

He headed for the door.

I turned to the Marquis and Theodore and simply said, "We are leaving."

"Wait," Theodore said and hurried to my side as I began to follow Gaston. "What is amiss?"

"There has been talk of a marriage between Gaston and Christine," I said.

"Oh bloody Hell," he sighed. "I take it this is not his idea."

"Nay."

"Nor yours," he added.

"Nay."

We had crossed the threshold and I paused to tell him, "We will not need the carriage."

"What should I say?" he asked.

"Nothing." I thought of what people had witnessed this night. "They will likely think we are fighting over her. Leave it at that. The Gods know the damn bastards need something new to talk about."

He smiled thinly. "Be careful."

"Do not worry," I sighed. "At this moment, there is nothing more dangerous than Gaston on this whole damn island."

"That is what I am concerned about," he said kindly.

I nodded. He was right to be concerned.

I hurried down the steps into the yard and then the street. There was no moon as of yet; it would rise much later. But Spanish Town was an orderly place, with someone assigned to light the lanterns on the corners.

I found Gaston, or rather he found me, before I reached the town square. He stepped out of an alley and I eyed him warily. He was all Horse, but the anger had passed and now there was just desperation in his eyes. I let him pull me into the darkness between the buildings. He stopped in a place that was as far from the nearest windows as could be managed, and then his mouth closed over mine.

Though carnality was far from my heart, or even my desires of the moment, I did not fight him in body or spirit. His hands began to move over my body roughly: more the fumbling of a young swain than the sureness he usually displayed with his seductions. It felt good to be touched, though. It felt good to not have to think for a time. My manhood, initially confused, quickly warmed and stirred to the idea.

I wondered if he had thought to bring salve in his belt pouch, I had not, and then he knelt before me and I stopped trying to think. I clawed at his shoulders and locked my knees as I leaned on the wall to peer up at what I could see of the stars as he pleasured me.

When I finished, he fastened my breeches, buried his face in my crotch, and wrapped his arms tight around my legs. I rubbed the stubble of his scalp as his sobs shook us both. I wanted dearly to know his thoughts, but I stayed silent and waited.

Eventually he stood and kissed me gently. I held him.

"I do not want to marry her," he whispered.

"I am not asking you to," I replied. "It is not my doing. I would not have you think it was."

"Nor was it mine," he sighed. "I would not have you think that, either."

"Are you still angry?" I asked.

He nodded.

"Are you angry?" he asked.

"Oui," I sighed. "But I am not angry with you."

"Nor I you," he breathed.

I did not feel he lied, but I wanted very much to have any further discussion in the light where I could see his face. "Let us go home," I said.

He nodded and led me out of the alley, his hand tightly entwined with mine. We crossed the nearly empty town square; and the Spanish design of it, and the lack of people, made me feel we were somewhere else, Porto Bello, or Puerte Principe perhaps, roving and making war again. I supposed we were. This seat of government and place of plantation commerce was surely not our home. We were interlopers here.

Though there was no moon and the light of the stars was dimmed by haze, he led us to the road leading toward the Passage and Port Royal, and we walked into darkness, trusting the road to be level and our footing sure. I thought of the battleground at the Governor's and wondered at myself. I was indeed angry over what had occurred, but I was not angry at any one person – or even all of them, necessarily. I was angry that I could not give him a child. I was angry that a child was required of either of us. I was angry that tradition and law required heirs. I was angry we lived in a world in which we could love one another such as we did, yet we were denied the ability to grant all of one another's desires or needs. As civilization receded behind us, I decided I was angry at the Gods.

Sixty-One

Wherein Unwanted Things Are Born

The night was black, hot, and thick with insects. They swarmed about us and buzzed incessantly in the forest. As it was too dark to see the trees, and the only sources of light that one might focus upon were the stars, it seemed as if they were the cause of all the sound, and that they buzzed as they twinkled. Despite the heat and stillness of the air, I was pleased we wore as much clothing as we did. It limited the amount of bare skin exposed to be bitten. The damn creatures did not seem to care if we were walking or crouched in the bushes to hide from any passing carriage, as Gaston insisted we do. And I found I was constantly waving my hand about my face and neck in irritated little swats, like a horse flicks its tail.

After perhaps a mile, I knew I needed some distraction, and so I broached the subject that hung over us like a pall, though I still wished to see his expression when we talked.

"Might we speak of it?" I asked. "Or something."

He sighed. "Tell me all that was said." He did not sound angry, just tired, as we trudged along the slightly paler black of the road – a charcoal perhaps, as compared to the ebon of the brush.

And so I told him all I could recall, sparing nothing, starting with my conversation with Sir Christopher and ending with my brief exchange with Theodore. Relating it all cleared my mind on several points, and as he did not speak when I finished, I began to relay my thoughts as well.

"I do not feel any of them began to engage in this... speculation... by design," I said. "It was all a matter of happenstance, or Fate, or a thing arranged by the Gods. And even if you were in agreement with it, it is not an inevitability. Christine might very well bolt again. Your father might regret his haste, as he regretted his pageantry in presenting you so. And Sir Christopher might come to feel he is asking a thing of her which she does not want.

"In viewing the matter objectively, as I feel some part of my mind was doing as events unfolded, I cannot say where it would be a bad thing. Christine is as she was before: still beautiful, intelligent, and... all things we might wish for in the mother of fine puppies – though I know not whether she wants to whelp any. And it would still aid her, in that giving her a name would free her from some of the constraints placed on her by society. It would appease your father as to the matter of an heir, and save us having to wait to see what horror he might send from France – though I doubt he could compete with my father on that front. And even if she feels she is enamored with me – which I feel she is, stupid girl – it will not matter so very much if she marries you. As in, she is not enamored of you, and thus I need not be jealous, and I will not have a damn thing to do with her, thus you need not be jealous."

He was still silent. I sighed as I followed the tumble of my thoughts.

"But... that is all objective reasoning," I sighed again. "My Horse, though I cannot name the cause of its unease, is quite distraught over the concept. I feel that it is because... we must, as in I cannot provide you an heir and one is required. And that they all view our love as some obstacle they must surmount in meeting their goals."

"That angers me," he said suddenly. He did not sound angry though, merely thoughtful. "And that this is a course being set upon us and not one we have chosen for ourselves. And oui, I wish we could bear our own puppies. It is not fair that we must involve some other when we are happy as we are."

The last was bitter, and I felt there was more he did not say.

"Should we not drag it all into the light?" I asked gently.

His breath caught, and his step slowed, and I was sure he was peering at me in the dark.

"Why did you do as you did in the alley?" I asked.

He stepped closer, and his hand found mine to tightly entwine our fingers. Then he began walking again with steadfast purpose.

"Gods, my love," I sighed. "Please speak of whatever is troubling you. You know I will never..."

"Oui," he snapped. "You will never betray me. It is me that is unworthy."

"How could you be unworthy?" I asked.

"I want her," he growled. "I do not wish to marry her, but I wish to fuck her very much."

I snorted with relief and immediately worried he would perceive it as derision. "That is not betrayal," I said quickly. "I want to fuck her, too. It is a thing of our cocks, not our hearts. She is quite fetching and very desirable."

He was silent, and I was not sure if it was due to stubbornness or thought. I let myself think my own thoughts to see where they led.

"I will not have us be like Pete and Striker," I said carefully.

"Non," he said. "I will not share you."

I shook my head, and sighed at my useless gesture in the blackness. Then I worried he would misinterpret that sound.

"I keep shaking my head or nodding as if you could see," I explained. "I am frustrated with myself over it. It is why I sigh."

His hand tightened on mine and he sighed.

"I do not wish to be shared," I said. "That is not what I meant. I do not want a situation to develop wherein you are yelling at someone on a beach ten years from now about your frustration over not having a woman – which it is your nature to favor. I would rather you bed one and know of it and…"

I did not wish to say *make a decision*, but I heard the words in my heart and they hurt, and I realized that was what had my Horse so spooked.

If he found a proper girl he could be attracted to, would you release him?

I must have stumbled or slowed, because I found his arms around me and we were standing still in the road.

"I do not wish to want them," he whispered. It sounded like a plea.

I took a deep breath. "Maybe… maybe you do not as you think you do. Perhaps you favor both men and women as I do."

But it was a false hope and we knew it.

"I will not betray you," he hissed. "I would rather… let us leave. We can return to Negril."

Clarity returned as I gazed up at the buzzing stars. I had sworn I would always do well by him.

"Non," I said, and kissed him gently. "This means too much to you. Not her, not women, but your title and all that it implies. We managed to talk ourselves into my marrying that bitch in the name of preserving the pretension of my title, how could we think to do less for you when it means so much more to you?"

He held me and rocked us from side to side a little: a gentle swaying a mother would use to calm a child soon to sleep.

Though I had spoken with calm conviction, my Horse was beginning to run with terror down a bramble-lined path into a darkness more encompassing than that in which we stood. What if he did find he favored them, such that ever after, being with me was a chore, and he stayed with me anyway, as I knew he would?

If he found a proper girl he could be attracted to, would you release him?

Christine had always been my formidable opponent, not his.

"I will never find anyone who loves me as you do," he whispered. "Or who can care for me as you do."

"I hope not," I said.

But what if he did?

I wished to lighten the moment, but all I could think of were very poor jokes about my being a fool, and they would only make us feel worse.

I remembered the rock I had overturned in my first confrontation with his father.

He does not favor men in general, but he favors me in specific a great deal. Because I love him despite everything. Because he has lived a life devoid of love.

Were we merely together because he felt he had no alternative? That no one else would love him as I did, so therefore he must make the best of it and accept me as I was, as a man? Could I let him go to see if he would choose me of his own accord?

I had to. The question was now in my heart, and I knew the only way to resolve it was to do the thing I was terrified to do.

And perhaps, a formidable opponent was best.

Flickering light far up the road heralded more riders and disturbed our reveries. We slipped into the brush to wait for them to pass. The approaching party turned out to be several riders and a buggy. They were proceeding at a sensible walking speed that allowed their torches to actually show them something of the road beneath their feet. We could hear them talking as they approached, mainly because two of their member – a man and a woman – were arguing quite ferociously about some incident at the party. Thankfully, I could not recognize their voices and the few details we heard did not lead me to believe the matter involved us. It seemed to concern his drinking and her flirting.

"I will never do that," Gaston breathed in my ear as they drew close. I could hear the humor in his voice.

I chuckled silently. "Oui, thank the Gods we will be spared this aspect of normalcy."

As they drew abreast of our hiding spot, the closest horse smelled us and tossed his head, but his rider was either half-asleep or drunk and merely cursed at the animal.

I was minded of all the times my mount had behaved strangely and someone, even myself, had ever complained of the animal's stupidity. Well, perhaps there were often wayward madmen lurking in the brush.

I remarked on this to Gaston when at last we felt we could emerge onto the road without scaring either man or beast and getting ourselves shot.

"Well, as you have said," he said with soft amusement, "our Horses are our truth. They see the madmen lurking in the bushes." Then his voice changed and I knew he had turned to face me. "They see them on this course, do they not?"

"Oui," I sighed. "And the madmen are very likely us." I thought of all I had been thinking before and knew that though it was all very true, and a thing I wanted the answer to, being as we were – mad – that I was a fool to pursue such an answer. The path surely led to one of us having a sizable bout; but then all things related to his inheriting likely did, and we might as well suffer them.

"So shall we reassure our Horses that all will be well and go on, or choose another path?" I asked.

His thoughts must have been following my own. "I feel there are madmen lurking in the bushes of any path we will ever take that actually leads somewhere."

I chuckled. "I concur."

He found my hand and we began walking again.

"She must want children," he said. "Or be willing to birth them and leave them with us. She can do whatever she likes after she gives us children."

"I agree. Do you wish to discuss that with her, or do you want me to talk to her?"

His grip on my hand tightened. "I will talk with her. If… If she is still enamored of you, I would rather you stay away from her. She must know she deals with me on this. That she is marrying me, not you by proxy."

"Oui," I sighed. "I would not have her think otherwise, and my arranging anything would be viewed oddly by her father anyway. It is possible he feels I harbor more than fondness for her."

Gaston snorted. "I do not wish for her to love me, but it bothers me that she still might be in love with you."

"No more than it will bother me if she falls in love with you," I said.

"I cannot envision that," he said sadly.

I shoved him a little and teased, "Are you implying I am more lovable than you?"

"Oui. You are handsome and charming."

I smiled in the dark and my heart swelled a little. "Thank you, but that only helps in making a good impression. You are very handsome and you can be quite charming too, once you know someone. Now where shall we house her?"

He sighed heavily. "Do we need another house? Can she not remain at Sarah's when we rove?"

"Women…" I tried to best consider how to phrase it. "There can only be one captain in a house. Neither Sarah nor Christine are the type to wish to be first officer."

He swore.

"But, that brings up another matter," I said. "This must occur soon if we are to rove. I am assuming your father will leave when his ship returns."

"Oui," he sighed.

"Do we wish to rove? Or, would you like to return to France?"

"I cannot until the other matter is resolved," he said thoughtfully.

"Oui, and now I feel your father will surely do that, but…" I sighed as I realized we had not discussed a rather important matter. "We could wait here until those documents are sent, and then go there with Christine if you wish. Or, despite your reinstatement as the Lord Montren, do you wish for us to go to Christendom at all? Or do you see us as staying here for many years and then going there after your father has passed? How do you view that matter?"

"I do not know," he said with surprise. Then he was silent for a good distance. "I suppose I should discover what he thinks will occur. But… I feel I would rather remain here in the West Indies for as long as possible."

I was relieved to hear it, even though it was what I had assumed. "All right. That agrees with me. We will need to procure a house for Christine, then."

We spent the rest of our journey home discussing a new house like Sarah's, and how to improve the bathing room.

Sarah's house was dark as we approached. We decided we should let ourselves in the back gate in case they had barred the door already. We hoped the dogs would not wake everyone. Thankfully, they did not bark, but much wagging of tails and snuffing occurred. We were going to climb up the cistern, but I decided I wanted water and went to the cookhouse. There was a single lantern in the atrium. The Marquis sat beneath it, playing with a deck of cards. I sighed. Gaston eyed me curiously from where he stood near the stable. I motioned for him to come to me, and once he did, he too saw his father and sighed.

The Marquis did not seem surprised when we walked out of the shadows, and I realized he had his back to the main door and his chair situated such that he could easily glance up at our room.

"Sorry to keep you waiting," I said lightly.

He smiled and shrugged, but his eyes were on his son. "Are you well?"

Gaston nodded. "We needed to talk."

"I would like to speak with you," the Marquis said. "Alone."

My matelot crossed his arms and squared his stance.

I shook my head and went to whisper in his ear. "There are things you might need to hear that he will never say in front of me."

He sighed and nodded, and kissed my cheek.

I left them alone and climbed the stairs to our room with my water bottle. Once there, I gratefully lit a lamp and doffed my clothing and tossed it into a heap in the corner. I rummaged through the medicine chest for the unguent Gaston prescribed for insect bites. I applied what I hoped was the correct one – it smelled as I remembered – and threw myself on the bed to lean against a post and drink my water, and wait.

I tried not to think of how much of this activity there would be in my future. We had left Gaston with friends on my marriage night, and still he had become distraught enough that he had asked that they take his weapons and bind him so that he did not come and find me. What would I do on his wedding night, get drunk and cry on Pete's shoulder?

At last my matelot slipped in the door and came to kiss me. He appeared tired in the soft golden light.

"Well?" I asked with a smile. "Does he approve of her? Does he worry I will impede the matter?"

"Oui and oui," he sighed, and searched about for a place to set his hat, at last deciding on a chair in the corner. "I thanked him for naming me Montren again. He said he felt he had failed with his other sons, and that perhaps the only reason I have turned out as well as I have is because he had little hand in it." He awarded me a rueful quirk of his lip as he hung his jacket on the same chair.

I chuckled sadly. "At least he sees it. Are you proud he feels you are now so worthy of his respect? I should think…"

"Oui," Gaston said with surety, "and I told him so." He shrugged as he folded his shirt. "It made me very happy." He did not sound as if it did at all.

"But then the discussion turned elsewhere," I said.

He turned to regard me and sighed as he scratched a bite on his neck. He went to the medicine chest and – to my relief – used the same unguent I had.

"We discussed Christine," he said. "He feels she is an excellent candidate. He thinks we should pay a call to the Vines' tomorrow. He too, thinks we should see to this quickly."

He sighed again as he stood and propped his leg on the chair to unlace his boots. "He wishes for us to return to France with him. I told him I am not ready yet. And… he seemed to understand that."

"So what is wrong?" I prompted, when he did not speak as he finished doffing his breeches and folded them as well.

He regarded me sadly. "He understands that you are very important to me, but he wonders if another could become just as important. If someone else, a wife for instance, could help mitigate my madness as you do."

I sagged back on the bed to gaze at the ceiling. I could not look at him. "That is… reasonable advice, I suppose."

"It made me… sad," Gaston said. "That he should view that as the only reason you are important to me."

I raised my head to gaze at him again. He was scratching his chest absent-mindedly, and gazing out the window.

"I had thought our discussion was going well," he continued. "But the last time I had a pleasant-seeming discussion with him was that night, and by morning…"

He looked down at his chest with bemusement, and then tears; and I saw the Horse take him. I knew, as if I could see his very thoughts, he saw the scars that marred him from shoulder to thigh as he thought she might.

I cursed my foolishness. They were so familiar to me now – so much a part of him – that I had not considered how they would appear to another, or even that he must reveal them.

I went to him and took his shoulders. He regarded me with a child's wide eyes.

I spoke gently. "If she is so damn concerned with vanity that she cannot see beyond them as I do, then to the Devil with her. She will not be a proper dam to our puppies."

"But what can I tell her?" he asked desperately. "I will not have her know..."

I put fingers to his lips. "Tell her nothing. Tell her you will not discuss it, and if she cares for you she will not ask, as you told me when you first revealed them."

"That will not appease her," he said. "You loved me enough not to ask and still it troubled you. She... will have no reason not to ask... others – not that they know, but... And what of my madness? What will we say of that?"

"That you are mad," I sighed, "and that if she feels you are behaving oddly, she should tell me of it and I will deal with you."

He nodded slowly, but he was becoming more agitated. "I will not have her tend me or be around me when I am mad. You are the only one my Horse will trust. She will not decide if I am to be bound or drugged or..."

I silenced him with a kiss. "No one but me will ever do that again," I whispered against his lips.

"My father will not, either," he hissed.

"Non, of course not," I said soothingly.

We could not go to France. I must have a long talk with Christine.

I led him to the bed and bade him lie down. "We are tired," I whispered. "Can you sleep? Or should I make it all go away?"

"Please make it go away."

I found the oil, and massaged his back and arms until he drifted to sleep beneath me.

I wondered what we would tell Christine. My ire rose that we should have to tell her anything at all, but I was too tired for it to grow into anger. I could not see where she would know how to handle him: she was just a girl; what could she know of madness? But perhaps his father was right, and I was giving myself airs to think I was the only one.

Exhausted and melancholy, I arranged our weapons and pulled the netting about the bed before curling next to him.

I woke to a light rapping on the door. At my call, Dupree answered and apologetically explained that it was quite late in the morning and the Marquis wished to speak with us.

Gaston obviously drifted in the bowers of the restorative sleep he often experienced after a bout: he had not stirred at the knocking or voices. I relieved myself and drank water. He had still not moved. He looked so peaceful in repose. I caressed his cheek and brow with a fingertip. At that, he stirred a little, and I widened my gentle touch to include his neck and shoulders until he opened an eye to regard me with annoyance and curiosity.

"You are very beautiful when you sleep, but it is late in the morning," I whispered.

He snorted and rolled onto his back to reveal his piss-hard member. "Am I beautiful at no other time?"

I grinned. "It is much like your eyes: they are ever green, but the shade and hue changes with your mood and the light. Such is your beauty: it is ever there, but it varies so that I am often struck anew by it."

"You never cease to amaze me," he said with a smile, and caressed my cheek. He fingered his member.

I kissed his palm. "I will gladly take that."

He frowned and looked down at his cock, only to smile and make the happy humming sound I so adored.

I was soon mounted atop him, gripping the headboard and staring out the window at a wheeling gull as I pleasured us with slow measured strokes. His hands ranged over my body; and my cock, though it had risen quickly for the occasion, bobbed happily between us without the pressing ache of need. It took a long and peaceful time, as it ever did when the prick involved is filled with as much piss as seed; and I savored it, thinking of the Marquis waiting below. We were not at his beck and call, and he would never own Gaston.

When at last my matelot came with a long happy grunt, he quickly rolled me beneath him, and pinned me while he plundered my mouth and exercised a strong hand upon my member until I exploded on my belly.

We laughed, only to have him sober quickly and hold me with great earnestness.

I sighed in his arms, wishing we could have staved off the matters of the day a little longer.

"You must speak to her," he said. "You must tell her she will not find love here. That if she wishes to wake to a man who loves her that she will need to look elsewhere. I will give her a name and she will give me children and then she can have her freedom to seek what she will, but I will not love her."

I wondered how I would say that diplomatically when I knew how very much his love meant to me. For a moment, I wondered how anyone could accept such conditions, and then I remembered that nearly all noblemen did when it came to marriage.

"I will speak with her if you wish it," I said.

"I cannot... tell her such a thing," he sighed. "I have difficulty speaking to her at all."

"You did not last night," I teased.

He rose to his elbows to regard me. "That was... we were discussing things of..."

"I understand," I said. "You were speaking of things you know, and telling some damn woman that she will not be loved in her marriage bed is not a thing I would wish for you to ever do so often that you will become comfortable with it."

He smiled grimly, and gave me a brief kiss before easing off the bed to find the chamber pot.

"Should I also broach your madness or scars before she makes a final decision?" I asked.

"Oui," he sighed. "I wish her to know that there are things… she will never know about me, and that I do not need another matelot. If that is unsatisfactory to her, then we will not marry."

"All right, let us dress and eat and go and find the Vines. Oh, and Dupree knocked earlier: your father wishes to speak to us."

He appeared rueful, and then he grinned. "I am pleased you made him wait."

I stretched languorously. "As am I."

I dug cleaner shirts and breeches from the chests for both of us, and we dressed like buccaneers pretending to be gentlemen once again.

The Marquis and Dupree were seated at their usual table in the atrium. They appeared relieved to see us. Pete and Agnes were playing with the dogs in the yard. No one else was to be seen, though the door to the room I now knew to be Sarah's office was open. There was a plate of fried fish and the grainy yellow cakes that I did not know the name of on the table, with butter and hot chocolate. With barely a nod of greeting at his father, Gaston and I sat and helped ourselves to the food.

I ate a piece of fish and washed it down with water before asking the Marquis, "In all your speaking to Sir Christopher last night, did he mention where they were residing this week? I believe they have a house in town as well as several plantations."

He raised an eyebrow, but responded pleasantly enough. "We are to see them today. They were staying at a plantation near… Spanish Town, is it? They planned to attend mass this morning, and then come to their house here in Port Royal, where Gaston and I are to pay them a call."

I nodded and swallowed a mouthful of the grainy yellow cake. "We feel I should speak to Miss Vines before a final decision is made."

"I do not see where that is necessary, Will," he said diffidently. "Gaston should speak to her, and then arrangements will be made between Sir Christopher and me."

"Oui, that is how it should be, and I do not wish to interfere in that," I said carefully. "However, there are matters that must be discussed with the young lady prior to either her decision or ours being finalized."

"Such as?" he asked sincerely and without rancor.

"Well, some mention must be made of his madness and scars. She does not know of them, and we feel she should prior to her agreeing to marry him. And then, she must also be told that certain explanations will not be forthcoming, yet… Well, I must concoct some story about that night to stave off her curiosity without telling her anything we do not wish for her to know."

The Marquis was frowning. "Telling her of his madness should be done, I agree, but I do not see why any mention need be made of that night. If, in time, Gaston feels he wishes to tell her of those events, that is his prerogative, but…" His words trailed off. He was looking at his son.

I looked to Gaston and found him furious. As I was quite incredulous that his father could think the matter could be viewed so nonchalantly, I was not surprised my matelot was angry. Nor was I surprised when Gaston stood and doffed his sword belt and then his shirt.

Dupree gasped in dismay at the sight of him. The Marquis was silent, but it was the silence of a man stunned beyond words.

"How am I to explain this?" Gaston growled.

His father shook his head and pressed his hand to his mouth, and then he was standing and stumbling to the door. He disappeared into the street. A concerned and confused Dupree followed him, carrying his master's cane.

Gaston sat heavily, his eyes pressed tightly closed.

"What are these yellow cakes called, or rather what are they made of?" I asked. "Do you know?"

"Corn meal. Corn. It is a grain of the New World," he said slowly.

"Ah, now I will know how to ask for it. They are quite tasty."

"I love you," he said.

"I know," I said.

He smiled weakly.

"Puppies?" I asked.

He chuckled and massaged his eyes and temples. "Oui." Then he shook his head and regarded me. "How could he not have known what he wrought?"

I shrugged. "Did he see you after his rage and madness passed? And Vittese obviously did not tell him."

"I should have killed him," he grumbled.

"Which one?" I asked.

"Vittese," he said with a frown. "Though perhaps I should kill my father, too."

"That will solve nothing. Your father's death, not Vittese's"

He nodded and stood, and we went to visit Bella and the puppies. He left his shirt off, and at the sight of him, Agnes stared.

"Um, Mi… Gaston, might I sketch you again?" she asked.

He sighed and smiled. "Aye."

Pete joined us in the stable, and Agnes soon did too, with her sketchbook and charcoal in hand. She had my amused matelot move twice before she was happy with his positioning in the light from the doorway.

As she settled in with the paper in her lap, she asked, "So, was Christine there?"

I sighed. "Aye, she was, and we spoke, and she is relatively well, though I feel she is not happy living with her stepmother, or vice versa."

Gaston and I exchanged a look.

He spoke. "Agnes, there is talk of my marrying her."

She looked up sharply. "Truly? Would she live here?"

"What?" Pete asked.

"Well," I said. "Gaston's father announced him as the Comte de Montren to everyone of note on Jamaica last night. And as he is naming Gaston his heir, he wishes, like all damn noble fathers do, that Gaston marry and produce his own heir."

Pete swore and shook his head. Then he shrugged. "StrikerBein'MarriedHasn'tBeenSoBad."

"Because the three of you were able to come to an arrangement that suits you," I said. "We will not manage the same thing."

Agnes was frowning and looking from Gaston to me and back. "So you will not both marry her in the buccaneer way?"

"Nay," I said with a smile. "Gaston will not share me. He does not share well," I teased him.

He snorted.

"Neither does Christine," Agnes said, and turned her attention back to her paper.

"Was she truly enamored with me?" I asked the girl.

She nodded and sighed. "She always said that if she must marry, she wished for it to be as her parents were, that she be in love with him and he with her. And she did not want children until after she had seen some of the world." She frowned with thought. "That was why she did not wish to marry. She says the only thing men want from women is trysting and children."

Gaston and I exchanged a look and sighed as one. We had no reason to doubt the girl, and it fit with what we knew of Christine; and though it was possible Christine's desires had changed this past year, it was more likely they had not.

"Well, then, it is unlikely she will marry Gaston," I said. "Because all we want from a wife is… children."

Pete smirked.

"Aye," Agnes sighed, "because you do not even need a woman for the other." She began sketching. "I feel sorry for her. Christine will never get what she wants, and she is too stubborn to do what she must. But then…" She frowned and shook her head and concentrated on what she was seeing again, her hand scratching across the page.

"Fortune has a way of visiting the strangest things upon people, Agnes," I said. "You may yet find that which you seek."

She smiled ruefully. "'Tis true. I never thought I would live such that I could spend my days playing with lenses and puppies and drawing naked men. My poor mother probably rolls in her grave."

"LifeCanBeDamnGoodWhenYaLeastExpectIt," Pete said with a chuckle.

An hour later I owned a very fine drawing of Gaston with a puppy cradled in his arms, and I felt much better about the world; though the Gods had thought it clever to throw Christine in our path, Their plan would surely fail.

Striker finally woke: as was ever his wont, he had drunk far too much at the party and been only vaguely conscious since. Pete, Gaston and I wished to go to the beach and spar, and Agnes wished to come too, along with the dogs, and Sarah did not wish be left at home alone, despite it being during her lying in, and thus the entire pack of us – including a grumpy Striker – went to frolic in the surf. It proved to be a very enjoyable afternoon. We decided that on the morrow we would dress Agnes as a boy and teach her to swim. Sarah wished to learn as well, but it was determined we should wait until after she birthed.

The Marquis was sitting in the atrium when we returned. "Might I speak with you?" he asked Gaston.

My matelot nodded and followed his father into the parlor.

I sat at a table near Dupree, who was fanning himself and appeared somewhat troubled. Agnes and Sarah retired upstairs to change out of their wet clothing. Pete and Striker pulled up chairs near mine.

"What is going on?" Striker asked. "You were the talk of the party last night. Everyone, and I mean everyone, seems to think you will put your wife out and marry Miss Vines."

Pete snorted derisively and laughed.

"Aw Lord," Striker sighed. "What have I missed now?"

I smiled. "All of the maneuvering that people witnessed last night involved the possibility of Gaston, the Comte de Montren, marrying Miss Vines."

"Oh, bloody Hell," Striker said. "Can we not go a year without some God-damned disaster?"

This set Dupree chuckling behind his fan.

I had to laugh with him. "Nay, it does not appear so. Yet, I feel the Fates will be cheated in their mischief this time."

Dupree was frowning at me.

"Unless there is a new development…" I said.

He shook his head with guilt.

The parlor door opened and Gaston stuck his head out. He was furious, and nearly spat my name. "Will."

I went to him, and he took my arm and pulled me inside.

The Marquis appeared dismayed at my entrance.

"What has occurred?" I asked my matelot.

"He is trying to make amends," Gaston snarled. "So he has gone and spoken with the Vines. He has spoken with her, for me!"

I looked to the Marquis. "What did you say?"

He sighed heavily. "I told them that as fine as their daughter obviously is; that a marriage would be unwise at this time: that I had been foolhardy in speaking as I did last night. That there were… aspects of the matter that I was unaware of, and that, though I dearly wish for my son to marry, he is not yet prepared to do so."

Relief flooded my heart. I sat and looked to Gaston.

My matelot was still furious. "It was my decision to make! You do not speak for me!" he growled. "If anyone speaks for me it is Will, not you!"

"I am sorry," the Marquis said heavily. "I did not wish to anger... to hurt you further. But I seem to be unable to do anything correctly where it concerns you... or your brothers... or..." He shook his head, and regret seemed to pool around him in the dim room like smoke.

I felt sympathy for the man, but Gaston still wished for blood. I stood and laid a quieting hand on my matelot's arm, hoping he would calm or at least hear me.

He met my concerned gaze, and the realization that he was not in control flickered in his eyes. He pulled away and looked about with frustrated anger.

"Let us go and talk," I whispered.

He took several deep breaths and nodded slowly.

"Puppies?" I asked.

"Non, I will scare them," he snarled.

I was so very proud of him.

"Pete?" I asked.

He shook his head. "If I give Pete this anger, he will kill him."

"Our room?" I asked.

He nodded.

"Will you go up first, and allow me to follow, or should I accompany you?" I asked.

His gaze flicked to his father and he snorted. "I can see myself up." He left us.

"We are used to managing our own affairs," I said quietly.

"I am used to repairing the havoc my impulsive nature sometimes wreaks," the Marquis said softly with a rueful smile, "but... I have done so much harm in this instance I can never mend it, can I?"

"Not quickly, perhaps not ever, but surely not quickly," I sighed.

"I do not feel I will ever be granted the time: not by God, or nature, or even... him."

"You are not gravely ill in some fashion, are you?" I asked with concern.

"Non, non... Nothing so... But I am not young, and after the deaths of his brothers, I feel my age in ways..."

"Must you return to France this winter?" I asked.

"Oui," he said sadly.

"Will you be able to return here?"

He nodded thoughtfully. "But... Fate is fickle and life fragile, is it not?"

I smiled. "Especially when none of us are peasants who never raise a sword, do not travel, and expect to die of old age in their beds."

He gave a snort of mirth. "I am going to Hell."

"If that is true, then we all are."

I left him, and went to our room.

Gaston was thankfully sitting quietly on our bed: naked, with his legs crossed like a tailor and his elbows upon his knees, so that he was a sculpture of triangles. He appeared calm, and his eyes were soft and sad.

I knelt beside the bed with my elbows on the mattress and gazed up at him. "What exactly did he say before you called me in that made you so angry?"

He shook his head. "It is a jumble. I do not know. His presumption. That..." He regarded me with guilt.

I raised an eyebrow.

"I will never lie with her now," he whispered. "Not that she would ever consent to it, but now even her choice about the matter is gone."

I smiled and pulled his hand to my lips.

He sighed. "You are ever too kind, and it is... It is such a stupid and trivial thing: I do not truly want her so much as... It is as if he took it away from me: the possibility of it." His frown turned thoughtful. "It is as if he took everything from me. He seeks to give me what he wants, but not what I want. He can never give me what I want. And... taking anything from him threatens the few things I have: things I value; things I have worked very hard for."

I crawled on the bed to sit before him and take his hands in mine. "It does not threaten my love for you. And it is too soon to tell how this play will end. Neither of you can expect to put all of it behind you in a matter of weeks. This will take years to resolve, if resolution is indeed what you wish for."

"You are correct, as always," he sighed. "I have just lived with it all so long that I wish for it to be finished. And yet... it scares me. I am afraid I will have to abandon my dreams. Though I have wrestled with that since his arrival. Last night, when they called me Lord, and... It was not as I had always imagined, yet it was. I always wished to grow up and have the schoolmasters and other children respect me. As terrifying as it was, it felt good to stand with him on those steps and feel them all gazing up at us. I just wanted you there beside me, though... not... near, but with me." He shook his head sadly. "I did not know to envision someone with me when I was a child: that I would want such a thing. And now, it will not be worth it without you."

My heart ached and I cursed my foolish worries about choices and opponents and all matter of silliness unworthy of his love.

We kissed. That tentative caress led to the next until we stormed Heaven so that we could drift to sleep in its bowers.

I woke smelling smoke: not the oily smell of the lantern, or the greasy smell of wax, but wood burning. It was not emanating from our room. I quickly disentangled myself from Gaston, who woke when I moved. He smelled it as soon as his eyes opened. It was drifting in the window over the alley: the one facing my wife's house. We scrambled clear of the bed and netting and peered out into the night. We could see little in the darkness, and then I looked up and saw the moon was obscured by thick smoke, and then the flicker of flame from one of the ground floor windows of her house caught my eye.

We managed breeches alone. Gaston went out the window and onto the cistern and down: it was the fastest way to reach the alley. I ran out onto the balcony and yelled until Pete and Rucker threw open their doors. Then I was following my matelot.

The blaze was racing up the stairwell in the center of the house. We found Henrietta and Vivian in the back room. The poor housekeeper was struggling to tow my damn drunk wife out the back door into the yard. Vivian was screaming that she wanted to see it burn. We pulled them out and across the alley.

"What happened?" I yelled.

Vivian was twisting in my grasp, trying to see the flames.

Henrietta was in tears. "She be drunk," she wailed.

I shook Vivian until her head wobbled.

She glared at me when I stopped. "She is not getting this house!" she roared and laughed. "You can do whatever the Devil you want, but that bitch is not getting my house!"

I shoved her at Agnes and Sarah before I hit her.

Then we fought the fire. Within minutes everyone in town seemed to have gathered, and bucket lines were formed to the yards and cisterns at the surrounding houses. One group doused the roof and walls of Sarah's house with water – as it was downwind – to try to keep sparks from taking hold there. The rest of us battled the flames themselves with dirt and sand scooped from the yards. Gaston and I stood side by side in the searing heat and threw bucket after endless bucket at the conflagration that seemed to take on a life and purpose, as if it wanted to consume the house, and us with it.

Her lighting the fire in the stairwell was both a blessing and a curse. It meant that by keeping the wood wet on the outside of the ground floor we could keep it from spreading out into the yard or trying to leap directly to the house on the other side, where there was less than a foot between the walls. But, the stairs also gave the flames the chance to climb to the upper floors, where we could not fight it directly. Eventually, we were forced to withdraw as the building began to collapse in on itself. Then all our efforts were turned to keeping its neighbors from catching. By this time, all the nearby cisterns were dry and water had to be passed from more than a street away.

Gaston and I staggered in the front doors of Sarah's, planning to get to the roof and continue slinging water, but Agnes grabbed us as soon as we cleared the foyer. The place was thick with smoke and busy men. When I recognized the girl, I wondered why the women had not been moved elsewhere.

"Gaston!" she cried. "You must come." She tugged at his arm, pulling him toward the parlor door.

He opened his mouth to speak, but no sound came out. He had little voice to begin with, and the smoke had taken the rest.

"Lady Marsdale!" Agnes yelled. "She is birthing. We cannot find the midwife."

"Go," I rasped and pushed him after her.

I was up the stairs and shouldering my way past the bucket line to reach our room a moment later. I hauled the medicine chest downstairs myself, not wanting to interrupt anyone else's work to ask for help. They were saving our house from a blaze my Damn Wife had lit.

The women were all huddled in the parlor, which was relatively free of smoke. I supposed if the house did catch, we could get them out quickly enough. The room reeked of rum, and I wondered who had let her drink, and then I saw that my matelot's arms were free of soot from the elbow down – where he had washed them in rum. The rest of him was as black as Samuel, and I knew I looked the same. They had Vivian on the floor in the corner, and Gaston was examining her. She kept cursing at him and trying to hit him with her free arm – Henrietta was holding the other, tears still streaming down her round face. Agnes and Sarah had her legs: my sister was actually sitting on her pinned limb, and I thought that best, as her own distended belly would not get kicked that way. I set the chest next to Gaston and dove atop my wife's flailing arm.

"What happened?" I asked Henrietta.

"Oh, my Lord," she cried. "She's been drinkin' since she saw ya. She were na' drinkin' before, na' like this. An' then we heard o' ya' courtin' the other young lass…"

"What?" I asked.

"The one they say ya danced with at the party. The one ya be courtin' afore my Lady arrived."

I swore vehemently, and the woman winced.

"Nay, nay, damn it!" I growled. "I am not courting Miss Vines. There was talk of Gaston doing so."

"Ohhh…" Henrietta said. "That weren't what the gossip in the market were sayin'. Ohhh," she wailed. "Me and my big mouth. I never know when ta keep it shut. I shouldna' o' told her what I heard."

I could not dispute that. Still, the poor woman had not lit the fire or urged her mistress to drink. "It is not your fault," I rasped as kindly as I could manage.

All the while, Vivian was still struggling between us and cursing, and then she stilled and grunted.

"There be another one," Henrietta said. "They be comin' afore she lit the fire. I couldna' leave her to go for the midwife."

My matelot had his fingers inside Vivian and his other hand resting on her nightclothes-swathed belly. He stilled and his eyes widened.

He tried to say something but I could not hear him. I leaned closer and he managed to whisper, "She is having the baby." He seemed truly surprised by this.

I looked at Sarah and Agnes. "Is there any water left?" I asked.

Sarah smiled weakly, and Agnes moved to sit on Vivian's right leg, which she had been holding, and handed me an ewer.

I took a drink of it. Gaston took a long pull on the remains of the rum bottle.

"Have you seen a child born before?" I asked him in French.

He shook his head and considered Vivian's sex spread open before him with dismay.

"Has anyone here seen a baby born before?" I asked in English.

I was greeted with concerned wide eyes and shaking heads.

"Have you?" Gaston asked accusingly, as if I were withholding some vital piece of information from him.

"Non," I sighed.

"You bloody arses!" Vivian yelled. "Find the midwife!" Then she lifted her entire chest off the ground and roared at Gaston. "And stop touching me!"

I slammed her back to the floor and growled in her face. "Shut up! You are having a baby."

"I know that, you imbecile," she hissed.

Gaston handed me the leather-wrapped stick he used as a gag for amputations. I pinned Vivian's arm under my leg and battled her thrashing head to get it into place. I had to hold her nose closed to force her to open her mouth enough to get it between her teeth. She fought even that, holding her breath until her belly contracted again and drove the air from her in a whoosh.

I swear we fought the baby for as long as we fought the fire. The child did not seem to want to be born. Gaston said he could feel its head, but the opening it must pass through was not as wide as it should be. Vivian at last stopped fighting us and simply lay there, exhausted, as the contractions tightened her belly. We removed the gag, because even when the contractions came, she did not seem to need or want anything to bite down on.

The golden light of dawn was streaming in between the shutters of the narrow windows when Striker and Pete staggered in the room and said the fire was out. They saw what we were about and quickly left – though they promised to see if they could find food and water for us. They finally reappeared with some boucan, mangos, and two buckets of water. We wiped away the grime with dry cloths first, and then with a damp one. Then we began to take turns napping.

I noticed Henrietta, and even Vivian when she was lucid, eyeing us with concern. I thought it due to our only wearing breeches. Then I saw they were really staring at Gaston, and I knew it was because he was only wearing breeches and his scars were now shown in vivid relief with all the soot still ground into them. I considered my chest, and saw with relief that many of the bruises that still lingered from our Horse play were disguised by the smudged soot. I went to find cleaner clothes. The house was thankfully empty of the men from the bucket line. Striker, Pete, Rucker, Theodore, Dupree and the Marquis sat around at tables sipping wine in the atrium, exhausted and soot-smeared.

"Is there any possibility of finding the midwife?" I asked them.

"Nay," Theodore said sadly. "We have tried. It was a night for babies, apparently."

"Well the damn child does not wish to be born," I said.

"CanYaBlameIt?" Pete rasped.

I looked about at the atrium: the upper floor was smoke stained, and below, planters and even chairs had been broken in all the commotion. I sighed and went upstairs. Our room was a water-soaked shambles. Our clean white netting and linens were black, as were the white-washed walls, floor, and ceiling. I collected and counted our weapons and other valuables, and found none missing. Someone had thankfully stacked many of them in the farthest corner. I found a pair of tunics in one of the chests. They smelled of smoke, but they were clean and dry.

When I returned to the atrium, Theodore asked, "Do we know how it started?" as if he already did know.

I met his resigned gaze levelly. "Let us say my drunken wife knocked over a lamp while stumbling about in a panic when she realized she was due to birth."

He nodded thoughtfully. "That sounds good. I would hate to see her charged with arson."

I snorted and sighed. "I suppose this will cost a good deal of money. The water vendors will have quite the festival."

He nodded and awarded me a rueful shrug.

"Lovely," I sighed, and returned to the parlor.

I could not initially decide if I was dismayed or relieved to find it a place of activity once again. Apparently the babe had at last decided to move, or perhaps Vivian had at last decided to release it.

I helped support her as we pushed her up to sit somewhat, and Gaston extolled her to push when her belly tightened. The contractions were much closer together now, but it still seemed to take an eternity and my aching limbs complained during every second of it. In the aftermath of such a drinking binge, and hours upon hours of laboring to deliver, Vivian was barely conscious.

At last Gaston got a very surprised and happy look upon his face, and he pulled a slimy red mass from between her legs. I was appalled, thinking for sure it was dead. And then he swiped at it with a cloth and rubbed its chest a little and it gave forth a weak cry.

"Ah, look, it be a little girl," Henrietta cooed as she helped Gaston wipe it clean.

I suppressed a curse.

"Drown her," Vivian breathed. "No one wants a girl. No one ever wants a girl."

She was wrong: the Gods had surely done much to see this child born.

Sixty-Two

Wherein We Claim Jamaica

Gaston laid the child on Vivian's still-distended belly, with the little head nestled between her breasts. He tied off the cord and cut it. He then regarded the cord with a tired sigh and tugged on it experimentally. "I think we have to wait for the afterbirth now, since it did not arrive with the child," he sighed.

"I am not finished?" Vivian asked, her voice as shaky as her hands as she tried to turn the squalling infant around.

I gingerly helped her move the baby so that she could view its face. She gazed on it for several moments, and the baby seemed to look back at her.

Then my wife wailed, "Oh, God. She is ugly. She is a girl and she is ugly. Oh, God!"

The baby began to squall in earnest.

"Ah now, sweetheart," Henrietta cooed and pulled the baby away. "Let us clean her up a bit now. You'll see. She's a sweet little one." She cuddled it to her ample bosom and crooned.

The infant quieted somewhat, until Agnes tried to wipe one of her feet with a wet cloth. The squalling began anew.

"We'll get her clean," Henrietta continued in a singsong fashion, as if she was oblivious to the cries. "And then after you be done birthin', you can nurse her."

Vivian began to squall much like her child, and turned to bury her face in my shoulder.

I held her, as I had for much of the last several hours, and looked to my matelot, who appeared as miserable as I felt – and Vivian and the child sounded. He was staring at her sex as if the afterbirth might crawl from her of its own accord. I wondered how long it would make us wait.

Henrietta and Agnes now had the baby on the settee, and they were wiping it clean while making shushing sounds that could barely be heard over the little one's screaming. I felt someone was missing, and I looked to my left and saw Sarah sitting forlornly on the floor staring at Vivian. She met my gaze and burst into tears.

"Pete and Striker are outside," I told her.

She nodded between sobs, and slowly crawled to a chair to push her way to her feet, and stumbled out the door.

"So will you deliver Sarah's child?" I asked Gaston in French.

He awarded me a look that said I must never jest about such things – or even make mention of them. I could not help but smile.

"You need not remind me you wanted no part of this," Gaston said ruefully.

"Non, non, I do not blame you," I said with a smile to reassure him. "I blame the Gods."

"Oh, God," Vivian cried as her sobs stopped and she tensed in my arms. "When will it end?"

"Push," Gaston told her kindly. "Just push. Let us get this out."

"I will never, never do this again," she sobbed once the contraction passed.

"Ah now, my Lady," Henrietta said. "All women say that, an' here we be."

I peered down to find Vivian glaring at her, as if she would strangle the woman if she only had the strength.

"I want to go home," Vivian said with another sob.

"You burned your house," I said.

She began to wail again until another contraction gripped her. This one did as we needed, though; and Gaston was able to pull the afterbirth from her. It was bigger than the baby. I thanked the Gods it was soft and squishy, and apparently able to come through her opening much easier than a bony little child. If we had to wait another hour, or even another minute, I would have wailed.

I was at last able to disentangle myself from Vivian. She lay on the floor in a heap, and offered little protest as Agnes and Henrietta got her wrapped in a clean blanket.

Gaston had been handed the baby, and as he gazed down at the tiny face with wonder, I knew we would likely be doing this again – not with Vivian, but with some other hapless woman. He had a puppy. The child apparently liked him as well, because she quieted; but perhaps that was due to the warm blanket she was now wrapped in and the tip of Gaston's finger in her mouth.

I moved to kneel beside him and gaze at her. She was ugly. I had not seen an infant so fresh from the womb before. She was red and wrinkled and squished; and I recalled Striker likening one to a flaccid cock.

My matelot was reluctant to let her go when Henrietta came to take her to Vivian. My Damn Wife was initially reluctant to accept her, but then she held the little bundle and something akin to motherly love seemed to light her features. Then she became insistent on unwrapping the girl so that she could see all of her, and counting her toes and fingers. Once they had the child in the blanket again, Vivian attempted to nurse her. I could tell that was going to take some practice.

"The first few times it be just ta give her a taste and tell your bosom it be time to make more," Henrietta was assuring her. "She not be truly hungry yet."

I pulled a worried Gaston to the far corner of the room and bade him lie down to nap. He did not close his eyes until the child stopped crying, and the quiet sounds of suckling drifted to us along with Vivian's surprised gasp. We at last slept.

We woke to Agnes' gentle prodding. "The midwife is here," she whispered when I opened my eyes.

Gaston was quickly on his knees and peering around Agnes at a woman with a wide back and frazzled hair escaping her bonnet, who knelt beside Vivian. A nervous Henrietta sat next to them. My matelot pushed his way to his feet and went to join them, and I reluctantly followed. I did not see what the woman could say that should make us lose sleep: the baby was already here and seemed well enough. And then we came to stand above them and I saw my wife's bitterly held composure.

"This is my husband, Lord Marsdale," Vivian said. "And that is the... physician who delivered her."

"The Comte de Montren," I said quickly.

"He is a count, too?" Vivian said with annoyance.

The midwife was looking up at us with wide eyes and struggling to push her squat body off the floor.

"Nay, nay, my good woman," I said with a gentle hand on her shoulder. "We shall sit. You need not stand. And how are you called?"

"I'm Mistress Engle," she said.

We dropped down next to the women, and Mistress Engle seemed not to know where to look. She was avoiding us with her gaze with such dedication that I quickly checked to insure we were clothed.

"How is the child?" Gaston asked.

The babe seemed content to my eye: she was deeply asleep even though she was lying naked between her mother and the midwife.

"She is fine," Vivian answered tiredly. She looked as exhausted as I still felt: her face was soot-smeared and her eyes were puffy and dark.

"Does she appear as she should?" Gaston asked Mistress Engle.

The midwife was biting her lip. "I was just tellin' your lady that the babe's a bit small." She shrugged and asked Vivian. "Has there been any bleedin' after? Your woman said that the afterbirth came out all right and that you did not seem to bleed much."

"There did not seem to be any bleeding, other than the fluids of the womb, but I have not seen a child birthed before," Gaston said.

"That's good, my Lord," Mistress Engle said with a compressed smile and her eyes firmly on Vivian. "There will be lots o' bleedin' now, but it is as it should be. More like your monthly. May I take a look at you, my Lady?"

My wife nodded reluctantly and moved to spread her legs. The midwife gave Gaston and me a nervous glance. I awarded her a compressed but pleasant smile, and stayed where I was.

My matelot gently pulled the baby on her blanket toward him and rewrapped her. His face held concern.

I leaned to him and asked, "What?" in French.

"She is not saying all that she sees," he muttered.

"I see that," I whispered. "Is her opinion of import?"

He nodded.

I stood and motioned for Henrietta to rise and follow me. She slowly got to her feet and followed me across the room on stiff legs.

"Has she been paid?" I asked her of the midwife.

She shrugged. "Not yet, but a small coin'll do since she missed the birthin'."

"Do you have a coin?" I asked, as patting my waist revealed that not only did I not have my belt pouch, I did not have my belt, either.

Henrietta smiled. "Aye, my Lord."

"Good. When you escort her out and pay her, see what else she will say to you that she will not say to us."

She smiled shyly. "I were already goin' ta do that, my Lord."

I grinned. "Good woman. Well, now you know to tell Gaston and me, no matter what it might be."

"Aye, my Lord."

We returned to the others. The midwife apparently thought Vivian had weathered the birth well enough. She stood, and with a gracious but clumsy curtsy, bid us farewell, and Henrietta ushered her to the door and out.

Vivian was smoothing her clothing decently about her again. She looked to me, presumably because I was standing, and asked, "Is there anything to drink on that sideboard?"

"Not for you," I said. "We will find you some water."

She swore. "What? You will deny me wine? My head aches and I need to sleep."

"I will be happy if you never have another sip of a spirit," I said. "Be it beer or wine, and especially not rum. Do you have any idea how much your little tantrum cost last night?"

She looked away. "Do you?"

"Not yet," I sighed, "but I dread being informed of it. Your house was destroyed, and this one must be cleaned and refurnished, and every cistern for a block in all directions is empty."

"Oh, well," she said. "It looks as if you will have to build that bitch another one."

"You stupid..." I sighed. "I am not seeking to marry Miss Vines. There was merely talk of Gaston doing so. Gods, I should divorce you."

"I thought you were," she snarled.

"So did I," I snapped, "but I realized I stand to make my father far angrier by keeping you for now."

She regarded me with sharp surprise. "What?"

Henrietta had returned to stick her head in the doorway. She appeared quite glum as she waved me over.

"Never mind," I said tiredly. "We will discuss it when we have both had sleep, and I know the entirety of the damage you have wrought."

Gaston handed Agnes – who had been listening to my exchange with Vivian with great curiosity – the baby, and came to join me in speaking to Henrietta in the atrium.

"First," I told the woman. "Your mistress is not to be allowed anything to drink except water or tea, or chocolate. No spirits: no rum in any concoction, no cider, no brandy, no wine of any type, and no variety of beer."

"Aye, my Lord," Henrietta said with wide eyes. "She'll not like that a bit. An'... I do not know if I can keep her from it once she's up and about. Unless you wish for me to watch her every moment."

"I expect she will not like it at all. I expect she will become quite mean," I said. "Most drunkards do. We will not expect you to bear the burden alone." I looked to Gaston, and he nodded with an amused smile. "And we shall see she does not go out and find her own," I added. "I just do not want you to bring her any when she asks."

"And she will beg before we dry her out," Gaston said.

Henrietta nodded sadly. "It's for the best, I know that, my Lord. But, by God, she will get mean. And she gets the sweats and..." She sighed. "She tried to stop after she got with the babe and we moved into the house. She said she didna' need it now that she had her own house and no one to make happy but herself. But she... it made her so sick, and what with the sickness in the mornin'... Well, she just decided she would drink less, an' she drank wine instead of rum."

She looked away sadly. "Maybe that's..." She looked to us again, her teeth worrying her lip. "The midwife said the baby is sickly because it were not blessed by the angels." She made a curious gesture of touching her upper lip. "She says it's a whore's baby." Henrietta winced at the word. "That many times women who live in sin have sickly little babies that are unblessed."

"What?" I asked.

"This here," she pointed at the indent beneath her nose.

"The philtrum," Gaston said with a frown. "There are old beliefs that it is the mark of an angel's finger on the lips of a baby, from when the angel seals the new soul in the body."

"So what does that have to do with...?" I began to ask, but he was already gone, back into the room.

"She don't have it," Henrietta whispered, as if the angels would hear her.

Gaston returned with the child and Agnes. As I did not hear Vivian yelling in their wake, I assumed she had fallen asleep again, despite the lack of wine. He turned the little one's face toward me and pointed at her lip. There was no indentation.

"Well, do all babies have one, or is it a thing we grow?" I asked.

"I want a second opinion," Gaston said. "One that I trust. I have not seen enough babies to know."

"I seen them real small," Henrietta said. "But I never seen one sickly, an' I never looked at their lip afore. An' this little babe, she be very wee indeed."

"Shall we locate another midwife?" I asked. "Is there another midwife? And, is that Mistress Engle the one who will deliver Sarah's baby?"

Agnes nodded. "I do not like her. She is simple."

Gaston shook his head and sighed. "We will address that later. Right now we are going to the Theodores'."

"Oh," I said.

And so, still wearing only filthy breeches and tunics, we left the house with the baby.

In the harsh noonday light, I was appalled to see the damage, and amazed it was not worse. Sarah's house was black with smoke, but not charred, and the other neighbor was slightly singed – some of their roof and sideboard would need to be replaced – but in between them was a smoldering tangle of black wood, one-third the size of the structure that had stood there yesterday. I supposed I should speak to Theodore while we were there about the cost.

At the Theodores', Hannah regarded us with alarm, and Mistress Theodore met us in the foyer to whisper, "He has only just gotten to sleep."

Gaston nodded and whispered, "We are here to see you." He proffered the child.

Rachel frowned, but quickly took the babe and led us into the back room where her child, Elizabeth, was crawling about on a blanket on the floor, next to a rocking chair and a sewing basket. Rachel laid our infant on the table and unwrapped her carefully.

"He said she had the child," she said. "And how is the little one?" she cooed. Then she was frowning as she examined the baby. Next to her, Hannah was frowning as well.

"She is very small," Rachel said. "Elizabeth must have been twice this one's size." She looked to Hannah for confirmation, and the forbidding Negress nodded with a grim smile.

"Her head's too small," Hannah said.

"Aye," Rachel said with a sigh.

"Do all babies have a philtrum?" Gaston asked, and pointed at her upper lip and then his own. "This little indent here."

Hannah and Rachel frowned at one another and then looked at the baby with new concern.

"Aye," they said in unison.

"Well, not all babies," Rachel said. "This one doesn't. I haven't seen that before. And…" she added with a new frown. "She's sleeping very soundly." She pinched the infant's thin thigh, and the child did not stir.

"So she is deformed and sickly," Gaston sighed with a thick voice.

"She might not be sickly," Rachel said kindly. "Has she… Has her mother fed her the first milk?"

We nodded.

"Has her mother had rum, or…"

"She was on such a drunk she is still not sober," I said ruefully.

Rachel nodded. "My mother used to say that if you want a child to sleep and you cannot get them down any other way because they're sick, then you drink some wine before you nurse them. It gets the baby drunk and they sleep."

"It goes into the milk?" Gaston asked with horror.

She shrugged. "That's what they say. But I have not heard of it with a mother's first milk. It takes days before a woman's breasts swell with true milk. The first milk is different, but if the mother was pickled all through her pregnancy…" She sighed.

"So we have a drunk and deformed baby?" I asked, wondering why I should not be surprised that the Gods would make such a jest of the matter.

"She's not ugly," Rachel said. "She's just not as other babies are."

Gaston was distraught. "That damn woman." He rubbed his eyes angrily and asked Rachel, "Can we feed her anything else until we wring the rum out of her mother?"

She smiled. "I'm still nursing Elizabeth. You can leave her here for a time and I'll feed her. She won't need much right away, and by the time she does, my breasts will produce more."

"You would do that?" he asked.

She nodded. "Only for you and this little one, not for her mother, but aye, I will do that."

"Thank you," he breathed and embraced her.

Hannah was still frowning at the infant, and she touched one little hand with a long brown finger and shook her head sadly.

"Now you two go and get some sleep," Rachel said kindly. "And keep her mother out of trouble. We will see to this one. Does she have a name?"

"Nay," I sighed. "It has not been discussed."

She frowned. "If… well, if she is sickly, you should think of a name soon and get her baptized."

I nodded sadly and followed Hannah to the door. Gaston stayed behind for a minute.

Hannah regarded me in the cool and quiet of the foyer. Her voice was low and for me alone when she spoke. "Master Will, you need to tell your… God, that you wish to keep that child, if you wish to keep her on this Earth. Otherwise, she is just a guest."

I took a deep breath and considered her. "I understand."

She nodded solemnly and left me.

Gaston appeared a moment later, and we stepped out into the bright light and heat. I told him what Hannah said as we began to walk home.

"I feel the same," he said sadly. "She ails. I cannot tell you the medical reason why, but I can see it. I feel it is the rum. If it can truly get into a woman's milk, could it not get into her womb? If it can, the child has been pickled." He swore. "But... What did Hannah mean we should do? Pray, or baptize her? I do not think either will solve the problem."

"Perhaps we should pray in my fashion," I said.

He smiled grimly. "Perhaps we should, and name her."

"And claim her," I sighed.

He frowned at me. "If you do that, you will be stuck with that damn woman forever."

"Do you want the pickled baby?" I asked.

He turned to regard me with hope and regret, and I sighed.

"Will, I do not..." he started to say, but I pressed a finger to the indentation above his lips.

"You need not say anything," I said. "Your face could inspire me to sign a thousand baptismal records."

He sighed, and smiled at me with great regard. "My heart aches."

"As does mine," I said softly.

He shook his head. "Non, not that way: I wish to kill her damn mother."

I laughed. "Well, perhaps that will be necessary someday."

Vivian was, of course, quite incensed we had left her child with Rachel Theodore. She cursed us a great deal. Gaston began to lose himself, but as he had with his father, he chose to leave the room with control and dignity despite the Horse glinting in his eyes.

When much of the yelling abated, I told her all that had been said by the midwife and Mistress Theodore. And then I added, "I believe we originally agreed you should like a wet nurse; well, now you have one for a short time. When you no longer sweat rum, I suppose we will have to bring the child back, though."

"I do not want one now!" she screamed, and threw what she could reach at me. "And I did not make the baby sick!"

I checked what remained of the room's furnishings carefully for any stashed bottle of spirits, and then hauled Gaston's medicine chest away and left her alone. Agnes and Henrietta had already retreated from her wrath.

Pete, Striker, and Sarah were sitting in the atrium eating soup. It smelled delicious and made my stomach rumble, but I had much yet to do.

"Is Gaston in the stable?" I asked.

They nodded.

"LookedAngry," Pete said. "WeLet'ImBe."

"That was wise," I sighed. I gestured at the parlor door, behind which Vivian was still yelling and throwing things about. "The baby is at the Theodores': Mistress Theodore is still nursing. We must dry my damn wife out. It will not be pleasant. If you would rather it were not done here…" I stopped: I did not know where I would take her if it were not to be done here.

Sarah shrugged.

"That room does not lock," Striker noted, and looked about as if considering the usefulness of the house's other rooms. "I've had to dry men out before; it's always the quartermaster's duty when the drunkards show up to rove. If you don't watch them, they get into the stores."

"What would you suggest?" I asked.

"Put her irons in the hold," he sighed. "We don't have a hold. I guess there's the stable."

"Nay, it is a happy place," I said. "I will not have her sully it."

Pete chuckled.

"Leave her where she is and put her in irons," Sarah said.

"We'll have to drill a hole to anchor the chain," Striker said.

She shrugged with a long sigh and looked about her soot-stained house. "That is the least of my concerns."

"I am guessing we do not have the necessary irons on hand…" I said.

Striker grinned. "Nay, the need has not arisen here."

Sarah smacked him playfully.

"You can buy them at the blacksmith's," he said with a grim smile. "All the planters need them."

"And a sad thing that is," I said, and went to find Gaston. He was sitting in the stable with the puppies. He appeared much calmer. "I am going to the blacksmith's to buy leg irons to chain her in the parlor until she sobers," I told him.

He smiled quite glumly. "That should solve the problem, unless someone brings her something."

"I doubt anyone here is so inclined," I said. "And I will threaten to beat Henrietta if she should allow the damn woman to talk her into it."

"Would you?" he asked with a frown.

"At the moment, oui."

He decided to accompany me, and we went to the blacksmith's and bought a set of anklets suitable for a woman, and a dozen feet of chain and a bolt to attach it to. Vivian had exhausted herself by the time we returned, and at first she did not wake as we drilled the hole at the base of one of the wall beams. Then she did wake and asked what we were about. Then she saw the chains. Pete had to sit on her as we wrapped her ankles to keep them from chafing, and applied the anklets, and locked them to the chain and the chain to the bolt. She had nearly screamed herself hoarse by the time we left her.

Henrietta had hovered by the door the whole time, her big eyes filled with tears. I towed her out with us.

"I will see to her later," I assured the woman kindly. "She will not be abused or go without food or water. I would rather you did not tend her for a time, though."

She frowned. "I will not bring her anything, my Lord. You can trust me."

"I believe that, Henrietta, but I am ordering you to stay away from her for your benefit. You have long cared for her, have you not? It hurts you to see her thus?"

She nodded with a little sob.

"Well it will hurt less if you do not see her, and you will like her better when it is done if she has not spent days cursing you."

"I suppose, my Lord," she said.

"I am quite serious, Henrietta," I said and shook her shoulders gently until she looked up at me. "I will dismiss you if you go near her without my permission. And God forbid what I will do if she receives a drink from anyone."

She swallowed and nodded quickly. "I understand, my Lord."

"Now, go and see if you can assist Samuel, if you please. It might take your mind off the matter."

This suggestion seemed to relieve her, and she hurried off. I hoped Samuel viewed her arrival in his cookhouse as a blessing and not a curse.

I went to join the rest of the household where they sat about the remaining tables in the atrium.

"Well, that is seen to," I said. "I will see to her. I have ordered Henrietta not to." I looked to Agnes sternly. "I do not wish you to go near her, either."

The girl regarded me with wide eyes. "Why would I do that?"

"Smart girl," I said, and dropped into a chair next to Gaston.

"She does not like me," Agnes said.

"She will if she thinks you'll bring her rum," Striker said.

"I am not stupid or naïve," Agnes said primly.

Several of us fought the need to smirk.

"Now that we have destroyed the parlor," I said. "What should we attempt next?"

Sarah chuckled mirthlessly. "Well, our rooms on this wing are not so very bad, but..."

"I have seen our room," I said. "I imagine all the rooms on that side of the house are black."

She nodded. "They need to be cleaned and repainted."

I looked to Gaston and he nodded. "We will set upon it in the morning."

"I have been wondering where everyone will sleep," she said. She indicated the Marquis and Dupree, as well as Gaston and me. "Thankfully, Uncle is still at the plantation, as his room is in ruin, too. If she is not to be near Lady Marsdale, Henrietta can sleep in the servants' quarters. And I know Will and Gaston are used to far worse conditions, and I suppose they will sleep in the stable, but my Lord, I do not know where we will put you," she said to the Marquis. "I would have said the parlor, but..."

We looked to the Marquis: Dupree was just finishing his translation.

He shrugged. "We rested in the dining room today. On the floor," he added, as if it amused him that he had done such a thing. "However, I would not deny the house its use..."

"Non," Sarah said quickly. "We can move the table and find cots. That will be fine. We can eat here."

"WeGotHammocks," Pete said. "MightAsWellMakeMoreHolesTaString 'Em. NotLikeWeWon'tBeFixin'ItAllAnyway."

"I am sorry," I said to all.

"It is not your fault," Sarah said. "Fires happen even when extremely drunken women do not tip over lamps."

Sam and Henrietta brought us corn cakes and more of the soup I had seen the others eating earlier, and we ate and began to talk merrily of all that needed to be done to repair each room of the house.

We at last succumbed to lingering exhaustion, and left the pool of warm lantern light about the tables. I went to check on Vivian while Gaston went to salvage what he could from our room.

Vivian had been unable to do much to destroy the furniture, but I was thankful I had left nothing of value in her reach. I found her curled on the end of the settee, with her arms about her knees. She made no move when I lit a lamp on the far side of the room.

"Go away," she muttered when I approached. Her eyes opened, and she squinted at the lantern light and winced.

"Do you need anything?" I asked. "And spare me the sarcasm such a question can well engender in these circumstances."

"I am thirsty," she said bitterly after a long pause. "And there is no chamber pot."

"All right," I said. "Are you hungry? I am sure you must be quite starved. Would you like some soup or bread? That is all we ate." She had not eaten since probably before the fire, and she had vomited several times during the birthing.

She shook her head, and pushed herself up to sit. "I am filthy and bleeding. I would like a clean gown and rags."

"I do not believe any of your clothing remains," I said with a sincere shrug. "Perhaps Agnes or my sister can loan you a gown and the other."

"And," she added. "I will need Henrietta to help with my hair and..."

"Nay," I said.

Her eyes hardened, but she bit her lip to keep her initial words in. "Why?"

"She loves you," I said. "Perhaps enough to do what must be done, but she has been raised a servant, and I cannot trust that that will not win out. You will need to attend to yourself, or I will assist you if there is a thing you cannot do alone. I will find a brush or comb for your hair."

"Damn you," she spat.

I shrugged. "I will bring you water in a cup you cannot break, and a pot."

Her curses followed me out the door.

"Has she gotten the shakes yet?" Striker asked with concern as I joined them.

"Nay, not yet," I sighed. "I think she is finally no longer drunk, and now she feels its bite."

I asked the girls for a spare nightgown and comb, and rags for the bleeding, and went to find water in a tin cup and a chamber pot. Agnes met me at the door to the parlor with a brush, a comb, some ribbons, and a gown and ladies' rags. In the parlor, I set everything where Vivian could reach it.

"Should I leave the lamp?" I asked.

"Go fuck yourself."

I sighed. "I will leave the lamp turned down low for a time, so that you might see what you are doing and place things so that you might find them in the dark."

"As long as you leave, I care not," she said.

I sighed again. "I know it is very small consolation, but I do not hate you. I am sorry I did not tell you of my change in plans; that I left you worried and concerned for your future... such that you would believe the rumors that spread through the servants after the party. I understand why you burned the house. And it was just a house. And... I feel you meant no harm to the child, if indeed the drinking is what caused the harm."

"She is my baby," she sobbed into the arm of the settee. "She is all I have. She is my little Jamaica, my little piece of Jamaica. She is not yours. You had nothing to do with her. Nothing." She turned to glare at me. "I dressed like a whore and went out every night after you sailed, and fucked any man who would buy me a bottle, until I missed my bleed. I made her. I decided who I would fuck. Me. Me. Not you. Not my father. She is mine, and you have no right to take her from me."

I was surprised and amused, and yet saddened as I heard a thing in between her words that confirmed what I had long sensed about her: that she was as scarred as I, though perhaps not in the same way.

I righted a chair and sat. "You do not know who the father is? Her father is some nameless buccaneer? You did not have an affair?"

She raised her chin and shook her head with dignity.

"You are not stupid and indiscreet or..." I said with wonder. "I had thought, or rather, I had heard you had an affair with some planter's son who looked like me. I thought you were a complete idiot. But no one has said a word about what you really did, which if they had known would have been the talk of the town. So you were quite careful and sly."

She snorted disparagingly, but she was frowning at me with speculation and hope. "Do you still not hate me?" she asked sarcastically.

I smiled. "Nay, I do not hate you. This confession here has raised you considerably in my estimation."

She shook her head. "You are daft."

"Nay," I chuckled. "Mad perhaps, in that I do not choose to always see things as others do. Let us get you sober, and then you can have... Jamaica... back, and we... "

"Do not mock me," she said.

"I am not," I said reassuringly. "I think Jamaica is a fine name. Jamaica Williams. We can call her Jaime. Unless you had some other name for her."

"Nay," she said with wonder and a pained frown. "I always thought of her as my little Jamaica. Wait, you will give her your name?"

"Aye." I decided I would not tell her this was due to my matelot and not her: that would only make her angry again.

She rubbed her temples angrily. "Damn it, my head hurts so. I will not remember all this in the morning. I will think it a dream."

"Then I will say it again in the morning," I said kindly. "Drink the water." I stood and handed her the mug. "I will bring more. I will leave the lantern for now. See to yourself as you can. You will be miserable for days, and giving you anything to mitigate it will merely make it worse in the end, but it will pass."

She gazed up at me with teary eyes. "I do not understand you."

I smiled. "Well, many would say you are in good company. I would not, though, because generally people who do not understand me are people I do not like. Perhaps you will understand me in time."

She shook her head with a rueful smile.

I took the medicine chest and left her. I found Gaston in the stable. He had taken our weapons and all else we might need for the night from the chests in our room, including a hammock, and he was in the process of stringing it from the beams in the half of the stable designed to be a stall, where someone would have to enter the structure to see it. I decided the place would do nicely, even though it was enclosed and had no breeze. However, we would need to acquire some of the netting if we wished to stay here.

I began to assist him and quickly relayed all that Vivian had said. He regarded me with first surprise and horror, and then perplexity.

"Jamaica," he said at last, as if the word were suddenly unfamiliar to him. "Can one of her names be Angelique?"

"Angelique? That is a pretty name. I.. Is that what...? I thought her mother should name her, I did not know you wished to."

He shook his head. "I was just trying to think of a name for her. It holds no great meaning for me. I like Jamaica. It is fitting. And it is a pretty name for a girl."

"Good, then she can be Jamaica Angelique Williams." It felt strangely ominous to name another so, with the name they would go by throughout their lives.

He smiled. "As soon as your damn wife is able, we will need to go and have her baptized."

"I would rather not," I sighed. "If there is a Heaven, I do not see where it should be required that we pay a priest to say words over her in order for her to reach it. If God truly requires that for one so young and innocent, He can hang Himself."

"But Will," Gaston protested. "It has nothing to do with God. It will mean you legally claim her as yours in the Kingdom of Men."

"I know, I know," I sighed. "And that is not why I am reluctant. It does have little to do with God, and all to do with placing her on the tax roll for the parish and legitimizing her as my child, but… I feel I am angered that I have to pay a priest for that, too, and by so doing, pretend God has a hand in the matter when all know it to be a lie, another shadow on the cave wall. There should be some office of the Crown that keeps such records."

"There is," Gaston sighed with a rueful smile. "It is called the Church. And your good King Henry made that even clearer in your country."

I grinned. "You sound like a Protestant. Hell, we both do."

"Non, we sound like atheists," he said.

"Except for that part about God," I teased.

"I have only been in one chapel where I felt the presence of… some great power not of this world, and that was at the monastery," he said. "I have been in great cathedrals. I stood in them in awe; but not in awe of God, but in awe of the men who built them."

I smiled at him with great regard that we ever thought so alike. "That is always what I feel when I stand in them. And when I stood in the Sistine Chapel and saw that wondrous art, I saw the hand of man, not God."

We finished arranging our new home and I went to look in on Vivian one last time for the night. I found her sleeping on the settee. She had donned the clean gown and combed and plaited her hair. I took her soiled gown and rags away, and the chamber pot, which she had filled. When I returned, I was sure she was awake, but she held still and made no move to turn toward me. I left the empty chamber pot, a fresh mug of water, and some boucan and an apple for her, and turned out the lamp.

Gaston was naked and coating himself in grease to keep the insects at bay when I returned. I quickly joined him in that endeavor, and it soon became a thing of such pleasure we used the grease elsewhere.

When Heaven's light receded from behind my eyes and we at last sought to move from the sated tangle we had become, Gaston shook my shoulder and regarded me with concern in the dim lantern light.

"What?" I asked.

"You must speak to the Gods," he said earnestly. "About Jamaica."

"What?" I asked.

"Pray," he said. "That she lives. Claim her."

He appeared to be in a curious state, and I saw much of the Child about him, so I did not argue that I felt I had said as much in my heart and surely the Gods had heard me and understood my intent.

"Must I do this alone?" I asked gently.

He thought on it and shook his head. Then he was prodding me to move until we sat like tailors facing one another. He took my hands. As I gazed into his eyes I could see he had fully adopted his childish mien now, and I wondered at it.

"What should we say?" I prompted him.

He gripped my hands tightly and closed his eyes; when he opened them he gazed upward toward the ceiling. "We wish to claim Jamaica Angelique Williams, the girl born of Vivian this morning, as our daughter. We promise to care for her, and we wish for her to remain with us and become healthy."

"Oui," I said, because *amen* seemed oddly inappropriate.

He smiled and regarded me with great love, and then he was crawling into my lap and pushing me back on the hammock to kiss me earnestly and sweetly. We cuddled together and I felt him drift to sleep in my arms. I lay awake until I was sure he slumbered soundly.

Then I whispered. "I want You Gods to understand that he comes first in all things: I will not give him up for the happiness and health of any other, including myself."

Sixty-Three

Wherein We Provide Succor and Solace to Girls

We woke to an insistent rapping on the stable's doorframe. I had a pistol in my hand before I recalled where I was. Gaston had done likewise, and we regarded one another sleepily. Light was streaming through the doorway. I thought there was something important I should attend to, but I could not remember what it could be.

"Come in," I grumbled.

Gaston awarded me a scandalized glare and pointed at his nakedness.

"Unless you are a lady," I said quickly.

But it was too late: Theodore stood before us.

"Or a gentleman," I added with a grin.

Theodore quickly turned his back as Gaston scrambled off the hammock to dress – and throw my clothes at me.

"To what do we owe this pleasure?" I asked our friend as I pulled on my breeches and tunic.

"Well," Theodore said with great somberness, "I was sent to fetch you. There is a screaming infant at my home, and my wife wishes to speak to you about the matter."

"Has something occurred?" Gaston asked quickly. "Does she ail... more than we know?"

That was not my concern, though I supposed it should have been. "Was your wife screaming when she asked you to fetch us?"

Theodore chuckled with little humor. "Thankfully, nay, and as to the baby's health, well, I feel she screams because she is an infant and they all seem prone to do so for lengthy periods, such that I wonder how they can sustain such noise." Then he asked with concern, "Does the child ail? Mistress Theodore has been so enthralled with the little one's well-being she has said scarcely a word to me."

"We feel the child might have been pickled in rum in her mother's womb," I said.

Theodore sighed. "Oh Lord, well… That probably explains my wife's request, then. Where is Lady Marsdale?"

"We are keeping her chained in the parlor until she dries out," I said.

He gave a lengthy sigh, and turned to face us. "I suppose that is for the best. How is she?"

"Not well," I said, as I remembered what I should attend to. "And I need to look in on her. Perhaps you should go with Theodore and I will be along shortly," I told Gaston.

He nodded grimly, but we did not part right away, as we both had need of the latrine.

As we walked to the back of the yard, I watched concern tighten his features, and wished I could say something to ease it, but all the platitudes I could think of were things that would have angered me if I had heard them spoken of even a dog or horse of which I was fond.

"You will do all you can for her," I said at last, just before we returned to Theodore. "And no matter what occurs, she will know that there was someone here who cares for her."

Gaston paused and turned to regard me with love. "Thank you." Then he shook his head with a bitter smile. "I know so little, Will."

"Do not chastise yourself over it," I said gently. "You know you know far more of medicine than probably anyone else on this island."

"That is what is pathetic," he said. "How can we all be so damn stupid?"

"We hide in caves," I said, and shrugged with a small smile that I hoped he would find reassuring and not mocking.

He smiled. "Take care of her damn mother."

"I will see you soon."

I followed them to the door and watched them leave, before reluctantly entering the cave in which Vivian now dwelled. My nose recoiled at the odor of the place, but my ears were thankfully not assaulted by her cursing, and it was too dark to see most of what caused the stench. I opened a shutter and gained enough light to find her lying on the settee, trembling and seemingly oblivious to my presence. I mused on how she was descending into deepest darkness in the name of being dragged into the light.

"You are obviously miserable," I said gently, "but other than giving you rum, what can I do to aid you?"

"Bring my baby back," she hissed.

"Not until you are well," I told her.

"And after the baby is well and weaned, I can drink again, correct?" she snarled.

"Nay."

"You bastard! You cannot keep me like this!" She rattled the chain.

I could not but smile. "My dear, you are my wife, and I think no man in town, surely no magistrate – or even clergymen – would find fault with a man keeping his wife sober – by whatever means. Especially not after you burned a house... by accident. And as for my feelings on the matter. I care not if you drink yourself to death, as long as you did not cost me a cent while doing so. But I think that happy scenario will be quite unlikely, as you will never be trustworthy while drunk – no drunkard is: reason flees with the spirits, and if you happen to feel guilt or shame you will simply drink until those feelings depart. So, if you are to remain the Lady Marsdale, or even live by my support under another name, you will be sober."

She cursed me vehemently as I collected the chamber pot and soiled rags. As much of it called into question my father and mother, I cared not, and even found some amusement in it.

Henrietta and Sam had bacon and eggs prepared, and were beginning a stock for the soup. I troubled them for a cloth-wrapped bundle of bacon I could shove in my waistband and a tin cup of broth, and then filled another unbreakable vessel with water. Vivian would not look at me when I returned. I set the cups and empty pot where she could reach them and left her.

I saw Gaston approaching the house as I walked out the front door, and immediately felt guilty that I had taken so long to leave. Then I saw how very concerned he appeared.

"How is she?" I asked as he reached me.

He did not choose to enter the house; instead he pulled me into the shade of the balcony and spoke quietly. "Rachel says that a healthy babe only eats and sleeps in the first weeks; and they do not truly hunger in the first days, so there is only the sleeping. Jamaica is so miserable that she does not. She cries and nothing else; and she is exhausted. We feel it is because she is drying out, much as her mother will do. Rachel wished to know if I could give her anything to ease her pain and let her sleep for a time." He sighed heavily. "I do not want to give her laudanum, though. It will be worse to take from her than the damn rum if she grows accustomed to it. I have other medicines that will make her sleepy, and still others that will ease her stomach, but none will remove the pain of being without the rum."

"So give her rum," I said. "Maybe a little, until she gets stronger, and then we can wean her from it."

He considered me for a time. Or rather he gazed upon me as he considered my suggestion and his own thoughts. At last he said, "I will give her laudanum."

I frowned curiously. "But..."

"Things do not die when placed in laudanum," he said, and entered the house. "Rum kills..."

I followed him to the stable, where we had moved his medicine chest. "So you will wean her from the laudanum when she is stronger?"

He nodded. "I am hoping I need not give her so much that it will be difficult."

He filled a small vial and we departed for Theodore's. We ate the packet of bacon as we walked.

I could hear Jamaica as soon as Hannah let us into the Theodores' house. Her cries were weak but constant – and I could imagine very grating. The never-ending complaint of a being in pain who feels none will hear her: more plaintive curses at the Gods than pained wailing. Rachel greeted me with a smile that spoke both of her tiredness of hearing the babe she coddled and shushed in her arms and of her continued commitment to the matter.

Gaston carefully mixed a tincture of the laudanum with water in a small glass bowl he had brought and took it to Rachel. There he paused and regarded the child and the mixture in his hand with consternation.

"Hannah, fetch one of Elizabeth's spoons," Rachel said with a smile.

Gaston sighed with relief.

Hannah returned with a little silver spoon: so small it would only hold a sip, yet still seemingly too large to fit in tiny Jamaica's mouth. Gaston gingerly accepted it and scooped up some of the laudanum-laced water and ever-so-carefully dribbled it between the child's lips. There was a great deal of sputtering and it took several attempts before she seemed to swallow a mouthful.

Gaston sighed and sat as we waited for the drug to take effect. "We need a better method of dosing her," he said.

"A baby's mouth is made for a teat. If you feed a babe without a teat," Rachel said, "you can use a water skin, but that wouldn't work for so small an amount."

Gaston shook his head in agreement. "Nay, the skin would absorb the laudanum."

The drug had taken effect on little Jamaica, and she was now limp in Rachel's arms. Fear clutched at my heart. The silence was ominous, and she looked as Gaston did when I worried that he had taken too much: close to death.

Gaston felt the same as I, because he stood and took the child from Rachel to carefully hold her so that he could place his ear to her chest. "Her heart beats strongly," he said quietly with some relief. "But slow."

"I had hoped I could feed her," Rachel said.

"I know," Gaston said with worry. "I wanted to give her as little as possible, but such lack of precision in dosing her will make it difficult. All the funnels I have will be too large. We will have to inquire of the glazier to see if we can have a very small one made."

"I would almost rather have her crying," Rachel said with concern.

"I know," Gaston said and handed the baby back to her.

"For now you can sleep while the baby does, Mistress," Hannah said kindly.

We left them to sleep, and I told the Gods I very much wanted the child to wake. Gaston was quiet, and I offered my hand and he took it. I knew there would be no solace I could offer him save laudanum if the child were to die because he gave her too much. That worried me more than the child's death.

Thankfully, unlike the cobbler we had encountered, the glazier seemed quite entertained by the notion of making something new, and spoke with great interest about the specifications of a tiny glass funnel. We left a deposit for his work, and arranged to come back that afternoon. Then we purchased an armful of netting for our new sleeping arrangement.

At our home, we found Theodore sitting in the atrium speaking with Sarah and the Marquis. Gaston nodded politely and slipped away to the stable.

"Your house is quiet for a time," I informed Theodore as I followed my matelot. "The babe sleeps. I believe your wife might be sleeping as well."

He appeared relieved at this.

"Wait," the Marquis called after me.

I paused and turned to find him hurrying to my side.

"What is the matter?" he asked with genuine concern.

With a sigh I explained briefly our concerns for the child: that she was damaged in some fashion, and perhaps not long for the earthly plane. "Gaston will not take it well if she dies," I finished.

He nodded thoughtfully. "Is that because he is a physician, or... Well, from my understanding, I do not see where he should feel some kinship with the child."

I gave a rueful smile. "He wants children... very much. And though this little girl has no relation to either of us, I have decided to claim her so that... we have a child. And, oui, some of it is due to his being a physician as well."

It looked as if he would say more, but he kept his lips pressed together.

"You think us fools," I said lightly.

He frowned and smiled sheepishly. "Non, not... I feel you will think I am a selfish old man: a noble in your definition."

I smiled. "You cannot see why we would do such a thing."

"Non, I cannot. I had children because a man, a nobleman, needs to have heirs."

"Honestly," I said, "I cannot quite grasp his fascination with them, either, but I will do this to please him. He views them with delight, though. I feel he wishes to raise them in a manner he was not raised..." I shrugged. "And somehow make right of that in his heart."

He seemed struck by that, not as if I had chastised him, but in awestruck contemplation. "That is truly noble," he said at last. "So does he intend to live with them?" He asked this last as if he could comprehend all else I had said, but not that.

"I think they will be underfoot more than good hounds," I said with a grin. "I cannot imagine it, either."

"That method of raising them seems to do well by the peasants," he said. "They appear to have far less trouble with their children meeting their expectations."

"Do they?" I asked. "I suppose... Well, I have always felt that is because they have low expectations. Now which of us sounds like a wolf?"

He chuckled.

He looked about, and spying Theodore and Sarah going over a ledger, said, "So you will keep that wife?"

"Oui, it appears so," I sighed. "Despite the trouble she has caused. It will not be due to fondness or duty."

"I imagine, though your good man there," he gestured at Theodore with his cane, "has not divulged any confidence, that there is significant cost associated with your wife's... escapade."

"I do not know the full accounting of it, but oui," I sighed.

He nodded and turned to meet my gaze. "I will pay it."

"Why?" I gasped. "You need not..." And then I recalled that all the money Gaston and I had in the bottom of the medicine chest came from the man before me.

He made a clucking noise. "Your affairs are inextricably linked with my son's, are they not?"

"Oui," I sighed. "We share all things, the good and the bad."

"Then your debts are my son's debts." He gave a little shrug and moue.

"They are, here, amongst the Brethren, but I am truly surprised you would view it so," I said somberly.

He awarded me a lopsided grin. "As am I, but I find I do, or perhaps should."

I was unsure as to whether his beneficence truly resulted from his accepting me as his son's partner, or whether it was his old oozing wound of guilt that he thought to staunch with even more gold, but I was pleased: because even if it was the latter, he was choosing to perceive me as someone inextricably linked to his son.

"Thank you, my Lord," I said sincerely and bowed. "We have the funds, but... well, your beneficence is appreciated."

"I know, and you are welcome to it." He clapped my arm and walked back to the tables.

I found Gaston where I expected, lying in the straw with Bella and her puppies.

He gently wiggled a slumbering loaf as he looked up at my entry. "Perhaps all little ones sleep so soundly."

I dropped down to join him. "She will be fine."

He sighed. "How is... Lady Marsdale?" He said her title as if it pained him.

"My damn wife will be fine, too." I laid a hand on his shoulder so that he turned to regard me curiously. "Your father has said he will pay all the debts associated with the fire."

"Why?" Gaston asked.

I shrugged. "He says it is because our affairs are linked and thus my debts are yours."

"Do you feel he is sincere?"

"Oui." I told him of my thoughts on it possibly still being guilt.

Gaston shrugged. "Gold will not remove my scars or... undo all else he has wrought, but it is appreciated. Now if he would only give us gold when he feels guilt, and do naught else."

I chuckled. "Oui. Speaking of that, should we pay a call to the Vines to smooth ruffled feathers, or simply let the matter be marooned and never discussed again?"

He shook his head. "I do not know precisely what my fool father said. Perhaps you should go. I would not have them think poorly of us."

"I will consider it, then; but I feel no great urge to do so now. If we do anything at all, we should see to cleaning rooms. I would feel guilt over that matter if I saw anyone else working on them, but I have not spied Pete and Striker this morning."

He nodded, and stood to address the netting. I moved to help him, and we decided how best to tack it to the ceiling so that it fell about our hammock.

Sometime after we finished with that task and returned to the puppies, I was lost somewhere between dozing and mustering the energy to crawl atop my matelot and nuzzle his neck when Agnes appeared in the doorway. Spying us, she swiftly stepped inside and squatted to speak in a whisper.

"I have been in the market with Pete and Striker," she hissed.

"Well, that explains where they are," I said in a conversational tone.

She frowned. "I was approached by someone there: someone we all know: Christine. She wishes to speak with you, both of you, but she is afraid you will betray her again and she seeks assurances."

I sat up. "Betray her? How have we... Oh... She is making another escape?"

Agnes nodded. "She is dressed as a boy again and skulking about the market. She would not tell me her plans; she only said that she wished to seek your advice, but that she was afraid..."

I looked to Gaston, who had also risen to sit and was now quite alert. He nodded.

"Tell her we will not betray her," I assured Agnes. "We did not mean to last time, but we did not know how much forethought she had given to the matter and we were led to believe she had bolted in blind panic and we feared for her safety. We will not make that mistake twice. If she will meet with us, we will tell no one. We will not give her up to any who come looking for her, either."

Agnes nodded. "I will tell her and see what can be arranged. She does not want Striker and Pete to know, of course, and Striker was angry when I said I had to return home... for female reasons – because we were looking at bedding and the like and it bores and confounds him. So I will have to be careful."

I grinned at the thought of Striker and Pete attempting to buy linens.

"Should we accompany you, then, and meet with her there?" I asked.

"Nay, nay," she said as she worried her lip with her teeth. "I am afraid she will bolt if she sees you arrive with me. Let me see if I can send her here."

She slipped away, leaving the yard by the back gate. Gaston and I regarded one another.

"Well, this is an interesting development," I said. "I suppose I shall not pay the Vines a visit."

He shook his head with a rueful smirk as he flopped back down next to the puppies. "Why can nothing be simple?"

"We would likely be as bored and confounded by it as Striker is with linens," I sighed.

I peered out: the sun was quite high. "I suppose I should see to my wife."

Sarah and Theodore were no longer in the atrium, but the Marquis and Dupree were. They were reading an English copy of *Don Quixote*; or rather, Dupree was translating it as he went, and the Marquis was leaning back in a chair with his eyes closed, either napping or listening. I could not tell which – though he was not snoring. His eyes did not open at my approach.

"Where is everyone?" I asked Dupree.

"Mister Striker, Mister Wolf and Miss Agnes are at the market," Dupree said quietly. "Mistress Striker has retired for a nap. Samuel is in the cookhouse, and Henrietta is upstairs collecting the soiled linens. We are apparently awaiting a water wagon to fill the cisterns so that the cleaning might begin."

"Well, I do not feel so very lazy then," I said with a smile.

"And..." He frowned. "You should probably know. Your... wife, was calling out earlier, and Henrietta went to see to her."

I swore and went to the parlor. I found Vivian pacing such as the chains would allow, with her gaze on the floor to keep from tripping, and her arms crossed tightly under her breasts to support them. She started at my entry.

"You have turned my maid against me," she snapped.

"I hope so, for her sake," I said and crossed the room. I gently took her chin to turn her face to the light so that I could gauge her eyes. She did not appear inebriated and she jerked away angrily. I could not smell any alcohol upon her breath when she cursed me.

Her sudden movement to escape me caused her to lose her balance and begin to fall, as she could not move her chained ankle fast enough to recover. I caught her and pulled her upright. The whole of it enraged her, and I was soon besieged by a flurry of ineffectual blows that I handily managed to stave off, until she attempted to put her knee in my groin and stomp on my bare feet with her tiny ones. Then I grabbed her wrists and held her from me. She roared with frustration and tears filled her eyes. I released her and she took another swing, this one a good solid jab and not a flailing slap. I threw my arm up to block it, and she flinched from my raised hand though I had harbored no intent to strike her.

"Go on!" she hissed when I let my arm fall. "I have been struck by better men than you!"

I made a guess and took a step back, beyond her reach. "You are saying your father is a better man than I? A man who would sell his daughter to the highest bidder to cover his gambling debts?"

"That is not what I meant!" she snapped. "I did not mean he was... better! I meant he could hit harder than some damn sodomite!"

"Oh," I said with feigned enlightenment, and then I could not stop the grin from seizing my lips.

"Do not mock me!" she roared as her tears came. "You bastard. What do you want from me?"

I considered the question sincerely and wiped the smile from my face. "I want to see you sober. I want to converse with the little girl hiding in there behind all that rum and ire."

"Why! Why?" she screamed. "You will not like her! No one ever liked her! She was useless! She will always be useless! A fat cow who cannot even deliver a boy! A fat whore with a deformed and sickly baby! I know what happens to women who cannot birth boys. My father beat my mother for me and all four of my sisters. I was responsible for her bad hip! Not one boy! She finally fell down the stairs and broke her neck!"

She stood panting and then the realization of what she had said came and her hand flew to her mouth to stop the words that had already fled. She regarded me with horror. "Do not pity me!" she hissed. But the rage was departing her and she sank to the floor in a cloud of gown.

"I do not. I do not!" I said loudly enough to draw her gaze back to mine as I squatted in front of her. "I feel sympathy for you, aye, but not pity. When you are drunk you are worthy of pity, you are quite pathetic, but now and... I think the girl under all that rum is not a person to be pitied."

"You do not know anything," she growled.

"I think I do: I know what it is to be beaten," I said softly. "And I swear to you on all I hold holy that you shall never be beaten by me. Nor will Jamaica. Gaston and I suffered enough in our childhood; we would be evil or ignorant men indeed to inflict what we faced upon another. We will not allow it."

I could see her searching my face and eyes for any sign of deception: I did not flinch.

"Well, you have not struck me yet," she said at last and fidgeted with her gown.

"Aye, and you have given me what many would consider good

cause," I said lightly.

She actually smirked, but then the tears came anew. I felt I should comfort her, but thought I dare not touch her.

"What can I do for you?" I asked gently.

"I am somewhat hungry and thirsty," she said and pawed her tears away. "Henrietta brought me nothing because... I was angry with her for not..."

"Bringing you something to drink," I offered.

She snorted. "Aye."

"I will see what Sam has," I said and went to the door.

"Might I have some chocolate?"

"As much as you want," I told her, and went to find some.

Gaston was leaning in the stable doorway as I crossed the atrium. He came to join me as I went to the cookhouse and asked Sam for chocolate. There was none hot, but Sam assured me he could make some quickly.

I pulled Gaston back to the stable doorway and quickly told him all she had said.

He sighed when I finished. "I so want to hate her."

I chuckled. "I know, but as we suspected, she is as scarred as we. That should not prevent you from hating her, though."

"It does if it gives reason to her actions," he said.

"Why is it that neither of us turned to drink?" I asked. "I drink... to excess more times than I wish to remember – more times than I can remember – but... it is different. I have seen others like her: people who drink to drown their sorrows: people who drink so that they do not feel. There are times when I feel the need to do so, but not every day. Even when I am lost to melancholy I do not drink in that manner."

He frowned in contemplation. "I do not know."

A soot-covered Henrietta approached with an armful of blackened linen.

"I have seen your mistress," I said. "I am taking her some chocolate."

She nodded grimly. "I am sorry that I went in, my Lord. But she was yowlin' such that I thought people on the street would hear her."

"I understand," I said. "Do not fret; you did well."

"Thank you, my Lord."

The chocolate was done at the same time the water wagon arrived. Gaston went to help with that matter and I hurried to take mug and pot to Vivian.

"How is Jamaica?" she asked as I set the things in her reach. She was still sitting on the floor.

I hovered, torn between going to help with the water and answering her. I decided they could do well enough without me and sat. "She is... as miserable as you from the lack of rum, it seems, and she can do nothing but cry. And as she is so small and weak, there are concerns... She did not wish to sleep. So Gaston gave her some medicine to calm her."

She seemed pleased to hear this, and then she snorted. "Can he not give the same to me?"

"Non, he cannot. It is laudanum: it can cause a greater craving than spirits. We are only giving it to the baby because she will not live if she does not eat and sleep. You are strong."

"She is truly that close to death?" she asked.

I nodded.

She started crying again.

"She is being well cared for," I said. "And… you can help with that as soon as you are … well."

"I made her ill," she sobbed. "She is better off without me."

I cast about for some kind thing to say and settled on, "The rum made her ill. The rum has made you… not yourself."

She snorted at that, but her words were soft. "I do not know who I am without it, or wine, or…" She sighed.

I thought it quite possible she had been drinking since she left the nursery. "How old were you when you were last sober?"

She smiled grimly. "Eleven."

"And how old are you now?"

"Sixteen."

I had been a boy fleeing his father's house and Gaston had been exiled here at her age.

"Five years," I remarked gently, "well, it is no wonder you do not know who you are without it. Let us find out."

She shook her head. "The last five years have been better than the first ten."

I shrugged. "You might be surprised at who you become in the next ten. I would have been at your age. And nay, I am not mocking you."

She was studying me, but her eyes were narrowed and her brow furrowed with thought that I felt had little to do with me. "I have never imagined I will live that long," she said at last.

"To the ancient and decrepit age of twenty-six?" I teased.

"How old are you?" she asked.

"Twenty-seven," I said with amusement.

She smirked and sighed. "It is older for a woman, you know."

"Aye, I do. Now drink your chocolate and try to rest. I will come back later. I should help with the cleaning – since we now have water."

She nodded, and I left her there sipping her chocolate.

I emerged to find Striker, Pete, and Agnes had returned, and Sarah had risen from her nap. The atrium was quite busy as my sister inspected the purchases the men were bringing in from a cart, and Henrietta, Samuel, and Gaston had begun to haul water from the cistern upstairs.

I caught Agnes' arm as she hurried past with more purchases from the market and whispered, "Did you find her?"

She nodded curtly. "She is supposed to go to the stable."

I wondered if Gaston knew that; and then I wondered if Bella would receive her. I hurried to the stable and peered in: I saw no slender lads inside, but the dogs were snuffling and growling near the fence. I thought it amusing that Agnes had not realized the dogs did not know Christine as we did.

I poked my head out the gate and found Christine there, leaning on the wall looking at the charred remains of Vivian's house. She had her hair stuffed up under a kerchief and hat, and her breasts were bound flat under a loose men's shirt; and as I had the first time I saw her dressed as a boy, I wondered how anyone could be fooled, but they had been, and even now I thought it likely I could introduce her to the Marquis and he would wonder how I knew some peasant lad and why I was bothering to show him off.

"She burnt it because she thought I was going to put her out and marry you," I said jovially. "She did not wish for you to have it."

Christine started and whirled to face me. Her eyes lit at the sight of me, and then narrowed. "But…" she began with consternation.

"It is but further proof that drunken young ladies should not listen to the gossip of servants, if such a thing should need further proof. Come in; let us introduce you to the dogs."

She hesitated before picking up her sack and slipping past me through the gate, and I knew it was due to her fear of me and not the snuffling beasts with raised hackles. I pushed the dogs away and admonished them to behave and sniff her as they would but not to bite. She held out her hands and let them learn her smell.

I led her to the stable. "Bella, the bitch, has puppies, and she is good with us, but she might not take kindly to a complete stranger. We will have to go slowly."

She nodded.

"Will," Gaston called down from the balcony above. Then he saw Christine and he took a long breath.

She smiled weakly and waved.

"Who is that?" Striker called from next to Gaston.

"Chris, an old friend of Agnes'," I said.

"Well put him to work so we'll know where she is," Striker said. "I don't need her disappearing again."

I chuckled, and Gaston shook his head.

"I should see to Jamaica," Gaston said. "I was going to ask if you would accompany me, but… you should probably stay now." His gaze flicked to Christine.

I shrugged, but my gaze held firm on his. "If you wish."

He nodded thoughtfully and shrugged. "I can go alone."

"Then go," I said. "We will see if we can get a room clean. Remember the funnel."

He nodded. "That is why I need to leave now."

Christine watched him hurry to the stairs and down, and then eyed me with curiosity.

"We named the baby Jamaica," I said with a grin, and took her sack and put it inside the stable. "Mistress Theodore is her wet nurse for the time being."

"What baby?" she asked.

I snorted. "My wife's. She gave birth the morning after the fire."

"Ohh," she said. "Might I ask: is it yours?"

"It is now," I said with a surety I found surprising.

"Ahh," she said with feigned nonchalance.

I found I did not wish to speak with her about the great number of things we should probably speak of – not alone. I led her upstairs and we joined the others in cleaning, starting with the Marquis' room. To my amusement, our number included Dupree and the Marquis in very plain breeches and shirts. Only Sarah was spared hauling buckets or swabbing the walls, ceilings, and floors. We only had one upset, when Agnes became quite daft in her pleasure at seeing Christine in the house.

Striker pulled me aside shortly after I shooed the girl out.

"Is that Agnes' boy, that skinny little shite?" he whispered.

I groaned. I did not dare tell him, as I could not be sure how he would feel about hiding Christine; and yet, if I did not tell him, I could not set the matter straight concerning Agnes' preferences.

"Nay, he is a friend," I said firmly. "That is not the type of... person she seeks as a suitor. She is merely very happy to see this friend. And why do you care?"

He shrugged, but then his nonchalance turned to a speculative study of me. "Why don't you care? What interest do you have in the girl anyway? Philanthropy? Do you plan to feed and clothe her for the rest of her life so that she can draw things: like you're her patron or some such thing?"

"Perhaps," I said. "And once again, why should you care? Has she been a bother to have about the house?"

He sighed expansively. "Nay, nay, Sarah is fond of her, but I'm ever being asked if she's available. People act as if she's my ward. And your uncle, good Lord. He wishes for her to be married off as soon as possible."

"Why?" I asked. "And where is that bastard? He was not at the party. He has not come to see if we burned away. Has Sarah been corresponding with him?"

"She sent him a note when you arrived, another concerning the party – which she was sure he was invited to – and another after the fire. She is actually becoming worried, but we need to attend to this before going in search of the daft bastard." He shook his head. "I think it's likely he's off visiting some plantation – God knows where – and all of the notes have not reached him yet, or his reply has not reached us. And..." He lowered his voice and wrapped an arm around my shoulder to whisper. "We think he is a lonely and horny old bastard, and that's why he wants the girl married off and out of the house. She frustrates him."

I swore.

Striker shrugged and spoke defensively. "You have not seen how he eyes her."

"I am not angry with you for the supposition, I am angry with him for being... an aging man with needs, I suppose." I chuckled. "The girl is not available unless for some unforeseen reason she takes a fancy to someone – which I do not see happening."

"Why?" he asked with amusement. "Though I should wonder, she lives well enough here without having to put up with some damn arse."

"She favors women," I said flatly.

He frowned, as if he did not comprehend my meaning, and then he snorted. "How does she know? Has she been with a man?"

I punched his shoulder hard enough to make him curse. "I cannot believe you said that," I hissed. "You daft bugger. How do you know what you favor? How do any of us? She knows."

"Truly?" he asked with sincere curiosity and rubbed his shoulder.

"Truly," I said.

He was frowning. "Well, that explains some comments Sarah has made... I am a daft bugger."

I grinned. "Aye, but we choose to tolerate it."

He snorted.

"I suppose I will have to broach the matter with my uncle in some fashion," I sighed, "but perhaps we will be lucky and he is already off with some lonely widow."

"God, no," Striker said quickly. "Then he will bring her here, and Sarah will have to deal with her."

"Oh, well, perhaps he has contracted malaria and died."

"Not that I wish the man to come to harm, but..." Striker sighed.

"I will go and look for him anyway, after..." I gestured at the cleaning – and spied Christine. "We have much to do here first, though."

"Aye," Striker said and hefted his mop. "If he's dead, someone will surely send word."

Gaston returned an hour or so later. He appeared happy and far more relaxed than he had in the morning.

"How is she?" I asked, as he joined us in the guest room where Christine and Rucker were mopping the walls while Pete and I worked on the ceiling.

"The glazier made an excellent little funnel." He indicated the size with his fingers. "She had woken by the time I arrived, and I was able to give her a very small dose, and then she ate and slept again; but this time, not like one dead."

"That is wonderful news," I said.

He smiled broadly, but it fled as he glanced at Christine. He came to me and leaned close to whisper, "What has she said?"

I shook my head. "We have not spoken at all."

He nodded grimly and took my mop. "You should see to the other one."

I brushed a kiss on his cheek and went to look in on Vivian. I found her sleeping, and tried not to disturb her as I emptied the pot and brought her more water and chocolate.

Two of the rooms, the Marquis' and the guest room, were cleaned and drying and we were working on ours by the time Sam told us supper could be served. It was with great relief that we stopped working and retired to what little water was left in the cistern to wash and prepare to eat. As the Marquis was still occupying the dining room, Sam laid the meal out on the atrium tables as he had in the morning. Thus Christine was able to sit next to Agnes without causing any fuss.

I took Vivian a bowl of stew, and she actually seemed pleased to see me – and the food – though she still appeared quite tired.

"How is the baby?" she asked after her first mouthful.

"Gaston was able to relieve her discomfort with precision this time, and she ate before she slept."

"Can I see her?" she asked.

I shrugged. "If you feel up to it, we can take you to the Theodores' tomorrow…"

"Nay," she said quickly and quietly. "Not there. Can she be brought here?"

"Perhaps, if Mistress Theodore and Gaston feel it wise. Do you not wish to see Mistress Theodore, or do you not wish to be seen?" I asked, and joined her on the settee.

"Both," she said irritably. "I can imagine what she thinks of me without seeing it in her eyes; and as you have noted, I burned all my clothing. Not that any of it would fit now."

"How should we remedy that?" I asked sincerely. "My intent was not to keep you in this room forever, and you do need clothes. Can Henrietta buy you something in the market, or should we send for a dressmaker?"

"Lord, no," she said and studied her bowl with embarrassment. "Henrietta can find me a dress, I am sure. And shifts, and shoes, and…" She sighed and stabbed at a piece of meat with her spoon.

"We have cleaned the guest room upstairs. I suppose, after it is painted, we can move you up there. It will be brighter than this cave of a room. And you can have a decent bed and a place for your things, and the baby when you are able to care for her."

She regarded me hesitantly. "I am growing fond of this cave."

I smiled at my choice of words and hers. "We can have a bed brought in here, too, if you would prefer; but it has been my experience that men – and women – should not live in caves."

"You believe that sunlight is good for the constitution or some such rubbish?" she asked. "It gives me freckles."

I chuckled, both at her literal interpretation of a thing I considered only as a metaphor and the thought of her having freckles. No gentle-born lady had freckles past her days in a nursery: they avoided the sun as if it might give them the plague. It was another shadow on the wall of the cave in which they dwelled: freckles and tanned skin were the mark of peasants or children; they could never be seen as either.

"Do not mock me," she said with more sadness that I would do so than ire.

"I am not. I... It would be difficult to explain, the idea of caves has more philosophical meaning for me."

"Now you are patronizing me," she said bitterly.

"Nay, nay. Why are you fond of this cave?"

"There is no one else in it," she said flatly, and turned her attention back to her stew.

"Well, if you move to the guest room, you need not see anyone you do not wish there, either; and the house can have a parlor again."

"That would be acceptable then. Must I remain chained?" She did not turn to meet my gaze on the last.

I snorted. "Only if I cannot find a way to lock the doors and window."

She swore quietly.

"I will not have you wandering the house at night – or the streets – seeking rum," I said lightly. "When I feel some assurance you will no longer seek it, then you may have your freedom." I stood to leave.

She looked up at me. "What if that day never comes?" she asked with a degree of challenge.

I grinned. "Then we shall have to lock you away in a tower like a princess in a children's tale. Or shoot you."

She rolled her eyes and awarded me a dismissing wave.

I wondered what we would do to keep her from spirits while we roved: whose care would we leave her in? Then I wondered if we should rove, or if Gaston would wish to leave the child.

I found Gaston sitting with his father, happily eating his stew.

"What do you know of that boy?" the Marquis asked before I could finish sitting.

I looked to the Marquis and raised an eyebrow. He gestured toward where Christine sat with Agnes.

"Why?" I asked.

"If the girl is to be your ward, you have to consider such things," he said quietly.

Gaston coughed and quickly leaned away from the table.

I patted his back as I responded cheerfully. "I do not view it as a matter of concern... for reasons I do not care to discuss at this time. Despite how it might appear, there is no cause for concern that they will engage in any lascivious behavior."

Actually there was, if Agnes had her way; but it was my understanding that Christine had rebuffed the girl's overtures, and I doubted she would have a change of heart now.

"Whether they do or not," he continued to admonish; but this time I noted a sly cast to his mien, "it is the matter of appearances you must be concerned with, if the girl is to ever be married off properly. Surely you, who I would imagine has ruined a number of girls, should know that." He grinned.

I thought it likely Christine's disguise had not fooled him any more than it fooled me, once he had a good look at her.

"I have, and I do," I said. "Oui, we will do our utmost to maintain appearances until we discover what the girl wishes to do about the matter of marriage."

He nodded thoughtfully. "I suppose I spoke too soon, then: you seem to have the matter well in hand. And... I suppose not all girls are dutiful daughters who follow their father's or guardian's wishes about such matters."

I smiled. "I do not consider that a poor thing; as not all men wish to have the kind of wife a dutiful daughter makes. And from what we have seen, this one might very well be following her father's wishes: perhaps not in her tactics, but in applying herself to the battle."

He shrugged. "I feel you are correct; but, seeing the tactics she is capable of, I would caution that the dutiful type is easier."

"We will keep that in mind," I said.

Gaston had been following the whole of it. I had felt his thigh tense with alarm when he realized as I had that his father had seen through Christine's disguise.

"And what would you advise of dutiful sons in the matter of marriage?" he asked his father.

The Marquis was surprised at the question, and set his spoon down to rest his head on his hands and consider his answer. "That, as long as the bloodlines are sound, they choose whichever horse strikes their fancy. The race is both longer and shorter than we ever expect, and one cannot know, merely by looking at a horse or its dam and sire, how it will ride in the end. So it is probably best to pick a horse one can at least feel happy about at the start. There are always regrets, but, by the Grace of God, they will be because one could not ride long enough."

"I already have an excellent horse," Gaston said without challenge.

His father gave a sheepish grin. "So you do. I feel a mare might prove better for such a long journey, but..." He held up his hand quickly to ward us off. "As things are as they are, it would appear you are only seeking a broodmare. In that instance, I would highly suggest a dutiful one. And, since mares in general are such a rare thing in these isles, I would be happy to send you one – one far better than you have seen before." He pointed over his shoulder at the parlor. "When you feel you are ready to take up the matter of breeding."

"I feel I am ready," Gaston said carefully, "but it is not a thing I wish to have sprung upon me, and... There must be time, or an avenue, to become acquainted with the girl and apprise her – in our way – of what we feel she should know."

"That will be difficult to arrange – with you here, and the suitable candidates in France – but I understand," the Marquis said. "And..." He glanced at me. "I know you will not be returning to France soon. Though I sometimes feel the press of my years, I should by all accounts live a while longer." He sighed. "My greatest concern is that... You will not survive this roving you plan to do. Or I will meet some misfortune upon sailing home."

Gaston nodded with a frown.

"We have much to consider concerning the matter of roving this year," I said.

"Oui," Gaston said with relief. "I wished to rove and be useful, but I was not a Comte before."

His father nodded approvingly, and some of the tension left his shoulders.

Gaston was regarding me anxiously.

I smiled warmly. "Though I would see you serve as physician, I have no great need to rob Spaniards. We have a sickly child to concern us, and a mother who needs watching."

He sighed with relief and jerked his chin toward where Christine sat. "Let us see what this one wants."

"After I eat," I said. "And I suppose we will have to find a place for her to sleep that will not compromise anyone."

In thinking of not roving, I felt some relief myself. Perhaps we could return to Negril. But then I realized Gaston would not wish to leave the baby in town, and Vivian did need watching. I tried to picture the four of us living in our hovel on the Point, and dark clouds of foreboding hovered on the horizon as I began to see how the Gods might find some amusement in that.

Sixty-Four

Wherein We Are Nearly Outmaneuvered

Christine needed no prompting to follow us to the stable after dinner. And so, after Bella decided she was acceptable, we sat about in the straw in the front part of the structure where the dogs were, each of us with a back to a different wall: our guest closest to the door, and Gaston closest to the puppies. Christine seemed to have little interest in the puppies themselves – a thing I found odd – and she eyed our hammock in the stall with curiosity, only to quickly look elsewhere.

"So, what might we do for you?" I asked Christine in French.

She took a deep breath and her gaze traveled from one of us to the other. Gaston was regarding the puppy in his lap: she spoke to me. "I am here to discover what prompted the Marquis' visit to my father, or rather the message that he brought. Has Gaston rejected me, or has his father found me unsuitable?"

"I cannot give you an easy answer," I said. "You were not rejected, so much as a speedy marriage was. A situation you should well be able to sympathize with."

Her eyes hardened and she quickly turned to studying the straw. "I rue that day," she said with guilt that seemed sincere. "I made a mistake, I admit it. I should have accepted your gracious offer and… saved us all a great deal of trouble."

"Perhaps," I said quickly. Though I did not wish for her to berate herself, I could never tell her I would not have married her anyway. "But what is done, is done. We are not here to discuss the past, but the future. What do you want now?"

"I wish to be married to… a man who would offer me the freedoms you did." She regarded me from beneath her lashes in a shy fashion, and I sensed earnestness but not coyness.

"To be married?" I asked carefully. "Why not simply escape your father again and travel in your current guise?"

She sighed. "If need be, I would do so again; but I would rather not be sought; and if I am to be exposed by some folly, I would rather have them attempt to return me to someone sympathetic to my aims and not my father," she said with frustration.

"I can see that," I said, and glanced at Gaston. He appeared to be ignoring us: a thing I found frustration with, as I wished for some subtle indication of his thoughts. I supposed his wishing to ignore her was indication enough.

"If the matter were as simple as your being provided with a name in marriage so that you might be free, we would possibly be happy to oblige," I said carefully. "But we have need of the name Gaston can offer; or rather we have need of a bride. Gaston wishes to produce heirs, and children must be the first priority in the application of his availability for marriage."

She nodded tightly and fidgeted with the straw. "I surmised that: now that he is a lord." She took a deep breath and raised her head to meet my gaze again. "I am willing to bear children."

I dearly wished to say, *the Devil you are*, but I held it in. "Well, he would need several children, preferably male, of course."

She shrugged with feigned nonchalance. "We are young: we can produce the necessary heirs and then travel: the three of us."

"The three of us?" I queried.

"Oui," she said with a knowing smile. "Do not members of the Brethren share all things, including wives?"

I glanced to Gaston, and found him regarding her with dismay. She did not see it: her eyes were only for me.

I awarded her a diplomatic smile. "Some do. But, that is not the matter of concern at the moment. I do not see where we will be able to travel once the children are born. I think children, even the one we have now, will likely be the end of our travels."

"Why?" she asked, with a mix of incredulity and curiosity.

"Because we wish to raise them," I said.

Now she was fully incredulous. "Why?"

I thought I would have sounded the same quite recently, but I found my answer ready and reasoned. "To insure it is done properly, and they are treated with respect and care, and they are taught ethics and morals we value."

She slumped dejectedly against the wall, her face contorted with a perplexed frown that was quite cute.

I glanced at Gaston and found him regarding me with pride and pleasure; and that expression was a thousand times more endearing than anything the girl could ever muster.

I turned back to Christine. "We will give you what assistance we can: secure passage for you and even give you some money, but..."

"Non," she said quickly. "What if it is as we originally discussed, when... What if we marry; and I produce the children; and then I can travel, as a lord's wife who will not be considered missing; and you can raise the children? Do you find me an unsuitable mother?"

Gaston was studying the puppy in his lap again, but this time I could see tension and agitation in the set of his head and shoulders and the careful precision with which he smoothed fur with one fingertip.

"Non," I told Christine. "We have long thought you would be an excellent dam: you possess many qualities we would see in children. And perhaps that arrangement would be suitable, but we must discuss the matter."

She smiled at me warmly: a fetching and triumphant quirk of her lips.

"But... it would not be as some of the Brethren do," I said slowly, and let my tone harden. "You would be Gaston's wife and bear his children only."

She raised an eyebrow at that, and spoke coyly. "There are ways to insure that only his seed is sown."

My smile was diplomatic and perhaps patronizing. "Aye, and my never laying a hand on you is the easiest of those. My matelot does not share."

Gaston sat the puppy carefully aside.

"Not even with you?" Christine teased, oblivious to him.

"He does not share *me*," I said with an amused grin, some cruel aspect of my spirit relishing the shattering of her girlish fancy.

"Oui, you cannot have him," Gaston growled.

Christine's coy smile fled and she turned to look at him with surprise. He was a forbidding statue in the shadows, with hard green eyes. She took a short hard breath, and fear and shame set upon her face.

"So," I said lightly, as if we were discussing the sale of a horse. "I do not believe we can achieve the arrangement you desire. We will still offer you what aid we might."

Anger suffused her. "Do not trouble yourself!" She stood and snatched up her bag and slipped into the night.

"Well, we have made an enemy this night," I said, still feeling triumphant.

He pounced upon me, his mouth hard on mine as he bowled me over and then onto my back: his hands closed tight around my wrists, pinning them on either side of my head as he straddled me. I did not kick about because I was scared I would hit the nest of puppies.

He brushed teasing kisses across my lips, only to pull his head away as I strained to reach him. My manhood began to strain as well, trapped as it was between us.

"You are mine," he hissed.

"Am I to be ridden this night?" I panted.

His eyes brightened and he made the happy humming sound: only in his present Horse state, it became more akin to a purr.

"Oui, let us see how very far my stallion can run," he said huskily. "Farther than any damn mare, I would think."

I chuckled at his entwining of his father's metaphor with ours, until he kissed me such that I ached with need and could not remember humor or metaphors or much of the last day.

"Strip and get on the hammock," he whispered as he released me. "There is a thing I would try."

I gleefully complied: my skin afire and my cock throbbing with anticipation. He left me for a time, slipping out into the atrium. I hoped he was insuring that we were alone and I could at least make some noise once he began whatever tortures he wished to employ. He returned with several candles, and lit them from the lamp before blowing it out. I grinned up at him as he regarded me in their softly flickering light, my smile widening at the sight of his feral one.

He shed his clothing, and dug salve, rope, and our gag out of our bags. He bound my wrists and ankles to the four corners of our hammock, and turned to greasing our members. He made coy work of his: taking pleasure in my enjoyment of the sight. I nearly spent myself when he finally took me in hand. He tapped my balls to distract me, and I moaned and twisted in my bonds, my cock cringing from the sudden pain. Then he was astride me, positioning my cock beneath him such that my squirming would bring him pleasure. Then he awarded me a deep and sweet kiss to savor before placing the gag in my mouth.

I squirmed with surprise and the first icy tickle of fear when he picked up one of the candles. And then there was only the inextricable blend of pain and pleasure as he spilled wax upon my arms and chest in little dribbles. It did not bring the deep immediate ache of a strap, or the hard pain of his teeth, but an initial shock of a burn followed by an irritating and mounting discomfort. I did not buck beneath him, I began to run in a sort of rhythmic squirming that he found great delight in as he kept me at it for a seeming eternity, until I felt I could no longer move and I could feel nothing but the burning upon my chest.

I was surprised to find my cock still hard when he at last set the candle aside and moved to impale himself upon me. His hole seemed cold and deep compared to the fire on my skin, and I mustered all the strength I had left to dive deep up into him. He gave a long low groan of pleasure and held me still with one commanding hand upon my chest. Then he began to move, and I did nothing but lie beneath him and accept his pleasure until I came. I did not feel I laid siege to the Gates of Heaven, so much as they opened for me without effort and I was washed on a wave into the light with little fanfare and great peace. I was barely aware of him bringing himself off to squirt cold jism upon my chest.

He released me very tenderly, rubbing my numb limbs and kissing me before rolling me onto my side. I was roused from my blissful lassitude when he tried to pull the wax from my skin. It was a new and irritating pain. He stopped, and I drifted again until he pushed a cup to my lips. I drank, tasting the laudanum and not caring. And then I was very far away and warm and happy, and I knew he was beside me and always would be.

I woke alone, a thin blanket covering my nakedness, and someone hissing my name.

Memory returned slowly, and I smiled at the ache in my body. My chest was mottled pink with burns, but there was no wax. I was missing the sparse hair that had covered it, though. I even found quiet amusement in that.

"What?" I asked. I was sure the voice was Agnes.

"You must come quickly!" she hissed from somewhere beyond the door. "There is trouble! Gaston sent me to fetch you!"

I pushed myself upright and awake, and sought my clothes. "What trouble?"

"Sir Christopher is here." She paused and there were sounds of commotion from the atrium, including a women's voice yelling and cursing. "Oh damn! They found her. She must have tried to climb off the balcony. The idiot!"

I had donned my breeches and tunic, and I hurried past her. The atrium seemed filled with people. The Marquis and Dupree stood to one side, with Pete, Striker, and Rucker. Across from them, stood Sir Christopher, Governor Modyford, and Theodore. Two men held a furious and struggling Christine between them in the foyer. She was still in her boy's garb, but with her hair a cascade of unbound gold. I could see Gaston in the shadows of the door to the parlor, and Sarah likewise hiding in the doorway of her office.

Fear roiled in my belly, and excitement burned the drug from my body, but not my head. I felt quite disoriented, as if I had suddenly been transported to another time or place. I had woken to such scenes before: whether they were of my orchestration or not, they always ended in either someone dying or my running away in the night, or both.

Pete was laughing; Striker was regarding Christine incredulously; the Marquis awarded me a resigned sigh and roll of his eyes as if to say, now see what having her here has done; Rucker was, as ever, quite curious as to what would occur, as if this were all some entertainment staged just for him; Theodore appeared quite concerned; Sarah did not appear surprised so much as angry – at me; and Modyford gave me a sly smile. My greatest concern, Gaston, looked as if he were ready to fight or flee if I should but give the word.

"There you are, you brigand!" Sir Christopher shouted at the sight of me.

"What is this about?" I asked with bravado as I crossed the atrium.

"You have trifled with my daughter's affections and brought her to ruin!" Sir Christopher railed.

"He has not!" Christine roared. "And I am not ruined! How dare you!

Summon another damn midwife if you must be sure, but do not speak that way of me."

Her father colored and snapped, "You be quiet! This does not concern you!"

"What?" she yelled.

"If you will not be silent I will have them take you outside," Sir Christopher said.

"So they can make lurid comments and ogle me as they have already?" she roared. "You are the one bringing me to ruin, Father! You are the one casting aspersions on my character!"

This seemed to flummox him, and he stood indecisive for a moment, his mouth opening and closing, and then he crossed the distance between them and slapped her quite smartly.

That was enough for my matelot. He stepped from the doorway and downed one of the men holding Christine with two quick blows, and moved to step between her and her father. Then Gaston had her safely behind him, and her father and his other man were backing away.

Christine touched her cheek gingerly, and regarded her father with angry eyes filling with sudden tears. He, in turn, seemed suffused with guilt over what he had done, and oddly, turned to seek Modyford's support.

"My Lord," Modyford said smoothly to me. "I must ask: have you had carnal knowledge of the young lady?"

"Nay, I have not," I said firmly.

"Who will believe that?" Sir Christopher bellowed.

I knew he was correct. "Quite possibly no one, sir. So the matter must rest between me and the Lord."

"That may be," he rumbled, seeming to be coming to a boil again. "But what am I to do with a ruined daughter?"

"I do not know, Sir Christopher. What would you have of me?" I asked, sincerely curious as to what he sought. Most fathers in his presumed circumstance kept the matter as private as possible and quietly found someone to marry the girl. They did not show up at a married man's house – with the governor – and make demands. Something was amiss. I tried to push the remaining fog of the drug from my head and think.

"I wish for you to make her an honorable woman," Sir Christopher said.

"Sir," I said with incredulity, "I am a married man. What do you suggest?"

"Bah," he said. "Everyone knows your marriage to that trollop is a fraud."

"Do they?" I asked with amazement at his audacity. "We were legally married in the eyes of God and man, sir. She has borne me a child."

"It is not yours," he said, but there was fear in his eyes, as if he was amazed at what he spoke.

And then I caught his eyes flicking to the governor again.

A hand closed on my shoulder, grinding the rough fabric of my tunic into my burned skin. I looked, and saw the Marquis' signet ring on that hand, his blue eyes quite somber above it.

He whispered in French, "They are plotting something."

"I know, I know," I murmured.

Sir Christopher seemed even more uncomfortable now that the Marquis had made his presence obvious. Modyford watched us with speculative eyes.

"Who stands to gain from your marriage being annulled?" the Marquis asked.

"Vines, if I pay him a dowry, but he is quite wealthy."

I looked to Gaston: he was whispering earnestly to Christine. Her face was a mask of anger, but she was responding with tight little nods.

My gut clenched. I knew what those two might be plotting: it was a way out of this thicket, one which we did not wish to take, but it would see us through. I had to ignore them for the moment, and tackle the real question of how we got here.

"Does Vines have such influence with your governor?" the voice of reason at my shoulder asked.

I looked to Theodore. He shook his head subtly, almost as if he answered the Marquis' question for me, though he could hear none of what we said. His eyes told me he did not know what this was about.

"I think not," I murmured. "But Modyford may well have enough influence over him to arrange this… show." And that was what I had been seeing: Sir Christopher was playing a part.

"Who would exercise such influence on the governor?" the Marquis asked. "Surely not her mother's family. Despite her uncle, she holds too little value for anyone to care."

And then I knew. I gasped at the surprise of it. "My father," I hissed.

"Ah," the Marquis said, as if the matter were now resolved and he was pleased there was some order to it after all. "It must not be politically expedient for him to tell you to put her out."

I was nauseated with the implications of my father conniving with Modyford.

Sir Christopher had been conferring with the governor, and now he squared his shoulders and turned on me with feigned outrage again. "What is your answer, sir? Will you do the honorable thing?"

"I will remain honorably married to my wife," I said.

"I will marry your daughter," Gaston said.

My gut twisted as if it would leave my body.

"What?" Sir Christopher sputtered. "That is…" He glanced at Modyford, who frowned.

The Marquis stepped forward, Dupree at his shoulder to translate. "And we will pay no dowry: not for a girl who runs about in men's clothing, despite her uncle, the Duke of Verlain, being an old friend."

Modyford tweaked his pursed lips thoughtfully, and nodded. "Well, then, that is settled, Sir Christopher. Your daughter will be properly married."

"But nay," Christopher sputtered and turned beseeching eyes upon his daughter. "I do not wish for you to marry someone you do not favor. I did this for you. You wished to marry Lord Marsdale."

Christine shook her head with a mix of confusion and anger. "I no longer wish to marry Lord Marsdale. And you have gone mad. And you have ruined my name. I will marry anyone to leave your house. Lord Montren has made me a very fine offer, and I will marry him. If I am the harlot you have made me out to be, you have nothing to gain or lose, no matter who I marry."

Gaston was regarding me with anxious eyes. I smiled weakly and nodded, and he seemed greatly relieved.

Modyford was walking toward the door.

"Governor!" I called.

He stopped, and turned to me with a curious look.

"Is my sister safe?" I asked.

Everyone became very still, and Modyford frowned.

"I know of no one who intends to harm her," Modyford said carefully after some thought.

"That is good to hear," I said. "I am pleased you are so well apprised of the situation: as the last we spoke of such things, I only had poor news to give you, and could only implore you to aid in her protection while we sailed."

This caught him off guard; and I saw the mask of diplomacy shift a little, first with fear he had been caught, and then angriness at it. "Due to your concern I made inquiries," he said quickly. "I have come to believe your concern was unfounded."

I smirked. "Give your regards to my father, would you? Tell him we wish to hear from him, and not merely feel his presence in our lives."

He took a deep breath and his pleasantly amicable mask settled into its accustomed position. "If I should ever have the honor of corresponding with your father, I shall relay that."

He looked to Sir Christopher, who appeared quite confused over our exchange. "We should be going. You should perhaps have your daughter's things boxed and sent here so that she might have a dress to be married in."

Sir Christopher gave his daughter one last beseeching look, but she kept her eyes steadfastly on the tiles of the floor. He left with his head hanging low between his corpulent shoulders.

Everyone descended on me as the door closed in their wake. I sat heavily under the onslaught of their questions and my own dismay. Gaston came to sit beside me and take my hand, and pull it beneath the table to hold it tightly with both of his. I did not wish to meet his eyes: I wished to think.

There was a livid purple bruise about my left wrist. I imagined there was a matching one on my right, which Gaston now held in his lap. I was scared to view my ankles, and as I now sat, could think of no way of doing so without drawing attention to the matter.

Sarah was before me, and she pounded the table with both hands. "What is happening, Will?"

I met her angry and scared gaze. "It is possible Father wishes for me to abandon the current Lady Marsdale in favor of another, and he made arrangements with the Governor to insure it."

I looked to Theodore.

His expression was grave. "That is possible. I did not make mention of it before, because the governor is prone to gossip and finds delight in it, but he has often asked me of your intentions toward your wife. This morning it was his first question as they came to fetch me here. I said I felt you had made a decision, and that it was to keep her. Modyford was not pleased with that answer, and I thought it very odd until I heard that Vines knew his daughter was here. He had her followed when she left his home. I was quite surprised the governor would wish to become involved in the matter, and the only explanation I could muster was because you are a lord. But, in viewing the matter from this new supposition, I think it offers their behavior far sounder reason."

Sarah slumped into a chair across from me, her face a mask of horror. "If it is true, then aye, I have no protection when Striker roves. I should have expected such... but..."

"The governor seems as prone to curry favor with lords as he does to gossip," I said. "We should have expected it, but... would he have contacted our father, or did his inquiries alert our father?"

"Nay and perhaps," Theodore said quickly. "I do not think he would have contacted your father directly."

"My father had me followed?" Christine demanded.

"Aye," Theodore said with a shrug. "He was quite proud of it. He thought it likely you would attempt to run away again after this matter of the possible marriage to Lord Montren, and so he apparently arranged things so that you would have the opportunity to escape, and he had someone in place to see where you would go."

"He would not have," she said with a perplexed frown. "He could not have," she added arrogantly. "I saw none of his men and I was quite careful."

"Miss Vines," Theodore asked with a pleasant smile, "could you recognize all the men the governor might employ?"

"Nay, of course not," she said quickly. "But my father is not the governor's man. The one time the governor asked my father to intervene in a matter of the council, my father considered it at length and only decided to do as the governor bid because it was truly the course of action he himself would take."

"Your father wished for you to marry me," I said. "Because that is what he thought you wished. You called him mad this day. Was he acting as he normally does?"

"Nay, nay," she said quietly.

"So," Sarah said, "our father quite possibly contacted Modyford and asked him to… discover whether you planned to put her out? Or was it to insure that you put her out? I can see why he might not wish to write and ask for such a thing. Committing such a request to writing with his seal might not have been in his best interests, and he is ever so careful about putting ink to paper if he cannot control that paper. So much so…" She frowned. "That it makes me wonder what means he might have used to convey the information to Modyford."

Theodore shook his head. "Many people in England and here employ couriers or men trusted to relay things best not committed to paper. Any ship traveling to England usually contains several such men. Many of the captains and officers make a handsome sum of money providing that service. Your father likely has employed someone to bring messages here." He sighed heavily. "That I was not involved in the arrangement of such services, and have not received letters or directives from such a person, indicates that your father does not feel I am his man."

"Now that you know of the possibility of it, can you make discreet inquiries?" I asked.

Theodore nodded. "Oh aye, now that I know if it." There was anger in his eyes.

"Why would he want her out?" Christine asked. "Your father, not mine."

I sighed. "From what we have been able to suppose, the marriage was arranged so that my father could pay some, if not all, of her father's debts in exchange for her father's compliance in the House of Lords or elsewhere with some matter. Perhaps that relationship is no longer necessary. Or, perhaps, my father truly wishes for me to produce an heir that is actually of my blood – as damn near any grandfather would – and feels that her reputation will always cast doubt upon that: but because of the arrangement with her father, and his lack of trust of me – in that I might divulge his request to others – he did not wish to ask me to put her out directly. I have been waiting for some order from him concerning the matter, but he has not chosen to correspond – that we have received – with Sarah or me since her arrival here. Of course, if I put my wife out without his agreement to it – in writing – he can use the matter against me to weaken my claim to my inheritance."

"I remember you mentioning that things were complicated with your father in that regard, but I did not realize…" Christine said. She appeared embarrassed.

"As always," Sarah said bitterly, "we cannot know what our father thinks."

"Well, we can no longer rely on the governor or militia to protect you should your damn cousin arrive," Striker said. He appeared as grave as Theodore. "I should not sail."

"We were fooling ourselves to think they would offer protection," I said sadly. "Gaston and I needed to sail, and Pete and you needed to sail, and thus none of us were going to stay with her, so I concocted that arrangement with the governor in order to protect her. But truly, there is no protection from an earl unless it is from a duke or king. My father could sail here and snatch her up and return her home at any time. Though I do feel that Shane sailing in, even bearing my father's name, might meet with more difficulty. The aspect of the matter I was truly relying on last spring was that, with Shane being wounded, they would not travel. And that Shane is the type of man who wishes to harm another in person and not send an assassin."

"Wait," the Marquis said to me as Dupree was halfway through translating.

Though I could see that Striker and Sarah had much to say, I could see the confusion in Christine and the Marquis' eyes.

So I started speaking, in French, before the Marquis could ask his question. "My father wishes for my second cousin, Jacob Shane, to inherit. Shane stayed and became a part of my father's dealings when I fled my father's estate at sixteen – primarily because of Shane. But that is another tale I do not feel like telling. Suffice it to say that both were dismayed to realize I still lived when I returned to the family estate three years ago. Without me, my father could have adopted Shane. As it was, Shane had decided to marry into the family, and when our sister Elizabeth was betrothed, he set his eye on Sarah. My return disrupted his plans in several ways, and he became quite angry with her. When he found I was involved in the aborting of his plan, he attacked her, and she defended herself by shooting him. In the resulting chaos, he dropped a wine bottle and lamp and severely burned himself. My father was quite distraught, more so that his beloved Shane should be so injured and marred, than that his daughter had been attacked. It was suggested that Sarah leave for a time. So she came here with my uncle – who was also quite disturbed at his brother's behavior, and thought she should be married off in order to protect her – and thus she met and married Striker. We have heard no word from my damn father as to whether he approves or accepts their marriage." I shrugged. "*We* have heard no word from our father."

The Marquis nodded sagely. "How long ago did this occur?"

"The incident in England was just over a year ago, I suppose," I said. "Sarah – and my bride – arrived in January of this year."

He spoke to Sarah and me, and motioned for Dupree to translate for the others. "I feel he could not have traveled this year. I know how long it took to arrange my voyage here. Does he know you are with child?"

Sarah shrugged. "If he has spies on this island, he has surely heard. For that matter, I am sure our uncle told him."

He smiled grimly, and his gaze went to Striker. "Prior to the last few years, when I have had much reason to examine my conscience and view matters differently than I had before, if one of my daughters had hastily married a man I did not approve of, and she was with child such that it could not be annulled, I would have..." He shrugged eloquently. "Seen that she was widowed."

Sarah pressed her fingers to her lips and looked away.

Striker smiled affably. "Aye, I have often thought that, and we have discussed it."

I was not surprised or appalled; I had thought such a thing myself. I grinned. "On two occasions my life was threatened for my relationship with some man's son. And we will not count the times concerning daughters."

The Marquis shrugged and regarded Gaston and me. "There was a time..." Then he grinned. "But as things stand, I am still amazed you have not shot me."

"Your realizing that has done much to increase your longevity." I said lightly.

He chuckled.

"Well," Striker said, "there haven't been any attempts on my life, yet. If he wants me dead, perhaps he thinks roving'll save him the trouble."

"Perhaps that is how he will attain it, if it is a thing he wishes," the Marquis said after hearing the translation. "Men are easy enough to place in harm's way when military endeavors are involved."

Striker frowned at that, but he at last shook his head. "I was asked to do dangerous things in Porto Bello – after I married her, but... among the Brethren, a captain is expected to lead from the front, and we gain extra shares for acts of valor. I took Morgan asking me to do as I did as a sign of his respect. And if I don't rove..."

"It is a matter of prestige," Sarah said sadly.

"If Modyford has recruited Morgan to the cause, it would be very easy to throw you to the fates again and again," I told Striker, "but I do not feel Morgan would be easily enlisted unless he dislikes you for some other reason – just as Vines had to have his reason. But as for our father seeing you dead by other means, if that is his desire, you may well be safest roving. Here, even with Pete ever at your side and weapons about, you would be a very easy target for an accomplished assassin. But roving, I cannot see where his agent might find a member of the Brethren easy to buy on such a matter; and placing a man in our ranks to fire carelessly in battle or some such thing, that will take him time – not that he has not possibly had such time. Sadly, if they truly wish us dead, the only way to prevent it is to kill them first and hope they have not left funds to pay for the deed with someone else."

"So we wait," Sarah said with sudden resolve. "And do what we will." She brushed the tears from her eyes and smoothed her skirt over her belly as she stood.

Striker went to embrace his wife, his mien one of forced cheer.

Pete stood still, a resolute statue of bronze with crossed arms. He met my gaze. "Iffn'AThingHappensICanna'Stop. I'llBeTheLastLivin'Thing YarFatherSees. TellMeHowTaFind'Im."

I nodded. "Should I write it down for you to keep, or should we work on your memorizing it over the coming days?"

He shrugged. "Both."

"If I am not dead, I would accompany you on that errand," I said.

Pete grinned. "Aye, I'dLookFurYa."

Gaston, who had been notably silent through all the discussion, squeezed my hand and said, "Jamaica must be baptized."

"Oui," I said. "I must lay public claim to her."

Sarah was regarding us. She shook her head and spoke English for all, even though she had overheard our French. "To thwart him? You will make yourself miserable to anger our father? You would have been happier to do what he wished. And though I would never play his advocate, his actions, however contrived, were in your favor this time."

"We had decided the matter before today," I said with some irritation. "I will claim the child as mine. And who I marry or remain married to has little to do with my happiness."

She frowned and quickly shook her head irritably. "That is not what I meant. I am sorry if you perceived it that way. I am saying that the one you are married to will cause you – and likely the rest of us – trouble until she dies. I did not realize you intended to keep her."

"We will not keep her here," I sighed.

Sarah glanced at Christine, who was studying the tiles thoughtfully.

"Gaston's wife will not live here, either," I added.

This brought a frown to Christine's forehead, but Sarah sighed.

Then she cursed in a manner that would have done her husbands proud. "I am sorry, I do not mean... I should relish the company."

"It is your house," I said. "I learned long ago that houses only have one mistress, if they are happy houses."

But this brought to mind the fact that we could not deposit Vivian and Christine in the same dwelling, either.

I looked to Theodore. "We will need to rebuild the other house. Until my father says otherwise, it is still to be used by the Lady Marsdale."

He nodded glumly. "I was beginning to sense that." He stood and smiled. "If you will excuse me. I have much to think on and do."

I stood and embraced him. "We will sort it all through."

"Aye," he sighed. He gazed at me earnestly when I released him. "I am sorry I have given you such poor advice."

"I am sorry you feel you have ever done such a thing," I said. "I surely do not feel that you have."

He snorted. "You are too kind." He sighed and regarded Gaston. "Should I return the baby?"

Gaston shook his head. "Nay, I will return her."

"What?" I asked.

"Jamaica is visiting her mother," Gaston said.

I recalled he had been standing in the parlor doorway when I had been summoned into the fray. That door still stood open now: along with the shuttered window opening into the atrium. Vivian had surely heard everything.

I would need to speak with her. I was damn glad Gaston had seen to her this morning – but then he had been responsible for my not being in a state to do so. It was with effort I kept myself from examining my wrists and ankles. I was relieved the others had either been so distracted by events to not notice, or polite enough not to make remark of it.

What was I going to wear to disguise them for going to the church to arrange a baptism? What was Vivian going to wear? What was Christine going to wear? How fast did we truly need to react? Were messages even now being written and a ship readied to sail to carry them? How much time did we have?

"Then I will speak with you later," Theodore was saying and bowing.

I returned the gesture and remembered to smile.

Gaston's arm was tight about my shoulder and he was dragging me to the stable. I did not protest.

"Did I do wrong?" he whispered urgently once we were alone. "I did not perceive the matter as my father or you did."

"You did not do wrong," I assured him, and wrapped my arms around him as much for my comfort as his. "I know you sought to rescue her, and me. Neither of us would have wished this outcome, but the Gods move in mysterious ways. Perhaps all will be well. We have so much to do. And damn it, I am finding it so hard to think now that the crisis is past."

He cursed quietly, and held me such that he ground my rough tunic against my tender skin.

"That hurts, that hurts," I whispered.

That served to elicit more cursing and tears, but he released me.

"Oh, stop," I murmured as I pulled away and leaned on the back wall. "It was glorious, and I woke happy."

He stood trembling, and I was alarmed to see how very lost he was.

I tugged him to me by his tunic, and took his face in my hands. "I love you. We will be fine," I murmured.

"What have I done?" he gasped.

"Nothing, yet. You need not do it."

"But..."

"Let us be calm and think of what we have to do that we wish to do. Later, we can consider the other."

He took a ragged breath and nodded between my hands.

"First," I said lightly, "and I say this not to cause you guilt, because I will not have you feel guilt over the matter, but however shall we disguise my wrists?"

I looked down. There were indeed livid purple marks around my ankles as well.

"And ankles," I added.

He smiled grimly. "Boots."

"Oui." I nodded. "And I suppose I should dress as a gentleman for church; but damn, I cannot see wearing a shirt or coat for all the days these will take to heal."

"You cannot tell anyone," he said with sudden desperation. And then he spoke with the Horse's growl. "It is not their concern."

"Non, non, never," I assured him. "My love, can you calm yourself?"

Fear dimmed the Horse's fury in his eyes. "Non," he gasped, and sank to his knees to wrap his arms about my waist and press his face into my hip.

"Do not worry, my love," I whispered, and rubbed his head.

A shadow fell over us, and I looked up to see his father. He met my gaze with concern. I shook my head and waved him away. He left with a nod.

After a time, Gaston's breathing steadied.

"What should we do, my love?" I murmured. "We should return the baby to Rachel, non?"

He nodded mutely.

"And I must speak with Vivian," I added. "So perhaps you can do the one while I do the other?"

He nodded again, but he did not move.

I gently prodded his arms from around me and lowered myself to sit beside him. He would not regard me: his mien was sad and guilty as he gazed upon the puppies.

"I wish you could keep me on a leash," he said quietly.

"To keep you from roaming, or to keep you safe?" I asked lightly.

He shook his head. "Both. I feel the need to do as we did while sailing to Île de Vache last year."

"To be chained to me so that you might frolic in the field without care?"

He nodded. "But I cannot – now."

"I wish we were chained together as well," I sighed.

His gaze was earnest. "Am I behaving so poorly?"

"Non, non," I said and kissed his cheek. "I feel I would find comfort in it: not to keep you with me, but that we were safe together."

He seemed to find brief respite from the fears gnawing at him, and then his brow was knotted once again. "Then, I gave myself to my Horse; now, I feel the need to do the opposite. I feel I am very much in the light; and it is bright, too bright, perhaps, and I wish to hide in the shade for a time."

I sighed, as I could feel the call of what he sought. "I understand: we either need to expand our metaphor to explain such a need, or we have been viewing it wrongly. Whichever, I know not if this morning is the time to consider it. And I regret that. I feel I wish we were sailing, without... our needing to be at the beck and call of the needs of others. I guess we yearn for escape."

He nodded and truly seemed relieved. "We keep loading things in the cart."

I grinned. "Oui. Neither of us is familiar with pulling such a load. So let us take time to frolic when we may. Like last night." I poked him teasingly.

He smiled and nodded, but his gaze became serious. "I am afraid I will fall."

The image of our being collapsed upon one another on a steep road, chained to a slowly rolling cart full of screaming women and children, being dragged ever closer to a cliff, filled my mind's eye.

"I am afraid of falling, too," I sighed. "We must find a way to manage all this, and pick a road that is not steep."

He frowned. "France would be the definition of steep, non?"

I nodded with great agreement.

"Negril is level, roving is level, but this damn place is all hills," he noted thoughtfully.

"Oui, with people who keep tossing loose gravel into our path." I shrugged. "But… I cannot see how we shall return to Negril soon, and I feel we would regret abandoning all to go roving. So we must level the ground here. Or at least build a brake upon the cart to keep it from running us down as we continue to load it with babies and women."

"It would be lighter without the women," Gaston sighed ruefully and stood.

I chuckled and joined him in standing so that I might embrace him again. "Feeling better?"

He nodded. "I felt I was being pursued, and I wished to run very far and fast," he sighed.

"By a runaway cart?" I teased.

"By the Fates."

"Ah," I sighed. "I feel we are being pursued by the Gods."

Sixty-Five

Wherein We Are Considered Mad

The atrium was empty when we emerged: I viewed it with relief, as I did not wish to encounter anyone in our initial errands. Gaston went upstairs to find my boots and coat, and I went to the cookhouse in hopes of finding Henrietta. She was not there, but Sam told me she could be found working with some of the others on the rooms: where, of course, Gaston had just gone. I swore and sprinted to catch up with my matelot. Thankfully, I discovered everyone working on painting the cleaned rooms and not cleaning ours. Gaston had slipped by them, seemingly unnoticed.

And then I found Striker speaking quietly to Gaston in the far corner of our room. He regarded me guiltily when I entered. Gaston appeared perplexed.

Striker gave one last look at Gaston – who nodded some understanding – and crossed the room to join me in the doorway. He patted my shoulder reassuringly before slipping around me and back to the other room.

I regarded my matelot with a raised eyebrow, and he shook his head with bemusement.

"What was that about?" I asked Gaston quietly in French as I joined him.

He smiled ruefully and sat on the corner of the bed. "He wished for me to know that if you are suffering bouts of madness, and I am having difficulty with you, that I might trust them."

"Damn, does he feel I will suffer so at your being married?"

He snorted and shook his head. "Non, he feels that will lead to more trouble, as I have obviously already had to restrain you before that decision was made." He touched my bruised wrist.

"Gods," I barked with amusement. I collapsed to sit next to him. "That is ironic." It was also deeply disturbing.

"I was worried when he came to speak with me, but..." Gaston shook his head. "I am sorry, Will, but I would rather have them think that than know what we have been about."

"Because then they would consider us mad," I sighed, but I nodded. "I agree. There is somehow less embarrassment in their thinking you have lovingly cared for me by binding me in my madness, than in my surrendering to you as I do."

"Oui, or that I have tortured you lovingly," he said, "as that is a thing they will surely never understand. It is still a thing I..."

I put my fingers to his lips and then followed them with my mouth. He returned my kiss with great love.

"I suppose I must pretend to be very sane these next days," I sighed when we parted. I recalled our sailing home from Porto Bello: all who had known of the debacle there had eyed our every expression with speculation. It had worn on us.

And by the Gods, we needed nothing else wearing on us now.

"It will not help," Gaston said in sad echo to my thoughts.

"We must be careful when we play so in the future," I said.

He nodded resolutely. "Thank you."

"For?"

He shook his head and his rueful smile returned. "For playing with me."

I grinned. "Non, thank you."

"Does your chest hurt?" he asked.

I nodded. "This tunic is quite rough against it."

"Then let us find you a softer shirt." He stood and began pawing through a trunk. He stopped and turned back to me with teary eyes. "I should marry her, Will. Though she lacks the deportment of a dependable broodmare, and... We have said it will be done; and it aids her, even though she is a stupid... And, it will save us having to wait to see what my father might send. I can allay his fears if I get her with a child now."

I nodded, and went to kiss him lightly. I had known it would be his decision when I saw him make the agreement with her. I found I thought it inevitable, somehow: the Gods had chased us down and tossed her into the cart.

"It need not be as horrible as we fear," I said. "Look at Vivian."

He regarded me with a perplexed frown, and then gestured at the smoke-stained room around us.

"Well, I am just saying she is not so very bad as we thought," I sighed.

"I will forgive her if Jamaica lives," he said solemnly, and handed me a soft cotton shirt.

Despite our dressing quickly in boots, proper shirts, and coats, I was not so very sure Vivian would forgive us – whether Jamaica lived or not – by the time we at last arrived in the parlor. I realized we had left her alone for quite a while this morning. She was pacing, and greeted us with panicked, teary eyes and invective. The child was wailing: wrapped in a blanket and propped carefully in a chair.

"She is hungry!" Vivian shouted at Gaston when she stopped cursing. "I dare not feed her! How dare you leave her here this long? I cannot bear her crying. And I cannot please her. I am a horrible mother!"

I swore quietly and moved between Gaston and her. He did not need her screaming at him this day.

Gaston seemed more surprised than anything at her words. He shook his head, said, "Non," quietly, and scooped the child up and hurried out the door.

"I am sorry," I said with sincere guilt. "We should not have left you so long alone, and..."

She met my gaze with a scared little girl's eyes, and sank to the floor with a ragged sob. "Your father wants me gone. Why are you keeping me? Why?"

"So you heard everything?" I asked, though the answer was obvious.

"Aye," she gasped.

I sat on the floor in front of her, and wiped tear-matted hair from her eyes with my thumb. "You will be well," I said softly. "We will have Jamaica baptized, and then no man may put the matter asunder. They had no right to suggest it, even now."

"Unless your father decides he wants me dead," she said.

I would have denied her if I could, but I could not. "You probably only need worry if you do bear me a son," I said with a kind smile.

She snorted, then the horror of the matter gripped her again and she put her hand over her mouth and whispered, "They kill people."

"I know," I sighed. "I am sorry you were dragged into this."

She shook her head with frantic little motions and clutched my arm. "Nay, I am better here. I mean... I can be better here. I mean my life can be better here."

"I am pleased to hear you feel that about it," I said.

She nodded, and gazed upon me in a fashion I found uncomfortable, as I had seen its like before, and it heralded emotions I did not wish to have directed at my person.

"You kept me," she sighed.

I sighed. "Vivian, you are a dear girl and you are my wife. Aye, I kept you. But... It is not due to love. Please do not misunderstand."

Her eyes hardened. "Why the Devil would I ever think that?"

I smiled and spoke lightly. "See that you do not. I have one girl already enamored with me, I do not need another. That will have me put you out if nothing else will."

She snorted. "Miss Vines is infatuated with you?" She considered the matter with a cock of her head. "Aye, her father seemed to think so."

"I feel I did much to dash it last night," I said. "But I... cannot always understand the workings of a woman's heart."

"We are far meaner scorned," she said, as if I were some youth in need of a lecture.

"Aye, aye," I said with a grin. "Hell hath no fury, I know it well." I stood. "Have you eaten? Do you need anything?"

She nodded and then shook her head. "Your... Lord Montren saw to my needs this morning. He said you were indisposed," she said accusingly. "Too much drink?"

I grinned. "No drink. Too much fucking."

She smirked. "So you did ruin her?"

I let the full measure of my incredulity show upon my features. "With my matelot, you silly chit."

She colored and looked away. "Oh, of course. I forget that the two of you..."

"What, do you feel we are lovers in name only?" I teased.

"Surely not now," she said archly.

I chuckled. "Come now, we have much to do today, and it is no longer young. I am going to the church."

"You have arranged the wedding already?" she asked with surprise. "I wondered why you were dressed."

"Nay, I know not when that will occur," I sighed. "I wish to have our daughter baptized. I will see if the good father can see us this afternoon."

She nodded reluctantly. "Has Henrietta found me a gown?" she asked.

"Oh, bloody..." I sighed. "I forgot to speak to her about that matter yesterday, and I have not located her this day. I will do so at once."

Vivian rolled her eyes.

I left her, and went in search of Henrietta. When I found her, the woman complained that anything she could find on such short notice would not be to her lady's liking. I told her I did not care, and to do the best she could.

Gaston returned as I was shooing Henrietta out the door. I led him back onto the street and toward the church.

"How is the baby?" I asked him quietly in French.

"Well enough. She is nursing." He regarded me with a guilty mien. "We must endeavor to take better care of them."

"Did Rachel chastise you?" I asked.

He shook his head. "Non, I was just thinking that...we are ever sitting about pondering... things. We have others who rely on us now."

"Oui," I said softly. He was correct, but the things we pondered were often his madness, or my own. Things that – like his loss of control in the stable this morning – made us incapable of seeing to anyone else while we dealt with them. Still, either we were responsible husbands and fathers, or we were not. I supposed that would be the true test of whether we could accomplish hauling anything else in the cart.

"It will take time for us to become accustomed to it," I said. "I recall it took me many months to care for you as I felt I should: I was ever berating myself for some manner in which I had not put your needs before my own. I was so very familiar with only seeing to myself."

"Oui," he said. "I had to learn the same in caring for you. But Will, I would not have us put their needs before our own; I feel we merely need to be more mindful of them."

Still thinking of our long adjustment to one another, I asked, "Do you feel caring for them will chafe, as I did?"

He shook his head quickly. "I do not feel chained to them as I feel chained to you and the cart. They are merely in the cart. And…" He gazed upon me earnestly. "I enjoy caring for them. It feels as it does when I tend the sick or wounded. I feel I have some use and purpose."

"Even Vivian?" I asked quietly.

He gave a self-deprecating snort. "Even her. She is not my enemy."

I thought of her gazing at me as she had for that moment and I sighed. "I hope Christine will not be mine."

He frowned, and then his fractious anger flared again. "I will not allow that."

I awarded him a raised eyebrow. "How do you mean that?"

His glare became a thoughtful frown once again as we came to stand before the church.

"If she hates me, there is little you can do to alter her heart," I said. "And the same is true if I come to revile her for some reason."

"I will give you no reason," he said. "She will not be your opponent." He regarded the church and turned back to me. "I will place no other before you."

I recalled all my foolish fancies after the party, of her being a worthy opponent by which to see if he would truly choose me. Once again, I cursed my stupidity. My heart ached, and I caressed his cheek.

"I know," I whispered.

He kissed me, there, on the doorstep of the church. I grinned. *What God has joined together, let no man put asunder* echoed through my mind, and I chuckled at the irony of it all. Gaston frowned at my humor.

"What the Gods have joined together, let no woman put asunder," I said.

He smirked. "Amen."

The pastor was quite pleased to see us, as always. He made great suggestion that he should see me in church more often; and then offered the same advice to Gaston, once my matelot was introduced as the Lord Montren. He very nearly bounced with glee when we told him of our need to arrange a baptism and a wedding; though his pleasure was diminished somewhat when we said it would not be a grandiose public affair that would show his true ecclesiastical talents. Despite that disappointment, he was apparently at our disposal at any hour or day, as long as it was not during Mass. We told him we would return later this day for one of the ceremonies, if not both.

We walked home – hand-in-hand – in companionable silence. Gaston seemed calmer. I felt anxious; but I did not know the why of it, and felt discussing it would only worry me more.

"I will see if Henrietta has returned," I said as we paused at the front doors. "Perhaps you should find your bride and determine whether she is amenable to a ceremony today." I sighed. "If ever, as this morning was a matter of duress."

His sigh echoed mine. "I almost wish she would run away."

I kissed his cheek. "We will endure…"

"And conquer," he finished with a weak smile.

Henrietta had not returned, and so I sat in the atrium – pleased to be in the shade in my heavy clothing – and waited while Gaston located Christine, who was closeted in Agnes' room. The girl allowed him to enter, and I watched the door close behind him with dread. I would have pondered it if the Marquis had not approached.

"Might we speak a moment?" he inquired.

I nodded for him to take the seat next to mine. "We have been to the church. The ceremony can occur at any time."

He nodded. "Is that wise?"

I turned to him with surprise. "Do you not wish it? We know she lacks the finer qualities of a broodmare, but Gaston feels all may sleep better if he can produce an heir sooner rather than later."

His gaze was speculative: his lips quirked in a fox's grin. He snatched my left hand and shoved my sleeve back to reveal the bruise. I pulled my arm away.

"This morning was not the time to make mention of this," he said quietly. "But they were noted, and wondered at. I thought…" He sighed, and abandoned whatever trail of thought he had been pursuing to gaze at me directly. "Is he responsible for those marks?"

I did not respond. It was a difficult question, especially if I was inclined to answer it honestly. And I knew not what he ascribed them to. I surely would have been as surprised as Gaston if I had been the one first presented with Striker's supposition of my madness. I could not see where the Marquis might leap to the same conclusion, though; but I had not thought he would see through Christine's disguise, either.

He sighed again and shrugged at my level gaze. "Did they not result from your being bound hand and foot? Did he set upon and bind you?" he asked with more diffidence.

"Set upon me…?" I asked.

"Does he attack you and seek to hurt you in his madness?" the Marquis asked with a mix of frustration and sympathy.

"Non," I said quickly. "It is not… what you think. He does not *attack* me in his bouts of madness."

"Then how did those bruises come to be?" he asked.

"It is not your concern," I said without rancor. "Truly, do not trouble yourself over the matter. It concerns no one except Gaston and me."

He shook his head. "I feel you may love him beyond…"

"All reason," I supplied.

He smiled. "Oui, beyond all reason; and thus, you might not see the danger he could pose to another: a bride, for instance."

I shook my head. "I do see that danger, and it is not posed by this matter, exactly."

"I thought you could… manage him," he said with an admonishing tone that raised my hackles.

"I assist him in managing himself," I said with a warning in my voice.

"By allowing him to…" He gestured vaguely at my extremities.

I swore. "Oui, by allowing him to do as he did. That would be one method of assisting him, oui." He would not let this die, and I could not tell him the truth, yet I must tell him something. "On occasion he wishes to exercise control… To feel powerful. I allow him to exercise that control over me. It is a *private* matter between us. It requires great trust. It is not a thing I can ever foresee him doing with some stupid little girl."

He was frowning, but he sat back in his chair and nodded thoughtfully.

"Do not ever make mention of this again, to anyone," I said.

He continued to nod, and then stopped to meet my gaze and ask. "Is it an aspect of his madness he is ashamed of, or is it a matter you would keep hidden?"

I shook my head and looked away with a heavy sigh. I should have shot the man days ago.

It was an astute question: one that bore examination. Gaston had allowed me to be portrayed as the madman to keep our secret hidden from Striker, and here I was allowing Gaston to look the madder of us for the same reason. Were we truly protecting a sacred thing between us, or selfishly covering our own shame?

I did not like that question. It burned in my heart, fanning the anxiety that had been simmering there.

"Both," I said tiredly.

He sighed. "I had thought that… his marriage, well, that marriage itself, would provide him with another caretaker; either as an adjunct to you, or as a – I will admit it – more suitable replacement. But now I feel… you are correct. No stupid little girl could love him as you do."

I turned to him and found him smiling.

His smile changed to a grin. "Women are generally far more sensible creatures," he teased.

Despite my cynicism and anxiety, I smirked. When that eruption of humor passed, I said sadly, "I am mad in my love for him."

He nodded, and clapped my shoulder. "He has been blessed to have found you."

"Thank you," I whispered.

He left me alone in the shade, and I found it was not nearly dark enough. I retreated to the stable. I intended to collapse into the straw and cuddle a puppy, but they were nursing, so I paced. Gaston entered before my thoughts could overwhelm me. He was not blind.

"Will?" he queried and stepped into my path to peer at my face.

"Your father noticed the marks," I said, and then I told him what I had said in explanation.

My matelot's face hardened, but he chewed his lip and stayed quiet.

"I am sorry," I said. "I wished to say nothing, but I felt I must. I did not wish for him to seek explanation elsewhere."

"You did not say it was about sex?" Gaston asked – or rather his Horse did.

Mine answered: I backed him to the wall, my fist pounding the wood next to his head to punctuate each sentence. "Non. I did not say how I beg you for it. I did not say how I writhe beneath you in pleasure, or how much delight you take in it. I said none of that! I kept our secret. From my shame, or yours, I know not which; but we are both the madder for it now!"

I was surprised at myself, perhaps moreso than he was. For one frozen moment I thought he might strike me: I thought I might strike him. Then his hands were on either side of my face and he was gazing into my eyes earnestly, as I often did when seeking to calm him.

"I am sorry," I gasped. "I am sorry."

"Perhaps I *should* take to binding you," he said with wry amusement.

I wrapped my arms around him and he held me.

"What is wrong, Will?" he whispered in my ear.

"I do not know. It has been eating at me since..."

"You woke?" he prompted.

"Non, non, I woke happy. Since I walked into that chaos this morning."

"I have already been bucking about," he said. "It is no wonder you are, too."

"I know." And I did. I had every reason to experience feelings of unease under the circumstances, but I felt unease at that. "It is... I have faced what I faced this morning before. I should not be so distraught. It is not as if it has led to..." And then I understood; and I shook my head and pulled away to meet his gaze. "I have faced that before, and it has ever led to a duel or my leaving some place. I always lost something or someone or... And now..."

"You are not losing me," he said. "We are not leaving, and I may not even marry."

"Why? What did she say?"

He shook his head and sighed. "She does not wish to marry this day. She was appalled at the suggestion."

"Did she give reason?" I asked.

"Non, she said she would marry me next week, perhaps." He shrugged. "We discussed where she should sleep until then. She does not wish to share Agnes' room."

Anger still flamed in my heart, and his words gave it a new direction to burn.

He caught me before I reached the door. "Will?" His voice held equal parts concern and warning.

I fought turning my anger back upon him. "Trust me. I have learned to trust you when you are thus."

He nodded and let me go.

Agnes and Sarah were standing in the doorway of Agnes' room, speaking to Christine, as I charged up the stairs. My sister regarded my arrival with a concerned frown, and I wondered what Striker had already told her. It only served to fuel my anger, and the knowledge that I would say or do little within the next moments to change their perception did little to damp me.

"Do you intend to proceed with the marriage or not?" I demanded of Christine.

"Aye," she said sharply, her own surprise at my sudden appearance turning to ire. She looked past me to Gaston in query. "I would prefer it be next week."

"I would have a reason," I said. "I would know if you are merely delaying the matter so that you might formulate some other escape from your father. If that is what you wish, we will be happy to oblige you, but do not toy with us."

"I toy with no one," she spat. "I will marry Lord Montren, but not this week, not that it is any concern of yours. If I am not to marry both of you, then the matter lies between him and me and has not a thing to do with you," she said with a spiteful sneer.

"Non," Gaston said.

Christine turned to look at him. The ire left her fine features as she beheld his stony face and stance. "I am sorry, my Lord," she said, "but I am either marrying you, or I am not."

"Non," he said. "You are marrying me, but above all others, he is my matelot, and all things concerning me concern him. If that is not acceptable to you, then leave."

She flushed. "I do not wish to argue over this."

Despite my Horse's wishes, I kept the smugness from my face. "I ask again, with all that is afoot, why is today unsuitable?"

Her cheeks became even redder. "I am indisposed this week," she growled.

Having become ill-accustomed to the ways of ladies these last years, it took me several moments to divine her meaning. When I did, I shook my head with annoyance. "That is of no concern. It surely will not affect the ceremony, and as for the consummation, you will merely need extra linens and an ewer of water."

"Will!" Gaston hissed.

I saw by his horrified expression that her having her monthly bleed would indeed have more impact on the matter of the consummation than the addition of a bathing tub in the wedding room.

I sighed. "You need not consummate the marriage until she is done with it then, but I still see no reason for it to delay the wedding."

Gaston nodded. If Christine could have struck me dead, she surely would have. Agnes was appalled and glaring at me as well. Sarah was attempting to stifle her mirth.

"I have not yet had the opportunity to try such a thing," Sarah said. "Is it truly not... ill-advised, other than the mess?"

I grinned. "I have known several ladies who swear it alleviates the cramping often associated with the matter."

"I look forward to testing that supposition, then," Sarah said, and walked toward her room.

"Striker may be appalled by the notion," I said. "Many men are."

She snorted. "He can be persuaded."

I turned back to Christine. "We plan to go to the church this afternoon for the baptism of our daughter. It would simplify matters if you were to accompany us and marry Gaston today. Can you find a gown? Perhaps you can borrow one of my sister's."

Furious, she stubbornly looked to Gaston. "My Lord?"

"As he said." Gaston turned away and walked toward the rooms being cleaned – where I noted his father and Striker stood watching us.

I turned away as well. Christine's parting glare told me we were far from the end of the battle. For a panicked moment, I considered telling Gaston to end the matter: it surely could come to no good; but then I remembered my words concerning Vivian, and I thought of how that had begun. Christine would not be about forever, and Gaston seemed intent on making her place very clear to her. I truly had no reason to be concerned: it was just my Horse shying at... madmen in the bushes.

I sighed and wrapped my arms around Gaston when I reached him. He was just telling his father that there would likely be a wedding that afternoon. Striker and the Marquis regarded me with concerned curiosity. I ignored them, and brushed a kiss on my matelot's cheek before entering the Marquis' room to see what progress was being made.

Rucker gave me a hearty smile and hurried past me to fetch more paint from downstairs. Pete and Dupree were painting. I knew the Marquis and Striker had also been involved in the endeavor, as they were somewhat spattered, but I felt their labor had been less intense than that of the two men working now. The Golden One's bronzed skin was nearly as white as Dupree's shirt, due to the splatter from applying the paint to the ceiling with a mop. I considered stripping and throwing myself into the labor in order to divert my attention, but then I remembered I could not expose my chest, and that recollection only served to make me wish to divert my attention even more.

"I am sorry we are so little help this day," I said. "We are to baptize the baby and get Gaston married this afternoon."

"Oui, my Lord," Dupree added. "Will we be attending?"

"If you wish," I said.

Pete set his mop in the bucket and wiped his face before awarding me a wry smile. "YaBeWellWithThis?"

I did not lie, or perhaps I did. "Aye. Well enough." I smiled.

He grinned, but his eyes were narrowed, and I felt as I sometimes did in his presence: that I was being perused by some ancient spirit.

"AllO'ItBeEnoughTaDriveAManMad."

"And if one is already mad?" I asked.

His grin widened. "ThenYaNa"AveFarTaGo."

I smirked. "Nay, I do not feel it is a destination, but a state of being. One either stands so that they perceive the world as all other men do, or one does not. And of late, I have ceased to be convinced that the sanity purportedly held by many is the truth."

He frowned at me, as did Dupree.

"I do not think I am any madder than any other man," I clarified.

Pete leaned on the unpainted wall and crossed his arms. "Some'AveBeenWorried. YaGonnaHurtYarself?"

"Nay," I replied with a dismissive snort. Though, I wondered if allowing another to hurt me would be part of the answer he sought.

"YaGonnaHurtAnother?"

"If they are my enemy, I should hope so," I said with a grin.

He grinned. "YaKnowFriendFromFoe?"

"Not always, it seems," I sighed, "but unless I am faced with betrayal, I mean none I now call friend any harm."

"ThenYaBeSaneEnough. AndWhenYaNa'Be, YaGotAMatelotTaCare FurYa."

"So you will gauge my sanity based upon my actions?" I asked.

He shrugged. "ThereBeNoOtherWay. YaCanna'KnowWhatAMan Thinks. An'ItDon'tMatter. WhatAManDoesMatters."

I supposed there was more truth to that than all the allegories of caves I could muster. Still, I wanted to know his opinion.

"What if a man does a thing that seems mad to others, but is actually quite reasoned from his perspective?" I asked.

"IsThatNa'TheWayO'AllThingsMenDo?"

I shook my head and smiled. I was asking an ancient God: Pete was all Horse and ever stood beyond the cave.

"I sometimes shy at things others do not see," I admitted quietly.

"TheyBeThingsAManShouldBeScaredO'?"

"I think so."

"ThenYaBeSane. DoesNa'MatterIfAnotherSeesIt. IBeWorriedAbout YaIfYaNa'BeScared."

"But I embrace... things... that other men fear," I added.

He grinned. "DoTheyKillYa?"

I shrugged and smiled. "Nay."

"ThenAnotherManWouldBeMadForGettin'Near'Im." He cocked his head with a knowing smirk. "ButYaBeSaneEnough."

"So, you would say the madness occurs only in those first moments when one reaches out to take hold of a thing others fear? And if one survives that first grasp, then he has crossed some demarcation of madness and becomes sane?"

He chuckled. "Aye."

I shared his mirth. "I agree with that." It matched well with much of what Gaston and I had thought on the matter these last weeks.

Striker, Gaston, and his father had joined us in the room. Dupree was busy translating for the Marquis. Striker was eyeing me with concern. My matelot was smiling.

"All reasoning applied to the matter leads to the conclusion of our sanity," Gaston said with quiet amusement.

I joined him near the door, and kissed him lightly. I glanced at the Marquis, who was frowning at Pete now that Dupree had finished.

"I feel we shall never convince any save Pete of that," I sighed.

Gaston shrugged. "At this moment, I care not."

"Should I remind you of that, when next you do care?" I teased.

"You may try," he said somberly. "I doubt you will be successful." He shrugged again and led me out to the balcony. "Henrietta has returned."

"Ah," I sighed. "Then we must abandon our sophism and venture out again."

He shook his head and frowned. "I feel we are crawling into the deepest recesses of the cave the others sit in."

"Non," I said quickly. "It will be as it was when I married Vivian," I whispered. "You shall play a part. We shall be shadows upon their wall, but we know what we truly are."

His gaze met mine for a moment before he began walking toward the stairs: I saw fear in his heart. I caught him and turned him to face me. The fear in his eyes was gone, but it had been replaced by resignation.

"What?" I asked. "As fractious as our mounts are this day, please do not leave a thing unsaid."

He shook his head and frowned with thought. "I am afraid we will cast many shadows, because there are different truths."

"The Devil with allegory," I said quietly. "What are the truths?"

He met my gaze earnestly. "I love you."

"But?"

"I want her," he whispered. He flinched from what he saw in my eyes.

"I understand, I understand," I said quickly. "Do not... Oui, my Horse does not like it, but I understand. As I have said before, I want her too. She is beautiful. I do not wish to speak with her now, but if the opportunity presented itself for us to fuck willingly, I would rise to the occasion. I think that is a thing of our Horses."

"Non," he said with a quick shake of his head. "My Horse does not want her, my cock does."

I nodded as I gave the matter thought. "You are correct. They are two different entities; they merely operate in concert on occasion to assail our reason: that is why I suppose I have ever seen them as one."

"My Horse does not like her, Will, but my reason says this is a thing I should do, and my cock wishes for it very much, and I feel great guilt over it. Which should I follow?" He shook his head irritably. "Not my cock, obviously: it has no mind and no say."

I sighed. "I feel this is why I was querying Pete. My Horse wants little to do with her, either; and my cock... as you say, has no say; and my reason says it is a thing that should be done. And I worry – as we have discovered in many things – that denying the truth our Horses perceive will lead us to ruin, but I do not wish to deny you a chance to... attempt things you have ever wanted and perhaps should try."

"Should I?" he asked. "I cannot conceive of lying with you without my Horse and my heart being involved. But her... I simply wish to fuck her until she gets with child. And that seems wrong."

I chuckled and he regarded me sharply. I shook my head. "My love, there are many who would say you are not a man for those sentiments." I sighed at his frown and sobered. "Most men are creatures of their cocks, with occasional periods of reason. Just as most women are creatures of their hearts, with occasional periods of reason. We are centaurs – though I have lived many years as a man like any other – but we are different, now. For me it is easier, as my cock favors men; but for you, there is a dichotomy in your soul about the matter, just as there is in Striker. In order to have the love our Horses desire, our hearts and souls desire, we must rein in our cocks with the iron hand of reason. I have become so accustomed to doing so because... It would be dangerous to live among the Brethren if I behaved as I did before coming here.

"When I traveled Christendom, I would have set about seducing Pete when first I saw him, whether I had a lover or not; and if I had a lover, I would have assumed he was doing the same. It was that way with Alonso: we would tease one another and even wager on who would be successful first. The only aspect of the matter that ever gave me pause was if I encountered a man who insisted on bestowing, and then my old fears, and thus my Horse, always trumped my cock."

Though he had frowned with the Horse's jealousy at the mention of Pete, my matelot had remained silent, and moved away to lean against the wall with a thoughtful mien. He nodded. "My Horse rules my cock in the matter of you."

"I know," I said, and went to him to lean with my hands on either side of his shoulders. I pressed my forehead to his. "And I thank the Gods for it," I whispered. "Let your cock play for a while, my love. Reason has a very strong hand in this matter – and I do not mean to hold the reins, but very good cards. We know that. You can make a child. You can give your father an heir. It aids another, who, though she is a silly child, does need help to find happiness in this life. We will... endure and conquer. Our Horses... They are strong. They can carry this for a time, oui? They can pull the extra weight in the cart. As long as we know it will end. We will need to treat them with great care and respect and give them many treats, though."

He smiled at that last, and moved enough to kiss me. "I will not have you angry with me," he said somberly.

I was minded of another time when we had stood thus against a wall, him with his back to it and me bracketing him. I had said I feared he would hate me for my cock's desires. "I will never hate you for what you desire," I said. "Never."

He gave a heavy sigh and embraced me. We stood thus for a time. I wished to hold him forever. Though my words had been said to calm my Horse as much as his, I felt I lied to the animals, just as I had ever done when my mount became startled and I knew damn well it should be, as I knew a fight loomed, or it would rain, or I too could see the snake – or madmen – on the road ahead. But sometimes men must press on to confront or pass obvious danger in order to reach some safe haven or obtain some goal that will make the whole of it worthwhile: things horses cannot understand.

And so we at last parted and went to collect women. Henrietta had returned from the market and shops with new stays, linens, shifts, stockings, shoes, and every other accoutrement her lady might need, and an old gown that she thought might fit Vivian; but she was afraid to show it to her mistress as it was drab, wool, and not at all stylish. I took the bundles from her and went to the parlor.

"This is the best Henrietta could do today," I told my wife. "To do better, we will need a seamstress to take your measurements and make you several gowns."

She eyed the dress with dismay, but to my surprise, did not squawk or make complaint. She took it from me with a resolute nod.

"Will you remove these chains so I might dress," she said quietly. "And send Henrietta in... or else I will need your assistance." She sighed.

I tried to remember where I had put the key. "Let me fetch the key, and I will send her in. I am accomplished at assisting young ladies in disrobing, but rarely the other way around."

She smirked, and then regarded me curiously. "So you intend to go to the church now? Is Jamaica not sleeping?"

"Need she be awake for this?" I asked.

"I suppose not." She shrugged, but then that nonchalance fled her and her expression became earnest. "It will be just us, correct? Just you and me, and... Lord Montren, I suppose."

"Well, actually, we were hoping to make only the one visit to the church and see to Gaston's marriage at the same time."

"Nay!" She sat, as if that would stop me from moving her, like a donkey does when it decides it will work no more. "I will not be seen by that bitch. Not like this. Not when... She will gloat. Do not make me do this," she wailed.

I cursed quietly and sighed. "Nay, nay, I will not force you to... face her. It was incredibly foolish of me to think that... Never mind. We will go alone: just the three of us. We will fetch Jamaica from the Theodores' and go to the church."

I left her, and went to find Gaston. He was speaking with Christine, Agnes, and Sarah at the top of the stairs.

"Apparently your sister's dresses do not fit her well," Gaston said with a tired sigh.

Sarah rolled her eyes. "She is taller and wider across the shoulders."

"And all of mine are not... They are just not." Agnes sighed, and did not explain her gowns' specific inadequacies.

I excused us, and put my arm about Gaston's shoulder to walk down the balcony a short distance before whispering in his ear. "Vivian does not wish to see her. She would go to the church alone with us and not be seen by anyone. As... you do not wish to brave your bride's monthly flow, do you feel your wedding can wait until the morrow, when perhaps another dress can be found?" I pulled away enough to regard his face.

He was grimacing, and he had colored slightly. "Oui."

I nodded, and began to pull away, but he clutched my arm.

"Will," he hissed. "The thought of blood in the bed, and... I cannot see... I can see... my sister, when I think of..."

"Oh Gods!" I pulled him into my embrace. "I am sorry, my love. I was not thinking at all."

"I had..." He sighed and held me tighter to whisper. "I did not think of it at first, either. I merely felt very uncomfortable and disturbed by the notion: the crowing of my cock was louder, though. And then... I did think of it, and now I know it will be difficult enough despite the urging of my cock."

"Well, the more time you have to prepare yourself, the better," I sighed and kissed his cheek.

"And I know how... Lady Marsdale feels," he said. "I can feel them staring at us even now. Gods, Will, we have told her nothing. In all the..."

I swore. In all the chaos this day, we had forgotten the things we most wished to address with any prospective bride: his madness and his scars. "Well, this delay is surely a boon granted by the Gods to compensate for our forgetfulness in the face of today's drama."

He pulled away and nodded with a rueful smile. "We would have remembered on the way to the church." He met my gaze. "You must speak with her," he said.

I did not see how that would go well. "Now, or after we attend to the baptism?" I asked.

"Now," he sighed. "I would have the matter decided now. I will... Is there much that must be done with... Lady Marsdale?"

I smiled. "She stumbles on your title as much as you do on hers: call her Vivian and be done with it. I said I would send Henrietta in, but we need the key to her chains, and I do not remember..."

"I put it with the one for our manacles. I will fetch it."

"That is a relief," I said. "Fetch Henrietta as well, unless you wish to assist Vivian with her stays."

He shook his head and hurried down the stairs.

I turned to find three women regarding me with curiosity in his wake. "It appears we will see to the baptism this day, and address the matter of the wedding when it is more convenient to do so. And I must speak with Miss Vines, alone," I said.

Christine frowned, but Agnes and Sarah nodded and began to walk away.

"Wait," Christine said. "Why?"

Sarah and Agnes paused.

"There are things Gaston wishes for me to discuss with you," I said. "Before you marry. In the... madness of events this day we... forgot to address some very important matters which might bring about a different agreement." I sighed and shrugged.

Her eyes narrowed. "I will not make any agreement with you."

I sighed again. "That is not my suggestion, Miss Vines. My suggestion is that you hear me out, and using the information I shall impart to you, choose to alter your agreement with Gaston, or not, as it suits you."

"You should listen to him," Sarah said, and led Agnes away.

"Fine," Christine said, with her hands on her hips. "Speak."

I looked about. I could, of course, suggest that we enter Agnes' room and talk, but with all else that had occurred, I did not feel comfortable with such a breach of decorum. All others on this floor of the house were engaged elsewhere; and if I kept my voice low, no one who might be below the balcony would be likely to hear.

I closed the distance between us. She stood her ground with more bravado than confidence: staying firmly rooted in the doorway, even when I was less than an arm's length from her.

I gazed upon her feigned haughty mien and wondered what I could say, or for that matter what I wished to say. I did not wish to divulge any secret of my matelot's to the little bitch standing before me; yet, I knew this adopted demeanor was a mask to hide her pain and anger. Beneath it lay a girl I had once thought I could fall in love with. That girl was still there, and my initial appraisal of her had not been misguided. I felt she would feel compassion for Gaston's woes, but I also felt that I would see little of it, as she was angry enough to kill the messenger this day.

She waited impatiently while I considered and discarded several versions of the truth. She had begun to turn away with annoyance when I at last decided what I would say.

"Gaston suffers from a malady of the mind. He possesses a great sensitivity of spirit and very poor control of his emotions once they are aroused. This malady is often seen as madness by those who do not know him well. We even refer to it as madness; but, depending on what you might know of madness, that definition might not be accurate in your interpretation. Suffice it to say that he has always suffered from it, and that it has led to his being abused by nearly everyone he has known, especially while he was young. And that has resulted in his being badly scarred, both physically and in his heart."

Compassion replaced the anger in her eyes: as I had hoped it would, both for Gaston's sake, and for the sake of validating my appraisal of her character. The tension drained from her, and she leaned against the doorframe with a thoughtful mien.

I continued. "His mother suffered the same malady, as did his sister, and we feel any child of his is likely to as well. That is why we wish to raise them personally, to insure that the effects of it are mitigated as much as possible, and that they are never ill-used because of it."

She nodded, but did not raise her eyes to meet mine. "I understand about the children now. How will this affect... a marriage?"

I shrugged. "If he becomes distraught or is behaving in a strange manner, you should urge him to seek me, or you should seek me. He can be quite... dangerous when he is in that state."

"And what if you are not available?" she asked with a little of her earlier rancor. "Can I not aid him?"

I thought of the Marquis' thoughts and wishes on a wife being a more suitable caretaker, and I suppressed a sigh. "Not unless he trusts you, and that trust will take time to gain."

She frowned, but acquiesced, only to frown anew. "How is he scarred? I have seen no evidence of..."

"It is easily hidden beneath even a buccaneer's garb. He bears deep whip scars from his shoulders to his knees."

"Whip scars..." she breathed. "How? Was he imprisoned? I thought the buccaneers never used the lash."

"It happened before he came to the West Indies. If he someday wishes to share that tale with you, then he will," I said firmly. "Until then, you must not ask. It was a very dark day for him, and recalling it... often leads to his madness." That was not necessarily as true now as it once had been, but I hoped it would stave her off.

She did not appear to be pleased about letting that matter drop, but she changed her questions readily enough. "What does he do when he has gone mad? Or is suffering from his madness, I suppose?"

I sighed. "When he has completely lost himself, he lashes out at all around him, caring not if they are friend or foe. And to those that even in his madness he does not wish to strike, he will often say things that wound far worse than any blow he might have landed."

"Is it as if he is possessed?" she asked, finally meeting my gaze.

"Aye and nay," I sighed. "In a manner of speaking, he is, but not by some otherworldly demon, but by the darkness that lurks in his heart: a darkness placed there by others. When he is thus, he sees all around him as the ones who hurt him. That is why you will not be able to help him or control him if he loses himself to it."

"How do you control him?" she asked with a touch of challenge that raised my hackles.

"Damn it, girl," I sighed. "This is not a game or contest. He loves and trusts me now, even when he is at his worst. It has taken us years to achieve that. He has stabbed me and struck me and we have fought one another with swords. He has said things to me that made me wish to die."

She crossed her arms and awarded me a look that said I had just thrown a gauntlet before her.

I leaned close to hiss. "If you truly loved him, you could, of course, weather all that as well as I have – and gain his trust. But you are not marrying him because you love him, and he is not marrying you for love, either. And if he doubts your sincerity when he is in that state, he will likely kill you."

She flinched and turned away. "If I am to marry any man, I wish to be a good wife and do all for him that I can."

"Good, that will be appreciated if you still wish to marry him."

"I do," she said with conviction.

I wondered what reason she employed in that decision: because it struck me as being madness. Where was her Horse trying to go? Where did her mind think the path lay? And what the Devil did her pussy want? I felt she was as much at odds with herself as we were on the matter, and yet she was calming her Horse and marching on. Or was her Horse the part of her that wished to pick up that gauntlet?

Answers to those questions were boons I felt the Gods would never grant.

Sixty-Six

Wherein Motivations Are Exposed

Gaston anxiously awaited me in the foyer. Without speaking, he led me outside and down the street, well beyond the hearing of anyone we knew. I soon determined we were actually on our way to the Theodores', and not merely avoiding eavesdroppers, and he seemed oddly reluctant to ask the obvious question concerning my meeting.

"She still wishes to marry you," I told him. "She is sympathetic to your malady, and to your being scarred because of it."

He nodded, and continued to regard me with the eyes of a man fearful of bad news.

"What?" I asked.

"Why are you angry?" he asked. "What else did she say?"

I sighed. "She wishes to assist you in your times of madness, in the name of being a good wife. I instructed her that she should seek me if you behave in any extraordinary fashion, but... Well, I feel she views my warnings of the danger you pose as a challenge."

He was shaking his head emphatically. "Damn her! Is she a fool?"

"Perhaps. Or mad in her way. As Pete said, we cannot know, can we? We cannot know her heart, or Horse, or... We can only see what she does. And I did not understand the warnings of others concerning you when first we met, either."

We stopped in front of the Theodores', and Gaston sighed and closed his eyes. "I wish you could be there to guide me. Then I could give you the reins and have nothing to fear."

"We could do that..." I said carefully.

"Non," he growled. "She will not have it her way."

I smiled, and pulled him to me so that I could whisper, "I love you."

He shrugged me off irritably, but his smile was genuine when at last it came. "You must stay near."

"If you wish, I will wait outside the door," I said sincerely.

"That will not be close enough," he sighed regretfully.

"You can curtain the bed," I offered, "and I can sit inside the room..." I could not picture her accepting that in the least.

He shook his head sadly. "It will be a thing I must brave alone."

"Do you truly feel it will be a test of your riding skills?" I asked with concern. "Do you feel when presented with... a woman, with... *that* in the offing, you will lose yourself?"

He met my gaze with earnest eyes. "I do not know, Will. I only know that the more I consider the matter, the more riled I become."

"What if she is not your first?" I asked.

"She will not be my first!" he hissed.

I openly cursed my stupidity. "I am sorry. That is not..."

"I know!" he snapped quietly. "I know what you meant. But Will, why should it matter whether the next is Christine or any other? I feel it will be just as bad."

"But, with any other, your Horse might not take offense at my presence," I said carefully.

He took a deep breath and looked away to study the wall and worry his lip with his teeth. "I will not... with a whore," he sighed at last. "I will not."

"Well, that limits our options then, somewhat," I said lightly.

"What were you thinking?" he asked accusingly.

"Nothing!" I hissed. "Prior to a few moments ago, I had not given the matter any thought at all, and when first presented with it, I thought we might locate a rather clean and expensive whore."

"You would have me bed some damn woman?" he asked, thankfully with more curiosity than rancor.

I shook my head. "I would have you wet your wick in one with me at your side, so that you might be calm and assured when it is time to bed your damn bride, so that you might make a child. The hand of reason, my love, the hand of reason."

He sighed long and hard, and sat on Theodore's front step with his back to the door. I could envision Hannah with her head to the same door, listening to the madmen outside, and I thanked the Gods she did not appear to speak French.

"Let us retrieve the child," I said calmly, "as that is what I assume we are here to do, and go and fetch my wife, go to the church, have the baby baptized, return them all to their proper places, and then discuss this tonight in private."

"I am sorry," he whispered.

I squatted so I could meet his gaze. "I am not angry, my love," I murmured.

Though he was calm now, he had come close to tears. His hand shook as he reached for me. I took it and kissed the backs of his fingers.

"I am a fool, Will," he said earnestly. "I cannot... act like a sane man."

"Non, non," I said. "You can act like one, you cannot think like one: there is a difference. We will sort this through. Now, come. We have a baptism."

I stood and pulled him to his feet.

"I cannot act like one without you," he said as I knocked on the door.

Hannah was indeed just beyond the door, as it opened before I could speak. She nodded politely, and, like any good servant, ushered us in without any telltale expression that she knew we had argued on the step.

Theodore sat in his office. I wondered what he had heard. His mien was thoughtful, and when his gaze met mine, he smiled ruefully. I stopped in his doorway, and recalled why our friend might be in such an introspective state: the trouble the events of this morning had revealed was not ours alone.

Theodore waved Hannah away, and my matelot and I entered the room and seated ourselves in the chairs before the desk. I noticed the usually neat and clean teak expanse was cluttered with paper and chalk boards, many with little notes and diagrams upon them.

"We need to locate your uncle," Theodore said without preamble.

I nodded. "And what shall we discover when we do?" I asked. "If he has been communicating with my father? My sister said he received a letter."

"Aye," Theodore said with a knowing smile. "I never saw it, as it did not pass through me. And I should have realized..." He sighed. "All your father's prior correspondence has come to me to distribute, or rather, the correspondence we know of. So, I need to know who delivered that letter to your uncle, and it would behoove us to discover what else he knows."

"I do not trust him," I said. "He is gullible, and... my father thinks him a fool. Thus, any information my father might have imparted to him, even if my uncle will relay it to me honestly, is suspect."

Theodore nodded, and his mien became somewhat guilty. "Must not his room be cleaned at the house? I imagine it is quite smoke damaged and..."

Surprised, I grinned. "Aye, and we should have thought of that... hours ago. Of course, since he is not here to see to the matter himself, it would be a kindness on our part to undertake the cleaning for him. Perhaps tonight, after the baptism. We could procure a good bottle of wine and actually do some work by putting my uncle's room... in order, since we have been shirking our duties concerning the cleaning all day. Would you wish to assist us?"

"I think that I will find studying the effects of such a fire to be very illuminating," Theodore said with good cheer.

"We shall make a fine time of it, then," I said. "I would also invite you and Mistress Theodore to the baptism."

Gaston frowned at me, and I patted his arm reassuringly as I continued.

"My wife will not be pleased, as she wishes to see no one, but I feel if you were to meet us at the church, perhaps..."

Theodore nodded. "I feel Mistress Theodore would like that very much, and... it would behoove you to have witnesses beyond the clergy. Are you going there now?"

"Aye, will this pose a problem?" I asked.

He shook his head. "Nay, I should truly abandon this... supposition I have been engaged in, else it will surely drive me mad." He gave Gaston a guilty glance.

My matelot awarded him a good-natured smile and a shrug.

We went to collect the child and inform Rachel of our plans. She handed Gaston a sleeping bundle, and frowned at her dress and apron, and then at her husband, before sighing and informing us she would change into something more suitable for church. We agreed to wait on the baptism until they arrived, and we hurried out the door.

As we walked home, Gaston cradled the tiny bundle in the crook of his arm and pushed her blanket away to reveal her face. He touched a cheek with his fingertip and smiled in a manner that warmed my heart considerably. I put my arm about his shoulder to steer him while he was thus enraptured. I did not feel any other would view that little girl with such adoration, nor did I feel any would ever view my matelot as I did.

I was beginning to feel Christine should be added to the list of people I should have killed long ago.

Vivian was ready when we arrived, and Henrietta looked none the worse for it: no teary eyes or strained expressions on either of them. There was an awkward moment when Vivian went to reach for the child and it became obvious Gaston would not relinquish her. My matelot appeared somewhat guilty over the matter, but resolute, and my wife took it well enough and made much of saying it was probably best he carried Jamaica, as she was not accustomed to doing so.

"She should hold her at the baptism," I said quietly in French, as I took Vivian's arm and ushered her out the door.

"I know, I know," Gaston sighed.

Vivian peered about self-consciously once we were on the street, as if someone might be there to spy upon her, and then her gaze fell on the ruins of her house and she gasped. The hazy golden light of late afternoon made the black skeletal remains appear even worse than they had at midday. It was as if we gazed upon a graveyard. She released my arm and went to stand before it with her arms tightly crossed and utter dismay upon her features.

"We will have it rebuilt," I told her gently.

She shook her head. "And then what? Shall I live there as I did before? Or will we all live there? I will not share it with..." She looked to Gaston guiltily. "His wife. I will share it with him, now... but not her." She looked away with a little frown, as if she realized how childish she sounded. "And I do not..." She sighed heavily and began to lead us toward the church.

"What do you not?" I prompted.

"I do not wish to live in it alone," she said over her shoulder. "I will drink if I do."

"Do you wish to live with us, then?" I asked. "We feel Gaston's wife will be in France as soon as it can be managed."

She stopped and turned, her arms akimbo. With her simply plaited hair and drab, shapeless dress, she appeared far older than her years. She sighed expansively and nodded her head in a tight little gesture. "Aye, I would live with you then, and the baby, as I see..." She looked pointedly at Gaston and shrugged.

"Will and I will share a bed," Gaston said.

"Obviously." She rolled her eyes, but her response seemed to contain more annoyance that the matter should be discussed at all than that it should exist. "I will sleep alone quite happily, thank you."

"We do not choose to live in town for most of the year, however," I said.

"I do not wish to live here, in town, either," she said. "There are too many people here who..." She trailed off with annoyed shake of her head and a resolute set to her jaw.

"Who know of you and your exploits, both purported and witnessed," I said kindly and gestured at the rubble behind us.

She nodded tightly. "I do not... I do not wish to face them without the fortification of strong spirits. I do not know how."

"I understand," I said, and went to take her arm again.

"We live in a hovel on Negril Point when we do not live here or rove," Gaston said. "We will not... We could not build a house like you had, there."

She shrugged. "That house was my... fortress. I feel distance from... others, will make for even thicker walls than those fine ones once made."

"Then we will manage it all, somehow," I told her, and began to lead us to the church.

I looked to Gaston over her head. He met my gaze and nodded thoughtfully, and then sighed with relief as he fell into step beside us.

I could barely imagine how we would survive upon the Point without one of us wishing to strangle her or her not taking a knife to us while we slept; but there was reason to hope we would find a way to manage it. Gaston would have his child, Vivian would remain sober and safe from the cares of the world, and I would have him and still have managed to thwart my father while doing everything a proper gentleman should – after a fashion.

At the church, Gaston handed her Jamaica, and she carefully carried the little bundle inside after pausing to gaze down at the little face with nearly as much adoration as my matelot had shown. And I wondered if what I perceived of her feelings toward the child was merely a thing of women, in that all women gazing upon an infant looked much the same, or whether she truly felt for the child as much as Gaston did.

She was dismayed to see the Theodores inside, but as Rachel gave her no looks of reproach, and even greeted her with a kindness I found strange coming from the woman, Vivian calmed somewhat and we managed the baptismal ceremony with little incident – though the pastor was disapproving of our choice of name, insisting repeatedly that we choose a Christian name. He finally relented beneath five glares and my argument that we were making it a Christian name this day.

As I had when I married Vivian, I found myself saying much in my heart to the Gods, even as blasphemy and lies passed my lips as to how I would raise this child. We named Gaston as godfather, and as I heard him say the necessary words to satisfy the ceremony, I continued to muse on how very much more we truly intended to do for this babe than so many others would do who stood where we stood and said what we said. Our participating in this ceremony was perfunctory, but the pact we made with this child was truly heartfelt and encompassed more than what little – and self-serving – direction the Church was giving us concerning her upbringing. In truth, my standing there at all – and all that that implied – was very much more than many children ever received.

When it was over, I found myself taking the child from her mother's arms and holding our little Jamaica so I could gaze upon her cherubic face. I doubted any about me would see adoration upon my features, but perhaps they saw my wonder. We were truly responsible for this little person, and for the first time I felt that charge, as deeply as I had felt I was married to Gaston on the day we were named matelots by our friends. The weight settled heavily upon my shoulders, and to my relief I felt myself rise to the occasion; and I knew I would walk taller for it, as I did with Gaston.

"Thank you," Vivian whispered as I returned the child to her arms, and I knew she was not thanking me for giving her the baby for the walk home.

"Nay, thank you," I said, and kissed her forehead. "We will make it work somehow."

Her eyes were moist. "Swear it," she said.

"I swear it."

"On?" she demanded quietly.

"On my love for Gaston," I said.

She smiled. "You are the only man I have ever met who would have the balls to say such a thing in a church. If you are so very brave, I believe you can truly make it all good somehow."

I bowed and grinned. "Then, my Lady, I thank you for the trust you have placed in me."

She snorted with mock annoyance, but her smile was genuine as we walked to the door.

Outside, Rachel and Theodore were waiting. "We might as well take her home," Mistress Theodore said.

Vivian seemed reluctant to part with the baby.

"Do you want to keep her yet?" Rachel asked my wife.

Gaston frowned at this suggestion, and Vivian tried to shrink into my side.

"I am… I am… I am afraid I will be a poor mother," Vivian said at last and handed the child carefully to Rachel.

"We all have to learn to handle little ones," Rachel said in a kinder variation of her usual direct manner. "I'll bring her around tomorrow, and you can start learning."

Vivian nodded tightly. "If you think it… best." She looked to Gaston and bit her lip.

My matelot looked to Rachel.

She sighed and said, "Any rum you might have left in you cannot be worse than what we're giving her now."

Gaston nodded glumly and shrugged.

"I will locate a bottle and see you… soon," Theodore said, after a glance at his wife proved she was not approving of whatever he might have planned involving a bottle.

"It is for a good cause," I assured her quickly.

"It always is," Rachel sniffed, and began to lead them home.

Theodore was battling a good chuckle, and he smiled warmly at us in his wife's wake. "Soon, then; I feel I should dine at home first."

"That might be wise," I agreed.

I offered Vivian my arm, and she clung to it as we began to walk home. Gaston fell into step on her other side.

"Mistress Theodore is often a direct woman; you should not take it personally," I told Vivian. "She does not seem to revile you."

She sighed, and tried to speak as if I was naïve, but her delivery was somewhat hesitant. "How a woman behaves in front of men is not always the same as how she behaves towards other women."

"I know that well," I assured her. "But I truly feel she means you no harm. I am merely warning you that on occasion she has scolded even Pete."

"Who is Pete?" she asked.

Gaston and I exchanged a perplexed glance over her head.

"The Golden God that lives in our house," I said.

Her eyes widened. "Oh, him…"

"It is good to know you are not blind," I teased.

She snorted dismissively, but there was color in her cheeks. "Oh, I have seen him, to be sure; I simply did not know his name. Captain Striker is a delight to the eyes as well."

"Aye," I said enthusiastically.

She rolled her eyes, and then sobered to glance at Gaston with a quick frown.

"I do not favor men, but I know they are handsome," Gaston said levelly.

This deepened the furrows on her brow and caused her gaze to flick to me.

"What?" I asked.

She shook her head and considered several tacks before blurting, "Neither of you is disagreeable to the eye, either. And... do not interpret that as anything other than a compliment. I want nothing to do with either of you, or any man, for that matter. I have had my fill of men," she finished quietly and sadly.

I shook my head, and squeezed the hand she had upon my arm. "I hope, for your sake, that you will have a change of heart on that someday. I am quite open to your taking a lover, if the opportunity should present itself and it will not complicate other matters."

She frowned, and flushed with her eyes steadfastly on the ground before us. "I cannot... could not..." She shook her head. "Will not do as I did before. I cannot see even allowing someone to touch me without a good deal of rum."

Her gaze shot to Gaston, and her color deepened.

"I tell him everything," I said.

She rolled her eyes. "I thought as much."

"I do not think you a whore," Gaston said.

She flinched at his tone, but she nodded and found the courage to ask, "What do you think me?"

"A drunkard," he sighed.

"I have had my reasons," she said quietly.

"So have I, and so has Will," Gaston said without recrimination. "We all have reasons to hide from pain. Some men, or women, take to spirits such that the cure becomes a disease. You are one of those people."

She was gazing intently at him. "I remember you are scarred," she said "I think I remember that from the birth."

He nodded.

She looked to me, her tone curious. "But I have seen no scars on you."

"I was raped and beaten by my cousin," I said with an ease that surprised me. "That is why I left my father's home when I was your age."

She winced and looked away quickly. Then she frowned. "Shane?"

I sighed. "Aye."

"He hates you," she said quietly.

I frowned, and then I recalled she said she knew him. "What did he say?"

"That you were a sodomite," she said with a shrug of embarrassment. "He reviles you for it."

"Because I can admit what I am and he cannot," I said with contempt.

She began to nod, and stopped to shake her head and speak with surety. "Nay, because you will inherit and he will not." She looked up at me with a perplexed frown. "I am thinking of all that was said this morning, about your father and…"

"Did you ever speak to my father?" I asked.

"Nay, well, aye, but as a formal introduction. He had to see what his money had purchased," she said bitterly. "We did not speak. And my father…" She sighed. "He did not speak with me, either. Shane spoke with me. He wished to seduce me."

Gaston swore.

"Nay! Nay!" she said quickly. "I am not that big a fool! He was drunk. We were drunk. There were others present, though. He led me to a corner and whispered of it. He said you would never do me justice; that I was wasted upon you. He even said you would never get me with child, and I might as well see to the matter myself where I could, as you would not challenge it if you were smart." She shook her head with guilt and embarrassment. "Even as drunk as I was… I knew he did not want me, and it made me angry. He merely wanted to ruin me before I was sent to you."

Anger and bemusement rose within me that he should still be such a damn fool, and then it exploded as the true import of some of her words came to roost. "He did not think I would challenge an illegitimate birth if I were smart?" I growled.

Her eyes went wide with horror at what she found in mine. She grasped at me and I thought she might kneel. I grabbed her shoulders to keep her from sinking, and it was only with great effort I kept myself from shaking her. Over her shoulder, I saw murder to match my own in Gaston's eyes.

"I am sorry!" she wailed. "I did not mean… You have been so good… I am sorry. I did not do it because of him. I did not know there was bad blood between you. I did not know. I did not know. I did not believe you would… I thought maybe if I had a boy, then… But…"

Though the street was not crowded, people were stopping to stare. I pulled her to my chest and put a hand over her mouth. I was gripped by such a rage I wished to strangle her, but a small and clear voice whispered that it was truly not her fault.

Gaston took me by the shoulder and began to tow us home with great purpose. Her panicked protestations stopped and she walked between us sobbing. When we were at last safely within the foyer, Gaston hissed, "Stable!" and pushed me away. I numbly did as he bid. I hoped he would not kill her, but I knew I would not lift a hand to stop him.

I collapsed on our hammock, shaking with rage made all the more painful by its impotence. I wanted to kill Shane. How could he still harbor so much hatred of me? And for my birth as opposed to his? For my inheritance, not for all that had passed between us, not for all the love and pain and blood. Nay, because I was something I could not help and could not change, and he was something else. All that had occurred must be viewed through that lens, no matter how warped or cracked.

Everything over which I had felt pain was meaningless. He had never loved me. He had never been my friend. I had been a deluded and lonely little boy. I was a fool. I should have killed him. I should not have let him scar me as he had, so deeply upon my heart that nothing would ever remove it, nothing could ever heal it.

I did not struggle when Gaston joined me on the hammock and held me so tightly my skin burned and my bones creaked. I knew it was he. Even in the state I was in, where I could see or feel nothing but pain, I knew he was there and he loved me. I clung to him.

Sometime later it was dark, and there was a light rapping on the doorframe. As if I listened through a fog, I heard Gaston say, "Come in; there has been a revelation, and Will is quite distraught."

"A revelation?" Theodore asked from near the hammock.

"Aye," Gaston sighed, "from the Damn Wife concerning the Damn Cousin. She spoke to him before she left England, and she has corresponded with him since."

"Oh Lord," Theodore said.

Having not known this last, I decided I would not yet be coaxed from the safe burrow of having my face buried in Gaston's shoulder. However, I did ask, "Does she live?" in French.

My matelot snorted, and spoke English for Theodore's benefit. "Aye. She is sincerely contrite. She did not know... who her enemies were." He sighed. "I have chained her in the parlor again. I did not want her sneaking out to wander the streets for rum, or harming herself. I judge her to be distraught enough to do either."

"Well, we would not want that," Theodore said sadly.

I felt Gaston shake his head. "She received a letter from the Damn Cousin through a man named Washington, and she sent her reply through him. Do you know of him?"

Theodore sighed. "Aye. He is a freight agent. He is a quiet sort, and respected for his discretion. Will's father, or his damn cousin, has chosen wisely." He sounded resigned and sad. "Might I ask the nature of this correspondence, or is that a subject best left for another time?"

"Will and I have not discussed it yet," Gaston said.

I shrugged, and he rubbed my back.

"Before she left England," Gaston said with little emotion, "the Damn Cousin sought to seduce her, and even suggested she should get with child because Will would not be up to the task. He told her that Will would not challenge any child she produced if he was smart. After she arrived here, she did as he suggested, not because he suggested it, but because she wished to be done with the matter of producing heirs as quickly as possible, and... she was very angry at the men in her life, and drunk, and thus lacking in judgment, of course. She received a letter from the Damn Cousin after her arrival. He appears to have been seeking information. She, being drunk and foolish and angry with Will, wrote him back and told him all she knew about us. She swears she did not tell him the child was illegitimate. She claims that, even inebriated, she was not that stupid."

"She did tell him she was with child, though?" Theodore asked.

"Aye," Gaston said.

"What could she have known to tell him, or rather, them, I wonder?" Theodore asked. "Unless Will spoke to her a great deal..."

I felt his gaze upon me, but I did not respond.

"I cannot see where she would have much to say," Theodore continued. "Apparently they had already established another agent to handle their correspondence."

"She mentioned speaking of Sarah and Striker," Gaston said.

"But that is a thing they were apprised of, anyway," Theodore muttered. "As they were with the child; and as they surely were of my friendship with Will. It is likely they have someone other than Washington spying for them."

"Perhaps it is the uncle. As for the wife, I am sure she complained bitterly of Jamaica," Gaston sighed, "but as for anything else she might have said, I too wonder at that. Will had already apprised his father of our relationship. She knew of it when she arrived."

Their words were tumbling through my own turbulent thoughts: shadowed and flickering motes of information, like leaves blown in a whirlwind of dirt. And then there was clarity. All became very clear when I peered through the lens of Shane's ambition: painful but clear. It was as if I could see the bullet embedded in my flesh and pluck it out.

"She would have been smug," I said. I raised my head and found the stall dimly illuminated by a single candle. Theodore was a shadowy form beyond the netting. "She would have been pleased to tell him she was married and the marriage had been consummated and she was with child. Depending on her phrasing, he might have read much into that, which might have pleased him, or it might have angered him."

"You say the cousin suggested you should accept an illegitimate child?" Theodore asked. "Does that not seem at cross purposes with the Earl's wishes?"

I smiled sadly. They could not see the matter as clearly as I now did. "Shane and my father do not think with one mind," I said. "They are set upon separate and colliding paths like poorly-aspected planets. Shane wishes to inherit: nothing more, nothing less. He said what he did in order to lead her to anger my father."

"Oh," Theodore said with surprise. "I see."

Gaston laid a finger aside my jaw and turned my head to face him. He studied me with concern, only to nod at what he found in my eyes. I kissed the tip of his nose.

"So, though your father seems willing to go to great lengths to defend him, we might assume they are actually working at cross purposes," Theodore was saying.

"Not always," I said. "My father wishes to have an heir he feels is worthy of the title. Shane wishes to be that heir. They are pitted against one another, but they are also pitted against me, in that I stand in the path of both their purposes. We, or rather I, have known that for a long time now; I just fail to see it in the proper light from time to time, due to my... entanglement with Shane. I let emotion cloud my reason."

Theodore nodded. "I now recall the circumstances of your sister angering him. It was due to his bid to marry her and your arrival thwarting the matter and making it known to your father."

"Aye," I said. "Who did not wish for him to marry into the family, as then he could not inherit. We cannot assume they now include one another in their plans any more than they did then."

"Now what shall we do?" Theodore asked.

"Search my uncle's room," I said with surety. "He might well be my father's unwitting agent. He surely is not Shane's, though. Or rather, he would not knowingly do Shane's bidding, but perhaps there is far more duplicity afoot in that regard as well."

Theodore began to leave the stable; he paused and turned. "I was asked to tell you your dinner awaits."

We thanked him, and lay there silent in his absence for several moments. I listened to puppies and did not meet Gaston's curious and concerned gaze.

"I was never anything to him," I said quietly, when it was obvious my matelot would not move until I spoke, and it became apparent to me that I should not leave the safety of his arms until I bled my wounds. "I was ever an impediment to his ambition, and all that passed between us was merely a divertissement. I have long labored under the delusion that he once cared for me in some fashion; and upon learning it was wrong to care for another man, he turned against me and our love, our friendship – or whatever it was I felt we had – in the name of propriety and being a good son: a good man. But nay, I was not even so much as that."

Gaston pulled my head back to his shoulder and kissed my forehead. I held him, and sighed long and hard, as if I could expel the poison in my heart with that breath; but, I could not: it lingered, clutching at me with painful claws.

"I will endure," I muttered.

His hand on my head tightened, pressing my face deeper into his flesh, as if he might push me inside him. For a time I took comfort in it, and held him harder, wishing I could sink within the safety of his ribs. Then I could stand it no longer. I could not crawl inside him, and so I must move. I pulled away to gaze down at him.

"I love you."

"We will conquer," he murmured.

I smiled sadly. "They will not care."

He shrugged. "We will care."

I wondered at that, but I did not voice my concern. I kissed him lightly, and crawled off the hammock. I could hear others out in the atrium.

"I suppose we should inform Sarah of..." I sighed: I did not know what I wished to tell her concerning Vivian's correspondence. Oddly, I did not want my sister to think poorly of her. "I suppose I should speak to Vivian."

He nodded and sighed. "I believe she is sincerely distraught over angering you."

I did too, and then I wondered at that. "I am a trusting fool. I have lost all ability to navigate intrigue. It is as if I have retreated to some state of innocence about men and women and their motives since arriving here. Or perhaps, I only deluded myself as to my prior deftness in such matters." I thought of all the times that people such as Teresina or Alonso had surprised me. And Shane. "Non, I am a trusting fool. I always have been."

"You are not a fool," Gaston said thoughtfully. "You see… snakes… and wolves readily enough, and know them for what they are; but with all others, you grant the blessing of good will, and then if they do move to bite us, you dispatch them quite nimbly. It is one of the things I love about you."

"Thank you," I whispered with an aching heart.

He moved to sit beside me. "Will, are you well?"

My mind was still cluttered with sharp and stinking debris of battle: things I dared not look at, stumble upon, or brush against. I shook my head sadly. "Are you?"

He sighed. "Nothing serves to steady my footing as much as seeing you slip."

I smiled. "I will be well enough. Help me up."

With a chuckle, he stood, and pulled me to my feet.

"What else might I do?" he asked.

"I wish to drink," I sighed. "Will it trouble you?"

He nodded amicably. "We have laudanum."

I reflected on the numbness either would grant me. "Non, wine will do."

He kissed me deeply, and I found it a balm for many things.

Our guest and housemates, save Vivian, were all seated about the tables. Sam and Henrietta had served roast pork and real bread. All was cold now – if the bread had ever been warm since crossing the threshold – but the smell was still delicious and made my stomach snarl with a ravenous hunger I had not known I possessed. I ignored the curious looks and sat to fill a plate and then my belly. Gaston handed me a flagon of wine, which I drained without delay. I forced myself to take my time to savor the bread. I slathered it with butter and ate it slowly with great relish.

Sarah chuckled. "The baker received a shipment of good flour yesterday. He has told Henrietta there will be bread for weeks now."

"That is lovely news," I said around another mouthful. I looked about the tables. All eyes were still upon us: the most curious being Christine's. I suppressed a sigh with another hunk of bread. "We will be cleaning our Uncle's room this eve," I said when I swallowed again.

"As we have done little else to assist with the labor this day." I looked pointedly at Sarah.

She frowned. "It too should be cleaned and painted, but it can wait until he bothers to return in my opinion."

"Aye, Will, you've had a good deal to occupy you today," Striker said with his own furrowed brow.

I shook my head. "We wish to organize his belongings before he should return."

Sarah's brow smoothed abruptly. "Oh."

I nodded. "We have learned the name of an agent either Shane or our father has used, and now we feel it best to see if there are others."

"Do you need any assistance?" she asked quickly.

"Nay, the three of us should be sufficient," I said, and gestured at Theodore, who was such an honest man he appeared a little guilty once again.

Dupree had been translating. The Marquis now grinned. "Will you be speaking with this agent?"

I looked to Theodore, and translated the question.

"He is truly well-respected and well-employed," Theodore said with a trace of regret.

"It would apparently pose some difficulty to speak to him as we would wish," I told the Marquis, even as Dupree translated Theodore's words.

"That is a pity," the Marquis said. "Is there any Mister Theodore might employ who could spy upon the man?"

I translated that for Theodore.

He sighed. "I have been thinking on it, but it is such a small damn town," he said bitterly, and took a sip of his wine. "There are likely people watching me to see if I make inquiries."

"Well," I said, "let us search for other avenues of attack."

"We'll find lanterns to speed your work," Striker said, and Pete chuckled.

"I will meet you upstairs," I told Gaston and Theodore. I stood and loaded another plate with a nice piece of bread covered in butter, and some lean pork. I took another long drink of my refilled flagon and left it with Gaston, and then filled another cup with water from the pitcher on the table.

The parlor was dark, and I had to set the food down and fetch a lit match cord from the nearest lantern so that I might light a lamp. I did not look for Vivian until I had light to do so. I found her crumpled on the end of the settee, staring at me with eyes wide like some small and startled forest creature. She did not move, except to follow me with her gaze as I crossed the room and set her meal upon the table near her.

"I am not angry with you," I said as I sat beside her. "You did not know. I believe he planted such suggestions in the fertile field of your anger – not that you might not have had them before – in order to cause further discord between my father and myself; which is exactly what has occurred. What is done is done, and much of it by my own hand.

"Shane has ever wished to... be me, to have all that was mine. He used you. I will trust that you understand that you were used, and that you will never communicate or correspond with my cousin, my father, or any agent they might have ever again. If you do, *then* I will be angry."

She nodded, the movement dislodging a fat tear from her eye. I gently wiped it away with my thumb. Her face was smooth, with no lines of emotion I might read etched upon her features, and even her eyes reflected the lamp such that I could not see past the shine of her tears. Thus, I was surprised at the suddenness of her movement as she reached for me, and had to fight the urge to pry her arms from me as she embraced me fervently. I held her as she sobbed.

"I never wished for any of this," she finally gasped. "When I was little I wanted to run away and live with the fairies. I did once. I snuck out of the house. I did not find any fairies in the woods, though; they were just dark and scary and cold. One of our peasants found me. He took me home, and I was beaten and locked away in the attic for a long time. I was happy there. I was alone. I wanted to stay there, but they watched me closely after that, and I never got another chance; and then I was out of the nursery and I discovered wine. I could sit in a room full of people and think my own thoughts and not even know they were there when I was drunk."

"We will hide you away," I assured her.

"How is it that you do not drink as I do?" she asked, and then pulled back to regard me with accusation. "And I smell wine upon you."

"Aye," I said, and realized there was an answer to that question. "Shane gave me reason to drink; but, he also taught me the dangers of drinking to excess. I could not avoid him if I was too drunk. And ever after, despite the pain of my memories, I have always known that drinking so that I was always numb to the world would have been my death: drunk men do not duel well."

She nodded, and sat up so that she was not pressed to my chest. "No one ever cared that I was drunk. They were happy it kept me quiet. And if I said things I should not, I was slapped and put away – with no wine – until I promised to keep a civil tongue. And then I came here and discovered rum. It is..."

"The Devil's brew," I teased. "It is tenfold stronger than any wine or ale."

She nodded again. "I did not tell him about Jamaica – about how she was conceived. Even drunk on rum, even with what he said..." She shook her head.

"I believe you," I said kindly. "They did not need to hear she was not mine from you. All in town spoke of you having an affair, remember?"

"That stupid boy," she sighed. "He thought he was in love with me."

"Young men are often stupid that way. I can well attest to it." I stood and leaned down to kiss her forehead. "Try and sleep."

"So you are searching your uncle's room this night?" she asked.

I smiled. "Do you listen to all that is said in the atrium?"

She shrugged. "It is often more amusing than my thoughts. I wish I spoke French."

I was very glad she did not, especially since she would live with us. But then another thing occurred to me, and I squatted before her to ask. "What have you heard said of me?"

She frowned, her eyes narrowed, and then she nodded. "They… Captain Striker, his friend, your sister, and the others, they often drop their voices to whispers and I do not hear what they say. I do hear that your name or Lord Montren's is often mentioned before the whispering starts. And I have heard mention of madness concerning both of you several times." Her gaze became speculative at this last.

I sighed: it was as I thought, and I realized I should not have asked. "That will entail a lengthy discussion, and I do not feel like engaging in it tonight. Suffice it to say that many here feel we are mad, and Gaston is renowned for it."

"In what way?" she asked with concern.

"In that we do not always think or behave as other men do."

She snorted. "That is obvious."

Chuckling with relief that I had dodged that thrust, I left her to her meal and went to join Gaston and Theodore.

Striker and Pete had indeed procured several bright lanterns, and now my uncle's room was filled with light and people. I had to work my way around our wolves, the Marquis, Dupree, and Rucker in order to reach Gaston and Theodore by the desk.

"I do not believe we will all be required," I said lightly.

"We're bored," Striker said.

"You are in the way," I chided. "And this will either be over quickly or become quite dull."

With heavy sighs – from all – Striker, Pete, the Marquis, and Dupree withdrew from the room.

I stopped Rucker before he could join them. "It is likely, with all the time you spent with my uncle, that your recollections may prove useful."

Rucker nodded. "I keep hoping I will recall something of use. I am adept at remembering names and faces, but there have been so many people we spoke to after arriving… And in these last months, your uncle and I have had a parting of the ways. He found my questioning the practices of the planters with whom he chose to cultivate friendships quite tedious, and even once accused me of being impertinent."

"I suppose you were questioning how they could treat other men as cattle in the name of money from a crop no one needs," I said with a grim smile.

"Just so," Rucker said.

Theodore chuckled. "I can still clearly recall how appalled you were when first I described the function and accounting of a plantation. You had labored under the concept that they were farms."

"Aye, and not more akin to mines as you instructed," I sighed.

I looked about at the massive teak furniture: all would have been perfectly acceptable in any English manor house, especially the heavily curtained bed. The recent layer of soot masked unpleasant odors, and I wondered if my uncle still suffered from the flux on occasion. It was perhaps a miracle, and definitely a testament to his strong constitution, that he was not dead. He was unwilling to take any of our advice as to the drinking of boiled water, the eating of the native food, or even sleeping in a cooling breeze.

"Dear Uncle Cedric was raised to be a good English wolf," I said, "and despite his tendency to be a kind master to the flock closest to him, any man he feels to be beneath him in status and who he does not know the name of is relegated to the category of sheep to be fleeced or eaten. Peasants, soldiers, and tradesmen are faceless and often troublesome commodities. The nobility is a thing apart and should ever be that way."

"He is like any planter here," Theodore said. "Even if they were not noblemen when they arrived, they are now after a fashion."

"Aye," I said, and grinned at Rucker. "It has been a great disappointment of mine – after Mister Rucker's fine tutelage on egalitarian philosophies of governance – to find that sheep truly like to be herded, and will do much to maintain their state."

"Sadly, I feel your experiences match my own," Rucker said.

"Gaston and I even bemoan the lack of independent spirit on the part of the buccaneers," I said. "Here they are living as free men, and all many of them wish to do is join the ranks of the wolves, and the rest seem quite content to be whipped into packs like obedient dogs. And yet, we are the madmen," I muttered.

"Society does change," Rucker said. "And those changes are always led by men considered mad."

"I will take some reassurance from that," I said lightly. "Probably to my grave."

We began with my uncle's desk, with me examining each packet of letters and Theodore and Rucker identifying the sender and Uncle Cedric's relationship with the person. Gaston poked about elsewhere in the room. Those of us reading the assorted notes and lengthy treatises drank steadily, as had been my wont all evening.

Many of the letters contained arguments from Jamaica's notable planters against doing much of what I had instructed be done at the plantation: growing local food and educating the men there, both white and black. And in the margins of many of these, my uncle had written *Marsdale* and circled particular points in the text. From this, I suspected my uncle planned to have quite the debate with me over the practices in question. As these supposedly learned arguments had much to do with damning lesser men for their lack of industry and ambition, and relegating the Negros to a status less than human, my ire rose, and I wished to not only fight my uncle over the matters, but win.

By the time we had determined that my uncle was everything I said he was – and perhaps more or less, depending on one's perception of how men should be treated, traditions upheld, and innovation skeptically queried – we were quite intoxicated, and my sober matelot had located the cache of correspondence we sought under a loose board in the corner.

I cheered heartily when I recognized my father's hand on the top letter of the packet Gaston triumphantly tossed onto the bed next to me. The elation at the discovery quickly turned to anger and dismay when I saw that one of the letters in the pile was addressed to me and another to my sister. As my vision was now blurred with wine and ire, I handed the former to my matelot; and he quickly broke the seal and read it.

"It is in response to the letter you wrote him after your marriage," Gaston said.

I struggled to remember what I had written him at that time. I believed it had been a very concise missive, and essentially only relayed that I had indeed married the bride he had sent.

His face grave, my matelot sat on the bed beside me as he continued reading.

"What?" I prompted.

Gaston shook his head. "He is pleased – or was pleased – that you married her as he instructed; but he admits she might not have been the best choice, and he did not expect you to actually wed her. He hopes for the best, but... alludes to that which we already know: that you might wish to put her out if she proves unsuitable."

"Gods," I spat, this new anger burning through even the wine. "Why did my uncle keep it from me?"

"Perhaps he was waiting for you to return to town," Theodore offered slowly. "Or... he did not wish to hand it to another to be delivered to you."

I picked up a letter addressed to Sarah; it was also still sealed. "He did not know the content," I said. "Or did he?" I began sorting through the rest of the letters. Uncle Cedric had received four missives from my father in the months since his arrival. I read them all and passed them to my compatriots.

I soon realized my uncle had not been hiding these letters from us due to maliciousness – or rather, not due to his. He had surely buried them away beneath the boards in a gesture of fondness, if not love. My father's words to him were not diplomatic, or kind, or even genteel; and I was sure my uncle must have felt the letters addressed to my sister and I contained much the same language. The pages my uncle had received from my father were filled with the words *disappointing* and *regrettable*: I was called a useless libertine, a wastrel, and a fool; Sarah's behavior was likened to that of a wanton trollop; Theodore was referred to as a sodomite-loving ingrate; and Gaston... I shuddered at those words: Shane had never used terms so vile toward my person.

I winced as Gaston and our friends gasped at some the passages. Rucker appeared deeply troubled, but Theodore seemed to find relief in what he read. It was very obvious he had been dismissed due to his apparent tacit approval of my relationship with Gaston, and so he no longer need wonder what he had done wrong.

Cold fear was clawing at my gut and heart. We had worried that Striker might be in danger – a thing that was surely true, judging from my father's kind words regarding him. But nay, Gaston was the one my father undoubtedly most wished to see dead. We had most probably been saved attempts upon his life only because we had been roving or safely tucked away at Negril. Our limited days in Port Royal had surely been a blessing. And this time when we arrived, there was the Marquis. Anyone my father might have employed must now be awaiting new instruction. I did not believe even my father would commission the murder of another nobleman's son; but the arrangement of an accident, or a duel, was another matter entirely.

And even more disturbing was the fact that my father knew a great deal about us. His spies had told him of our home at Negril: he wrote of the shame of the heir to Dorshire squatting like a peasant in a hovel. Someone had relayed to him the purported events on Tortuga, the charges of witchcraft from our sailing the summer before, and even that we had apparently quarreled in Porto Bello. He viewed Gaston's madness as a symptom of the perfidy of sodomy. My moral failings in the matter would have been tolerable if I had been discreet, but he was outraged and appalled I had dragged my title – and thus, through our relationship, his – through the muck and moral mire that was the West Indies.

I was sure he wished me dead, too.

At last all had finished reading. We sat dazed and silent in the aftermath.

I took Gaston's hand and he squeezed it reassuringly. He had become stiller with every page, until his body was quite rigid and his face frozen into a mask of amazement, but now he sighed heavily and gazed upon me with concern. I smiled weakly.

"Your father despises sodomy, sodomites, and all things pertaining to said topic quite passionately," Theodore at last remarked.

"Aye," I said. I thought of the pleasant and diplomatic letters I had received. The only indication I had ever had that my father felt as he did to such degree was his haunting comment on the Christmas Eve I had returned home. When I had asked if he had known all the evil Shane had wreaked upon me, he had admitted, that, yes, he had, and he allowed it because he *thought it might put me off men.*

"He has a number of spies, it would appear, or one who is very close to you and has written him often." Rucker observed.

"Aye," I said. He had informants among the Brethren, or perhaps not. "I will have to reread the letters and consider all he mentions. It could be that he has men in Port Royal who are well-versed in plying the Brethren with rum. By the Gods, I do not wish to consider one of our own working for him directly."

"You might wish to do that very thing," Theodore said sadly.

"I know," I sighed. I stood and collected the pages. I thanked the Gods I was full of wine, else I would surely have stumbled and fallen this night as hard as I had at Vivian's news. I had been viewing my father's motives as incorrectly as I had Shane's.

Gaston was watching me with concern. I shook my head and went in search of Sarah. She had thankfully not retired for the night, nor had any of the others, though it was quite late. They were apparently awaiting news from our search, and to pass the time the Marquis was playing chess with Pete; the Golden One was winning. My descent of the stairs was greeted with eager eyes.

I tossed Sarah her letter. "He had a packet of mail from our father hidden under a floorboard."

She quickly tore into the missive. I sat opposite her, and watched anger tighten her features. All eyes in the atrium shifted back and forth between us – save the gazes of those who had read what I had: they watched Sarah alone.

"He is disappointed in my behavior, both toward Shane and my hasty marriage," she said as she threw the pages down. "He deems it regrettable and unfortunate, and asks that I abandon it. Then he goes on to say that if whatever madness gripped me in England has passed, I should be pleased to hear that, though I have permanently scarred my cousin, he yet lives and should recover. And though he feels we can never be allowed about one another again – a thing he expresses great disappointment in, as it serves to complicate matters concerning *his* households – he wishes for me to return home."

Her gaze met mine. "Will, it was dated in April. What the Devil was our uncle doing holding it?"

"There was one for me as well," I said. "I believe our dear Uncle Cedric wished to protect us. Father's letters to him are not so diplomatic as these sent to us."

"You have read them?" she asked.

Theodore dropped the pile of pages on the table before her. "Much of it is not fit for a lady's eyes."

At that, the three ladies present reached for the letters.

I looked to the gentlemen. "You *are* in danger," I told Striker, and then turned to the Marquis, "and your arrival and claiming of Gaston as your son has probably saved his life."

All appeared stricken by this news. I looked about, and saw Henrietta and Sam waiting near the cookhouse, attentive to any need their masters might have. I saw the shutters to the parlor, and thought Vivian undoubtedly listened from within. I was gripped with the fancy that every shadow held someone lurking, listening, watching. And I had thought our lives complicated enough by our ever seeming to hold the attention of the Gods.

Sixty-Seven

Wherein We Surrender the Field

I went in search of paper and ink. Gaston followed me to Sarah's office.

"I must give Pete the information he requested," I said as I explored the desk.

Gaston wrapped his arms about me as I fumbled at selecting a quill. I knew he sought to comfort me, and though I knew his love to be a balm for all things, it could not remove the sting of this, because I felt nothing I could name so that it might be cured.

"It does not hurt," I murmured, and stroked his arm. "Or perhaps it is more accurate to say it does not hurt at this moment. It is actually something of a relief to have the suspicions I have long held confirmed. And now I feel we are besieged. We have been living in a halcyon world of blissful ignorance and yet we are in mortal danger. I wonder if he thinks killing you will put me off men."

I pulled away from him to sit heavily in the desk chair. He knelt before me, with his elbows upon my knees. His gaze was earnest and his expression thoughtful and concerned. He was my touchstone, my anchor, all I held sacred and holy.

"I must protect you," I said.

He shook his head.

"Non, non," I said quickly. "This battle is not worth your life, or Striker's, or Vivian's, or anyone's. It is for a thing I do not want. Non, worse yet, it has been fought for a thing I might never have. For all I might wish for them to suffer an epiphany such that they are moved to apologize or make amends, or perhaps simply feel in the deepest recesses of their souls that they were wrong, they will not: that day will never come. I doubt even the fires of eternal Hell could burn away their righteousness and ambition. I cannot win. Even if I put both of them in the ground, I cannot win."

Gaston smiled sadly. "Would it not be enough to send them to their graves to spend eternity knowing they had lost?"

"Would flogging your father to death change anything?" I asked.

He gave a rueful shake of his head and sighed. "I feel I have won far more by not killing him."

"I think your father is a thousand times the man mine is," I said.

"We did not think my father would ever do as he has done," he said thoughtfully. "Perhaps yours may one day surprise you."

"If he does, it may be to no avail. You were willing to forgive your father because you felt you had sinned. I do not feel I have ever done anything to garner my damn sire's hatred. Thus, I do not know if I can ever find it in my heart to forgive him." I sighed at the implication of my words. "Of course, that makes me as poor a man as he is, but then I am his son."

"Only in that you will stand by your beliefs to Hell and back," Gaston said with a smile.

"That is true. I wonder if it is a thing of the blood," I said sadly.

Gaston shook his head. "What do you wish to do?"

"Supply Pete with the means to avenge us should it become necessary and... retreat." As I said it, I was gripped by clarity of purpose, much as I had been gripped by clarity of insight regarding Shane: I now saw what I must do quite clearly. "I must renounce. It is the only way to thwart them – the only possible way to remove us from harm's way. The only other is to kill them, but in that they would win in another fashion: I would still never inherit and we would be forced to run from the authorities, a thing which will undoubtedly be quite difficult with a cart full of wives and babies. Unless we retreated to France and that..."

He shook his head. "I am sorry I have removed that option... for now."

"Non, non, I meant no recrimination by it," I said quickly.

He sighed. "I was thinking their deaths could appear accidental, a fire perhaps, but then I realized that would mean you would inherit and..."

I grinned and kissed his forehead. "We can no more live in England than in France. And I do not wish to be the Earl of Dorshire. Truly, no matter what good I might do with it, I feel I would have to... be chained in a seat in the cave again in order to accomplish it. I will not do that. I would rather stand in the light, with you."

He gazed upon me with great regard. "That is what you have always said. I still find wonder in it. Thank you."

"You are most welcome, but as I once noted, I am really quite self-serving in the matter."

He chuckled. "So you will renounce."

"Oui. I will surrender the field. Sadly, it will not end Sarah's and Striker's battle with him, but it may well save us, because..." I sighed, "as good as we are, we cannot protect against everything. We already lead perilous lives."

"They will be far less perilous now that we will no longer rove," he said.

"Thank the Gods for that."

We gathered paper, ink, and quills. As we walked out of the office, my gaze fell upon the parlor door. With a sigh, I pointed, and handed Gaston my portion of our writing supplies. He nodded and went to join the others, and I slipped into Vivian's cave.

She was standing at the end of her chain, as close to the shutters leading to the atrium as she could manage. She started at my entrance, and appeared quite guilty.

I smiled. "As you have heard, we have discovered much of my father's feelings on... several matters."

She nodded soberly. "They have been reading parts of the letters aloud."

"I am going to renounce my title," I said quietly. "You will no longer be Lady Marsdale."

She took a deep breath and nodded. "Will I continue to be Mistress John Williams?"

"Aye," I said.

"Then I am fine with that," she said. "I feel it is for the best," she added quietly, "for all of us."

"I thought you might," I said with a sigh of relief, "but I also thought I should tell you of my decision before announcing it to the world."

"Thank you for that courtesy."

I left her, and returned to the circle of light and family in the middle of the atrium. The Marquis sat at one table, with deep furrows upon his brow and his head in his hands as Dupree read a letter to him. Sarah was likewise quietly reading another to Striker and Pete: they all appeared quite angry. Christine and Agnes were huddled over another missive, both looking quite confounded. Rucker and Theodore were sharing more wine. I went to sit between them and Gaston, and snatched the bottle when it came near. At that, Theodore waved for Henrietta and requested another.

I selected a quill and sheet of paper and wrote the pertinent information – including a rough map – Pete would need to locate my father. I passed it to him when I finished. "My father is the Earl of Dorshire. That alone should allow for you to locate him, but he either resides at the address I have given in London, or at the family estate of Rolland Hall."

Pete nodded thoughtfully, and began to slowly read the names with Sarah's assistance.

"I would like a copy of that information as well," the Marquis said. "I wish to write your father."

"Please do," I said, and proceeded to make another copy.

Once that was completed, I composed the following letter:

> Dorshire,
>
> I have learned that you have no need for me to inform you of the milestones of my life, or even to comment on the scenery I might pass. So I will not waste ink or paper in relating things that others will tell you, and I will use this space to relate things they cannot.
>
> I have stolen and read the letters you sent my uncle: without his consent. I now believe you are a threat to my life and to all I hold dear – and all for a thing I do not wish to own. Please rest assured that I despise you and all you represent as much if not more than you despise me. I wish to have nothing further to do with you in this life or the hereafter. I would gladly consign you to the bowels of Hell if it were in my power to do so.
>
> That being said, I hereby renounce all claim to the title of Viscount of Marsdale, and all claim to inherit the title of the Earl of Dorshire, and any monies, privileges, or other properties associated with said titles. Furthermore, I abandon all claim to any money I might have been due to inherit from the family estate separate the title, and any and all other property.
>
> I doubt this letter will suffice to dispatch the matter legally, so I will pursue having a formal notice prepared and witnessed and sent to the House of Lords.
>
> Please adopt Shane and name him your heir with my blessing. I cannot think of two people more deserving of one another.
>
> The Get of Your Loins,
> Will

Gaston chuckled quietly as he read it. When he finished, I passed it to Theodore, who remarked, "As your barrister, it is my duty to inform you that you are drunk."

"Is it poorly written?" I asked.

Theodore shook his head and laughed.

"Is it poorly done?" I asked.

He sobered and shook his head sadly. "Nay."

"What?" Sarah asked.

I passed it to her and she began to read it quietly to Striker and Pete.

"Everyone might as well hear it," I said.

And so she read loudly enough for all to hear, with Dupree translating for the Marquis. There were appreciative chuckles all about as she finished.

"If you send something to the House of Lords, he will hate you all the more," Sarah said as she returned the letter. "But if I could, I would do the same. Unfortunately, I am his daughter, not his heir."

I sighed. "Perhaps my making much ado of the matter will place him in a position from which he dare not strike at you. And, though he likely wishes to harm Striker, he does not wish you dead, merely his dutiful daughter again."

"I would rather be dead," she said.

I dusted the now-dry page and folded it carefully. "I must step aside, or they will kill me."

"You actually believe that?" Christine asked. "Aye, he hates what he feels you have become, but surely..."

I met her gaze levelly. "Did you not read what he wrote? I am a thorn in his side, an embarrassment, a mark of shame. This is a man who allowed his godson to beat and rape me repeatedly under his roof in the hopes that such abuse would put me off men. He said as much to my face, when I returned after running from him and my cousin for ten years."

Christine regarded me daftly, as if my words were somehow beyond her comprehension. Agnes' mouth fell open, and she quickly threw her hand over it. Dupree had gasped when I spoke, and the Marquis did the same when it was translated. The rest knew the truth of it already, and they regarded the table gravely, as if mourning someone who had passed. Gaston's arm stole about my shoulder, and he kissed me lightly on the cheek.

I could look at them no more. I set about dripping wax to form the seal, which I supposed would be my thumb, as with this letter I should no longer use the Marsdale crest. The Marquis' signet ring intruded into my watery vision. It was not on his hand. I looked up and found him regarding me with great compassion.

"I will write him, but this will give him a thing to think about," he said.

"Thank you." I took his ring and used it to seal the letter.

He held my hand when I returned the ring. "I will not forsake either of you," he said gravely.

My heart ached and I smiled weakly. "That means more to me than I can express."

Gaston did find a way to express it: he embraced his father and they held one another tightly for a time.

I handed Theodore the letter. "I believe the Marquis wishes to write him as well. They should go together."

Theodore nodded thoughtfully, and considered the paper in his hand. "Do you wish to pursue the formal renouncement and send it at the same time?"

"Aye, can you draw one up and arrange for suitable witnesses?"

"Of course," he said. "Perhaps the governor."

"Aye, he would do nicely." I stood. "Well then, we have much to do on the morrow." I looked to Sarah. "Perhaps you should write him as well."

"And what should I say?" she asked sadly.

"The truth," I sighed. "What good will lies do us now?"

"TruthAn'LeadAn'Steel," Pete said thoughtfully. His mien was one of contemplation and ancient wisdom.

My spirits were lifted: I doubted my father could defeat Pete at chess, either – once someone taught the Golden One the rules of this game.

"Do you feel I should do as I plan?" I asked him.

Pete regarded me with a furrowed brow. "DoYaNa'Want'EmDead?"

"Aye, I want them dead, but I wish to live a long and happy life with Gaston and any children he might choose to collect," I said. "I feel murdering them would not lead to that."

He nodded sagely. "Aye. YaBeRight. MustBePlannedCareful. Now. ThisBeAGoodFeint." He pointed at the letter Theodore held. "Puts'EmInCheck. Makes'EmAngry. Keeps'EmOffTheirBalance. Gives'EmSomeGround. IfTheyRun, SoBeIt. IfTheyCharge." His lips quirked in a grim smile. "WeMustBeReadyFor'Em. I'llThinkOnIt. Winnin'sGonnaBeALongGame."

"Thank the Gods you are on our side," I told Pete, and then turned to Sarah. "You should consult him before you write."

"I hear that," she said with a proud smile.

"I concur," the Marquis said with an appraising look at Pete.

Dupree was still whispering in his master's ear with a perplexed grimace, and I knew Pete's enunciation had confounded him once again; but apparently not so that the Marquis misunderstood the Golden One's wisdom or intent.

Christine stood abruptly and left the table. Agnes glared after, and then in a move just as sudden, stood to reach the bottle Rucker and Theodore were sharing and capture it for her own. She sat and took a long pull.

"You should be careful of that, young lady," Rucker chided. "It will make you stupid."

"I am already stupid," Agnes muttered bitterly.

I walked to stand behind her and leaned over to whisper, "You are not stupid for loving anyone, even if they are too stupid to return it."

"Thank you," she whispered.

As he was closest to her, and looked quite sad and lost in his own thoughts, I clapped Striker's shoulder and whispered to him. "I am still proud to call you brother, but I am damn sorry you are embroiled in this."

He smiled, and looked to Sarah and Pete, who were speaking quietly next to him. "It is worth it." He looked up at me. "How are you?"

"Somewhat drunk," I said, and gestured with the bottle I still held. "But, sadly, that will pass." I looked to Gaston, who was standing at my side. "But we will endure and conquer."

"But first we will sleep," Gaston said, and led me to the stable.

He made me remove my coat and boots before allowing me to sink to the straw and cuddle puppies. I was not so drunk that I could not see his mien was somber and withdrawn, and very much the physician.

"I will be well," I assured him, as he came to sit next to me after removing most of his clothing. "How are you?"

"The Horse wants them dead," he said sadly.

"Mine wishes to run to the farthest reaches of the world," I said, and felt melancholy grip me in echo of his sad tone.

"I must protect you," he whispered, and kissed my temple.

Like a retreating tide, the wine that had fortified me pulled away and sucked my bravado with it: I cried in his arms like a babe.

Sometime later, he pushed all the puppies into a pile next to their mother and led me to bed. I fingered the blanket lying there, the one I had been covered by when Agnes roused me this morning.

"It has been a very long day," I remarked. "Did Sir Christopher and the governor truly arrive this morning?"

He nodded, and urged me to shed my shirt and breeches, which I did.

"It feels as if days have passed," I sighed as I lay down.

"Oui," he sighed in echo, and joined me on the hammock.

He kissed me lightly on the lips, and then his mouth trailed down my neck and chest. I was quickly forced to put a stop to it with deep regret.

"I would not deny you anything, my love," I whispered, "but I am quite tender and you have not shaved. Neither have I, but..."

He shook his head and pressed fingers to my lips. I kissed them; and with a rueful smile, he moved to lie beside me.

"I feel no need this night," he said. "I merely wished to comfort you."

"Hold me, then."

He complied, and I curled against him and let exhaustion claim me.

I woke alone to rain beating on the roof, and an aching and dazed head and dry mouth. Thankfully, today there was no rapping at the door or urgent whispering of my name. I moved enough to find the pot and water, and then returned to the hammock to lie like I sometimes had as a boy, with the blanket wrapped about me and pulled up around my ears to thwart the chill of the world.

I dozed. I felt Gaston's weight on the hammock before I had any other awareness of his entry. He was smiling at me with amusement, as if he had been calling my name and I had not answered. He had shaved. He wore a paint-splattered kerchief and tunic. His kiss warmed me in all the ways a blanket could not, yet my manhood did not stir so much as it sighed. We curled together, and he sighed with either relief or contentment.

With him beside me and not before me, I saw my sea chests stacked just inside the doorway. They still stank of smoke, and Bella was eying them with annoyance.

"What have I missed?" I asked.

"We will be staying here until we return to Negril," Gaston said. "So Pete and I brought our things down."

I nodded. "One of the wives will have our room, and the other will have the guest room? And we shall stay in the stable like good studs?" I chuckled.

He did not find amusement in it. "Oui: Christine will have what was our room. I would have put Vivian in it, but Striker..." He trailed off with a disgruntled snort.

"What?" I turned enough to see his face, and found him more troubled than angry.

"Striker suggested that we... I might be more comfortable to ensconce the one who would be fucked farther from my father's room."

"Well..." I said with a small smile.

"Oui, he is correct," Gaston said. "But..."

"You have not married her yet," I said kindly.

He sighed, and there was resolve in his eyes. "Her things arrived this morning. We put them in our room – her room. She slept there last night without them. Agnes and she have quarreled." He shrugged.

"Have you seen to Vivian, or visited Jamaica?" I asked to distract him.

He gave a rueful smile. "Vivian is well. I have not dared go to see the baby: Theodore slept in Sarah's office last night."

"It is good he is at heart a sober man," I said with a grin. "Because he drinks with relish."

Gaston chuckled and kissed my nose. "As do you."

"I am sorry..."

He kissed my lips. "Non."

I caressed his smooth cheek.

He grinned and kissed my chest. "Better?"

"Oui," I breathed.

He smiled, and then guilt suffused him. I laid my hands aside his face and held his eyes to mine.

He sighed. "I fear we will need that whore."

I nodded. "Perhaps we can ask Theodore if he knows of some lady or widow who entertains gentlemen discreetly."

"That would be better," he said with relief and some thought. "I cannot see... The brothel whores disgust me."

"I know. I have always thought it an irony that many men will tell you that a true man who favors women can crow at the sight of any woman, but I think rising for women of that ilk is not showing an appreciation for women, so much as it is simply affirming one is not dead: if such can give a man rise, he might as well fuck a sheep; they seem far cleaner."

He nodded with a wry smile, and then frowned. "The thought of mingling my jism with another man's is… disturbing. And that disquiet does not rise from jealousy."

"Would you mingle yours with mine?" I teased.

"That is different," he said quickly. "You are mine and…" He sighed. "I cannot explain it."

"We mingle our fluids all the time," I said.

"Oui, because…" He regarded me seriously. "It is love. If you and I were to fuck the same woman it would be acceptable; but if it is not you, I wish her to be clean and… I would rather she be virginal."

"You need not explain," I said. "It is a thing of intimacy, and I am quite pleased you wish to share that with no one else: that you hold it in such regard."

"I do," he said earnestly. "You are the only man my Horse ever wishes to be intimate with."

"Thank the Gods," I teased.

He smiled at last.

With all the talk of jism and intimacy, my cock had at last stirred, despite my aching head and empty stomach. I ran my hand down his chest and belly to find his member flaccid, but he held my hand there and covered my mouth before I could pull away with regret. His hand was soon upon my organ, and shortly after that he was within me, and we laid siege to Heaven with slow deliberation. When the holy light at last broke upon me, I finally felt I was ready to rise and meet the day.

"I so needed that," I murmured as I crawled from beneath him and out of the hammock.

He lay there, sated, and smiled up at me happily. "As did I."

I considered my clothes. It was still raining. I tried to recall if anyone in the house was not part of some faction that considered my bruises to result from either my madness or Gaston's. I thought it likely Christine and Agnes were innocent of speculation, and perhaps Rucker. Would they notice or care if I did not choose to hide behind finery on this rainy day? I decided I did not care.

"I will dress when and if we go to the church this day," I told Gaston as I stood in the stable doorway and surveyed the rain-soaked limestone of the empty atrium.

He began to laugh. "Else you will strut about naked?"

"Aye, and proudly," I teased, and located a pair of breeches and a tunic. The canvas was still rough upon my tender chest, but the thought of being swathed in damp linen the entire day made me find it preferable.

"So, what shall we do?" I asked. "What need we do? How late in the day is it?"

"Past midday. The rooms are clean and ready. Father has moved upstairs. I asked Vivian if she wished to move to the guest room, and she said non." He shrugged. "Christine has asked if she should dress for church. We should possibly brave the Theodores'."

I smiled at his evasion. "What did you tell Christine?"

He took a deep breath and regarded the ceiling. "That I would think on it, and see how you were feeling."

"How do I feel?" I asked with a grin.

"You feel it is entirely too much effort this day," he said without emotion.

I chuckled heartily. "And I am hungry."

He dressed, and we scurried through the rain to the cookhouse. Our servants were not there, but we found dried meat and some apples, and my stomach felt they would suffice.

We crossed to the relative dryness beneath the balcony and went to the parlor. Vivian seemed pleased to see us. I was in fine spirits, and found amusement in surprising her, by dropping to kneel on the floor in front of the settee where she sat and resting my elbows upon her knees.

"I want you to move upstairs," I said.

She rolled her eyes, but sobered to contemplate me. "Will it be mine alone?"

I nodded.

"With the baby," Gaston added.

I shrugged. "Yours and Jamaica's," I amended.

She grimaced at that. "But..."

"You will learn," I said firmly with a smile. "Perhaps you should accompany us today to the Theodores'."

"Oh, Lord," she sighed. "It is raining, and... I should move upstairs."

"I do not see where any of those issues are mutually exclusive," I said with a grin. "We will move you now."

"Will you move the chain?" she said dryly.

I sighed as I looked to the bolt we had put in the wall. "Do you feel it is necessary?"

She froze, fear deep in her eyes as they peered into mine, and then she looked away with guilt and pink cheeks. "Aye," she breathed.

My humor fled in the face of compassion. "Do you still crave it?"

She nodded. "I think about it all the time," she whispered.

I looked about the room. "Aye, well, you have little else to do. That is why you should tend your own child, perhaps. It will give you something to do and focus your thoughts."

"I am afraid I will do something stupid," she said.

I was too, and in the face of that, my first thought was flippant: *And then Gaston would strangle you.* But I held my tongue and looked to him instead, to see who he agreed with.

He was regarding her with compassion, and at my gaze he sighed and rolled his eyes, and came to sit beside her on the settee.

"Babies are somewhat forgiving," he said kindly. "They must be, because many of us live and many of our mothers were fools."

"I do not wish to be a fool," she said seriously.

"Then you must learn," he said.

She nodded tightly.

We released her, and I went to borrow a cloak and pattens from one of the women. Sarah was in her office busily writing at her desk, and as she was so huge with child that rising from a chair presented difficulty, I decided to leave her well enough alone. Even over the rain, I could hear Henrietta chatting with Christine in the doorway of what had been our room. I did not wish to speak to the bride, and thus appear healthy and capable of attending church. Thus I stealthily went in search of Agnes. The girl greeted the knock on her door with hopeful teary eyes, and seemed disappointed when she beheld me.

"We need to borrow a rain cloak and pattens for Vivian." I smiled kindly. "And Gaston said you quarreled with Christine."

She grabbed my arm and towed me inside. "She is such a bitch!" she spat. "I am not staring at her every moment, and I did not touch her in the night. I lie awake all night so that I do not. We have not been friends since I told her. I should not have told her. Now all that I do is suspect."

I pulled the girl to me and embraced her until she ceased to struggle and began to cry: all the while murmuring reassuring things.

"I understand your pain," I said when the worst of it had passed.

"Is it ever this way?" she asked.

I sighed. "If the one you favor does not favor you, aye; even if they do not share your sex, but especially if they do."

"It is so unfair."

"Aye, it is," I said. "I feel Christine is a very confused girl on many fronts."

"She attests I am the one confused," Agnes said bitterly, her ire returning. "She says I cannot possibly know I favor women, as I have never been with a man."

I grinned. "That is a commonly held sentiment, and it is utter shit."

She gave a heavy sigh and spoke with more sadness than anger. "We were so close... before. She was so kind to me. We did everything together, and I dared not tell her and... And then I did when I thought she would marry you."

"My dear," I said quietly, "you would have been miserable not telling her."

She nodded.

"Take comfort in that it is unlikely it will go as poorly as it can between boys," I said.

She frowned and turned to look at me. "Is that what happened with... your cousin?" she asked with trepidation.

I nodded. "For the most part, but, Shane favors men as much as I. We... actually were lovers for a time, and then... my father poisoned him against me." I realized that was true: I had thought it to be the other boys we had associated with; but nay, it must have been my father. "Shane became obsessed that what we did was wrong, yet he would not stop doing it, and it caused great turmoil in his soul and he turned that anger to me. He blamed me for causing his lust. So he would drink until he could battle it no more and then he would come for me."

Tears welled anew in her eyes, and she came to embrace me.

I sighed and held her, as it seemed – instances of bravado aside – I could still not speak of the matter without threatening to moisten my cheeks. And despite my new perspective toward Shane's ambitions, and my protestations that what had passed between us was only a divertissement to him, I could not hide from the old knowledge that he had been tormented by his change of heart: tormented such that he chose to torture me to ease his own suffering. My father had wounded both of us.

"And now you have Gaston," Agnes was saying as she released me.

"Aye, and I thank the Gods daily for that."

She awarded me a perplexed frown. "You always say things like that, as if you are a pagan or a heretic."

"I am very likely both." I grinned. "I have long been enamored of the Greek and Roman view of the Gods as opposed the Christian one. I cannot say I believe in them as some men believe in God or Christ, but I feel there are beneficent entities watching over us."

"Many call those angels and saints," she said without challenge.

"Aye, I prefer to think of them as the Gods of old."

She smiled. "Like Pallas Athena, or Jupiter, or Apollo."

I nodded. "Just so. Have you read Hesiod or Ovid?"

"Nay," she sighed.

"Speak to Mister Rucker and see if he can procure copies."

This brightened her mood. "Aye, I will."

She did indeed have an oilcloth cloak and pattens and was happy to lend them to me. I returned downstairs and found Vivian and Gaston waiting impatiently. My matelot raised an eyebrow as I approached.

"We had to discuss why she quarreled with your bride," I told him in French as Vivian donned the pattens.

His frown slipped away and he nodded with understanding. "Why?"

I gave him a brief account of Agnes' complaints. He sighed when I finished, and Vivian was glaring at us.

"If I am to live with you two," she said as she swirled the cape over her shoulders. "Promise me you will not ever be yammering on in French."

We headed into the mud filled street, and I wished I had pattens as my bare feet sank in ooze to my ankles. "I will promise nothing of the sort," I said.

"Then I will be forced to learn French," she said over her shoulder. Her tone was as haughty as it had been when she drank, but I sensed amusement under her words.

Gaston's grimace was quite sincere, though.

"We must keep some things private between us," I teased her.

She snorted. "You keep a great deal private between you already. And Jamaica will speak English."

My matelot was actually becoming angry.

I waved him off. "Lady…you are in no position to make such a

demand. The child will be well-educated and speak both languages."
I wondered how long it would take me to relinquish calling her Lady Marsdale, much less anyone else.

She rolled her eyes and paused to award me a flippant curtsey. I chuckled, and Gaston sighed with annoyance.

We went to the Theodores' yard and knocked on the back door. Hannah frowned at us with surprise when she opened it. "My Lords, Lady," she said quickly, and then looked down at our muddy feet and sniffed.

"There is only one Lord among us now," I told her as she produced a bucket for Gaston and me to rinse our feet. I pointed at my matelot.

She gave us a perplexed frown that seemed to question why we would bother her about such a distinction rather than why the distinction need be made. Then she knelt and assisted Vivian in removing her pattens.

"This is Hannah," I told Vivian, as I doubted they had ever met.

Hannah nodded respectfully and Vivian nodded tightly and seemed to relax, until Rachel stepped onto the back portico. Then my wife tensed again, though her eyes were hungry upon the baby Mistress Theodore held.

"Lord Montren, Mister and Mistress Williams," Rachel said smoothly.

I smiled. "I take it your husband arrived home safely."

She snorted. "No thanks to you." She handed Jamaica to Gaston. "And I would speak to you of that."

Gaston gave me a sympathetic look that still seemed to say that it was better me than him.

I followed Rachel into Theodore's office.

"He's sleeping," she said quietly.

"I am sorry we did not escort him home last night," I said quickly. "And I am sorry... my business gives him cause to drink on occasion."

He had obviously told her I had renounced, but I could not be sure what else he shared with her. Thankfully, she answered that for me.

"It was not you that gave him cause to drink," she said, "but your father."

"Aye," I said with a smile. "He has that effect on me, as well. Many people, I would imagine."

She nodded, and there was compassion in her gaze. "That is not..." She sighed and bit her lip. "I would ask you a thing a wife should not," she said at last.

"I will not judge you for it, and I will answer if I can," I said seriously.

"Thank you. How is he when he drinks? He does not drink about me, and... Though we have been married several years now, it has not been as long as a wife needs to truly know a man's habits – the ones he practices when he is not about his wife."

I smiled. "Lady, in my experience, your husband drinks either when he is distraught or to enjoy the company of his fellows. He is not a poorly behaved drunk: he does not become belligerent. He is either prone to melancholy or ebullience depending on the circumstances that set him upon the bottle. I have seen him sing and dance a fine jig while intoxicated. He does not gamble or seek to consort with women in that state." I grinned. "Or men, either."

She sighed with relief and then regarded me quizzically. "He dances?"

"Aye, he once impressed Pete with his prowess. We were quite surprised."

She chuckled. "I would pay to see that."

"As I can no longer expect an inheritance, I might be willing to make such arrangements."

This gave her even more amusement.

"Truly, you should come with him when he visits," I added seriously.

She shook her head. "Nay, a man does need time with other men. And... In truth I would rather it be with you and yours: when he has gone off to cavort with planters, he has returned reeking of perfume. I trust him with my soul, but it bothers me that he should be forced to even know of the trollops the fine gentlemen of Jamaica consort with."

I grinned in agreement. Her words piqued my interest and reminded me of what I needed to speak with Theodore about: I could not see him or other gentlemen visiting the brothels on Thames and Lime.

"So is she here to learn to be a mother?" Rachel asked, and jerked her head toward the back room and Vivian.

"Aye, she is sober now; and contrite concerning her past deeds; and we will watch her closely to see that she does not stray. However, I do not feel she is quite ready to take the child home as of yet."

"She best not be," Rachel said archly. "I will judge when that will happen."

"Be kind," I said quickly, and Rachel paused in leaving the room to regard me sharply. "She is... She drank because she feels she is a poor person. She has ever been chastised for her failings and..."

Rachel nodded, and I saw compassion in her eyes again.

"You were wonderful with her at the church," I said.

She frowned. "Do you think I would be mean?"

"Mistress Theodore, you have given Gaston and me a good start on occasion, and there is no one we would less like to be scolded by."

This set her chuckling again. "I did not think I had such power."

"Lady," I teased, "you are one of only two women that Pete will not cross."

As her laughter retreated up the hall, I heard a chuckle. I stuck my head through the doorway at the back of the room and spied Theodore lurking in the shadows of the stairs. He appeared bleary-eyed and tired yet, but awake and in good spirits.

"I heard voices," he said.

"How much did you hear?" I asked.

"How much should I have heard?" he queried.

I considered that, and smiled and joined him on the steps with my voice low. "Your wife loves you a great deal, but she was curious as to how you comported yourself while intoxicated."

"Oh..." he said with a sage nod and then a smile. "And you told her."

"You dance a fine jig."

He grimaced.

"She said she would pay to see that and we might make arrangements later," I teased. "She also said she would rather you cavort with us than your other clients, as you on occasion returned from those outings reeking of perfume."

He grimaced with renewed vigor. "Will, I never..."

"Of course not: she does think so, either. However, it does bring me to a question I wish to put to you."

"What?" he asked with a very-arched eyebrow.

I sighed. "Gaston wishes to... learn of women... with me as his guide, prior to his having to consummate a marriage. The whores we have seen here do not intrigue us. Would you, in your conversations with the fine gentlemen of Jamaica, happen to have heard where finer quality whores might be found?"

He sighed, and stood to lead me back into his office. "I have... *heard*... of two options. The first is Widow Marsh. She is a handsome woman of middle years with three lovely daughters. They live on her deceased husband's plantation outside of Spanish Town. In their loneliness they have been known to entertain gentlemen at their house. They will serve a fine meal, and one of the girls has a fine voice and another plays a harp. They are not whores per se, but they enjoy the patronage of several of Jamaica's finer citizens, such that the plantation need not plant or harvest anything and they wear the finest gowns from London and the finest perfumes..." He nodded obliquely and flushed.

"Can arrangements be made of a more discreet nature, without the fine meal and harp playing?" I asked.

He shrugged. "Unfortunately, I doubt it. I feel the girls are truly her daughters, and she is quite watchful of them; and she is also interested in maintaining a certain reputation."

"Well, that will not do," I sighed. "I cannot see Gaston squirming through a recital."

"Neither can I; which brings us to Mistress Garret," he said with a shrug. "She resides alone in a small house here in town. She takes in sewing from the milliner, grows herbs for the apothecary, provides certain services to the women of Port Royal, and other services to discreet gentlemen."

"What services does she provide the women?" I asked with amusement.

"She is something of a midwife and apothecary for women's matters of health." He sighed heavily. "She knows which powders can lead to a miscarriage, or the ones that supposedly can engender love."

"Oh," I said as understanding dawned.

"If she is lucky she will not end her days on a stake and pyre," he said with a trace of sadness. "I have warned her that she treads on dangerous ground, but she feels it is some obligation she must uphold."

"Do people call her a witch?" I asked. "And you have warned her?"

"Some do call her that," he sighed. "And aye, on occasion, when I found the needs of the flesh quite gripping, we shared more than a passing acquaintance before my marriage."

"Then I take it she comes with your recommendation," I teased.

He grimaced. "Aye... and nay. She is... older. She is a handsome enough woman, but no beauty." He winced. "Well, let us say that I am sure there was much to commend her in the bloom of youth; and surely no one would now call her decrepit, but she is not a young nubile thing like you would find at Widow Marsh's. She finds pleasure in her work, and she is quite capable of providing pleasure. She should be capable of instructing a man in the matter."

I suppressed a sigh: I did not wish for her to instruct him alone. I nodded as I considered what he had not said. "Does she present herself like a doxy? Does she seek to cuddle any man in reach? Does she smell of other men?"

"Nay, nay," he said quickly. "She is quite forthright, and presents herself more like... a woman who has seen her share of the world. And she is clean and keeps a tidy home."

"Why did you not marry her?" I teased.

He snorted. "She refused."

I was surprised, and shook my head. "Theodore, if you would rather we..."

"Nay, nay," he said with a dismissive wave. "It is her business – quite literally. I was... lonely when I attempted to court her. It was the foolishness of a man who felt he might never return to civilized society. She saw it with a very clear eye, and told me not to return. Truly, I thank her for that to this day."

He sat at his desk and produced paper and quill and proceeded to sketch a crude map showing the way to her home through a back alley. Once it was dusted and folded, we went to join the others.

Theodore paused with surprise when we entered the back room and found Vivian actually nursing Jamaica. I smiled at the sight: mother and babe both appeared quite content; and Gaston was looking on with relief. Despite my father, I felt buoyed by hope that we might attain that which we sought; and that what we sought would indeed be a pleasant way of living – the Gods willing, of course.

Sixty-Eight

Wherein We Learn of Women

An hour or so later, we slogged home in quiet contentment. Vivian seemed more at ease with the baby, and Rachel seemed pleased with my wife's progress. Gaston was relaxed. I had even managed to forget the other matters confronting us for a time – until we neared the house, and it all came rushing back to me like a wave on the beach.

"Let us move you upstairs," I told Vivian as she shed her wet and muddy cloak and pattens in the foyer.

She sighed, but Gaston nodded his agreement.

"I will find tools," he said, and slipped away across the rain-soaked atrium.

Vivian stood still and listened to someone walk across the balcony overhead. "So I will be in the room next to… his bride."

I nodded. "And next to the Marquis."

"That I will not mind, but… Does she know I must be chained?" she asked quickly.

"I would think so; unless someone failed to mention it these last days." I sighed. "And, with all that has occurred, that could very well be the case."

"I suppose there is no helping it," she said quietly, and slipped into the parlor.

I followed her. "We can disguise hauling it up there and attaching it."

She nodded and sagged onto the settee. "Thank you. I am sure she will hear it, though, as I walk about."

"We could bar the windows and door," I said lightly.

She smiled grimly. "And that would be less obvious? It is no matter. It is what I deserve."

"What?" I asked. "You know damn well we do not do this as punishment. And it is your decision. You are the one who feels you cannot trust yourself."

"I deserve the shame," she said so quietly I had to puzzle through what I thought I heard.

Gaston returned and I pulled him outside to the foyer. "Let us test her," I said. "We cannot keep her chained forever, and she is greatly ashamed of it and rightly so... But still... I do not wish for Christine to be crowing over the matter."

He frowned, but finally shrugged. "And if she drinks?"

I shrugged. "Then we will have to keep our wine and rum in a locked chest under our hammock at Negril."

He sighed.

I returned to Vivian. "We will forego the chain. Either you truly wish to reform, or you do not. If you feel the need to seek alcohol such that you are willing to forego your freedom and your child, then I do not think chaining you will truly rectify the matter. It is merely a temporary stay of an inevitable disaster. You must choose this course by your own will."

"I am too weak," she said sadly.

"Nay," I said. "I feel you are far stronger than you have allowed yourself to imagine. And my dear, would it not be better to give yourself less to hide from the world rather than more?"

She nodded slowly, but there was much doubt in her eyes, and I thought she might chew a hole through her lip as we gathered her few belongings and escorted her upstairs.

Christine stepped into the doorway of her own room as we opened the doors to Vivian's. She glanced at my wife with open curiosity. Years of experience in dealing with jealous women prompted me to push Vivian inside the room before their eyes could meet. Thus Vivian was spared the pitying glance Christine awarded me.

"Will we be going to the church this evening, my Lord?" Christine asked Gaston in French as I followed Vivian into the room.

"Non," he said quickly, and walked toward her and out of my hearing.

I closed the door, and Vivian dropped her armful of belongings on the bed.

"Why is he marrying her?" she whispered. "To appease his father? Have you both not seen where that will lead?"

I chuckled. "Aye, you have proven to be quite charming."

She whirled, her eyes hard as if I was teasing; but at seeing my expression, hers softened and she spoke softly. "So have you."

That thing I did not wish to see in her eyes was there again: the first glimmer of infatuation, or perhaps love.

"Should I send Henrietta up?" I asked quickly.

She looked away just as quickly and shrugged. "I suppose."

"You will be fine here," I said. "If you should need us, we will be in the stable."

She turned back to me with an eyebrow raised.

"That is where we have strung our hammock since the fire," I said.

"You could move to the parlor," she said.

"Nay, we actually prefer the stable. That is where the puppies are."

She waved me away.

I found Gaston waiting for me at the stairs. He appeared glum, and led me wordlessly to the stable. As we neared our sanctuary, Henrietta peered from the cookhouse and announced that dinner would be served in the dining room. I asked her to attend to her mistress when she could, and to take her a plate of whatever we were to dine on. Then I asked for kettle of hot water.

"I must shave before dinner," I said when we were at last alone and Gaston was eying the kettle curiously.

He gazed upon me with speculation as he sank to the straw with the puppies; my words apparently burned away his dour mood. "Did you have something in mind that will require it?"

I grinned, and tossed him the folded map Theodore had drawn. "It seems there is a Mistress Garret, who performs a variety of services, including on occasion entertaining gentlemen. Theodore was once her client."

My matelot regarded the map dubiously, showing less interest in the activities it might suggest than in whatever he had first thought my intent to shave might entail. "What did he say of her?"

I relayed all Theodore had said while I shaved. Gaston, with some reluctance, joined me at the bowl and glass and removed the dusting of rust from his jaw.

"So she might well be a witch," he said as we dressed in our finery.

"I doubt she consorts with the Devil," I said. "Her knowledge of herbs might be of interest, though."

He nodded. "She might be interesting to meet." He sounded and looked as distant as a ship in fog.

I pushed him back onto the hammock and dropped to my knees before him. He gasped lightly when I pressed my lips to his quiescent member.

"You need not," he said and put his hand to my head to push me away.

I got my teeth on either side of his cock and worried it through the fabric.

"Please," he whispered with a weary resolution that stood in complete juxtaposition to anything resembling passion; yet he flopped back onto the hammock in surrender to my intent. I unfastened his breeches and found his cock far more enthusiastic than he appeared to be. In truth, his manhood and I made short work of the endeavor.

I crawled astride him to peer down at his closed eyes and somber face. If I had not just tasted his pleasure I would have thought him beyond it.

"My love?" I whispered.

He smiled sadly and opened his eyes to regard me with great love. "Thank you."

"We need not go," I said.

"That is the thing of it: we need not do anything, but we must," he said earnestly.

I could not gainsay that, so I held him until Sam knocked to summon us to dinner. With mutual sighs, we stood and fixed our clothing.

"We will meet her, and if for any reason you find her distasteful or unsatisfactory, we will leave," I assured him. "And she might not be willing to receive us this night, anyway."

"She will most likely be indisposed," Gaston said.

"Our luck being what it is," I agreed.

All members of the household were present for dinner: save Vivian, and the most notable exception of Pete and Striker. I raised an eyebrow at my sister as Gaston and I seated ourselves at the table.

"They are out in the taverns collecting gossip," she said, with a slight frown that either indicated her concern over the wisdom of their endeavor, or her misgivings as to why the activity should be necessary.

"They are well liked and better suited to do so than Gaston and I."

She nodded. "In addition to our larger concerns," she sighed, "Striker wishes to discover if anyone has sighted the *Queen*."

"What is the date?" I asked.

She smiled and shook her head admonishingly. "It is the fifth of December, the year of our Lord, one thousand six hundred and sixty-eight."

I snorted at her inclusion of the year. As I turned to allow Sam to ladle soup into my dish, I saw the Marquis and Dupree displaying perplexed frowns. I did not think it would be over the difference between the Julian and Gregorian calendars – as Gaston was often prone to complain about – and so I gave Dupree an inquiring glance.

"The *Queen*, my... sir?" he asked.

I smiled. "The *Virgin Queen* is the name of our ship."

He seemed to find relief in that; and the Marquis amusement in it once it was translated.

"My ship will return soon," the Marquis said thoughtfully.

Gaston nodded glumly, and I caught his glance at Christine.

"Must you sail as soon as she arrives?" I asked.

He shook his head. "When will your fellows sail?"

I looked to Sarah.

"If they sail," she said in French. "The admiral wishes to rendezvous at Île de Vache at year end, but so many are planters now, with cane harvesting to oversee, it is not known if he will manage to collect the number he seeks until February. And regardless, my husband cannot sail until our ship returns, and did not intend to until I have birthed – though the last is a thing surely imminent."

"Are you well?" Gaston asked her quickly.

She nodded readily enough, with a small, apologetic smile. "Do not worry. I am well enough; I am merely very tired of being pregnant."

"If Striker and Pete do not sail, will he have Cudro take the *Queen* roving in his place?" I asked. "Or will you keep the ship here and send her on merchant voyages?"

She sighed heavily with her fingers to her lips, and I could see she fought sudden tears.

"I am sorry," I said quietly.

"Non," she shook her head. "I do not want them to go. I know it may be no safer for them here, but..." She stood. "Please, excuse me," she said in English; and she left us.

I followed her. "Sarah?"

She paused at the base of the stairs. "I am fine, Will," she said with annoyance that I did not feel was aimed at me. "I know I cannot..."

"What?" I prompted when it was obvious she would not finish her thought.

"I do not wish to lose him, or them, to our damned father, the sea, the Spaniards, the flux..." She trailed off with a sob.

"Aye," I said softly, and put my arm around her. "Of course not."

She cried on my shoulder for a time, and I mused on not knowing what to say to comfort her, as I did not know an answer to her dilemma. Even if our father were not a threat, I could not see her men not sailing. Striker came from a long line of captains and sailors: he would not stay ashore by choice, even for her. And Pete... I could not envision the Golden One living a peaceful life of prosperity without some adventure, but perhaps I was mistaken.

She at last released me and pulled away to mop her tears and compose her face. "It is funny the paths our lives have taken," she said with feigned good humor.

"Did you wish to be the lady of a fine manor?" I teased.

She met my gaze and raised her chin. "I am."

I chuckled. "Will you return to dinner?"

She shook her head. "Nay, please have Henrietta bring something to my room."

I watched her laborious ascent of the stairs with unease, and went in search of our housekeeper.

"Mistress Striker will require her meal in her room," I told her, "and... Please look in on her often, even if she should seem annoyed by it. She may be very close to her birthing."

Henrietta nodded gravely. "I've been thinkin' that meself, my Lord."

I shook my head and smiled at her frown. "I am no longer a lord."

"Ah, I'm sorry, my..." She grimaced.

I patted her shoulder. "Find us if..." I sighed. "Gaston would be there in addition to the midwife."

"Of course... sir."

Everyone had finished their meal by the time I returned to my seat. Rucker was expounding on the various stages of sugar production for the

Marquis. I ate my soup in silence while Sam cleared the table, avoiding all curious glances save Gaston's. I smiled grimly at him but waved off his inquiry.

"Shall we have a game?" the Marquis inquired of us, when my meal and Rucker's discourse were concluded.

Gaston looked to me.

"Sadly, non," I told his father. "We have investigative matters of our own to attend to in town."

The Marquis nodded his understanding. "Then perhaps Mademoiselles Vines and Chelsea and Monsieur Rucker will indulge me."

They nodded agreeably, though Christine seemed reluctant and her curious eyes were upon Gaston and me as we rose and left the room, and Agnes appeared quite distracted.

We returned to the stable to don our weapons. Judging from his mien, my matelot was still less than enthusiastic about our plans for the evening; but I was beginning to feel a little thrill at the thought of the coming escapade.

"How is Sarah?" he asked in French.

"Quite possibly close to birthing; and, of course, concerned over all else facing us," I said, and relayed her words.

There was a rap in the doorframe and we were surprised to see Agnes.

"How is Sarah?" she asked me.

I sighed. "We were just discussing that very topic. She worries about a great many things, and she may be close to the birth. I have instructed Henrietta to look in on her often, but perhaps you should spend time with her if she will tolerate company."

Agnes sank to the straw and picked up a puppy with a sigh. "I do not know if she wishes for my company either."

"I did not mean you in specific," I said quickly.

"I know. It is just…" She shook her head.

"Did you two have a quarrel?" I asked.

"Nay," she said quickly and then seemed unsure. "Nay." She sighed again, and fiddled with the straw and puppy, and then picked up a folded piece of paper lying in the straw.

I realized it was the map to our evening's destination, which I had handed Gaston when he was sitting with the puppies earlier. "That is ours."

Agnes was frowning at Theodore's crude map. "Why do you have a map to Mistress Garret's?" she asked. "And who drew this? There is no sense of the distances at all."

Gaston slumped against the doorframe with huge sigh that surely spoke much of how he felt the Gods mocked us.

"Why do you know of Mistress Garret?" I asked the girl.

She flushed, and her gaze met mine with guilt. "We… Christine wished to see her."

This brought Gaston's gaze to her as well.

"Not for… anything," Agnes stammered quickly. "Because… we

should not. It was one of our outings dressed as boys. Christine had heard whisper of her, of Mistress Garret, that she was a witch, and she wished to see her. The woman saw we were girls the moment she laid eyes on us, but I do not think that required witchery. She asked if she could do anything for us, and when we said no, she looked Christine in the eye and said she hoped she would never see her again, and then she looked at me and said there were things she could teach me. Christine was quite upset over the incident."

I thought Mistress Garret sounded ever more intriguing. "Did you return?"

Agnes shook her head sadly. "I was afraid and... I was not sure what she could teach me. I had heard... She was handsome, but as old as my mother, and..."

"You heard she entertained ladies?" I asked

"Nay, nay, men," she blurted. "And I knew that was not a thing I wished to learn, and I was afraid of witchery."

"She could probably teach you herbs and remedies," Gaston said. "It is not witchcraft. You should know better."

Agnes cringed. "Is that why you are going to see her?"

I thanked the Gods for their providing such a likely excuse and the word *aye* was almost to my lips when Gaston blurted, "Non." I cursed myself for pausing to thank entities that possessed a perverse sense of humor, and regarded my matelot with surprise. He had realized his error and was now as flushed as the girl. She was studying us intently. Gaston cursed, sighed, shrugged, and turned away.

I sighed. "Gaston wishes to have me instruct him in the ways of women and their pleasure, prior to his marrying Christine. And... we heard Mistress Garret might be amenable to being the model for such instruction."

"Oh," she breathed. Her gaze darted from one to the other of us and then to the puppy in her lap. "You can teach that?"

"Aye," I sighed. "I am an accomplished instructor in the matter."

"Oh. Does Christine know?" she asked without coyness.

"Nay," I said quickly. "And she must not."

Agnes flinched and became defensive. "I would not tell, and it is not as if she speaks to me now, anyway."

"Good," I said, and snatched the map from her. Gaston had sagged against the wall again, this time in mortification. I took his hand and towed him out the door and into the rain, which seemed to have no intention of abating.

As we entered the dark and muddy street, I cursed my stupidity in not perusing the map at length. I led us in what I felt was the correct direction, until I at last spied a lantern beneath an eave. I held the damp parchment close to the light and memorized what I could before the ink soaked away. Soon after, we paused in an alleyway, just outside a lamp above a door I hoped was Mistress Garret's. Our stopping there had more to do with a garden tucked in beside the small building than Theodore's map.

"What if she is not alone?" Gaston hissed.

His Horse had emerged as we tromped here through the mud and muck, and in the face of its opposition, my meager enthusiasm for the endeavor had dwindled considerably.

"Most courtesans douse the light outside their door if they are engaged," I said with little surety.

"What if she does not know that?" he asked.

"Then pray to the Gods she has the good sense not to answer the door," I sighed.

She did answer the door, and I knew at once she was the woman we sought. She was handsome and had surely been a beauty in her youth. Now the lines on her face spoke of laughter and a quiet dignity. Her thickly coiled hair was straw-colored like mine, and streaked with silver. She was thinner than I had expected; there was nothing plump about her, and I thought that a relief, as I would not want Gaston to contend with sagging flesh. She greeted us with a knowing look in her gray eyes and welcomed us in from the rain.

The small room in which we found ourselves was filled with shelves of drying plants, pots and vials. There was a table in the center and a seemingly clean bed along the wall.

"Mistress Garret, I assume. We were recommended to you by an old business associate," I said carefully.

She nodded and looked us over. Her gaze was speculative on me; and concerned when she regarded Gaston, who had turned his attention to the plants beside him and seemed quite intent on ignoring her.

"I serve many needs," she said smoothly. "What might yours be?" she asked me.

"My... friend is to be married and he wishes to learn of women prior to his wedding night," I said.

She nodded and regarded Gaston anew with a small quirk to her lip. "I can see to that."

"He wishes for me to be present," I said.

Her small smile fled. "Are you confused about the matter, too?" she asked.

"Nay," I said quickly.

She awarded me a look that I could interpret in no other manner than patronizing, and my heart hardened toward her considerably.

"I'll instruct him if he's to learn anything here," she said. "I don't do two at a time. You can pay extra to watch, or you can wait outside. If you don't want to stand in the rain, there's a tavern 'round the corner, or you can bring him back another night."

Though her words were much as I had expected, I was still disappointed and I knew not how to counter her.

"Is this used to stop bleeding?" Gaston asked as he plucked a root off a shelf. His Horse was now deeply hidden behind his physician's mask, and I could but smile.

She started, and turned to him with a frown.

"He is a physician," I supplied.

"Aye," she told Gaston.

"How is it used?" he asked.

Her frown became perplexed, and then she crossed her arms. "Are you going to buy it?"

"Aye," Gaston said with annoyance. "And what other concoctions do you recommend to ease a woman in childbirth, and why?"

She regarded him in perplexed silence for a moment before looking at me askance and coloring ever so slightly. "I must apologize. When you said you wished for him to learn of women, I misunderstood."

I smiled.

We were soon seated at the table with wine, while she taught Gaston a great deal about what herbs treated various women's ailments. I soon began to think waiting in the tavern around the corner might be a good idea.

When we at last departed, she had more coin than I imagined she usually earned in a night, and we had oilcloth-wrapped packages of assorted roots and leaves. We ran home through the rain in silence. It was too dark for me to read his expression, and he did not seem to want to gaze upon me.

We found everyone had retired for the night, and whether Striker and Pete had returned I did not know. Gaston led us into Sarah's office, and found paper and quill to make notes and labels for his purchases. He ignored me, so while he was thus engaged, I slipped upstairs and peered at Vivian's door. There was light showing through the slats. I knocked quietly and received no answer, so I opened the door a little until I could spy her sleeping in her bed. I waited until I was sure she was indeed sleeping and not merely pretending to do so. With a sigh of relief, I closed the door.

There was light streaming from Christine's room as well, and I wondered if she could not sleep or if she also felt the need to sleep with a lamp.

Gaston had not completed his notes by the time I returned, so I sat in the other chair and waited.

At last he stopped his furious scribbling. He pushed the packages around on the desk a bit and fiddled with the quill. "I cannot," he said at last without looking at me.

"With her perhaps," I said. "I was not pleased with her, either."

He shook his head. "Non, her terms were unacceptable, but... It was not that alone."

I smiled. "She was not as arousing as Christine could be even to the dead, so do not..."

"Non," he said quickly. "It was not her. The thought of... entering her... I... my cock found interest even in that with her. But..." He snapped the quill he had been fidgeting with in an accidental nervous gesture, and gazed at it forlornly.

I went to kneel before him so that I could gaze up at his face. He met mine with guilty eyes.

"You know you can tell me anything," I murmured.

"It is akin to the thoughts I called horrible concerning you," he whispered.

I nodded as understanding suffused me. "Has all this exhumed some dark place where you buried things concerning that night and your sister?"

He nodded and gave a little sigh, and then as much to my relief as it was a show of his, he relaxed and opened his hands to lay them upon mine. I entwined our fingers and squeezed reassuringly.

He took another deep breath. "When she said she would not allow you to stay, my Horse became quite angry, and yet I was filled with fear that you would leave me with her and something horrible would happen to me – and thus I wished to throw her down upon the bed and take her anyway, with you there to protect me, because I was... gripped with this hatred of her, that she was another woman out to harm me, and... I wanted to take what we came there for, and prove that they had no power over me, and... All I could do was concentrate on the herbs and what they meant and it passed, or... I was able to don a mask and calm my Horse and..." He sighed and gazed at me with pleading eyes.

"My love, I am so very proud of you," I murmured.

He frowned.

"I did not see it, my love," I said with pride, "neither did she. For all that, you handled yourself very well indeed."

"Is how I ride the animal truly more important than what it wishes to do?" he asked earnestly.

"When it involves others, oui," I sighed. "And... provided you did not act on it, is what it wanted to do so very evil when it still remembers how you were wronged and has nothing to compare it to?"

"Perhaps not," he said doubtfully. "And perhaps, you are correct and I am seeing a new pocket of pus from the old wound," he said with more surety.

"Now that it has been discovered, we must drain and treat it, non?" I said gently.

He nodded resolutely. "But Will, I cannot with Christine. She is... a thousand madmen in the bushes. I will panic and buck and not be able to ride myself without you... or even with you," he added sadly, and tears filled his eyes. "I am too mad to be the heir my father needs, even with all this control I now have. And I feel guilt that I should be concerned with that in the face of your renouncing. I should be able to walk away from mine for you just as you have done."

"Oh, hush, my love." I brushed the tears from his cheeks. "The circumstances are different and you know it. You are tying yourself in knots."

He nodded. "Oui, it is all a tangled mess. It is as much a Gordian Knot as my impotence was."

"And we cut that free," I said. "We will sort this one out, too."

"But that is it, Will," he said with new tears. "I do not wish to solve this one. I have you. I should not need them."

I understood, but I knew he was viewing it incorrectly. "This is not about you or me, or rather, us. This is about a wound you carry. We must heal it, or now that it is festered it will spread its rot and it will harm us. I do not doubt your love for me. I do not doubt your devotion. And this is not about your madness per se, or pleasing your father. If you are still wounded from that night in another manner, then it must be healed."

"How?" he asked with exasperation. "I look at them, and I want them, and I cannot trust them, and they will spook me such that I trample them."

"All of them?"

"Any that give rise to my lust," he spat.

"My sister?"

He froze and glared at me. "Will, she is your sister."

"Oui, she is my sister," I said gently. "As Gabriella was your sister; and Sarah has led one of our friends astray and…"

He cursed and looked away. "Oui. All of them," he said bitterly.

I cast about for how I might make it easier for him. "My love, we stand in the light. These are merely shadows from the cave. They cannot live in the light. We can just look at them. They cannot reach us and they are not real… If you do not act upon them, then they are not real: they are just shadows and they hurt no one, not even you."

I watched him think on it, and I thought on Pete's words about a man's actions being the measure of madness, and then I mused on all we had told the Marquis, and that moment of giddy joy when I had first felt that perhaps we were sane and the world was mad. I felt it to be true even more strongly, now. Tonight it did not make me giddy, though; it merely made my heart ache. I was moved to embrace the only person I felt I would ever stand beside.

"What?" he whispered as he held me in return.

"You are not alone," I murmured. "And neither am I. And the world is mad, not us."

He gave a brief bark of pained amusement and held me tighter. "If this is sanity, then the world is a very dark and scary place."

I chuckled into his shoulder. "Have we not established that?" Then I added somberly as the thought struck me, "Are we not the get of it? Has it not made us as we are?"

He pushed me away enough to gaze upon my face with a frown. "Non, it has given us the wounds we carry, you are correct; but it did not make us, any more than our fathers did."

I smiled, both at his sentiment, and that he was in sufficient possession of himself to think it.

"Let us sleep on this," I whispered.

He nodded and sighed, and pulled me into his arms again. In time, we gathered his new herbs and retreated to the stable. There we doffed our damp and muddy finery, and cuddled together beneath the blanket, to retreat even further from the world into a womb that held only love, light, and warmth.

In the morning it still rained, and I wondered at it. Rain for days was not unheard of in the winter months, but it was usually a thing the Gods reserved for autumn, and thus another reason we avoided Port Royal in the storm season. I supposed we should be thankful there was no gale; but as the downpour had not abated enough to allow the sun to shine, it was becoming as cold as I could remember the West Indies being, short of a true storm.

We huddled in our hammock, venturing out only to relieve ourselves and procure water and bacon from Sam – who was happily holed up in the warm cookhouse. We told him to have Henrietta take food up to Vivian and returned to bed. Gaston seemed quite content to remain in my arms beneath the blanket and nowhere else, even though Sam had graciously offered a place by the only hearth the house possessed. My matelot seemed to be possessed of the mood I had the day before, and I could think of no reason we truly needed to brave the wet and mud: Jamaica and Vivian would be fed and cared for, and even Bella had her fat puppies dug deep in the straw beneath her: we need only see to ourselves for a time.

We told stories of the coldest we had ever been, and considered purchasing another blanket or going in search of a brazier; but for the most part, we dozed and made love. When Gaston was awake and not engaged with me carnally, he was contemplative and not inclined to speak. I let him have his silence, knowing he had much to think about for which I could not offer answers. I concocted a dozen plans for getting rid of Christine, and ruminated on whether my fancies were wishful thinking about things I thought inevitable – both his marriage to her and the need for her to be gotten rid of, if it should come to pass. And I considered whether the marriage could be avoided and how, and whether that was born of selfish desire – or love for my matelot and an intrinsic understanding of his needs and frailties. I at last concluded that I did not wish for him to marry her; but that it was a decision he must make for himself; and if he did marry her, she would have to be sent to France with his father as soon as possible – with or, most likely, without, a child in her belly.

Our retreat and reverie was inevitably disturbed by a knock upon the doorframe. At my call, the visitor announced herself to be Agnes.

"Come in if it will not disturb you," I called, "but we are naked and beneath a blanket and not inclined to dress."

"I am well with that," she said, and escaped the rain to sit in the straw huddled beneath a blanket of her own.

Bella nosed her proffered hand, but seemed disinclined to offer up a puppy from their warm nest, and Agnes did not attempt to dig one out.

"Is anyone about?" I asked.

She shook her head. "Everyone has stayed in their rooms. Well, some came down to break the fast, and the Marquis and Mister Rucker are discussing something in the dining room with their feet by a brazier, but beyond that, all is quiet."

"Did Pete and Striker come home last night?" I asked.

She nodded and toyed with straw and did not meet my gaze.

"Are you wandering about the house from boredom, or did you come here for a reason?" I asked.

Her wide mouth formed a grim line. "A reason. How did it go with Mistress Garret? Did Gaston learn all he needed of women?"

Gaston tensed behind me, but I chuckled. "He learned a great deal of women, aye."

"Such that he needs no more lessons?" she said, her long fingers burrowing in the straw.

I abandoned my humor. "Not necessarily. Why?"

"Well…" she said to the straw. "I was thinking that… The pleasuring of women is a thing I would do well to learn of, and perhaps…" She flushed. "I should determine whether I am truly confused about matters of men and women and what I favor, and…" She counted off another point on her fingers. "As you have said I need not marry, then I need not maintain my maidenhead, and…" She sighed and counted off another finger. "Many feel that a girl in my situation has already provided such service to her… patrons."

Gaston swore very quietly behind me and planted his forehead between my shoulder blades.

"Um…" I managed to say while questioning whether the Gods were beneficent or cruel. "Are you suggesting you serve as a model for Gaston's instruction?"

"Aye," she squeaked, and heaved a sigh that must have drained all the air from her thin body. She at last met my gaze, though, and I saw earnestness and fear in her huge brown eyes.

"My dear Agnes," I said kindly. "That is a most gracious offer, and I will be happy to instruct you in such matters without carnality. You need not…"

"You do not find me attractive?" she squeaked with tears.

"Nay, nay, that is not the matter at all," I said quickly. I felt completely off balance for the conversation, as if somehow the blanket wrapped about me and Gaston clinging to my back would topple me so that I fell in a clumsy heap of social inappropriateness. "It is just that you need not provide such service. I would not have us take advantage of you in that fashion."

"But you are not taking advantage if it is a thing I want," she protested. "I would learn, and you are the only two men I can think of that I would be willing to learn of such things from."

Gaston moved so that he wrapped an arm around me and brought his mouth to my ear. "Oui," he breathed.

I squirmed enough to be able to see his face.

He nodded resolutely, and his eyes were calm. "My Horse does not hate or fear her – as long as you are with me."

My cock sprang to life as the implications of his words and hers took root. I nodded.

I turned back to Agnes. "My dear, we will accept your offer, gladly. And... If one of us was in a position to marry you, we would. We have long considered it, but circumstances are such that... well, I could not put Vivian out and Gaston's father..."

She shook her head. "Thank you, but I do not know if I wish to marry either of you, anyway." She stood and wrung her hands. "What should I do?"

My thoughts were scampering about like excited dogs, and yet I still possessed the clarity to realize our current sleeping arrangement would not be amenable to three; and, as Gaston had been at me twice this day, there was another matter that must be tended to. "Let us all move to the bathing room, where there is a brazier and water."

"We will bathe?" she asked incredulously.

"Aye," I said and reluctantly slipped from beneath the blanket to find a pair of breeches. "For your first lesson in the matter of sex involving men – though I know that is not what you truly wish to learn – if you plan to tryst with a man who you have any reason to believe has been busy with other men, you must always make sure he washes his prick."

Gaston cursed quietly – due to his presumably having forgotten this detail in his excitement – and rolled out of the hammock wrapped in our blanket.

"And for that matter," I continued, as I surveyed the empty atrium and the short distance to the bathing room, and decided I would gain nothing by donning more clothing. "You should always inspect a cock before allowing it entry. There is no sense in playing with a member that shows signs of the pox or other ailment."

"How will I know what that looks like?" she asked.

"It is usually quite obvious," I said, "but ours are healthy and yet different, and so they should provide you some basis for future comparison if that should ever be required."

Gaston had donned breeches and nothing else as well, and left our blanket on the hammock. I was pleased in this, as it would stay dry and thus we would have a warm place to return to.

We sprinted to the bathing room, and I hurried to get the brazier going while Gaston happily discovered that the upper cistern had indeed been refilled since the fire. He filled the tub partway, and the sudden stream and pool of water seemed to suck up what little heat the room had possessed. Even as the brazier finally caught, I thought my choice of locations for this endeavor might have been foolhardy. Agnes handed us her damp blanket, and Gaston and I huddled together on the floor beneath it, waiting for the coals to produce heat.

"Have you had any carnal experiences at all?" I asked Agnes as we waited.

She shook her head sadly.

"Even poor or unwanted ones?" I asked carefully.

This shake was quicker than the last, and her expression was one of surprise that I should ask, without a trace of fear or defensiveness. I was relieved.

"Do you pleasure yourself?" I asked.

She shook her head again, but this time she ended the gesture with a sigh. "I have touched myself," she admitted. "But... I do not understand the way or why of it. It made me uncomfortable."

"How?" I asked. "Well... how did you touch yourself, and can you describe the nature of the discomfort?"

"I touched my privates," she said and flushed anew. "You once told me to do so," she added quickly. "You said I could discover how to please another that way."

I wondered when the Devil I had done that, and then remembered her watching over me after I had taken the beating in the tavern. I had been quite drugged.

I grinned. "Aye, I did say that. And you found no pleasure in it?"

"It made me... ache... Not like when I have my monthly, but with..." She shrugged helplessly.

"With desire?" I offered. "With need?"

She frowned and nodded. "I suppose that is how it is spoken of. It was interesting for a time, and sometimes I would do it just to feel that, but it seemed to serve no purpose and I have felt I was doing it incorrectly."

I smiled in sympathy and recalled that it was different for women. Their sex did not seem to possess a mind of its own that knew damn well what it needed.

"The pleasure comes when you tease or push that desire to the breaking point," I said.

"So I did not do it long enough?" she asked with concern. "It became painful if I did it too long."

"Aye, aye," I agreed. "It is a matter of intensity and varying the sensation. Do not fear, I will teach you. If you are pleased with nothing else this endeavor might offer you, I am sure you will be pleased with that."

This seemed to warm her enthusiasm, much as the coals had finally begun to do for their corner of the room. I invited her to doff her clothes and join us beneath the blanket. Though we still wore breeches, I was thankful at this stage that my ardor had cooled as I made a place for her to sit within the tangle of our legs. Gaston was hard against my side, though. I pressed closer to him, and his arm pulled me closer still.

She did as I asked; and no surprisingly sumptuous beauty emerged from her shapeless dress. Though she was now nearly two years older, she was still every bit as skinny and under-endowed as she had been when first we met. Her hipbones could bruise a man, and her breasts could barely be cupped; yet there was much of a woman about her, and she would not be confused with a boy by any but the blind.

Shivering, she slipped into the space I had made for her, facing Gaston with her shoulder to my chest and her knees pulled up. I wrapped her in the blanket. Her skin was icy, and I chastely rubbed her arms and legs to warm her until she relaxed enough to lean against me.

For some strange reason that only our Horses understand, I was brought to recall a memory of long ago: not of the last time I frolicked with both a man and a woman, but of a cold and rainy day in a barn with Shane when first we had pleasured one another.

I turned my head to find Gaston and saw worry in his eyes – for me. He knew me well enough to read my slightest shudder, and I took great comfort in that and the memory receded.

"The first time I ever… played… with another was on a cold and rainy day such as this," I said to both of them. "We had been riding when the rain came, and we hid in a barn and doffed our clothes and attempted to warm one another."

Gaston nodded his understanding – he knew the story – and kissed my cheek.

"Was it with a girl or a boy?" Agnes asked.

"A boy," I sighed. "I was thirteen and he a year older."

"Is that when you learned you favored men?" she asked.

"Nay, I had realized that before then," I said with a smile. "The boys had begun to speak and brag of women, and all I thought of was them."

"Aye, I know that well," she said. "This is nice; neither of you are hairy." She frowned at her words. "I mean to say, when I think of men, I think of them as being hairy and sweaty, and I find revulsion in the thought of them being near me. I do not find either of you revolting, and… Being held is nice. No one has held me like this since I was little."

Tears filled her eyes and I pulled her close in empathy.

"Oui, it is nice to be held," Gaston breathed. "No one ever held me that I could remember until Will."

"My mother held me," she told him. "We were too poor to have a governess."

"You were blessed, then," I said.

She smiled and wiped away her tears only to have her eyes fill again. "I loved my mother and father. I miss them."

"I am glad I have found my father again," Gaston said. "I never knew my mother. I did not truly know him until these last weeks."

She looked up at me. "Your father is a beast; was your mother kind?"

I snorted. "Nay. I had a governess I was fond of, though. She would hold me when I was little."

She ran an inquisitive finger up my arm to my shoulder, and then she frowned. "What happened to your chest?"

Gaston stilled.

I sighed and decided something akin to the truth was the only thing readily available. "We were frolicking and managed to spill a large amount of wax on me."

She grimaced in sympathy. "Did it hurt?"

I nodded with a small smile, and quickly kissed Gaston on the lips. He sighed.

"Does it hurt now?" she asked.

"It is tender, aye."

She nodded, and her inquisitive finger ventured to Gaston. "And do your scars hurt?"

He held his breath for a second at her touch, and then shook his head.

"They are different in sensation for him," I told her, and put a finger next to hers to run across the pattern of his scars. "He still feels beneath them, but it is a duller than what he feels on the unmarred skin. Avoid this." I ran a finger wide around his scarred right nipple.

"It feels odd," Gaston added. "It is not pleasurable."

"His other one is fine," I said, but as his left nipple was pressed against my shoulder, we could not reach it and he did not seem prone to move to allow us to.

"Do you have any places that feel odd to the touch?" I asked as I caressed her cheek.

She stilled like a scared rabbit beneath my finger and closed her eyes. "I do not think so."

I explored her face and neck with gentle fingertips, and she sighed. She stilled again as I wandered to her collarbone and then between her raised knees to the space between her breasts. I thought she might faint from lack of breath as I slowly worked my way toward her left nipple, and I finally touched it just to get her to gasp. Soon, she was leaning back against my upraised leg, with her hands grasping at Gaston's arm and my shoulder, and her legs spread as much as the space would allow, and we found her pleasure faster than I had imagined.

When she stopped gasping, she raised her head to regard me with wide and wondrous eyes and proclaim, "That is why people do it."

Gaston erupted in mirth.

As she was not the first woman – virgin or otherwise – I had been the first to bring across that threshold, I was not nearly as surprised. I cuddled her close and kissed her forehead before tilting her head back and teasing her lips with mine until she opened for me to explore her mouth: a thing she seemed amenable to me doing: a thing which gained me a poke in the ribs and a tight hand about my balls from my matelot.

I pulled away from her mouth with amusement and turned to him. "Would you not have me enjoy her at all?" I murmured chidingly in French.

I was initially faced with the Horse's stubbornness; but though it was fractious, he seemed to have it in hand, and my balls and turgid member received a far more pleasant caress and my lips an apologetic kiss.

"I had not seen you kiss another," he murmured before kissing me deeply.

When he let me breathe, I found her watching us with narrowed eyes.

"I would like to see you make love," she said as if it were a curiosity.

"You will," Gaston muttered in English, which set me laughing.

He disentangled himself from us and stood to put a kettle to boil on the brazier and transfer some glowing coals to the tray beneath the tub. I despaired of that much water ever growing warm. I stood and stretched, as much to readjust my member in my breeches as to straighten my spine and legs. She lay on the floor in the blanket and regarded us.

"Are you aroused?" she asked. "May I see it now?"

I gave my matelot an inquisitive glance, and he snorted with annoyance at either his jealousy or my teasing him of it. I dropped my breeches and kicked them away, and she knelt to peer at my member with the same frown she wore when studying a thing beneath a lens before sketching it. I watched Gaston's breeches join mine in the corner with hungry eyes.

"Have her please you," he said huskily in French.

As always, I would deny him nothing, especially not when he asked in such a manner.

I bade her stand and she came to me with outstretched hands. I caught her wrists and said, "With any lover, be it man or woman, it is best not to start with the organs of desire."

She nodded her understanding and redirected her hands to my neck. Then she proved she had indeed been an apt pupil, by stroking and exploring me gently much as I had done her. She even mimicked my movements in playing with her nipples, and I was surprised at her adeptness in discerning action from sensation.

Gaston watched us all the while with a lustful gaze that kept me far harder than her ministrations. At last he slipped behind her. She started a little as he put his arms around her, and her eyes went quite wide as he adjusted their positions, and I knew he had nestled his cock between her buttocks. Then his hands were running down her arms while he nuzzled her neck, until he at last reached her hands and guided them to my member. He whispered in her ear of how I liked to be touched while I held her hips and tried not faint from dizzy pleasure.

She squeaked with delight and surprise when I came on her belly. Then she explored the stickiness of my jism with a child's amusement. Gaston used my come to lubricate his slow exploration of her body until she was panting and grasping at me with sticky fingers and I was kissing him over her shoulder. She came such that her being pinned between us was all that kept her from sinking to the floor.

"May I take you?" Gaston asked her.

She nodded mutely, and he lowered her to lie on the blanket. I sank down the wall to lie beside her on my side, with my head propped upon my arm. We watched Gaston empty the kettle into a basin and dutifully bathe his member.

"This first time it will be uncomfortable and might hurt," I said gently.

She nodded, "I know," as if it was a small matter, but I could see the fear begin to grip her.

I ran my hand over her body and sank my fingers between her legs. She squirmed a little as I explored her readiness. Gaston returned to us and gazed in wonder as I pulled my well-lubricated fingers from her.

"You are as ready as you will ever be," I teased her lightly in order to tell him he might proceed.

They each nodded at what they heard, and Gaston eased himself between her legs. With amusement I recalled the last time I had seen him between a woman's thighs: at Jamaica's birth. I studied his face and found as much fear there as Agnes' still held.

I wiped my fingers on the blanket and then caressed her face and turned her head so that she looked to me. "Close your eyes," I whispered. "And relax."

Then I looked up at him again, my eyes asking the questions I did not wish to voice in her presence. All I could think was how very fast touching her cold flesh had taken me back to a barn I did not wish to remember. Was a girl spread before him carrying him where he had feared it would?

He took a deep breath and nodded that he was well enough. He did not take his eyes from me as he positioned himself and slowly entered her. Then he held still, and I held his eyes as I would a rope to keep him from falling even when she gasped and tensed at the discomfort of his presence.

At last he looked away and fought a sob. I glanced to her and found her eyes still tightly closed and her teeth upon her lip. I caressed her cheek and then his, and wiped his tears away before they fell upon her. He kissed my fingers.

"I do not like this," Agnes whispered.

I looked to her and found her eyes open. Thankfully she was only staring at me. My hand went to her cheek again and I kept it there to keep her facing me while I kissed her forehead.

"Do you want him to withdraw?" I asked.

She shook her head as much as I would allow. "He can finish. Will it take long? I feel I am on a spit."

I chuckled. "Aye, it does feel much like that. Some come to enjoy it."

"Do you?" she asked.

"Aye, very much."

She began to turn her head to Gaston and I glanced at him and found that though his eyes were puffy, he was in control of his emotions again. I let her see him.

"Do you like it?" she asked him.

He shook his head and smiled at her. "Not as much as Will does. It is odd and... aye, as if one is impaled."

"Gaston is usually the one within me and not the other way around," I said quickly.

"Oh, so you do not take turns?" She seemed surprised.

"Nay, not... evenly," I said.

"Do you need to move?" she asked him, with a frown that said she did not think that would be pleasant at all.

"I will go slowly; and you will tell me if I should stop," he said.

She nodded, and he began to move. She grimaced a little, and clutched at my hand, but then her expression became one of perplexed curiosity and she studied the ceiling and wall with her tongue in her cheek, as if she were attempting to determine if she liked the taste of the endeavor.

"With the moving it is not as bad," she noted. "But it is not as fine as the touching."

"It rarely is the first time," I assured her as I turned back to Gaston.

He was finding his pleasure, or rather his cock was; and I thought once it gripped him he would make short work of the matter. I was correct: he came a few strokes later.

She gasped with surprise as he thrust deep and grunted.

"I can feel it moving in there," she said.

He withdrew and collapsed on the floor beside her.

"If I fetched my paper, could I draw you making love?" she asked.

Gaston regarded the ceiling with bemusement.

"I suppose," I said slowly, "but perhaps we should rest for a time…"

There was a knock on the door and we jumped.

"Sirs, are ya in there?" Henrietta called.

"Aye, aye," I said quickly. "We are bathing."

"On a day like taday? Sam said ya were but I didna' believe 'im."

"Henrietta, what do you need?" I asked.

"It na' be me, it be the mistresses," she said. "Lady… Mistress Williams be askin' for ya, an' Miss Vines, an'… well sir, I think perhaps Lord Montren should be speakin' with your sister."

"We will be out soon," I sighed.

Gaston had already stood and found his breeches.

I waited until I heard Henrietta walk away before speaking. "Well, if we all so desire, it appears we must continue this another time."

Agnes toyed with the edge of the blanket thoughtfully. "I would be amenable to that. Even this last part. I would try it again." Then she looked to Gaston. "Do you feel Sarah is ready to birth?"

"That is what I suppose I must determine," he said. He stopped at the door and looked down at me with hundreds of unsaid words.

"I am well," I assured him. "I will see to Vivian. You go to Sarah."

He leaned down and kissed me deeply. "I love you."

"And I you, more than I can say."

He nodded and my words seemed to calm him somewhat. He looked to Agnes. "Thank you."

She nodded with a small smile, and he left us.

"You should probably wait after I leave before slipping out," I said.

She nodded her understanding. "I think I will take a bath. I am still sticky with you." She grimaced.

I kissed her lightly, found my breeches, and slipped out the door. I wondered if the Gods had delivered us a blessing or a curse.

Sixty-Nine

Wherein We Choose to Play

Gaston was more than a step or two ahead of me; he had already donned a tunic and was standing outside Sarah's door. I saw the door open, but with the rain I did not hear what was said; I only saw that he entered.

Now, standing half naked in the cold, I found I could easily consider the whole interlude a pleasant dream. I wished to speak to him of it, more to confirm it had indeed occurred than for reassurance that he was well with it – or that I was, for that matter.

Reluctantly, I went to the stable and found a tunic before dashing to see Vivian.

"Where have you been all day?" Vivian demanded as I entered her room. "Henrietta told me you were still sleeping this morning, and now you have been in the bathing room."

"Well, it would appear you have no need to ask where I have been," I said with some amusement. "We did not hear you were seeking us until a few minutes ago."

She glared at me. "My breasts are full and I would like to feed my baby."

"Let us go, then," I said. "I am sorry you have been waiting." And I silently cursed my thinking the baby and she were fine without us this morn.

She did not move. "Have you been fucking all day?" she asked vehemently.

"Would it make you angrier if I had?" I asked, my ire rising. I was beginning to feel she wished to fight far more than she wished to see her child. I was curious if she was drunk, but I smelled no rum or anything else that she might have used to mask it, and her words and eyes were clear and cold. "Is that what you want, to be angry?"

"Nay!" she roared. "I do not wish to be angry. That is why I am angry."

I took two steps to the door and stopped. On the one hand, I had never seen any man – myself included – win an argument with a woman when she was thus; on the other, leaving would solve nothing and we were asking ourselves to live with the woman: she was going to have to learn to convey her thoughts and feelings in a rational manner.

I turned back to her, grasped her shoulders, and met her angry gaze. "Think about your answer. Why are you angry with me?"

"Because you were not here," she said quickly.

"Why did that make you angry?"

"Because you are..." She stopped and looked away.

"Because I am what?" I asked.

She pulled away and I allowed it. "It is nothing. Let us go."

"Nay," I said. "I will go, and you can stay here with your full breasts and pout all damn day, or you can speak your mind."

She crossed her arms and sat on the bed. "You will not like what I have to say, and it matters not. It will change nothing."

"I already do not like what you have been saying, so in that respect, it matters not," I said. "But I would know why you are angry with me for not being here when I did not know I should be here. Aye, I should have looked in on you sooner, but I thought Henrietta was available to do that. I forgot that you had begun to feed the baby. You could have simply asked Henrietta to wake us. But no, you did not do that. You sat up here and became angry, did you not?"

"I am not being childish," she said bitterly.

"Call it what you will," I said, "but if I had not sworn I would never beat you, I would consider putting you across my knee."

She shook her head and looked away stubbornly with teary eyes. "I do not wish to fight with you."

I thought myself a fool for staying, but here I was. I guessed wildly in the name of goading her. "You are angry that I was fucking and you were not."

She swiped her tears away and glared at me. "Not everyone wants to spend their lives fucking."

"You are angry that I was lying safe and warm in someone's arms and you were not."

She flinched and flushed and looked away with pain in her eyes.

I sighed. "Damn it, girl..." I could not envision us ever being with her as we had just been with Agnes. And I did not know if I wished to continue what we had started with that girl. But I surely knew Vivian would wish for far more love than we had shown Agnes. She wanted love: she needed it. I could not ever place one foot on that path without breaking her heart. "I am sorry I cannot love you as you deserve."

"I know. I know," she sobbed. "I know you cannot. You are kind to me, and we are married, and yet I cannot have… you. Not that I want you. Not that I do not. It is ironic. It is just… I am alone."

"That need not always be the way of it," I said softly, and came to sit beside her on the bed. "I wandered lost and alone for years before I found Gaston, but I did find him; and someday you will surely find someone, or he will find you; and then we will do what we can to see that you can be with him. Until then, you will have our daughter to love and be loved by, and you will have our friendship."

I moved to take her hand and she scooted further away.

"Do not seek to comfort me: it makes it worse," she said quietly. "I do not know if I can bear ten years of loneliness – not without rum."

I had surely not borne it without wine. I sighed. "You might surprise yourself."

She snorted. "I might kill myself."

"What would you have me do to make it better?" I asked. "Other than supply you with rum?"

"I do not know," she sighed.

"Let us at least work towards bringing Jamaica here," I said. "And I am sorry we made you wait so long. It was not solely because we are thoughtless cads. We have problems of our own, and I do not say that to give excuse or evoke your sympathy."

"His madness?" she asked with a frown.

I nodded. "It strikes in peculiar ways at times, and he needs to be alone with me to sort through it."

She nodded. "I am sorry. I will try to remember that the next time I am feeling… sorry for myself."

I truly wished I could comfort her. "Thank you. And I promise we will try and remember others are relying on us. We have already chided ourselves on the matter and still… We are used to seeing to ourselves and no one else."

She smiled sadly. "I have never had to care for anyone. That is why I am afraid I will do poorly by the baby."

"It takes time to learn," I said. "It took many months before we became used to seeing to one another and not ourselves alone. I think it is harder for those of us who have been poorly cared for. We do not have fine examples to emulate. I know what I do not wish to ever do to a child, but I know so little of the things I should do as a father."

"I understand," she said, and sighed and stood: my worries were still etched upon her face. "Let us go."

Rachel was thankfully pleased to see us and said our arrival was well-timed, as both Elizabeth and Jamaica were hungry. She soon had me shooed out to her husband's office while they dealt with the children.

Theodore was thankfully alone, and I supposed that was due to the weather and not the lateness of the day.

"I have something for you," he said proudly, and pointed to a document sitting at the edge of his desk. "I found a model for it in one of my books."

I went to peruse the paper, and found it to be my formal renunciation: all couched in the language of the law, and made to sound so very proper that no one might ever guess the hardship, blood, and tears that gave rise to its intent.

"Thank you," I sighed. "It is quite lovely."

He regarded me speculatively. "Is it still what you wish to do?"

"Aye, aye," I assured him. "It is just so very… proper. I suppose there is a part of me – a very foolish part of me – that would have those receiving this to know the why of it."

He shook his head regretfully. "That has little bearing on the law."

I smiled. "I suppose it does not."

"And it would just serve to embarrass your father and make him even angrier than this will alone," he added kindly. "This, they can at least speculate about."

"I know."

"I will arrange a meeting with the governor after the rain stops." He set the document aside, and lowered his voice to ask with feigned nonchalance. "So, were you able to see to that other matter?"

I grinned. "We met with that individual – who appears quite well if you are curious – and found an arrangement could not be made to our liking."

He leaned forward with great curiosity and whispered. "Why?"

I leaned forward as well, so that my whisper did not have far to traverse the teak. "She was not conducive to my remaining with him throughout. And though I am sure she could have instructed any man quite adequately, that was not the true cause of our concern, and so Gaston plied her for information on women's ailments and their treatment and we left her with a goodly sum of coin for her trouble."

He appeared both relieved and thoughtful, and then concerned again. "May I ask what the true cause of your concern was?"

I sighed, not knowing what I should say and feeling I had already spoken too much in the name of allaying his fears regarding his recommendation. "Gaston has discovered that he harbors quite… mixed feelings regarding women. He does not wish to suffer a bout of madness in their presence, and thus wishes for me to remain with him and insure that does not happen or guide him from trouble if it does."

"Oh Lord," Theodore sighed and sat back in his chair with a sympathetic gaze. "What will you do?"

"I believe we have the matter in hand," I sighed. "Another candidate for… Well, we now have another…" I was at a loss for the word to describe the services Agnes was offering.

"Should I ask?" he asked archly.

I sighed. "Agnes: which does and does not change the nature of our relationship with the girl, but perhaps you should be apprised of it."

His eyebrows climbed quite high toward his receding hairline.

"It was her suggestion – do not ask how it was arrived at: I will be puzzling it for days – but through happenstance, she learned we might have such a need and she possessed several reasons of her own for wishing to engage in the... activity." I said ruefully. "I did not wish to use her so, and I will be loathe to have any learn of it and think we have taken advantage of her."

He nodded thoughtfully. "I would never assume either of you to have forced yourself upon the girl in any fashion."

"I should hope not," I said with a touch of rancor.

He feigned wincing from my tone and smiled. "I have no judgment on the matter as long as it meets with the satisfaction of all the parties involved."

I sighed. "Well... it has so far."

I recalled Gaston's tears and – the rest of our charges and responsibilities be damned – I truly needed to discuss the matter with my matelot as soon as I returned home.

"So tomorrow, then?" I asked.

Theodore nodded. "If there is no rain. I never relish traveling to Spanish Town in the mud."

"I never relish traveling anywhere in mud," I said.

We went to the back room so I could collect Vivian and found her quite engaged in nursing. I was somewhat dismayed: as much as I enjoyed Theodore's company, I did not wish to stand around in his house this day.

"Might I leave you here for a time?" I asked Vivian.

Though she tensed at the suggestion, such that it disturbed the baby from her business, Vivian did not blanch, and her nod, though tight, was indeed a nod. I looked to Rachel.

"She is welcome to stay as long as she wants," Rachel said graciously. "The children will nap and we can have chocolate and talk."

I turned back to Vivian and found her now quite pale. She managed a thin smile for her hostess, though, and I was proud of her.

Then she glared up at me. "Do not forget I am here."

I bowed.

She rolled her eyes.

I hurried home, only to find the stable empty. There was no one to be seen in the rain-soaked atrium or yard. All was dim, yet not dark enough to require lanterns, and all seemed dark and forlorn. I gazed along the line of closed doors upon the balcony and wondered which one I should knock on to find my matelot. The house had swallowed him, or rather the denizens of those rooms had. Fear and melancholy struck such that they nearly drove the breath from my lungs. I stood wet and gasping, wondering at myself and this sudden onslaught of madness.

Gaston found me some interminable time later: frozen to the center of my soul and huddled beneath our blanket in the straw with the puppies and three dogs, who could do little to warm me. We shared one glance and I was pulled tightly into his embrace and held until I stopped shaking.

"What has happened?" he hissed with worry, when I had found the composure to stop clutching at him.

"I am sorry," I whispered. "I am sorry. It is only me. I... slipped... for but a moment. I returned and could not find you. I could not even look. I was gripped... I felt lost... loss. That I had lost you. It was foolishness... madness, really. I will be well."

"You will not lose me," he murmured.

"I know. I do. Truly. I just..." I sighed as I puzzled through my feelings and our metaphors. "My Horse... must be concerned."

He pulled me to my feet and then to the hammock and stripped my wet clothes away.

"If it is to rain like this, we need another blanket," I said, as he wrapped our naked bodies together in our single expanse of warm wool.

He snorted in my ear, and then his mouth was upon me, cajoling and sweet, and best of all, warm, until at last the cold gripping me began to abate. My cock remained ominously still, and thus I was able to note with amusement that his had risen yet again. I did not argue that he need not prove his love to me, or for me. My Horse wished for the assurance; and I knew, in a distant manner, that I should not deny it. It was as if I watched our lovemaking unfold from the vantage of a high tower, and judged it a good thing to witness but not an activity I need actually engage in. And that vantage gave me the curious and ironic presence of mind to wonder why I was not concerned that I felt so very far away.

"I am not well," I breathed, as he discovered my inert member.

He began to pull away: I stopped him. He continued for a short time, and then pulled out abruptly, only to return to hold me with every other part of his body that could.

"I am warmer now," I said. "I felt frozen before." I kept turning about my thoughts – disconnected and jumbled things – seeking some design they might form. "My Horse seems happier now. I still feel oddly distant: as if I am not in my body."

He squirmed over me so that we lay face to face: his held compassion and love. "That is often how I feel when my Horse takes the bit."

"Truly? As if you watch events but do not feel them?"

He nodded. "Sometimes."

"It is odd. I always envision the madness gripping either of us as a potent thing. A thing that envelops all senses and bears us down or drags us off."

"Sometimes it drags you off and then you watch it," he said with a thoughtful frown.

"As if our Horse throws us from its back and we must catch it again. You have always likened it to hanging on to a rampaging animal, though."

He shrugged. "Sometimes it is."

I sighed. "It makes me feel the fool for all my pretensions of control… Of viewing it as a thing of light and the cave and…"

He hushed me with a kiss. "It is all metaphors and it is none, Will. You know that; you are merely lost in it now."

I did. I sighed and nuzzled his neck; and he held me; and I listened to the rain, and his heartbeat.

"Your sister is feeling contractions of her belly on occasion," he said quietly. "She has not begun to labor yet, but she might be quite close. She has sent for the midwife, and I would attend that meeting." He sighed heavily. "I would know more of women."

I nodded. I understood what he said. "Have you seen Agnes since?"

"Non," he said quickly, and then he did not speak but I could hear unsaid words.

With the clarity born of my distant perspective, I said, "I do not feel that that in specific has troubled me." I raised my head enough to meet his worried gaze. "How did you find it?"

He frowned and looked away with, thankfully, what appeared to be more thought than guilt. "I wish to experience it again without my head being so full of… memories. When it came time to actually lie with her, all I could think of was my sister, and how this or that element was different or the same."

"You cried," I prompted gently.

He nodded. "I cannot give a single reason for it. I seemed to be flooded with emotions from that night: many different emotions I cannot truly name. It was as if they were released to wash over me like a wave, and I felt tumbled beneath them. I do not know if that will happen again. I am relieved it happened there with you and with one such as Agnes."

"As am I," I said softly.

He shook his head the way a dog or duck shakes off water. "My cock enjoyed it well enough. It was squishy."

We smiled in memory of Pete's name for that part of a woman's anatomy: *the squishy hole.*

He sobered quickly. "She is very thin and not… When I envision a woman, I see more rounded features. But… I found her pleasing." He met my gaze with guilt. "In ways I do not find you," he sighed. "It is different."

I smiled. "If you found Agnes and me pleasing to the eye, or even your cock, in the same manner, I would be concerned for one or the other of us."

He gave another fleeting smile before frowning again. "Pleasing her seems to be much as it is with you, other than her not being enamored with my entry."

"That could change," I said with a shrug. "Even though she does not favor men, she might come to find pleasure in your presence there. Though women are larger and… squishier, it does not mean they need not become inured to it."

"I will not do it again if it will spook your Horse as it has," he said earnestly.

I thought on it with curiosity. "I cannot say if it will or not. We cannot know if it will unless you do it again." I was feeling more myself, or rather more within myself, and I was able to look upon a single thought and feel great conviction towards it. "I will stipulate one thing. I would not have you touch her again unless I am present."

He nodded. "Of course."

I was able to recall why we wished for that, anyway. "Did you feel any urge to harm her?"

"Non, none. She is Agnes. My Horse has ever viewed her as... safe. She is not alarming or threatening." He frowned. "I did not like watching you touch her at first, and your kissing her was... not appreciated, but that was because it was you and I felt jealousy. Later, when I instructed you to have her pleasure you... that was my Horse wishing to see you pleased; and since I was involved in the activity, I was not jealous. I do not feel you harbor any feelings toward her other than fondness, or her you."

I kissed him lightly. "I will endeavor to allow you to guide all that occurs in our future trysting with her."

"My Horse would prefer that." He smiled thoughtfully. "My cock could not care less."

"It is a thoughtless organ: they all are," I said with amusement.

"How did you find it?" he asked me with curiosity.

"It was a thing I did for you. She was... a tool, with which you could be pleased in a different manner; with which we could resolve your concerns regarding bedding a woman." I sighed as I listened to my words. "I do not mean to sound so very cold: I am fond of the girl, and I am happy we gave her pleasure, but..." I shrugged. "She is just a woman."

He sighed, and his face contorted with concern. "I wish I could reassure and soothe your Horse as you can mine."

Emotion swelled within me, and though I would assign it the name of love, it felt far more complex and nuanced, and I did not think man possessed names for some of the colors swirling within the sudden storm roiling within me: describing such things fell within the ambition and purview of poets. I hurried past the feelings to a memory: of us on a road in the dark.

"When this matter first arose," I said hesitantly. "When we first considered Christine... for you. I looked to the challenge with some anticipation. I wished to have a worthy opponent. I wished... to see if you would still choose me if you had one such as her available. It was as if my Horse required proof. I have since abandoned such notions. I know your love for me transcends... the desires of your cock. And, I felt my Horse knew this as well, but perhaps it is still concerned."

He frowned and rolled on his back to study the ceiling with his lip between his teeth. "So… your Horse will feel more reassurance if I bed them?"

The storm I had hurried around struck with a ferocity that left me nearly as breathless as my earlier bout upon not finding him. I loved him. I loved him more than life itself. I could not lose him. I could not share him. I felt the fool for admitting what I had. Then I felt the fool for feeling that. I tore at myself with red hot tongs of regret. I wished to retreat to the tower again, but I was held fast in the thick of it. I gasped.

He turned to face me with concern.

"I am a fool," I hissed. "Oui, the more women you bed, the more reassurance I might find." I spat with bitterness and sarcasm.

He rolled atop me to gaze earnestly into my eyes. "Will…" he admonished with a growl.

I shook my head with shame. "I know. I know. You would not bed them all even if I gave you true license to do so. You do not wish to… and…"

"Should I bind and gag you?" he whispered.

He was only partially teasing, and I stood in the thick of the storm and thought on it.

"Take the reins," I whispered. "I am plunging about. I feel it now. Gods how I feel it. I am trying to hang on. Should I let it throw me again? And what part do you find mad?" I asked with sincere wonder. "I truly felt I wished to compete with Christine. Was that the madness you see? Or…"

He silenced me with a deep kiss, and I accepted it gratefully. It steadied me. I felt pulled away again, safe and distant, as if he had extended a hand into the howling winds and plucked me out. The storm raged on, though. I wondered if this was how I made him feel when he was thus. I wished to know that very much, so much that I found myself clutching at him to keep that particular wind from dragging me back into the maelstrom.

"Can you calm yourself?" he whispered.

"I do not know," I said. "I thought I was recovering. I thought: and now this… It is a storm like you speak of. You hold me clear of it, but I feel if I think, I will be sucked back in."

He regarded me with a physician's concern and my matelot's love. "I am going to drug you."

I nodded eagerly, but as he climbed from the hammock I was gripped by the knowledge that I was forgetting many important things and I could not spend the day abed – as we had already done – as we had already angered someone by doing.

"Vivian," I hissed. "She is at Theodore's. She does not wish to be abandoned there. She does not… She is lonely. She is… She wants to be loved. I cannot care for her as she needs. I would break her heart and you would kill her."

He smiled with patient amusement as he returned to me. "I will fetch her home."

He pressed a small cup to my lips, and I drank.

"Christine is lonely, too," he sighed. "And I cannot care for her, either. It will kill you and my Horse will kill her. But I did tell her that we would train her more in swordplay if the weather breaks."

I nodded, waiting for the drug to ease my heart.

He returned to lying beside me beneath the blanket, and pulled me into his arms.

I was sure there was something else I should tell him. That thought left me anxious that I would not remember before the drug took hold.

"Theodore has drawn up the document for the renunciation," I said at last with relief. "He wishes for us to go to Spanish Town when the weather clears."

Gaston nodded. "Perhaps we can do both on the morrow. Was there not another thing we should do in Spanish Town?"

I looked to see if he was merely attempting to distract me, but he seemed sincere.

"I suppose we should visit Ithaca," I sighed. "Not that I will ever inherit it now. And we can go riding." That thought pleased me, and as the drug began to wrap me in a sheltering blanket even more comforting than his arms, I let myself think of riding.

"Your uncle," Gaston said with a frown. "We need to track him down."

I could not remember who he spoke of. I snuggled against him and reveled in the world slipping away. I rode Diablo, feeling the wind in my face and the play of muscle beneath my thighs. The road was wide and level before me, and I could go anywhere and never look back.

I woke to Gaston whispering my name and rubbing my shoulder. Bright light sprayed between every crack in the stall walls and flooded the open doorway. I could not hear rain. I needed to piss, and my mouth was dry. I thought it likely my head would ache soon.

"How is my mad matelot this morning?" Gaston teased as he prodded and rolled me out of the hammock.

"It is morning?" I asked, as he guided me to the chamber pot. "What morning?"

"The next: you only slept through one night," he assured me.

He handed me a bottle of water once I had relieved myself, and I sat upon a trunk to down it. Even before I wiped my lips from that, he was handing me a hunk of meat and another of pineapple. I was not especially hungry and so I sucked on the fruit as I watched him lay out clothes and pack our bags.

"Are we traveling?" I asked.

"I let you sleep as long as I could. The others are waiting," he sighed. "We are to go to Spanish Town to meet with the governor. We have sent for the horses. I have made arrangements concerning Vivian and the baby. I have told Christine that we will see to the marriage once we return. I have told Agnes you are not well. Your sister is not likely to give birth within a day or so – I hope. I have a list of the plantations where your uncle has stayed from your sister and Rucker. Some are a day's ride from here. I would rather not visit Ithaca, but we should probably see if he is there first. I would spare us the frustration, though. They will learn you will never be its master soon enough and undo anything we tell them."

I listened to all that and dressed in the good breeches he handed me. His last words brought me to sit upon the trunk again, as my heart suddenly seemed too heavy for me to carry.

He turned, and pushed boots on my feet and began lacing them. "How are we?"

I did not know how to respond. His words and the events of yesterday – the events of the last week – swirled about me, gaining speed and threatening to become a maelstrom again. I stood in fear amidst them.

He looked up, and upon seeing my face, quickly stood to gaze into my eyes. "Will?"

"I am not yet well," I whispered.

He frowned and studied me with speculation. "Can you ride?"

"Which mount?" I asked with a tight smile. "I feel I would be fine upon the back of a real animal, but the one inside me I must be very careful with."

He sighed and smiled a little. "Will riding the one help put you at rights with the other?"

I nodded. "It usually does."

"Do you wish to go to the governor's?" he asked. "We can tell Theodore to postpone it."

I tried to think on all that would be entailed: a pleasant ride in the company of friends; having to smile and be friendly to the governor and anyone else who might be there; signing the document; having them wonder at it; having them think me a fool; wondering what else my father had arranged with Modyford... The winds began to howl.

I took a deep breath. "I feel I must go, but... You must hold the reins."

He nodded. "I want us to return to Negril as soon as possible." He sighed. "Will, I am doing what I must, and I am well enough at the moment, but I am very close to only standing because you cannot." He indicated how close by holding a finger and thumb a very small distance apart.

"Then we are in trouble," I said as lightly as I could manage. "Gods help us."

"It is so steep here," he said with a sigh of discouragement.

"I will not think of that, or anything," I said. "And you should not, either. I will dress."

He smiled. "Let me shave you first."

I watched motes of dust dance in the shafts of light above us as he worked. I tried very hard not to think, especially about the fact that I could not think. I had nearly broken a sweat with the effort of it by the time he finished.

"I must be distracted," I said as I accepted the shirt he had selected for me.

"I will think of something," he muttered as he donned his weapons.

I donned mine as well, and slipped on my coat. We said goodbye to Bella and the puppies, and went to join Theodore, the Marquis, and Dupree in the atrium. I wondered at the need for us all to go, and then quickly decided that the Marquis' presence on this mission was greatly appreciated. But all that thinking just brought the winds closer, and so I stopped it, and walked briskly to the street.

Though the rain had stopped, the street was still filled with mud. Someone had thankfully arranged for a carriage, though. After we climbed in, Gaston asked his father his thoughts on the Sun King. The Marquis regarded him with a raised eyebrow, but began to explain his feelings about Emperor Louis XIV's policies and reign. Dupree translated for Theodore. I quickly discovered that – as well-intentioned as Gaston's ploy had been – talk of kings led me to think of wolves, and sheep, and the plantation, and my father... Thus I spent much of the journey to the wharf watching the mud being flung from the carriage wheel.

The wake of the ferry proved to be an equal distraction, and though I was aware of several pairs of eyes upon me, I was able to throw that concern to the maelstrom. I wondered if the winds circled fast enough, if they could throw thoughts I did not wish to encounter out and away as mud was flung from wheels. The Bard had told me there was a calm center in the largest storms, the ones the Indians call hurricanes. As I seemed to picture the winds howling around me, perhaps I stood in such a center, and I could be safe here as long as I did not move; and in time the winds would wear themselves out, having flung all of the awful thoughts away.

Our horses, Diablo and Francis, were as fractious as ever. And who could blame them? Being solely ours, and with our being present so seldom, they spent their days doing nothing but eating, sleeping, and frolicking: they were spoiled through and through. My sorrel, Diablo, tried to bite me as I approached. I wished to embrace him for it: here was a true distraction.

The farm they resided on had chosen to saddle them for us, and I supposed that was acceptable as we wore our better clothes, but I thought we would have to make arrangements to return the tack once we changed into our buccaneer garb, which Gaston had thoughtfully packed.

Our companions had arranged for horses at the livery, and soon we were all mounted to ride the short distance to Spanish Town. I longed to run. I looked to Gaston and he grinned. We pushed out hats far onto our heads, put heels to our steeds, and left those near us in a spatter of mud and curses.

We rode for the sheer glory of it; and when Spanish Town loomed all too soon, we glanced at one another, and with the grins of foxes signaled our mutual accord; and so we wove our way through side streets to another road leading out of town and continued to ride. Our horses were far from winded and our spirits far from sated when Gaston pulled Francis up. I reluctantly reined Diablo in and turned to join him. My matelot did not need to tell me we must return, and I did not need to tell him I did not wish to: there were many things we need not say. He reached for me as I passed, and I leaned to kiss him. Then we cantered back to town.

Theodore and the Marquis appeared quite relieved to see us as we rode into the yard of the Governor's House.

"I would not miss this," I chided, as we joined them on the portico.

Theodore snorted derisively.

We were allowed to scrape our boots and then ushered into the governor's office. He was present, as were Sir Thomas Lynch, Henry Morgan, and two other men Theodore quickly identified as councilmen. All greeted us graciously and viewed us with barely disguised curiosity.

"You need for us to witness a document?" Governor Modyford asked as he took a seat behind his desk.

The Marquis and I took the two chairs before him, with Dupree at his master's side, Theodore hovering nearby, Gaston leaning with his back to the doorpost, and the other guests arrayed about the walls, standing or seated.

Calm rolled over me like a fog. It was as I often felt before a battle. I found comfort in it, clarity: all things were held at a safe and muffled distance save those right before me, the things I could do something about.

I nodded politely to the governor's question, and Theodore unrolled the document he had prepared and flattened it with paper weights at the corners before sliding it across the desk to the man. I watched Modyford struggle with surprise and dismay as he read it.

"My Lord, you cannot be serious," Modyford said when he finished.

Lynch moved to regard what he could of the document. The governor was forced to slide the paper to the side of the desk to keep the other man from leaning over him. At which point, Morgan joined Lynch in reading: a thing the former was not pleased with at all.

"I am very serious," I said.

"Why?" Lynch blurted.

"I believe my father does not wish for me to inherit," I said coolly. "There is another he has long favored over me; and I believe, working either separately or in concert, that they will do what they feel necessary to insure I do not inherit. So I have decided it is in my best interests, and of far more importance, the best interests of all whom I hold dear, for me to step aside. It is not a battle I wish to wage or win. I feel the cost will be far too high."

Wearing a perplexed frown, Lynch sat in a chair beside the governor's desk. Morgan seemed torn between amusement and bemusement as he strolled to the window to look out over the garden. The other councilmen seemed as confused and stunned as Lynch. And Modyford regarded the wall beside his desk with pursed lips and the furrowed brow of consternation.

"I..." Modyford began and glanced at me. He sighed. "I have no reason to believe your father does not wish for you to inherit."

"He has told you such a thing?" I asked levelly.

Modyford snorted and mopped his brow. "Nay," he said after some consideration. "I feel as I do because I know a little of fathers and sons."

"And what does that knowledge tell you of my situation?" I asked.

He sighed. "That even though a man might become frustrated or find much to disapprove of in his son's conduct, his son is still his son."

"Aye," I said. "A thing in this instance that both parties find unfortunate. I will repeat, or perhaps rephrase: I do not wish to become the Earl of Dorshire, or remain the Viscount of Marsdale, even if said titles would not cost me all that I hold dear; because I believe, in the end, they would. Since you avow you have not communicated with my father, I would say it is very likely I know the man far better than you possibly could. I have little doubt he will do whatever he wishes to insure his title is not disgraced. I also know, without doubt, that he finds me a disgrace. Thus, even if he wishes for me to inherit, I feel he will destroy those aspects of my life he feels to be in error. I will not allow or condone that. I am removing myself from contention; and I care not whether you find me a fool for doing so. I only wish for you to witness the document."

"And that is a thing I will not do, *my Lord*," Modyford said with the raised chin and hard eyes of a man who expects to be struck.

I stood, and he tried his best not to flinch as I leaned over his desk to slide the paper to me. I snatched a quill from his cup and dipped it in ink. He gave an exasperated sigh as I signed the document, *John Williams*.

I looked about, none but my friends would meet my gaze. I passed the pen to the Marquis, and with a grin and flourish, he signed with his title. Gaston approached and did the same. Then Theodore took the quill from him.

"You do not wish to do that, Mister Theodore," Modyford said as Theodore inked the pen.

Theodore smiled grimly and signed before meeting the governor's gaze and saying, "I believe, under the eyes of God, I must."

Modyford frowned, as did Lynch.

All were silent as Theodore dusted the signatures and waved the paper dry. I felt the silence like a band tightening about my skull. I no longer stood in a place of quiet and clarity in the center of a maelstrom; the howling winds were within me, and they wanted out.

I looked to Gaston, and he nodded at what he saw in my eyes.

"There are larger interests at stake," Modyford implored as Theodore rolled the document.

"Larger interests?" I snapped.

"We all must mature and put aside boyish pursuits at some day in our lives," he said. "As men, we must bow before the needs of king and country. You are a lord: that is a sacred duty. The king does not need his lords squabbling amongst themselves when there are enemies abroad."

"Spare me!" I snarled. "So now you represent the king? Who has promised you what, Modyford? How grandiose is your political ambition? Or is this all in the name of what gold you can line your pockets with?"

"Will!" Theodore snapped, and I felt both the Marquis' and Gaston's hands upon me.

"My Lord, you go too far!" Modyford said with pompous outrage.

"Do I?" I roared. "I am a man who merely wants to be happy in this life! Is that too much to ask? I love this man!" I pointed at a startled Gaston. "And I believe my father will kill him. Should I not – as a grown man and not a boy – do all in my power to safeguard the object of my love? Is that not what a man does?"

"Oh Lord..." Theodore breathed: his whispered words loud in the booming silence.

"Will," Gaston implored and tugged gently on my arm.

I did not wish to take my eyes from Modyford's, primarily because he did not wish to hold my gaze. I wished to think it was because it weighed heavy on his soul.

"My Lord," Lynch said. "Do you not realize sodomy is illegal, even here, as this is an English colony?"

Morgan swore vehemently.

Gaston towed me toward the door before I could even begin to counter Lynch.

"Thomas!" Modyford roared in our wake.

"Nay," Lynch yelled in return. "This is insanity. How long will you support these damn pirates?"

"We need them!" were the last words I heard of Modyford's before Gaston had me through the doors and outside.

Gaston got my back to a wall on the portico and took my face in his hands. "Will?"

I was gasping with unexpressed rage made all the worse by hearing the ghostly echo of the confrontation repeated quietly in French by Dupree.

"I want them dead," I hissed.

"Of course you do," Gaston said with a worried frown. "But you will not, oui? You will let me have the reins and guide you to safety, oui?"

"Oui," I sighed, and tried for his sake to find that quiet center of the storm.

"We should go home to the sister's," the Marquis told Gaston. "Forget seeking the uncle for now. There is much to discuss."

My matelot nodded; and beyond him, Theodore appeared relieved.

I nodded weakly, and allowed Gaston to lead me to the horses. I mounted numbly. I did not wish to think, but I could not find distraction or solace in the ride back to the Passage. I felt as I imagined a condemned man felt: there was very little hope in my heart that anything would be resolved to my satisfaction; yet I still held great faith that I was loved and always would be in this life and any that might follow, though it could provide me little comfort at the moment.

The journey home seemed interminable, and when at last we walked though the doors all I wished for was the drug and sleep. Striker stepped from Sarah's office with a grim visage that mirrored our own, and I quickly despaired of crawling into our hammock before more troubles were laid before us.

"Sarah said you went to the Governor's," Striker said to Gaston. He glanced over us and sighed. "From the looks of it, that did not go well."

"Nay," Gaston said. "He refused to sign the document."

Striker did not appear surprised. He nodded. "We've been nosing around and we have some things to tell you. Let's all sit down."

"Everyone," Pete added from the office doorway. "EvenTheWomen."

"And your wife is here, too," Striker told Theodore.

"She should be," Theodore said sadly.

Pete and Striker pushed the tables together in the atrium to form one long one. I sat on one side of it while Gaston and Theodore went to fetch the women. The Marquis sat opposite me, concern tight upon his features.

"I believe this is an occasion for wine," the Marquis told Dupree, who hurried off to fetch that.

"And water," I added belatedly.

The Marquis called after his man and requested that as well, before turning back to me and asking quietly in French, "Are you well?"

I shook my head and awarded him a sad smile. He reached across the table and patted my hand. I was tempted to squeeze his before he withdrew it, but I did not. I felt too confused to engage in unfamiliar gestures. So I squeezed Gaston's hand instead when he returned and took the seat beside me. He kissed me lightly on the cheek.

The women did not appear happy to be there: none of them. Sarah had been crying. Agnes was pinched with worry. Christine stood defensively with her arms crossed until Rucker made such a show of offering her a chair that she had to accept it. Rachel awarded us all an anxious and uncomfortable glance as she sat. Vivian was, of course, both livid and scared to have been called downstairs; but she had taken the seat Gaston had offered her on my other side, and now she clutched the sleeping baby as if it might protect her or she must protect it.

I offered her my other hand, and she squeezed it gratefully.

"What has happened?" she whispered.

I could only shake my head.

"What happened at the Governor's?" Sarah asked.

Theodore sighed and glanced about until he saw none of us who had been there would speak. He sighed again. "The governor refused to sign the document of renouncement I prepared. They all did. The governor was quite… adamant… that Will not sign it, either." He went on to describe all that had occurred and was said.

This ended with Rachel's and Sarah's heads buried in their hands, Vivian regarding me with dismay, Christine studying the table with a frown of incredulity, Rucker grimacing, Agnes looking perplexed, and Pete and Striker chuckling.

"Lynch will not arrest you," Striker said. "He would not dare; Morgan and Modyford would have him shot for disrupting the fleet sailing this winter."

I nodded.

"I agree," Theodore said, "still… Modyford will not always be governor. He wishes for greater things. And Morgan's life and influence will likely be short-lived."

"Aye," Striker sighed. "It will all change, and those who wish to follow the old ways will move on soon enough. But we have larger problems. Not that the damn man not witnessing the paper isn't a problem."

"What have you learned?" Gaston asked.

"There's a bounty on our heads: yours and mine," Striker told my matelot with forced cheer.

My heart felt as if it had stopped for a moment. There was a surprised hush about the atrium, broken only by Dupree's whispered translation.

Gaston sat back in his seat with a thoughtful frown and a grip upon my hand that hurt more than my lurching heart.

The Marquis abruptly stood to pace and swear – most of which seemed to involve my father's ancestry, or lack thereof, and potential love of farm animals, and sadly even a purported love of cocks and sodomy.

It was a sorry reminder of how much I might be reviled by those who did not share my interests: how the things I enjoyed most would be epithets used to cut another. But expressing my love for Gaston was illegal; was it not? I was sure my father thought he was doing me a great favor: saving me from ruin and even damnation. It made me hate him all the more.

"Father!" Gaston said sharply.

"No one puts a price on my son's head!" the Marquis growled.

"What is he saying?" Striker asked.

"Well, he was cursing," Dupree said with an embarrassed cock of his head. "And this last: no one puts a price on my son's head."

"They didn't know," Striker said quickly.

"Father, sit down and listen," Gaston commanded.

The Marquis opened his mouth to speak and closed it again, and then did as his son asked.

"We went to the taverns and started spreading coin and rum,"

Striker said. "We heard tell of it soon enough, that someone, actually two men, had been approaching men known to do an underhanded thing now and again, and telling them there was a reward if Gaston and I should come to harm in battle, brawl, or duel. They all said there was no reward if any of the women around us were harmed."

"Well, that is good," I said.

"Aye," Striker agreed. "It's not the only good in this tale, but it is the best piece of it. From the looks of it, many of the men approached wanted nothing to do with it, at least the ones that talked to us. And they did not say that because we beat them, either. One said he was scared of Pete, another of Will, and another said that he thought it would lead to nothing but trouble even if he could get enough men together to take a pair of us, because by the time you have that many men, someone will talk and they didn't want to be running for the rest of their lives. All we talked to apologized for not giving us warning, but many of them we didn't know well and some of the others were scared we would kill the messenger." He gave his matelot an admonishing look that indicated that might have nearly happened, anyway.

"So we learned the names of the two men spreading the word," he continued. "One was the barkeep at the Three Tunns. He apologized, too, but said he was paid good money just to talk others up, and he didn't think any he talked to stood a chance of harming us, anyway. But he would not say if he had any takers. And he's well-liked, and beating it out of him would have caused trouble." Striker sighed sadly.

"TheOtherOneWeren'tSoLucky," Pete said.

Striker smiled grimly. "Aye, he's rotting on the Palisadoes. He was a known rat bastard. He admitted he had several takers, though; but he had no names, and only one of the men he described we thought we could recognize: an arrogant, thin, one-eyed man with dark hair."

"Hastings," I gasped.

Striker nodded. "Trouble is: he said the man had a patch on his left eye, and Pete swears Hasting's patch is on the right, and I can't remember for the life of me."

I could not, either. I could clearly picture Hastings in two different situations, and in my memories, his patch was on the right in one, and on the left in the other. I frowned at my matelot.

"He is not blind in either eye," Gaston said.

"Oh, shit," Striker said with a nod of understanding. "He just wears a patch."

"Why would a man wear a patch if he isn't blind?" Rachel asked.

"For seeing in the dark," Striker said. "When we sailed with Myngs, there was a man I knew from the King's Navy who did it. And Hastings is from the Navy. When you walk into a dark place after you've been in the sun, it takes a long time before you can see anything. The same is true if you're in the dark and walk out into the light. So men on a man o' war that have to be on deck and then below for a gun deck or chart room sometimes take to wearing a patch they can move from one eye to the other. That way one eye is good for the dark, and the other for the light."

"They cannot shoot well at range, but they do well in boarding," Gaston said.

I thought on the type of man who would hamper himself at all times in order to be able to quickly adapt from one situation to another. It would take stubbornness and foresight I did not feel I possessed. But then we were talking of the man who had murdered Michaels, possibly for no other reason other than because he could, and had taken great relish in our hanging Burroughs.

"I feel we should kill him, anyway, even if he is not the man that bastard meant," I said.

"Aye," Striker agreed with a shrug. "I don't like him either. Sadly, he's the only one the man could describe well-enough for us to suspect."

"What else did he say?" Gaston asked.

"They received their money and instructions from that agent, Washington," Striker said. "So we paid him a visit."

Theodore groaned.

Striker snorted. "We didn't lay a hand on him, though Pete sure as the Devil wanted to. He was a smug bastard. We told him we knew he was in on it, and if any of us were harmed, those that lived knew where to find him."

"Do you feel he will pray to God that we all live?" I asked.

"Nay," Striker sighed. "I should have let Pete kill him."

"And face hanging?" Theodore asked.

"ThereBeWaysWhereinNoneBeTheWiser," Pete said with a derisive snort.

"But not now," Theodore countered. "Now everyone who would make a decision as to your guilt or innocence knows that we are all embroiled in this feud. And they might not arrest a buccaneer for sodomy, but they will hang one for killing a supposedly honest man and respected citizen. So whether you are seen or not, if that man dies, they will come to us for answers."

Pete was obviously not pleased with that perspective of the matter. "IffnWeKill'EmAll, CanWeHideInFrance?"

Dupree frowned and began to dutifully translate.

"Nay," I said to Pete. I looked to the Marquis and switched to French. "He wishes to know if we could seek sanctuary in France if we kill my father."

The Marquis shook his head. "I could not protect you. It would be a matter of state for one nobleman to harbor another's killer. The Emperor could well demand you be surrendered, or he could laugh about the matter. Either way, it would be above our heads and very dangerous. You could seek sanctuary with the Church, but..." He smiled. "I do not see that suiting you."

I chuckled sadly and shook my head: I could not see spending my days in a cathedral because I had been forced to rid the world of my father. I was sure that in that situation, some damn self-righteous bastard would work to keep Gaston and me apart – for our eternal salvation, of course.

Dupree was translating the Marquis' words for Pete.

The Golden One scratched his jaw and grunted. "ThatBeWhatIThought."

"All the men questioned said we women were not to be harmed," Sarah said. "You will stay home this year and we will attempt some manner of resolving this. If no damn man on this island will sign that document, then perhaps Will should travel to England and present it in person."

"Sarah," I chided, though I well understood her wish. "I have seen such things before. I would not be allowed to reach the House of Lords. If they know I leave here for England..." I shook my head as the enormity of what she suggested settled across my heart and shoulders. "We do not have an army or the political clout to guarantee my safety. And though I doubt they would have me murdered on the street, they could well have me arrested on some charge, or even... restrained for my own good under the auspices of my being mad. That is done even to hush sane men. We honestly do not know enough of Father's allegiances and enemies in the court to know who to approach to thwart him, or to beg for aid."

"Then we shall discover that information," Sarah said with a desperate shrillness to her voice. "I am sure the Marquis will assist us. He can surely get mail in and out of England that our father's men would not know of."

The Marquis nodded as this was translated.

I looked to the rolled document Theodore had laid on the table. "That is surely the only way that will ever be seen." I turned back to her. "But all that will take time, possibly years."

"Then we shall wait years," she said. "Not that you need worry as much: Father will surely rescind his bounty on Gaston, once he knows he is a Marquis' son."

There were many surprised faces about the table.

She flushed with embarrassment. "I am sorry."

Pete was shaking his head.

"Stop that," Sarah growled at him. "You do that every time I say you should stay. What great battle plan do you have, then?"

He stood. "Gettin'TheChessBoard." He sniffed with hurt: either feigned or real, I could not tell.

Striker awarded his wife a look that said there was much he would not say, and she covered her face with her hands and gave a ragged sob. Then she pushed herself to her feet and waddled after Pete.

"Pete has a plan?" I asked.

Striker nodded. "He won't tell us of it, but he's been thinking on it for days. Sarah is sure she won't like it. I'm pretty sure she won't like it. I'm not sure I will."

I was curious, and I looked to my matelot and found him curious, too.

Pete returned with the chess board balanced on one hand and his other about Sarah. He handed the board to Striker and helped Sarah return to her seat. Then he took the board and set it in the middle of the main table, where the most people could see it. He leaned on the wood and rested on his elbows, so he could reach it from where he stood at the head.

"ThisBeUs." He pointed at the chiseled white pieces on his side of the board. "ThatBeThem." He pointed at the black. "All'EreBePieces."

"All right," Striker said and stood to get a better view from where he was at his matelot's side. "So Sarah is the queen?"

"Nay," Pete said with a disappointed sigh. "SarahBeTheKing. The KingNotMoveMuch. 'EOnlyMovesOneSpaceAtATime." He demonstrated this with the white king. "TheGameBeLostWhen'EBe Captured."

At Dupree's worried expression, Gaston and I began translating. After our first awkward mutual utterance, we began to take turns.

Pete picked up the queen and pointed at me. "WillBeTheQueen. TheQueenCanMoveInAnyDirectionAsFarAsSheWants. SheBeTheMost DangerousPiece. WillBeTheOneO'UsThatCanBeALordAn'APirate."

He pointed at the Marquis and Theodore. "YouBeCastles. YouCan MoveFar. ButOnlyOneWay."

"GastonAnMeBeBishops. WeMoveADifferentWay ButWeCanMove JustAsFar."

"What am I?" Striker asked.

Pete snorted and tossed him one of the knights. "YaBeAHorse. TheOther OneBeTheBrethren. YaDon'tMoveStraightOrFar. ButYaBe Dangerous 'CauseTheOtherManFergetsHowYaMove. 'EBe Thinkin'StraightLines. But TheBrethrenBeAboutCrookedPeople. Men WhoWouldRobTheBlindBut Na'TakeMoneyTaKillTheirOwn. TheyDon't UnderstandThat." He pointed at the black pieces.

Pete looked about the table to see if we understood. I grinned at him with enthusiasm, for I felt hope again.

He nodded at what he had seen in our faces, and shrugged. "TheRest A'YaBePawns. ButThatBeGood. PawnsBeImportant."

"Now," he said, and snatched the white knight from Striker. He arranged the black pieces about the board, leaving the white pieces in their starting rows. "TheyBeenMovin'. FurMaybeAYear. AllTheWhile, WeNotBeenKnowin'WeBeenPlayin'. WeBeWayBehind."

"TheyGotMorePawnsThanWeGotPieces. WeKnowThatBeTheEarl." He pointed at the black king. "An'ThatBeTheDamnCousin." He pointed at the black queen sitting next to the king, in their starting positions behind a short row of pawns. "WeKnowOneO'TheCastlesBeThatBastard Washington. AndOneO'TheHorseBeModyford. WeTookAPawnLastNight. WeNa'KnowWhoTheRestBe." He waved his hand over the other black pieces.

I looked at the black spread about the board and the white in its neat rows with the pawns in front. "They are already boxing us in."

"Aye," Pete crowed triumphantly.

He began to scoot the white pieces around, forming a phalanx of pawns around the queen, a knight, and both bishops, in the middle of the board. He arranged it so each piece could move easily from behind the pawns and potentially strike all the black pieces spread about the board, except for the king and queen. Then he arranged the pawns about our king so that it could move in two directions to escape, and placed the castles and a horse to guard it.

"ThisBeUs." He pointed at the white phalanx in the center and then Gaston, Striker, me, and himself. Then he indicated the women, Rucker, and Theodore. "ThisBeThemThatStayInPortRoyal. OrGoTaFrance." He moved one of the castles all the way to the white starting line, where it put the black king in check.

The Marquis nodded approvingly as I finished translating.

Pete pointed at the phalanx of white again and began striking out with the pieces there, capturing one black piece after another until only a few pawns, the castles, and the king and queen remained.

"WeNeedTaTakeTheirPiecesOffTheBoard. WeGottaFind'EmFirst Though. WeGotTaFlush'EmOut. WeGotTaGuardEachOther'sBacks. LikeBoardin'AShip. WhenWeGetDone. WeSeeIffn'EStillWantsTaPlay. If'EDoes WeGoFor'Im."

Sarah pushed her way to her feet again and began to leave the table.

"Sarah?" Striker queried.

"Look at you all, grinning like ghouls," she said with tears forming in her eyes. "You will leave me here and go roving in the name of gaining a tactical advantage?"

"He does not want you dead," I said. "You will be safe unless we lose. Striker is safest amongst the Brethren."

She shook her head with frustration, her voice becoming shrill again. "Since our damn father has apparently been misguided enough to lay edict that I not be harmed, even though my husband is to be taken from me, Striker is safest at my side."

"As long as he does not leave this house," I challenged. "Do you feel he will live well with that? Will you? And it will only be until Father decides his other methods have failed and he must attend to the matter himself. Not one damn man will raise a hand to stop him if he arrives here with a small army of mercenaries on one of the king's good men of war. Pete is correct. We stand our best chance doing what we do best and killing them first. Meanwhile, you and Theodore and the Marquis can wage a more covert battle to discover who wants our damn father dead or disparaged as much as we do.

"And," I continued as more aspects of the matter revealed themselves to me. "We do not lose if you are taken. We stand a better chance of rescuing you if we are not here when and if our father arrives."

"Aye," Pete said with a feral smile. "WeGetCaughtWithOurPants

Down, WeBeDead. TheyTakeYouWhileWeBeRovin', WeJustRoveIn EnglandNext. WeGetYaBack."

Sarah ignored Pete, and glared at me as if she wanted me dead as much as our father, and turned away to the stairs.

"Sarah," Striker called and looked to Pete and hissed, "You go. You're better with her when she's thus."

"Naw. IBeTheOneThatMade'ErAngryThisTime," Pete whispered back with a rueful shrug.

Striker swore quietly and followed his wife.

Vivian tugged at my sleeve. "So you will go roving and not go to this Negril place with me?" Her concerned gaze was locked on the chess board.

"Nay," I sighed. "I am sorry, but if this is the plan we follow, we will not go to Negril."

"But..." She gazed up at me earnestly and bit her lip. "Can we not simply go to France? Without killing anyone?"

Gaston sighed.

"Oui," the Marquis said with enthusiasm as Dupree finished. "You could avoid all this. You would all be welcome."

Dupree thankfully translated for those who did not speak French, as I was busy watching my matelot, who had become suffused with guilt. I laid a hand on his shoulder, and he shook his head sadly.

"Naw," Pete said. "StrikerNa'LeaveTheSea, An'IDon'tSpeakFrench."

"You do not speak English," Vivian said, and cringed at what she saw in Pete's eyes.

I laid a hand on her shoulder and looked back to my matelot. He had met his father's earnest gaze.

Gaston shook his head sadly and stood. "I am sorry, I cannot." He left us and retreated to the stable.

I looked to the Marquis apologetically and said, "Not yet."

"I do not wish to..." Theodore sighed. He met my curious gaze. "There is the other matter. Gaston should not go to France."

I struggled to remember what he spoke of, and then I did. I looked to the Marquis. "And though we now trust you greatly, he cannot set foot on French soil until the matter of his competence is resolved."

The Marquis frowned with surprise as if he, too, struggled to remember what I spoke of; and then he shook his head irritably and began to protest.

"What if something befalls you before it can be righted?" I asked. "There are presumably those who would not wish for you to have an heir."

He sighed and slumped back in his chair to nod with solemn understanding. "You are correct. I have put him in a sad position should he return to France without me; and there are those who were pleased when my sons died, as it meant I did not have an heir."

"Please make clearing his name your first order of business upon returning." I stood to follow my matelot.

"Of course," the Marquis said with irritation, and then he gazed up at me and frowned with compassion. "You need not worry about that."

"Then can I go to Negril?" Vivian asked, oblivious to all but her own concern – though in fairness, she had not understood the French conversation.

"Nay," I said quickly. "Not alone."

"I can take Henrietta," she said with determination.

I could not picture that, and then I could. "Nay! It is too dangerous. The Devil with all this." I indicated the chess board. "You could be raped, robbed, and killed by the crew of any passing ship that happened to see the smoke from your cook fire. And all the water must be hauled up from the bog. Nay. Nay."

She took a ragged breath, her eyes desperate. "Then can we rebuild the house I burned?" She cringed and looked away with shame. The baby was waking, probably sensing her mother's unease. Vivian jiggled the baby to quiet her, and only succeeded in disturbing her more. I thought both of them would be wailing at any moment.

"Nay," Theodore said. "The property belongs to Will's father."

Vivian swore and looked up at me with pleading eyes again. "But I cannot. I cannot live here. I just cannot." The baby began to wail.

I struggled to think of another solution. "I am sorry. I fear you will have to. We will try to come up with an alternative, but this seems best."

"Nay," she sobbed. "Are you trying to drive me to drink?" She stood and hurried to the stairs.

I watched her climb them and run down the hall to her door, which she slammed upon entering. It did little to mute the baby's now frantic cries.

"Does she hate us?" Agnes asked.

"Nay," I said. "She fears all hate her."

"She can come and live with us," Rachel said, and gave Theodore a look that would brook no argument.

He nodded pleasantly. "That will be lovely."

Rachel smiled at her husband with great love and kissed his forehead before following Vivian up to her room.

"I am sorry, Theodore," I said. "For everything."

He smiled. "I am not." He turned to look at me. "I will not have any regrets no matter how I am judged in the end."

"Thank you," I breathed. I looked at the others. "Thank you all."

I felt I had stood at a table with them and said that before. I felt I would ever be saying that, because anyone who befriended us would always be inconvenienced in some fashion.

Rucker grinned. "Nay, thank you; after a life of reading about the battles of kings and queens…" He raised the black king piece. "I find amusement I am finally party to one."

I smiled. "At least we serve some purpose."

"We should have more pawns here who can shoot," Agnes said as she shoved chess pieces around the board.

"Aye, you should," I said. I could hear the winds howling in my head again.

My gaze fell across Christine. She was studying the table with a frown, her finger tracing the same whorl in the wood over and over again. I wondered if she heard winds howling in her head.

"Will?" Theodore queried.

"What?" I asked and turned to him. For a frantic moment I wondered how long I had been watching Christine's finger.

"Are you well?" he asked.

I glanced around. Pete, Rucker, and the Marquis were watching me with concern.

"Nay," I said. "I am… I need to see to Gaston. It has been a very trying time for us. We really wished to retreat to Negril."

This elicited frowns, and even Christine looked up to gaze at me with concern.

I was afraid I would say something else I should not. I nodded at them and walked away, forcing myself not to run to the stable.

I found Gaston sitting with the puppies. He looked up at me with sadness and calm, and I dropped to sit beside him and take his hand.

"I am afraid," I whispered. "That we will lose. That I will lose you, and on the way to losing you, we will lose everyone."

He nodded solemnly and handed me a puppy. "I am afraid the Gods do not know we play chess."

Seventy

Wherein We Seek Peace

We shed our fine clothes and donned our buccaneer garb, and lay in the straw and smelled puppies and allowed Bella to clean our faces and hands. The winds receded as I concentrated on the reassuring smells of milk breath and dogs. After a time, I calmed, and then I realized my matelot had retreated even farther than the stable, into the mien of the Child. I wished to go with him, but I did not know how.

"Can horses sit?" he asked, as he placed a puppy on my chest, and arranged my hand about it with earnest concentration: as if the little bundle being sheltered and not rolling away were the most important thing in the world.

"Non," I said. "Not by choice. If their arse is upon the ground and their front legs are straight, it is because they have fallen or they are ill."

This seemed to sadden him. "And they do not lie down to sleep?"

"Non, very few horses lie on their sides upon the ground to sleep. A grown horse lies on the ground only if it is ill or birthing. Foals and even colts will sometimes lie on their sides to sleep, but often they will lie like a cow does, with their legs folded beneath them."

He nodded thoughtfully. "How do centaurs sleep?"

"How do you want them to sleep?" I asked.

"I am very tired, Will," he sighed, such that it made my heart ache. "I would like to lie beside you for a time. Like colts do, or goats, or bulls, I suppose, with my legs beneath me so that I can rise quickly if there is need."

"Then you should rest, my love," I whispered. "Lie beside me and watch over us, but rest. I will watch too, and I swear, if danger approaches I will find my feet."

"I know you will," he said with a warm smile, and moved to lie beside me with his head cradled in the hollow of my shoulder.

I saw us as centaurs, kneeling side by side in the traces on a steep road, with dark forest all about and wind howling in our faces. But we had one another's warmth; and though the cart creaked in the gale, it did not roll. The vision gave me strength and set me at peace.

"I think we should geld the puppies when we return," he said sometime later. "And Taro. I love puppies, but we cannot have them all the time. There will be too many for us to feed, and I will not give them away to have them misused. I am afraid of what will happen to these if we do not return."

"So am I," I breathed. I felt my peace and calm begin to crumble, but I knew he needed to speak: that it was part of his request to lie beside me. "What else are you afraid of?"

"I am afraid of leaving children behind," he said thoughtfully. "I do not wish to have a child born of my seed that I will not be there to grow. I should not get Christine with child before we sail. Not until all this is behind us."

"You should perhaps not fret on that," I assured him. "There is no guarantee you will get her pregnant even if you do marry her before we sail. Not every seed finds fertile soil in a woman. Not all babies are conceived as Sarah's was. It can take weeks or months, even for the diligent."

"I have thought that," he sighed. "I feel my father shall be disappointed. I wish he did not need to worry, though." He pushed himself up to one elbow to gaze at me earnestly. "How feel you of Pete's plan?"

I sighed and allowed myself to think on it, to recall what I had felt while Pete revealed it. "I think he is correct. I do not think we will be safe here. We must fight. And I am dismayed to admit I feel this will be but the first battle of a war. I attempted a treaty, and I feel it has failed. But... That is not true, as the enemy has not even received my offer yet: it has only been rejected by his agents, and they are, perhaps, misguided."

"So we will feint in order to keep his forces busy while an ambassador delivers the treaty and sues for peace," Gaston said. With the Child's mien about him, it seemed as if he were a precocious boy discussing the dealings of men.

It made me feel as if I were a very old man explaining the workings of the world. And I felt other things as well, listening to my soul in this quiet place with him. "Oui, but... If I listen to my heart... I feel the treaty was the feint. I feel the war is inevitable, and that is perhaps the major source of the gravel strewn before me. I so wish to go to Negril and escape it all, but I am afraid Negril is not far enough – no place will ever be."

"And the sea will not be bad," I added. "We have often felt the road is level there."

He nodded. "But Negril is better. There, the road slopes down, and the cart rolls forward of its own accord, and we need not haul it. We can play in the fields."

I closed my eyes and prayed we would be able to come to such a place again. I did not tell the Gods I wished for it: I begged.

I felt him brush my tears away, and I opened my eyes to find him gazing down at me in the golden afternoon light, as if he were an angel come to grant my prayers.

"All will be well, Will," he said kindly, as if he were indeed inspired by the Gods and filled with Their wisdom. "We are dangerous men. None can take us if we are prepared. We will kill them first."

I grinned at the incongruity of his words with my thoughts. "I love you. You are my angel of the flaming sword – and hair." I pulled at his red tufts that always glowed like fire in the evening light.

He smiled. "Do you feel the others will accept this course?"

There was a hopeful tone to his question, and I was minded of Sarah saying we had grinned like ghouls when Pete presented his plan. Did we relish war? Perhaps we did, because my matelot was correct: we were dangerous men, and we knew how to solve problems with blades and pieces. It was the rest that was confusing.

I thought of how the others had reacted. "Sarah is angry," I noted. "I should not have spoken to her as I did."

He shook his head, and his words were not so very childlike. "Non, you saved Striker the trouble of saying it, and Pete's words also angered her. It is better she is angry with you."

"Oui, I suppose so. Vivian was quite distraught." I realized Gaston had left the table before I spoke with her. "But Rachel has offered for her to live with them."

He sighed with evident relief. "That would be very good. That is one puppy I will not have to worry about, then."

I smiled. "Oui, if my silly wife does begin to drink again, they can toss her on the street and still the child will be well cared for." I sobered. "I think it will truly be better for Vivian, too. She cannot live in a house with Sarah and Christine. They will all fight like cats, and she would be back on the rum in no time."

He sighed and sagged down to rest his head on my shoulder again.

"What?" I asked.

"I suppose Christine will live here," he said.

"If you marry her," I said, "and... Well, I suppose even if you do not. We could send her to France with your father, but not if she is to bear you children." I snorted. "I keep thinking we should do that, anyway, and you can find her later and have children."

"If I do not marry her we could send her to France?" he asked hopefully.

"Will you marry her?" I asked with true curiosity; and not merely as a prompt to know his thoughts.

"I do not know. I must decide. I know I must decide soon." He sighed. "I would bed Agnes again. Soon."

"Tonight?" I asked.

He rose so he could peer at my face again. "If you can bear it."

I did not rush to reassure him: I considered my heart. "I stand at the center of a storm of howling winds. I feel they will close in on me at any time, but I am safe for now."

He nodded sagely. "It is a fearful place. I always envision you there with me, anchoring me against the winds."

I imagined we were two centaurs lying together upon the road again, in the center of a storm howling all about us. I smiled. "You have not been resting. We have been regarding the road ahead a great deal, but not resting. I will watch for a time."

He looked to the open doorway beside us: the Child hovered at the edges of his face and nearly slipped away. "It is getting late, and I need…"

I put fingers to his lips and shook my head. "We will not sail tomorrow. We have no ship until the *Queen* returns. And even if she did arrive tomorrow, we would not sail until Sarah births. You need do nothing this night but rest. Unless your Horse has other desires you feel you must sate."

He shook his head quickly and emphatically, a child's gesture, and lay beside me again. "I only need do that to… show me what decision I must make."

"Let it go for now," I whispered, and rubbed his back.

My Horse was now very calm, and I wondered at that, until I realized a decision had been made: several of them, and they all sat well with the animal. I thought they might cause trouble with others, but I did not care. We would escape to a place where the road was level and we could battle that which opposed us, and for a time lighten the cart of several women in spirit if not in actuality.

When Sam came to tell us dinner was served, Gaston did as I bade, and chose to remain curled up with the puppies in a state of innocent bliss while I went to fetch our meal. I was not yet ready to face most of our housemates, either, and so I was relieved to see the dining room empty. Sam and Henrietta were dismayed, but I told them to keep the food warm and people would surely trickle in as they hungered.

As I filled a plate with corn biscuits and pork, Henrietta approached me with her hands wringing her apron.

"Might I have a word, my… Mister Williams?" she asked. She smiled wanly and continued at my nod. "Mistress Williams has moved off to the Theodores'."

I was surprised. "Already? Well, I suppose that is good. We must visit in the morning."

"She told me to tell you to get your arse out o' bed and over there afore noon," she said diffidently.

"This was Mistress Williams and not Mistress Theodore?" I asked with a chuckle.

"Aye, sir," she said with a perplexed nod. "Would Mistress Theodore speak that way to ya', sir?"

"On occasion."

She seemed to have to think on that. "So, sir, I been wonderin'," she said with her lip in her teeth. "Who do I work for now? Should I be goin' ta the Theodores' or stayin' 'ere, or are me services needed at all?"

"Do you think you are needed here?" I asked.

"Aye, sir." She nodded emphatically.

"Well, then, we must discuss the matter with my sister."

"Do ya think she might be willin' ta pay me the same salary?" she asked with an anxious grimace.

I vaguely recalled I had agreed to pay the woman a sum my sister deemed foolhardy. I smiled. "That will have to be discussed."

"I thought as much," Henrietta said with a resigned nod.

"My sister was raised and trained to manage a manor house; I was not," I said by way of apology. "She has feelings about what is proper and…"

"Ya need not explain, sir," Henrietta said. "It were just that with the money ya would 'ave been payin' me, I were thinkin' I could save it all and maybe marry an' 'ave me own house someday."

I sighed. "Henrietta, this is Jamaica; men outnumber women here. If you wish to marry and have your own household, you can find men who earn more money than I was willing to pay you, or own property, or both, who would be delighted to court you."

"Truly, sir? And you would be well with that?"

I sat the plate down and took her by the shoulders. "Henrietta, I will never endeavor to stand in the way of any person's happiness, and you are a free woman."

"Well… I just never looked on it that way afore. I thought me bein' as I am, I would need ta 'ave a bit o' money ta offer a man."

I shook my head. "My dear woman, some men prefer plump, and here, they are not choosy to begin with. And you have a pleasant demeanor and you can cook. Men will duel for you in the street. Announce that you are available and let them court you. Or tell Mister Theodore and have him tell you if he knows of any eligible and acceptable men."

"Truly?"

"Truly." I nodded emphatically.

She smiled and curtsied. "Thank ya, sir. Ya 'ave made me a happy woman this day. The future looks bright as dawn now."

"I am pleased to hear it."

She hurried out, and I sighed. I thought my sister would likely shoot me for losing a perfectly good housekeeper.

As I tried to leave the dining room, Agnes arrived.

She glanced around before sidling up to me. "Are things well? Since… yesterday?"

"Aye, aye," I quickly assured her. "And if you are willing, we wish to continue our adventures in that matter, but not tonight. It has been a very tiring and confusing day, and... we are too tired to... play."

She nodded with seeming relief. "I was afraid you had experienced regret."

"Nay. Have you?"

She shook her head. "I have been thinking on it a great deal, and I feel I wish to try the part I did not like so much again." She frowned. "Would that mean I am wrong in thinking I favor women?"

"I..." I truly did not wish to engage in this discussion. "Nay. Perhaps. But... Well, you will likely have to experiment with the other as well, before you can decide that."

She nodded agreeably. "Do you feel Mistress Garret might entertain women? She is old, but..."

"I do not know," I said with some surprise at her even thinking of such a thing. "Do you have coin with which to make such an inquiry?"

She opened her purse and showed me what she had.

"That should be more than sufficient," I assured her. "Haggle. Whores can be flexible in the matter of price. Tell her what you wish, allow her to name a price, and then counter if you find it beyond your ability or interest."

"I will," she said with enthusiasm and turned away.

"And damn it, girl, do not go over there at night."

She appeared crestfallen.

"Truly," I added. "It would not be safe in that section of town for a young lady. And she might have other clients and there could be confusion, which I am sure you wish to avoid."

"Aye, there would be trouble if I had to shoot someone," she sighed. "I will go in the morning."

"And eat something," I admonished.

She acquiesced glumly and went to the table.

I hurriedly retreated to the stable, pondering whether the puppies were the only truly innocent beings in the whole damn house.

I mentioned nothing of my encounters to Gaston. He had built a nest in the straw and was now burrowing in it. He greeted me with a warm and happy smile, and was quite content to lay his head upon my lap and allow me to feed him. He was very much as he had been when we sailed to Cow Island with a chain between us to keep him from wandering off. I was not worried, though: I had faith that, if the need arose, he would be on his feet beside me and not frolicking in the meadows leaving me to hold the cart. This was what he had meant by needing rest, and I was glad I could provide him this solace.

The only thing that concerned me was that he felt he needed it so badly. It made me acutely aware of how very strained our lives had been these last weeks. But in viewing it from that perspective, I realized we were doing miraculously well: better than I ever would have dreamed possible the day we read his father's letter, just over a fortnight ago. And we had not known then even half of what would face us.

"I am very proud of you," I whispered, when at last we cuddled in our hammock.

He took a deep breath and I felt the Child slip away as he spoke. "So am I. It is all due to you."

"Then I am very proud of me," I teased.

"You are loved," he whispered, and kissed me lightly. "Thank you."

I pulled him closer and drifted to sleep, safe in his arms from the world.

His Horse apparently rose with the dawn – in all His glory – as I was brought to rising by warm lips and a hard cock. As we were piss hard, we did not make short work of it; and as he was quite feral, it was not a languorous affair. I felt I had run five leagues when he at last found his pleasure and brought me to mine.

When I made mention of this as he hopped out of the hammock, he frowned thoughtfully and said, "We have not been attending to our morning regimen."

"Oui," I sighed, as I recalled my thoughts of last night. We were doing well, but we truly needed to do more to mitigate our reaction to the turmoil we faced. His Horse was much calmer when he exercised to the point of exhaustion every day – trysting aside.

He pulled me to the edge of the hammock, and held the pot for me so that I could piss without moving further. Then he jumped atop me again to cover me with kisses like a happy dog. I laughed for the joy of it. He was surely in a fine mood, and I hushed the little voice in my head that said it was because he was still teetering on the edge of madness. Of course he was. So was I, and I needed to frolic for a time as much as he.

"We should go to the Palisadoes and spar," he said gleefully.

I grinned. "Oui, I will enjoy that very much, but we have also been instructed to go and visit Vivian before noon."

"Does one preclude the other?" he asked as he left the hammock again.

"Non, but one should perhaps be done before the other, as I do not wish to feel I must hurry to return from our frolicking in the waves."

"Just so," he said with a thoughtful nod. "Will they be awake now?"

"Do babies sleep?" I asked, as I assessed the morning light blazing through the doorway to illuminate Bella and her pups. Due to our trysting, we were now well past the cock's crow; and I could smell bacon.

We dressed in our usual attire and strapped on our in-town weapons, before snatching handfuls of bacon and a bottle of water and hurrying to the Theodores'.

Hannah met us at the back door with some amusement. "You gentlemen are early this morning."

The baby and her caretakers were indeed awake. We entered to find Vivian feeding one child and Rachel the other, both with small blankets draped decorously over their shoulders so we did not see their exposed breasts. My wife was smirking, apparently at something Rachel had said, and they eyed us with as much amusement as Hannah had.

"Some buccaneers do rise with the sun," I chided with good humor as we took seats at the small back room table.

Rachel snorted and gave me a mischievous smile. "Buccaneers or not, you're men, and it's been my experience that men who rise with the dawn do not leave a warm bed."

I raised an eyebrow. "Lady, it has been my experience that when a man does rise with the dawn… in a warm bed… that warmth and exposure to Heaven's beneficent light can put him in such a mood that he walks lightly and smiles the whole day through."

She smirked. "Usually they roll over and go back to sleep."

"Not this one," I said, and pointed a piece of bacon at Gaston. He flushed and smacked me upon my thigh beneath the table, such that I knew it would bruise.

Rachel and Hannah laughed, but Vivian's mouth was slightly ajar with surprise, and her face was as crimson as my matelot's.

I grinned at her. "And how are we this fine morning?"

She looked away quickly and closed her mouth into a bemused smile. "Well enough… without all that."

I recalled our conversation of the day before regarding her loneliness, and I sighed with guilt. "I am sorry."

"Nay, nay," she said quickly and quietly. "It is good to see people happy." She gave a thoughtful nod.

"I want you to know how pleased we are that you decided to accept the Theodores' gracious offer," I said with a nod to Rachel, who nodded soberly in return.

Vivian smiled at Rachel. "I think we will be happy here until you return. I will learn to cook and sew," she told me with surprising enthusiasm.

"Aye," Rachel said. "Idle hands lead to idle thoughts, and idle thoughts lead to drink. We will make an honest woman of her."

I frowned askance at her, amazed at how very Protestant she sounded. I supposed it was her Jewish upbringing: they ever seemed to be pious and industrious people.

"Though I think in this case that is very true," I told Vivian, "I have known many wealthy women who did not drink, though they had people about to do all that they required."

Vivian frowned in thought, and then smiled at me with wisdom far beyond her years. "I am not to be one of those women."

"Nay, you are not," I said kindly. "The Fates have conspired against you at every turn."

She shrugged. "I was not happy before. So now I will try something new."

"I am so very proud of you," I said.

Vivian nodded, and then for a moment fear haunted her eyes, and they flicked to Rachel, who was busy with Elizabeth.

"It will not be easy, but I shall try," she whispered.

I leaned close and whispered. "Good girl. People who care for us and want what is best for us are not always easy, but there are times when we need the guidance that others can provide when we have lost our way."

"I know," she whispered sincerely. "And I am grateful for it. I just do not wish to repay her kindness with disappointment."

I felt compelled to remind her she was a lord's daughter; and I wondered at it and kept the words safely behind my teeth. Instead, I said, "All will be as it needs to be, have faith in that and in the leanings of your heart. Trust yourself." I grinned. "You burned your house for a reason."

She gave a cute and rueful grimace. "So I did."

"You see, even in your darkest hour... the G... Someone... was watching over you."

She nodded soberly, and frowned with a question that she opened her mouth to voice; but Jamaica did something which gained her mother's attention, and when Vivian finished adjusting the babe and spoke, I did not think it was the words she had been about to say.

"I hope Someone is watching over this one," she said quietly.

I felt Gaston's hand upon my thigh and knew he had been listening. I ran a finger down Jamaica's little arm, which protruded from beneath the blanket. "This one will be well cared for. All her parents were surely raised by wolves, but she shall be raised by centaurs and a..." I glanced at my matelot with a raised eyebrow.

He gave a thoughtful frown as he regarded Vivian. "What do you English call the little animals that burrow under hedges?" he asked in French. "The ones that roll into balls and have spines on their backs?"

I chuckled. "Hedgehogs?"

"Oui, that," he said with surety and little humor.

I stifled a true laugh as I turned back to Vivian's perplexed and annoyed frown. "Oui, that."

"What?" she asked with a defensive tone.

So I began to explain, to the other women as well, how we saw the world as being full of wolves and sheep and all other manner of animals, both mythical and mundane.

"I am not a hedgehog," Vivian said with annoyance when I finished. "You two get to be something fine like a centaur, but I am a hedgehog? Though why anyone would wish to be half something and half again something else is beyond me."

I knew I could never make her understand that was precisely the point, so I laughed.

Rachel and Hannah were trying not to laugh. Gaston heaved a heavy sigh with his face buried in his hand.

"What is my husband?" Rachel asked.

"A raven," I said. "He is smart and ever bringing news."

She smirked. "Then I wish to be a raven, too."

I nodded agreeably, though I pictured her as a goat: like the great matriarch of our little flock at Negril.

I looked to Hannah in order not to leave her from the discussion, and an immediate image came to mind. "I see you as a crane: a great dignified bird wading through mud to find a fine morsel here or there."

Hannah regarded me with surprise and nodded her head with sudden tears. "Thank you, master. You do me great honor by saying such a thing." She stood and looked to her mistress. "I should see to the soup."

Rachel nodded, but her eyes followed the woman's departure with concern. She turned to us. "She says so little of herself."

I wondered at her surprise over that, and then I realized that Rachel had not been raised with a great chasm between her and those who served – and her people were not accustomed to owning slaves. Yet she kept the woman in bondage.

"Would she remain in your employ if she were free?" I asked.

Rachel frowned tightly. "I do not know. But…" She nodded to herself. "It is a thing that should be discussed." Then her eyes were hard on me again, this time with mischief. "Jonathon is correct: you are ever causing trouble."

I snorted that she would think such a thing on the heels of the other. How easily were lives disrupted; and was I truly the Gods' sole instrument in it?

"You have not yet begun to see me cause trouble," I teased.

We stayed for a time in order for Gaston to cuddle Jamaica. Theodore at last joined us with sleepy eyes, and I smiled a great deal and continued to be pleasant, as I ever did when my Horse chomped at the bit, but I was quite pleased when at last we left.

"I need to run," I told Gaston as we walked to Sarah's.

He was thoughtful. "You do not find peace in the babe as I do," he noted.

I sighed, as he was not apparently on the same trail of thought I was. "I am sure I would find peace with the child if I did not need to contend with her caretakers whilst you cuddled her." At his hurt expression I quickly added. "Non, non, my love. I mean no admonishment. I am…"

His fingers darted to my lips and he nodded. "You are ever our bulwark."

I attempted to rein in my exasperation, as he was surely the last person I should trample with it. "I… find it confusing that they can be so warm and caring for one person, or many people, but not for another. Though they do not treat Hannah poorly… I just… It wears on me like a burr beneath a saddle, yet not so much as I should throw them off. It minds me of all the other well-meaning wolves I have met, and… I cannot hate them, yet I find myself compelled to revile what they do on occasion and…"

He smiled. "I love you, because you perceive things in that manner."

"I do not always," I sighed. "And that… Well, sometimes I am too tangled in my own thoughts and... Now, this day, that... Our being with them... My... agitation at this moment... Is not because that woman is a slave and they see little wrong with it. It is... People. It is the cave, or our no longer dwelling within it. The light casts smaller shadows out here for motives to be hidden within. I can no longer gaze happily upon the cave wall and not see... And I never could, but... I am not suggesting we purchase Hannah and free her. What would she do? And where would Theodore find another housekeeper? And what of Vivian? Should she be turned into a thing she is not... a common woman – in order to cure her drinking? And how dare I be concerned that she is a nobleman's daughter and what that might imply... Damn it all, it is the very essence of that which I wish to avoid. It is all some giant tangle of... wrongness, and I am overwhelmed by it. "

His hands were aside my face, and he was gazing at me with great concern.

"And I am not mad for all that," I whispered.

He shook his head in a small emphatic gesture. "Non, you are not. You are my Will, just as I love you. You are so strong. If I dwell upon such things, or even allow myself to consider them this day, I will be mad. Let us go to the beach and run until we forget."

A strange new thought occurred to me, and I was overwhelmed by melancholy. "We can tire our Horses, but we can never run far enough. We cannot leave this world, and it is wrong."

I saw fear in his eyes, and panic wrapped icy fingers up my spine. I was flailing around. I was going to drag us down. "I am sorry. I am sorry."

I closed my eyes and held his shoulders. He was solid beneath my hands. We would not fall. He was all I had in the world and he would not forsake me. We would survive. We would endure. I could not see how we would ever conquer, but it did not matter. Simply being with him was enough.

I took a deep breath and opened my eyes. He was still there: the fear had sunk beneath his concern in the emerald depths of his soul.

"I will stop looking about," I said. "I will gaze only upon you: my light. Until we are through this... thicket; storm; what have you; until the road is level again."

He sighed with relief and held me tightly. "And I will do the same," he whispered.

I sighed. "Of course, if we are only gazing upon one another, we will surely blunder into something." I shook my head at my continued foolishness and gave him an apologetic smile.

He was quite somber as he shrugged. "Whatever it will be, it will not stop us. We will trample anything that stands between us and a level road."

His words still echoed in my ears as we stepped inside the house and found nearly everyone in the atrium. I could envision them all with large hoof prints on their heads.

"Gaston," Pete said quietly. "Sarah." He jerked his chin toward her room surreptitiously.

My matelot hurried up the stairs without a backwards glance. As everywhere I looked, other eyes were on me in pleasant greeting, I wondered if I should follow him to escape; but they all seemed to be in fine humor, and I wondered what they had been about.

"So where have you been so early this morn?" the Marquis asked jovially.

"To visit my wife and child," I said and took a seat near him. "What have you been about?"

"Samuel announced we would have turtle soup for dinner, and Pete was telling us of turtles," he said.

I glanced at Dupree; the poor man did not look as happy and at ease as all the rest.

"I am understanding more of Monsieur Pete's speaking," Dupree said when I caught his eye.

I smiled, and not merely to paste a pleasant mask upon my features.

"And what will the rest of the day hold?" I asked the Marquis.

He shrugged expansively. "Do you have any suggestion? Pete has mentioned the turtle pens. Mademoiselle Agnes was thinking of drawing them."

Dupree was translating his master's words to the others as we spoke.

"That sounds like an amusing diversion," I said. "Gaston and I need to retire to the beach to practice our fighting skills, as we have been somewhat remiss in doing so of late."

"I think that would be a more entertaining amusement," Christine interjected in French.

The Marquis and Rucker nodded agreeably, as did Pete and Agnes once Dupree finished translating.

"Well..." I cast about. My matelot was still upstairs. "If Gaston is not needed here, of course."

"Of course," the Marquis said.

"We should change for the beach," Christine announced in English, and gave Agnes a pointed look before heading up the stairs.

I caught Agnes' frowning gaze and asked. "Is she not a bit premature? How is Sarah?"

The girl shrugged and looked to Pete.

He shrugged. "SarahDidNa'WantTaLeave'ErBedThisMornin'. ButShe Won'tLetUsSummonTheMidwife."

We would not escape them. I silently cursed my luck and considered finding some wine.

"This time at the beach will not take all day, will it?" Agnes asked quietly.

"Nay, you would all be quite burned if it did," I said, wondering why she asked.

"I had a thing I would do in town," she said with a look that told me

I knew of what she spoke.

I nodded agreeably, only remembering her wish to visit Mistress Garret after the girl had run up the stairs. I sighed and went to see what was available on the dining room's sideboard.

I had a bottle in hand, and the atrium was filled with our friends wearing clothing they did not mind soaking in the sea, when I met Gaston on the balcony outside Sarah's room.

"They are coming with us," I said quietly in French. "It is not my fault. I sought to tell them we would not accompany them elsewhere and... the Gods are fickle. And chide me not on this," I indicated the bottle. "It is for the best."

His face shifted from dismay to wry amusement and he took the bottle from me for a long swig of his own.

"How is she?" I asked.

"She has begun to labor, but the contractions of her belly are very far apart and she has not lost her water."

"So, should you stay?" I asked hopefully.

He shook his head regretfully. "Striker can stay with her now, but I will likely be attending her for much of the night. She has dismissed the midwife."

"She has? I did not like the woman, but..."

"Sarah feels the woman might be in league with your father's agents, or reporting to them," Gaston said with a shrug. "And I think the woman is a fool. If Sarah must be attended by someone other than me, it would be better if it were that Garret woman – though she could also be in their employ." He shrugged again, as if the whole damn town potentially being in my father's service did not trouble him.

It made me ill to think of it, and I took the bottle from him to take another pull.

"I should go and run hard now," he said with a tired sigh, "and then perhaps I should sleep for a time this evening so that I can remain awake tonight."

I nodded. "Well, that will change our other plans."

He frowned, as if he could not recall what I spoke of; then he frowned as if he did. "I suppose," he said regretfully. "You have not spoken to her yet, have you?"

"Not this day." I recalled I had not told him of my meeting with her the day before. "I did speak to her briefly yesterday, and she expressed an interest in continuing our... explorations. She has also hatched a plan to engage in her own adventures with Mistress Garret."

He paused in leading me to the stairs and awarded me a troubled frown. "How?"

"She wishes to meet with the lady and determine if she can be hired to... teach a woman of women."

"Oh," he said, and turned back toward the stairs. "I suppose that is a good idea."

"I dare not suppose anything," I said. "It will only cause me to dwell on disasters surely in the offing."

And thus eight of us left the house for the beach. The girls were dressed in their boy attire, and I cursed that Agnes should still appear so very boyish in breeches, and Christine still be so very attractive. I drank my wine, and considered people likely to be trampled. My matelot's supposed bride was definitely at the top of the list – especially as she seemed compelled to chat with Gaston throughout our journey to the Palisadoes, while the Marquis watched them with guarded and speculative approval, and Agnes glared at the former object of her affection.

"Are you well?" Rucker asked me as we walked through the gate in the Palisadoes wall.

I decided I had enough wine in my belly to calm me; and I handed him the bottle, and he took a thoughtful pull.

"I am troubled," I said.

"By her?" he asked.

I started. "Am I so obvious?"

He smiled. "She is a beautiful young woman who will marry your man. I would be concerned if you were not."

I sighed. I longed to confide to him that there was so much more to it than that. "It is complicated, and there are aspects to the matter I should not speak of, but... Aye, she does trouble me, and it is not for fear of losing his love. She is a child, and views this as a competition, and she does not understand... him. And, truly, this behavior on her part is not in keeping with what we knew of her from before, and thus it is... confusing and troublesome, particularly in light of all else that has occurred regarding my father's machinations."

I found myself frowning at this new curve in the trail that might or might not be a figment of my fancy.

"Do you feel she has her own agenda, or another's?" he asked astutely.

"I do not know," I said. "But... it is a thing I must determine."

There was a line to be drawn between looking only to my matelot in order not to spook my Horse and knowingly letting us stumble into a pit.

As I was full of wine – though not drunk – I cajoled Pete to spar with Gaston while we watched. I sat next to Christine so that I might spar with her. She seemed displeased with my intrusion.

"Do you seek to give me instruction on the match?" she asked, settling into her stance as a jilted lover with ease.

"Do you still seek to be a swordswoman?" I replied, gauging how much wine I had truly imbibed and measuring her as an opponent.

"Aye, and I engage in my calisthenics every day," she said, giving me a chance to escape.

I decided I was up to the challenge and I would have satisfaction. "Good, as you should. So why do you possess this sudden fascination with marriage?"

She took her eyes off the combatants and turned to glare at me: sidestepping my opening thrust, though she appeared surprised by it. "I do not possess a fascination with the prospect of marriage; I am dismayed by it, but I have no choice in the matter."

I shook my head and countered. "According to whom? From where I stand, you could simply leave. We would be pleased to furnish you what money we can, and you could go and do as you wish. Aye, you risk being returned to your father if you are discovered..." I shrugged; and switched hands, as I my goal was to drive her onto different terrain and not necessarily run her through. "I can tell you how to find men who can forge documents such that you need not worry over that, either. Pick yourself a name and become someone else. Many people do it."

She looked away. "I am a woman."

I frowned: it was a sturdy block, and one that I had expected somewhat, but now found disconcerting in its simplicity. "Who once purported to have far more interest in the world than could be contained in child-bearing and house-keeping. I believe you told us you wished to lead armies and explore new lands."

"Childish fancies," she said bitterly.

It was a solid move, but one I did not find in keeping with her style: which was why we were sparring here, to begin with. I could recall quite clearly how she had spoken with such passion of her desire to escape the lot to which she had been born: a year ago. And mere days ago in the stable, before my father's machinations had been known, she had been quite fixed on escaping to a more interesting life. Had her infatuation with me prompted all that alone?

"Has your womanhood suddenly blossomed in your heart such that you can no longer deny its essence, or has your spirit been broken?" I riposted.

"Neither," she said firmly, as if the idea could be easily beaten aside. "I have merely matured and realized my place in the world."

I switched hands and footing again, and struck with earnestness. "Then I am disappointed that you should grow to be so ordinary," I chided. "Perhaps you are not what we wish for in a dam."

I had scratched her. She stiffened, her attempt at world-weary resignation cast aside to reveal smoldering anger. "You can never understand."

"You best make me," I said.

"Nay, I need do no such thing," she snapped.

"Ah, but in that you are mistaken," I said coldly, relishing driving her across the yard. "We have wolves sniffing about our doors: I will not let my matelot walk into one's jaws. Either you lied when you first told us of yourself or you have found reason to become someone we do not know – and that is a thing I must understand. Or you are at the mercy of another agenda: perhaps another's agenda."

She took a quick breath of surprise and turned to regard me with a furrowed brow. She began to flail about in a desperate attempt to hold me off. "I would never. I am not my father and I know nothing of... How dare you?" she hissed. "I did not lie. I cannot ever have those things I wished for. They were a dream: a lie; a fancy. That is not how the world is. Damn you! That does not make me weak."

Beyond the wine and my ire, I sensed something in her last words: an opening. "What does make you weak?"

She clamped her jaw closed and shook her head tightly before looking away. "I am not weak. I am just a woman, and I have the desires of a woman. That does not make me weak or fickle."

"What desires have you discovered of late?" I asked, and then realized how very far I had stepped: it was as if I had charged into her feint and lost my balance.

She regarded me smugly. "I desire a man: one who values my lack of convention; one who will desire me. I thought that man to be you, but that was merely girlish infatuation. It need not be you. Your matelot will do nicely. Are you afraid he will find more favor in my arms than in yours?"

Suddenly, I was the one falling back before her rain of blows, barely managing to maintain my composure. "Never," I said; and it was a lie despite all my faith in him, and she saw it.

"If you truly loved him, you would not stand in the way of his being happy," she said: her blade at my throat.

It was with great effort that I kept my hands from about her throat. I stood and walked to the surf to cool my heels and lick my wounds. I need not ever worry. I knew that. Her ever being with him would lead to disaster long before he might come to love her. Nay, what hurt was that I thought I had killed and buried my foolish fears over the matter days ago. Yet, here I was, off balance and feeling the bite of a much older blade, one from which I carried many scars: one she had wielded with great resolve, whether her choosing it had been by accident or with forethought.

And that knowledge brought clarity to my heart and stilled the winds for a moment. It was my decision, and there were times I should truly listen to my Horse.

Gaston joined me soon after, his face suffused with concern.

I smiled weakly. "I sought to determine her motivations, as I feared they might stem from another... as they do not seem to be in keeping with what we first knew of her. And... for my trouble, I have discovered I am too damn drunk to duel with a woman."

He looked from me to her and back again with a frown and his eyes hardening with the Horse's anger. "What did she say?"

She was watching from up the beach, her eyes narrowed.

I sighed. "That she has discovered her womanly desires and she feels you will do nicely. She is thinking with her pussy – and her head, I must admit. Women are so like cats. Men are stupid when under the sway of their cock, but a woman... Non, a woman develops craftiness and uses wiles when lustful that make a mockery of all that is good about them.

"There is a part of me – ironically my Horse, I feel – that wishes for you to marry her just to prove to the insolent little bitch that you will never love her as you do me. I want to fight her: to stomp her into the ground. But… It will entail entirely too much effort for too little satisfaction, and I will not have us carrying her about for the rest of our lives, as she will surely be a heavy load. I do not wish for you to marry her. I am asking that you do not."

He nodded tightly and soberly, and then the tension flowed from his shoulders and face like the receding waves at our feet. He smiled. "Good."

I was relieved, yet there was still guilt that I should make such a demand. "I…"

He shook his head in admonishment and his smile broadened.

I sighed, and let my tension flow away with his. "So now what shall we do?" I chuckled.

"Sail," he said. "My father can send a more suitable bride: one that you can accept; one I might be ready for." Then he sighed and looked away at the horizon. "I do not wish to tell him… or her."

"Oh, I will tell them," I said.

He chuckled. "There are days when we should not allow you to drink."

"One must pay more attention to one's seat upon one's Horse when drunk. As fractious as my animal is this day…" I sighed. "It is for the best. Sometimes we should not soothe ourselves past the madmen in the bushes. We should choose another path."

He nodded thoughtfully. "What of Agnes?"

"What of her?"

"I would still… experiment," he sighed. "I feel, even if the need is not imminent, that it is a thing I must overcome."

"I agree. I have no difficulty with Agnes."

He got a handful of my tunic and pulled my mouth to his. I savored it: even more so because she was watching – and then I felt the fool for that. But as we walked back to the others and I saw her speculative glare, I knew she would ever think I had withdrawn from the battle because I was afraid of losing. I hoped the Gods would see fit to show her the error of such hubris in time.

Seventy-One

Wherein We Are Reunited With Hope

We made our way home in the bright noontime light. Gaston avoided his father and supposed bride, and frolicked in the surf with Pete and Agnes: they took turns lifting her up and tossing her into deeper water – a thing she shrieked at but seemed to find much delight in. Christine appeared angry, and glared toward the threesome every time her former friend squealed. I watched them and her with amusement and great relief. The Marquis, Dupree, and Rucker fell into step beside me, and we spoke companionably of unimportant matters. I knew well Gaston's father was not blind, but with the others about, he thankfully asked me nothing.

When we at last entered the house, we were all quite surprised to be greeted by Striker, Vittese, and several men from the French ship. Vittese appeared momentarily delighted at our arrival; and then a disdainful mien fell over him once again, as he avoided all other gazes and bowed properly before his lord. His face still bore bruises and a crooked beak from Gaston's beating. The Marquis greeted him warmly, and stepped into the dining room to speak with him privately.

Striker shrugged at us. "They sailed in this morning. They've been waiting out the rain down the coast." He led Pete upstairs to Sarah's room.

Gaston and I exchanged looks of resignation and sadness. It seemed the end of an idyll; and I knew well I would have been quite surprised at that perception of the Marquis' imminent leave-taking, a mere fortnight before. My matelot sighed heavily and climbed the stairs to look in on

Sarah. The rest of our company deserted me to change from their damp attire.

I stood alone with the French sailors, who had followed the girls with hungry eyes and were even now making little comments.

"Those are ladies," I said sharply.

One of the men snorted contemptuously at me.

I wondered if the entire crew of the ship the Marquis had sailed on were daft. The words that I was a lord filled my mouth, and I bit them back. I was no longer that, but I was yet a wolf when I chose. I drew a blade. "Get out! Wait in the street like the dogs you are."

The snorting one seemed disinclined to move, but one of his companions whispered something in his ear that made him frown at me; and the three retreated to the street, much to my disappointment. I was in the mood to run a man through.

I retreated to the stable, melancholy nipping at my heels.

I wanted to escape to the sea. I tried to tell myself all would be well once we were amongst the Brethren again; but then I remembered, there would be some among that number who wished us dead. And the rest... Well, we had not always done well with the rest, anyway. The whole damn world seemed filled with fools and bastards, and it filled my heart with dread. I doubted we would ever be well anywhere except alone.

I sheathed my blade, sank to the straw and cuddled a puppy. I did not feel inclined to cry so much as sink beneath the very dirt and disappear.

I was startled by a knock on the doorframe and looked up to find the Marquis watching me with concern.

I composed my features quickly. "Tell your man the others are in the street. They were viewing the girls in a lewd manner."

He snorted understanding and his disapproval. "I will give instruction that all should be kept away from this house while they are in port. There is no need for them to be here, anyway."

"We shall miss you," I said.

He sighed sadly. "Oui. I do not wish to leave." He brightened and shrugged. "But it will not be this day."

"Good," I said with a sincere smile of my own; and then I sobered. "There is a thing we should discuss."

He nodded and glanced behind him. "Can it wait until tonight? I need to go speak with my captain."

I guessed Vittese was within hearing. I nodded. "Or later, if you will not sail on the morrow."

He grinned. "I will remain until all business I need attend to here has been completed."

I wanted to tell him he need not wait on a wedding, but I held my tongue and smiled in parting.

I was not long alone in his wake; another shadow fell across the puppies: Agnes. She had freed her hair to flow across her shoulders, and she was dressed in a finer gown than I had ever seen her in before.

This one actually followed the shallow curves she possessed.

She fidgeted in the doorway. "Um… Would you…" She looked up over her shoulder and sighed. "While Gaston is busy with Sarah… Could you… leave?"

"And go where?" I asked.

She sighed as if I were daft, and stepped into the stable to lean toward me and hiss, "Mistress Garret's."

I remembered. "Now?"

"It is not night," she said with some exasperation.

I sighed. It would be a distraction. "I suppose. I will need to speak with Gaston, though."

She nodded. "He is speaking with Striker on the balcony."

I sighed again, and carefully deposited the puppy with his fellows before pushing my way to my feet. The ground floor of the atrium was thankfully empty of all save Agnes. Gaston was standing on the balcony speaking with Striker in hushed tones. I went to stand almost beneath them, and Gaston leaned over the rail to gaze down at me. His eyes flicked to his father's room.

"He will not sail today," I assured him quietly in French, "or even on the morrow, but he is going to speak to his captain now. Agnes wishes for me to accompany her about town. Do you have need of me?"

He frowned at Agnes, but he shook his head. "Your sister is well enough. I might sleep for a time."

"Good," I said. "I hope to join you when I return."

He awarded me a warm smile. "Please do."

It was the balm I needed; and I smiled, and walked with a somewhat lighter step as I led Agnes to Mistress Garret's.

We spied the woman working in her garden as we came up the alley. I stopped and stepped into an alcove between two buildings. Agnes stood where I had left her, in a state of agitation, and wrung her hands. I snatched her into the alcove with me.

"If I approach her for you, she will become confused as to your, or our, intent," I chided gently.

"What if she doesn't like me?" Agnes whispered.

"She is a whore," I said kindly. "She will not show it."

This wrinkled Agnes' nose quite cutely. "But…"

"Agnes," I said sternly, "if you harbor any conceit of this being a romantic engagement, then we shall return to the house. Do not fool yourself. You must be here to engage a professional woman to perform a service for you, not to meet a potential lover; else you will be greatly disappointed."

She frowned and hung her head with a blush upon her cheeks.

I took her shoulders and turned her to face me. "My dear girl, I know it is difficult," I said kindly. "If you wish to do this, view it as an opportunity to enhance your confidence towards the matter and ally your fears as to your true desires. Once you have accomplished that, then you should fraternize with the other young ladies about town and the plantations. You might be surprised at how many you will find with desires to match your own."

I could see doubt flit across her face, but then she squared her shoulders and marched down the alley.

I leaned on the wall and allowed my dismal prognosis regarding her chances of finding lasting love to mingle with the day's disenchantment with humanity. Even if she did find some girl willing to become as enamored of her as Agnes was likely to become of any woman who would look her way, the lover would likely be forced to marry by duty or circumstance, and Agnes would learn to live as all who did not love as society dictated: meeting in secret and ever forced to hide her true feelings.

Agnes walked past me at a rapid pace. I hurried to catch her, and she pulled away from my hand on her shoulder. I fell into step beside her and peered curiously at the curtain of hair hiding her downcast face.

"What happened?" I asked.

"She said no," Agnes sobbed and kept walking.

"Truly? Did she give reason?"

Agnes stopped and tossed her hair back before meeting my gaze defiantly – as if I were somehow involved in her misery. "She said..." Her eyes darted from mine and her voice became quiet. "She does not favor women and... she was appalled at my suggestion."

I cursed quietly and pulled her into my arms. "What a stupid woman."

Agnes sobbed on my shoulder for a time, and then she pulled back with renewed rancor. "I just want to love them! Why is that so wrong?"

"It is not!" I softened my voice. "My dear, even though the whole world may seem allied against you, what you desire is not wrong. They are the fools. They are the ones who live in fear of anything that might distinguish them from the herd. They are poor vessels for the intelligence... ingenuity... uniqueness... the immense capacity for love, that the Gods have gifted us with."

"Then why is it so hard?" she asked earnestly.

"Perhaps it is a challenge: a gauntlet thrown before us."

She shook her head sadly. "I feel I am already different enough."

I put my arm about her shoulder and steered her toward home. "My dear, that just makes you special."

She slipped her arm about my waist and leaned into me. I planted a kiss upon her head.

There was no one about in the atrium when we arrived, and she seemed reluctant to release me, so I led her to the stable. We found Gaston there, sitting with the puppies.

"We have met with opposition," I said and released her.

She sat next to him in the straw and pulled a puppy into her lap as I explained what had occurred.

Gaston's eyes filled with sympathy and he pulled her into his lap.

I dropped to sit with them, and for a time we sat in companionable silence. Then Agnes fidgeted a little before her hand slid up my matelot's chest and her face rose to regard him with hopeful eyes and tremulous lips. He glanced at me, and I smiled indulgently and moved so that I could guard the door. His mouth covered hers and she sighed and clutched at him. A few minutes later they had her skirts up and she was astride his lap, earnestly taking his direction as to how to raise and lower herself upon his member.

He seemed calm, and not at all possessed by old memories or his fears, and then he regarded me over her shoulder and I saw he was merely hiding it all for her benefit. I went to join them, and sat astride his thighs behind her. She gasped with happy surprise as my hands stole between them to play where they would. I nibbled her neck, and then leaned around her to share a deep kiss with Gaston, who clung to me like a drowning man.

Between my melancholy and earlier indulgence in wine, I was only mildly roused by our antics. Thus I set myself to fondling her and reassuring him without a care for my pleasure, until at last she came with sweet little gasps and sucked him dry with the strength of her satisfaction. We shifted her off him, and entangled the three of us to cuddle contentedly.

"At least I can have this from time to time," Agnes whispered. "Unless... you will not wish to after you marry."

"I am not marrying Christine," Gaston sighed in her hair.

She stiffened and shifted so that she could regard both of us curiously. We sighed as one.

"She will cause us nothing but trouble and hardship," I said. "She is jealous of me, and..."

Agnes nodded sagely. "She wants a man of her own, and it shames her."

I did not ask whether Christine had entrusted her with such information, or she was guided by intuition: I felt the words rang true enough not to question their source.

"She does not know yet," I murmured.

Agnes shrugged. "She would not listen to me, anyway."

Gaston was feeling quite heavy against my chest, and I peered down to find his eyes closed.

"We should rest for a time. Gaston will be attending Sarah this night," I said.

The girl nodded and rose spryly, quickly straightening her clothes. Then she leaned down and covered us in a curtain of mahogany hair as she kissed us each sweetly on the forehead. "Thank you."

Gaston roused himself to take hold of her arm and then her neck and pull her mouth to his for a true kiss. "Non, thank you."

She grinned proudly as she pulled away.

When we were alone, he turned to me and pulled my mouth to his. I kissed him deeply and thoroughly until he sighed.

"How was it this time?" I asked.

"Better," he said softly, and looked away. "But..."

"But?"

He shook his head. "It did not remind me of Gabriella this time, but... My Horse is... angry somewhat, even with Agnes."

"How so?"

He sighed. "Angry that my cock should take such pleasure in her, and... angry that she should presume I would want her. I do not know if that is a thing that will pass with time. And... If you were not here, I fear I would... become overwrought with guilt. That would truly anger my Horse."

He moved so he could gaze up at me without craning his neck. "I feel you will always need to be present. Does it bother you? Today you did not..." His hand brushed my flaccid member still tucked away in my breeches.

I shook my head. "I am too... distraught in general this day."

He regarded me with concern.

I shook my head again. "Do not trouble yourself. I am well enough. Let us rest for a time."

We made our way to the hammock and curled together to sleep.

We were roused by a great deal of noise: boisterous men giving happy greeting. I had been startled so abruptly from a sound sleep that it took me several moments to recognize who I heard; and then Gaston and I exchanged a look of surprise and tumbled from the hammock, hurrying to the atrium to greet our good friends: Dickey, Liam, Bones, Nickel, Julio, Davey, and Alonso.

Among all the embraces and back patting, we learned Cudro, Ash, and the Bard had stayed in the Chocolata Hole with the *Virgin Queen*, as there was haggling to be done with the Port Royal officials and merchants. Striker ran off to assist them. Pete frowned after him while taking a pull on a rum bottle, and then he turned and found me.

"NoneO'UsShouldBeAlone," he hissed in my ear. "YouTwoWatchTheHouse. Don'tTrustNoOne." Then he was gone, in pursuit of his matelot.

In all the joviality, it took me a moment to understand his concern; and then I did, and once again, I did not think much could drive the melancholy from my heart. I still could not believe any here would seek the bounty on our heads, though.

But then, as the household – except for Sarah and the Marquis – joined us, and we sat about with several bottles and the men began to regale us with tales of their smuggling, I began to consider each of them in turn.

Dickey's character was surely beyond reproach. Becoming a buccaneer and then our Master of Sail's matelot had erased all trace of the effete young man with whom I had sailed from England. His lanky body was now filled with hard-earned muscle that seemed to steady him, and his eyes were confident and happy. And even the boy I had known had proven to be stalwart and principled, a man of loyalty to his friends no matter the circumstances. And, even viewing the matter cynically, I did not see the Bard and Dickey severing their ties with the R&R Merchant Company to be in their best interests – unless they sought to establish their own.

Liam, our Scots musketeer, could not even possess the ulterior motive of a business venture. He had money and land, and all I knew that he had last yearned for was his deceased matelot: the death of whom still seemed to haunt him despite the fine spirits, such that he was not our principle tale-teller, as had ever been his wont. I could not gaze upon his sad pale blue eyes and crooked nose and think he would ever betray us: he carried the Way of the Coast in his heart like a cross and shield.

As did Julio the Maroon, in his fashion. Julio was ever a man of principle, and though not involved in our business venture, he did own land that we had helped him gain despite the dark hue of his skin. I did not see him as a man who would betray his fellow for gold, and we had surely never done a thing to earn his enmity.

The same – that we had done nothing to earn his enmity – could be said for his matelot, Davey, the stubborn goat of a sailor I had rescued from the slavery of being a pressed crewman on an English merchant vessel. However, I could see Davey doing a great many things for gold, and I questioned what loyalty he held for anyone. Some would say it was because he had been shat on throughout his life and learned nothing else; and perhaps it was even a thing I would say when under the sway of a kinder spirit; but this night, I was not so inclined to be generous.

Bones, our lanky and ever-indolent musketeer, was inclined to inspire and sop up generosity. I could not see him rousing himself to the level of industry required to hatch a plot, and I had seen nothing of his character to indicate he would do such a thing against those who treated him well.

His partner, Nickel – I could see nothing from their behavior to indicate they had at last truly become matelots – was likewise a good sort, and though there was depth to the former planter's son that he hid behind pleasantries and genteel behavior, I did not sense that it ran contrary to what he revealed upon his face. He would have likely made a fine priest, as had been planned for him; but he had chosen to escape that destiny and sail for adventure. Young men were often inclined to acts of disaster in the name of establishing a name for themselves, but I saw none of that about him, either.

And that left Alonso: my former lover, two years my partner in crime and all manner of things in Florence; a Spanish noble not ready to accept the yoke of maturity. He eyed me even as I looked upon him, and fear rimed my gut with ice. Alonso needed money, though he did not profess it. He had left behind all he had in Panama, including a wife, his good name, and any standing with his family, when he had joined with us in Porto Bello. He had ever been a nobleman's son, living as he saw fit to maintain the finery to which he was accustomed. I still could not believe the rough and crude life of a buccaneer appealed to him as he now claimed, when I had seen the care with which he had once selected his clothing and jewels. He had killed for money: killed men we had been acquainted with and who had no reason to fear us. And Gaston's death was in his best interest, as he still sought to win me back.

I would have dismissed that last conceit if he were not still gazing upon me this night much as he had three months ago, when we returned from Porto Bello. He felt he loved me yet: the damn fool. I had hoped it would pass these last months, once he was clear of the damnably boring and frustrating existence he had led in Panama, and thus no longer in need of foolish romantic notions concerning a former lover. Now I saw clearly that, even if he knew nothing of a bounty on Gaston's head, my matelot was still in danger.

I considered shooting Alonso then and there; but the others spoke fondly of him now. And I knew it would not sit well with them without reason, and my speculations would not yet be enough. I would need to watch him closely and seek my opportunity.

Their smuggling venture had apparently been quite lucrative, yielding a great deal of good Cuban tobbaco, wool, and wheat in exchange for paper, shot, hardwood, and iron. They had been greeted warmly by all they encountered along the coasts of Cuba and Hispaniola, save a few local militias; and they had even managed to ally any concerns on two of those occasions with a little gold and rum. As for the rest, they had retreated rather than fight – even though they lost some cargo on one such adventure.

Alonso had been a fine asset, being the one able to slip into the towns to locate merchants willing to trade. He had often been accompanied by Julio posing as a slave, or Cudro posing as a Dutch merchant. This had led to several adventures of a different sort, which he and the others related with great relish. Apparently, small Spanish towns were just rife with wayward maidens and lads ripe for the plucking, along with the occasional lonely widow or soldier. That part of his new life I could see Alonso taking to quite well. He had never been as discerning about his lovers as he was his attire.

And there was a time when I had been much like him; but that life now seemed a dream, or rather a nightmare I was relieved I could not remember in its entirety.

Other than a good-natured pull or two, Gaston and I eschewed the rum and wine flowing about the tables, and listened with feigned good cheer – at least on my part. But, as my matelot's grip upon my hand was fierce, I thought his ease with the situation also false.

Agnes happily sketched the men while Rucker plied them with questions. Christine sat in the shadows somewhat apart from the rest and listened to their tales with barely-concealed longing, in mockery of her dismissing her need for adventure as a girlish fancy.

Gaston at last decided he should look in on Sarah, as Striker and

Pete had not yet returned. He kissed me and left, and I watched him walk to the stairs with a suddenly lonely heart. I was not long alone, though; Liam appeared at my side and motioned that we should retreat further from the others.

"You have seemed still in the grips of mourning this eve," I said carefully when we were alone enough to be able to speak without fear of being overheard.

He nodded slowly. "Aye, it's been right hard. It not be the same without him. Near twelve years and then… I feel like I be missin' me shadow. An' I see no end in sight. I thought the rovin' would distract me some, ya know? But nay, it just made it worse." He frowned and studied me speculatively. "I canna' see takin' on another."

I nodded my understanding. From what he had told me at Otter's death, his beloved Dutch matelot was the only man he had ever been with, and Liam did not feel he favored men so much as companionship.

"So what will you do?" I asked.

He sighed. "That be the thing o' it. I been plannin' on speakin' with Striker 'bout my na' goin' rovin' this time, but… the thought o' goin' to the Point alone is a dismal thing. An'…" He frowned at me again. "There be a thing we 'eard tell of. An' it makes me think I should na' abandon me friends."

"What?" I breathed.

"There be some talk among the crew of a prize on yur matelot's head. An Striker's." He studied me intently.

"Aye," I sighed. I sighed again as I realized how very lucky Pete and Striker had been this autumn: if the men on the *Queen* had known of the bounty before they sailed, every buccaneer on the island had surely been apprised of the matter for months, and yet no attempt had been made on Striker. Perhaps it was not luck: perhaps no member of the Brethren would ever stoop to such a thing.

"We have only recently learned of it ourselves," I said. "It is my father's doing."

He frowned at that. "We thought it might 'ave been the French. None on the *Queen* say they know the how or why o' it, but I don't trust the lot o' 'em. Why would yur father do such a thing?"

"Because… He disapproves of my lack of discretion in taking a matelot, and he dislikes my sister's choice of a groom."

"Bloody Hell," Liam said with a sad shake of his head. "Ya would think ya wronged 'im somehow."

"He feels we have," I sighed.

"That be a sad thing." Then he sighed and shrugged. "Better this than the French, though. Men would be more likely to take money from one of their own to do a deed than from some damn… lord." He gave me an apologetic grimace.

I snorted. "I am no longer a lord. I am denouncing my inheritance in order to save my matelot. If my father's concern is that I am dragging the title through the mud, then he should be less concerned if I have no title. Of course, my father can be a hateful and conniving man, prone to vengeance, and he might not care. And... we have learned the offer of the prize money came from several men about town. They have supposedly not told anyone the source of it."

He sighed heavily. "What will ya do?"

"We plan to sail. We cannot cower like rabbits in a hole, and we feel the best tactic will be to lure our opponents out. And, we hope to be safer amongst the Brethren than here ashore, amongst bored planters' sons and hired brigands."

"Aye, aye," he said with a somber nod. Then he sighed. "Ya be needin' me ta sail, then."

My gaze, which had been wandering as we spoke, passed over Agnes, and I frowned. All here would go save the women.

"Perhaps not," I said quickly. "We are leaving much of value behind, and it would be a relief to have someone we can trust to watch over them."

"Ah," Liam said with surprise. "Yur sister, huh?"

"Aye, and my wife and child."

He frowned.

I smiled. "Much has occurred in your absence." And so I set about telling my own tales of our last weeks in Port Royal, leaving very little out save the circumstances of Gaston's estrangement from his father.

When I finished, he was shaking his head and smiling with bemusement. "Bloody Hell, it be no wonder ya want to get back to sea. It be safer there. But what with Theodore, an' your wife an' babe, and yur sister an' her babe, an' all bein' in danger even a little, I'm not sure I be man enough to do it; at least not without more hands an' eyes than the Good Lord saw fit ta give me."

"Do you know of any others we might trust who do not wish to sail, or at least do not express great exuberance for it?"

He frowned and nodded thoughtfully. "Aye, Julio an' Davey. Playin' a slave again wore hard on Julio, an' 'e's been speakin' o' settlin' down an' plantin', and Davey loves him fierce and 'e's a bit tired o' the sea 'imself. An' the damn diseases they got in Porto Bello 'ave left 'em wary. An' then there's Nickel an' Bones. The rovin' life o' a buccaneer don't suit Nickel, an' he would learn another trade – though 'e don't want ta go back ta Bermuda and join the clergy, neither. An' Bones, well 'e would be right happy holdin' up a wall wherever ya prop 'im."

"The only one of that number I do not trust is Davey," I sighed.

Liam shrugged. "Ya only see the worst o' 'im 'cause that's all 'e shows ya. Ya scare 'im, an' he be filled with envy at all 'e thinks ya 'ave."

I sighed. "Men in envy of my life often set out to ruin it."

He thought on that and grinned. "Davey na' be an ambitious man. An' Julio can keep 'im in line. I'll vouch fer 'im."

"Then I leave it to you to make the offer. We can pay you all for your troubles."

He made a disparaging noise and awarded me a chiding look before shrugging. "I don't care. The others might, but damn 'em if they ask for more than they need." He considered me speculatively. "What should I be tellin' 'em?"

"Whatever you feel you must. I will trust your judgment."

He took a deep breath and smiled grimly. I remembered well that he had often been concerned he was perceived as too much of a gossip to be trusted.

"Thank ya," he said.

I considered those about the atrium again. I thought it likely what I had just set in motion would leave us with far fewer pawns than perhaps Pete had counted on in the field, but it gave me great confidence we would have something to return home to.

Gaston had not returned, and I looked about in time to spy Henrietta hurrying up the stairs with a steaming kettle.

"I believe Sarah has begun to birth," I said.

"Truly?" Liam asked as if it were a horrific thing.

"Aye, someone should fetch Striker and Pete," I said.

"I will," Liam said. He stood and went to speak quietly with first Julio and then Nickel. Julio assured Davey he need not go, and the three of them headed to the door .

"Where ya off to?" Alonso called after them, in English that sounded suspiciously like Liam's.

"Ta go fetch our damn captains and more rum," Liam said with forced cheer. "Striker's wife be birthin'."

This brought a round of cheers and a startled look to Agnes. She closed her sketch book and scurried up the stairs.

I stepped from the shadows and called after her, "Come and fetch me if I am needed."

She nodded as she hurried across the balcony, and then she was gone into Sarah's room.

There was movement beside me, and Alonso threw a heavy arm across my shoulders. I did not attempt to shrug him off.

"And how are you?" I asked without turning to regard him.

"Fine, truly fine," he breathed, turning the air redolent with rum. "And how have you been?"

"Truly fine," I said, and pulled away to return to the seat beneath the balcony I had occupied while speaking with Liam.

He followed, and took the other chair, stretching his long booted legs before him and leaning his wide shoulders against the wall. His months roving on a Brethren vessel had stripped away the paunch his indolent life as a Spanish colonist had begun to give him. And he was shorn now, his great curling mane of mahogany hair reduced to a thick wavy carpet of velvet upon his skull. It suited him. He looked as handsome as he had when first I laid eyes upon him.

"You do not look fine," he noted in Castilian. "You forget how well I know you."

"You forget how little you knew of me when we professed to know one another well," I said with a grin.

He appeared pained. "Si, of certain things, perhaps; but I do know you, Uly."

I sighed. "Then you should know me well enough to not call me by a name I have long discarded. I am no longer a hapless wayfarer in search of my home – heroic or not – so Ulysses no longer suits me."

"You will always be Uly to me," he said. "In my dreams."

I shook my head in bemusement. "It truly pains me that you feel I am so fickle that you might actually succeed with your suit: you a man not prone to foolish fancies."

"Ah," he said with a knowing smile. "But you are ever a man of such things. You are prone to romance; and it is true, it is a thing sorely lacking in my life. Why should I not seek to address its absence?"

I sighed. "You should seek to address its absence elsewhere."

"But is not my troth romantic?" he asked with a grin.

"In the manner of fools everywhere, perhaps."

"And how is your matelot?" he asked.

"Well enough."

"I have learned more of the customs here in these West Indies," he sighed. "I understand that men do not dally and tryst as we did in Florence: they hold only to one man. At first I thought it boring, but now, I see where it might possess other possibilities."

I smiled and shook my head, not sure if I wished to see where he was going with this line of thought and not truly caring. "It allows for a great many possibilities; jealousy such as you cannot comprehend being one of them."

He shrugged. "I believe we have already witnessed that between you and your man, have we not?"

I was minded of the eyes upon us on our voyage home from Porto Bello. Rumors of my duel with Gaston, and the cause of it, had spread among the fleet in variations too numerous to count; so all thought they knew our business, when of course none had any understanding at all. And then I was minded of dueling with Christine this day. I was not fit to seriously spar with Alonso any more than I had been to engage her, even though the wine had since drained from my head.

"You have glimpsed but a shadow on the wall; silhouettes seen through the gauze of a curtain: no more than that," I sighed. "One of the *possibilities* of matelotage is the privacy of intimacy. I will not discuss it with you. You, of course, will think what you will. I have larger concerns."

He frowned. "Such as?"

I decided that though I did not wish to spar, aiming a pistol at his head and telling him to back away was very much within my abilities.

"My father has threatened our very lives," I said, and turned to regard him.

His brow tightened; and though he attempted to appear confused, he knew of what I spoke. I did know him as well as he thought he knew me.

"He has offered a prize for the death of my brother-in-law and my matelot," I continued. "I have not yet been able to tell him I am willing to renounce my title in order to end the matter, and he does not yet know that Gaston is no longer estranged from his father, and now holds a title of his own. I fear either that information will reach him after an attempt is made upon us, or it will fall on deaf ears when it does. And it is no matter if it reaches him or not, truly, as once such a thing is offered, it is very hard to rescind it."

"So what will you do?" Alonso asked, his face serious and his gaze on those still seated in the middle of the atrium.

"We will kill whom we must," I said calmly. "Or we will die."

He awarded me a perplexed frown, but would not meet my gaze. "You feel your father wishes for your death as well?"

I smiled grimly. "If Gaston dies, I will take my life. How is that for a romantic notion?"

He flinched, and at last met my gaze with speculative eyes, but he said nothing.

My smile widened. "If you ever intend to win your troth, I suggest you insure nothing happens to either of us."

"U... Will, how could you..." He seemed sincerely appalled, but I did not believe it.

I stood. "You forget, I know you very well; and, I know what we are both capable of. Even if you would not wield the blade yourself, I know you would lose no sleep over turning a blind eye to someone else doing it. You would consider it a fine turn of fortune." I leaned close to whisper. "I killed for you, and I very likely would have sacrificed myself to save you. And I did not love you a tenth as much as I love him. So, if you know me: know that. And, if you love me: love that."

I saw pain and then anger in his eyes. There was a time – I could not deny it – when it would have pained me greatly to have hurt him. I turned away before he could see I remembered that.

I joined Dickey, Davey, Rucker, and Bones at the table. Christine had moved from the shadows some time ago to sit with them. Rucker and Dickey were curious, and glanced to the place where Alonso still sat. Christine awarded me a smug knowing look that said someone had made mention of whatever they thought they knew regarding my relationship with the Spaniard. Davey's gaze was accusatory, and I considered smashing the rum bottle I had picked up over his head. Instead, I took a pull and sat with them, pasting a smile upon my tired face.

"Is all well?" Dickey asked.

"No one has died as of yet," I said. "On the other hand, the people who need to die have not as of yet. So it appears we are in limbo."

Rucker chuckled appreciatively, and Christine looked away with a troubled frown, but the others regarded me expectantly, awaiting my explanation of such an utterance.

I was rescued from having to make that explanation – or at least decide what and how I should make it – by the arrival of Striker and Pete, Liam's party, and a number of men from the *Queen*, including Cudro, and to my surprise and Dickey's delight, the Bard. The expectant fathers hurried upstairs, and Cudro descended on me to pull me to my feet and into his arms for an embrace that caused my spine to protest heartily.

"And here is my matelot, Ash," the big Dutchman boomed proudly when he released me.

I grinned at Ash and embraced him. Except for his beak nose, he looked little like the sallow-faced planter's son we had met less than a year ago: the one who had little understanding or use for matelotage. He now seemed as proud of it as his partner. I was pleased for both of them; Cudro had at last found someone youthful and pleasing enough to take on; and Ash had been able to prove he was any man's equal, as he was now a captain's partner.

The Bard was next in my arms.

"So you have decided to set foot on land? Has our ship sunk?" I teased.

He awarded me his usual sardonic grin. "Nay. I thought since Striker was having a baby, I should witness it with my own eyes, else I would never believe it. And Striker says all the excitement has happened here, anyway. We've been missing it at sea."

"Aye, well… aye," I chuckled. I looked about and found myself surrounded by fine friends. "We have discovered trouble here, and I am afraid it is my doing."

"We've known you were nothing but trouble since we first sailed with you," the Bard said.

"I suppose that is true," I said with a shrug; and then I realized that it was true. Gaston and I were ever the source of trouble, and yet these men had stood by us time and again.

"Well, let me tell you of this latest patch, then," I said and sat.

They all found seats; and I proceeded to tell them all I had told Liam. I once again omitted the details of Gaston's estrangement from his father; and I also did not make mention of Jamaica's dubious parentage. I did include Pete's chess analogy, but as most of them did not know the game, I was forced to simplify it somewhat.

As I spoke, I saw Julio and Nickel speaking with their respective partners: in the end they all nodded at me when I happened to gaze upon them – except for Davey, who frowned and sighed. Christine also spent a great part of my tale glaring at me or the table. The others laughed or stared off in contemplative silence by turns, depending on what I was relating at the moment.

Cudro sighed expansively when I finished. "There would have been a time when I would have said damn any buccaneer to Hell for taking your father's blood money, because they sure as the Devil aren't true buccaneers." He shook his head. "But now…" He sighed again.

"Too many arrived as Nickel and I did," Ash said. "The Way of the Coast means little to them, if they know it at all."

There were sad nods all around.

"They're all the Crown's lackeys and one bad turn from being pirates now," the Bard said. "Well, we can protect the four of you while you're on the *Queen*; but with this warship Striker says Morgan has, the good Admiral will be wanting a big target and as many men as he can muster. Who knows how far the tale of this bounty has spread. All it will take is one stray ball in a heavy battle."

"That can 'appen anyway," Liam said, and all nodded sad agreement.

"But it will happen a bit more frequently if our own men are aiming at them," the Bard said.

"Is this a thing that can be addressed the way you took on the French?" Cudro asked with a thoughtful frown.

I had not even begun to think of a strategy; and I had forgotten about the *Oxford*; and I had cared not where we might rove. I considered Cudro's question.

"Well," I sighed. "A prize on a man's head is a difficult thing to counter, as few will step forward to claim a reward for not doing a thing they would not want to admit to having considered."

Ash chuckled. "Ah, aye, excuse me there, Will. I could have shot your matelot in the back during that last bit of gunfire, but I did not. Please pay up."

We laughed.

I sobered a bit as my long-confused and exhausted mind took to the matter. "A rumor could be spread that the bounty is a lie: that it will never be paid, but… I think many would question it. And the truth, that this is a matter between lords… well, that would carry little weight or sympathy with most. The men on the *Queen* know that you all know of the plot, correct?"

They nodded.

"We told them that any man considering harming the rightful captain or an owner of the vessel could be hung for mutiny," Cudro said. "And that we would probably skip the hanging part and just let their matelots do what they would with any damn fool stupid enough to try it."

"It put the fear o' God in some o' 'em," Liam said. "An' others were just as surprised as we be ta learn o' it. There were a lot o' grumblin' that any among us would even think o' such a thing."

"That's why I don't fear for you on the *Queen*," the Bard said with a grin.

"Hell," Cudro said with a shrug. "Most would not be fool enough to attempt it ashore. They know we'll question the direction any ball or blade will come from, and that we're looking for anything suspicious. If we could spread that among the fleet…"

I shook my head. "Aye, it would probably suffice. No man would dare collect if he thought it would destroy his reputation with his fellows – unless they are some damn fool like Burroughs was. We cannot protect against idiots too blinded by greed or impaired in their judgment to know that what they do is wrong. But... I fear larger forces working against us."

"Modyford," the Bard sighed. "His being involved in the business does not bode well for ours; much less your lives. If the governor asks, or even if he doesn't, Morgan – who does not like you – or Bradley – who likes you even less – or any of the other captains, are willing to be involved and turn a blind eye, you are likely done for."

"They cannot be bought," I said, more to myself than to them. I was denouncing the only coin they might consider: my inheriting, and thus my interests eclipsing my father's someday.

"We'll need to keep the four of you tucked away," Cudro said.

I sighed and nodded my agreement, but I could not see how we would accomplish it. "Gaston wishes to serve as surgeon. That could keep him tucked away, but not Striker. As captain, he must be with our men."

"Not if he's not captain," Cudro said.

"Not if he is ill," Julio said at almost the same moment.

Cudro and Julio nodded their agreement at one another's suggestions; and the rest looked about to see who might be giving such provocative ideas merit.

"Ill how?" Liam asked.

"He would pretend," Julio said.

"Beneficence," Alonso said, from where he stood just beyond the tables.

I recalled who he spoke of, and sighed and frowned at him. Alonso shrugged.

"What?" Liam asked.

"Rodolfo..." I sighed again. "We called him Beneficence because... It is not important. His father bought him a commission, and Bene wanted nothing to do with the military. Truly, none of us could see him wielding a weapon other than his tongue. He was an effete little bastard and afraid of horses. So... While we were all drunk one night, we concocted a plan whereby he would become wounded such that he could not serve. So I shot him in the leg in a duel the next day. He took to using a fine ivory cane, and – as he had predicted – it did little to dampen his career as a libertine."

"If Striker can't act ill, that might work even better," Cudro said seriously. "And it would give him an excuse to step down as captain."

I glared at Alonso, and he responded with an oblique smile.

"Striker won't like either course," the Bard was saying with a chuckle. "But it could keep him alive."

"We'll tell Pete o' it and 'e can knock some sense inta 'im," Liam said. "'E can either na' be captain or 'e can get shot."

I laughed. "Unless Pete has a better plan that he has not told us."

"I don't want anyone thinking I have any motive in this other than keeping Striker alive," Cudro said earnestly.

All shook their heads and made disparaging noises and he calmed somewhat.

"So, we'll tuck the four of you away with the wounded somehow," the Bard said, "and the rest of us will seek out the traitors."

"Na' all o' us," Liam said.

"Nay, Will has asked that those of us who wish to… stay behind and guard those here," Julio said.

I nodded. "Once my father learns I have not put her out, my wife will likely become a target, as will my child. And though he would not have Sarah harmed, he might have already requested she be taken away for her own safety once Striker and Pete are no longer about. And I am sure he has no love for this child being born. They are all treasures we need safeguarded, and I thank those of you who will stay, even if you intended to do so for other reasons."

The five men who had agreed nodded.

"All of you?" Cudro asked, and gazed on each of them in turn. "Damn, we'll miss you, but I see what Will is saying."

"I wasna' gonna sail anyhow," Liam said sadly. "My heart's na' in it anymore."

There were nods all around.

"So there is this household and Mister Theodore's that must be protected?" Julio asked.

"Aye," I said. "It would likely be more convenient if they were all in one dwelling, I know, but… Women do not always live well together, and it is best there is only one mistress of each house."

"Where will I be living?" Christine asked abruptly. There was venom in her gaze.

I had forgotten she was present. I sighed. "That must be discussed."

She stood, kicking her chair over behind her, and marched up the stairs to her room and slammed the door.

All had been silent during her ascent, and now Liam asked quietly, "Is she na' the one Gaston agreed ta marry, or am I gettin' all confused?"

"She was," I said, trying not to speak so that my voice carried to the second floor. "But, I have asked him not to. We hope to send that one to France with his father."

Rucker smiled and met my gaze. I shrugged for his benefit.

"Might I ask why?" Dickey asked.

"I do not like her," I said, and elicited a number of chuckles.

"But he likes your wife?" Alonso asked in English.

I sighed. "My wife is a drunkard – as I believe I mentioned – but now that she is dry, she has become somewhat endearing; and, of course, Gaston adores the baby, Jamaica."

"Ya na' be lyin' with 'er since the babe, right?" Liam asked.

"Nay," I said quickly.

"An' yur matelot na be…"

"Nay, nay, nay…"

"All right."

"She is still my wife, though," I said seriously. "And it is not her fault my father despises me."

"So we got ta look after two ladies and two babes?" Davey asked, as if he were being asked to muck a stable.

"Well, they are... ladies, aye, but they are not..." I sighed. "They are Mistress Striker, and Mistress Williams. And they will look after the babes. There will also be Miss Agnes." All nodded as they knew her. "Mister Rucker here."

"I am not the target of assassination... I hope," Rucker said quickly. "And I hope not to be a bother."

"Can ya shoot?" Liam asked.

"A little," Rucker admitted.

"We'll work on that, then," Liam said and clapped his shoulder.

"There is also the housekeeper, Henrietta, the servant, Samuel, and... Oh, damn, possibly my uncle. Though he might be dead, for all we know. And he also might need to be shot... We will discuss that later," I added in response to their frowns. "At Theodore's, there is Theodore, Mistress Theodore – some of you might remember her as our former housekeeper, Rachel."

"The Jewess?" Liam asked.

"Aye, her," I said.

"She's gotta sharp tongue," he sighed.

"Aye, but she bakes a wonderful cheesecake," I said. "They have a daughter, Elizabeth, who is little more than an infant. There is also a housekeeper, Hannah."

"Can Theodore shoot?" Liam asked.

I thought of our friend swooning during the altercation at the Chocolata Hole, and suppressed a sigh. "I believe he can be roused to defend his family, but I know not of any martial skills he might possess."

"We'll be workin' on that too, then," Liam said.

"My sister and Agnes can shoot, and they have the dogs," I added. "Vivian... Mistress Williams... should be taught. Actually, all of them, including Mistress Theodore, Hannah and Henrietta should be taught, and Sam."

Liam nodded sagely. "Well, we'll be right busy even if no one ever does come after 'em."

Davey groaned, but Julio, Nickel and Bones were laughing.

I realized how much trouble I was causing, and smiled. It would be interesting to see what we would return to.

The front door opened and the Marquis entered, leaning in equal parts on his cane and Dupree. I was almost alarmed at his state until I saw his face light with surprise and then delight at seeing the atrium full of men.

"Ah! Your ship has returned too!" he called in French. He was drunk.

I stood in greeting; and Cudro, Alonso, Dickey, Ash, and the Bard did as well; with the rest following us to our feet with expressions of confusion.

"My Lord," I said, and bowed appropriately.

He made a loud disparaging noise. "God, I have had enough of that today. It has been refreshing to be without it these last weeks. Sit! Sit!"

Those of us who understood French sat, with the rest following. They no longer appeared as confused. My bow and greeting had apparently done as I had hoped, and shown them who we addressed. Now they were all nervous, and many sat straighter and looked as if they might hide their bottles. Though they had been about me for years when I held a title, I had never let them view me as a true Lord; and so for many, this was likely the first time they felt they had been in the presence of nobility.

The Marquis made his way to my side and dropped down to share my chair, and I made way for him as much as I could without being pushed onto the floor. Once seated, he snatched the bottle Dupree had been carrying and handed it to me. "Fine fine..." he muttered.

It was a truly delightful cognac, and I savored the burn as I passed the bottle to Cudro, who smiled widely once he had a whiff of it.

"Ah, a man with a good nose," the Marquis said. "Now who are all these gentlemen?"

"Gentlemen," I said for all, "allow me to introduce Gaston's father, the Marquis de Tervent." Then I began to go around the table, giving each man's name, duty, and some other tidbit about him. The Marquis said some small thing to each, which I translated, and they all began to smile and relax again.

Then he asked of the success of their voyage, and the Bard and Cudro began to relate what they would, with me translating, much to Dupree's relief.

Some time later, a door opened on the balcony above, and Striker strode down the stairs carrying a small bundle. All hushed in anticipation. Striker's happy and awestruck smile spoke volumes.

"I have a son," he said.

The atrium erupted in cheers, and the little bundle started so that everyone smacked one another and bid for quiet. Then Striker laid his son on the table and carefully unwrapped him to reveal a baby every bit as pink and wrinkled as Jamaica had been – but larger. And he did have the little indent beneath his nose; and his head seemed huge in comparison to hers.

"He's ugly as sin, but he seems to be fine," Striker said proudly.

"'E's not ugly! 'E's a baby!" Liam protested.

The Marquis smacked Striker lightly and pronounced, "He is beautiful," once Striker's words were translated.

I looked at all the happy faces and felt a warmth of the soul I had not remembered. Then I glanced over my shoulder and was relieved to find Gaston leaning on the railing, gazing down at us like a beneficent angel. I grinned at him, and he smiled with all the love I would ever need. I thanked the Gods – for many things, but most of all for him.

Seventy-Two

Wherein We Run Toward Ruin

"How is Sarah? Is she accepting visitors?" I asked Striker as he wrapped his son in his blanket and prepared to return him to his mother.

"Aye, aye, come up. Gaston says she is well," he said quickly.

I had assumed as much; else Striker and my matelot would not have appeared so calm.

I followed him up the stairs and down the balcony and found my sister – though obviously exhausted – anxiously awaiting the return of her son in the middle of a cloud of clean white linen and netting. As Henrietta was scrubbing a spot on the floor at the foot of the bed, and Agnes was bundling up soiled bed clothes, I surmised the birthing had not occurred in the bed.

Striker placed the babe in his wife's arms and snuggled beside her. Pete was leaning on the sash of the outer window, looking over the room with regal pride. Oddly, he appeared as tired as Sarah: as if he had been the one who gave birth.

Gaston embraced me as soon as I was within reach. He looked worn down but happy.

"I see it went well?" I murmured in French.

He grinned. "Much better than before. I learned much last time, and from that Garret woman." Then he sobered. "But... Now that I have seen a healthy babe..."

I nodded quickly, not wanting to dwell on it here. He understood, and we exchanged a look that said we would discuss it later.

"So, will we be doing this again?" I teased Sarah as I went to the foot of the bed.

She snorted and smiled beatifically down at her son. "I cannot think of it now; but aye, I feel I would survive another. Striker wants an army." She grinned at her husband.

I glanced at Pete and found him momentarily dismayed by the suggestion.

"You do not want an army?" I asked him.

Pete sighed. "TheWorryin'Na'BeEasy."

"Ah," I said, as now I understood why he appeared exhausted. "Well, those of us not engaged in this lovely activity have been hatching plots to give you more to worry about."

"Aw, Lord," Striker said, as all eyes came to me, even Sarah's and Henrietta's.

"Liam, Julio, Davey, Nickel, and Bones did not wish to sail again – at least not this next voyage. So I have asked that they remain here to guard our treasures…" I indicated the bed. "Whilst we rove, and they have agreed."

Gaston exhaled a truly relieved sigh.

Striker frowned, and I could see him mouthing the names and considering them. Sarah was frowning as well; but with her, I sensed it was more from putting names to faces than from the suggestion itself. I turned to Pete and found him nodding thoughtfully.

"We'llMissThosePawnsOnTheBoard," he said, "ButGoodTa'Ave 'Em'Ere. ITrustMostO"EmAsMuchAsAnyMan, An'LiamTenTimesThat. DaveyBeStupid, ButJulioBeSmart. An'BonesBeLazy, ButHonest. An'NickelSeemsAGoodSort."

"I don't know this Bones and Nickel," Agnes said with a frown of her own, "And Davey is an arse, but Julio is always a gentleman, and Liam was always very kind to me."

"Aye," Striker said with a smile. "They have all agreed? That is good news. So they will guard Sarah and your wife?"

I nodded.

"Excuse me, sirs," Henrietta said and pushed herself to her feet from where she had been scrubbing. "Will they be livin' 'ere?"

"Aye," I said. "Here and the Theodores'. They will need room and board. The matter of other compensation has not been discussed. Liam was, of course, bothered that I should mention such a thing; but if they are not getting prize money or planting during these next months, they will need something."

"Aye, of course," Striker agreed readily.

"Well, sirs," Henrietta said diffidently. "Where will be housin' 'em? We'll need a barracks."

I chuckled. "I would imagine in the guest rooms." I looked to Sarah and she nodded. "Gaston and I will not be here, and neither will the Marquis or Miss Vines."

"Where will Christine live?" Sarah asked.

"Well," I said with a short huff of a sigh. "We were hoping France."

Except for Agnes, they all regarded us with curiosity.

"I will not marry her," Gaston said.

"Oh," Sarah and Striker said as one.

"Good," Pete said. "SheNa'Know'ErPlace."

This garnered him a raised eyebrow from Sarah.

He crossed his arms. "SomeWomenNa'Know'OwTaBeMarriedTaTwo Men. An'IfYaWereLike'Er, IWouldaStrangledYa."

Sarah smiled glumly. "I suppose that is true. I do not feel Christine wishes to marry, anyway."

"She doesn't," Agnes said above her own crossed arms. "Not truly."

Striker shrugged and looked to me. "So, we will exchange one set of house guests for another, and we shall sail. I'm pleased you were able to arrange all that while we were busy."

"There is more," I said.

Gaston chuckled. "What else have you done?" he whispered in French.

I sighed. "We have been discussing a manner of keeping the four of us safe while roving. Our friends learned of the prize on your heads from men on the *Queen*."

This brought a round of curses, even from Sarah.

I smiled. "They have assured all who sail on our vessel that such a thing ever being considered will not be taken lightly. But... It is likely that word of it has spread throughout the Brethren and the fleet. We will be at risk in any engagement where some damn greedy fool feels he can drop one of us and claim it. Though I imagine, if one of us does fall, there will be dozens of claimants, even if the gunman is a Spaniard."

"Aye," Pete grumbled. "WeDieO'TheFluxAn'SomeBastard'llClaimIt."

"Well, not you or Will," Striker teased. "There's no price on your heads."

"There might as well be," I said soberly. "I have informed Alonso that if Gaston dies I will take my life."

Henrietta crossed herself. It reminded me of her presence, and though I had no reason not to trust the woman, she could be a bit talkative, perhaps at an inopportune time.

I addressed her. "Perhaps you should see if my sister requires anything after her labor," I said politely.

"Oh... I suppose, of course," she stammered. Her eyes were on me, though, and full of concern. "That's na' a thing ya should..."

I sighed. "Henrietta, taking my life will not send me to Hell any more or any less than anything else I have done in my life. Truly."

Her face constricted in a grimace of concern and disapproval, but she pulled her gaze from me and looked to her mistress.

"I would like some water, and perhaps some chocolate," Sarah said.

Henrietta nodded and left us. I felt every other eye in the room upon me in her wake.

"Why did you need to tell Alonso that?" Striker asked.

"Because he thinks he would benefit from Gaston's death," I said. "He thinks he might win me back if Gaston is gone."

Sarah and Agnes grimaced cutely with incredulity: perhaps at Alonso's hubris, perhaps at mine. Pete made a disparaging noise. Striker smirked.

I did not wish to turn and look at my matelot; but I listened for the door in case he exited it to go and kill Alonso. Gaston's arms slipped around me from behind and he kissed my neck sweetly.

"Let'sJustKill'Im," Pete said.

"I considered it," I sighed. "But our friends have grown fond of him, and he protests that he would never be party to such a thing."

"Aye," Striker said. "Cudro and the Bard spoke highly of him. Do you trust him?"

I took the time to truly consider that question in light of whether they could trust him, not I. "I do not think he would do anything to harm you. I do not believe he would make an attempt on Gaston's life directly. I would not leave him here to guard the women. He is not at heart an honest man, and has a wolf's principles. But... he does have his merits if his goals are concurrent with one's own. He does value loyalty, and it is a thing he aspires to."

I shook my head at their frowns. "He was the best I could manage at the time."

Striker smirked, and Pete snorted quietly.

"He's a handsome devil, and charming," Striker said.

"Which one is he?" Agnes asked. "And he was your lover? Is that what you are saying?"

Sarah also appeared perplexed.

"Aye, aye, Alonso," I sighed. "You might have met him briefly before the *Queen* sailed. We were lovers in Florence, years ago. We encountered him in Porto Bello and he joined our number and came here."

"That was my doing," Striker said with a frown of regret.

"Aye," I agreed. "I would not have brought him... Not after it became apparent he still truly believed he loved me. But we had greater concerns. I told him then, though, that I would kill him if he did anything to come between us."

"Is he stupid?" Sarah asked.

"For which?" I asked with a wry smile. "Being in love with me, or thinking I will return to him?"

She shrugged and grinned. "Both, I suppose."

"Aye, that is a question," Striker said, as if it were of great philosophical merit.

Gaston's embrace tightened about me, and he whispered in my ear, "I still think I should fuck you in front of him."

Despite a decade spent living the life of jaded libertine, I felt the color rise in my cheeks.

This garnered a great deal of amusement about the room.

I ignored them, and turned in his arms to face him and push him back to the wall. "As we will all be trapped together on a tiny ship, I feel that will be inevitable," I whispered huskily.

He grinned. "Good." But then he sobered, and concern haunted his eyes. "You will not take issue with it..."

"Non," I said seriously. Our last discussion of the matter had somehow ended in both of us being mad, him having another ragged scar across his chest where I nearly killed him, and my jaw being broken. "But... we should talk on this elsewhere and later."

He kissed my lips gently.

I turned back to the others and attempted to collect my wayward thoughts. There were many things that must be discussed. I felt all our remaining hours in Port Royal would surely be spent talking to someone about something – or rather, trying to convince them of it.

"Be all that as it may," I said dismissively of Alonso. "Cudro and the Bard feel we will be safe upon the *Queen*, but not in battle. To that end, we discussed how to safeguard us. We think it best if we are all tucked away somewhere so that any who wish to harm us cannot do it by means of an unfortunate line of fire or some other accident. Gaston has expressed a wish to be surgeon. I can be his assistant. Wherever we go on the Spanish Main, there are likely to be wounds and ailments in good supply to keep us busy."

I looked to Gaston, who had moved to stand beside me. He nodded soberly.

"But that does not address the two of you," I said to Striker.

"I can't hide as captain," Striker said.

"That is why it might be best for you *not* to be captain," I said with an apologetic grimace.

"Aye," Pete said. "IBeenThinkin'That."

"Good," I said to him. "We were wondering what your fiendish tactical mind was planning."

Striker was frowning at the babe sleeping in Sarah's arms. Pete was frowning at his matelot.

I continued quietly. "We thought you could either not accept the nomination as captain, or we could concoct some ailment or wound that would require you to step down – and leave you in Gaston's care, with your matelot at your side, of course."

Sarah's face contorted into a concerned grimace, and she caressed her husband's face. He looked up at her, and I saw the love pass between them as if it were a palpable thing.

Striker nodded and turned to look at Pete and me. "It will be suspicious if I do not sail as captain. Let us sail, and get wherever Morgan wishes to plunder, and then... We will concoct whatever won't be questioned, and I'll step down."

Pete appeared relieved, and Sarah's eyes closed and she kissed Striker's forehead.

"I need to live a lot more than I need to be a captain," Striker told everyone with a mildly chiding tone. Then he grinned. "I'm not a fool."

"Cudro wants all to know that he has no design upon the position," I said. "He just wishes to keep you safe."

Striker snorted. "If I didn't trust the bastard, I wouldn't have let him sail off with our ship for two months." He looked to Sarah. "But I should probably tell him that myself."

Sarah nodded, and Striker stood and leaned down to kiss her, and then what little skin of the sleeping bundle was available to lay his lips upon. Then he strode to the door, and Pete followed him.

Gaston began arranging his medicine chest so we could carry it downstairs.

"Do you need me to stay?" Agnes asked as she stepped to the table and lowered the lamp.

"Nay, go, sleep..." Sarah sighed. "Ask Henrietta of my chocolate."

Agnes left us.

"We will all return," I told Sarah.

She regarded me sadly. "I am sorry I was angry with you."

I frowned. I had known her angry about events, and at me for being the bearer of news she did not wish to hear; but not at me in the way which she was now implying.

"I forgive you, for whatever you were angry about."

She smiled. "I felt my life was caught in some war between you and Father. I have felt that since you returned to England. That I was a pawn in someone else's game."

My breath caught as I realized how everything must have appeared from her perspective.

Gaston paused and turned to gaze at her.

"I am sorry," I said. "I can see where that would be very easy to feel."

She shook her head and waved the past away. "If things had not occurred as they did, I would not be here now, loved as I am, with this beautiful child in my arms. So I regret nothing. And... I have thought on it, and I do not blame you. Truly, I have never blamed you. You are as much a victim as I. Our father is the damn culprit. I do not even blame Shane as I blame him."

"For so long," I sighed, "I did view Shane as the culprit: I thought him the root of all the evil in my life. But nay, you are correct, it is our father. And... somehow, that hurts more than Shane, even though I once thought that bastard loved me. Father never loved me. So, ironically, there was no betrayal, in that there was nothing to be lost; yet there was, in that a thing that should have existed, never did."

"I betrayed myself," Sarah said. "I saw love where it did not exist. Father does not love; he admires things that please him. Or rather, he is kind to things that please him. He is indifferent or cruel to things that do not. I used to please him; whereas, you never did. I used to think he loved me; at least you spared yourself that."

A tear glistened on her cheek in the lamplight. I felt its echo in my eyes.

"We will let you rest," I said, and went to help Gaston with the medicine chest.

"You had best all return," she said as we reached the door. "Do not make me have to follow the lot of you to Hell."

I chuckled. "I try not to believe in Hell."

"That is probably for the best," she said with quiet amusement.

We left her with my nephew, and walked down the balcony. Below us, the courtyard was alive with revelry. Striker was speaking from the head of the table, offering toasts. The Marquis and Dupree were still with them. Alonso had stepped into the light to sit with the others.

I looked to Gaston. "Shall we join them?"

He smiled. "For a time."

Agnes stepped from the shadows of her doorway into our path as we reached the top of the stairs. She gave me quite a start, and I reached for the pistol at my belt. Gaston appeared likewise surprised.

"What is it?" he asked quickly.

She looked concerned: her long face pinched with worry and her fingers constantly weaving. "I was thinking..." She sighed.

I sat my side of the heavy medicine chest down; and, with a sigh, Gaston lowered his as well.

"Well..." she stammered. "During our... *experiments*... could I get with child?"

I knew Gaston blanched, even though I could not see him clearly in the shadows. I swore silently and spoke kindly. "Aye, you could. It is a risk ever-present in such activities. If such a thing were to occur, you need never worry about you or the child being cared for."

"I am not concerned about that," she said quickly. "I do not wish to give birth. I have seen it twice now, and it is not a thing I wish to do."

"There are ways to avoid pregnancy," Gaston said quietly. "Draughts and old remedies."

I could hear the discomfort in his voice.

"Should I take them now?" she asked.

"You would take them after you feel you are with child," he said sadly. "Or, before, but after, and they will act to..."

Her face contorted with surprise. "I do not want to miscarry the child," she whispered. "Is there not something I could take before..."

He sighed heavily. "There are supposedly concoctions, but even Mistress Garret could not swear to their usefulness. The only sure way is to poison you or the child such that you miscarry."

She shook her head emphatically.

"That and abstinence," I said.

"Oui," he said with bitter humor.

Agnes sighed. "I had thought... I don't know what I thought. Stupid things."

"I am sorry," Gaston said.

I could feel him not looking at me.

I was appalled – with myself. I sighed. "I am sorry. I was... being an irresponsible bastard. Pregnancy was so commonplace a result of my prior life – and I never saw the children or cared – nor did the men I associated with – that I did not consider the consequences here."

She awarded me one of those little nods women give men when they want them to believe all is forgiven, but truly they are close to tears.

"If I become pregnant," she whispered to Gaston. "I will have the baby."

I could not look at Gaston. I picked up the medicine chest and made my way downstairs with it heavy across my thighs and my toes feeling for each step.

I was urged to drop my burden and join in the festivities as I skirted the happy men in the atrium. I gave them a grim smile and vague assurances of returning and continued on. Gaston at last caught up with me, and took one of the handles with a smile that said he was not at all angry. Confused, I transferred my attention to the other handle and let him lead us into the stable.

Light and noise poured through the doorway into our quiet sanctuary. Bella thumped her tail and licked her lips in greeting as she nursed her pups. We stepped into the shadows of the stall and deposited our burden under our hammock.

"I am sorry," I hissed.

Gaston's arms were about me and his lips upon mine. I accepted his kiss.

"Stop," he whispered when our mouths parted. "I want children."

"Oui, I know that…"

"I did realize I might get her with child," he said.

I frowned, a gesture wholly for my own benefit as he could not see it.

"Was that your intent?" I asked with surprise.

"Non, non," he sighed. "Perhaps… I think perhaps I had some forlorn hope that if that one became pregnant, I would not have to marry the other one."

"My love," I said with bemusement. "That is a thing you should tell your matelot."

He sighed and sat on the hammock. "Will, I did not want to admit it, even to myself. And then… We had so little time and… I realized we would not know in time, even if my seed did take. And before that… when first the opportunity presented itself, I just wanted to. I only thought of the other… when I had my cock in her." He sighed heavily.

I laughed quietly and embraced him. "My love, that is when many men think of it."

"Oui, but Will… I only thought of it then because I remembered thinking the same with Gabriella, and how… the babe would not live if the mother died, which my sister surely would before she could carry a child. The consumption had torn her lungs to pieces and…"

My humor fled and I held him tightly. "You wanted a baby even then?" I murmured.

He nodded against my chest. "It was one of my regrets about becoming a monk. Yet, I knew I should not. I knew they would be mad. I knew I was too mad to marry. Yet, I thought of it even then."

I tried not to envision his thinking such tragic thoughts on that awful night. I listened to the men in the atrium: happy in their togetherness; happy in the birth of Striker's son. "I wish I could share in your great need of them," I said softly.

"I am grateful you do not," he said, and I could hear some amusement in his voice. "If you did, we would never have met. You would have found some woman suitable enough to make children with, and you would have stayed with her and them."

I shook my head. "I have known a number of men who were enamored of children though they favored men…"

He pulled away a little and shook his head. "I am not speaking of that. It is not a matter of what you favor; it is a matter of you favoring children. You do not, so you did not seek to add them to your life. If you had, you never would have made it here."

"Ah," I said stupidly. "And does it bother you that I do not favor them so very much now? Though, I must admit, I am touched by Jamaica. Still, I think I will feel more for her when I can converse with the child…"

His fingers were on my lips. "I am grateful that you place me above all else," he said seriously.

"Ah, as I will ever be inclined to do your bidding."

"Just so," he said and pulled my mouth to his.

"So…" I said with a grin. "Will you continue to fuck her when we return until she becomes pregnant, and then marry her?"

He sighed. "I had not thought that far into the future. I did… just now… tell her that if she does become pregnant I will marry her."

I could feel him regarding me in the darkness.

"Good," I said. "I feel I will much prefer her to any your father might send. She was our first choice, anyway."

I felt him sigh with relief.

"My love," I chided. "You can speak to me of…"

"I did not wish to burden you further," he said quickly.

"We cannot always be worrying about that," I said. "We are both such… hardy, yet fragile creatures… that will ever be a concern, yet if one of us carries something alone that he should not, that… that could lead to disaster."

He took a deep and long breath before whispering. "I need to leave this place, Will. Soon."

"I know," I said softly. "If ever you feel you cannot remain a moment longer, tell me, and we will go at once and sort the rest through after we are calm. And they can sit and wait, or leave us behind, or whatever they wish to do until we are ready to return, even though it might take months."

"We cannot do that," he said.

"Oh, oui, but we can," I said sternly. "Damn them all. I do place you above all else."

"I am loved," he said.

"You are loved," I affirmed.

"I will never place any above you," he said and kissed my cheek.

I considered that: as in light of all else we had said, it did not sit well with me.

"Perhaps you should," I whispered. "Perhaps… If we are to approach this matter of children with the diligence they deserve, with the loyalty and love we never received, then perhaps one of us should place them above all else. And that disturbs me greatly – as I do wish to be loved by you above all else – yet… I cannot see bringing them into the world to satisfy your need for them without doing as we have discussed, and giving them everything we lacked."

His breath was ragged, and his arms closed about me until I could barely breathe. "Will, I so love you," he whispered in my ear.

I smiled. "I have great faith that your heart is so big I will never feel any lack, no matter how many children we have."

He gave a short huff of amusement, and then we were startled by a knock on the doorframe.

"Hey, you two fucking already?" Striker asked with a drunken slur. "Get out here and drink. Or at least get your damn father to bed. He's drooling on the table."

"We are coming!" I yelled, as much with amusement as annoyance.

"Well, hurry up and finish!" he called, and left us, muttering, "Can't leave you daft buggers alone for two minutes…"

Gaston released me and pushed himself to his feet. "I suppose we should get my father," he said with amusement.

I chuckled. "And then we should return here and fuck."

He bowled me back onto the hammock and kissed me with great promise. "Oui," he hissed as he stood again.

Though my cock thought his father could wait, I followed my man out of the stable and into the light. The Marquis was not drooling on the table, yet; though he did appear quite tired. But at our appearance, he found new life and cheered our approach heartily. We took a chair from the dining room, and stuffed it in between the Marquis' and Cudro's, and Gaston sat at the front and I straddled it behind him. My cock at least found some amusement in being pressed between us, but I knew it would soon begin to ache with dissatisfaction unless I drank it away; and I was possessed of the sure knowledge that, despite our fond wishes, we would not be departing to meet its needs any time soon.

We drank more than we should, and laughed hard and grinned like fools, until at last even the most boisterous among us began to grow quiet and the lamps guttered from a late-night breeze. Now the Marquis was leaning on us and barely awake. Striker sat between Pete's legs, with his own upon the table and a satisfied smile not even the Devil could dispel upon his face. The rest of our number, save Dupree, Rucker, Alonso, and Liam, were likewise draped on one another or entangled in some fashion. I felt sorry for the four lonely men; but it was a sentiment quickly dissipated when I saw Alonso glancing my way with longing: like a cold wind blowing away a warm fog of happiness.

I stirred, and roused Gaston from his torpor. Thankfully he needed little urging to rise, and we hauled his father to his feet with us. Dupree was sleeping in a puddle of his own drool, and we left the poor man there: the Marquis was enough to handle in our condition and his. We put him between us and maneuvered him up the stairs and into his room to deposit him on the bed. He was unconscious before the down of the mattress had finished sinking beneath his weight. We removed his sword belt and shoes, and draped netting about him. Gaston leaned on one of the bed posts and looked as if he were considering how easy it would be to crawl into bed with his father rather than making his way to our hammock. I took his hand and dragged him to the door.

"We have much to do tomorrow," Gaston said as we made our way down the stairs.

I could not remember what he spoke of, but I knew enough to know I did not want to think about it. I shushed him and led him to bed. I felt eyes upon us as we rounded the table, but I did not glance back. I was going to have to kill Alonso. I hoped it would not be on the morrow. I doubted it was one of the tasks Gaston spoke of.

At last we cuddled chastely in our hammock. I faced the door and held a pistol loosely cradled in my hand. I drifted away yearning for our days on the Point, where we had forgotten why we needed to sleep with weapons.

I woke with an aching head from a disconcerting dream, in which I stood at the edge of a battlefield outside of some Spanish town, naked, without weapons, and all were laughing at me. Upon opening my eyes, I felt I was late for some event, but I knew not what.

Gaston slept like one dead; or rather, like he often did when suffering a bout. He did not respond to my gentle prodding or whispering his name. I let him be, and went in search of water. Samuel had prepared corn cakes and turtle soup for dinner the night before, which no one I knew of had eaten, and now he had warmed the lot of it and presented it as breakfast. I took a bowl, plate, and bottle of water to the stable and waved them under Gaston's nose. There was still no response; so I ate half the soup, drank half the water, and left the rest where he could see it and the dogs could not reach it, upon one of the chests.

By then I had developed a list of things I must do. Of foremost importance was speaking with the Marquis; but as the man would not be rising early this morn, that task would be accomplished later in the day. This was perhaps good, as it would give me time to compose my thoughts, which all involved explaining why Gaston could not marry Christine and should marry Agnes, before the Marquis sailed. Then there was Theodore, who must be told about last night's arrangements, and of course Vivian would expect us to visit. Though Gaston could not accompany me at this time, I thought it best to see to that bit of business now, as I doubted anyone at the Theodores' was sleeping off a drinking binge. Gaston could visit Jamaica later.

I donned my arms and stepped to the doorway, and saw the men strewn about the atrium. Alonso was awake. I was surprised, but then I remembered how very well he could hold his wine; and though he had been drinking rum last night, he had not drunk so much that he had become lost to it. He smiled at me in greeting.

I smiled back and glanced to the stall where Gaston slept like a helpless babe. I did not think Alonso was such a fool. I did feel we must begin to think of such things, though, and make the necessary preparations.

I crossed the atrium and climbed the stairs and knocked on Agnes' door. It took several minutes before she responded groggily. I announced myself, and she told me to enter.

With a chuckle, I stepped into her room and found her curled in the bed clothes regarding me with sleepy eyes.

"Is something the matter?" she asked.

"I must leave the house and I need..." I sighed. "I need someone to watch over Gaston. He is still sleeping. We drank last night. Everyone drank last night."

"Is he ill?" she asked and sat up with a concerned frown.

"Nay, not... he is just deeply asleep, such that..." I stepped to the door and peered out. Alonso was still sitting where he had been, sipping wine. "He cannot guard himself in his current condition."

"But..." she said.

"The men we would have guard him are unconscious with drink... save Alonso," I sighed.

She frowned cutely, and then understanding slowly dawned upon her. "I cannot protect him."

"I feel your presence in the stable should be more than sufficient," I said. "And you can wake him if something untoward does occur." Though, I questioned my belief in that.

She nodded and climbed from her bed. "I suppose I should dress."

"Sam has food," I said.

Her stomach grumbled and I chuckled. "I will fetch you a plate," I said. "Come down as you can."

"Might I sketch him?" she asked as I walked out the door.

"As much as you wish. In his current state, you might be able to pose him somewhat."

"Is he naked?" she asked hopefully.

He was not, but I grinned. "I will see to it." Then I paused and turned back to her. "But do not think other activities..."

She shook her head emphatically, with a chiding frown that I should even think such a thing.

Alonso regarded me curiously as I crossed the atrium. I considered making some excuse for Agnes' imminent arrival, but decided against it. Perhaps it would be better he knew I did not trust him. Or, he might not realize Gaston was asleep when I summoned a young lady to our room; and that should leave his morning filled with mystery.

The idea made me chuckle as I pulled off Gaston's tunic and breeches. Even this did not rouse him. If his breathing had not been so very steady, and likewise the beating of his heart, I might have been alarmed.

Agnes arrived, wearing a gown, but every bit as disheveled as she had appeared when exiting her bed. "Is that man out there this Alonso?" she asked.

"Aye," I said.

"He is handsome enough, I suppose." She frowned. "What will he think?"

"I do not know, and do not care. If he comes over here, glare at him until he leaves."

She reached in the side of her skirt and pulled her pistol out.

I chuckled anew. "Gods, I hope it will not come to that."

Agnes snorted as she sank down to sit with Bella and the pups.

I went to the cookhouse and fetched another bowl and plate for Agnes, and a large bone from the meat box for Bella. My appearance at the stable with these items was greeted with delight. I left them.

Alonso was standing now, somewhat in my path as I crossed to the front door. He regarded me with bemusement and crossed arms.

"Where are you off to?" he asked in Castilian.

"To visit my wife and tell the Theodores of our plans," I said with a shrug.

"To visit your wife, eh? And you leave your man with so small a consolation..."

I snorted. "That small consolation has a pistol, and she does not favor men. I have told her you are nothing but trouble, and should be shot if she feels the need."

Now he was truly perplexed. I laughed as I continued to the door.

He rushed to catch up with me. "Will! You truly do not trust me?" He was angry now.

I met his gaze without challenge and stated fact. "I do not."

"What have I done? To you?" he demanded.

"Expressed thoughtless stubbornness about a thing of great import, namely my feelings for that man."

He shook his head with evident frustration and stepped in close to meet my gaze with great earnestness. "I swear, on my mother's honor, on the Lord's cross, I will never do anything to harm your man. Nothing. Nor will I allow another to harm him. I will be his staunchest protector."

I actually believed him. "Why?"

He sighed. "Because I know you, and cleaving only to one lover is not in your nature."

"Then why would you want me back?" I asked, truly incredulous.

He shrugged, but his words were impassioned. "Because it is not in my nature, either. Because I enjoyed what we had before. We shared women and men. I loved hearing of your conquests, and having someone to tell of mine."

"Gods, Alonso! I cannot go back to that life. I would not, even if I could. Even if he were gone, I now know another manner of living, and I do not want that life anymore."

He threw up his hands. "There is no reasoning with you!"

"No, there is not. So stop. Go away. It is done between us. Find someone else. Return to Florence or some other city in Christendom where there are hundreds of libertines who lived as we did."

He shook his head. "No, I want you."

I considered shooting him, or drawing my blade: my hand was tight upon the hilt and had been throughout our conversation. But, in that moment, I realized I could not kill someone for loving me, no matter how misguided the love. It seemed wrong.

"If you wish to spend the rest of your days in unrequited love for me, then so be it," I sighed. "That is your choice. Either you will turn yourself from it in time, or you will not. I cannot help you."

"We shall see," he said, with the jaunty grin I had once adored.

I shook my head sadly and left him. As I walked into the street, I realized that I would still have to kill him if his love – once he realized it would truly always be unrequited – turned to hate, as love always seemed to do under that circumstance. Oddly, as long as he yet loved me, he was not a threat, merely an annoyance.

Hannah greeted me with a warm smile and led me in silence past Theodore's closed office doors: apparently he was with a client. The ladies and babies were in the back room, as usual. Jamaica was napping in a small crib upon the floor, and I squatted to examine her. I was acutely aware of the fact that she did not resemble Sarah's son. I made no mention of that to Vivian, though, as she was gazing at her daughter with pride.

"Where's Gaston?" Vivian asked. "Or should I refer to him as Lord Montren?"

"Call him Gaston," I said. "We had a busy night. Hush!" I chided Rachel before she could voice whatever was behind her smirk. "My nephew was born and the *Virgin Queen* arrived."

"Oh! A boy! How wonderful!" Rachel exclaimed. "How is he? How is Mistress Striker? What have they named him?"

I grinned. "He is fine. Sarah is fine. I do not know what they intend to name him; no mention was made of it."

"I would imagine Captain Striker was quite pleased," Vivian said with a glum smile.

"Aye," I sighed. "He was delighted to have a son." I shrugged in an attempt to let her know she should not fret over it. "The Marquis' ship also arrived, so he will be sailing soon. I assume we will also."

Vivian frowned at that. "How long will you be gone?"

"Probably six months or so," I said.

She sighed.

"I have... um... made arrangements," I said and looked to Rachel. "For the well being of all we value here. The details will need to be decided upon; but five good men from the *Queen* have chosen to stay here in Port Royal and watch over everyone while we are gone."

"Who?" Rachel asked. "Do I know them?"

I listed the names, as she did indeed know Liam, Davey, and Julio.

She nodded thoughtfully. "Do you truly feel it to be necessary? Will they walk around the houses with arms?"

"I do not know. I would prefer that Vivian not go anywhere in town without escort." I looked to her as I realized how she might have interpreted that.

She shook her head with pinched lips. "I will not be going to the market or..."

"There has been no mention of a price on your head," I said carefully. "But I feel that is largely because my father thought I would put you out."

She nodded. "I understand. I will not go to the market because... people will stare, and I do not wish to see them."

"All right. I... do not wish for you to think it is for any reason other than your safety," I whispered.

She smiled. "Thank you for saying so."

I turned back to Rachel. "Beyond Vivian's safety, our largest concern is that Sarah will be abducted once Striker and Pete have gone. The men will be living in her house; however, if any feel there is a need for someone to watch this house as well..."

"Of course," Rachel said. "We have another spare room."

"I also think it would be best if you all learned to at least shoot pistols." I looked back to Vivian. "You especially. I want you armed at all times. Agnes and Sarah carry pistols about in their skirts. They can show you how they suspend and conceal them."

"Will you teach me?" she asked.

"If we have time; if not..."

She shook her head with a stubborn look I was beginning to know well.

"Vivian," I chided. "They are good men. I will introduce you before we sail. None will judge you harshly."

I bit my tongue a little on that: Liam judged all women who might come, or had come, between matelots, harshly. Julio would probably be the best to handle her, but I worried that she might be inclined to bigotry due to his being a maroon. I sighed.

"And you must understand that they are not servants," I added. "No matter how coarse some of them might appear or speak, and no matter the color of their skin, or their nation of origin, I consider them my peers, which means they are your equals as well."

She frowned at that, but nodded, and then regarded me with guilt. "I am not so... high and mighty as I once was. And, aye, I know I am no longer a Lady." This last was a trifle bitter.

I snorted. "You will ever be a Lady, as you will ever be a lord's daughter, for whatever dubious worth such a thing possesses."

She awarded me a grudging smile. "True."

There was frantic knocking on the back door. Hannah let Samuel into the house. He looked as if he had run the distance here.

"Master Will!" he exclaimed with relief upon seeing me. "They said to get you. None of them knew where Master Theodore's was. The women be fighting."

I followed him without question, or even bothering to excuse myself, and we ran home. I saw no women fighting as I slid to a halt in the atrium, but I did see a number of worried men.

"What happened?" I asked.

Alonso chuckled. "The blonde one," he pointed upstairs, "came down and went to the stable after you left. There was quiet for a time, and then they were at each other like cats. The brunette is in the wash room with the maid. The blonde apparently has a good right."

I swore and ran to the stable. Gaston regarded me groggily from the hammock with a pistol in his hand.

"I heard yelling," he said.

"Apparently Christine and Agnes," I muttered and looked about. Agnes' sketch pad was sitting on the medicine chest, open to a very nice nude portrait of my matelot. The medicine chest and the trunks with our clothing were open. I frowned at that, but picked up the picture and showed it to him. "I left Agnes here to watch over you, as you were sleeping like one dead. Christine apparently came down after I left."

He looked at the sketch, and then at his nakedness, and frowned. "Christine walked in..."

"I suppose she did. I will discover what occurred. She struck Agnes."

Gaston swore quietly in French and struggled to sit up.

"Non," I said and pushed him back. I handed him the water bottle, and closed Agnes' sketch book and set it aside. "Stay here, drink, eat." I indicated the cold food. "And leave the matter to me."

He nodded with guilty eyes, and I kissed him lightly. He pulled my mouth to his for a true kiss, and I accepted it, even though his breath was horrible.

I grinned as he released me. "Drink the water, you taste of soured rum."

He grinned ruefully. "I feel as if I drank a keg."

"You did not, but..." I bit my lip and sighed. "It is the turmoil of the last days, my love; you have been fighting your Horse very hard, and you become very tired when you do so. I have seen it before. Rest."

"I know," he sighed. Then he was frowning and trying to rise again. "Have you spoken to my father?"

"Non, but with what has occurred, I am sure I will shortly. Do not trouble yourself. Lie down. Rest." I pushed him back onto the hammock, and this time he acted as if he would stay.

I left him. There were still no women visible in the atrium, but five people pointed me toward the bathing room, and another five toward the top of the stairs. The bathing room was closer.

I knocked on the door and Henrietta opened it. "Oh, Lord... Sir..." she sputtered.

I waved her off and stepped in to find Agnes regarding me with wide teary eyes above a split lip. "What happened?" I asked kindly.

"I said something stupid," she sobbed.

I smiled, even though my gut was curdling as I imagined all the stupid things she could have said. "Well, that happens, my dear. Start at the beginning."

"Christine walked in while I was sketching Gaston," she said. "She did not knock, and it is not as if there is a door, but she just walked in and I had no warning. She just stared at him for a long time with her face all screwed up in a grimace. And then she realized I was there, and she stared at me for a moment, and then at my drawing, and then she demanded to know what I was doing, as if she were blind. I told her I was watching over him while you went to the Theodores'. She became enraged. She began to look about for a blanket, claiming she wanted to cover his nakedness. He was lying on one, but she did not try to take it up. I told her it was no bother. I had seen him that way many times before." She shook her head ruefully. "She was not pleased with that at all. She said she could not believe he would show himself to anyone or want me drawing him when he was so scarred. And I tried to tell her that he liked it, because I showed him how handsome he was. And she slapped me. She called me a deluded little girl who liked ugly things and had no sense of beauty." She sobbed anew. "And so... and so... I told her he was not ugly, and you found him beautiful and I found him beautiful, and if she could not see he was beautiful then she was a mean-spirited bitch. And then she tried to hit me again, and I hit her. She said I was never to speak that way about her husband again. And then..." She looked up at me with guilty eyes. "I told her he was never going to marry her. And then she tried to hit me, and we began to punch at one another and pull hair, and I ran outside, because I was afraid she would hit me so hard I would swoon and I would fall on the puppies. And then she ran off."

I embraced her. "It is all right, it is all right. All will be well. It was bound to happen. She was to be told today, anyway. I thank the Gods she will not marry him." I truly thanked the Gods that Gaston had not heard what was said.

I found Henrietta watching us with quiet concern.

"It sounds as if it is a fine thing she will na' marry 'im," she said.

I nodded and passed Agnes to her. "I must speak with the Marquis and Christine."

I ran up the stairs and began to knock on the Marquis' door, and then I realized Christine was already speaking to him.

"Why will he not go to France?" she was asking.

I slapped the door twice and opened it. The Marquis was sitting at the edge of his bed, looking every bit as disheveled as we had left him the night before. Christine was pacing. A bruise was forming below her left eye, and her hair hung limply from where it had been arranged atop her head.

"Because he is mad," I said. "Civilization of that order is difficult for him."

The Marquis pointed at me, as if to say that that was what he would have said.

Christine turned to me, closing the distance between us like an angry dog. "I will marry him. You will not stop me."

"You stupid girl, I already have," I said.

"Why? Are you afraid a woman will show him how to be a man, and he will no longer take it from you?" she hissed.

I was incredulous, so much so it took several seconds for me to discover how to reply.

She turned back to the Marquis. "He just wants to keep your son as his boy and not allow him to be what he rightfully is."

"Gaston bestows in our relationship," I said at last. "Nine times out of ten, perhaps nineteen out of twenty, he is the one with his cock up me, not the other way around. Ask any man down below. They have seen us at it."

The Marquis covered his smile with the back of his hand and found the corner of the ceiling of great interest.

Christine whirled to face me, but she blushed. She attempted to cover her discomfiture with a disparaging snort. "Well, then, you are even less a man than I thought you were."

I chuckled. "You stupid cow. I know very damn well what I am. I am a man who will not allow the man he loves to be forced to share a bed with some witch who cannot bear the sight of him."

She flinched. "That is not… I do not know what that little bitch said, but that is not true! I was… You said he was scarred. You did not say… How did that happen?" she demanded. "It must have nearly killed him! I cannot imagine how much pain and suffering he must have endured. And there she is drawing him, like he was some thing of amusement to her, like a thing under one of her lenses!"

If she was sincere, I could see how Agnes and she had come to such an impasse of ideologies at that moment.

The Marquis had blanched.

"You will never know how that occurred," I said firmly. "You have not earned the right, and you never will. He will not marry you. You will cause entirely too much havoc in our lives, and not because I fear he will love you. Nay, it is because I fear he will hate you, and his madness will… You simply do not and cannot understand."

"It is not your decision," she growled and turned to the Marquis.

"It is not mine," he said quietly.

"It is mine," I said.

She shook her head and walked around me and out the door.

I looked to the Marquis. "He is still haunted by events of that night. He has discovered that... there are difficulties with women. He does not trust them. He fears his madness if alone with one under those circumstances. We have been addressing the matter with... the girl, Agnes, and as long as I am with him, he is... somewhat well with it, but..."

He held up his hand to stop me, and stood. When he reached me, he laid his hands along my face and smiled. "My boy, you need not explain. He cannot marry that one, even if..." He sighed and shrugged expressively. "Can he marry the girl? I believe you both suggested her, and I said no because of her lineage, or lack thereof. I am a foolish old man mired in traditions and... perhaps a lifetime of dreams I myself have destroyed. I am grateful I have a son who will acknowledge me, and not shoot me," he added with a moue and a smile, "and I will be happy with any wife he chooses to take, and I will be delighted simply to have grandchildren. I can see he gets on well with the girl, he is comfortable in her presence, and she is talented and intelligent. I am a God-damned fool to ask for more than he can give when I have done so much to..."

"He loves you, you know?" I said. "He truly wishes to please you. He wanted me to tell you about the matter of the marriage, because he was afraid you would be disappointed and..."

He shook his head. "I need to have a long talk with him before I leave."

"Oui," I said. "I will entrust him to you," I teased.

He grinned and embraced me. "Thank you. I appreciate that. Now, what is my future daughter-in-law's name? Do you know anything of her?"

"She has been using the name Chelsea as a surname, but I am not sure if that was her father's or one she has adopted. Chelsea is a place name in England, and also the name of a Lord I once knew in Paris. Her father attended a university, so there was either money or thrift involved there. Her father died and her mother married a planter, sight unseen, and came here. Her mother then died of the flux. I know little else, other than what you have seen. She is young."

"All good wives are," he said with a dismissive wave. "If they get too old, they begin to think for themselves."

I chuckled. "I am afraid this one has already set herself on that path, and it is a thing we value in her."

"Then good," he said with a little shrug. "Speak with them, and have my son come and speak with me. I believe I shall... attend to my toilette." He frowned at the empty cot beneath the window. "Where is Dupree?"

"The last I saw him, he was drooling on the table downstairs when we carried you to bed. I shall send him up if I see him."

He sighed with amusement. "I do not often drink to such excess."

"How is your ship?" I asked with a grin. "I hope full of more of that excellent cognac."

He sighed again, this time unhappily. "Sadly, I feel he has but few bottles of that. Non, the ship is well. The captain has provisioned and filled her with cargo and is quite anxious to sail."

"Well then we have much to do."

"Oui, oui, now go and find my man before I ask you for the chamber pot."

I left him, closing the door behind me. Agnes was ascending the far stairs with Henrietta. I went to meet them before they entered Agnes' room. Her lip had swollen quite pronouncedly. I was sure she would look lovely before the clergyman.

"I must speak to Agnes in private for a moment," I told Henrietta.

She left us, and I followed Agnes into her room.

"Would you consent to marrying Gaston?" I asked.

She sat on her bed and studied the floor. Her hands were surprisingly still at her sides, and her face was only creased by a single line across her brow. "What would I be expected to do?"

"Well... the Marquis wishes for grandchildren."

She nodded with resignation. "I would be the Comtessa de Montren? Would I have to go to France? I don't speak French."

"Aye; nay; well, I do not know; I doubt we will ever live there for any length of time; and it might behoove you to learn it."

She nodded again. "I suppose."

I knelt before her. "You have many qualities we feel we would value in a mother, and you care for him; and he, even in his madness, has little difficulty with you. I actually considered marrying you myself if I had put out Vivian. And, you were Gaston's first choice, but his father was interested then in obtaining a bride of noble French lineage. Christine's uncle on her mother's side is a Duke."

Agnes frowned. "My father's brother is a duke: the Duke of Chelsea."

My jaw dropped. "God damn it, girl! Why did you not tell anyone that months ago?"

She wrinkled her nose with annoyance. "No one asked! And it is not as if it matters. My father's family shunned him when he married my mother."

I sighed. She was correct. We had never asked, and it was probably not a thing one spoke of, if one had never been raised to be a noble and been reduced to the status of a bondswoman.

"I have met your uncle," I said.

She shrugged and spoke bitterly. "I have not. Can he draw? Father could draw, but he could not even afford art supplies, they left him so poor. They did not approve of that, either."

I smiled and kissed her forehead. "You need never worry about that."

"I know," she sighed.

"Will you marry him?" I asked.

She nodded. "That will anger Christine."

"Oh, aye," I chuckled and stood. "You might wish to choose a pretty dress, and perhaps a hat and veil to cover that lip for the church."

"We're getting married today?" she asked with horror.

I shrugged. "Everyone must sail soon."

"Oh, bloody Hell," she said.

I laughed as I closed her door. Gaston would be surprised, but I truly did not think he would be upset over this turn of events.

There were fewer men in the atrium now, but Alonso was still there. He stepped into my path as I headed toward the stable.

"You might wish to knock," he said with a teasing tone.

"Oh? And why is that?" I asked.

"The blonde is with him. There have been noises…"

I swore and dove around him to sprint to the stable.

Bella was growling and upset.

Christine was a bloody and disheveled heap in the corner beneath the hammock, sobbing quietly.

Gaston was a huddled mass in the opposite corner, rocking himself with his hands over his mouth and his horrified eyes upon her.

I wondered if the Gods were truly as cruel as They appeared to be, or if They were actually set upon some higher purpose that we mortals could not divine.

Seventy-Three

Wherein We Face Judgment

I dropped to my knees and crawled under our hammock to Gaston, shedding weapons as I went. He was not so lost he did not see or know me. He seemed relieved at my presence, and his gaze was pleading as I approached.

"They will come," he whispered in French. "I must be punished. Will, I cannot bear it again."

"Non, non," I murmured, as I reached him. He did not flinch from my touch, but he resisted my attempt to pull him into my embrace. "You are safe. I will not allow anyone near you. No one will hurt you. There will be no punishing. You have fallen very hard, though, my love. We must calm you."

I needed to restrain or drug him. I needed to get Christine out of the stable. I prayed the others would stay away.

I could hear them outside: not near the door, but in the atrium questioning one another as to what was occurring. If they came rushing in, all would be chaos. I doubted he would stay as he was in the face of others. Perhaps he would collapse and allow them to overtake him; but more likely, his Horse would rise in his defense, and then someone would be hurt, and possibly even the puppies would be trampled. Yet I did not feel I could leave his side to warn them off; and I harbored the lingering fear from events at Porto Bello that they would not listen.

Anxiety threatened to overwhelm me. That would surely be the end of sanity.

"Christine," I hissed.

I knew she listened: her sobbing had abated as we had whispered to one another.

"Can you crawl outside?" I asked.

Gaston erupted. "Non! She must not leave!" He began to dive past me: toward her. He had a dagger.

I grabbed his arm, and threw myself with him, so that we both landed almost atop her: me on my side somewhat beneath him. She squealed, and tried to scramble away along the wall.

"Let her go," I whispered. My hands were locked about his right wrist: the hand with the knife. He did not strain to bring it closer to her, but he would not let me pull it away. I had no leverage in the position in which I had landed.

Our faces were all very close: hers battered and scared: his full of the Horse in all its feral glory. I supposed I appeared very desperate, as that is how I felt.

"Non," his Horse snarled. "She will tell them and they will come."

"You cannot kill her," I said.

This seemed to give him pause.

I continued softly. "If you kill her we will have to leave… Jamaica. We will have to leave the baby."

He shook his head. "It is not my fault! She is a vile witch! I told her to go! She would not leave! She would not stop touching me! The lying whore! She would not look at me, but she would not stop! She said bad things about you! She is just like the other one! I will not bear them! They will not hurt me again!" But even as he ranted, he backed away.

I could well picture what he spoke of, and I cursed her foolishness; yet I still pitied the poor girl as I moved to kneel between them. She could not have known what she would unleash with her stubborn hubris.

"I know, I know," I murmured. "It is her fault. No one will blame you."

He backed to the far wall again, and regarded the dagger in his shaking hand as if he did not recognize it.

The blade was not bloody. I could not spare her a glance; but in what little I had seen, her clothes were torn, but most of the blood seemed to be about her face and not elsewhere along her body. I was not sure if he had merely beaten her, or if he had indeed raped her, and I wished to ask neither of them. I did not want to know, and it would solve nothing if I did.

He tossed the dagger away and curled on the floor to sob.

I crawled to him again. "Oh, my love. It will be well. I will take care of you."

I needed to drug him. I did not wish to bind him, not in front of her; and I did not feel he would submit to it, anyway. The water bottle was lying on its side near the overturned soup bowl: both appeared to be empty. If I was to give him laudanum, I would need water.

I needed help.

I got my arms about him again, and this time he allowed me to pull him across my lap.

"I am evil," he sobbed.

"Non," I whispered and stroked his back. "You are merely mad, my love. And this time another incited it."

I dared to glance over my shoulder. Christine was regarding me with horror and accusation.

"Go," I mouthed in English.

She began to move quietly toward the doorway to the stall. Her attempt at silence was futile, however, as there was straw all about. Still, even at assuredly hearing her move, Gaston did not tense beneath my hands.

Bella growled protectively above her pups, and I looked over my shoulder again. I was relieved to see she was bothered by Christine's approach and not someone from outside the stable. Christine viewed the animal with trepidation: surely feeling caught between two beasts. She began to angle her way across to the outer doorway, so she could stay as far from the dog as possible.

At least I had been spared having dogs growl at me after my violent encounters with Shane. My heart welled with sympathy for her; and then a strange thought came to me: even if Gaston had done what I hoped he had not, it was not the same. Gaston had not been her friend and lover for years before turning on her like a beast. He had not reviled and beaten her for days in advance. Christine had not been betrayed by a lover.

"Will?" Striker queried from the doorway; and then as he must have spied Christine. "What the Devil?"

Gaston tensed and his head came up.

"Get her out of here," I said.

"What happened?" Striker asked.

He was in the outer room now. Gaston could see him, as he was growling along with Bella.

"Get out!" I roared over my shoulder at Striker, as I threw myself atop Gaston, attempting to pit my weight against his.

"Stop it! Stop it!" I hissed in French to my matelot. "Lie still! I can protect you if you will lie still!"

He stopped struggling, and I heard the rustle of cloth and straw behind us. Terror gripped me. I could not see if they stood there ready to pounce. I could not see if they had retreated. Though he was still, Gaston was still poised to push me off.

"Pete!" I bawled.

"Will? WhatYaNeed?" Pete asked softly from the doorway. His voice sounded close to the floor, as if he were squatting or kneeling.

"Keep them out," I gasped. "Please. I beg you, keep them out."

"NawNaw. NoOneComin'In'Ere. SheBeGone," he told me, and then murmured at Bella, "An'YouLady. YaBeQuietToo."

The dog quieted. Gaston was still tense beneath me; and I dared to move enough to regard his face. He gazed up at me with contrition.

"I want to drug you," I whispered in French. "Will you allow that? I swear, my love, I will let no one hurt you."

He nodded tightly, the tears filling his eyes again.

"All right," I murmured in English, and turned to find Pete.

He was gathering up puppies and moving them to the far corner of their room, as far away from the doorway as could be managed.

"Thank you," I said. "Could you please have someone bring water? I need it to administer the laudanum."

"Good," Pete breathed as his gaze met mine. His eyes were as calm as he appeared, and they held that ancient wisdom I had so often found in them.

He slipped to the doorway, and I heard him ask for the water. They had all seen Christine now; I could well imagine what they thought. I dreaded having to face them. I knew once Gaston's madness abated, he would rather die than see them and know they knew what had occurred. Yet we had to sail with them. I wanted to run very far away.

Gaston clutched at me, and I looked down at him. His mien had shifted yet again, and now he was as fearful and grief-stricken as he had been when I first arrived.

"I am sorry, Will. I am afraid."

"There is nothing to fear," I whispered.

"I have sinned again. I do not want to be punished, but I know... I cannot..."

I hushed him, and smoothed his tears away. "Non, no one will punish you. You are safe."

"But I did it again," he sobbed.

"This one is not dead. It is different."

"Non." He shook his head emphatically. "Non, it is different. This is worse. I did not hurt Gabriella. I hurt Christine."

Pete returned with the water. He knelt in the doorway of the stall and handed it to me. "IBeOutside."

"Thank you."

He left us, and I turned to the medicine chest and found the laudanum.

Now that we were alone again, Gaston rolled to his knees and came to me earnestly. "She said..." He looked away, his breath coming faster and faster again until he panted. "She said she would prove to me that I wanted her. That she was better for me than you. She kept touching me. But she would not look at me. And the Horse became very angry. I told her I would give her what she wanted and she would not like it. And she tried to run. And I hit her. And then I hit her to keep her quiet. And then I... threw her down. And..." He met my gaze with pleading eyes. "It was not better. It was not like when you surrender to me. It was..." He looked away again. "But I liked it. And... I am evil."

My hands shook as I tried to mix the laudanum and water in a little cup. I could see what had occurred very clearly. It sounded so much like some of my encounters with Shane. And so I pictured Gaston attacking me, eyes hard and blazing with anger and lust; throwing me to the ground; taking what he would. My cock stirred, and I gasped.

Gaston was not evil, but as I well knew, I was surely mad.

"You are not evil," I said as I handed him the cup. "Many men would have done as you did when faced with a woman behaving as she was."

"Then they are evil," he said, and downed the cup.

"Perhaps," I sighed. I met his gaze solidly. "I love you, and I cannot believe I would love an evil man."

I waited for him to refute me with some remark about how I was blind or foolish, but he was not himself enough to argue, and I realized I was attempting to put my thoughts in his mouth. It was not fair to him or our love: he was regarding me with hope and the need to believe me.

"Truly," I murmured for us both. "You are not evil. I could not love evil as I do you."

He let out a long shuddering sigh, and the fear gripping him seemed to depart with it.

I guided him out from under our hammock and found his clothes. He dressed numbly, leaning on me for support. I bade him crawl into the hammock, and I located our blanket and covered him. He clung to me, the drug not seeming to take him under. As always when administering it, I feared giving him too much, and so I had probably given him too little.

"Sleep if you can," I whispered. "I must speak with the others. Can you be alone for a time?"

He shook his head and proffered his wrists. With a sigh, I found the rope he had used to bind me during our escapade with the wax. I bound his wrists before him and then tied the rope to the hammock. He seemed to relax once bound, and closed his eyes. I continued to sit with him, smoothing his hair and rubbing his shoulder, until he became supple enough that I thought the drug might have finally taken hold.

I mused on how much I did love him. I loved him so much I would forgive him anything: but, forgiving him this was not some sin against my fellow man – or woman in this instance – as, if all had happened as he said it had, I truly would have forgiven another man for doing the same. It was wrong and unfortunate, and I would hate any man for doing such a thing to a woman I cared for – and possibly even kill them for it – but it was forgivable if I cared for the man more than the woman. Such is the creature of mercurial ethics that I am.

Still, even with such reasoned peace of mind, I was afraid to walk out the door and speak with the others. But I could not hide from them forever. One of us must face them now, and it must be me as it could not be him. I was our bulwark in these matters.

Thankfully, there were fewer present than I had assumed; and none of them women, who I feared most. Only Striker, Pete, Liam, Cudro, the Marquis, Dupree, Rucker, and, to my dismay, Alonso and Theodore sat at the tables at the far end of the atrium.

I crossed the distance reluctantly, feeling other eyes upon me, but not knowing from where the feeling emanated: I could see no one upon the balconies or peering from the rooms.

"How is he?" the Marquis asked in French as I approached.

"Drugged and sleeping," I replied in the same. "He is overcome with shame, and fears he will be punished."

The Marquis sighed heavily and looked away with guilt.

Pete pulled up a chair for me and offered me a bottle of wine as I sat. I took a long pull and studied the table: the wood of it, not the men around it.

"He is drugged and sleeping," I repeated in English. "He is... He has not been well. He has been teetering on the precipice of a good bout of madness for weeks. She provoked him quite thoroughly. Due to events of his past, and his feelings concerning women and such things, she waved a flag before a bull in every regard. She was angry that he would not marry her, and blamed me, and apparently wished to confront him in private and make him reconsider. He says she would not leave him be, until he at last lost his temper and his sanity and... gave her what she had requested in a manner that he is now filled with shame and regret about."

There were quiet sighs about the table, accompanied by Dupree's whispered repetition of my words in French. I dared look up and let my gaze travel to each of them. I found no condemnation, not even from Striker. All seemed concerned or curious. I sighed with relief.

"Stupid girl," the Marquis muttered in French with a sad shake of his head as Dupree finished. He looked to me. "You told her he was mad, non?"

"I told her," I said, "but it has little meaning when one has not seen..."

"She has seen it now," the Marquis said with a shrug and moue.

"I doubt she feels wiser," I sighed. "She will in time." I recalled her angry and accusing eyes upon me in the stable. "How is she?" I asked in English.

There were a number of shrugs, such that much of the table seemed to twitch.

"She be with the womenfolk," Liam said, as if it were a great mystery and would remain so.

"All of them," Striker said.

I glanced at him, and then Theodore, who sighed.

"The ladies of my house wished to visit," Theodore said apologetically. "To see the baby... and due to curiosity regarding your abrupt departure." He shrugged. "Actually, your wife did not wish to accompany us, but Rachel was quite insistent. And once we arrived, well... They are now closeted with the others."

"Lovely," I sighed. "The last thing Vivian wants is to be trapped in a room full of women; but I suppose her spirits will be buoyed in that they will be paying very little attention to her."

Cudro snorted. "Aye, because the last thing any of them will want now is to be in a room full of men. They'll be looking sideways at us for weeks."

I nodded, and spoke from experience with such matters. "Aye, they will rally around her, hear her presentation of events, and hate him... and us. It will take months to sort the whole thing through." Though, I tried to assure myself that not all women sided with the one wronged: some viewed such things in a far more cynical and pragmatic light than a man ever would.

"Damn good thing we're sailing," Striker said.

I snorted with sad amusement as my gaze met the Marquis'. "Aye, but it upsets other plans." I repeated my words in French before Dupree could.

The Marquis sighed. "Did you speak with her?"

I nodded. "I wish I had not. If I had gone directly back to Gaston, I might have been able to..."

He shook his head quickly. "We cannot change the past." He shrugged eloquently. "We can abuse ourselves endlessly over it, but..." He sighed and smiled.

I chuckled grimly. "He will, you know. I will have to watch him every moment to keep him from harming himself."

I shook my head as I thought of spending our voyage to wherever we would plunder chained to him. It would not be wholly unpleasant, and perhaps I could rest as well. We would be safe upon the ship amongst our friends. I should have known we would be safe even here; but truly, though my fears in the stable had been exaggerated by my Horse's panic, our friends had not always acted to warrant my trust at such times.

"So, did she agree?" the Marquis asked me.

"Oui," I said. "And her uncle is a Duke. Her father was shunned by the family for marrying her mother, and so she has never made mention of it."

He sighed and shook his head. "God knows, I should not care if she has noble blood: all who have it seem to be fools." He indicated himself.

Cudro, Rucker, and even Alonso – who spoke some French – were regarding us with even more curiosity than those who did not understand our words.

"Agnes," I said for the benefit of the French speakers. I continued in English. "It has been decided that Gaston will marry Agnes and not Christine."

"Ah," Liam said. "That why they be fightin' earlier?"

"Aye and nay," I sighed. "They did not know of our plans when that occurred."

Alonso chuckled. "Women always have their own agenda. You should know that."

This brought amusement all around.

"Aye, I know," I said with a grim smile. "And we should remember that theirs have likely changed in light of this."

The Marquis nodded sadly once my words were translated.

I addressed him in French. "We had hoped Christine could return with you to France. She has expressed an interest in traveling and seeing the sights of Christendom. Now she might well return to her father."

He frowned at that. "How much trouble might that cause for you?"

I looked to Theodore and switched to English. "What do you feel would be the outcome of her returning to her father at this time?"

Theodore sighed heavily, and his brow furrowed as he considered it. "There will be no legal matter, but he might feel compelled to challenge Gaston to a duel or engage in some other stupid act of revenge to save face. He could conceivably put another price on your heads," he said, then shrugged off his attempt at humor. "It is best in these situations for a marriage to occur to appease the family, but that is apparently no longer an option. I have never thought it a good one, as I feel it is a poor way to begin a marriage."

"There are places where marriage by rapine is an honored tradition," Rucker noted.

"Brave damn men," Cudro muttered.

Theodore chuckled. "I surely cannot imagine it."

"Women be like men." Liam said soberly. "Ya beat any one 'ard enough an' they'll get quiet."

"With some that's when they become the meanest," Striker added with equal sobriety.

Smiles fled faces.

I frowned as I considered how Christine would weather this. I felt strongly that Gaston had not beaten her hard or long enough to do anything but make her angry and dangerous. She would not run as I had done. This abuse was a new and raw wound, and not marks laid upon scars and scabs. She was not inured to it or anything of its like, and would not feel she deserved it. Even if we had not wished for her to leave before, we had to send her away now.

"So, you wish for her to go to France," Theodore was saying. "Does she know this?"

I shook my head.

"Well, it is often best to present a distraught individual with the option you wish them to take while they are... distraught," he said. "Else they often develop their own plans and become quite fixed upon them in their time of distress."

He was correct. Some of my greater intrigues had been culminated during such times, as I had caused them to bring about the hasty making of decisions. "Are you volunteering?"

This elicited a number of chuckles, as did his sorrowful expression.

"I suppose," Theodore sighed. "As your barrister."

"I feel I will be the messenger most likely to be stoned," I said.

"Is there anyone else they might be more inclined to listen to?" Theodore asked hopefully.

I looked to Striker.

"Oh, bloody Hell, nay!" he said quickly.

I looked back to Theodore. "You are very likely the finest candidate we can muster."

"Perhaps ya should take a white flag," Liam offered quite seriously as Theodore stood.

"Nay," Theodore sighed. "I feel that will make my case too obvious."

We all watched him walk up the stairs and across the balcony as if he were a condemned man. He knocked upon Christine's door, and it was opened for him, but he was apparently not allowed entry. He stood and spoke so quietly I could not hear a word, with someone I could not see, and the panic I had felt in the stable began to grip me again.

I stood and went to look in on Gaston. He appeared to be sleeping. I did not touch him for fear the drug's grip was truly too shallow and he would wake. So I knelt and soothed Bella instead.

"Will!" Striker called a few minutes later. I emerged from the stable in time to see all the women, Christine included, marching across the balcony and down the stairs. Christine was wrapped in a blanket, but I could see from the color of her skirt that she had changed her gown. She appeared furious and ready for battle.

I attempted to gauge the mood of the other women. Sarah had the pinched look she got when angry or frustrated: it made my stomach clench, as it was a masterful mix of both our father's and our mother's disapproval. Agnes appeared thoughtful and concerned; and I saw some hope in that. Henrietta was all atwitter: her hands wringing and her eyes teary. Vivian looked more concerned with quieting the child in her arms than with what was occurring around her; but I supposed the child was agitated because she sensed her mother's unease. Rachel's face was a hard mask of disapproval that I was sure could make Theodore's balls retract, as it was very nearly having that effect on mine, and I would not be sharing her bed that night.

Theodore appeared very composed, his face betraying nothing; but when he met my gaze he gave a small sign, just the slight turn of his head that said he found some aspect of what we faced curious.

I crossed my arms and remained standing when I reached the tables at which the men sat. The women were arrayed beyond the tables, and the men seemed disconcerted by this, as if they had been caught in the middle of a battleground. As one, though, all the men turned their backs to me to face the women.

"Where is he?" Christine demanded.

"Drugged and sleeping, and you will never be in his presence again," I said firmly.

"So he is afraid to face me?" she spat.

"'E be mad, woman! Are ya daft?" Liam asked.

"Aye," I said. "What part of madness do you not understand? He has suffered a bout. I warned you of this."

She looked away with anger. "So that is how it is?"

"Aye, that is how he is when he loses himself. He will recover. He will rue forever what occurred this day. He is sorry even now. He was sorry when it occurred, but he could not stop himself; that is how madness behaves."

"So that is it?" she asked, more of the walls than any of us.

"How are you?" I asked Christine.

Her face contorted with incredulity as she turned back to me. "How am I?"

I sighed. "Is anything broken? Do you require a physician?"

"My maidenhead is broken!" she snapped, eliciting gasps and grimaces from the women and men alike.

"I am truly sorry," I said sincerely. "I truly am. If I could change what occurred, I would, but I cannot."

"What occurred, Will?" Sarah asked. "Besides the obvious. Why? We would understand. We are... concerned."

Christine awarded her a glare of great venom, and the lead in my gut relaxed somewhat. They were not united against us, thank the Gods; but my sister's actual question bothered me.

"He is no threat to the rest of you," I said with more of my Horse's rancor than I knew was prudent. "Gaston has been under great strain these past weeks," I continued quickly and with more care. "She apparently sought to confront him because we had decided – due to the strain he was under – that he should not marry her. From what he was able to tell me, she was quite determined to press her case as to why he should marry a woman and not remain with a man, and... She drove him into madness."

"How dare you?" Christine roared. "This is not my fault! I am not to blame! You damn bastards, all of you!" She had backed away, to face the women as well now. "Will speaks of being raped – a thing none here witnessed – and you all hang your heads for his shame! I am raped – and my attacker does not deny it – and you all blame me!"

"It is not the same!" Sarah said with such force the babe in her arms startled. She handed the child to Rachel and began to emphasize her words with her hands. "Will was raped by our cousin who is an evil man! I know! I had to shoot him lest he do the same to me. I had to run here to avoid him. He does vicious and horrible things to all around him. Gaston is not an evil man. He is good and kind to everyone. He is just mad. It is my understanding he was born mad." She turned to look to the Marquis and myself for corroboration.

Dupree had been translating rapidly, and thus at her last words, the Marquis stood and faced Christine to speak with great passion. "Oui, he was born mad. His mother was mad. I had to keep her locked away to prevent her from hurting herself or anyone she thought an enemy in her madness. Gaston appears far saner only because of Will's kind caretaking. I wish to God I had cared for my wife as Will cares for my son. But make no mistake, my son is still mad."

"Then he should be locked away, too!" Christine roared in French.

"You have no right allowing him to hurt people just because he behaves well. If he is so very mad that he is blameless of what he does, then he should be kept in a cell!"

"Nay!" I snapped in English. "Any sane man can be provoked to violence. And we did all we could to keep you from harm. We knew he would not do well with you: that you would cause trouble for us. We sought to ward that off. Gaston has not been about women for his entire life, between boys' schools, a monastery, and living here amongst the Brethren. He did not know when he offered to marry you that he would..." I stopped, unsure if I should say more, but all eyes were upon me now. "A woman is responsible for his scars." This earned me curious looks from Striker, Pete, my sister, and even the Marquis. "She did not wield the whip, but she was responsible for it being used. Until he was confronted with the prospect of marriage, he did not know he still harbored such anger and resentment about the matter. Now he does, and we have sought... We have found he might be with a woman, and thus produce the heirs his father wants, if she is a woman he feels he can trust and... if I am with him. Neither of which was possible with you."

Christine was shaking her head, her face a mask of incredulity once again. "I am so very relieved I did not marry you," she said with sarcasm.

"You stupid girl!" I snapped. "I would not have married you, anyway. Gaston would not allow it. He suffered a bout at the prospect of it the night you ran away. He fought with me, and then from the guilt of that, went and took on an entire tavern."

"And got Will good and beat in the process," Striker added.

"Aye," I said tiredly. "Thus he suffered his punishment by being forced to watch me lie about in pain." I glared at her again. "You must understand. He is truly contrite over what has occurred. He did not do this to you with malice. It was not a thing planned. We were attempting to save you from facing his madness, as we judged you would drive him mad."

She was very still, and then she moved. "Then this should hurt him!"

It seemed I saw the pistol emerge from beneath her blanket at the same time I felt the kick of the ball hitting my right shoulder. I was not prepared, as I would have been if dueling. During a duel or battle, all appeared to slow around me before I was wounded. This had been so very fast. I fell back, the world spinning and all about erupting into chaos.

"Not again," I gasped as the pain hit. Why was I always getting wounded when Gaston was mad and we were at our worst for handling the matter?

Cudro and Agnes appeared above me.

"Gaston," I said. Then I remembered he was drugged and I cursed.

Cudro and Alonso lifted me onto the table. Liam pressed a rag to my wound. I could hear yelling all around, but I could not understand the words. Someone took my right hand and implored me to hold on in

French. I looked down and saw it was the Marquis. I looked elsewhere and saw Gaston through the bodies. He was coming, leaning on Agnes. I reached for him with my left hand, and then he was there above me at the head of the table, his face pressed to mine, our fingers tightly clasped on my chest.

"Show me," he gasped at Liam.

They cut my tunic open to expose my shoulder, and Gaston probed at the wound.

I tried to ignore the pain. I did not try to look at the wound. I studied my matelot's profile. As always, my blood steadied him. He was slowed greatly by the drug, but he was sane, with a strong hand on the reins.

"It is not bad," he whispered in French. "It is just in the muscle. It must have been a small ball."

I nodded, reluctant to tell him it was a lady's piece, as I did not know what Agnes had told him of my assailant, or for that matter what had become of my assailant. Perhaps Pete had killed her. He had been moving toward her very rapidly when I fell.

"Can you tend him?" Striker was asking.

Gaston grimaced with thought. "I cannot wield the instruments. I can tell someone what must be done and guide them."

A discussion of who that someone would be followed, and Cudro ended it by volunteering. He had stitched Gaston's head once before, that day of the tavern beating. Gaston nodded his assent and began to give instructions.

He sat in a chair beside my head. I was sorry when he released my hand, but another set of fingers were quickly entwined with mine, and I looked down to my left and found Vivian's worried face. She squeezed my hand nervously, and I squeezed back. The Marquis still held my right. At Gaston's instruction, Agnes retrieved things they would need from the medicine chest, which someone had fetched from the stable. I felt surrounded by love and industry on my behalf, and the pain and its cause were very distant things.

"Drink," Gaston said, and Agnes held a cup at my lips.

"Non," I said and turned my head away. "I wish to stay with you. I fear…"

"I am giving you as much as you gave me," he whispered in my ear. "You will not go far."

There was grim amusement in his voice, and I nodded and drank.

Agnes gave me the stick to bite on, and I bit it and turned my head away to rest against Gaston's arm as they began to work. Sometime later, they had removed the ball and the piece of my tunic that had entered with it, and sewn the wound closed after dousing it in rum. I had felt all they did, but thankfully from a safe distance. They had no need to hold me down, and I had no need to scream or bite the stick in two.

There was some discussion as to what to do with me, and it was decided I should be moved to the Marquis' room. I did not feel the need to argue with anyone about the matter, as long as Gaston would remain with me. Despite the drug, I was still anxious over that one aspect of my predicament. Gaston himself allayed that fear while fanning another, by instructing Agnes to find the manacles in our bags in the stable and bring them to us. I looked to him with curiosity after his request, and saw fear haunting his eyes. The crisis had passed, and his control was receding.

"We will be fine," I murmured.

"Who shot you?" he asked.

"The Gods hate me," I sighed.

He frowned, his eyes hardening.

"Non, my love, please," I breathed.

"I will do nothing," he said firmly. "I will stay with you."

"Christine," I said.

He grimaced with pain and buried his face in my neck.

"I am sorry," he gasped.

Cudro leaned over me. "We need to move you now."

"Oui, where is Christine?" I asked.

He shrugged. "Pete hauled her off. I think they trussed her up in the parlor. She won't be shooting anyone else." He frowned at Gaston, who did not seem inclined to release me.

"Can you walk upstairs with me, my love?" I murmured.

Gaston nodded tightly and let me go. I did not see the Horse's anger in his eyes, only guilt and shame. Cudro helped me to my feet. Gaston was unsteady once he rose, and Liam quickly threw an arm about him. We made our way to the guest room. Once there, I was propped on pillows at the head of the bed with my right arm in a sling. Gaston crawled on the mattress to kneel at my left side. His hands were quickly clutching my good one, and his eyes were on my belly and nothing else. His breath was coming shorter and faster than I would like, and as my shoulder still ached, I wondered if we should both have more laudanum. I was going to suggest it when Agnes arrived with the manacles.

She stood there with the bag and regarded us with concern and curiosity.

Striker had followed her in with the medicine chest, and stopped behind her with annoyance, as the room had a number of people in it and she was blocking his path.

"Striker," I hissed, relieved he heard me over the all the muttering of the others. "Help her with those, please."

He pushed her aside and deposited the chest at the foot of the bed, before taking the bag from her, hefting it, and looking at Gaston warily. Then he turned to the others. "Out. All of you. They need to sleep."

Cudro and Liam walked toward the door, but Vivian sat in a chair in the corner. The Marquis shooed Dupree out, but he also seemed inclined to stay, as did Agnes.

Theodore regarded me with concern. "My question can wait."

"Your judgment is sound," I said.

He smiled and followed Liam out the door.

Striker shrugged at those remaining, and carefully crawled up the bed sit next to Gaston. Agnes sidled up on my side, and watched him with interest. Striker frowned at her.

I considered it through the pain and the drug. Gaston had asked her to bring them.

"She should learn," I said.

Striker shrugged and motioned her closer. Gaston kept his eyes on me, but he proffered his wrist, and Striker explained to Agnes how to wrap it with the leather so the iron bracelets did not chafe. He then had her do mine.

The tension left Gaston's shoulders after the cuff was locked around his wrist and he tested its weight. After I was chained to him, his hand slipped into mine and he sighed.

Striker dangled the key before me with a questioning look. Agnes began to reach for it, but I shook my head.

"Nay, Striker should have it," I told her. "We will sail before these are removed." I looked to Striker, and he nodded solemnly.

"Thank you," Gaston whispered without looking at either of them.

Striker smiled and patted my matelot's shoulder before crawling off the bed. He glanced at those remaining, and looked to me with a raised eyebrow. "You two need anything else?"

"We will be well for a time," I said. "I do not think they will trouble us."

"Will must sleep," Gaston said. He was still not looking at the others, and his fingers were tight about mine.

"Well, we will address the matter," I said to Striker.

"Rest. Try not to get shot again," Striker said with a grin and left us.

I squeezed Gaston's fingers. He sighed, his eyes remaining upon my midsection.

I looked to our guests. Vivian was sitting anxiously at the edge of her chair, the baby held close to her chest; thankfully little Jamaica was sleeping. Agnes was regarding Vivian and the Marquis with surreptitious annoyance. The Marquis only had eyes for us, and I could see him boiling over with things unsaid. They made me very tired.

"We truly need to rest now," I said. "I do not feel my death is imminent."

"I will be quiet," Vivian whispered. "Please let me stay."

"You might need something. It's not as if either of you can move like that," Agnes said.

I looked to my matelot, and found his gaze had become locked upon his father. Gaston took a long shuddering breath as the Marquis approached.

"I love you," the Marquis whispered to him. "And I am proud of you."

Gaston released a hoarse cry, and collapsed across my belly to sob. His father sat on the edge of the bed and rubbed his back.

"I am so sorry I have caused you such pain," the Marquis whispered huskily. Tears rolled down his cheeks, and he looked to me with worry.

I gave him a reassuring smile and nodded. Despite how distraught it made Gaston, I felt his father was doing the correct thing. Gaston's Horse needed to hear those words from him. It would not hear them so well later, when he was calm.

"I will leave you to care for Will, now," the Marquis said.

Gaston clutched at him with his free hand as the Marquis stood.

His father squeezed his hand. "We will talk again before I sail. Do not worry. Now you should rest."

Gaston released him with a small nod. The Marquis smiled at me and left us. My matelot moved, and raised my arm so he could slip between it and my side, and thus rest his head on my good shoulder.

I considered asking Agnes for more laudanum, but speaking seemed more than my tired body wished to do, and so I closed my eyes and let the exhaustion carry me under, beyond even the pain's reach. I hoped I sank beyond the reach of capricious Gods for a time.

Seventy-Four

Wherein We Stand in the Face of Madness

I dreamt I could not wake. My shoulder ached, yet the pain could not convince me I was not dead. There were moments when I was sure I lay in the guest room watching pipe smoke curl across the ceiling while people played cards, and there were others when I thought that peaceful image to be a thing I was attempting to console myself with while I actually lay weighed down and trapped beneath my sins in an anteroom of Hades, listening to devils gamble for my soul. For the longest time I could not rouse myself to dispel or confirm either notion. I drifted on the smoke and the tide of consciousness, ebbing to and fro.

Eventually a salient sensation gave me a hold on reality, both figuratively and literally: my fingers were being squeezed. I clung to that contact, and slowly pulled myself from the morass.

Gaston held me in this life. He was a great yet reassuring weight along my left side: his head on my shoulder; my arm behind him; his leg over mine. I squeezed his fingers. He responded by squeezing back and nuzzling my neck, then he pulled away and rested his head on the end of my shoulder. I smiled and opened my eyes, turning my head enough to see his green orbs a nose-length away. Our breath mingled as I studied him. He appeared calm and in control, though sorrowful.

"How are we?" I breathed.

"Better, because of you," he sighed with a sad smile. "How are you?"

I took a moment to think on it. "I am pained, but relieved. I feel we have weathered another storm. At least I pray it is behind us."

He frowned. "I am not well, Will. The storm still rages, I am merely lying with you in a quiet hollow beneath the winds. Once we move…"

"Non," I sighed quickly. "Outside, not inside. I do not feel I am well, either."

He smiled wryly. "You are surely not, but it is an ailment I hope you will be afflicted with until the day you die."

I found his humor a well-needed balm; yet I wondered at it. He seemed quite well indeed despite his concerns. I failed to keep this new thought from my face.

He frowned. "Will?"

"I am sorry," I said quickly. "It is the pain."

He nodded, and his eyes flicked to the others with fear. "I…"

"I will handle them," I whispered, nearly relieved to see some sign of his madness. "What do you require?"

"A pot and water, and more laudanum."

I nodded, and slowly turned my head to the right, amazed anew at how a wound in one place could cause so much pain in another. I was sure I could not move my toes without intensifying the ache or eliciting some twinge in my shoulder.

I was greeted with a sight that I was sure would be the way of things for many months in our absence. Liam, Bones, Nickel, and Agnes were playing cards. All were smoking pipes, their faces intent behind the drifting smoke. From what I could see of the piles of coins, Nickel was ahead. If any had heard us speaking, or realized we were awake, they did not show it.

I spoke loudly enough for them to hear. "I pray that when I die, if I should go to Heaven, I will be greeted by fine friends playing cards."

Liam chuckled and turned to face me. "That'll likely be the story. As ya be the luckiest bastard that e'er lived, and iffn that will serve ta get ya to Heaven, ya will be the last ta go. And by God, iffn ya can get there, the rest o' us will too."

Bones laughed heartily at this.

Agnes had stood and crossed to the bed. She laid fingers on my forehead as if I might be feverish. I supposed she did not know what else to do to determine our condition.

"We need water, and a pot, and more laudanum," I told her.

She nodded, but she was frowning at Gaston. I turned to look, and found his eyes closed as if he pretended to still sleep.

"He will be well in time," I assured her.

"Before you sail?" she asked quietly.

"I think not," I sighed.

"Then we will not marry before?" she asked.

Gaston tensed.

I smiled at her. "Do you still wish to marry him?"

She shrugged and frowned upon me with curiosity. "Aye, why would I not? Does he no longer wish to marry… After Christine and all?"

"I do not know," I said honestly. "We have not been able to discuss it. However, I feel it will need to wait until after we return."

She shrugged again. "I am well with that. I just..." She shook her head. "Will you need help with this?" she asked as she retrieved a chamber pot from under the bed.

"Nay, we will manage," I said.

"Then I will fetch water." She turned to the door.

"Agnes," I said sharply enough to halt her. "What were you thinking?"

She sighed and looked to the others before turning her back on them and coming to lean close to me. "What if you do not return?" she whispered. She glanced at Gaston with guilt. "I do not wish to be a bother, but... I have thought on it, and decided I would rather be a married woman than a girl no one knows what to do with for the rest of my days, whether I am provided for or not."

Gaston's grip upon my fingers had tightened to a painful intensity, and I knew without looking that it must have been obvious to her that he was not sleeping.

"That is probably wise," I sighed. "We must discuss it, and see what Gaston feels."

She nodded and left us.

I looked to the others, not sure of what they had heard. I spoke loudly for them. "While I am relieved and pleased to have awoken to fine friends watching over us, we would now appreciate some time alone."

"Aye, let's end this," Bones said as he tossed his cards down.

"You only wish to stop because you are losing," Nickel said with a smile as he scraped the last hand's coins into his winnings.

"Ya think o' a better reason?" Bones asked.

"Ya might be the second luckiest man I know," Liam sighed.

"Only at cards," Nickel said. "Will trumps me in all else."

With a round of chuckles, they nodded at me politely and left the room. The sun shone quite brightly through the door.

"Did we sleep through the night?" I asked Gaston when we were at last alone.

"You did," he said softly, and sat to reach for the pot. He nestled it in the bed linen between us and drained himself with evident relief. Then he assisted me into rolling toward my left side so I could do the same.

I waited until he had finished leaning across me and off the bed to slide the pot under it before I spoke.

"You cannot face them at all?" I asked kindly.

"All is shame and guilt and fear," he whispered as he moved to sit with his legs crossed tailor-style beside me.

"Agnes will return shortly," I said. "I hope," I added, as the pain and thus my desire for laudanum was increasing with every passing moment.

"I must face her," he sighed. Then he frowned. "Why does she think we are to marry?"

I frowned, as I struggled to remember why he would not know of that, and then I realized there was much we had not discussed. "Oh Gods," I breathed. "Your father will accept her. He... apologized for causing trouble by not accepting her in the first place. And... her uncle is a

Duke, after all. So I asked her if she would be willing to marry you. I am sorry. You were sleeping, and... Then things transpired with Christine as they did, and..."

His fingers were on my lips and he smiled ruefully. "So I can simply marry Agnes now? And he will accept me even after..."

"Apparently," I said with a smile.

"How did you manage..." he asked with wonder.

"Your father wishes for you to be happy, and he wishes for you to be able, and... Well, he would rather you marry a girl you wish than not at all."

"But, non," he said with growing consternation. "Why does she not revile me after what I did?"

I smiled. "None do. Well, except Christine. No one reviles you. They all feel you were provoked. They blame Christine. And Christine..." I sighed. "She shot me because she realized no one would allow her to shoot you. She was enraged that all should hold you blameless due to your madness."

"But..."

Agnes hurried in with an onion bottle of water. She seemed pleased Gaston was sitting and willing to meet her curious gaze. "How are you feeling?" she asked him.

"Confused..." He said with great honesty. "You do not hate me?"

"Nay, why would I hate you?" she asked as she came to perch on the edge of the bed.

"Who struck you?" he asked.

Her lip was quite livid and swollen.

"Christine," she said with a frown and glanced at me.

"He slept through your fight, and then was still drowsing before Christine so rudely woke him, and so he has missed much," I said. I vaguely remembered telling him of the girls fighting, but he had been so very sleep-addled I wondered if he recalled any of it. Then I realized there was much of the explanation of her fight with Christine that I would not have him hear at the moment. I stopped her before she began to speak. "Agnes, please fetch the laudanum. There is much that must be discussed, but I would rather speak with Gaston alone, first, please."

If she fought me on this, I thought it likely I would shoot her and he would not marry her, either.

She went to the medicine chest and looked through drawers. "I do not remember where we put it. We threw everything in here after tending your wound."

I was squeezing Gaston's fingers. He was still watching her with a mixture of awe and confusion.

"So if you still need to speak alone, I suppose I should tell the Marquis he must wait a bit longer," she said. "When I left to fetch the water he asked of you and I said you had woken."

Gaston sighed raggedly and slumped over my belly, much as he had when his father spoke with him when I was brought to this bed.

"Do you remember your father speaking to you, here?" I asked.

He nodded. "I have been thinking I dreamed it. And..." He shook his head. "So everyone... I did not wish to look at anyone when we tended your wound. I thought they all spoke to me because of you... that..."

"No one hates you," I said kindly. "You are loved. Even now."

He sobbed.

Agnes had found the bottle and she now stood beside the bed gazing at him with sympathy. She extended her hand, but stopped and glanced to me. I nodded reassuringly, and she sat and rubbed his back.

"No one hates you," she whispered.

"Why?" he growled, and he rose to look at her with the Horse's eyes at its worst. "Why? I raped her! I would do the same to you!"

She left the bed and stood beside it. Her eyes did not leave him, but they did not fill with fear, either: rather her surprise transmuted to curiosity.

I tightened my grip on his hand, but as he was already grinding my bones to dust with both of his, I felt there was little danger he would release me and reach for her across my body.

"You damn women!" he was growling. "You do not care! You only want to be fucked! You do not care what trouble it will cause!"

She began to frown.

"Agnes!" I snapped. "This is his madness talking."

She nodded.

"Oui, I am mad," he snarled at me. "But you are madder! Why do you wish for me to marry one of them? Why?"

"Because I love you," I said calmly.

"Why? Why are you so intelligent and wise in all things but that?" he roared. "Why can you not see me as I am?"

I smiled sadly. "My love, why can you not accept that you are worthy of love?"

"Non," he said and shook his head with a child's stubbornness.

"Oui. Now quit thrashing about and let her give me that damn laudanum. Tell her how much to use."

He closed his eyes tightly and sobbed, rocking back and forth as he attempted to control himself.

I glanced back at her. She was watching him with wide but sympathetic eyes. I was very proud of her. We, in the end – and the beginning – had chosen well. It remained to be seen if she would feel the same, though.

"Agnes," I said kindly. "He will recover. Please bring that over."

She nodded, and came to the head of the bed and perched on the edge again. She began to pour the drug into the mixing cup, and I could see it was far more than either of us should have.

"Nay, half that," Gaston said quickly before I could speak.

She nodded, and poured some back in the bottle, and proffered the new amount for his inspection. He nodded. She mixed it with water and gave it to me.

"Now the same for me," he said calmly.

She did the same thing and handed him the little cup. He downed his dose quickly and returned the cup to her. She set it and the bottle next to the water on the night table.

"I will tell everyone you are still... not well enough for guests, yet."

"Thank you," I murmured.

"I am sorry," Gaston said and pawed tears away.

She shook her head and chewed on her lip. "So..." She frowned and sighed. "Nay, now is not the time. I will go." She stood.

"For what?" I asked.

She flushed. "To speak of arrangements," she sighed. "I am being... selfish." This brought a deeper frown and blush.

"What arrangements?" I asked.

"For the wedding," she said with a sigh. "I would not have you think I am a silly chit, though. It can wait." She turned and headed for the door.

"Here," Gaston said with a ragged breath. "See if Theodore or my father can arrange for the wedding to be here in the house. I do not wish to go to a church." He stopped and gazed at her with concern. "Unless you feel it must be in the church and..."

"Nay, nay," she said quickly. "I will see what can be done."

"Thank you," he breathed. "I am not so... Will knows what to do when I am like that. I am not like that as often as I used to be... before Will."

She nodded. "You are like a very angry dog. I will just stand still if it happens again."

"I would not hurt you," he said quickly. "Truly... not even the worst parts of me wish to harm you. But I say things sometimes..."

She nodded. "You are just barking. I trust you." She came quickly to the bed to lean across me and kiss his forehead. Then she leaned over and kissed mine. "Everything will be fine," she assured us. When she was back at that door, she paused and turned to add, "I will keep everyone out and see to things." Then she was gone.

I smiled with relief.

Gaston regarded me with tears filling his eyes yet again.

"See," I chided gently. "You could not even drive her away. You are cursed to be surrounded by stupid people."

With a sob, he threw himself down beside me and buried his face in my shoulder to cry.

I murmured sweet things of great import but little coherence to him until the drug at last took us both.

I next woke from a pleasant dream I could not remember. I thought it odd that I was sure it was so very pleasant, and it seemed to permeate all I perceived. I gazed with bleary eyes upon the flicker of lamplight upon the ceiling, and found it warm and cheerful. Likewise, I found comfort in the snoring and the murmurs of unseen voices from the dark beyond the door. My matelot lay next to me, on his back with his limbs spread wide in trusting sleep. And that same trust was what had walked with me into the world of the living from the land of dreams. Though my shoulder ached fiercely, my mouth was parched, my head throbbed, my stomach rumbled, and someone plotted in the night nearby, I felt no discomfort or worry of the heart or soul. All was well with the world, and I need but address each little problem one at a time.

"Hello?" I croaked.

The door swung open, and Agnes stepped into the light, followed by Theodore and Striker. I smiled at them and they seemed very pleased to see me.

"Water," I rasped.

Agnes sat on the edge of the bed and raised my head to help me drink from the tankard of cool water she proffered. I gulped it greedily, thinking it was the best I had ever tasted. To her surprise, I drained the cup dry.

"Should I get more?" she asked.

"In a moment," I said with more my usual voice. "What is being discussed?"

Striker and Theodore pulled up chairs and sat: Theodore like a proper gentleman, Striker straddling his with his chest to its back, as ever seemed to be his wont.

"Morgan has sailed for Cow Island. The *Oxford* should already be there," Striker said.

It took several moments to remember who Morgan was and what an *Oxford* was, and then determine why either had any bearing upon me. "So we should sail soon."

"Aye," Striker said and pointed at my matelot with a questioning look.

"He will be fine," I assured him.

"To be elected surgeon?" Striker asked.

"To be married on the morrow?" Theodore asked.

The calm of the dream still lapped at me, and I thought of my matelot's earlier behavior – with Agnes, and more importantly before she returned.

"We will manage," I said with surety.

"And how are you?" Theodore asked. "I told the priest you cannot possibly go to the church... But can you go downstairs?"

"I will manage. Now, however, I wish for a little food and more of the drug."

Agnes gave me another dose: carefully measuring the amount Gaston had indicated before. Then she hurried out in search of food.

"So they will marry?" Theodore asked once she was gone.

I nodded. "She saw him at his... well, not worst, but she surely saw his madness, and still she wishes to proceed. And so does he."

Striker sighed with relief. "She will be so much better than that damn blonde."

"What happened with Christine?" I asked.

"Pete hit her good," Striker said with a sigh, "and then trussed her up in the parlor. The Marquis had his men take her to his ship, bundled up on the floor of a carriage. She is good and angry."

"We all think it is best if she simply disappears," Theodore said.

"I would not have her dead, unless there is no way to calm her…" I said with unease.

"Nay, nay," Theodore said quickly. "From the island: disappears from the island. The Marquis will take her to France with him. And then… Well, he did not say what he would do with her there. I suppose it will depend on whether she calms." He sighed. "I am curious as to what I should tell Sir Christopher, though."

"I do not know," I said sadly. "I suppose he should be told the Marquis is taking her to France – after they sail."

"To what end?" Theodore asked. "If Gaston will have married Agnes, it will be obvious he will not marry her."

"We will have to speak with the Marquis, but I would have you tell that fat bastard Vines that the whereabouts and deportment of his daughter is the Marquis' business now."

"He would not take that well," Theodore said with a smile. "And I am sure he will be contacting her mother's family in France."

I sighed. "I suppose I will never know now how her mother came to marry that fool. But, aye, you are correct, and… so we should speak with the Marquis and ask what he intends to do with her in France. If he is turning her over to her family there, it will not matter. But I cannot see where we will want her telling the French court of this matter."

"Why?" Striker asked. "She would just be ruining herself by doing that. And why should you care what they say about Gaston in the French court?"

"Well," Theodore chided. "The Marquis might care what is said of his son there, as it would reflect poorly upon him."

I looked at my sleeping matelot and knew there was another reason we might care. "Gaston might go there someday."

Striker snorted with amusement until he met my gaze. He sobered. "Would he really want that?"

I sighed. "Not the life at court, but the life like his father's: that will require it, on occasion."

Striker frowned and studied my matelot.

"I know it is difficult to envision," I said with a smile. "But someday, when we are older."

"Nay," Striker said. "I don't doubt it. It's just… I don't like to think about… when we're older. I think about my son, and I think about watching him grow to be a man; but I don't see myself in those fancies as being any older or different than I am now." He smirked at his foolishness.

Theodore chuckled. "You will likely be a wealthy merchant with a fine plantation and a seat on the council when you're older." He frowned suddenly. "Unless this other matter cannot be resolved."

Striker grimaced and finally grinned. "If that's my future, I'm not sure I want the other matter resolved. Pete would never stand for it." But I could see he lied somewhat. His eyes had brightened as Theodore said it.

I let him have his delusions. "And what do you envision of your future?" I asked Theodore.

He was still frowning, and seemed lost in thought. He sighed at my question. "I used to think I would be a wealthy barrister with a plantation and a seat on the council."

"Has your friendship with me truly ruined that?" I asked.

"Nay," he said with a sad smile. "But my principles and convictions surely have." He chuckled ruefully. "Even if this matter is resolved with your father, I have now made enemies."

"It can't be that bad," Striker said kindly. "Modyford wants to return to England."

"Aye, but who will take his place?" Theodore asked archly. "I would bet money on Lynch, and he dislikes the Brethren and anyone who associates with them."

"You can come to France with us someday," I offered with a grin.

Theodore sighed. "I would have to learn French, and study the law all over again." He pursed his lips thoughtfully and finally smiled. "But who can say what the future holds." He stood. "I should return home. I will see you on the morrow for the ceremony."

I was saddened by his apparent mood, as I stood between the ebb tide of my pleasant dream and the incoming wave of the drug. I felt as if we were all things tossed ashore to be burned in incessant light; and I was minded of a thought I had once had, that no one arrived on Jamaica except through that means. We were all flotsam cast away from somewhere to bob upon the sea until we reached this distant shore by happenstance.

Striker was thoughtful as we watched Theodore leave.

"It can't be as bad as all that," he said to me after the door closed. "We've all been well enough these last months. They've been hatching their plots, but we've seen none of it."

I wondered why he wished to cling to the bliss of ignorance. "I had not returned to town and failed to put the wife out," I said. "Nor had I tried to renounce my title. Now they must hatch new plots, or await orders from those who do. It merely buys us time."

Agnes returned with a bowl of soup and some bread. Striker stood and moved so she could come to the bed and sit to help me eat. I felt somewhat helpless: my right arm hurt too much to move, and my left was pinned by my matelot. And the drug was beginning to pull me under.

"I can't believe it will all end because I married your sister," Striker said. "I knew things would change, and I almost lost Pete, but... everything is well now."

"I am sorry," I said.

"I don't blame you," he said.

I knew he did not. I blamed myself, and my father.

"When do you wish to sail?" I asked.

"I want to board tomorrow night, and sail the morning after." He grimaced in anticipation of my response, and I thought he had probably been wincing at people's reactions every time he spoke of it.

Tomorrow night seemed an eternity away with the drug tugging at me. Yet, I knew there was much we must accomplish: things that must be packed and possibly purchased. I would be of no use, and Agnes would not know all my matelot wanted.

"Let me have the key." I watched to see if Striker would hesitate. He frowned, but pulled it from about his neck and brought it to me without pause. I silently cursed my doubt. Since that fateful night in Porto Bello, he had not crossed us once. I wondered what he must do to earn my trust again.

Agnes accepted it from him, as I did not have a hand to grasp it with.

"Thank you. Put it in my sling, please," I told her and looked to Striker. "He will either be ready to sail and be surgeon tomorrow, or he will not. If he is, there is much that must be done and I do not want us to need to find you."

Striker frowned at Gaston and then looked to me. "I spoke to Farley."

I sighed. "Will he sail?"

"Aye. I told him Gaston wished to be surgeon, but I was not sure if he could manage it this voyage."

I thought on it, slowly, as the drug was washing over me now. We liked the young physician. "I would not have him lose the money he might earn for the position if he sailed on another vessel, but it would be best if he were there in case Gaston cannot perform the duties for whatever reason. Yet, Gaston must be surgeon if..."

"Aye, I agree, Farley even agrees," Striker said with a smile. "He says he's looking forward to sailing with Gaston again – to learn from him. Perhaps you can make some arrangement: pay him the money he would have earned. You don't need it; at least I assume you don't. He has a young wife. I feel he'd be agreeable to that. And aye, your matelot must be surgeon if you and he are to stay out of the fighting. Though there are those who'll question you sitting about behind the lines, especially since we'll have two surgeons."

"They will do as they will," I sighed tiredly. "We are ever being questioned."

He sighed heavily. "Well, not to add to it, but... If he's to be wandering about tomorrow, keep him from Sarah."

"What?" I asked, and even Agnes gazed up at him with surprise.

"She forgives what he did on account of his being mad," Striker said carefully. "But she keeps calling him "that poor mad man", and feeling sorry for you having to care for him. If she sees him running about as if nothing occurred..." He sighed again.

"I understand," I said sadly. "We must meet her expectation of madness – and probably those of others as well, like Rachel – in order for them to forgive what occurred with Christine." I sighed. "I do not know how he will be upon rising. I do not know how rapid his recovery will be.

I feel he will be able to do as he must for short periods, but he will not be well. He can act in a normal fashion even when teetering on the brink."

"I know," Striker said. "It's your sister who doesn't understand."

I sighed again. Everything was distant now, beyond the drug: even thoughts of my sister getting that pinched look of disapproval about her mouth that my mother used to. I felt I could not both hold my head above it and talk at the same time; yet what was the point of holding my head above it at all, if not to talk? And that thought distracted me until Agnes offered me another spoonful of soup. I drank it and looked to Striker, who was watching me with concern.

I sighed and smiled. "I am drugged and not at my best for serious matters. I do not know how *I* will be tomorrow," I said ruefully. "I feel the marriage must be a very small affair. I would like Theodore to witness, and you and Pete." I looked to Agnes. "Is there any you wish to have present?"

"Sarah," she sighed. "But I understand."

"I am sorry, Agnes," I said. "You are taking this all so well, and I am so very pleased. Thank you."

She smiled and fed me more as she talked. "It is all right, and you are welcome. I will be a Comtessa. I will have a name and be a Lady. It is not a thing I would have coveted, but once I thought on it, I began to see it as some strange vindication for my father. And, I will not have to bear men like Fletcher courting me any longer. Thus, I am not worried about the wedding. Sarah is the only female friend I have now; that is why I would have her attend, but it is no matter. She is not familiar with madness. I am not, either, but I cannot see how she would understand how he was today."

"What happened today?" Striker asked.

Agnes had shoved a spoon in my mouth before I could answer. She did not look at Striker as she spoke, and I could see her choosing her words carefully as she shrugged. "Gaston was distraught, and he yelled a bit. It was not a thing to worry about."

"Then why would Sarah take it poorly?" Striker asked, his cursed doggedness getting the best of him again.

She met my gaze with concerned eyes; and I could see she did not know what to say and had realized she should not say much.

"He was in the grips of madness," I said quickly. "You have seen him when he raves. He could scare the dead."

Striker smirked. "Aye, you're right, Sarah wouldn't know how to face that at all. If she's yelled at, she gets angry. And Gaston raving like he does would scare her." He frowned. "I think some of that is due to your damn cousin."

I grimaced. "Aye."

He began to frown at Agnes with perplexity. As she had her back to him, she could not see it. I wished to ask him what he wanted, but I had more soup in my mouth, and I hoped he might actually let whatever it was go until another time.

Apparently he could not. "I thought you didn't want to marry, Agnes."
I stifled a sigh.
"Not someone like Fletcher," she said. "I will gladly marry Gaston. And not because of his title," she added quickly.
"But *someone* told me you preferred women," Striker said.
She flushed.
"I told him," I grumbled. "I wished for him to leave off bothering you."
Striker rolled his eyes, Agnes sighed.
"I feel I prefer women, but I cannot marry another woman, even if I met one that I wanted who wanted me, and…" She turned to look up at him and speak with spirit I would have applauded had I two free hands. "As Gaston has Will, I need not worry about him always being up my skirts, or expecting me to love him as a wife would."
I laughed at Striker's discomfiture.
"All right, I can see that," Striker said diffidently.
"She goes well with us, does she not?" I teased.
She smiled.
He snorted. "Aye, she goes well with the two of you. What of the other one?"
"She is not as you think, and once you get to know her – sober – she will surprise you." But that made me consider another thing, and I regarded Agnes seriously. "I would like it if you would attempt to befriend Vivian. She is lonely, and… not so very bad."
Agnes nodded with reluctance. "I will try."
"Thank you, I know it appears I ask much based on what any of you have seen of her."
Agnes nodded in fervent agreement, and I chuckled.
Striker was leaning on the bedpost, staring at some distant thought. "If it's as you and Theodore think it is – which I don't doubt, I just want to doubt it – then they will all need to stand together while we're gone."
"Aye," I said solemnly.
"We will be well enough," Agnes said with a frown, as she put the now-empty soup bowl on the tray.
Striker gave a heavy sigh. "I pray you are," he said tiredly as he walked to the door. "Tomorrow, then."
I nodded, and he left us.
"What should we do if they do arrive to take Sarah away?" Agnes asked with a frown.
"Run and hide," I said. "Help with a fight if it is but a small one, but if they come in force, or with the governor, or… You would be best to slip away and hide. Keep some coin on you, and…" I did not wish to consider what she spoke of any more to give her advice, and I felt the drug was making my tongue run away with me and trouble her with things best discussed calmly. But then another thought gripped me, and I knew I would not rest unless I voiced it.
"If they do come in force, they will seek Sarah, and possibly Vivian, but not you. If you can escape with either child, you would do all a great

favor."

She nodded with wide eyes that showed she well understood what I meant. "Do you think they will come?"

I spoke to reassure us both. "It is like a card game. We gamble that they will not arrive or order an attack here before we return; and truly the cards are in our favor. They will have little time to mount such an attack in person, since they cannot learn of what has transpired here for over a month, until Modyford can send a ship to England: so two months. And then it will take another two to bring their message back. However, if they are already in route, and were merely waiting for the storm season to end, then…" I sighed.

We could guess much and guarantee nothing. If we truly loved them, we would not leave them. Yet, I knew we could probably not save them by remaining. And if we ran elsewhere, the trouble would follow us.

She touched my brow with concern. "We will be fine," she assured me.

"You had best be," I said, with an attempt at good humor. "Let us not dwell upon it tonight. The drug is making me weary and addled and I must rest."

"I will stay and…"

"Nay, nay, please go and sleep. I can wake Gaston if the need arises, and if there is plenty of water in that pitcher, then he can reach all that we might need and… I have the key if he cannot."

"All right, then," she said and kissed my forehead. "Sleep and try not to worry."

At my behest, she left the lamp burning low, and I lay there and watched the light waver upon the ceiling. I no longer felt the pleasant echo of my dream – whatever it had been. I was now gripped with a horrible thought that I knew would haunt me if the Gods in Their capriciousness were cruel. I would rather sacrifice all of them than lose Gaston.

I dozed, the drug allowing no other recourse despite my ugly thoughts. At least it held the mad maelstrom of the past days at bay. I did not feel threatened by my madness, but by the world's.

Gaston finally woke some inestimable amount of time later – I only knew it was before the dawn and close to the time when my head cleared from the last dose of laudanum. With a squeeze of my hand and a light kiss – once he saw I was somewhat awake – he went about draining himself and then drinking an equal amount of water in silence. He fingered the laudanum bottle with longing, and then placed it farther from him without pouring a dose. I considered asking him for more, but I too decided against it, as there was much we must discuss.

At last he sat cross-legged on the bed beside me, eating a piece of bread, and he seemed prepared to speak.

"I love you," I whispered.

He smiled. "How are we?"

"The pain is distant but coming closer every moment. But we must speak first. There is much I should tell you, but I must know how you are. Do the winds howl very near?"

He took a deep breath and frowned, and at last shook his head. "I am well enough to stand with you." He seemed surprised.

"All right, let me see if I can remember it all." But I told him first of my speaking with Agnes at the end, and my concerns and revelation.

He came to lie beside me and hold me tightly with great love. "If I truly felt we must sacrifice them all, I would not leave." he whispered. "I do not feel that is Pete's intent."

I had been thinking on that. "Non, he made Sarah the king. I think he is willing to use her as bait, not sacrifice her. But, I also think he might be willing to lose the game and keep his life – and Striker's: just as I am willing to lose if I can keep you."

"I too place you above them," he murmured sadly. "Even little Jamaica... as she is... sickly and..." He shook his head.

"It is troubling, non?"

"Oui." He kissed me lightly. "But necessary. If... trouble overtakes them, they will return to Heaven. You and I..." He took a deep breath. "So what else has been discussed? Apparently I am to be married." He smiled ruefully.

"Oui, and we chose well."

He nodded. "If I think of them – the women – they are all tangled together, even Agnes, but I can reason with my Horse concerning her. She did not run. If she had run..."

"I know," I murmured. "I was very proud of her."

"So, must I go to the church?" he asked with resignation.

"Non, they have arranged for the marriage to be here."

He sighed with relief and then looked away with consternation. "I do not know if I can consummate it; even here beside you on this bed. I do not think..."

I grinned and stopped his words. "You need not worry. Striker wishes for us to board tomorrow, and sail in the morning. You only need worry about standing before an election," I added. "Farley will sail with us, and Striker feels we can offer him the money you will earn as surgeon, and he will be content not to compete for the position."

"Of course," Gaston said agreeably. "And by tomorrow I should be fine to stand before them – for a time. I suppose I cannot hide if I wish to be surgeon. I have been thinking on that. I must be among the men on occasion. But I can do that. I must be surgeon if the plan is to work." He sighed, and then tensed once again. "My father..."

"Is still here and waiting to speak with you as far as I know. Can you see him?"

He nodded. "Oui." He smiled. "I am doing well." But those words seemed to trigger the winds rising in his eyes and he looked to me with guilt. "It is wrong, Will. I should not be doing well. I have done a horrible thing, and you are injured because of it, and... I cannot feel so..."

I saw very clearly the path he was beginning to charge down. I was not sure if the calm of a moment before had been the result of his having firm hands on the reins in an island of repose within the storm, or if – and this was a thought I found quite surprising – his Horse had been well with matters and what I saw now was his thinking all should be otherwise. He had been so very calm... I had nothing to lose.

"If you descend into madness to punish yourself, you will cause me even more pain," I said sharply.

Startled, his eyes met mine with anger and then surprise.

"I am too drug-addled to engage in great discussion of the matter," I said. "But, suffice it to say, that I will be damn angry with you if you give your Horse the reins and beat it into the bushes when I am wounded and we have much to recover from. If your Horse is willing to sit well over the matter, you should not drive it – or yourself – mad in an attempt to assuage your guilt."

I saw the play of emotions across his face and the Horse in his eyes, and I smiled with a snort of amusement. "I am as surprised by the idea as you, my love," I said softly.

He lay still for a time, and then he snorted with amusement. "All our talk of my becoming my Horse, and masks, and caves and shadows, and... You are correct: I can drive myself to it. That is what I did in Porto Bello that night." He shook his head sadly. "I have... I must think on it." He shook his head irritably. "I use it as an excuse."

"You are mad," I sighed and squeezed his hand. "And when you are at your worst, it is truly the reason and not an excuse, but... There are times when I feel you anticipate it: there are times when I do."

"You are correct," he said sadly. He rolled over to gaze up at the ceiling. "I choose to let it... myself... run – these days. I do not know where the madness begins or ends, and where the Horse stands, and what truth is, and..." He gave a ragged sob.

I knew it would hurt horribly to roll over toward him, and once there my right arm could not reach for him. I felt helpless again. I moved my heavy wrist, reaching around for his hand, and not finding it, crawled my fingers along the chain until I came to the other cuff and then at last his fingers. "I love you."

"That is real," he sighed.

"Hold on to it," I said. I recalled our floating together in the sea like this, just our hands touching. I smiled. "We are mad because we choose to live in truth and not shadows. We are our Horses. We only become confused when we attempt to make sense of it all."

"I could have escaped Christine," he whispered. "But... I wanted to show her how... foolish she was to want me. I wanted to... hurt her. I wanted to drive her away."

"So did I," I said.

"That is wrong, Will," he breathed.

I frowned. I could very clearly remember the look in her eyes when she fired the pistol. She had looked like that when we dueled on the beach. "She wanted to hurt me. I would rather this than what she intended."

"I wanted to kill Gabriella," he sighed after a time.

"Why?" I asked.

"Because she was going to die, and I could not. I knew, Will. I knew what I did was wrong that night. I knew it, and I thought he might kill me, and I wanted him to."

I did not feel he had presented it in quite that manner before. It meant much, and I thought we should discuss it, but then I thought we need not. I spoke the truth of the moment. "I am pleased he did not."

"So am I," he said with wonder. "And I feel guilt for that as well."

"Have we not discussed how guilt serves us poorly?"

He gave a rueful chuckle. "So if I am not to wallow in my guilt or drive myself to madness, what would you have of me?"

I smiled. "Love me, and drug me again, and think of all you will need before we sail. The key is here in my sling. I feel it is close to dawn."

"I see light through the shutters," he said as he rolled to me and pulled the key on its thong from my sling. He kissed me lightly. "I suppose I will visit the apothecary."

As he unlocked the manacles and set them aside, I remembered there were things I had not wished to tell him for fear of provoking his madness. He paused in leaning over me to fetch the laudanum to gaze at me with concern. I sighed and smiled ruefully.

"Avoid Sarah," I said sadly.

"Why?" he asked, a frown of worry tightening his face.

"According to Striker, she is willing to forgive the actions of a madman, but she might not be so kind in her regard of a madman who recovers his sanity in a timely fashion."

He hung his head, and I was able to pull his face to mine now that my arm was free.

"It is a conundrum," I whispered. "You are mad, but it seems that you are only to be forgiven the acts of madness by some if you are ever mad."

"There is no puzzle to it," he said sadly. "If I was always as mad as my mother was, then my life would have been much simpler: Heaven or Hell. But instead I am cast into limbo."

He pulled away and mixed the laudanum for me.

I changed my mind. "I would not have you face the day alone," I said and turned my head away as he proffered the cup. "I will take the pain."

His eyes were as firm as the hand that came to grasp my jaw. "You will drink so that I do not have to worry about that, too."

I took the dose.

"It is early yet: I need not leave you," he sighed, and slid his arms behind my neck and curled about me so that my head rested against his chest and shoulder.

I wished to keep talking, to reassure him, but the new drug washed in over the receding tide of the old and carried me under quite thoroughly. All I could do was cling to his arm and pray the Gods would continue to let us float.

Seventy-Five

Wherein We Say Farewell

I woke from a dream in which I heard the Gods speaking to me; though I could understand nothing They said. In what I believed to be the waking world – though I did not wish to open my eyes and determine the full glory of its existence – people were speaking French: one of them was my matelot; the other my sleep-fogged mind slowly identified as his father. At first I could understand nothing of what they said, either; and then the words began to make sense.

"Unfortunately, we might only be able to fully resolve the matter by having you stand before a French court, or at least a judge," the Marquis was saying. "I do not know, though; and it might be possible to arrange that in Petite Goave where the Governor is. I will let you know as soon as I discover the details." He sighed. "I chide myself on not seeing to the matter before I sailed, but... I knew not how I would find you, and I felt addressing that matter would be awarding more to my hopes than I thought I could bear if they were not met."

He sounded tired, and I carefully peered through my eyelashes. At the angle my head had slumped in my sleep upon the pillows, I was thankfully able to see him sitting at the table. However, I could only see Gaston's leg, where he sat upon the floor with the contents of his medicine chest arranged about him.

"I will be content as long as it can be resolved," Gaston said calmly. "We cannot be sure what the future holds, and even with this new trust between us, I do not wish to place myself under your control should I set foot on French soil. I must be my own man if I am ever to return to

France."

His father sighed and slumped back a little in his chair. "I understand. I do." He sighed again. "I have much to do... in regards the past as well as the future. I will be composing letters the whole way home." He frowned. "Do you think I should post Will's letter to his father upon reaching France? I am hesitant to do so until I can arrange to see that the papers of renunciation can be delivered."

That was a good question, and I felt I should answer it, but I also felt I wished to spy upon more of their conversation: not solely for my own benefit or through a lack of trust, but because I felt if I disrupted them by announcing my presence, it was possible they would not speak as they should. So though I felt guilt, I stayed still and silent, though not so still that it would appear I was no longer sleeping: or so I hoped.

"We can ask Will when he wakes," my matelot said. "But I feel they should arrive at the same time, else his father will try to stop the other."

I agreed, and my heart warmed at knowing I could indeed trust his judgment.

His father nodded. "The ambassador to England is an acquaintance of mine, but I have an old friend who is much closer to him than I. I intend to write my friend first, and ask how I should proceed." he sighed. "I must determine what I will say, though. It is a good thing I will have many weeks at sea."

"What is there to determine?" Gaston asked with curiosity and no challenge in his tone, and I saw him moving packets of herbs about, from one pile in the arrangement before him to another.

The Marquis took a deep breath and chewed on his lip. "If... Well, I must tell them that an English lord has endangered my son. I could deliver the letter and document without that explanation, and merely ask that they see to it there; but the ambassador will surely wish to know why, as it might be a thing that costs political coin, as it were. So I must tell them why. But then, they will wish to know why an English lord would do such a thing, and then I will need to tell them... something. If I tell them that this Lord Dorshire merely dislikes your association with his son, they will suspect something more; and if I tell them the truth, they will think things that are... incorrect."

"You do not wish to tell them we are lovers," Gaston said. His words were not cold, but they were not warm and conversational either.

The Marquis sighed and emotion flowed across his face as he considered his next words. "Non, I do not *wish* to tell them that. Because I feel they will interpret it poorly." He held up his hand in a bid for patience. "I have seen man-lovers about court. They are prodigal libertines, ever up a skirt or down a pair of breeches with little concern for propriety."

"And you would not have me viewed as that?" Gaston asked with less of an edge to his voice.

"Non, I would not. Because, as I have seen, much to my surprise, that is not the way of it here. But, of more import in dealing with the ambassador, the man-lovers of the court – at least those I have seen, and the ones I feel he might be most familiar with in kind – do not engage in relations or entanglements of a duration to warrant long-term concern by... anyone, save the Devil when it comes to their immortal souls. If the ambassador or my friend perceived you and your relationship with Will as being of that type, they would wonder why his father cared a whit. If Will was the typical libertine, his father would have to destroy dozens of men to keep his son from ruin."

I could see the Marquis' point, and as I had once been one of the men of which he spoke, it skewered me deeply.

"I see," Gaston said sadly. "Can you not convey what you have seen here?"

"That is what I must determine the wording of, and..." He sighed and chuckled. "At the same time I am telling them you are a man-lover who is quite devoted to your man, and he to you, such that his father wishes you dead, I must tell them I am claiming you as my heir once again. You see my quandary."

"Oui, but... I am not a man-lover. I love Will, but he will be the only man I ever lie with. I suppose that will make no sense to them, either. Unless you say that I am mad, which..." Gaston sighed.

His father laughed. "Oui, it is a conundrum."

"Oui," Gaston sighed.

The Marquis sobered. "And, it is a thing I do not understand. I see you, and a blind man would know you loved one another, but... Men love one another, as brothers and the greatest of friends without..."

"Will loves men," Gaston said quietly, and my stomach constricted.

"So you... engage in this... to please him. He said something of the sort the day we met." The Marquis snorted. "And then, well... He said a thing that amused me while arguing with Mademoiselle Vines."

"What?" Gaston demanded.

My heart joined my stomach in clenching such that I was not sure if it would function.

His father cleared his throat and gave a little moue. "That you are the... bestower... in your relationship."

"Oui," Gaston said slowly, and I could feel him gazing in my direction. "Most of the time, but on occasion I do receive him."

His father grimaced. "Why? I mean, I can understand where... perhaps... poking into... Well, that it would not be so very different than bedding a woman in certain regards, but... the other...?"

Gaston snorted. "Have you ever had a truly satisfying shit?"

His father nodded with seeming reluctance and a grimace of distaste.

"It is like that," Gaston said, "Over and over again, with an experienced hand about your member at the same time."

His father flushed and studied the floor with a compressed smile that finally became a chuckle. "I see. So there is some pleasure to it."

"Oui," Gaston said with amusement I could hear. His next words were sober, though. "I saw boys at it in the schools you sent me to. They usually paired older to younger, with the younger being considered... like a woman, I suppose. Some of my fights were to fend off advances of older boys because I was small and considered handsome. I wanted none of that. And when I came here, obviously I saw men about it all the time. They paired, but neither was the weaker even if one was always the receiver. And still I wanted none of it. I did not want to be someone's boy. I did not feel any desire to..." He sighed. "I did not feel any desire. There was no need. Until Will. And even then, I was not enamored of our eventually trysting so much as I wished to please him so that he would be satisfied and stay with me. And now..." He sighed. "I find I prefer him, because it is more a matter of my heart than my loins."

My heart felt as if it would burst, and it took nearly all my concentration to remain still and silent.

"But..." His father said with dismay. "You have been with a woman, now, non? Your bride, oui? I understand your love for him, I merely..."

Gaston sighed. "Women are complicated for me. It is due to... Gabriella... But, I feel, even if there was not that and my madness to contend with, I might find I preferred Will."

"Well," his father sighed. "That would mean you love men more than women, would it not?"

"Non," Gaston said with a sigh. "It would mean I prefer the tightness of an anus; and that, for my life here, I prefer the constant company of a man as opposed to a woman who I must ever leave in port. And though I wish for children, I am pleased to not have to concern myself with the matter every time I wish to tryst."

His father had flushed anew and now laughed. "I can see where that might have a benefit. For the life you lead here," he added seriously.

"If I come to France," Gaston said with equal somberness. "Will will be with me, and we will share a bed wherever we reside."

"My son," the Marquis said, "in France, as in England, sodomy is illegal. I do not know if the English prosecute the matter with diligence, but in France it is a matter under the purview of the Church and the church courts. They overlook individuals with those proclivities if they are discreet, and in the city or at court, but a nobleman having a lover in his bed at all times would be..." He shook his head sadly. "Especially in the country. We have loyal servants, I feel that if you have a wife and children, and Will has a room down the hall, they will overlook the fact that one bed or the other is not often slept in. But discretion will have to be maintained outside of the household."

I wished to cry, as it was a truth I well knew.

He continued patiently. "If you wish to be a nobleman, to be as you were born to be, then you must accept that there are sacrifices in the name of that responsibility. I know Will is willing to walk away from his birthright because... well, he should; and judging from what I have heard, he will never gain it anyway. But... My Lord, Gab... Gaston. We have mended our differences, have we not? I wish to welcome you back with open arms and give you all that I have. It will do neither of us any good if you are charged, condemned, and burned at the stake."

I could remain silent no longer. I did not need to hear Gaston's reply. I knew it in my heart, just as I knew he must hear mine before he said a thing that he might later wish to rescind.

"We will do as we must," I said.

The Marquis started, and Gaston's head appeared at the foot of the bed to gaze at me with teary eyes through the bars.

I switched to English. "This means much to you, my love. Details need not be decided now. Do not throw it away. We can manage something when the time comes, or perhaps not, and you will choose not to accept it. Perhaps you can accept it and we can avoid living in France. I do not know what the future holds, and neither do you – as you once told me. For now, reassure him. You need make no protestation for me. I do not doubt your love."

He awarded me a wry smile. "How much did you hear?"

I grinned. "Let us say I wish I could discuss things sexual with my father in such a fashion."

He snorted with amusement and turned back to his father. "Will says we cannot know what the future holds, and we need not wrestle with such matters now, nor should I make some stand. He will abide by whatever needs be done." He sighed heavily. "I suppose I will, too."

His father appeared very relieved, and he looked to me to award me a nod of gratitude and respect.

"I love him... beyond all reason," I said gravely.

He nodded again and turned back to his son. "I am sure something can be arranged that will... perhaps not be the best for all involved, but will suffice."

Gaston nodded. "We will face that matter when the time comes."

His father pursed his lips and frowned. "Is this why you do not wish to return to France with me, now? In addition to the matter of your legal standing."

"Partly," Gaston said. "I need Will *with* me. We have enough to battle now, without having to worry about nosy servants and priests. And, I cannot face... court... or even possibly unfamiliar people day after day at this time. I feel I will in time, but not now."

The Marquis nodded gravely.

"And even..." Gaston sighed. "Even at the best I can imagine being in regards to my madness, I do not wish to live in a home where I must watch my back at all times. It will drive me to madness."

The Marquis frowned. "I will consider that. How things are arranged, and how they might be changed to... So that you need not concern yourself with troublesome things every day."

That concerned me. I thought there would likely be much we would wish to have a hand in regarding the family lands and how the people were treated upon them and the like. I would not have us insulated from them. And then there was another matter of things we would wish to have a hand in the daily affairs of.

"Children," I said. "Once they are produced, we will wish to raise them, as we have said."

"Oui," Gaston said quickly.

I smiled at the Marquis. "We will not find it suitable that they are raised by nannies and tutors in another wing of the house, and only brought around to see us before their prayers." I tried to remember other households I had visited over the years. "Perhaps… There can be a set of family rooms, or a wing, that would have very few servants and we could live there with our wives and children, and thus none would be the wiser as to the actual sleeping arrangements as they should occur."

And then I remembered that our wives might have sleeping arrangements they wished to pursue separate of us as well. I suppressed a sigh. We were fools to think we could attempt what we sought. However would we make us all happy?

The Marquis was thoughtful. "That is done… on rare occasion."

I smiled. "I know; I have seen it: on rare occasion."

He smiled. "You are correct, though; something can surely be arranged."

Gaston made no comment, nor did he seem to wish to consider the conversation any longer. He pulled himself off the floor and came to sit beside me and check my bandage.

My shoulder had ached since I awoke, but it had seemed a distant thing in comparison to the other matters being discussed – or rather, my interest in them. Once my wound was exposed to the air, though, I became quite aware of its primacy on the horizon of my concerns.

"How am I?" I asked in French: my matelot's face did not appear peaceful, and I was not sure if it was due to the conversation or the state of my wound.

"It is angrier than I would like," he sighed, and smelled the soiled bandage he had removed.

The Marquis had moved his chair closer. "Is he not well?" He grimaced at the sight of my shoulder.

I craned my neck – despite the pain it caused me – and saw the puckered wound was indeed red and swollen.

"I will prepare a poultice," Gaston said, and left the wound uncovered. He looked back at it as he stood. "If that does not draw the inflammation out, I will be forced to open it to drain the wound. It will take longer to heal then."

"So you will not be able to sail?" the Marquis asked with a touch of hope.

Gaston shook his head. "Non, he can heal on a ship as well as here." He went to the door, and after peering out to see who might be about, left us.

His father sighed in his wake.

"Would you stay if we did?" I asked.

"Non, sadly, I should not. I have been away too long, and… As we were discussing before you woke, there is much I must attend to in your aid. Including that damn girl," he sighed and gestured at my shoulder.

"How is she?"

"Furious. Vittese has locked her in a cabin with no windows in order to keep her from attempting to escape."

I frowned. "We will not have her harmed."

He snorted dismissively. "What would you have of her?" he chided. "Would you have her go and tell her father what has occurred? The governor perhaps? As your good Monsieur Theodore noted, under the usual circumstances of trouble of this nature, they would simply hide her away for shame and perhaps demand a duel or some sort of dowry; but I feel in these circumstances she cannot be but a thorn in your side, if not a knife in your back."

He was correct. We had made her an enemy, and it was likely that even if her father did not demand satisfaction for the matter, she would make another attempt to harm us herself – and such an attempt could take many far more lethal or troublesome forms than a little pistol shot. Or, someone would seize upon some way to use her to our disadvantage even without her consent.

"So what is to be done with her?" I asked. "Strangle her and dump her at sea? Sadly, that would truly be in our best interests."

He rolled his eyes. "I hope it will not come to that. I truly do. If she does not calm during the voyage, I know not what we will do with her. I would rather hand her over to her mother's family in France, or even send her to her aunt in Geneva. But I cannot have her tearing through the courts casting aspersions on Gaston now. I pray she will come to her senses and realize that she can make the best of this situation if she will but take the money I give her and keep her mouth shut."

"That is my hope as well," I said. "Could her uncle cause problems for you?"

"He could, but I will slander the girl and her family before I allow that to happen," he said with a shrug. "Her mother did marry beneath her, and I am sure there is either a scandal or some other machination involved in that which her kin would rather not have examined, as I have heard little talk of it before now."

I envisioned Christine standing between snarling wolves; and then I remembered the look in her eyes when she pulled the trigger, and then a dozen other examples of her smugness and anger about my matelot and me. She was not some little lamb, but a she-wolf who could bite and snarl with the best of them. I vowed I would cease to be tempted to feel pity for her.

"You know something of her," the Marquis was saying. "Will she come to her senses?"

"She will cool like tempered steel," I said sadly. "And be all the sharper in the end."

He sighed. "I do not wish to resort to murder."

I snorted. "I will kill her if need be to protect Gaston."

"But sadly," he noted, "you will not be on hand when such a

decision must be made."

"Has Vittese killed for you before?" I asked.

He paused before nodding tightly.

A thought occurred to me, and I sighed. He regarded me with curiosity.

"We are little different than my father," I said.

The Marquis snorted. "Non, that is not true."

He did not elaborate; and he was no longer meeting my gaze.

I smiled. "And how are we different? I see no difference, other than I stand here and he stands there – on the other side of a fence he has made between us."

"This is a war," the Marquis said with a nonchalant shrug and a fidget with his cane that belied it. "A feud. And we did not start it. You are correct, he made the fence." He shook his head. "I love... loved, all my sons; yet, even when I saw them heading toward ruin, I did not resort to attempting to break them or destroy their friends and associates. Even with Gaston – though... I might have killed him that night in my rage – I did not wish to see him harmed or tortured in an asylum in order to save me the trouble he caused."

"Hold," I said. "I did not mean to imply that you were as base or conniving a man as my father: you are not. But, we are wolves at heart, and we do what we must when we feel it is warranted. But whereas you and I act from love..." I shook my head. That line of reasoning was unsound. "My father does what he does for love of another, too, I suppose."

The thought pained me nearly as much as my shoulder. There was that betrayal Sarah and I had discussed. A father should do all in his power to protect his son, not his godson. But I was not the son he wanted; and his wanting Shane over me merely proved him to be a fool.

I shook my head. I had walked these paths before and found they led nowhere.

"You are a better man than my father," I told the Marquis. "Never doubt that."

He frowned at me with sympathy. "Your father... I wish he would experience some epiphany as I did, and realize he should seek to redress your grievances and act toward you as a father should. I have hopes of that: that once he realizes others – his peers – are involved, he will realize the error of his ways."

I tried to envision that. "I do not think I could ever trust him. I would always feel he made amends or acted kindly in order to secure the good opinion of others and not mine."

"Is your father not a Christian man?" he asked.

"By birth, I suppose. Do I feel he has ever expressed a Christian sentiment – said or done a thing that the Savior himself would commend – outside of a church or the presence of clergy? Non."

"That is... unfortunate," the Marquis said, and then glanced toward the door. "My son is not a religious man, now, is he? I know he once considered becoming a monk, before..." He sighed.

"That night broke his skin, his voice, and his relationship with God," I said without rancor.

He winced. "Can that be mended?"

I thought of all our talk of Gods. "I feel he is at peace on the matter."

The Marquis seemed uncomfortable about saying whatever he would next. He finally sighed and said, "Being a member of the Catholic Church is part of a French lord's life."

I nodded. "We will do as we must."

This did not seem to satisfy him, but Gaston entered before he could speak. My matelot set a kettle and a bowl on the table and handed me a small bundle of bacon. I ate while he sorted through herbs and selected several and began to combine them in a bowl with steaming water. I knew that mass would soon go into a muslin bag and then upon my wound.

"Might I have another dose?" I asked.

"This should not hurt," he assured me.

"It hurts now," I said.

He smiled. "Wait a moment."

I sighed.

"My faith has brought me great strength over the years," the Marquis said.

Gaston stopped mixing and looked to me and not his father.

I smiled wanly. "French lords must be good Catholics."

Gaston sighed and turned back to his work. "My faith gives me great strength, too; and someday, when I must, I will attend mass, take the sacrament, and confess."

"But," his father said with worry, "You... Have you confessed and been absolved since... that night... for what happened then and all you have done since? I am not asking as... As your father, I am concerned for your immortal soul."

Gaston stopped mixing again, and grasped the edge of the table. I could see his shoulders tighten.

"My lord," I said calmly. "Leave the matter be."

Gaston's gaze met mine, and I saw great love there, so much that my breath caught.

He turned to face his father. "Non. I have confessed and prayed and been absolved."

"That requires a church and..."

"Does it?" Gaston asked with surprising calm. "Non, I have not become a Huguenot. I know what is heresy and blasphemy, and I will not transgress in the presence of anyone who will bring the matter before the church. Now, however, this is the last day we will see one another for possibly several years. I do not wish to fight over this now. I love you. Have faith in me." He turned back to the bowl and began to place the mass in the bag.

His father smiled, and his eyes filled with tears. He stood and went to Gaston and embraced him. They held one another for a time until Gaston gently pushed his father to sit again and brought the poultice to me. I said nothing as he applied it to my shoulder and poured me a strong dose of laudanum.

"You did that very well," I whispered in English after I took the drug.

He smiled. "I love you. Now rest. I will take my father to the apothecary's."

A strange thought gripped me: he would be fine without me.

"What?" he asked at whatever he saw on my face.

I shook my head. "Nothing, I would have you take more than your father with you, though."

He nodded thoughtfully. "I suppose that is true. Now rest, and know that I love you." He kissed my forehead lightly, and then my eyes so that I closed them, and then my lips. It seemed a form of benediction, and I let it release me.

They left, and I dozed: troubled by errant visions of how we would one day be forced to live, and the stench of the poultice.

Gaston gently woke me sometime later, but not so much later that the drug had receded. I felt no pain, and the door seemed a distant thing.

"The priest is here," he whispered, even though we were alone.

He had dressed as a gentleman, and I saw clothing laid out for me at the foot of the bed as he helped me sit. My wound seemed a bit less red, but perhaps it was my imagination. I knew it only ached less due to the drug. He began to dress me in silence. I kept thinking that there was much I needed to discuss, but I could think of none of it. Still, his silence concerned me.

I cupped his jaw and brought his eyes up to mine when he finished lacing my boots. "Speak to me," I implored.

He sighed. "It is best if I do not think. I will marry her. We will say our goodbyes and go to the ship. Then we will escape."

I nodded and sluggishly cursed my foolishness. "I will leave you be."

He shook his head and smiled wanly. "Never."

We made our slow way down to the parlor. I could have walked there – possibly well enough – by myself, but with the drug making me dizzy, I leaned on him gladly.

Striker and Pete joined us in the parlor to stand in witness alongside Theodore, the Marquis and Dupree. The only others present were the bride and clergy, and we had seen no one as we descended the stairs. I wondered where and how Striker had driven them off. Agnes was dressed in the gown she had worn to visit Mistress Garret; and her hair was plaited and coiled in a manner that showed her graceful neck. Her lip was still swollen, but all had the good sense not to mention it, even the priest. He was the same unctuous individual who had performed my marriage and Striker's.

"My dear Lor... Mister Williams," the priest said with a quick glance at Theodore. "I hear, and see, you are wounded. After this joyous event, shall we tend to your relationship with your Father?"

I almost told him I was far too injured to attempt such a thing, and then I realized he meant the Christian God; and then I remembered much of the conversation we had engaged in with the Marquis. It was all I could do not to roll my eyes and sigh.

"I feel I will survive this wound," I assured him. "I do not feel I need make peace with God now, thank you."

This seemed to disappoint him, but I ignored him as Gaston helped me to a chair. Then my matelot went to stand beside his bride, and the priest thankfully made short work of the ceremony.

"So, even though this did not occur in an English church, this will be considered legal in English law?" the Marquis asked in French with Dupree translating.

"Aye," the priest said happily with a nod to Theodore. "I will record this marriage in the rolls and all will be as it should be."

I was beginning to wonder how much of a donation we had made to the church.

"Well, I would see you married again in a Catholic church someday," the Marquis said to Gaston as if he still questioned the legality. Thankfully Dupree did not translate this last for the others.

My matelot shrugged and awarded his father a patient, "We will do so when we are in France; this is the best we can manage here."

"I know, and I am well pleased with what has been accomplished," his father said quickly. "Thank you."

Gaston took a deep breath, but held back whatever he would have said after glancing about the room. He nodded curtly. "Now we must return Will to bed," he told his father.

We thanked the priest, and Theodore escorted him out.

My matelot turned to Agnes and embraced her to whisper something in her ear and she nodded solemnly in response. Then he came to me and helped me rise and walk to the door.

"If Theodore returns here," I told Striker as we left the room, "Tell him we will visit his house on the way to the ship."

"Good," Striker said. "I'd like to be gone in an hour or so."

I was pleased to hear it, though it left little time to settle our affairs. The thought of escaping this cursed place once again began to fill me with drug-muted excitement.

"I have told Agnes to give us some time to pack, and then we will meet with her to discuss how she will manage in our absence," Gaston whispered to me as we climbed the stairs.

His voice was taut, and I held him tightly more to reassure him than support myself as we reached our room. At last we were safely alone and the door closed behind us. Gaston got me to the bed and dropped to his knees to wrap his arms around my waist and sob in my lap.

"We will be fine," I murmured. "All will be well. We are not going to France... soon."

"I married someone other than you," he growled with the Horse's voice.

"And what does that mean?" I asked lightly as I tried to recall how I had felt when I married. I succeeded and sighed. "It means nothing. It is just a legality needed so that your children will be legitimate."

He sat back to regard me fiercely. "And what does that mean? If I get children on a woman, then they are mine if I say they are!"

I smiled. "You know I agree with you. And I love you for thinking as you do. But at this moment, I cannot discuss it. Now help me dress like a proper buccaneer, and let us escape these matters of civilization."

He opened his mouth to speak, but then the fight left him in a prolonged sigh and he let his head fall on my knees.

"I love you," he whispered.

We set our gentlemanly attire aside with relief and donned our buccaneer garb and weapons – to the best of my ability, with the rest readied upon the bed for him to carry. Gaston finished packing what little we would take, and stowed all else in the trunks that had been delivered to the room while I slept. Agnes arrived, and we gave her the fortune lining the bottom of the medicine chest in a bag and bade her find a place to hide it. Then Gaston spoke at great length about the dogs being gelded and all manner of things she should see to in our absence. Like the good girl she was, she took notes.

Then, with Agnes hauling part of our gear so Gaston could handle the medicine chest, we went to the stable and sat with Bella and the puppies for a time. When we returned, they would be dogs and would not remember us. We wished to capture as much of their peace and innocence as we could. Sadly, some things are very difficult to recall with the piercing poignancy that makes the memory truly worth keeping; I feel the grace granted by the puppies was one of those elusive wonders, and I mourned leaving them and it from behind a curtain of laudanum.

Striker found us, and we reluctantly gathered ourselves to say our goodbyes to the household. Gaston spoke to Liam at length, away from the others, and I made my way to the place where Striker and Pete were standing with Sarah. My sister handed Pete the baby and came to embrace me.

"So does my nephew have a name?" I asked.

"Aye, we had him baptized yesterday," she said proudly. "Peter James Striker." She grinned at her men before turning to me to whisper earnestly, "Take care of them for me."

I smiled with the incongruity of it, as I gazed upon the robust men of whom she spoke whilst I leaned on her for support; but I understood.

"I will do all I can to keep them from harm." I looked down at her and thought of other dangers. "You... If they should come for you..."

Her gaze hardened and her chin rose.

"Damn it, Sarah, go!" I hissed. "Give the baby to another and have them run, but you should go. Agree to whatever you must, do what you must to live, and we will come for you."

Her breath caught, and she looked away. "I pray it will not come to that."

"As do I," I whispered, and held her tighter.

I looked beyond her and saw Pete and Striker regarding me with stern faces, and I realized they had heard my words. I shook my head forlornly. Striker sighed.

Pete, quite teary-eyed, returned the child to Sarah's arms when I released her. "DoWhatWillSays. HeBeRight."

She met his gaze firmly. "They will not arrive before you return."

The Golden One's eyes narrowed with speculation and doubt, but he nodded and embraced her.

I was moved to touch the little foot protruding from the blanket between them. The winds were a distant thing in my head under the aegis of the drug: more like breezes swirling thoughts about just beyond my grasp; but though my thoughts were wind-swept and elusive, my visions were very clear. I imagined vivid scenes from tales of old, both biblical and mythical, of the carnage and fear-born wrath of kings threatened by prophecies of firstborn sons. I thanked the Gods Jamaica was not a boy, or even mine, and then I told Them that I wanted my little nephew to live very much; even if that required my sister putting him to sea in a basket.

Gaston came to fetch me, and leaving teary women and stalwart men in our wake, we gathered our things and made our way to the Theodores'. Striker, Pete and the others who would sail marched on to the Hole, but Gaston, the Marquis, Dupree, and I went inside. I heard Gaston speaking with Theodore, confirming the arrangements all had been making as I lay about wounded and drugged concerning Liam and the others and things that must be done. I ignored them and went to the back room to find Vivian and Jamaica.

I knelt beside my wife where she nursed our baby. I had planned to tell her what I had told my sister; but I realized it would only make her distraught and she did not need to hear it. She knew to run, and it was very likely she placed Jamaica before all else. Not that my sister did not; but Sarah knew of the dangers as a thing of speculation and distant concern, and had only once had violence threatened against her person. And she had managed that well enough. Vivian had known fear; she would not be brave.

Vivian regarded me with startled and concerned eyes, and I knew I must look quite the sight.

I smiled weakly. "I will heal."

I could see the side of the baby's face pressed against her mother's teat as she nursed. The little mouth stopped its rhythmic sucking, and Vivian jiggled her to get her started again.

"She does that," Vivian sighed. "It is like she forgets what she is doing."

I thought of how healthy and strong my little nephew appeared in comparison, and Gaston's sentiment about Jamaica returning to

Heaven if the worst should occur. I knew she might die while we roved, even if nothing untoward befell the rest of them.

I glanced away, and found Vivian watching me with concern.

"What?" she breathed.

I sighed and gave her a rueful smile. "There was a time when I wished you dead, but now… I would not have anything bad happen to either of you. Be careful, and take care of her. You are a good mother."

Her hedgehog bristles had risen in her eyes for a moment as I spoke, but when I finished, she smiled sadly. "You know, marrying you is the best thing that has happened to me."

I shook my head. "Well, then, my dear, let us hope the rest of your life is better."

She smirked.

Gaston had joined us. He regarded me with concern. I shook my head and moved aside so he could gaze upon the baby. Vivian jiggled the child and pulled her from her breast to hand her to my matelot. Little Jamaica proceeded to drool the contents of her mouth upon him. He smiled and wiped it away with the corner of her blanket.

I pushed myself up and brushed a kiss on Vivian's forehead, before leaving them to dote on the child. I wandered out the back door and down the steps to the cistern, and there I sat and stared up at the hazy and cloud-filled sky. It would be beautiful shortly, as the evening was already awash with golden light, and soon the clouds would glow with color. I was overwhelmed by the sense of impending beauty, such that the winds receded well beyond even where the drug could dull and shelter me from them. And I was minded of a night that seemed an eternity ago, when I had stood on a bridge watching a river lit by a sinking sun. It had been a portent that had led me West – after a fashion – to all I now found good in the world.

I smiled warmly at Gaston when he at last emerged with swollen eyes to lead me away.

"How are we?" he asked as he took my hand.

"No longer worried," I sighed. "We are loved."

He smiled and kissed me lightly, and we went around the house to meet his father, Dupree, Liam, Nickel, and make our way to the Chocolata Hole, our ship, and escape to level road. When we at last stood before a canoe with our things loaded aboard it, I embraced Liam and Nickel in parting and exchanged the usual pleasantries of such an occasion with good cheer. Gaston said goodbye to his father; and an observer might have thought one or the other of them were going to the gallows, for the sobbing that occurred there. At last I held the Marquis with great regard, and we said those things that are meaningless in light of all that had been said before. Then we were rowing away and at last being greeted heartily by those aboard the *Virgin Queen*. I felt free, yet still in the grips of destiny, as we waved goodbye to those left standing on the shore. We would see them all again, and any fear of a different outcome was wasted effort and showed a lack of faith in the Gods.

Roving
January-May 1669

III

Seventy-Six

Wherein We Regard Ambition

Despite the sense of peace in which I found myself enveloped, I was dismayed anew by the size of the *Virgin Queen's* cabin. Truly, I had remembered how very small it was, but as impossible as it is to capture a thing of wonder such as the innocence and peace of puppies and hold it in your heart as a balm against misfortune, it is equally difficult to recall things which you do not wish to remember in excruciating detail, such as the precise feel of the pain of being shot, or the size of a ship's cabin. The room was smaller than the stall we had slept in these past weeks: and it was filled with four hammocks. Ours was situated where our table had been on the last voyage. The Bard and Dickey still slept above us, with Cudro and Ash next to us, and Pete and Striker above them. Thankfully, all the pieces of netting were now well anchored at four points, so we had sagging beds and not swaying bags; but conversely, this meant there was room for nearly nothing else in the small space.

Gaston stooped to raise our hammock with his shoulder, and slid the medicine chest beneath it next to the bulkhead. The netting rested upon the box, as our bed was suspended so close to the floor I felt our arses would rest upon the planks when we were both in it. After a quick inspection and some cursing, my matelot determined we could not raise the anchor points without a great deal of effort, and the ropes were already quite short. So it appeared we would spend the voyage with our feet resting upon the medicine chest. I supposed it was better that than our heads.

He stowed the rest of our gear near the windows, and bade me lie in the hammock. I did so gingerly. Then he joined me, and not only did our arses indeed touch the floor, the sagging brought us together – a thing I usually took much comfort in – and put a great deal of strain upon my shoulder and the wound.

My matelot quickly clambered from the hammock and helped me out of it. Then he cut the ropes holding it to the wall. He guided me to sit upon the medicine chest, and I leaned against the wall tiredly and searched his face for signs of the Horse or fury and found only resignation.

"The shops will be closed," he said thoughtfully. "I cannot see how I can purchase a mattress before we sail. We will need to redo the bolts and rings, and you should probably sleep alone for now."

"Non," I said. "Go and steal one. Or borrow. Theodore or Sarah can buy another on the morrow."

He smiled. "True. Let me find someone to help carry one. Will you be well here?"

I sighed and smiled. "I will be fine anywhere in my current condition."

My matelot sighed. "I do not know if I should give you more or less."

This set me to laughing; and though he sighed with annoyance, he at last smiled.

Striker and Pete joined us.

"We need a bigger ship," Striker said, and I saw my dismay at our accommodations written on his face.

I chuckled. "And we wished to return to sea…"

"There will come a day when I will not," Striker said with a tired sigh.

Pete's lips quirked in a wry smile, and I thought he would speak; but then he looked about the little room and sighed as well.

"Will you help me carry a mattress from Theodore's?" Gaston asked Pete. "Will cannot lie in a hammock."

Striker snorted as he looked to the netting on the floor. "I told them that one was hung too low; but there was only one man in it."

"Who?" I asked.

"Your Spanish friend," Striker said.

I snorted. "All the more reason, then… Why was he in the cabin?"

"Cudro said the men didn't trust him at first." Striker shrugged.

I could well imagine that, and I sighed. I would not have wanted to be Alonso: sailing with men as bigoted as the buccaneers could be towards all things Spanish.

Gaston kissed my cheek and led Pete out onto the crowded deck, to go in search of a mattress.

"How is he, truly?" Striker asked.

"Who?" I asked, wondering if he still spoke of Alonso.

Striker grinned. "How drugged are you?"

"I feel no pain," I said slowly. "In truth, I feel little but peace and faith."

He laughed. "Your matelot: how is he?"

"As he appears," I sighed, not wishing to discuss the matter.

"He does appear sane enough," Striker sighed and smiled. "You, on the other hand."

I laughed, and it hurt, which only made me laugh more. "Aye, me, I am the one to question the sanity of."

He grinned, and then frowned with amused thought. "You do seem to cause all the trouble."

His words seemed to sober him, and he busied himself stowing their gear and muskets.

"I am sorry," I said. "I do not wish to leave them, either, but if we stay it may well be worse in the end."

Striker shook his head. "That is not... I married her." He stopped and turned to face me. "And I would not take that back for all the gold in Spain. It just..." He shook his head angrily. "It's like God is making a mockery of me. I resolve I cannot have everything I want – both Pete and Sarah – and then I can. And now, I want to be both a captain and her husband, and it seems I cannot have both those things, yet... I..." His frown deepened and he rubbed absently at a smudge on a wine skin he was stowing. "I hold out hope that I can. And because of that..." He looked up at me again. "I don't want to resolve to have only one or the other just yet. I'm truly hoping something will happen soon that will... So that I don't have to step down or hide."

I nodded with understanding. I had known how the idea of it would trouble him the moment it was conceived.

"Perhaps some strange event will occur that will make that possible," I said kindly.

"If I were a God-fearing man, I'd pray," he sighed.

I smiled. "Sometimes it is sufficient to tell Th... Him, what you wish – without fear or even a bended knee. And, if you do not, how will He know?"

Striker grinned. "I'll do that, then."

Cudro entered. "A word, if you will," he told Striker.

They began to walk out, and I asked, "Cudro, might I lie on your hammock for a time?"

He studied me for a moment, and then the remains of our hammock. "I wondered where they went off to in such a hurry. Oui, lie down, before you fall over, you damn fool."

I did, sinking into the netting with great relief that I could once again lie still for a time. I studied the patterns in the weave of the hammock above me, and told the Gods a great many things I would see before sleep claimed me once more.

I woke to Pete and Gaston wrestling a small mattress into position. They were attempting to be quiet and cautious, and I surmised sluggishly that they were concerned with waking me. A ludicrous gesture, in that the deck and bulkhead wall reverberated with the sound of men, and I had surely been wakened by the distant roar of it entering the room in a great wave when they opened the door. I touched Gaston's arm, and he regarded me with surprise and then relief. Pete grinned, and they shoved the unwieldy bag into place with less decorum.

"How are you?" Gaston asked as he knelt beside me. He appeared strained, and his eyes darted to the door as Pete opened it to leave us.

"Well enough," I said. "What shall we do?"

Gaston took a deep breath and nodded to himself. "What we must."

I chuckled, and he helped me to stand, and together we emerged from the cabin into the din and press of the deck. My shoulder soon ached as the laudanum ebbed and we were jostled about. I said nothing of it, and kept my good hand on Gaston as we were greeted by all we knew.

"So 'ow the devil did that 'appen?" one of the Bard's sailors asked and pointed at my shoulder.

Gaston stiffened, and I was thankful the deck was relatively dim and the man could not see me blanch.

"His damn drunk wife shot him," Striker said with a laugh from above us on the quarterdeck.

This brought a round of laughter, and I was clapped on my shoulder so hard I had to bite my lip to keep from crying out, as all made remark of how they had heard my wife was quite the drunkard and she had burned her house.

"But why'd she shoot ya?" the same sailor asked when some of the noise had died down. "She find out ya 'ave a matelot?"

"She knew that!" Striker yelled. "She found 'em fucking."

This brought even more laughter, as all seemed to take it for the joke it was. I squeezed Gaston's shoulder before the glare he was aiming at the floor could be directed at anyone – such as Striker. Thankfully, none seemed willing to ask more, and then someone told a tale of having a woman stumble upon his trysting, and we were able to slip to the quarterdeck where we were met by a ruefully shrugging Striker.

"You have a better tale?" he asked.

"Nay," I sighed, as we stepped around him and Gaston shouldered us to the rail. "Yours is far better than the truth; and I am in no condition to lie cleverly," I whispered as we passed.

"I thought that, which is why Pete and I decided we best do it for you," Striker said with a grin and handed Gaston a bottle.

My matelot had calmed, and he took a small swig – though he held it long enough to convince anyone further from him than I that he drank far more.

I leaned on the railing and gazed across the canoe- and longboat-crowded water to the shore. It was now truly dusk; and all was awash in beautiful light tinged gold and pink and purple. It hid the ugliness, and made what I could see of Port Royal appear very inviting. I snorted at such falsity.

Gaston gently tapped my good shoulder, and I turned to find Farley standing with us. He greeted me warmly, and I returned it in kind, as

I had come to admire his dedication to his craft when we sailed home from Porto Bello. He was a good man and fine physician, even if he had been trained in foolishness as Gaston said.

After we had exchanged our initial pleasantries, Farley found my matelot regarding him with consternation and his high pale forehead clenched into a frown. "What is it... my Lord?"

"Do not. I have no title among the Brethren. But thank you." He smiled. "I wish to be physician on this voyage, but I do not wish for you to go without. I do not need the money the post pays."

Farley frowned anew at that. "I... I am quite pleased you are sailing, and as you are the superior physician, you should, of course..."

Gaston spoke quickly; and just as quickly stopped. "I am concerned that I will suffer my madness and..."

"Oh," Farley nodded. "So... If you should not be able to..."

"Fulfill my duties, oui, aye," Gaston said with a nod. "It would be best for all if you are here. But, as I said, I would not have you deprived of the money that a man of your experience should rightly earn."

Farley nodded thoughtfully. "Thank you, I appreciate the sentiment, truly. I have a wife, now, and... What do you suggest?"

"So do I," Gaston said dully with a frown that transmuted to bemusement. He shook his head and met Farley's gaze again. "I will simply give you the money I would earn as surgeon."

"That hardly seems..." Farley began to say, and then he looked to shore and nodded to himself. "I will accept your generous offer. And feel that I am doubly blessed in that I will be paid to learn at your side again."

Gaston smiled with relief. "Thank you."

I stood there in my drug-induced limbo, unsure whether I felt relieved or dismayed that I did not seem to be needed this eve: Striker was lying for me; my matelot was speaking for himself; what good was I?

"When was he shot?" Farley was asking.

My matelot was frowning. I was not sure if it was in regard to Farley's question, or because I was becoming oddly shorter. The next I knew, they had their arms about me and I was being half-carried, half-dragged back to the cabin and placed upon our new mattress, which smelled pleasantly of lavender. They soon had my tunic off and were examining my wound. Farley's face held little beyond curiosity, but he did not meet my gaze. Gaston appeared concerned.

I grabbed my matelot's arm. "What?"

"You fever," he said quietly. "The wound is inflamed. I must drain it."

Fear gripped me, despite the drug and – what I now guessed to be the other culprit of my feeling of peace – a fever. From a medical perspective, putrefied wounds killed more men than blades or balls ever did. Prior to seeing Gaston treat wounds, I had viewed the fevered death of a rotting wound as the natural end result of dueling: sometimes it simply took a man days or weeks to die; sometimes he lost a limb. But now that I had seen firsthand the how and why of it as a physician sees it – that the wound becoming inflamed was not always necessary – I realized I did not wish to pass in that manner, and it seemed horribly unfair that I should survive the ball only to be felled by a fever.

"It is not so bad," Gaston said quickly in French, his eyes upon my face and his brow creased with a different form of concern.

I sighed. I supposed it was not. He was not crying or appearing desperate.

"You need to rest, though," he said calmly. "I do not want you to move from this bed."

"I do not wish to die," I said, knowing it a stupid thing to say.

He smiled grimly. "I will not allow it."

Gaston gave me another dose of the drug, and I passed into peaceful oblivion as he began cutting the stitches.

I woke to the lovely feeling of fingers massaging my scalp. My shoulder did not ache so very much. The room reverberated with Pete's and Cudro's familiar snoring. Pleasant golden light streamed through the open windows. I lay between my matelot's legs: my head upon his inner thigh. He was staring off across the cabin, seemingly lost in thought. The deck was slanted up away from me. I could feel the ship roll through waves, and almost envision their direction and that of the wind; but, the knowledge was elusive. And it sparked a deeper concern: we were under sail.

This knowledge bit sharply, and I started so that the fingers in my hair stopped and emerald eyes gazed down into mine.

"What day?" I hissed.

He smiled. "Only the next."

My thoughts were now quite clear; and regrettably, so was the pain in my shoulder. We were sailing west to Cow Island, thus the golden light was the sunset.

"Elections?" I asked.

He nodded. "I am surgeon."

The strange mix of dismay and relief that I was not needed returned.

"That is wonderful," I said.

He was frowning at me. I sighed. Could I truly hide nothing from him?

"You do not need me," I said. "And I am pleased, but dismayed."

His hands closed around my throat, and I saw past the apparent calm of his eyes and into the turmoil of his soul.

"How am I?" I asked.

He closed his eyes and sighed, but a true smile played about his lips. "You will live," he whispered when he met my gaze again.

"And you are pleased, yet dismayed..." I teased.

He growled, and gently shoved my head off his leg so he could quickly maneuver himself to lie beside me with his head upon his arm. He leaned down to kiss my lips.

"The wound is draining nicely," he said with a grin. "The inflammation is not deep within the muscle. I have been sitting here for hours thanking the Gods that They blessed you with a constitution that makes your other attributes nonexistent in comparison. And this morning, I stood on the deck before the men and thought how I must become surgeon… because of you." He looked away and pursed his lips thoughtfully. "And… Then…" His smile returned as he gazed upon me again. "I thought how I must do it for me. It is my rightful place: my knowledge is tenfold Farley's."

My heart ached to rival my shoulder. "I am very proud."

"I need you," he whispered. "But not to carry me, now. You make me stronger than that."

I caressed his cheek with my knuckles, and ran my thumb across his lips, and he lowered his head to claim my mouth.

I was proud of him. And I felt loved beyond all measure. But… some little thought clawed about in my belly.

Thankfully, Gaston became distracted by dosing me with a little laudanum, tending to my wound, and locating a pineapple for us to eat.

As I mouthed the succulent fruit, and the drug began to tug at my thoughts, pulling them deeper, or perhaps farther from the cave, I envisioned my Horse. It stood trembling beside the road. I did not attempt to soothe it, nor did I grip the reins, though I had the peculiar feeling the animal might bolt at any moment. Instead, I held still and listened and looked about. At last I spied the cause of its consternation: Gaston's Horse pulling the cart down the road without me.

Gaston was lying beside me again, eyeing me with concern.

"I am afraid you will leave me now that you do not need me as you did before," I said softly. "It is not a rational thing. It is my Horse."

He had been prepared to protest, but at my last words he nodded solemnly. "What might I do to reassure it?"

"Do not leave," I said with mild amusement.

"How frightened…" he began to ask, and then he looked away and took a quick breath as if realizing where we were. He moved closer, partially covering my left side, so that our noses touched. "We are not well," he breathed, as if it were a thing the world could not be allowed to hear. "We must not forget that."

I envisioned his Horse standing nose to nose with mine, beside the road: the level road of the sea, where we need not fear the cart rolling away or anyone strewing gravel beneath us. I wished to frolic in the field for a time, but we could not. He was chained to the road, and not to me: he was the ship's surgeon. That annoyed my Horse more than frightened it.

"You have chained yourself to something other than me and our cart," I said thoughtfully as I rolled this new concept about in my head, examining the rough edges and not seeing how it could fit anywhere I might wish to place it. I wanted to throw it away.

"Will…" he began to protest.

I shook my head and awarded him a reassuring smile. "Non, it is as it should be. It is your profession… And your father. And your future. And as we have discussed, there are things in our lives you should put before me now. It is good: very good. I am merely… It is new." I remembered not to shrug.

His brow furrowed, and he lowered his head until our foreheads touched. In the gentle swells of the laudanum, I imagined he was attempting to find another way to share my thoughts. I chuckled. He pulled back and frowned at me.

"I wish you could see into my mind," I said.

The frown fled as he regarded our position, and he smirked. "I wish I could shove my head inside of yours and live there: all of me."

I shook my head. "I do not think you should."

"Why?" he asked seriously.

"I do not feel it is a fine place, or that any other should be forced to dwell here."

"It is better than my mind," he said. "And there would not be this wall between us." He thumped his chest lightly.

I caressed his arm, feeling the hair upon his skin and the muscle beneath it. "I like these walls. Not that they keep us apart, but that they give us something to climb." I envisioned climbing atop him; and as my cock stirred despite the laudanum, I chuckled at my wounded body rather than curse it.

He was shaking his head at me, but a smile played about his lips. "You are drugged."

"I am happy and loved," I sighed.

He became quite somber again. "You are more important than…"

I put a finger to his lips. "I know."

And I did. Yet, even though I no longer felt the tingling of fear as I had before, I knew the drug was hiding it, just as it was masking the pain of my still-aching shoulder. I needed to heal, and learn to accept this new arrangement of our lives. I was sure Cow Island would give us time to do both, as long as we stayed aboard the ship.

And so I slept a great deal, and dreamed of frolicking centaurs, whilst we beat our way east up the ever-westward rushing winds of the Northern Sea. Gaston spent most of my forays into consciousness at my side; and we spoke of things that held little import in the world of men, and much interest for playful mythical beings: such as, upon watching Pete sleep for hours, we questioned why cats are indolent creatures – to which we eventually bowed to Pete's perception of the matter: that cats lie about all day in order to conserve their strength, so that they might perform heroic deeds.

At that, Gaston called me his lap cat and asked what feats I planned to perform, and rubbed my belly and massaged me quite deliciously. At some point in the happy fog I drifted in, the clouds parted enough for me to see that my matelot wished to be stroked; and so, when next we were alone save for snoring men, I rolled onto my good shoulder and presented him my backside – with a helpful wiggle of it, in case he might mistake my intention.

He did not move for a time, exhibiting his usual stillness before a protest; and then he was upon me, pushing my breeches down and caressing my buttocks such that I squirmed and sighed. He produced the pot of his favorite salve, and the air became redolent with almonds and musk. My manhood stirred and rose slowly: apparently weighing whether the promised acute, yet ephemeral, pleasure of coupling outweighed the subdued, but constant, bliss of the laudanum. In the end, it made no distinct choice, and merely ached happily for a time as my man filled me and rocked us with the waves until he washed ashore at the Gates of Heaven, while I watched him from a distance and smiled lovingly.

Though my matelot was concerned that I did not join him in the culmination of the activity, he was greatly relieved that I wished to receive him; and coupling became part of our daily regimen – or rather my part in it, as I was, of course, not joining Gaston is his morning calisthenics.

And so our voyage to Cow Island passed, until at last the Bard slipped us behind the reef of the western bay, in the last week of the year. We anchored with the other vessels of Morgan's fleet, including the *Oxford*. I was feeling well enough to venture onto deck; and, as I had not seen her before, I was quite surprised to see the warship towering over the Brethren's brigs and sloops. With her thirty-four guns on two decks, she was the largest craft I had seen in the West Indies save the galleons. I could well see why she emboldened Morgan so.

There was another ship I did not recognize next to her: a frigate, and French by her colors, the *Cour Volant*. Cudro and Gaston did not recognize her, either. Thus when Bradley rowed over to greet us, Striker's first questions were of this new vessel.

"You'll like it none," Bradley sighed and pushed his hat aside to scratch his head before casting an annoyed glance toward Gaston and me.

"Then you best tell me of it before my men scatter," Striker said.

This elicited a deep frown from the older captain, but then Bradley shrugged and spoke as if he were angry at the events in question and not Striker. "She's French and from Tortuga. Her captain's called La Vivon. Any here know him?" He glanced about, and Cudro frowned in thought and Gaston shrugged.

"I've heard of him; don't know him, though," our Dutchman said.

"Well," Bradley sighed, "They took an English merchant ship... for victuals." Bradley cursed with another shrug. "Nothing else, and they left a note payable on account in Cayonne or Port Royal. But Captain Collier." He gestured with his hat at the *Oxford*. "Saw it as piracy and he captured the *Cour Volant* for preying on an English vessel."

Striker spat, "God-damned navy bastards! I knew they would be nothing but trouble. What is Morgan doing?"

Bradley took a deep breath and let it out slowly while meeting Striker's gaze. "He wants the ship."

"Will they join us?" Striker asked.

Bradley sighed again. "He doesn't care."

Striker swore profusely, and there was much muttering among the men who had heard.

Bradley stepped close to Striker and spoke so that only those nearest heard. "Think, man, if you do not sail with us now, do not think you will be welcome next season. Come and speak with Morgan, but do it with a civil tongue."

Striker stepped back from him and looked about.

When his troubled gaze met mine, I gave him a helpless gesture with my good hand in lieu of shrugging. "You might as well hear him out."

"YaBestNa'TakeMeThen," Pete told his matelot with a glare at Bradley. "Take Cudro."

The Dutchman sighed. "If I must."

"AndADozenMore," Pete hissed. "MenWeTrust. GastonAn'I'llFetchYa BackIfTheBastardDoesAStupidThing. It'llCost'ImDear."

Bradley kept his voice as low as Pete's. "That isn't necessary."

Striker shook his head; his dark eyes were cold. He did not keep his voice pitched for the closest ears alone. "I don't know who to trust these days. You can't trust a man just because he says he's a member of the Brethren. And Collier isn't one of us. Maybe he's heard some tale of me. Maybe Morgan wants my ship."

Bradley swore quietly. "Lord, man, if we've sunk that low..."

"Then what?" Striker snapped. "You have a wife and plantation."

"So do you," Bradley said.

"Aye, aye," Striker said. "Mine married me because she respects me."

"Aye," Pete grumbled. "SheDon'tFuckDogs."

Bradley gave a hissing inhalation; and all was quiet and still for a moment in its wake. Striker awarded his matelot a look that said that perhaps those were unwise words. Pete shrugged.

Cudro exchanged a look with Striker and began calling upon men to lower our longboat and row Striker to the *Oxford*. As I eyed the half-dozen men he chose, I rued our not having Liam, Julio, and Davey with us; but I knew well they were best where they were.

"I would have you go," Striker told me.

Bradley paused in going over the gunwale and gave Striker a warning look.

I shook my head with a sad smile and told Striker. "I do not feel I would aid in the endeavor, even if not in my present state."

Bradley snorted and continued down the netting to his boat.

"I know," Striker sighed, and then whispered as he passed me to board our longboat. "But I'll never worry about you shooting someone who needs to be shot."

I chuckled and grabbed him to pull his ear to my lips. "I would dearly love to put a ball in Morgan's eye."

Striker grinned and sighed. "And that's why you shouldn't go."

"How long?" Gaston asked as Cudro and Striker began to climb over the side.

"Dusk," Striker said.

Cudro nodded. "I'll send Ash back if all is well and we need stay longer. I send anybody else…"

Pete, Gaston, and the Bard nodded solemnly.

As they rowed away behind Bradley's boat, I forced myself to concentrate on gauging the crew's reaction. There was much consternation among their ranks. Once again, I wished for Liam's presence: to talk to them in his way and learn their thoughts. I did not feel I was up to the task; and not only because of my wound. I was not one of them in that way. Sadly, I realized I had somehow become a wolf here. I supposed I should not expect them to view me as aught else when I was still a Lord in their eyes, and an owner of the ship, and I was ever in the cabin with my matelot. For all my talk of being a member of the Brethren, was I truly? Was any of us? As Gaston had once asked, how many of the men around us had ever been on the Coast we were purportedly the Brethren of?

It made me sad and weary; and I pushed away from the rail and Gaston, and retreated to the cabin. He followed me as far as the door, but seemed reluctant to retreat with me.

"I should rest," I said. "In case there is…"

He snorted. "There best not be need. What is wrong?"

I pulled him close and whispered my thoughts. His eyes were sad when he pulled away far enough to meet my gaze.

"I have never truly been one with them," he said distantly. "We are Arthur's knights, championing an ideal."

I sighed, feeling how very correct he was, and how very wrong that should be. "Sometimes ideals need more championing than people."

He grinned. "You are my Will." He kissed my nose. "I should…" He looked back over his shoulder and returned to gaze at me with a grimace. "As I am surgeon this voyage, and I have made a commitment to…"

"Oui, you should be present among them. You need not explain. I commend you heartily. I will rest."

He kissed my lips lightly and left me. I closed the cabin door. As I turned to my bed, I was dismayed to see I was not alone. Alonso lay sprawled in Cudro's hammock, his eyes curious and intent upon me. He had been in the cabin several times as we sailed here, but I had not been alone with him since before I was shot. I made no effort to hide my sigh as I sank to my mattress.

Alonso snorted and rolled his eyes expressively.

"I am pleased to see you, too," he said sarcastically in Castilian.

"I came here to rest, not spar," I said with a sincere smile.

He shook his head sadly. "I do not mean to trouble you, Will." This time there was no hesitation before my name.

"Perhaps not," I said. "And I… You should not. I wish I could trust that you will not."

"Who do you wish you could trust?" he asked, and sat enthusiastically. "Do you fear that I will trouble you with my actions?"

he teased. "Or do you wish that my presence would not trouble you?"

I was amused at his conviction in this truly annoying path he chose to follow. "You trouble me, you bastard; but it is not from fear I will find you enticing."

He sighed and shrugged expressively. "A man must dream."

I did not wish to address that further, and he did not seem inclined to leave; nor did I feel inclined to lie down and turn my back on him.

"How do you find sailing with so many who hate the Spanish?"

He frowned at this new topic, and reclined again on the hammock, positioning himself so that he could face me.

"At times I have been concerned," he said seriously. "But those who have pledged their friendship have been quite sincere. And if they have not swayed the others, they have at least given me the peace of mind to sleep at night." He smiled. "The first time I went ashore in Cuba, half the crew was quite convinced I would betray them, and I knew Cudro would kill me with little regret if I did anything to warrant their mistrust. But he knew what should be obvious: I had nothing to gain in betraying them. I was not a prisoner, and if I had wished to remain amongst *my brethren*, I would have stayed in Porto Bello. The only thing that could drive me to the Spanish now is fear for my life amongst these Brethren.

"And I understand their fears and hatred," he continued with another shrug. "I have heard Spanish men brag of what has been done to the pirate dogs should they be caught. And I know how very much my fellow countrymen believe this New World to be theirs alone – by the Providence of God. If they could but mount the ships and men, they would drive every English, French, and Dutch man, woman, and child, from these islands into the sea; put them in slave chains; deliver them to the Inquisition; or simply kill them. They view it as ridding the world of vermin and infidels for the glory of Spain and God."

I nodded, but his words begged an old question. "Why can they not mount the ships and men?"

He chuckled. "Those same men who brag mutter of that when deep in their cups. No one knows, or admits to it, but all guess. Men know how much gold and silver goes to Spain, but none of it returns. Spain sends warships to collect it, but they do not stay. We have great cities, but they were built by the generations of Spanish men living here, with no help from the King. Spain sends what she deigns, takes all she wants, and lays down edicts about what men here might do; grow; decide... Spain controls everything in this New World. You must have writs from Seville to do anything of import. It makes everything very slow, and smothers men with any ambition. Spain seeks to keep her colonies from rising to challenge her, but it is like a father who will not allow his son to leave home and face the world. Eventually the boy becomes indolent and resentful, and accomplishes nothing, even for himself."

"I have heard that," I said. "The first galleon we took could not have fought us with cannon – even if we had allowed her – because her gun decks were filled with smuggled goods."

Alonso nodded. "All salaries are fixed in Spain, and no private shipping or trade is allowed, so the Navy officers make money where they can. It is a sorry state of things, and one I am not proud of." Then he gave me a devilish smile. "But I had nothing to do with it, and now, due to God's Beneficence, I will profit from it. And have adventure."

I chuckled. "It is always surprising to see where God chooses to bestow His beneficence. I rather thank it springs from the hearts of men, as all things do."

He rolled his eyes. "Ever the blasphemer."

"It has not failed me yet." I shook my head with a smile. "If God in His beneficence has granted you the opportunity to prey on your former countrymen, has He abandoned them?"

"No, no," Alonso said with a shake of his finger. "He, in His infinite wisdom, has seized upon you pirates as a way of showing our King the error of his ways. Spain is corrupt and she has lost her way. Her citizens are being poorly used. I am an instrument of relieving their pain."

The quirk at the edge of his mouth, and the sparkle in his eyes, belied the sincerity of his words; yet I knew him well enough to know he did believe much of what he said: he was merely pretending to make fun of it so I did not view him a fool if I should not agree.

I awarded him a derisive snort. "How much conviction will you have for that conceit when you see the ill-used men of those colonies being mis-used further still: robbed, beaten, tortured, killed, all for gold? And by your hand as well, lest your new brethren question your loyalties and turn upon you."

His brow furrowed, and all pretense of humor or sarcasm fell away. "I do not know... Will. In what we did this last month, the smuggling, it was a thing that benefited the Spanish colonists we traded with. There was no harm to it. And I know what we will do next: I have spoken at length with Cudro and the others." He met my gaze. "I feel Spain cares not for a lost town here or there. It is not as if you pirates have taken a city of wealth. You robbed and ransomed Porto Bello after the Fair. The silver had already departed with the fleet: thus Spain did not care.

"Spain is more concerned about the Galleons and the Flota: the wealth going to Spain. However, they will surely be angered enough to send ships and men if you were to take Cartagena or Havana – places Cudro says your Morgan wishes to attempt with that warship. I feel he will bring Spanish wrath upon your little colony of Jamaica if he succeeds. If he does not, then..." He shrugged. "The King truly does not care." He seemed saddened by this.

I was surprised that he should have such interest in his former fellow colonists – or in anyone: it was not his way. But there was more in what he said. I frowned.

"So you view roving with us against such targets to aid in sealing our doom?"

He smiled grimly and shrugged. "You will do these things with or without me, no? And..." He grinned. "You will not take such cities with less than an army and a dozen such ships."

"True," I said. "And true. And I pray men other than Morgan among the Brethren still possess reason, and we will choose a reasonable target. But if you think we will fail, why are you here? Do you not fear dying with us?" I teased.

"I will claim I was a prisoner," he said dismissively.

I chuckled. "And if the Gods smile upon you, your former countrymen will have no one there who witnessed you running some Spanish soldier through."

"We must take chances, Will," he said with amusement. Then he frowned. "And there you go blaspheming again."

"It is only blasphemy if it is my religion," I said.

"Now you speak heresy," he said seriously.

"I have ever felt it to be the least of my sins."

He shook his head, and spoke with a trace of amusement in an attempt to mask real concern. "I fear you will burn in Hell from the moment of your Judgment, and there will be nothing for it."

"I find it strange you feel you will achieve Heaven, even after a lengthy stint in Purgatory," I teased.

"As long as I die in the company of a priest..." he said, and then frowned. "Which is a concern I have traveling with pirates."

I smirked. "Si, well, we all think we are going to Hell; so why should we seek to be shriven on our death beds? It is hypocrisy. You should live as if you cannot seek redemption short of having Christ's undivided attention in the moment before you cross the veil. Which returns us to my question: you will rob and kill men, Spanish men, your fellow Spanish colonists, of whom you seem to hold much interest in the well-being of?"

He frowned and looked away. "I must have faith in my convictions. I will..." He shrugged. "I have robbed men before. And in this raiding we do, Cudro says that it should be possible for me to avoid being involved in the truly distasteful aspects of the matter, such as torture. And I will not seek to kill anyone unless it is to defend my life or that of a friend." He nodded at me. "And... If my hand is forced, and I am ordered to commit some sin to prove my loyalty; I will view the sin as being that of the man that made me do it, and not my own."

"Now who speaks heresy?" I chided. "You are showing inordinate faith in the Grace of God. Well, you shall undoubtedly be fortunate wherever we rove, in that there will surely be priests available to take your confession."

He frowned with concern and curiosity. "How will you justify what you will do in this endeavor?"

I gave a grim smile. "If all goes as planned, I will not need to be involved in the killing or the robbing. I will be busy tending the wounded: a thing I do not feel even your God will fault me on, with or without His redemption."

"U... Will," he chided.

I snorted. "Stop. We have killed for money before. If you believe God's Grace will give you passage to Heaven, so be it. We all must make our peace with our deeds and what we feel we will find in death."

"How will you make your peace?" he asked with sincere curiosity.

I had no ready answer for that, and so I considered it. I envisioned my judgment as a court room, with everyone I had ever known lined up as witnesses. Surely I had not done poorly by so very many that the ones who hated me outnumbered those who did not. And, of course, there would be those who hated me through no fault of my own, such as my father or Shane. I thought it would be a very long trial. I sighed. "I hope, that when it is time for me to die, that if there is Judgment, that I will be judged fairly for all I have done, the good and the bad, and by my intentions for those things that appear bad but were not meant to harm, and that I will be found as having done more good than bad."

"Without Salvation?" Alonso frowned. "You are a heretic Pelaganist! Do you feel you have done more good than bad? If you were to die this minute, what do you feel that answer would be?"

I sighed again and smiled. "I feel as of this day, I may well need a very sympathetic jury. But I intend to change that."

Surely the words of those who loved me would count for more than the words of those I had wronged – with anything short of death, I supposed. Perhaps the deaths could only be countered by lives saved. What would the girl in the church in Puerte Principe count as?

"So, you think this is your answer to peace with God and entering Heaven?" Alonso scoffed.

I shrugged, and realized my shoulder did not hurt as much as it had before. "Alonso, we cannot know what awaits us until we are dead."

"That is the gamble of a madman," he said.

I laughed at his assuredly inadvertent choice of words. "Si, it is the plan of a madman."

The door opened, and Gaston strode in. He was as surprised as I had been to see Alonso.

"We were discussing religion," I said in French.

My matelot snorted and glared at Alonso, but his words were for me. "You were to rest." The ire in his tone was not directed at me, however.

Alonso threw his hands up and stepped carefully around Gaston in the narrow space. "We will continue this," he said over his shoulder as he opened the door.

"Undoubtedly," I said with a smile.

Gaston dropped to my side and regarded me with admonishment.

"Hush," I chided. "You will be amused at his conceits."

"I am sure I will be," he said unconvincingly. "Cudro sent Ash to tell us they would dine there and that all is well."

"So we will assume all might be well and wait?"

Gaston sighed. "Oui. Now what did that bastard say?"

I chuckled, and then seriously relayed all we had spoken of, and my thoughts on the courtroom in Heaven.

"Do you now believe in Heaven and Hell?" Gaston asked with concern.

"Non," I said thoughtfully. "Not as... Alonso does, but... I believe we are judged, if not by the Gods, then by our fellow man, and if not him, then by ourselves."

He lay on the mattress and gazed at the ceiling. "Oui."

My words tickled some memory into rolling over to reveal itself. "You once asked me of that: of sin. You spoke of a man being able to sin against mankind, or himself, or nature, but not God. I thought myself very unwise in comparison, as I had never considered such things as you had."

He frowned up at me. "Oui, I remember." His gaze returned to the ceiling and became distant. "That was before you made me remember. Before... before you, I would sometimes spend days and weeks staring at the sea, trying to comprehend the guilt that followed me. I thought of it as the gulls. It was always there waiting to pick me apart. I knew I had sinned, but I could not reconcile the guilt in the face of my no longer believing in God. And as I could not remember what I had done..." His words drifted off with a sigh.

He looked up at me again with a new frown. "He called you a Pelaginist?"

I chuckled. "Oui."

"Why does a good Catholic Spaniard know of Pelagius?" he asked.

"I do not know. We never discussed such things before. I... When I was with him, though I might have joked of... blasphemy, I was ever careful not to truly speak my mind on such things around those I could not trust. There are those who take it so very seriously, and I have seen men destroyed by the Inquisition. And around Alonso... He is devout in his fashion, and did not wish to discuss it."

I poked Gaston. "What do you know of Pelagius?" I teased.

Gaston snorted. "Among monks he carries a certain infamy. They argued about him. I feel many of them wished to believe his heresy: that a man need only live a good life to achieve Heaven, and that it has nothing to do with the Church, or receiving God's Grace. And you?"

"Rucker educated me well about all manner of heretics."

"There are many who would call the Spaniard a heretic." He snorted, and then sat to regard me earnestly. "What do you know of his Horse?"

I frowned as I considered that. I searched through many memories of Alonso, and found no evidence of what I would now consider to be Horse-like behavior. "I have never seen it."

My matelot frowned. "Is he like Pete?"

"Non," I said with surety. I could envision Pete as a great golden animal with ancient wise eyes. Alonso was a man upon a horse, and the animal was restrained with iron hands. It pranced, pawed, tossed its head, frothing and champing at the bit, yet Alonso's seat upon it was solid and unaffected by the animal's antics. "He is not his Horse. He is… always in control of his Horse, such that it never moves without him."

Gaston was thoughtful. "Like you? You once moved in harmony with your animal, such that you never lost control."

I understood what he meant, but I did not feel it was the same for Alonso. "Non, he does not enjoy riding it. Horses are things he needs in order to travel; they are not things of pleasure."

Gaston was frowning at me.

I shrugged. "I feel perhaps that people ride as they… ride. Or, at the least, it may be an indication of it."

"Ah," Gaston said with a somber nod. "So you truly feel he rides his Horse such that it never wishes to go anywhere without him?"

"Well… That would obviously make it a very docile animal, or him a very powerful man." I shook my head. "There is nothing docile about Alonso. Theodore's Horse is docile. Alonso's is…"

"A dangerous weapon." Gaston was frowning at the door. "Especially in the hands of a man who believes he cannot sin."

I had never viewed Alonso in that manner before. "The only thing I have ever heard him express remorse about is me."

Gaston shook his head tiredly. "We will surely have to kill him." He flopped back upon the mattress to gaze at the ceiling again.

I wondered what Alonso's Horse would do if it got the bit in its teeth, or threw him. The idea chilled me, because I realized I often did see his Horse, the power of it. Alonso's iron grip on the reins had allowed him the patience to carefully seduce me time and again, but then having to finally let his Horse act, he had not cared if I bled when at last he took me – and I had always seen that in his eyes at that moment. I had always thought it lust; and it was, of course, but now that I understood Horses, I understood a great deal more.

"Oui," I whispered. "He is a danger to me, not you. His Horse wants me."

"You did not know that?" Gaston asked with surprise.

I frowned down at him. "Non. Did you?"

He gazed up at me with incredulity.

I sighed. "I was concerned about the Man. I know what he is capable of. I thought I was a desire of his… misguided heart. I thought I was something he rationalized that he wanted out of guilt or nostalgia for our past. I did not realize his Horse was involved."

"I see it watching you," he said softly. "You never see how others desire you."

I knew he meant Christine. I sighed. "I never understand it."

"You are a wild and free thing that we all wish to ride," he said, and sat to face me. He kissed me lightly.

"Or capture and tame," I said bitterly.

He pulled away to regard me with concern.

"Not you," I said quickly. "Christine and Alonso."

He nodded. "But you are mine," his Horse whispered before his mouth claimed mine.

We proved he was very correct, as he gently pushed me down and rode me to his content.

Though the activity made my shoulder ache, and I did not find my pleasure in it, my Horse was as content with the endeavor as his was. It, we, I, was wanted. The knowledge had always been there; I had simply not viewed it in that light before. I could be wanted even when I was not needed. And even though I could be wanted by those I did not wish to have want me, I knew I need not bow to any save my matelot: not kings, or admirals, or fathers, or even Gods.

Seventy-Seven

Wherein We Are Challenged

Striker returned near midnight. He was drunk: all who had gone to the *Oxford* had apparently been plied with spirits in the hopes they would succumb to the siren song of alcohol-induced good fellowship. But whereas Striker had been seduced and beaten by the fruit of the vine – such that Pete had to carry him to their hammock – Cudro was thankfully conscious and coherent, and merely appeared tired from the battle. The Bard, Dickey, Gaston, and I followed him and Ash into the cabin to join Pete and Striker.

The big Dutchman sat heavily on his hammock and smiled indulgently at Ash, who crawled in behind him and curled up to fall immediately asleep. Then Cudro glanced at each present in turn, until he seemed satisfied at our number and composition.

"Morgan wants the ship, all right; but it's the *Oxford* he wants, not the *Cour Volant*. There is much uneasiness between him and the Navy man, Captain Collier. I feel – and this is not confirmed by the man – but I feel that Morgan would have used what enticements he could to get the *Cour Volant* to sail with us, and he would not have taken her outright had it been his decision. And it is evident he rankles that it was not his decision, just as Collier bridles that Morgan should be Admiral. Meanwhile, Collier's officers are greatly curious about how much booty they can reap from the Spanish."

The little room was filled with a collective groan.

"We're sailin' nowhere!" Striker yelled.

I was surprised he was still awake and not lost to the living until noon.

"With starvin' men!" he continued. "'Til they quit snappin' at each other's arses!"

Cudro nodded sadly. "The *Oxford* has provisions from Port Royal. Some of the other captains are angry that she should be provisioned and they should not. They've been sailing *in defense of the colony* for longer. And some think we'll sail now and find victuals fast enough for it not to matter. And some…" He sighed and shook his massive head. "Hell, no one is ashore hunting cattle. Those who would put men to the task do not wish to be the first, because their men will likely desert for other ships where no one is working, lest they be tasked with providing for all. And Morgan will not organize the matter, or give another leave to do it."

"We should leave," the Bard said. "There are better ways to make a living than taking this shite."

"We have ninety men aboard, and they want to rove," Cudro said. "Otherwise, I would agree with you."

"And it's our right!" Striker growled from his hammock, and flopped over so he could look down at us. "If Morgan can't lead, then someone should take his place!"

"ShutUp!" Pete snapped and grabbed his matelot's jaw. "YaBeDrunk!" He looked down at Cudro. "'EBeTalkin'LikeThisThere?"

"Nay," Cudro said with an amused shake of his head. "He was very diplomatic until he realized there was no reason to be had, and then he started drinking to drown his anger. I brought us home before he started talking."

"I'm not stupid," Striker snarled. And then in the mercurial manner of the drunk, he flopped onto his back to whine, "I know we can't win. They'll destroy us all. And if it isn't them, it'll be Sarah's damned father."

There were sighs and uncomfortable glances all around, and Pete clambered into their hammock to smother his matelot against his chest and murmur things we could not hear.

Cudro looked to the Bard and then me. "Morgan is calling for a great party on the *Oxford* in honor of the New Year tomorrow. He wants all the captains to attend. He says they'll decide then where we rove."

The Bard frowned. "You going? Or just Striker?"

Pete moved to the edge of the hammock, where he could lean over and regard Cudro. Striker was now lying still and quiet beside him. "'ENa'BeGoin'Alone," Pete said firmly.

"I wouldn't suggest it," Cudro said. "But Morgan wants him there."

"ThatBeBecause…" Pete stopped, and glanced over his shoulder at his matelot. When he looked back at us, his eyes were guilty and tired. "TheyThinkTheyCanMold'Im. AnIfTheyCan't…" He eased his way back to the floor: Striker remained still, a boneless mass suspended above us. Pete squatted with his back to the windows and kept his voice as low. "ISee'EmLookin'At'Em. Judgin'Whether"EBeLike'Em. Whether"EBeA ThreatTo'Em."

"Aye," I said as I saw what he meant. "The other captains are easy to control. They are wolves, but weak-willed ones. Like Bradley, they think that if they do as they are told, they will be rewarded. They think they want the trappings of an orderly society. But Striker is not a planter, and does not want to sit about and sip chocolate and discuss slaves and become the kind of man that they perhaps feel has always stood above them. He has different ambitions. Despite the wife, he still holds to a matelot and the old ways. He comes from a long line of pirates, not men who feel they were cheated from an inheritance, or robbed by some lord, or whatever battle the other captains feel they want recompense for."

Pete nodded. "YaBeRight. IHeardTheirTales. TheyAllThinkTheyBe OwedSomethin'. ThatTheyBeenCheated. ItWeren'tAlwaysThatWay. But ThemBeTheMenMorganGathers. MenLike'Im. ItNa'BeThatWayWith MyngsOrMansfield."

Cudro and the Bard nodded solemnly.

"Things have changed," the Bard said. "We need to move on, sooner rather than later. But... I can't see how we can just sail away, either. Cudro's right."

The Dutchman shrugged. "We could send the men who truly want to rove with Morgan to the other ships; and provision and go in search of lone vessels or the fleets this spring. But we would never sail with Morgan again. And though that seems a blessing, I've been thinking about how close the damn bastard is to Modyford, and what that will mean to our business."

The Bard cursed. "Aye. That's why I don't think we can just sail away, not unless we collect all that we have and move on to Tortuga."

A cannonball had formed in my gut as I listened to them, and I saw Modyford telling me he would not sign my declaration to my father. Gaston's hand was on mine, and I knew he was thinking the same.

"It is not how close Morgan is with Modyford that we must fear," I said sadly, "but how close Modyford is with my father. They are all ambitious men. I am sorry."

The Bard snorted. "No one blames you. It's just been our good fortune to know you." He grinned.

Cudro chuckled. "Aye, the Fates, you know they be fickle bitches."

Despite my fears, I found humor in that. "So what shall we do?"

"Well, we should at least see what is decided – if anything – on the morrow," Cudro said.

"Speaking of Will's father, and plans," the Bard said and looked to Pete. "What do you think will happen with Morgan and the others if things we planned occur, such as Striker stepping down?"

Pete glanced up at his now-snoring matelot, and the weight of a thousand years seemed to descend upon his shoulders and fill his eyes. "HeWon't." He looked to Cudro. "'ECan'tBearIt. ThereBeThings'EThinks 'EBeOwed Na'ByOtherMen, ButByGod. An'Bein'ACaptainLike'IsFather BeOneO"Em." His gaze traveled about the rest of us. "ButIffn"EDon't StepDown, Morgan'llKill'Im. MorganKnowsStrikerBeBraverThanThe

Others So'E'llSend'ImWhereTheOthersWillNa'Go."

"And eventually the Fates will have their due," I said.

Pete nodded. "WeMustMake'ImStepDown." Guilt fully suffused him now, and it hurt to gaze upon it.

"Before the meeting?" Cudro asked with concern.

"Nay," I said quickly, and looked to Pete for support.

The Golden One nodded. "AfterWeKnowWhatBeDecided." He shrugged his wide shoulders. "MaybeWeBeLucky. MaybeWeAllSailAway' CauseAllSee MorganForAFool. ButIDoubtIt."

I did too, and I did not suppress my sigh.

Gaston's fingers were reassuring about mine. "So we will meet again after this party," he said.

All nodded agreement.

"Good," he said. "Then Will and I will take the watch. The rest of you should sleep. You will need to be awake late into the night tomorrow."

Dickey had wrapped his arms about the Bard, and was holding him as if we faced battle on the morrow. Cudro shed his weapons and eased himself down to lie next to Ash. Pete followed Gaston and me from the cabin.

Though the deck was awash with snores in the moonlight, I could see and feel dozens of eyes upon us.

"There is to be a meeting tomorrow night on the *Oxford* for the captains," Gaston said: his broken voice carrying only to the men closest to us. "They will decide how we will provision and where we raid."

His words were quickly passed in murmuring waves amongst all who were awake, and the men closest to us nodded their thanks at this information.

We retreated to the quarterdeck; and though it was also full of sleeping or quietly talking men, we were able to find a somewhat private section of rail. To my annoyance, Alonso joined us; and to my surprise, Farley too.

"The men have been saying that no one is ashore hunting cattle," Farley whispered.

I nodded, and explained what I felt they should hear of the situation concerning the captains sparring for position, making no mention of anything we had said regarding Striker's place in all that.

"So we know nothing until after they meet tomorrow," Alonso said when I finished.

"Nay, we do not," I sighed. "And all we learn from the meeting may well be that we must make our own decision."

He snorted. "Is that not always the way of it?"

"Often," I admitted.

"WeBeKnowin'ThatNow," Pete said thoughtfully. "IBeGoin'With'Im Tomorrow."

I recalled Morgan's previous meetings with his officers – the ones I had attended – and how a voice of reason had often seemed needed. I sighed. "I should go; but I should not."

Pete snorted and nodded. "Aye. BestYaDon't. 'EDon'tLikeYaNone."

"Nay, he does not," I agreed. "I ever tell Morgan that which he does not wish to hear – or worse yet, that which he does not wish for others to hear."

Alonso laughed. "Aye, Will; you cause trouble wherever you travel."

"Nay," Gaston said coldly. "Will evokes consternation in those who govern poorly because he is compelled to speak truth."

"Si, trouble," Alonso said with a defiant shrug and grin.

I rubbed my matelot's shoulder, but his gaze remained fixed upon Alonso.

"What is this?" I murmured in French at Gaston's ear.

He sighed and turned to meet my gaze, but his words were still hard. "He is not allowed to make jests at your expense."

It was a pronouncement straight from his Horse, yet I could not stop my smile. "Should I tell him that?"

Gaston shook his head, and a rueful smile graced his lips. He gave Pete and Farley a nod and led me around two sleeping men to another place upon the railing. "I do not like his familiarity with you."

"Oui, oui," I murmured. "It seems as if he ever seeks to remind all how well he once knew me. And I look at him now and feel embarrassment that any should know."

"I want to shoot him," Gaston said thoughtfully. "But I suppose it is jealousy: a thing I should suppress."

I embraced him with my good arm and chuckled against his neck. "You are doing an admirable job of it already, my love."

He snorted, but his arms were around me and his lips upon my cheek. "Will you forgive me if I cease to do so?"

"Oui," I said without reservation.

There was a snort nearby, and we looked around to find Pete gazing upon us with a mixture of amusement and disdain.

"Aye, we are at it again," I said with a smile.

Pete sighed and joined us, choosing to sit and dangle his legs through the railing. We glanced at one another and dropped to sit next to him.

"What is wrong?" Gaston asked.

Tension left the Golden One's shoulders, and he glanced at Gaston before returning his gaze to the dark beyond the rail.

"IBeenThinkin'TooMuch," he sighed.

"It serves purpose," Gaston admonished kindly.

"Aye," Pete grumbled. "ButIKeepWonderin'IffnIBeWrongAboutThe Chess. MaybeWeShouldJustRun. But…" He sighed as if the weight of the world drove the air from his lungs. "IBeWonderin'IffnItBeBetterTa BeHappy… Fer'ImTaBeHappy, ThanFer'ImTaBeAlive. IWantTaLive NoMatterTheCost. But'EDon'tSeeItThatWay 'EValuesSomesThingsMore ThanLivin'. AndIDoToo… But…

"IBeenThinkin'LikeIDidAforeSarah. 'BoutTheWholeChessThing. IBeen Thinkin''EWouldDoWhatItIsWeNeedTaDoTaLive. ButIShould

ALearnedWithSarah, ThatICan'tBeThinkin'Fer'Im. 'EBe'IsOwnMan. An'ILove'Im. An'IWon'tLeave'Im. An'IKnow'EWon'tLeaveMe. ButIKnow 'EWon'tLetGoA'Things'EWantsMoreThanGoldOrLife. IBeOneO"Em. SarahBeOne'O'Em. ButBein'ACaptainBeOneO"EmToo."

I thought of Striker's words to me. "He is hoping something will happen that will allow him to keep everything: some miracle such as your loving him enough to take him back after Sarah."

Pete sighed with frustration. "Aye. ButICan't… ItNa'BeUpTaMeThisTime. An'IWouldIffnICould. 'EAlwaysBeTheOne Thinkin'FerUs. Thinkin'O'Money, An'WhoWeShouldSailWith, AnWaitin' 'TilItWasGoodTa'Ave'IsOwnShip."

He turned his great blue eyes upon us. "ButThatBeTheProblem. 'EWereAlwaysWaitin'FerSomethin'. Me – IWereHappyJustLivin'– With'Im. An'Now, IBeDoin'TheThinkin' An"EStillBeWaitin'. An'ItBeLikeItWasWith Sarah. INa'BeEnuff. SarahAn'TheBabeNa'BeEnuff." He gave a bitter shake of his head and looked away again.

His words made my heart ache, as I heard strange, twisted echoes of my thoughts in them.

"Is love enough?" I asked, and heard Gaston's breath catch. "I would have… I have gambled all that I am upon it… Because I have spent my entire life waiting for it. I have harbored no other goal or dream. But truly, can we define ourselves by love alone? Gaston is a physician by calling, and I cannot deny him that. And I know you do not seek to deny Striker, and…"

Pete was staring at me, and I thought I had likely angered him, but I did not see rage in his eyes, but curiosity.

"YaPutYurMatelotAboveAllElse?" he challenged.

"Have I not proven it?" I asked.

"YaDidNa'WantYurTitle."

He was, of course, correct. I soothed my ire at his challenge, and seriously considered his question and found at every turn that I discovered nothing my heart had not initially said.

I sighed. "I occasionally feel driven to philanthropy, and I am ever called to… minister to those in need of counsel, for good or ill, but I have often walked away from those pursuits these last years – for him. I do not even put my life above his. And yet, I know that is perhaps not as it should be. I feel at times that my devotion is madness, a benign one to be sure, but still, not as maybe the Gods intended."

I looked to Gaston, and found him smiling indulgently.

"I love you," he breathed in French. "And you are mad." This last seemed to pain him, and he looked away, startled.

I wished to speak to him of it, and felt annoyance at Pete's continued presence, and I grinned.

"At every turn," I said to Pete as I returned my gaze to him. "I am not as other men in that regard. Do you place Striker above all else?"

Pete smiled and scratched his blond stubble as he returned his gaze to the stars. "Nay."

"So what would you not do for him?" I asked with curiosity. Pete had already given up much of what I felt he might have valued – namely buccaneer tradition and roving like wild men as they had for ten years – in order to stay with his man. I could not see him leaving Striker, even if his matelot were to become an honest merchant and sit about Port Royal for years at a time. "My nephew? Sarah?"

He winced. "Naw, Na'Thinkin'O'Them. Should."

"I do not place little Jamaica above Gaston, either," I said.

"TheyNa'BeOurs," Pete sighed. Then the golden shoulders shrugged. "StrikerBeMine. 'EBeAllIEverLayClaimTo. So. Won'tStayWith'ImIffnI Can'tFuck'Im, OrIffn'IMustBeLyin''BoutIt. OrIffn''ENa'HoldTaMeBein' 'IsMatelotInOtherWays. INa'Be'IsFriend. IWillNa''AveAnyDamnBastard Thinkin'IBeAnotherMan'sSlaveOrServant, Na'Even'Is, 'SpeciallyNa''Is."

He sighed and the shoulders slumped. "ThereWereOtherThings. LastYear. AforeSarah. ThingsIThoughtMoreImportantThanLivin'. PridefulThings. ButILoved'ImMoreThanThem."

I heard his sad words, but my mind had become caught upon his current line of last defense.

"I have ever measured love by a man's ability to overcome the purported wrongness of fucking me. I do not view it in quite the same manner, now; but I feel that is a very good distinction to be made. If we are not loved enough to held to in all ways, then it is not truly love: if they are not proud of us, it is not love."

Pete nodded and continued watching the dark water.

Gaston was quiet with his head pressed to the railing. I squeezed his fingers and he returned the gesture and added a small sad smile.

"If ever I am not proud of you, shoot me," he whispered in French.

I nodded solemnly.

"What'd'ESay?" Pete asked.

I turned to him and found him frowning. I repeated Gaston's words.

Pete nodded and looked away with a sheepish grimace. "Shoulda' Guessed." Then he turned back to fix Gaston with a challenging stare. "WhatDoYa'PlaceAbove'Im?"

My matelot flinched, but he met Pete's gaze steadily, even as his fingers nearly ground my bones to dust. "You are correct: I am more like Striker than either of you. I want things... now... that I never dreamed of before I had Will. He has made it all possible, and I feel ashamed that I should want anything other than him."

"Do not, my love," I said in English. "I feel it makes you a far saner man than I."

"That hardly seems possible," Gaston said with a wry smile, and let up on my fingers.

"SoYa'Sayin'IBeMad?" Pete asked with a trace of amusement.

"Perhaps," I said with a grin. "Or I am saying we have very small lives. Perhaps we should develop other goals."

Pete was no longer amused, and he shook his head with consternation. "Iffn'TwoMenBoth'AveGoals, TheyNa'StayTogether."

I nodded. "Perhaps that is the madness of love ever bemoaned by poets and playwrights."

The Golden One sighed. "'ECanKeep'IsDamnGoals. StillDon'Know 'Ow'E'llReach'EmThough."

"Let us see what the morrow brings," I said tiredly, and then realized I was wrong. "Nay, let us make goals, and then see how the morrow shapes what course we must take to achieve them."

Pete smirked. "I'llLikelyBeShootin''ImTaKeep'ImAlive. EvenIfItMakes 'ImMiserable." He snorted. "BeBestFurSarahAn'TheBabe." He stood, and leaned down to brush a kiss on my forehead and then another upon Gaston's. I was minded of Agnes, and wondered why they felt compelled to ever do that. Then he left us, and we heard the cabin door open and close a moment later.

"I see why your Horse is distraught now, about losing me," Gaston whispered in French.

"I do not," I said with a smile. "I see why it is a foolish animal."

His green eyes were in shadow, and nearly as dark as the ocean beneath us. "I am ashamed," he breathed, "that I am relieved that I am all you value."

I considered that, and at last smiled. "I am relieved that you are ashamed."

He frowned briefly, and smiled.

"Let us not question our love," I said softly. "As we already know it to be mad, and a thing of our Horses, and thus of a truth we cannot question even at their wildest."

He kissed me with great truth, and I snuggled into his arms and wondered how this new year we teetered on the eve of would unfold. There were surely choices to made; but I felt they were all to be made by others, as I had already made mine.

The remainder of the night passed without incident; and we slept through much of the day, thus apparently sparing ourselves from the tension growing upon the *Queen*. When at last we emerged onto the deck in the late afternoon, we found our companions fretful: the deck was awash with grumbles, and very few were speaking to one another upon the quarterdeck.

Cudro awarded us a shrug, and glanced at Striker as we joined our friends. "We were discussing what we wish of the meeting tonight."

Striker's back was to us, and his gaze was fixed upon the western horizon. Pete was glowering at him. The Bard was sullenly studying the other ships. Dickey was eyeing his matelot with concern. Ash was regarding his own man in the same manner: his hands fidgeting as he stood at Cudro's side. I wondered how we had not been woken by whatever argument must have occurred. It was no wonder the men were grumbling.

"What we wish for; or what we will ask for?" I asked cheerfully.

Striker turned from the rail and came to me to hiss bitterly, "We can't ask for what we wish. All here want a different thing. What do you wish for?"

I met his dark eyes and felt I understood his anger. He was torn between his need to do well by his men and friends and his personal desires.

"I wish to live," I said solemnly. "I wish for us to do whatever will best further our survival. We have agreed that roving is a good course in order to discover our enemies and keep them from our home; but I do not wish to sail against a target that will be the end of us. In order to do anything, though, we will need to provision; and if we do not get these men off this ship soon, they might well be at one another's throats, or ours – with or without the enticement of a bounty."

Striker released a prolonged sigh and looked away before giving a guilty nod. "Aye."

I glanced about. Cudro was fighting a smile and studying the rigging. The Bard gave a sullen nod, and Dickey appeared relieved.

Pete met my gaze with a rueful smile. "YaBestBeCareful. OrYaBe Evokin"Ere. OrWhateverThatWordBe."

This earned him a frown from his matelot, and Gaston's amusement.

Striker at last determined we would not explain; and I was relieved to see him shrug the matter away and don his usual mantle of nonchalant leadership.

"If nothing else, the matter of provisioning must be decided," he said.

"Aye," Cudro said. "I still think that, unless we sail for a target on the morrow, we should put our men ashore to hunt even if none of the others do."

Striker nodded.

"Even if we don't sail with the others," the Bard added. "We will need to provision."

Striker sighed and nodded. Pete appeared glum, though.

"I'm going to dress," Striker said.

This prompted a groan from Pete, but he followed his matelot to the cabin.

As there was little else to be said in front of the men – who, I was sure, had heard far too much already – we stood about and waited. At last Cudro, Ash, Pete, and Striker – all wearing boots, hats, and shirts – were in the ship's boat and rowing toward the *Oxford* in the golden light of the setting sun. The warship's decks were full of men, and music floated to us on the breeze. Some of our men asked if they could join the party there, and the Bard said we should have our own and told the men to dip into the one barrel of rum we had. There were soon more smiles than frowns aboard the *Queen*, and our musicians were testing their instruments.

Then our boat returned: full of the same men who had set out on her.

A furious Striker met us on the quarterdeck, followed by a somewhat amused Pete and a resigned Cudro.

I asked the obvious. "What occurred?"

"The meeting in the main cabin is for captains only!" Striker spat.

"No quartermasters! No matelots! And it's not because the damn room is too small!"

His words spread throughout our decks, and one of our men closest to us handed him a tankard of rum. Striker took a good swig.

I thought of the rum and wine being consumed aboard the *Oxford*. "Is it a meeting, or a party?" I asked.

"Party, where Morgan gets to tell drunken men what he wishes," Cudro said.

"Aye!" Striker growled as he disappeared into our cabin.

I looked to Pete.

He smiled. "'EDidNaGoWithoutMe," he whispered as he passed us to follow his matelot.

I smiled, and turned back to find Cudro and the Bard eyeing Gaston and me. "Well, gentlemen, now what shall we do?"

The Bard cursed quietly.

Cudro shrugged. "Put men ashore in the morning, and wait and see what the damn fools decided. Then we can argue as to whether we follow their course or not."

His words had not been spoken for our ears alone, and they were picked up and carried throughout the ship. The men relaxed and soon our party was once again underway, with music, dancing, rum, and surprising good cheer.

After darkness descended upon the bay, the *Oxford* began to fire celebratory salvos from her cannon across the water. Some of our men considered doing the same, but the Bard and Cudro ordered no one to waste our powder. So we listened to the big guns roar on occasion without answering them.

Striker and Pete rejoined us sometime later. They were smiling and stripped down to their breeches, and there was fine teasing from all close to us as to their activity of the last hour. Much to the pleasure of the men, they took to the deck and danced a jig together, as they had the first night I spent upon the *North Wind*. When the applause subsided, they came to the quarterdeck, sweating and eyes shining.

"Fuck them," Striker said, and gestured toward the *Oxford* with a rum bottle.

We all looked to the huge ship silhouetted against the northern stars: her lines dotted with lanterns, and a barely-discernable, writhing mass of men occupying her decks. Her bow began to expand, as if I viewed her through a bubble in a glass bottle. And then I was flat on my back with Gaston atop me, watching the shrapnel tear past above us and hearing the roar of the explosion and the clatter of debris hitting the *Queen*'s side. Then there was much yelling by all as to what had occurred, and howling by the men who had been struck.

Gaston's wide eyes met mine, and I was sure he mirrored my surprise. I turned to find Pete and Striker next to us. They appeared just as dazed. We slowly sat and crawled to the rail to peer cautiously at the place where the *Oxford* had ridden at anchor. The great ship was gone.

"The drunken fools must have lit the powder cache," Gaston said.

I was minded of the last time I had seen a ship explode: the *King's Hope*, upon which I had sailed to Jamaica. We had destroyed her to hide our rescuing Davey from servitude. The comparison left my thoughts very cold and still; and I wondered a great many things: primarily, was the *Oxford's* destruction truly an accident?

We dispatched our boats and canoes to help search for survivors. They returned with information, nearly all bad. Morgan was alive with only a leg wound. He and the men he had invited to sit beside him at the dining table – Bradley, Norman, and the *Cour Volant's* captain, La Vivon – had been blown backwards through the gallery windows into the sea and lived. Several others from the cabin had also survived, but with such wounds that they were not expected to last the day. Beyond them, there were only a handful of survivors from elsewhere on the ship. Some three hundred men had perished, along with the captured crew of the *Cour Volant*. The dark waters boiled with sharks at dawn; and upon the waves, other sharks roved about, relieving the floating dead of their rings and other such valuables.

Gaston and Farley – with me offering what assistance I could – had spent the night removing splinters and applying poultices for those who had been struck by debris. Thankfully, none of our men were seriously injured.

Once the sun had fully risen, the Bard inspected our ship, and decided that, though she had thankfully sustained little damage, it would still be best if we careened: a task he had wished to see to at Cow Island, anyway. And, as it was now obvious we would not be sailing immediately for some target, we needed to provision, and surely none would argue it. And so we busied ourselves with putting men ashore to hunt and preparing the *Queen* for her repairs.

We were relieved to see two of the smaller vessels in the fleet doing the same. But no boats left the *Mayflower* or *Lilly*: the only ships, to our knowledge, whose original captains remained alive.

Striker sent a canoe to find which ship Morgan occupied and inform him of our plans. Our man returned with news that those aboard the *Mayflower* felt she was in need of careening, but that Morgan and Bradley were arguing. It seemed Morgan wished to sail for Port Royal on her.

"That damn fool," the Bard hissed quietly to our cabal as we stood on the quarterdeck.

"Well," I sighed. "He should tell Modyford their man of war is missing." I could not suppress a chuckle, despite the bodies of the dead. I reasoned those same men and more would have surely died if the ship had been used as Morgan wanted: to sail against a major Spanish port. At least this way they died drunk and happy.

"Even if he doesn't sail to Port Royal, it'll be weeks before we rove," Striker said.

"And when we do, it will not be against some damn target we have no hope of taking," I said.

"Amen to that," Cudro said, and turned back to organizing our men going ashore.

"When we do decide," Striker said thoughtfully, "there won't be as many of us making the decision. Even if the other ships all stay, their captains will be newly elected and probably not as foolish as Morgan's usual men."

"We can only hope," I said.

"I've been thinking. This changes things," Striker said, and looked to Pete. "About the plan. Morgan will not be so willing to risk me now; I'm one of the few seasoned captains he has left. So even if he is in league with the Damn Governor and the Devil Earl, I should still be safe from him placing me in harm's way, even if I remain captain."

I could see the hope in Striker's eyes, and I knew well Pete saw it, too.

"Aye," Pete grunted with evident reluctance. "SoItSeems."

"Unless Morgan blames you," I said lightly. "In which case, all Hell will break loose upon this bay, and we will not need to worry who seeks the bounty."

"What?" Striker crowed.

The eyes were upon me now: even Cudro returned, drawn by the volume of Striker's query. I smiled at the men with whom I did not wish to share this discussion, and retreated to the stern rail; our cabal followed.

When all were close, I asked quietly. "How likely is it that seasoned men – albeit, many of them Navy men not often allowed to indulge in debauch – would make the mistake of sparking the powder cache?"

There were frowns all about, and my matelot and Cudro swore. Pete's eyes narrowed with understanding, and he nodded and awarded me a look of praise.

"I've been wondering that, myself," the Bard said quietly. "All our men were drunk last night, and I would be damned if you could have found one of them that didn't know to keep their pipes away from the powder."

"Aye," I said. "Now, in all fairness, it could be that a mistake was made by one of the Brethren aboard that ship – a man or men not familiar with where the powder cache might have been. And they were firing salvos."

"That's unlikely, though," Cudro said. "But it could have happened: drunken men fetching powder with a lamp on a ship they did not know. But I can't see where the crew of the *Oxford* would have allowed any of ours near their precious guns."

"Aye, aye," I said. "Or perhaps it was some lust-struck pair struggling to light a lantern below decks and beyond prying eyes during the party?"

"Don'tNeedLightTaFuck," Pete said.

I chuckled. "Aye. Let us merely say that it could have been an accident, but it seems unlikely. So, if it was not an accident... Who did it?"

"I did not," Ash said solemnly, earning him several bemused stares.

"I did not, either," I said with a grin. "I think none here would have killed so many to solve our problems – not and leave Morgan alive. I truly feel it to be a matter of providence; but it is possible it was the hand of another. My fear is: that someone will think it our hand."

"We weren't there!" Striker protested.

"Aye," I said.

Realization came to his eyes.

"Coulda'DoneIt," Pete said. "CrawledOutTheWindowsWhenAll ThoughtWeFucked An'SwamOver. LitASlowFuse."

Striker swore vehemently. "But we did not. And why would anyone think we would? Unless..." He glanced over his shoulder at the men, and quickly turned back to us and cursed.

I shrugged. "Someone has shared what they might have overheard of our honest opinion of Morgan, and our possible targets, and..."

"It could have been the French," Gaston said.

"They were locked below," Striker said.

Gaston shrugged. "Perhaps they were attempting escape, and sought a distraction, and it went awry. Or perhaps they did it in anger and cared not because they thought they would be hung. I have considered blowing a powder cache in a ship I was on twice. Both times I was bound below decks and mad, and cared not for the fate of those aboard."

Though his words brought to mind unpleasant images of him in that state, I nodded. "Well, perhaps we should spread that rumor upon the fields, once our men begin to mingle with the others and we can appear to have heard it ourselves."

"Morgan will not blame us," Striker said doggedly. "Why would he? He needs every ship and man he can get."

I met his gaze calmly. "What if he considers you a threat?"

Striker shook his head and looked away. "I'd find it flattery. I can't see where he'd want the bounty. And if he were to try and take me, or Pete, or any of us..."

I smiled. "If he were to attempt such a thing, he will not be roving this year, or any other if I have my way. Nay, there will be bloodshed if he is a fool about it. But if he makes insinuations and spreads rumors, he could turn your men against you as well as the rest."

"Damn you, Will," Striker sighed with evident melancholy. He walked away.

Pete watched him leave with sorrowful eyes, but when he glanced at me I saw gratitude.

"I hope you're wrong," Cudro said before following Striker. "But we should spread the rumor about the French, anyway."

I was soon left alone with Gaston. He watched me with earnest eyes.

"What?" I queried.

"I was musing that you do not see yourself as others do. If your Horse could ever gaze upon you, it would fear nothing."

I snorted. "Intrigue is a thing I have been forced to learn. It is not a thing I take pride in. And the Gods know my father and others have played me for a fool for years."

He smiled. "And I rarely take pride in my ability to kill; but they are things that need to be done, and it is good we do them well when needed. And your father would not have snuck so very close if you had not become accustomed to sleeping without a pistol."

I knew he was correct, but I could not feel it in my heart. I could not rouse the ire to berate myself, either, which I supposed was a good thing.

We followed the others ashore, and I stood about and did little as the others prepared to beach the *Queen*. My shoulder ached considerably less, but I still only possessed one arm for the purposes of labor.

We were thus engaged when several boats arrived with Morgan, Bradley, and Norman from the *Lilly*. This party stood about some distance down the beach from where we worked, seemingly in no hurry to join us. I looked to Striker and saw that he had not seen them. I made a decision: this was a thing I was best suited to do. I might have lost my ability to see snakes in the bushes these past years, but Gaston was correct: I had not lost my ability to handle them. I walked down the beach.

"Is she badly damaged?" Bradley called as I came close enough to hear him above the surf.

"Not that we have seen," I said cheerfully. "But you know the Bard; he is a cautious man, and we planned to careen here, anyway."

He was moving stiffly, and his cheek was marred by a large bruise. Norman appeared to have fared a bit better – at least physically. He seemed to move with ease, but he looked exhausted, and I thought it likely he would need to sleep for days before the furrows in his brow smoothed. Morgan was not looking toward me. His leg was bandaged and splinted, and he was using a crutch.

The men with whom they had arrived were standing well back with the boats, and I wondered if I had interrupted a private conversation.

"We were relieved to hear that at least you three survived," I said.

Morgan whirled to award me an angry glare. "Where was Striker?"

I saw warning in Bradley's eyes. I met Morgan's gaze levelly, with resignation. "He went to attend your *meeting*, but upon learning it was merely a *party* – a party at which his matelot and quartermaster were not welcome – he returned to the *Queen*. Would you have had him die with the others?"

Morgan looked away, momentarily shamefaced. "Of course not." He rallied his indignation quickly, though. "I have just wondered how it is he managed to avoid…"

"Morgan!" Norman hissed.

"Apparently God smiled upon him last night for loving his matelot more than his ambition," I said casually. "Ask any aboard the *Queen*, they returned and spent a goodly hour fucking before joining the crew in dancing – before the *Oxford* exploded."

Bradley cursed; Norman shook his head with a small smile; and Morgan gazed upon me with incredulity.

"His fortune might well rival yours," I added. "To survive such a blast when so many died. Though I am confused as to why God chooses to smile upon you."

I knew even as the words tumbled from my lips that I should not have said them, but it had been far too tempting.

Morgan moved with a speed that belied his injury, and his face was inches from mine before my hand finished closing about the pistol in my sling. I did nothing else, though, as Norman and Bradley were upon us, with weapons drawn in probable need of their friend's defense.

"You shut your mouth!" Morgan hissed. "I need hear nothing from you now! You are a common man! By your own hand! You are nothing!"

I was surprised, but not so that I lost my balance or reason. "*Like you*, I have ever only been what I have made of myself, you damn fool: nothing more, nothing less. I have spent most of my manhood without my father's name. I have angered men far greater than you and lived by the grace of nothing more than my wits and friendships."

"Ah, bloody... Here they come," Norman muttered.

I kept my gaze locked with Morgan's. "Decide now," I whispered. "Before we have an audience. Am I a threat to you? I have ended many a man's ambitions in anger – with no gain and only detriment to myself. I do not want your position. I do not want you as an enemy. I already have enemies and battles to fight. I do not need another. But if you make me your enemy – or any I call friend your enemy – I will fight you with all I have. So decide."

His brow and eyes tightened as he considered me; and then he stepped back with a sigh. "We are not enemies," he said quietly, with a slight tilt of his head.

"I feel no need to call you friend, either," I said with a thin smile.

He nodded. "Then we have an understanding."

"I hope so."

There were men all around us now, and Norman and Bradley appeared quite concerned.

I heard "Will?" from three mouths, and I smiled broadly as I turned to face my matelot's hard green eyes. Pete and Striker were beside him.

"All is well," I said with mild admonishment for the benefit of the men behind them. "Morgan is merely distraught in the wake of our loss, and I said a foolish thing he took poorly."

"Nay, nay," Morgan said smoothly. "It was not so foolish. I am – as our good Will said – distraught, and I mistook his words. He was giving good counsel, as he ever does."

I was sure those who knew us best were not convinced in the least, but the rest of the men seemed mollified.

"That's our Will, always speaking his mind," Striker said with passably feigned amusement, and clapped my shoulder as he walked past me. "I was damn pleased to hear you three survived. How are the rest of the ships?"

Pete was now beside me, and I snagged his shoulder and pulled his ear to me to whisper. "He has made his accusation and I met it. The others do not back him."

"GoodFurThem," he muttered darkly.

I let him go and met my matelot's gaze again. "I am fine. Let us walk," I said quietly, and began to lead him back to the *Queen*.

He slipped an arm around my shoulders and fell into step with me. "Do not walk off without telling me," he admonished through clenched teeth.

"I know, I know," I sighed. "However, it would have gone worse than it did if you had been present. There would be blood on that sand."

"What did he say?"

I sighed again, and repeated all. "My quick tongue has ever been my blessing and my curse," I finished.

We were nearly back at the place where men were arranging lines to haul the *Queen* up onto the beach. He appeared thoughtful, and he did not stop or try and steer us away from the others. Instead, he returned to where he had been working when I left him, then stopped and turned to me to whisper in French with a small smile, "I find your quick tongue a blessing."

I kissed him, and he savored it with a small sound of pleasure.

"I am sorry to cause you worry," I whispered when we parted. "I thought it best I met with him alone to see what he would say. And I am glad I did."

He met my gaze with concern and admonishment. "So am I. But now, you will stay away from him? Even if you are his better in all ways a thousand times over?"

I grinned. "Oui, Papa, I will not play with the wolves, or poke them with sticks."

He rolled his eyes and turned back to assisting with the cable.

I slapped his arse, and returned to standing where I had before, watching others work. I did not feel so very useless now, though. I mused on the encounter, and smiled to myself. I was not as impotent as I had been feeling of late. I looked at the place where the *Oxford* had been, and wondered at the Providence of the Gods.

Seventy-Eight

Wherein We Suffer a Loss

I watched Morgan's boats push off from the beach a short time later. Ash and some of the others who had run to my aid were quick to return, but Striker, Pete, and Cudro were deep in discussion and made slow work of their walk. Gaston and I went to meet them. They ceased speaking as we approached, and Striker regarded me with a gaze hung between anger and curiosity.

"What was said?" he demanded.

I told him. Cudro whistled with quiet amazement as I finished, and Pete nodded from behind his matelot's back, but Striker looked away to study the waves and chew on his lip.

"And what was said to you?" I asked.

When Striker would not answer, and Pete did not seem inclined to, either – as he was staring upon his matelot with troubled eyes – Cudro spoke. "He is displeased we are careening and hunting. He would have the lot of us sail as soon as possible. He has instructed Bradley to remain here only long enough to repair those vessels in need of it, and for himself to return from Port Royal. Then we are to sail east to Savona. That is a thing they decided last night. Once there, they planned to regroup and sail south and plunder the coast of Caracas. Now..." He shrugged. "He will sail with Norman on the *Lilly* to Port Royal, with the French prize."

"So the *Cour Volant* is a prize now?" I asked.

Cudro sighed. "My words, not his. It might as well be. He's still claiming they committed piracy. He swears the French had a Spanish letter of marque – which is a foolish thing, as to my knowledge the Spanish do not issue letters of marque. But when we asked of it, the document they described sounds to be a certificate of trade from a Spanish governor. We have one." He shrugged again.

"Burn it," Striker said. He turned to me. "You're correct. He doesn't trust me."

"I am sorry," I said.

"We told them we were thinking it might have been the French trying to escape – and Morgan liked that well enough – but then he reveals that he intends to try their captain for piracy and I feel…" Striker turned away again and cursed.

"Aye," Cudro said sadly. "It seems we are helping to dig that poor French captain's grave, when all we're trying to do is save our own hides. But none of the French want to sail with Morgan – not after the damn duel with Burroughs last year – and now this. Now the French will likely avoid Port Royal, and that should anger Modyford when the merchants complain of the lack of French booty. But Morgan cares not; he's angry the French will not support him in lining his own pockets, so it seems he'll take their ships how he can. They're all a bunch of hogs rooting after gold."

"Aye, they might well all be hogs and not wolves," I sighed.

"It is a good thing he will not cross you," Striker said with a bitter tone that brought my gaze quickly to him, only to find him walking on toward our working men.

"What the Devil do you mean by that?" I asked.

Striker stopped and turned to me. His mien was guilty. "I did not…" He sighed and at last met my gaze. "I'm neither a threat nor a boon to the man. I'm a kicked dog."

"My good friend, I know not what to say," I said softly. "Do you wish for his regard?"

"Nay," Striker said with exasperation which seemed to be as much directed at the Heavens as at me. "I wish for things I can't have." He turned away again and started walking.

I let him go, and turned back to Pete, Cudro, and Gaston. I met the Golden One's blue eyes: once more he appeared age-old and weary. He did not speak, but his shrug was eloquent enough, as he too, walked by me.

"Have I done poorly?" I asked Gaston and Cudro.

Our Dutchman scratched his massive head. "That's hard to say. We'll only know in the fullness of time." Then he, too, left us.

I met loving green eyes and felt my doubts ease.

"You may well have saved his life and command," Gaston said.

I frowned. "Morgan's or Striker's?"

He grinned. "Both."

I sighed and followed him back to the cables coiled upon the beach.

Morgan sailed to Port Royal on the *Lilly* the next morning. I had been sitting on guard for hours, as it had been my turn, and I watched the sloop raise sail and race out and around the reef with the dawn breeze: golden light making her seem as if she were gilded with some intangible thing of far more value than wood and canvas. The somewhat less nimble French frigate followed in her wake: a dirge of a darker shadow, despite the fine color to the light. I awarded my poetic whimsy a snort of ironic amusement.

Gaston looked up sleepily from where he cuddled beside me in the nest we had made in the sand. In addition to taking the watch prior to mine, he had been bent and strained over cables for much of the evening, assisting in bringing the *Queen* to lie with her crew upon the beach. I had not wished for him to wake as yet, but the beach smelled of roasting beef, and there would soon be too much activity for him to continue to slumber like a babe.

"They are gone," I said in French. "Sailed away to wreak havoc elsewhere and apologize for the duplicity of others: seeking gold when it surrounds them and they are but blind to it."

He nodded and smiled, and pushed my leg flat so he could place his head upon it and arrange himself with more comfort at my expense.

Striker stirred from beside Pete, and rose to stretch. He did not meet my curious gaze before wandering up the dune to relieve himself. His sleep, if he had indeed slept, had been fitful in the hours I had watched over us, such that his tossing would have woken any man except his exhausted matelot.

I reluctantly pushed Gaston off my leg, and scratched his scalp before standing and stretching. My matelot peered up at me speculatively, and I cut my eyes in the direction Striker had gone and mouthed his name. He rolled over and lifted his head enough to see Striker at the top of the dune.

He sighed. "Tell him to stay down. Men will be clearing their weapons soon."

I sighed my understanding and arranged my weapons about my belt as I went to join Striker.

"You should not stand so tall," I said with a smile when he turned at my approach.

Striker frowned. "I will not crawl."

"Even when shot at?" I teased.

He shook his head with a sad smile. "I wish to say, especially not when shot at, but those are the words of a fool. I well know it."

"This business with my father will pass..." I hesitated, surprised at my next words: rather like, after spending months watching a foal grow, turning one day and finding it a horse. "When I kill him," I finished.

Striker regarded me with concern, and I wondered what he found upon my face. I knew discomfiture roiled about behind it, but I felt I was not truly showing that any more or less than nonchalance.

I met his gaze. "I think I have known that since this began, possibly longer. I have not wished to speak it, though. It will take care and arrangement, as I do not wish to hang for it, but that is how this will end."

"That's what Pete said," he sighed.

I nodded solemnly. "So, as Pete has also said, we must clear pieces until we can position ourselves to deal with them: my father and Shane. And... That will require sacrifices."

"I know all that," Striker said. "I know. But I can't. I can't just step down. Not because I don't wish to save my own arse. Not because I want to make things harder. But I can't see doing it after..." He waved his arm at the bay where the *Oxford* had been. "Not without..." He swore. "Well, it's not as if the bastard trusts me now, anyway. Or likely I will have much sway with these men when all is done. We'll likely have to leave Jamaica, for Christ's sake."

I could not see where he could manage surrendering his position without damaging his reputation, either, even if the *Oxford* had not exploded. "But you see how he will risk you; even if another does not attempt to collect the bounty? Even if you are not a threat, per se, you are surely a thorn in his side that he wishes to pluck."

"Aye," he said sadly. "I see it now."

"Then will you allow us to arrange some accident that will not maim you?"

He grimaced. "Can't I pretend to ail?"

"Enough so that you cannot be captain?"

His gaze met mine and his eyes implored. "Not yet. Not until..."

I nodded quickly. "It is necessary. I understand."

"Aye," he said and looked away quickly. "Speak to Pete, would you? He acts as if all I do is argue. He's angry with me about something."

"You really need to learn to speak to one another," I sighed.

"What has he said?"

I shook my head, but then I relented in the name of the knowledge that they would likely come to blows again before they did speak as they should.

"He loves you above all else – provided you always hold him before others as matelot, and not expect him to become... *an old friend*."

"Never," Striker said quickly, and frowned toward the place where Pete was still snoring.

"And he despairs that you will ever be happy," I added. "He feels you always seek things you do not have; when he feels, perhaps, that you should be content with the treasures you now hold."

Striker's eyes held on my face, but when I said no more, he turned with a sigh and walked several steps down the dune to sit – with his head safely below the crest. "I'll think on it."

I patted his head as I passed, and returned to my matelot.

Gaston sat and stretched as I approached, his gaze curious. "You win every battle here. This must be a fortuitous isle for you."

"It inspired you to fuck me," I said with amusement as I recalled our last visit here. Then the things that I needed to say drove my humor way.

"What?" he asked with concern as I came to sit beside him.

"I must kill my father," I whispered.

He nodded solemnly.

I gave a grim smile. "It seems all have known this except me. And that would be a lie: I have known it; I merely did not wish to gaze upon it; speak of it; imagine it."

"Is it truly so unsettling?" he asked with sincere curiosity.

"I wanted to kill your father, and now..." I waved vaguely at our recent weeks.

"Oui," he sighed. "But yours is..." He stopped, frowning in thought.

"Mine is simply a different animal, and we should not compare the two. Yet... I suppose in my heart of hearts I have ever harbored hopes as you did. That one day I would be embraced." I gave a rueful smile. "Killing him will end any hope of reconciliation."

He smiled at my humor, but his words were serious. "And must be carefully done. You spoke of as much with my father. He cannot shelter us, if it were to become known that we did such a thing."

I did not miss his inclusion of himself in my eventual act of patricide. I did not argue with him. I could not: our lives were one. He could no more avoid the consequences of anything I did than I could hold my right hand accountable but not my left.

Instead, I recalled what had been said to his father. I concluded that, when we first learned of my father's plotting, in my pain at the horror that had befallen us and the battles we must face, I had known I would kill my sire. It was simply a matter of when and how. And yet, despite my knowing, I had harbored a feeble hope of reconciliation. I remembered how bitterly I had argued with it.

Now, sitting on this calm beach in the dawn light, killing my damn father seemed a far more serious thing than it had, in the winds of the storm I had been fighting those weeks in Port Royal. I had guessed this to be the outcome long ago. My Horse had possibly even known it when I fled my father's house at sixteen. It had surely known he plotted against me then, though I had tried to hold the blind trust of a child close in my heart: telling myself over and over that if my father only knew what Shane had done, if I had only possessed the courage to overcome the shame and tell him, he would have put an end to my misery. But when I at last returned to England, he had made that treasured belief a travesty by admitting he knew all along. And then I had let him send me here.

"I do not hate him," I said. "I just want him gone, like a mad dog that threatens my stock and my person."

Gaston nodded. "Let us deal with his pawns and pieces, and then we will see what ours have managed, and then we will plan."

Melancholy and sorrow lapped at my thoughts, washing away the childhood dreams, smoothing all the little tracks and scuffs of memory for and against my bastard father, until there was nothing but a smooth, hard-packed expanse of inevitability.

Morgan returned in just over a fortnight. The *Lilly* slipped alone around the reef to join us. By then, my shoulder had healed such that

I could exercise it in moderation; and we had careened every vessel in the bay. Our efforts at provisioning had not met with as much success, though: all the men chose to eat well every day, but many of the new captains did not ask their crews to hunt or cut firewood for the making of boucan as they should. Thus, the *Queen* and one other ship full of seasoned Brethren – and not Morgan's new mercenaries – were the only ones with holds full of salted beef and boucan after two weeks. The *Queen* had lost some men over our insisting they work, but gained some from other vessels, where little thought and much faith was being exercised concerning the fleet's future. During all this, we had been quite vigilant, but if any plotted against Striker or Gaston, we did not learn of it.

Morgan seemed disinclined to host any manner of fête involving his captains in honor of his return: ashore or upon the *Mayflower* – which he lived aboard for only the three days it took to careen Norman's *Lilly*, before returning to the *Lilly* and naming her his flagship. From this, we inferred Bradley was no longer one of our admiral's favorite people; though Bradley did not speak directly of that, when he told Striker what he had learned from Morgan regarding the ill-fated French ship and her captain.

Morgan had not brought the *Cour Volant* back to the fleet, but she had not been given back to her captain, either. The admiralty court had been assembled within a day, and passed a verdict of piracy against the poor Frenchman. The *Cour Volant* had been seized and her captain thrown into the gaol to await hanging; but then Modyford granted the man reprieve, and then insulted Morgan by requisitioning the French ship for use in the colony's defense in the *Oxford's* absence.

So despite our admiral's maneuverings and complicity with English law in order to obtain the French vessel – further scuttling any hope of the French Brethren ever sailing with him again, after the debacle at Puerte Principe – he had failed. And he no longer had an English man of war, or even apparently the governor's favor at the moment. I did not wonder why he did not wish to make merry.

Nor did he wish to sit about the bay at Cow Island, where he would be reminded of the *Oxford's* demise. Nor did he wish to make men work, and thus run the risk of anyone else not liking him. Thus, he decided we should sail for the island of Savona on the southeast corner of Hispaniola as soon as possible. When it became apparent that not all our twelve ships were ready to do such a thing, he chose the Bay of Ocoa – to the east along the southern shore of Hispaniola – as a rendezvous point, saying that from there we could provision at the inconvenience of the Spanish until all were assembled to sail on to Savona.

From Savona, Bradley told us, Morgan would probably still wish to sail south and plunder the coast of Caracas; but we would not go so far west as our admiral had planned when sitting behind the *Oxford's* guns. From this, we learned our damn leader had indeed entertained the notion of attacking Cartagena. I thanked the Gods for the destruction of the *Oxford*: I only wished They had not taken so many lives to do it.

And so in the third week of January 1669, we left Cow Island. The voyage to the Bay of Ocoa should have taken less than a week, but we ran into stiff headwinds at the southern cape of Hispaniola, and they did not abate for three weeks. The fleet became separated, as some of our number chose to turn back for a time, others sailed farther south, and all kept their distance from one another in order to maneuver as we made our attempts to round the cape.

Thankfully, aboard the *Queen*, men were angry at the wind and sea and not one another. Striker and Pete had even reached some accord before we sailed, such that they appeared as comfortable with one another as Gaston and I: and we were very well, indeed. Our men, who filled our deck as usual, stayed clear of our sailors as best they could; and our cabal stayed clear of the Bard as he waged war against the elements. And we were all quite pleased we had a hold full of meat. We surmised some of the other ships would never make the rendezvous, choosing instead to plunder what they could to the lee of the cape in order to fill their bellies.

We judged it to be the ides of February when at last we sailed into the Bay of Ocoa. There were three ships to greet us: the *Lilly* and two other wind-nimble sloops. Striker went to speak with Morgan as soon as we dropped anchor. He was grim when he returned.

"They just arrived," he said upon joining our cabal on the quarterdeck. "And it is as we thought: the lot of them are starving. Morgan wanted an accounting of all we had: I told them we could share some of our salted kegs until other food could be found, but I would not surrender it all. He likes me even less now."

"He cannot demand our food," Cudro spat.

"Nay, because we can just sail off," the Bard said.

"Aye," Striker said grimly. "But that is the only reason he did not ask. He kept speaking as if we were all Jamaica's navy, and all belonged to all."

The men who overheard this were grumbling.

Striker turned to address them. "Worry not! I will not surrender what we worked hard for. I do wish to give them a little to fill their bellies so they can find their own."

This seemed to suit the men, and though some thought the bastards deserved it, others were willing to share.

"Morgan wishes to send sorties ashore, starting tomorrow," Striker told us. "With levies of men from every ship that arrives. He says our men are needed because they are fed and fit."

There was quiet swearing all about.

"All right," Cudro sighed after he finished cursing Morgan's ancestry in Dutch. "I'll discover who wishes to volunteer and go with them." He left us, and began asking about for men who wished to go ashore.

"How long before we sail?" the Bard asked.

It had often been a topic of discussion. We had decided to wait and see what we found here, and what developed of that. We had even discussed sailing on our own against the fleets. The men were poor, though; and Morgan had managed to bring them all a good deal of silver last year. Thus we were resolved to wait and see, but not if it became apparent we could do better on our own.

"A week," Striker said.

"Did Morgan say how long he intends to wait?" I asked.

Striker snorted. "The only ship he is truly waiting on is the *Mayflower*. If we're here more than four or five days, he might wait longer for her. I doubt he'll wait more than a few days beyond her arrival, though. He is determined to sail to Savona, and then south by the end of the month, with however many men we have then."

"Is there money to be made preying off little villages?" I asked with annoyance.

"Aye, if they don't know we're coming," Striker said. "And it's divided between few men. Of course, that's all we'll likely have."

Two more ships arrived the next day, and the shore party returned with some pork. This continued for three more days: ships and meat trickling in. On the fourth day, the *Mayflower* arrived, much to the relief of all: she was our largest vessel and carried over a hundred men.

Her arrival depleted the *Queen's* stores still further, though. The hunting had not been going well, either. The Spanish had now had ample time to tell one another of our predations; and thus everywhere our men landed, the livestock had been driven inland. Morgan called for a meeting on the *Lilly,* and we wished Striker and Cudro good fortune at it. They, of course, returned with vexing news.

Striker led our cabal to the cabin and closed the door. "I am to lead a larger party ashore tomorrow, to plunder what we can if we can't find stock."

Pete snorted derisively at this news, and turned from his matelot's plaintive stare.

"Should I ask why you were granted this dubious honor?" I asked.

Striker sighed and pulled his gaze from his matelot to meet mine with resignation. His tone was laden with sarcasm. "Norman is old, Bradley has just arrived, and, according to Morgan, I have a propensity for making sure men are fed." He shook his head. "Aye, it is as we feared. He is willing to risk me more than any other. But... He's also correct. And, if there was no price upon my head, and..." He sighed. "There was a time when I would have considered it a vote in my favor. But now, here we are, and... I haven't stepped down. And it's my own damn fault. I know that."

Pete sighed heavily and turned around to face his man again. "It'll Work. You'llStepDownTomorrow."

"Why?" Striker asked. "Even if I just refuse, I should have some reason." He did not sound as if he argued for the sake of it.

"'Cause..." Pete stopped and looked away again: his face troubled.

"I know not what excuse Pete might wish you to concoct," I said quickly. "But I think it would be a likely time, and perhaps our best, to arrange a hunting accident."

Pete winced; and I could see from where I stood that Striker had not been blind to it, but he turned to me with a grim smile.

"Aye," Striker said. "I've been shot before. Never to save my life, but I'm sure I'll live through it."

"ICan't" Pete said thickly. He would not meet my gaze or anyone else's, and all eyes were upon him.

"There is no need for you to be so burdened," I said lightly. "I will shoot him."

Striker pulled his gaze from his matelot again and grinned at me. "Thanks. You're a true friend."

I grinned in return. "Aye, you best remember it. You will owe me dearly for this."

At that, I turned to the door and motioned for the others to precede me. I was thankful when they did. I did not look back as I closed the door behind me, leaving Striker and Pete alone. We retreated as a group to the quarterdeck, but no one seemed inclined to speak. Gaston wrapped an arm around my shoulder and pulled me close to kiss my cheek.

When at last Striker and Pete emerged, they appeared none the worse for whatever had passed between them. Actually, they looked quite jubilant, and clung to one another in a way they seldom did. Striker addressed the men, explaining that he would be commanding tomorrow's sortie. Fully half our number volunteered to accompany him. Most claimed boredom, but I saw another reason in some eyes, and I wondered at the nature of it: did they wish to protect him, or engage in that thing we most wished to avoid, namely his death? I said nothing, and trusted in Cudro's knowledge of them to choose who best served our purposes. Gaston and I retired to the cabin, where my matelot proceeded to pack his medical bag with everything he might need to perform surgery.

"Where do you feel I should shoot him?" I whispered. "I was rather thinking a limb."

"It must incapacitate him," Gaston said grimly.

"Oui, I suppose it must, otherwise why would he relinquish command?" I sighed.

"Avoid his belly."

"Oui. Would a wound such as my most recent suffice?"

"Oui," he sighed, and turned to look at me. "Right side as yours was. I will proclaim it is worse than it will be. And..." He stopped and frowned as he studied my shoulder. "You should use a musket to make it plausible."

I sighed. I had not fired my musket but twice since my wound; both times had told me how tender the area still was. "I will manage. What of Farley?"

"We will find if he is truly our friend," Gaston said with resignation.

"Should we tell him anything at all?" I asked. Our good young physician ever seemed the serious type, but we had truly not brought him into our confidence on any matter save Gaston being elected surgeon. He had taken to that well enough, though.

"Perhaps we should tell him. What do you think?" Gaston asked.

"I think you are correct. Now is a good time to learn where his loyalties lie."

Gaston took a deep breath and a small smile graced his lips when next he met my gaze. "I am pleased I am having this discussion with you and not Pete."

I was too. I had not planned to offer as I did, but it was probably best things had occurred as they did. I would have a calmer heart, and it was not as if we could have let them go ashore without us, anyway.

I only wondered what opportunities would present themselves on the morrow. I doubted any would find my claiming I had discharged my piece by accident credible. The most likely scenario for success involved some exchange of gunfire with the Spanish. I hoped there would be Spaniards tomorrow, and not just cattle. Perhaps we would need to raid some village, and in that exercise Pete, Striker, Gaston and I could become somewhat separated from the others.

I told Gaston my thoughts on the matter, but spared Pete and Striker. That night, I dreamt of shooting everyone I knew, and having them shoot me, and all rose from where they fell and laughed at one another. I woke feeling restless in temper and spirit. My Horse was quite calm, though: this was a thing that needed to be done – with love – and I was well-suited to do it.

In addition to the four of us, Cudro had mustered himself, Ash, Alonso, and Maslow, a likeable fellow and one of our better musketeers. I was concerned when I saw Alonso was to go with us, but I said nothing of it. We had been polite to one another these last weeks, and though I had done little to avoid him, I had turned aside his efforts to have private conversations with me. He had found amusement in this.

The boats with the men from the various vessels came together near the ship anchored closest to shore. I counted sixty men. Striker asked around and determined the previous days' landing places, and he decided we would row farther east along the shore, before landing to the west of a village one of the other sorties had seen. We made for that area with companionable jocularity and competition between the rowers, and thus had a quick time of it.

Once ashore, the men from the *Queen* stayed close together, near Striker, as the entire sortie worked its way through the dense forest, toward the meadows that purportedly lay beyond. After a time, we found a small wagon trail and followed it carefully in the direction of the village. We saw no one and no livestock. I thought it was merely because we were wandering about in the forest and not near any place of habitation; and then we came upon a cleared field with a plow sitting in a recently turned furrow. We felt eyes upon us; but whether it was one frightened farmhand or the entire population of the nearby village armed with pitchforks and aging blunderbusses, we could not know. We retreated to the trees to at least make ourselves less obvious targets, and considered our options. We decided to proceed toward the village, but with even greater caution. Then one of our vanguard reported seeing cattle in a field to the north of the road ahead. As we were there to procure meat before all else, Striker led us toward them.

We did indeed find a score of cattle being driven across a meadow by two cowherds. They did not appear to be in a hurry, or necessarily driving the beasts away from the direction we had come: they were actually doing quite the opposite. Pete, Cudro, and Gaston viewed the open expanse and cattle with suspicion.

"Why are they driving cattle when an alarm has been sounded?" Cudro asked.

"Maybe there weren't no alarm. Maybe we just be makin' too damn much noise," another man said, eliciting many chuckles.

"Let's just get the damn cattle and be done with it," Striker said.

He sent two small parties of men – four apiece – to run along the sides of the meadow and check for ambuscades, while the rest of us used the relatively open ground to reach the cattle quickly.

The cowherds saw us coming and abandoned their charges to run into the forest. We let them go, and our men set to killing the beasts. Pete roared a minute later; and I turned to look about in time to see one of our scouting parties returning to us at a run, with what seemed a hundred Spaniards on their heels. Looking the other direction showed a similar sight. There was no time for cursing. Those who had not fired on the cattle chose targets among the Spanish, while Striker roared for all to gather up and get their backs to one another.

I had no time to count the Spanish facing us; but it was evident that, if they had all hit their marks upon first firing, they would have killed every buccaneer two or three times over. But they were not well trained – despite the uniforms on some – and thus we were able to form into a circle, and very few of ours were wounded after the first exchange. We began to fire in tight volleys, as pairs of matelots are wont to do. They began to run about in confusion, reload slowly, and make easy targets of themselves. Every time a buccaneer musket fired, a Spaniard dropped. Every time they fired, it gave one of our men more time to reload or aim. And soon their trumpet was sounding a retreat, and Cudro's magnificent voice was calling us toward the closest tree line.

Gaston and I were some of the farthest from that point of retreat; and we pulled back slowly, continuing to fire at any target that presented itself, until at last we were safely in the trees. Only then did Gaston hand me his musket and turn to the closest wounded man. And then Ash was beside him with a pale face. We ran with him to the back of our number, and found Cudro standing above a stricken and tearful Pete and a very bloody Striker. The world spun about me, and I leaned on a tree.

"He's not dead..." Cudro hissed uncertainly.

"We must get out of here," I whispered.

"Oui, aye," Cudro said. "I'll gather everyone. We'll need to carry some, but he's the worst. I saw it. They saw he was in command, and fired on him first."

I swore long and hard as I knelt beside Gaston who was frantically examining our unconscious friend. He tore away Striker's tunic, and had Pete and I put pressure on two of four wounds: one in his shoulder similar to mine, but on the left; and one just above the base of his ribs on the right. Striker's left hip had also been grazed, and his lower right arm was a bloody and broken mess; but Gaston simply tied cloth above the arm wound and ignored the other. I noted that, even before Pete and I leaned on our respective holes, they had not been spurting blood: merely leaking it. And thankfully my matelot did not look as he had after his cursory examination of Otter – who died.

"He can live," Gaston hissed to Pete.

The Golden One nodded tightly without taking his eyes off Striker's seemingly-peaceful face.

Gaston sat back and surveyed the circle of distraught men around us and the chaos beyond them. He looked back at Pete. "We will need to carry him. I do not wish to seek the balls or debris, or sew him here. I will bind the wounds and then we must go." He looked to me. "Find Cudro, and send any other wounded here."

I did as he bade, dodging through the score of men closest to us, glancing at the handful of wounded and telling them to get closer to Gaston so he could judge their wound before we moved. I found Cudro among the men not wounded, peering into the field. The Spanish were removing their wounded from the field: dozens of them, more men than we had brought. But they were also involved in some curious activity that had our men quite riled. Apparently one of ours was dead, and in the retreat he had been left where he fell. The Spaniards were circling about the body, stabbing it and yelling imprecations.

"We must go," I said sadly.

"That can't go unanswered," Cudro rumbled.

"All right, but they could cut off our retreat," I said.

"They aren't heading that way, but back to town," he said.

As they had not determined so many were lying in wait for us, I felt doubt at our scouts' abilities now; but judging the mood of the men, Cudro was right: the insult to our dead could not go unanswered.

I turned back to assessing the wounded; either sending them toward Gaston, or checking to see that someone had bound their wounds. I judged a score of men – a third of our number – had lost blood; but only Striker might be mortally wounded, and only three others were bleeding from chest or belly. The rest were grazed or afflicted with muscle wounds that could easily be bandaged, though some should be sewn. Of our eight men from the *Queen*: Pete, Gaston, Ash, Maslow, and I were completely unscathed; Alonso had a welt along the crown of his head and appeared quite dizzy; and Cudro had had a ball put a nice clean hole in his massive upper left arm.

When Cudro judged enough Spaniards had left the field, a contingent of our men surged out and shot the men still stabbing the body. They collected it, and returned to us. Then with one man carrying the corpse, Pete carrying Striker, and a handful of men supported by their matelots or friends, the lot of us hurried back toward our boats. I stayed to the rear – as Pete was moving slowly and Gaston with him – and covered our retreat. Maslow helped Alonso, who was at least able to walk, though not in a straight line without assistance. He could not shoot.

I told the Gods They best do a better job of opening the eyes of those now in our vanguard. I feared we would return to the shore and find leering and gibbering Spaniards dancing around our broken boats. I heard shooting ahead, and panic renewed its icy clutch upon my heart, until word was passed back through our ranks: we had stumbled upon Spanish horses and shot them for the needed meat. I decided I was ill-pleased with the Gods, but I kept mention of it safely behind my lips, lest They wreak some further vengeance upon us.

We found our boats safe where we had left them: whether through providence or Spanish incompetence – which may or may not have been due to providence – I could not know. As there was little to be done for the dead man, we hastily buried him there between the roots of a tree, and hoped the Spanish would not be so vile as to disturb him further. Then we were all upon the water, those who could rowing furiously for our ships.

Pete and I rowed, with Gaston tending Striker at our feet. Poor Striker had actually woken during our run to the beach, and promptly succumbed to darkness again. Gaston had drugged him as soon as we stopped. I watched my matelot probe and clean the shoulder and rib wounds. He did not seem overly concerned about them, though. It was the arm wound that caused him to grimace. The ball that struck the forearm had shattered one of the bones there. Gaston had to extract splinters to probe it further. The blow of the ball and the sharp edges of the bone had reduced the surrounding flesh to the consistency of ground sausage. I had seen him tend similar wounds: in every case, the man's arm had been removed, as flesh so rendered often could not heal; and if it did, the man would have no control of his fingers and possible eternal pain or numbness.

I wondered what Striker would do without a lower right arm. He surely could still command, but he would ever need someone to fight beside him. Thankfully, he had that.

All was confusion for a time when we arrived at the *Queen*; but Cudro and the Bard quickly put enough order to it to get Striker, Pete, Gaston and myself into the cabin. We laid Striker on our mattress, and Gaston finished tending the chest wounds. I assisted as I could, and Pete sat in grim silence with tear-filled eyes.

"He should live," Gaston told him when he had finished there. He wiped his hands and turned so he could look upon Pete's face. The

Golden One would not meet his eyes.

"The shoulder wound was much like Will's," Gaston continued. "And this lower one broke a rib, but did not damage the organ beneath overmuch. The problem is this arm wound."

Pete nodded. "SayIt."

"I need to remove it here," Gaston said quietly, and indicated a place just below Striker's right elbow.

Pete nodded again and took a long shuddering breath. "DoIt."

"Will you stay?" Gaston asked.

There was another nod from the golden head. "BestMeHoldin'Im Iffn'EWakes."

"Nay," Gaston said kindly. "I will not let him wake and feel anything."

"Good."

Pete lay on the floor so he could cradle Striker's head to his chest and not be in Gaston's way. He did not watch as my matelot removed the ruined flesh and salvaged what skin and muscle he could to make a nicely rounded stump. As Gaston finished this last, I wrapped the severed lower arm and hand in cloth and sat them aside.

"ThatNa'BeGoin'TaTheSharks," Pete said calmly. "WeBuryIt."

"All right," I said, and wondered when he would be going ashore within the next few days, much less Striker.

"Salt it," Gaston said.

Relieved at such an obvious solution, I nodded and slipped from the cabin. I immediately encountered curious eyes and waiting men. "He lives. The wounds are not so very bad, but... He has lost his right arm from here." I indicated on my arm. This elicited much muttering and discussion; but several men shouted encouragement, and a few waved hooks. The consensus seemed to be that he was a strong man: he would do well enough without. I agreed – for the most part.

I told Cudro of my need for salt, and he said he would bring it.

"And how is your wound?" I asked, and pointed at his bandaged shoulder.

"Good. Farley saw to us," he said. "Alonso is sleeping. Farley is watching him close. He wishes to confer with Gaston."

"All right, I will send him out if..."

Cudro nodded tightly. "No hurry. As I said, he's sleeping."

But as I turned to return to the cabin, I recalled that sleep for a man who has been hit in the head is not always a good thing. So I told Gaston of it at once, and he nodded reluctantly. I could tell he did not wish to leave the cabin. He kept turning and regarding the door with trepidation.

"Should I fetch Farley?" I asked in French. "Or should we say the Hell with Alonso: that he will receive all his God intends from Farley's training. Or..."

He put quick fingers on my mouth. "I wish to leave little to any God this day. Stay with Pete. I will manage. Be here."

"Always," I whispered.

He kissed me lightly and left us.

I looked to Pete. "Cudro is finding salt and cloth to preserve the…"

Pete nodded tightly. "TakeArHammock. ThisBedBeABloodyMess. ButItBeHisNow. GastonSayItBeBest'ELieFlat."

He was not looking at me as he spoke, and I sensed shame and guilt.

"There was nothing you could have done," I said softly.

He snorted. "Na'WishedItUpon'Im!"

"He can do all else he wanted with only one arm… And you beside him."

Pete made an incoherent animal cry of grief and guilt, and new tears slid down his cheeks.

I changed my tack. "He should not have had to pay so high a price, and you will be forever in his debt."

He took a deep calming breath and nodded tightly. "ThatBeTheWay O'It." He still would not look at me.

I cleaned the soiled bandages, and mopped up what blood I could from the floor. The stains on the bed were permanent: seeped deep into the feathers.

"Move here, so you might lie beside him," I said, once I had cleared Gaston's medical tools away. "Has he feared losing a limb?"

"AyeAn'Nay," Pete grumbled as he moved where I bade, and stretched out beside his man. "'EAlwaysThought'EWould. 'IsFatherWereMissin'Fingers AnPartO'ALeg. 'IsUncleLostAEye. 'EThinksThatBeTheWayO'It. ThatRovin'WhittlesAManDown."

He at last met my gaze. "StillNa'BeRight."

"Nay," I agreed sadly. "But perhaps that is the way of it. Violence whittles away at a man. The courts of Christendom are filled with tales of men who were once duelists, but now languish either broken and destitute with some relative, or merely broken but rich in some villa. A man can only be lucky for so long."

"Don'Wanna'Lanegwish. ThinkI'dRatherDie."

"Aye, that is ever what I told myself. But the languishing is for those who have nothing beyond the dueling – or in this instance, the roving. Let us be men who have more."

He sighed and smiled sadly. "ButAsYaSaid. WeBeMenWhoOnly'Ave Another."

I smiled. "Aye, let us not languish in the arms of what we have, then."

Pete's eyes narrowed in a frown, and then he nodded with solemn understanding. "YaBeRight. 'ELivesYet. An"CauseO'This, 'ELiveLonger."

"Aye, perhaps it is better that it occurred as it did: with mostly untrained ambushers in a field. If it had been in the taking of a fortress, they would have aimed cannon at him, or at least aimed better."

"TrueThat. StillWish'EDidna"AveTaLoseTheArm."

"Aye, of course you do not, but you are not to blame."

He nodded sincerely. "Aye." He looked to me with solemn eyes. "ThankYa."

I nodded, and did as he often did with Gaston and me. I leaned down and brushed a kiss on his temple and then another on Striker's forehead. "Rest now."

He nodded and smiled, and I took up the wrapped arm and left him.

Cudro was waiting on the quarterdeck steps. "Not sure if I should go in or not."

I nodded. "Best that you did not: Pete needs time alone."

We carefully salted the arm and wrapped it in oilcloth. Then, cradling this macabre bundle, I went in search of my matelot. I found him on the quarterdeck, in serious discussion with Farley. Alonso was beside them, asleep and oblivious to all.

"How is he?" I asked.

In response, Gaston raised Alonso's eyelids and peered at the sightless eyeballs.

"There does not appear to be any swelling within the skull," Farley said helpfully. "His eyes do not bulge and his ears do not seep, but he is unable to remain conscious."

Gaston shrugged sadly. "All we can do is let him sleep and give him laudanum if he suffers. We cannot see what has occurred within his skull." This last was said with annoyance.

"He could lie about comatose for days, or weeks..." Farley sighed.

My first thought was that Alonso would not trouble me whilst he lay about: I felt quite the bastard. I sighed. "Will you need help caring for him?"

Gaston looked to me sharply, and then frowned with guilt.

"Nay," Farley said. "I shall see to him."

My matelot stood and thanked Farley, and we walked a short distance to the rail. I clutched my bundle tightly, strangely afraid it would fall over by accident and Pete would blame me forever.

"How is Pete?" Gaston asked.

I shrugged. "He will overcome his guilt in time."

"Good," Gaston said with a measured nod. "Can we return to the cabin?"

I studied him, and saw the strain about his eyes and mouth.

"Oui." I led him there.

I handed the bundle to Pete, who tucked it protectively between himself and Striker, and then I gestured for Gaston to climb to the upper hammock. He stood where he had, rocking with the ship, and I knew he was already retreating from the world – feeling it safe to do so simply because I was leading him somewhere. By the time we were at last safely tucked into the nest beneath the ceiling, he had curled in on himself, and his eyes were full of the Child. After so many weeks of his sanity, I was actually surprised.

He began to examine my hands, feeling and testing every joint and crevice with first his fingers and then his tongue. I could imagine what he was thinking, and I did nothing to deter him, until at last he allowed himself to sleep with my right hand clutched tightly to his breast.

I lay there for a long time, alternately cursing and wondering at the Gods' fine sense of irony.

Seventy-Nine

Wherein We Face Dreams and Fears

I woke to golden light from a nightmare involving Gaston's bone saw, and surmised by how un-rested I felt that it was evening and not the following morning. My stomach roiled with hunger at the tantalizing smells of beef and pineapple, and I wondered if we had water about or if I must fetch some. Gaston slept like a babe in my arms, and I did not wish to disturb him by moving, but my cock was quite insistent that it be drained in a manner that did not require his love or person. I climbed carefully down from the upper hammock – so as not to wake him, and because I was unfamiliar with the hand and toe holds – and relieved myself through the open window; my stream arcing and glittering in salute to the setting sun.

Reluctant to emerge from the cave of pleasant and plebian thoughts of the body, I looked down at Striker and found myself dumped unceremoniously into the light. He was awake. Pete snored quietly beside him, but Striker lay still with his eyes open, gazing up at me. I dropped to kneel at his side, and quickly moved to lean over him, as he seemed desperate to follow me with his gaze, but he appeared to only wish to move his eyes. His apparent fear of movement minded me of floating upon the water: how, when unfamiliar with it, I ever felt the need to remain motionless lest I get dunked beneath the waves. Remembering the rolling, constant pain of my shoulder wound, I thought it likely he was afraid of being pulled beneath waves of a different sort.

"How are you?" I asked, once my head was directly over his so he only need look up.

"Hurts... everywhere," he whispered, as if it were a curious thing and not a matter requiring immediate attention.

Despite corroborating my thoughts on his reason for stillness, he did not look as a man in pain often does. His eyes were wide open and not drooping, and his color was good. Still, I quickly prepared a small draught of laudanum for him, and gingerly raised his head to dribble it past his lips.

"I thought I was dead," he whispered slowly when I returned to gazing down at him. "I saw them fire. There were so many. It seemed they were all coming for me. Like demons sent from Hell. I thought, this is it: this is how you will die, you damn fool. And then when I woke, I thought we were imprisoned."

I smiled and caressed his cheek. "Nay, only upon our own ship. It is not your day to die."

He awarded me a weak smile. "Thank God for that. And Gaston. How am I?"

I sighed, and tried to keep the grimace from my face. I lightly touched the bandage of each wound as I spoke of it. "You have a wound, here, like the one I had from Christine; and a broken rib and bruised organ here; and a grazed hip; and..." I sighed again, and gently raised his maimed arm so that he could see the stump.

He gazed for a time with curiosity and little comprehension at the lump of bandage around and beneath his right elbow, and then his eyes finally widened in understanding.

"Oh," he said, and turned his gaze to the ceiling before, giving a choked huff of amusement. "I always knew I'd lose something in the end. But the right. Damn."

I lowered his arm and he did not try to move it.

He tried to look to Pete without turning his head. "How is he?"

"Nearly overwhelmed with grief and guilt," I said.

"Poor bugger," Striker breathed as tears filled his eyes. "It wasn't his fault. He tried. I should've..."

I moved so that he could only meet my gaze, and admonished, "Do not you start."

He risked a little nod, but his words were defiant. "My pride brought me to this."

I snorted. "Damn it, Striker. What are we without pride? We are merely sheep to be shorn by any with shears. If you lose yourself to this, then your pride will have brought you to a pitiful end. It has happened by fate or providence, and now you must go on for yourself and for those you love and who love you."

I knew my words to be strong; but I felt that, as of yet, he floated in a curious state of grace above the pain and true dismay and grief; and thus he might actually hear me now, and be able to recall all I said later, when it would do some good.

I could see the drug tugging at his eyes, beginning to pull him away but not yet under. He nodded without fear for the pain. I roused Pete, who blinked once in confusion and then rolled quickly to his knees to shoulder me aside and peer down at his matelot.

I retreated back to our new hammock, and found a pair of serene green eyes waiting for me. I pulled him to me, and he returned my embrace with equal fervor. We held one another for a time, and I tried not to listen to the quiet whispers from below.

"How are we?" I at last felt compelled to whisper: I could not see his face.

"Better than before," he breathed in my ear.

"We have not slept long." I shrugged awkwardly. "Unless this is the next day."

"I think not," he sighed. "I kept envisioning it was you. I could not drive the image away."

"I understand."

"If that ever needs to be done... I do not think I will be able to. Anything else, I feel I could do for you, but that..."

"Hush," I said, as my mind's eye attempted to show me the image his words invoked. I kept my gaze steadfastly on the small pot of salve wedged in between the beams beyond his shoulder. We would need to replace it with our own.

"I do not even wish to think of it."

I felt him nod.

The cabin door opened, and I heard steps and then a surprised, "Ah, you're awake," from Cudro.

"Somewhat," Striker said, almost too quietly for me to hear.

Gaston and I released one another, and I turned and found I could not see below without climbing to the edge. The previous occupants had covered our new hammock with a thin blanket for privacy: a thing I had noticed before, but now appreciated fully.

Cudro was kneeling beside the mattress. "I've been to see Morgan and the others. They wished to see you, but I told them to wait until tomorrow."

"Good," Pete said. His eyes were thick and swollen, but he appeared calm.

"The men would see you, too," Cudro said. "They worry. But you don't look ready to see them."

"Nay," Striker said with a weak smile. "Tomorrow."

"Maybe," Gaston intoned, and climbed over me and down. "He will not leave this cabin. If he feels well enough, they can come in small numbers and give their regards."

"Aye, that was what I was thinking," Cudro agreed quickly.

"Election," Striker said as Gaston nudged Pete away and began to examine the bandages.

"No hurry," Cudro chided. "And they should hear it from you, after they see you'll live."

"Between you and me, then," Striker said with a wry smile. "You're captain."

Cudro chuckled. "Aye, sir."

"How many did we lose?" Striker asked.

"Just one," Cudro said, and told him of all he had missed.

"It is a damn shame about the man lost," Striker said with drug-borne amusement, "and all the wounded, but at least we brought home meat. With that, my command will surely be judged successful and worthy."

Even though we had not the drug to buoy us, we laughed with him in genuine pleasure that he could jest.

"Morgan has decided that we all sail for Savona the day after tomorrow," Cudro said when our humor abated. "Tomorrow, he will lead a party of men ashore to teach the Spaniards a lesson."

This set us laughing again. But I thought of the numbers I had seen, and then the numbers of their wounded.

"They already learned their lesson," I spat.

Cudro chuckled. "Aye, but you know Morgan."

"Sadly," I sighed.

Cudro stood. "I'll send word that you're speaking, and *might* be up to meeting with them tomorrow." Then he eyed the rest of us. "There's roast beef if you're hungry. It's not horse, I swear."

He left us chuckling; and I climbed down, and after confirming that all save Striker were as famished as I, went to collect food and water.

Cudro was busy telling the men he had spoken with Striker, and that the man would probably feel ready to see them once we were at sea tomorrow. This seemed to cheer them.

A concerned Farley crossed my path as I returned to the cabin with a pineapple, a water bottle, and several hunks of beef. As I had already stuffed meat in my mouth, I motioned for him to follow, and he happily joined us in the cabin, where Gaston told him of Striker's wounds.

"Have you heard anything about the others?" Gaston asked.

"Aye," Striker added weakly.

Farley sighed. "One of the men died – the one with the abdominal wound. The others were apparently treatable within the knowledge of medicine their surgeons possessed."

I chuckled quietly around a mouthful of beef. He was beginning to sound like my matelot.

"In all fairness, though," Farley continued. "From what I heard of the abdominal wound, his bowels were perforated."

Gaston sighed and nodded. "We could not have saved him, then."

"No others on the *Queen*?" Striker asked with a frown of difficult thought.

"Only Alonso," I said. "And how is he?"

"Still unconscious," Farley sighed.

"Head wound," Gaston told Striker.

"Damn," Striker said. "I am thankful I still have my wits about me." He frowned again, and smiled brightly. "At least, I think I do."

"You are drugged," Gaston reminded him. "So that you might sleep."

At that admonishment, we withdrew and left Striker with his matelot and the laudanum.

Striker did indeed sleep through the night, despite Cudro's suggesting the musicians play, and thus the entire ship's company making merry on deck even though there was not a drop of rum to be had. Gaston and I remained on watch throughout the night: sitting and talking quietly of stars with some of the sailors, after all had calmed and the deck reverberated with snores and not the pounding of dancing feet. As the first light glowed along the horizon, we woke the Bard and Cudro, and I moved our things to our new nest while Gaston saw to his patient – who was awake and in need of another dose. Then we snuggled together and slept. I did not dream of bone saws, and Gaston did not sleep like one dead.

We woke in the afternoon to a knock upon the door, and then Cudro ushered Morgan and Bradley into the little room.

I rolled and peered over the edge in time to come face to face with Morgan, who was stooping only slightly and eyeing the room with disdain.

"How many men sleep here?" he asked.

"All the ship's owners," I said coldly.

"Oh," he sniffed. "You should get a bigger ship."

I did not say the obvious, or anything else that came to my tongue, such as my wry concern that, if we did, we could not dare allow him to host parties upon it.

Pete had propped a bag behind Striker so he might view his guests. Bradley had already knelt beside the mattress; and Morgan lowered himself to the edge of Cudro's hammock to join in their conversation. I cursed that, as now I could only see the top of his hat.

"You could still command," Bradley was saying.

"Not for a time," Striker said. "Maybe next year. I am either in pain or drugged beyond it. Cudro will be captain while we rove, now."

"Good," Morgan said. "He's another owner of this vessel?"

"Aye," Striker said.

I bit my tongue, and I could see Pete doing the same.

"Perhaps next year you should get two ships, if there are two of you who can captain," Morgan said pleasantly. "Why deny Jamaica and the fleet both of your expertise?"

Striker smiled. "Aye. We will see to that. Worked well this year, though."

Morgan did not respond to that. Instead he said, "We gave the Spanish a scare today, to teach them that they best not trifle with us. They are keen to take on a small band, but when I landed over two hundred men, they fled."

"Did Cudro not speak of it?" Striker asked. "There were hundreds of them, with some in uniform. They must have come from all the villages along this coast."

"He said as much," Morgan said dismissively. "Not enough to take on a real army, though. Not enough to take on *you* and fifty buccaneers!" he guffawed.

"I was on the ground in a pool of my own blood before we started fighting," Striker said wryly.

"I'm glad we didn't go today to avenge your death," Bradley said.

"Thank you," Striker said. He grinned. "So am I. Just wish I didn't have to pay with my good right arm for the pleasure. But it's better than dying. And I've got Pete, so it's not like I need both hands anyway."

Pete smiled at his man, and it was as if I could see his heart swell.

Bradley's brow furrow as he gazed upon them, and then he dropped his face to study the floor. "Aye," he said softly. "You're a lucky man."

"So you will hold elections?" Morgan asked brusquely.

I saw Striker start to shrug and think better of it and grimace. "Aye, soon. The men wish to give their respects first, and I will tell them it's my decision."

"But when we arrive at Savona, he will be captain?" Morgan prompted.

"Aye," Striker said.

"Good then, I will relay orders to him and let you heal," Morgan said and stood. "Don't die, Striker, we have need of you yet."

"I'll remember that," Striker said with a wry smile.

Bradley hesitated in following Morgan from the cabin. "Get well. You have two surgeons, but do you need…"

"Oh, shut up," Striker said with an amiable smile. "You know I have the best on Jamaica."

"When he's sane," Bradley muttered.

"I've seen him at his best when he's mad," Striker said. "Now fuck off and sail."

Bradley left with a chuckle.

Pete leaned over Striker and kissed him, and I turned away and found my matelot smiling.

"I am loved," Gaston breathed.

"Truly," I said.

He covered my mouth with his, and soon we were engaged in an activity we had not partaken of in days.

Later that evening – after Gaston had tended Striker's bandages and pronounced him fit enough for it – the men began to enter the cabin in pairs and speak of how loved Striker was, and he in turn told them to place their trust in Cudro, and all seemed pleased with this. We had the election the next day, and Cudro was ratified as captain. A good man named Boller was elected Quartermaster.

The next morning, our small fleet of eight ships and five hundred or so men sailed for Savona. When we arrived there two days later, Morgan organized a sortie of one hundred and fifty men under Bradley's command to raid the coast near San Domingo; but they returned empty-handed to report that the Spaniards were well prepared for them. Bradley later told Striker he had informed Morgan that unless we truly intended to raid here, it was not worth the pitched battle that would ensue to gain a few bags of flour and a handful of cattle. Morgan had not been pleased.

Thus, our admiral held a meeting of his eight captains. Cudro seemed pleased when he returned. He slipped into the cabin to tell Striker of the decision before putting it to a vote before the men.

"Maracaibo," Cudro said.

I frowned, but Striker and the others nodded.

"One of our new captains was on a French ship with L'Olonnais," Cudro continued. "He says he can get us past the reefs at the lake mouth. No one has raided there since the French two years ago. They should be ripe and we will not have to go against a fort."

"Is this pilot supposedly as well-informed as the good man who told us Puerte Principe was wealthy?" I asked.

There was laughter, but we cursed as well.

"And is he a pilot?" the Bard asked.

Cudro sighed and smiled. "I know not on either question. We can only pray, as he's what we've got and Morgan likes the idea. L'Olonnais did well there with few men. And it's closer than trying for the Main. If all vote for it, we'll sail south to Ruba near Curaçao, and see if we can trade with the natives for food to tide us over – since it's a Dutch colony, now. Then we'll sail southwest into the bay and the lake mouth."

"We are sailing into a lake?" I asked.

"A lake bigger than the isle of Jamaica," the Bard said.

That would be large, but it did not mollify my concern, in light of how the Spanish had become so organized against us here on Hispaniola. "Could they not trap us in it?"

"There's no fortress at the entrance, and we shouldn't be there long enough for them to send overland for aid from Cartagena," Cudro said with a shrug.

Gaston was frowning, though. "It is purported to be another Spanish cesspool of disease."

"Do the damn Spanish keep their gold anywhere else?" the Bard asked with a grin.

"Apparently not," I sighed.

Gaston shook his head with disgust.

Cudro went to present the choice of target to the men and call for a vote; all save Striker went with him to cast theirs.

"I see no reason to vote against it, as there is apparently no alternative being offered," I said quietly to Gaston in French, as we stood on the quarterdeck and listened to Cudro explain the plan.

"Non," he sighed. "We go there and see if the pawns come out to play, and then we sail home. I am just afraid we will be throwing bodies over the side the whole way home, as we did from Porto Bello. We will have to search for quinine once the town is taken. We will not drink any water that has not been boiled, or eat food that has not been cooked. We should try and stay away from the water and swamps, but I know not how. This ship will be in the water, and as it is in a lake, it will be sluggish and free of salt..." He was muttering to himself now.

We called out "aye" at the vote and Gaston immediately besieged Farley, who had moved his charge to the now mostly empty hold.

I stood by them, and gazed down at Alonso, who still slept like one dead. I counted the days: it had now been seven since that fateful morning.

I knelt beside my former lover and took up his hand curiously. I squeezed a finger; he did not move. He looked very handsome in repose. I recalled watching him sleep on occasion. He looked older now; there were lines about his eyes and mouth that had not been there for me to trace with a careful finger, in those foolish days when I thought I loved him above all others.

My breath caught. I had loved him, though. At that time, I had loved him above all others. I should not allow what I felt then to be dimmed because it paled in comparison to the love I knew now: it had shone very brightly then.

In an act of whimsy, I leaned close to him and whispered in Castilian, "Alonso, it is... Uly. You need to wake now, or else you will waste away, and none of the young men or ladies will find you handsome anymore. And you will not be able to raise a sword or fire a piece to defend yourself. And you will die unshriven among uncouth barbarians. So wake, and regain your strength. Stop dreaming of earthly and heavenly delights. You have always wished to have them here and not in the hereafter, anyway. And... you will be missed. I would not see you die this way. I do not wish to see you die at all. I did love you once."

Feeling the fool, and alarmed Gaston would take umbrage even now, I sat back and looked around. My matelot was thankfully deeply worried about the lives of other men at the moment.

Alonso stirred a little: a small fitful gesture. I had not watched him sleep for any length of time since he succumbed after the wound, so I could not know if it was a thing he often did or not. But perhaps he liked being spoken to in Castilian. So I continued talking: not so intimately now, but reminding him of adventures we had had as if we were conversing over tankards of Madeira.

Some time later, I glanced around at the end of a tale and found Farley and Gaston regarding me with curiosity. I shrugged.

"I thought speaking to him in Castilian might... wake him. Sometimes, when Gaston is... not well, he forgets he knows English, and French is all he will hear."

"Oui, aye," Gaston said with a thoughtful frown.

"I have heard of wives waking a husband or a child afflicted as he is by speaking to them," Farley said. "I have been speaking to him, but, in English. I had forgotten it was not his native tongue. How foolish of me."

Alonso stirred fitfully again.

"Does he do that often?" I asked.

"Nay," Farley said with surprise. "He does not move."

"Well, maybe he hears me, then," I said.

"Perhaps you should come and speak to him..." Farley stopped as he saw the look that passed between Gaston and me.

I surmised I appeared questioning, and I saw resignation in my matelot's eyes.

Gaston smiled. "Aye, he should come and speak to him."

"Will that present a difficulty?" Farley asked curiously.

"You have heard we were lovers, have you not?" I asked, and indicated Alonso.

"Oh," Farley said and shook his head. "I am quite the fool. Aye, I have heard that."

"Alonso harbors foolish hopes that we will be reunited," I said.

"And I am prone to stupid jealousy," Gaston said, while showing me with his gaze how very stupid he found his old fears.

Farley smiled and looked from one to the other of us.

"Whatever for?" His tone was teasing, but tinged with trepidation. I could not recall our ever speaking to him of anything of a personal nature, other than Gaston's madness to a small extent.

"Because Will is my life, and I fear losing him," Gaston said simply.

Farley colored a little and nodded. "Of course. It is just... well, I cannot see where either of you would give the other cause. You seem very... close."

"It has been my experience that jealousy seldom needs cause," I said lightly.

Gaston smirked at me. "No part of me will be jealous."

I grinned. "I will hold all parts of you to that," I teased in return.

Farley was frowning now with perplexity.

I waved him off. "Thank you for caring for Alonso as you have."

"Someone must," Farley said with a shrug. "And I have few other patients, and... I enjoy his company." He seemed uncomfortable at that admission. "It pains me to see him as he is now."

"Do not worry; we will not think you entertain thoughts other than the platonic for him simply because you are amongst buccaneers."

He flushed and shook his head. "People here *leap* at conjecture..."

I laughed. "Tell me of it." I clapped his shoulder and led Gaston away to the quarterdeck.

"I will never again be jealous of Alonso," he said when we were relatively alone at the rail.

"I know. I feel I might be more uncomfortable with aiding in his recovery than you are, but... it pains me to see him in that state, and... I did love him once."

Gaston frowned at that, but then he nodded with a rueful smile and cast his eyes skyward. "I will not be jealous."

"Keep telling *Them* that," I teased.

He laughed, and pulled me to him for a lovely kiss that warmed my heart and cock. We settled in and watched the stars twinkle as we shared stories with the men on watch.

Our small fleet sailed south with the dawn. It would take several days to reach the little Dutch-claimed isle known as Ruba. Gaston and I settled into our routine of keeping the night watch, participating in the clearing of weapons and cleaning of the ship in the early morning, sleeping until the afternoon, rising and engaging in calisthenics or sparring, and then enjoying the tales and music of the evening hours with our friends. I added speaking with Alonso to my daily duties; and, of course, Gaston tended Striker. And thus two days passed.

On the third night, Farley hurried on to the quarterdeck, seeking me. He did not tell us what was about: he merely led Gaston and me to the hold, where we found Alonso blinking slowly at the dim lantern light.

"He called out for you," Farley said.

I knelt beside Alonso and spoke Castilian. "Alonso, how are you? Do you know where you are?"

His gaze found me and brightened. "Uly," he sighed. "I found you. I kept hearing you... in this dream. But whenever I turned, you were not there. So I was chasing you through this great house... It was not my father's, or Teresina's or... It had parts of every house I have ever been in: all connected together as if someone kept building and building for acres and..." He shook his head irritably. "It is not important. I found you now."

"Si, you have returned to us," I said.

"Where have I been?"

"Lost in that dream, perhaps – for the last nine days."

He was quite stricken at this information. "That must be why I feel so weak."

"Si, are you hungry? Thirsty?" I asked.

He nodded quickly, and Farley handed me a water bottle and went to fetch food. I helped Alonso raise his head so he could drink. He regarded me above the mouth of the bottle like a trusting babe. I found it disturbing.

After he had drunk a goodly amount, I set the bottle aside

"Do you remember what occurred?" I asked. .

He frowned slightly with thought, and peered about, though there was little to be seen beyond the small sphere of lantern light in which we sat. Even Gaston was a shadow among shadows leaning against the hull, out of Alonso's sight. He nodded encouragement to me, and watched Alonso with a physician's curiosity.

"Where are we, Uly?" Alonso asked.

"In the hold of the *Queen*: Farley has been nursing you here."

His frown deepened. "What *Queen*? Are we on a ship? Everything moves as if..."

I shifted my seat to a more comfortable position and tried to keep the alarm from my face. "What is the last thing you remember?" I asked calmly.

He shook his head slowly, his gaze on nothing as he looked inward. "I remember a great many things: people, places, events... But there is no order to them." He smiled sadly and met my gaze. "I cannot tell you what came last. Have I been ill?"

"Wounded," I said levelly. "A musket ball grazed your skull. Sometimes injuries to the head take strange courses."

Farley had returned with a plate of stew. He was regarding me curiously, as he did not speak Castilian.

"Do you know Farley, here?" I asked pleasantly as I motioned for Farley to sit with us.

Alonso studied him, and nodded with a smile of recognition and relief. "Si, I know him."

I turned to Farley and quickly explained all Alonso had said. He appeared quite concerned and glanced to Gaston, who shrugged and motioned for me to continue.

So Alonso recognized Farley, who he had met but recently. "Do you remember Cudro?" I asked.

He thought on it. "A big Dutchman? Wonderful voice?"

"Si, si," I said happily. "You seem to know people. Now, where... Where do you live?"

"I suppose here on this ship," he said speculatively, and then he sighed with relief. "Si, I remember: the *Virgin Queen*. I can envision her quite clearly."

"Good, good," I said. "Now, who are you? Not your name, but... how do you make your way in the world?"

He met my gaze with concern, and gave a glance to Farley. "I am a Lord's son, and I have done a great many things for money..." He sighed and looked away to consider the floor with growing agitation. "I know this ship is not business of my family's, or by her name, the King's either, and that it is a thing of the New World... somehow. I do not know why I know that, though. I do not know how I came to be upon her." His gaze returned to me. "I remember meeting you quite clearly, and all manner of things concerning you, and... Uly... No, you do not wish to be called that. We have moved on and changed names." He glanced at Farley with trepidation again.

"You can speak of anything you remember here," I said.

"U... Will, that is it, Will. I do not know if I can explain. I see things, I recall them, and those memories lead to a dozen others, but there is no order. I can make sense of them only by thinking of what they must mean. There was a woman..." He shrugged. "There have been many women. But one I married. I can recall the ceremony in the church. But... Was that before or after I met you?"

"After, but before we met again," I said carefully. I turned to Farley, and behind him in the shadows, Gaston, and told them in English this latest exchange.

Farley regarded Alonso with wonder. "This is quite the case for study. I have heard of nothing like it."

I glanced at Alonso and asked in Castilian, "Can you understand English?"

"With difficulty," he said in his own tongue.

I looked to Gaston. "Should I tell him?"

Alonso tried to turn and see who I spoke to. Gaston moved into the light with a sigh as he considered my question.

"Oh, I know him," Alonso said darkly in Castilian, and I was minded of Gaston's and my discussion of Alonso's Horse. I could see the animal very clearly in his eyes at this moment.

And Gaston's Horse rose to meet it. He stood at the edge of the light with his eyes hard and full of warning.

"Who is he, then?" I asked Alonso briskly, startling him somewhat.

"He is your lover," Alonso said sullenly.

"Well, you remember that," I said sharply. "Do you remember that I left you?"

"Si," he said, and looked away with guilt. "I do not know when or how. I just hoped..." He looked at me plaintively. "So, you have not returned to me."

"No," I said without rancor.

"Then... it was just the dream." He frowned, and asked with a tinge of vehemence, "Then why did you call me back?"

"Out of respect for what we once had," I sighed. "I did not wish to see you die in so ignoble a fashion. A man such as you should be shot." I shook my head at my choice of words and softened my tone. "You should die tragically or heroically, not wasting away with someone wiping your arse."

I left them. I did not want to see that pleading and hurt look upon his face a moment longer. Gaston followed me, and his arms closed around me from behind when I reached the relative privacy of the quarterdeck rail. I took deep breaths of the night air and tried to calm my suddenly furious Horse.

"I should have smothered him," I hissed at the night in French. "He does not own me because I once loved him. I do not owe him anything because I once loved him. I do not owe him anything because he is wounded or mad or... anything. I will not feel sorry for him!"

My matelot's arms were tight around me, like iron bands holding the slats of a barrel together. I could not breathe for how close he held me, and then I felt his teeth at my neck and I could not breathe for another reason.

My Horse pricked His ears and lashed His tail and craned His neck back to regard His dark companion: yes, He was hard against Us; grinding against Our arse slowly while His hands slid down Our arms to pin Ours to the rail. We would run. I felt the wind in Our teeth.

I sighed and lolled my head away to give Gaston better access to my neck. He bit and nibbled while he moved one of his hands to reach into his belt pouch. I used my free hand to unknot the cord for my breeches enough to push them over my hips. My naked manhood was trapped between my belly and the wood of the rail – wood worn smooth by hundreds of hands, so that it now seemed invitingly warm. We were within the light of the lantern kept near the whipstaff. I did not care. It was obvious he did not either when his slick hand eased between my arse cheeks. And then he was within me, and I was full of him, and he held me against the rail and ground into me with agonizing slowness such that I moaned and struggled feebly as each stroke rode his member over that little lump that plucked at every fiber of my being as if I were a harp. The rise and fall of the ship in the waves, the twinkling of the stars, the murmur and snores of men all about us, wove into a symphony until at last I could hold the crescendo at bay no longer, and with a hoarse cry I emptied my member and it spewed up and out to cover our entwined hands atop the rail. Gaston followed a moment later: thrusting hard and squeezing the air from my lungs and the last drops from my trapped cock.

"You are mine," he breathed throatily in my ear, and I chuckled because it tickled and it was so very true and I adored it.

Gaston rumbled amusement with me, and released my hands to make great show of wiping my jism upon my tunic – this action also tickled, and got me laughing with little breathless huffs. I struggled to pull my breeches up, and felt him doing the same, and then he stilled abruptly. Alarmed, I turned, and seeing nothing to our left except men playing cards, looked right, and found Alonso and Farley standing on the steps. Farley turned away abruptly with flame-cheeked embarrassment; but Alonso's eyes were black in the dim light, and his face smooth and unreadable. Then he too turned away and retreated to the hold; walking unsteadily, but with a stiff back and proud shoulders.

My matelot's head dropped onto my shoulder, and he sighed heavily.

"Good," I said, feeling triumphant. "Now he has seen what I offer you."

"But with his new impairment, will he remember you never offered it to him?" Gaston asked, sounding the reasonable physician once again.

"He had best," I said coldly, surprised at how deep my anger ran.

Gaston sat, and pulled me down beside him. We spoke no more of Alonso, and as I knew I would not stop thinking of it, I asked the men next to us if we could join their card game; and thus we whiled away the remainder of the night.

In the morning, Farley came to find us. At first he seemed reluctant to look at either of us, and me in particular – and he flushed a great deal. As he seemed he might be more comfortable with Gaston, I excused myself and went to the cabin.

I found Striker sitting with his back to the wall, crying. He quickly wiped his tears on his shoulder, as his remaining hand was in a sling. I looked about; we were alone: Pete was out seeing to their weapons.

I closed the door behind me and asked quietly, "Should I leave? Or do you desire company?"

He sighed. "Stay, though it has been nice to have a moment alone, but... I don't seem prone to put it to good use." He frowned. "Where is Gaston? I think it's time for another dose of the drug."

I let my lip quirk at that, and sat beside him. "To ease the pain of the body, or of the heart?"

"Both, damn it," he said irritably.

"It makes everything so very pleasant, does it not?"

"Aye," he said with a slow nod. "Much better than rum."

"You cannot float upon it for the rest of your life," I said affably.

He glared at me.

"It is far more precious than rum, and harder to obtain," I said. "And Gaston would not allow it even if it ran from springs on every island. He knows well its siren call, and he is quite stubborn about allowing only those in dire pain to hear it."

"I don't want to drown my sorrows in it," Striker said. "I just want the pain to stop."

I thought for a time, and he glared at me and began to appear smug. I nearly had the ranks of my argument formed when he spoke.

"You have no good reason other than it being evil or some such rubbish," he said.

"Well, Gaston says it will steal your very soul, and letting it go once you are quite inured to it can hurt worse than the pain you took it to avoid. But nay, beyond that, some things should hurt. Some things should be mourned. Limbs should be mourned, just like the passing of a fine friend or loved one. Hiding from the pain in a bottle of anything is dishonoring the person – or thing – lost. We should weep. We should let the grief pour from us and then... Well, then it is like a wound: once it is bled out and the pus drained, we should let it heal."

Striker dejectedly studied his lap. "You finished?"

"Aye."

"Go to Hell," he said flatly.

I chuckled. "I probably will, and I can only wish it will be for telling people things they do not wish to hear. There is probably a very pleasant room in Hell for those who commit that sin. I am sure the Devil loves us."

"Nay," Striker said with a thin but sincere smile. "He hates those like you. You tell truths, and the Devil hates the truth. He is a thing of lies."

"I can see that argument," I said. "But I was rather thinking He might adore us because we are ever causing trouble." I climbed to my hammock.

"I want to drown, Will," Striker said.

I peered over the edge at him. "Is it too hard to swim?"

He frowned and at last shook his head. "Not too hard, just hard."

"Do you have someplace you wish to go – some distant shore?"

"Aye," he said. "And I'm afraid I'll never reach it."

"Then float for a time until your strength returns."

"The drug helps with the floating," he said doggedly.

I snorted. "I will speak with Gaston."

"And say what?"

"I was going to tell him you did not need it anymore for your body's wounds."

Striker swore.

"Now I will suggest he wean you off it slowly," I said smugly.

"You bastard..." He sighed and smiled. "Thank you."

"And I will not tell Pete," I added.

He awarded me his middle finger in an age-old salute – though he could not extend the hand in the sling to give it great emphasis.

I chuckled, and rolled over to await Gaston. I was of a mind to tryst before sleeping. I realized he had been gone for some time, and I hoped Farley had not requested he come and speak to Alonso or some other damn fool thing.

I had just decided to go and fetch him when the door opened, and he entered with Pete and a strange look upon his face. Gaston quickly climbed to me.

"Hey," Striker said, "What about..."

"Wait," Gaston said. "I must speak to Will." Then he was atop me, smothering laughter in my shoulder.

"What?" I prompted, and poked him in the ribs.

He only swore quietly, implored the Gods for strength, and laughed harder. "I should not laugh. I should not laugh," he hissed at last.

I pushed his head away from my neck so that I could bring his mouth to mine. He responded readily to the kiss, returning it hungrily, and then he broke it off to laugh again.

"You must tell me," I said with amusement.

"Oh Gods," he sighed. He bit his lip and tried to speak, only to lose himself to mirth once again, and then he pressed his lips to my ear and blurted, "He enjoys spanking women."

"What? Farley?"

Gaston nodded frantically. "It began with serving girls, and then at the university he hired whores, and now he is somewhat..." More laughter. "Frustrated, as his wife finds no pleasure in it." More laughter. "He was curious about how I got you to be agreeable to being pinned as I did last night." This sobered him a little.

I frowned, trying to imagine what little the man could have seen. "That was tame for our... Horse play..." And then I wondered what Alonso had truly seen, and I felt a chill.

"Oui," Gaston said, and met my gaze seriously. "I did not speak of all we do, but Farley sensed your... submissiveness, and it fascinated and aroused him." At this, he frowned and sighed. "I told him it was merely you, the way you are; and that my wanting to... control you when you are thus is simply the way I am; and his wishing to do the same with women is the way he is; and that he should seek a mistress who desires such treatment. He despairs of finding one." This brought another smirk.

"So he is not aroused by punishing another, or..." I asked.

"Non, non, they must be willing." He was quite sober now. "He wants that feeling of mastery that only comes when another submits."

I sighed. "I have encountered a number of women who enjoyed that kind of play. I am sure he will find someone, though perhaps not easily on Jamaica."

Teresina had spanked her newer girls when they misbehaved. She occasionally asked Alonso or me to do the honor, as it added to the girl's humiliation and embarrassment. I had always refused, but Alonso had taken relish in it.

"What?" Gaston asked.

I shook my head. "If Farley saw all that in our trysting last night, I am wondering what Alonso saw."

He frowned at that, and then sighed and gave me a feral smile. "That you are mine."

"Always," I whispered.

He ran his hand down my body to my member, and toyed with it so that it rose to meet him happily. I closed my eyes and tried to push all other thoughts away, but I was haunted by the image of Alonso leering triumphantly at me, as he used to whenever I agreed to bed him after his patient seductions.

A throat was cleared below us. "You're not talking anymore," Striker said, and Pete chuckled.

Gaston swore and released me. I pulled him to my mouth and quickly whispered of my talk with Striker. He at last rolled onto his back and sighed with a slow nod. Then he climbed out of our hammock.

I lay there staring at the ceiling, which was just over a foot away. Wanting Alonso to see what I gave Gaston and not him was one thing, but I did not wish to think he fantasized about me, especially if those fantasies might ever involve my behaving with him as I did with Gaston. It took the life from my member.

When Gaston returned a few minutes later, I pulled him into my embrace and implored, "Make it all go away."

To my relief, he did.

I avoided Alonso and Farley for the rest of our voyage.

The little island of Ruba was filled with pleasant natives, Dutchmen we avoided, and Spanish horses. After convincing their owner we would not eat them – a problem he had apparently suffered in the past with damn-fool, starving pirates – Gaston and I were able to rent two animals and engage in a little riding, in which we found great pleasure. But sadly, our time there was all too short, and we were soon underway: to the nearby bay that led to Maracaibo Lake.

The mouth of the lake is rather like the waist of an hourglass: quite narrow in comparison to the bodies of water on either side of it, and filled with rivulets of sand in the form of long bars. As it would be very easy to see any ship making passage of it from either shore, and the Frenchman who had purportedly been here with L'Olonnais swore to Morgan he could find the correct channel even by moonlight – a thing the Bard swore about long and hard – it was decided we would enter the lake at night, so as to come upon the town of Maracaibo by surprise. Thus we anchored far from shore until the sun set, and then made our way into the channel.

When at last the order was given to weigh anchor, the Bard made slow work of it, and maneuvered us so that we could be last in the line of ships to attempt this "damn fool's errand of a disaster" as he dubbed it. Thus, though we could not have told shallow water from deep in the fickle moonlight, we clearly saw two of the smaller sloops stray a little off the *Lilly's* course and run aground. Then the *Mayflower* dropped anchor, and boats were exchanged between her and the *Lilly*. We were not at all surprised when a boat was sent to us with word that the fleet would anchor where it was and proceed at dawn's light. Thankfully the messenger was an experienced seaman, and laughed as hard at delivering this lovely news as the Bard did upon hearing it; so we did not think he would go and report our insolence to Morgan: we only hoped the damn fool would not hear our laughter carrying across the water.

Striker complained at being locked away from all the fun; and Pete helped him to the quarterdeck so he might sit with us. To avoid being seen from shore, we did not light our lanterns. Our men slept or sat about and talked quietly, over bottles of wine we had acquired on Ruba. The stars twinkled, the moon glowed: both making pretty patterns of the waves washing across the distant sand bars, and picking out details of the other ships, as if their masts or spars were touched with silver now and again.

I was gazing upon this peaceful tableau and listening to Striker tell of watching another captain ground on a sand bar off Campeche, when I noted something odd about the stars along the horizon of the high bank to one side of the passage. They were yellow, and large, and they moved upon occasion – and not in the manner of stars, even falling ones. These odd lights were well above the water, and I might well have thought them torches or lanterns, if the Spanish had a town here.

I nudged Gaston and pointed. He stiffened at the sight of them, and we sat like transfixed cats until Cudro asked, "What the Devil are you two looking at?" Gaston and I pointed as one, and then all our cabal sat and watched.

"It's a fortress," Striker said with drugged amusement.

"Nay," Cudro breathed. "They have no fort here. I've spoken with Frenchmen who were here. There's no fort." He sounded as if he were trying to convince himself.

"There was no fort," the Bard said. "But the damn bastards have had two bloody years to build one."

I could indeed see the hard straight lines of an edifice of man in the glimmer of moonlight now.

Cudro swore quietly and went forward to rouse men to take a canoe and go and alert the vessels closer to the purportedly non-existent fortress.

"We'll have to take it," Striker said with a tired sigh. "All that can, should rest. It will be a long day tomorrow."

I decided I truly despised long days of the type he spoke of.

"If they send men ashore to take it – from this ship – I should go," Gaston whispered to me in French.

I sighed and kissed his cheek. "Then let us rest."

Very few hours later, we began to put men ashore in the predawn light. The Spanish, of course, saw our vessels at about the same time we began to land men; and then the fort that was not supposed to exist began to attempt to bombard our ships. They apparently were well-stocked with large cannon and powder, but the Gods had smiled upon us in the night, and even the ships that had run aground were not within range of their guns. The fortress was intelligently situated such that no vessel would get past them and into the lake, though. One can never fault the Spanish on their ability to place and build fortresses.

It was midday before most of our men were ashore. As they knew we would attack by land, the Spanish had burned buildings about the apron of the fortress in order to provide a clear field of fire. Anticipating a long and bloody fight, Morgan held back until all the men who could be spared were ashore.

Gaston and I crossed on the last boat from the *Queen*. When we arrived, the sun was slanting west, and most of the buccaneer cohort had already advanced from our landing place to the fort. We followed until we found a good shady place, and there we sat with the other surgeons, awaiting the sounds of musket fire and grenades; the cannon bombardment of the sand bars had ceased a short time before. There was no sound of battle, though; and an hour or so later, a man ran back to tell us we had taken the fort without a shot being fired. The Spanish had abandoned it, but as a trap. They had left a slow match burning toward the powder cache; and it had been by sheer luck that a man in our vanguard had seen it, and pulled it away before the entire building exploded and rained down upon most of our men who had just triumphantly entered.

With relief in our hearts and upon our breath, we returned to the boat and the *Queen*, leaving others to tear down the defense walls, burn the gun carriages, throw the spiked cannon down into the sand to be buried, and take all the powder back to the ships. I thought it likely we would not have everyone back aboard until midnight. In the meantime, Gaston and I happily told Striker, the Bard, and all the rest what we had heard. We decided that Morgan's luck would most probably become the most famous thing about him.

As the town of Maracaibo now surely knew wild dogs were at their door, Morgan told all he wished to sail at dawn; and so we did. We did not attempt to liberate the two grounded vessels: we left a few aboard them, and took the rest of their men on the other ships and hurried to the town. We sailed in close to their wharfs, praying that they had no cannon here, and hoping to cover landing our men with our own guns if need be. All the panic and precaution proved unnecessary, though: our men found the place quite empty, thankfully without any traps.

I supposed I should thank the Gods for small favors, as now we would have weeks of sitting about, waiting for our enemies to show themselves while the buccaneers chased through the countryside seeking Spaniards to rob.

Eighty

Wherein We Confront Old Enemies

Within a day, all our company save those needed to man the ships had come ashore and taken houses around the grand square and surrounding streets. The church had been appropriated as a guardhouse, and sentries and patrols were arranged about the town. A hundred men were sent into the countryside to find Spaniards, and they returned the next evening with fifty mules laden with food, household items of value, weapons, and thirty prisoners: men, women and children. And so another hundred men were sent out the next day in a different direction, while the first male prisoners were questioned in the usual manner as to where they had hidden their valuables. If the torture was successful, a party of men was sent to retrieve the treasure, and so on.

It was likely this would continue for weeks, and we were initially reluctant to leave the ships; but Gaston and Cudro decided they could not very well haul our wounded to the ships, and thus a hospital had to be established in town. And so on the third day, we took a fine house just off the square, and began to fill the large lower rooms with cots and mattresses and the upper rooms with us, including Striker: he had not wished to be left behind, and Pete had thought it best that all those in danger be together. Unfortunately, there were not so many rooms that Gaston and I could have one to ourselves, so we shared with Pete and Striker.

Also unfortunately, the house had beds and not hammocks, but I was relieved to find them festooned with netting or lace to hold the insects at bay: the air teemed with biting things as soon as the sun began to sink, and I did not relish spending every day and night slathered in hog's fat. But though we would not be harassed by stings in bed, I did not think I would sleep well in the heat – especially not with the four of us sharing the bed, even though it was quite large. The lake sat in a bowl of distant, high mountains that were apparently too far away to send down a breeze to the shore at dusk or dawn. The air was heavy and fetid, and seemed thicker and hotter at night. It smelled much like Porto Bello had: full of rotting vegetation.

To add to my annoyance and unease, Alonso had moved to the house with us. I had thought it best he remain on the ship, where no one would mistake him for one of his former countrymen; but apparently he insisted on coming ashore. He moved well now; any trace of his being bedridden for a week had vanished. But according to Farley, Alonso's memory was still addled, and there was worry he might be having other difficulties of the mind as well – though Farley did not explain these to Gaston when the matter was discussed. Our fellow physician merely said he thought Alonso should be close at hand, where he might be observed.

As there was little else to do now, and much we thought we would be doing in the future, Gaston, Farley, and I left Pete with Striker, and Alonso to do what he would, and wandered out to search for treasures that men seeking things that sparkled would miss. We had found a small bottle of quinine in our house, and hoped to find more in the other wealthy homes. Thus we started with the house to our left and worked our way down the street, taking any medicinal substance we found. The buccaneers who were billeting in the dwellings questioned our taking things from them; but when we explained it was for the hospital, they quieted. Our intention was to make our way into the main square and find the apothecary, but we did not reach it on the first day, and returned home with arms and bags well-laden as the insects began to swarm.

We retired to the dining room to sort our finds, and found Alonso sitting at the head of the table with a bottle and goblet, his long legs propped on a chair: looking every bit the Lord's son he was, despite his rough tunic and breeches. He smiled at Farley, quickly passed his gaze over Gaston, and allowed it to linger on me.

I met his eyes levelly, and refused to look away even when he did not and the knowing smile he gave me churned my belly.

"You should make yourself useful, and assist us tomorrow," Farley was saying. "When we locate the apothecary, there will undoubtedly be much to carry."

"Oh, Alonso does not work," I said. "It is against his nature."

Alonso glanced away with irritation. "I apply myself dutifully to matters of import."

"To obtain things you want and serve your interests," I said.

"I would think surviving a tropical fever would be in his interest," Farley said pleasantly.

Alonso had returned his gaze to me. He smirked and spoke Castilian.

"Si, *Will*... I work very hard to take what I wish. I receive what I want in life as a result. God rewards those who take initiative."

I heard a personal insinuation in his words, and was not sure if it was my fancy or what he meant. I did not wish to consider his meaning either way, or converse with him at all; but his sentiment and arrogance reminded me of another conversation I had with him earlier this season.

"So," I asked in English, "tell me Alonso, did your God have you shot in the head by one of your former countrymen so you would not be forced to murder or torture your former countrymen – or did you arrange it yourself, in order to serve your needs of having a clear conscience in this endeavor?"

"Will?" Farley said with surprise.

Gaston snorted with amusement.

Anger flared in Alonso's deep brown eyes, and for a moment I saw his Horse again; and then he appeared hurt – quite convincingly.

I spoke Castilian. "Gods, you are such a liar; and to think I once admired you for it. It shames me." I turned away and went in search of food in the cookhouse.

Gaston found me there later. I was not sure how much time had passed. I had grown tired of being bitten while trying to gather food to eat, and lit the fire and damped the flu and sat in a cloud of smoke attempting to gather the reins on my racing thoughts. He sat next to me, and I handed him a piece of bread and cheese.

I gazed into his questioning eyes through tears that were not solely smoke-induced. "I loved him, and I loved Shane, and other men like them; in that they were liars to the very core of their beings. They were not creatures of light, but of the deepest shadows of the cave where they dwelled. They drew sustenance from the cave, from the shadows that other people call reality. They cannot exist without those shadows. They would have to become entirely different people if they stepped into the light and had to face their souls. And yet, I loved them and... I knew that about them even then, though I could not put names or order to it as I can now with our metaphors. I saw them as strong, that they could... manipulate all around them with such ease. That they towered above weaker men who... Men who lived within the realm of reality, which was a place I did not wish to dwell, or even dwell upon. I wanted the lies. I wanted the shadows where I too could hide.

"And I am ashamed; and I wonder at myself, and I wonder if perhaps I viewed them as being mad after a fashion for being as they were, and thus I wished to care for them. And that... I am not pleased with that thought. I wonder if... It is like the... It is like my feeling a man did not love me unless he was willing to take me even if he felt it was wrong. Somehow. It is... Like my feeling you will not love me – that you will leave me there alone on the side of the road if you do not need me. I feel... I have felt, that in order for any to love me, I must be needed. And I have felt that they needed me because they were mad... in that they dwelled in the shadows and could not see truth and... They must have been hiding from some great wound as I was.

"And now, it all appears so odd, looking back on it. I can see why I did what I did, ran where I ran, but it is as if it happened to another and... I want no part of it. Yet, I know denying it is only a thing of shadows and madness, too."

His eyes were as teary as mine, and yet he brushed my tears away gently with his thumb and allowed his to roll down his cheeks.

"I will always need you," he whispered. "I will always want you. I will always love you. And I know you know that. You have led me from darkness. You won once; do not mourn those who could not follow you, who could not see you, who could not love you enough to overcome their fear."

His words swelled my heart, but even so I considered them carefully. Was I mourning? Was this as I had told Striker, that some things must be mourned? And what was I mourning now: my long-lost innocence, or that some souls, the souls of those I once loved, were truly lost? And did I believe that any soul could be truly lost: that any man could not step beyond the cave into truth?

Yes – and that *yes* came from a position of hubris so profound it brought mirth to my lips. They could not be saved unless someone like me loved them, and I could not love them all or long enough to save them when they would not return my love.

Gaston raised a curious eyebrow at my bark of laughter.

"They were too blind to love me enough to allow me to save them," I said.

He did not regard me with admonishment or incredulity: he simply nodded.

"That seems too wrong a thing to say," I whispered. "It is such..."

He silenced me with a kiss, and I quashed my protest. I should trust him. He was truth.

Alonso did accompany us the next day, and he stayed well clear of me; and we did locate the apothecary, and quinine – and once I saw the price marked upon the label, I was pleased we were robbing the place. And though it was a good-sized bottle, it would not be one-tenth of what we needed if men began to sicken in the numbers they had at Porto Bello. So we took all we could, and vowed to continue searching the next day.

That evening, Cudro and Ash arrived. They had been on one of the sorties to the plantations to locate prisoners and valuables. Cudro appeared concerned when he entered, and upon seeing our pile of goods upon the table, he became alarmed.

"Good God, if any think you're hoarding..."

"It is all medicinal," I said. "Men should bloody well not clamor to have their share of it. And if by some act of divine providence we do not need it, then, aye, it can be shared out with all the rest."

"Gaston and Farley should probably meet with the other surgeons about it, then," he said. He sighed. "We don't need trouble. There is another matter. I have been told that you and Pete are to go on the next sortie. Morgan has instructed that all men not injured or surgeons are to go on the raiding parties."

My anger was fast to rise. "We were mentioned by name?"

Cudro sighed again. "Aye and nay. Bradley is in charge of assembling the sorties, but he has passed much of the matter on to the quartermasters for each ship. Boller came to me as soon as I returned. He's been afraid to come and speak to you of it," he chided.

I snorted. "So Bradley mentioned us?"

"Nay; I don't know," he sighed again. "Boller mentioned the two of you by name, and said…" He held up his hand to keep me silent. "Hastings told him that you two had been discussed, and it had been noted you were staying here and not raiding. That bastard Hastings is Bradley's quartermaster; but I don't know, and Boller sure as the Devil doesn't know, if Hastings was told by Bradley to mention you, or if Morgan mentioned you to Bradley. I think it's likely that Hastings is up to deviltry. And I was going to go and ask Bradley of it, but he's out leading a party recovering treasure."

"Then let us ask Morgan," I said, and walked toward the door.

"Nay, Will," Cudro said. "I will speak to him."

"Nay," I said, resolved. "He already dislikes me."

"All the more reason then!" Cudro rumbled.

"Nay! If Morgan is party to our doom, then he had best say it and we will be done with it!" I walked out into the night, Gaston thankfully at my heels.

"Will?" he queried with some humor as we entered the square. "Are you well?"

I grinned at him. "I do not know. Should I stop?"

"Non, I will follow where you lead."

That steadied me, though I was not sure how unsure my footing had been before. He was with me, and we were one; and thus, though I boiled with anger, I must watch myself.

We found Morgan holding court in the town hall. He was sitting on a table, bottle in hand, listening to some man's tale when we entered; and at first he did not see us. Then we were beside him, and he peered at me with surprise.

"Might I have a word with you?" I asked. "In private."

There were mutters of concern from the closest men, but Morgan stood and followed me as I snatched up a lamp and led him to the rear doorway. When we reached it, Morgan glanced back at his bodyguards and Gaston.

"If they don't go in, neither does he."

I shrugged, and glanced at Gaston, who smiled and stepped back. I could well be about to do a thing that could get us killed, but he trusted me. I smiled grimly as Morgan closed the door behind us.

We were in an office with a great desk along one wall and a table near the other. I set the lamp on the corner of the table, and we stood near the middle of the room, adjusting our positions until the light shone on both our faces.

"What is amiss?" Morgan asked seriously.

I was surprised at his lack of bombast, and then suspicious of it. Still, I vowed to give him the benefit of doubt as to his guilt in the matter.

"You know of the bounty my father has placed upon Gaston and Striker, do you not?"

He did not blink. "Doesn't everyone? Has someone tried to collect it?"

I snorted. "Not yet, or that we have learned of it. However, our captain, Cudro, was told tonight that Pete and I are to abandon our matelots here in town and go on one of the raiding parties."

"By who?" he asked.

"So you gave no order naming us?" I asked.

"Never," he sighed and grinned, and showed how much rum he had consumed. "You and that golden god are two of the last damn people I wish to cross." He frowned. "And Cudro is your man as much as anyone's. So who told him?"

I believed him. I sighed and moved to lean against the wall with unexpected relief. Morgan offered me the bottle with a wry grin, and I took it and a long pull. After I wiped my mouth, I said, "Bradley's quartermaster, Hastings, told our quartermaster, Boller, that our lack of participation had been noted, and that you had laid edict that all must participate unless they were surgeons or injured."

Morgan shrugged. "I did say that. I did not mean you two in particular. I will call on you to render your services if I need a thing translated prettily, and Pete… Striker needs him." He chuckled. "You know, I have given great thought to our little talk on the beach that day. There are many people I don't want as enemies." His humor flowed away, and he regarded me speculatively, but without rancor. "You do not wish to lead men?"

"Nay," I said and took another pull before returning the bottle to him. "Is that why you do this, to lead men?"

He snorted, but his words were serious. "I wish for fame and glory. One must lead men and have wealth and win battles to have those things." He frowned at me again. "And those are things you do not seem to want."

"Nay, I do not," I said with a shrug. "There are times when I feel compelled to assist my fellow man, but I have found it is often more effort than it is worth, because the men most in need of assistance often do not wish to be assisted, or even realize they need assistance."

"So why are you ever challenging me?" he asked.

"Because I feel you lead men astray – or in directions not in their best interests, but in yours."

He laughed. "Everyone does that, you fool."

I laughed with him. "I know. It does not mean I must like it."

He nodded thoughtfully. "I suppose not." He studied me again. "So you are truly no threat to me. You do not covet my position?"

"Nay," I said.

"Good." He sighed and turned to me again with his head cocked. "But what of Striker? He is well-liked, and he could lead the men if he just put himself to it. I keep wondering what he is waiting for."

I sighed. "I do not feel he is as ambitious as you. Aye, he wishes for fame and glory, but he does not entertain grandiose plans on the scale of yours. And... He has Pete, who sees grandiose plans and ambitions as a great deal of work."

"Ah," Morgan said as if it were a revelation. "I did not wish for any harm to come to him, but..." He shrugged. "I have considered that it might be in my best interests if he did not live." His statement was nonchalant, but his speculative gaze was quickly upon me in its wake.

I shrugged. "You think I have not met men who think as you do before?"

He chuckled and looked away. "Nay, I think you have, and I think you killed them."

I laughed. "Aye, when they crossed me."

"Ah-ha," he said with a smile, and gestured at me with the bottle. "That is why I have given great thought to crossing you of late. There was a time when I would not have, because of your father; but now I know I would have to have you killed first before I did a thing that angered you, and I see no need to stoop to that."

"I am grateful to hear it," I said with a grin. "You have far more men at your disposal than I could fend off."

"True that," he said without irony. "So, as of yet, neither of us want the other dead. And yet there are those among our company who do want you or yours dead."

"Aye. Can you offer aid?"

He frowned at me. "Why did you come here if you know men are hunting you?"

"To draw them out, far from the women and children."

"Ah, very good." But then he was frowning again and he sighed as he considered the bottle before setting it aside. "What aid could I offer that would not impede that plan? If I say that any man of our company harming another for a bounty will be hung, then..."

"Our quarry will hide until we return home, aye," I said with regret.

He nodded. "I will not question your having to kill a man in the name of defending your man or Striker, though. If you catch one making the attempt, I can speak afterwards of knowing of it. And if you find one you suspect before he shows his hand, like this man Hastings, you have my leave to duel him."

"Thank you," I said solemnly. "Having you on our side will make the matter much easier."

He met my gaze. "Do not argue with me so much in front of the men as you have in the past."

"All right, I will not. May I argue with you privately?"

He laughed. "Aye." He sobered. "Your counsel has proven useful."

"I am glad for that. Allow me to give some now. Gaston and Farley, who are the only surgeons among us trained as physicians, fear that we will see the swamp fever, malaria, as we did at Porto Bello. This place is just as fetid: the air is very bad. We have been collecting medical supplies from the Spanish apothecary and houses. If anyone makes note that we are hoarding booty; that is what that is about. We will do all we can to help those afflicted if the illness strikes, but it would be best if we remained here as short a time as possible – though I know damn well that most of the men here would rather risk death than go home without gold."

"Thank you for that information," he said with a frown. "Tell me if there is anything else we can do if it begins to strike."

I nodded and offered my hand.

He clasped it firmly. "I am pleased we have reached this understanding."

"As am I."

We walked smiling from the room and were met by a dozen curious faces. Gaston fell into step beside me as I headed to the door.

Morgan returned to the table. "It was nothing – just the damn physicians worrying about medical supplies. They put such import on everything, like we're all going to contract the plague."

I was chuckling as we walked into the street. I quickly relayed all to Gaston.

"Do you trust him?" he asked. "You saw his eyes; I did not."

"Enough," I said, "for now."

"I thought you might kill him," he said casually.

"With you hostage outside the door in a room of armed men?" I chided.

"I thought you might have expected me to do something... inspiring. I could have taken the two closest and joined you in the room. I saw a window past your shoulder when you entered."

I laughed. "I do not doubt you could have inspired the room of them, much less me. And then what would we have done?"

"Seen a great deal of this damn swamp as we headed for those mountains," he said thoughtfully.

"I love you too much to ask so much in the name of my temper."

He was still very serious, and I stopped to gaze at him.

"I remembered what you must feel when you see my Horse take the bit in its teeth," he said.

"Was I so very mad as all that?" I asked.

He shook his head, frowning in thought. "Non, it is as if I am expecting you to be. It is..." he sighed and smiled ruefully. "As if I am expecting one of us to be, and I feel quite well."

"Can we not both be sane at the same time?" I asked.

We gazed at one another, and the humor found our eyes and then our mouths, and we laughed. We embraced until it passed.

He whispered. "We are so very far from... where we once were."

"Oui," I said. "I am so very proud of us."

"Oui," he sighed, and kissed me gently.

Cudro, Ash, Alonso, Farley, Pete, and even Striker were at the dining table arguing when we entered.

"All is well!" I proclaimed. "It was Hastings. I have Morgan's leave to duel him if I can. And if we should kill anyone attempting to murder one of us, he has said he will support it."

"How in God's name did you manage that?" Cudro asked sincerely.

I did not know what I should say; and looking at them, there was much I realized I should not relay of that conversation. "He is afraid of Pete."

The others laughed uproariously; even Alonso. But Pete regarded me as if I were full of shite.

"Nay, truly," I told Pete. "And me."

This brought a smile to the Golden One's lips. "ThatMakesMoreSense."

"But truly, he does not wish to cross you, either," I added. "Now, since you are all down here, Gaston and I are going to use the bed. Alone."

"For what?" Striker teased.

Gaston regarded him seriously. "It is my birthday, and I prefer to lie on a soft mattress when Will impales me with his cock."

Cudro spit his wine across the table. I did not bother to see the rest of their reactions, or even wish to know Farley's and Alonso's.

I had, once again, been unaware of the date – and additionally, forgotten the day of Gaston's birth: an oversight for which I was immediately rueful. But the second part of his utterance drove even that from my heart. I wanted to think of nothing but doing the thing of which my matelot had spoken. And so I thought of nothing except how best to show my man how very pleased I was the Gods had seen fit to have him born on this day twenty-nine years ago.

It was a very fine night. We stormed Heaven with entwined and straining limbs, and him urging me ever upward with happy grunts and moans while I remembered how joyously good it was to be inside him.

In the morning, I was still in a fine mood, even when I learned that Hastings had gone on the day's sortie. We found it interesting that he had attempted to arrange to go somewhere with Pete and me; and wondered if he thought to kill one of us first, or if he had another who was to strike while we were away. I did not think Hastings was the type to have an accomplice, or to be one, for that matter. We stayed in the house, anyway.

The next day, we learned Hastings had returned; and leaving a dozen of the *Queen's* most loyal and seasoned buccaneers with Cudro and Striker – who whined pitifully that he could not join us – Pete, Gaston, and I went in search of the eye-patch wearing quartermaster of the *Mayflower*. We found him in the town square assisting with the torture of the prisoners. He feigned disinterest in our arrival, and then surprise when I caught his eye and asked to speak to him.

"What can I do for you, good sir?" he called loudly enough for most of the square to hear. And he needed to call out, as he did not seem inclined to approach us.

He was wearing his patch on the left, and I wondered if he truly had a bad eye, or whether it was as Gaston and Striker once suggested, and Hastings moved the patch from side to side to provide for seeing in darkness or bright light.

"You can meet me on the field," I called back jovially.

Hastings feigned astonishment for our audience; but even at twenty paces, I saw his eye narrow for a moment with sincere surprise. "Whatever for?"

"I will see you dead before I will allow you to collect any bounty on Gaston or Striker," I said pleasantly. I would have been astounded if he had accepted my challenge.

The square began to buzz with mutterings, and men moved from the shade to stand closer and listen.

"Are you mad?" Hastings asked. "What are you speaking of? I don't know of any bounty."

I grinned. "Then the men of the *Mayflower* have had the unfortunate judgment to elect a deaf and daft quartermaster." I looked around at the crowd. "How many of you have heard there is a bounty on Striker's and my matelot's heads?"

Amidst laughter, nearly every hand in the square raised.

"How many think you can do it?" I called out.

There was more laughter, much head shaking, and no hands raised – though several fellows pushed their friends' arms up, for which they received hearty curses and punches from those so used.

"Why would you think I would?" Hastings asked with sincere curiosity and speculation as he walked closer.

"Because you enjoy killing," I said.

"There are more than enough Spaniards for that," he said slyly.

"Aye, but I think you are the kind of man who enjoys killing those who do not expect it. You take pleasure in murder."

For a moment he regarded me with sincere astonishment and wonder, and then the mask of feigned innocence and indignation returned. "You're a damn fool!"

"Then prove me wrong," I said.

He shook his head adamantly. "I'm no fool. I know of your prowess. I'll not waste my life over some damned allegation. Say what you will. Think what you will. Slander my name. I don't care. I have no quarrel with you."

I grinned at him. "Ah, but you do. You can own it or not as you choose. Just remember what I said. I will see you dead."

He shook his head and walked away to return to what he was doing, ignoring the men making catcalls and daring him to take my challenge.

I led Gaston and Pete back to the house we had appropriated.

"Well?" Striker asked.

I snorted. "He knows we know. And now all the Brethren here know he knows, and we know, and…" I shrugged. "That is all I sought to achieve this day. Now we will see what he does next."

We continued our daily routine as if nothing had occurred. Two days after my confrontation with Hastings, we found the town physician's house. We were overjoyed, as it contained a treasure trove of medicines: more than the apothecary had held. We took the valuable quinine and the flower pods necessary for laudanum back to our house, choosing to inventory the rest of the materials later in case we had need of them.

Thus, when our bedmates decided Striker was well enough to engage in carnal activities and they wished to have the room, Gaston and I were pleased we had a place to which we could retreat and a task to occupy us and keep us awake – as we dared not sleep alone in some other house with no one to watch over us. So we left our wolves to their pleasures, slipped away from the party over which Cudro was presiding downstairs, and carefully returned to the physician's house by the light of the moon. We justified our risk as necessary to flush out Hastings or any other would-be assassin; sitting in the light with our friends was surely not going to accomplish it.

Once at the physician's house, we shuttered the windows, lit a lamp, found paper and ink, and began to arrange and list the herbs and concoctions Gaston felt we might need. I was actually not surprised to hear the noise of the back latch a little later. My matelot had heard it as well, and we turned the lamp very low and left it in the office as we padded through the doorway to the back room: the surgery. We crouched in darkness and saw the door open, but we did not see anyone enter before it closed again. As we were behind the surgery table, which had drawers beneath it, I thought it likely someone had entered, but they were keeping themselves as close to the floor as we were. A moment later my suspicion was confirmed: we heard the strike of a flint, and the weak light of a candle glowed beyond the table.

We each had a pistol and knife, and Gaston motioned left and I went right, and we came around the table at the same time, and found a young Spanish boy who squawked in honest fright at the sight of us. Gaston dropped his weapons and dove atop the lad before he could escape. Much struggling and cursing ensued, until the boy finally realized he would not escape us and another form of defiance was in order.

"I will tell you English dogs nothing!" he spat.

"I would find concern in that if I had asked you a question," I said in Castilian, which surprised him greatly.

He closed his mouth tightly and regarded me with eyes full of bravado. Now that he was still, I judged him to be young, but not a babe: perhaps seven or eight years of age. While Gaston held him pinned, I searched his pockets and found no real weapons, only a small knife like boys will carry and the flint and tinder. He was clutching something in his hand, though; and after prying it open, I found a note. It contained one word, apparently a Latin name; and I showed it to Gaston, and he frowned.

"It is a concoction sometimes used to treat the flux by balancing the humors," Gaston said. "It is useless."

I sighed and looked back at the boy. "You have the flux?"

His eyes widened, but he clamped his jaws even harder.

"Tell him I can give him something better to treat the flux," Gaston said.

"This man is a physician," I explained, to which I received a look of vibrant incredulity. I sighed. "He can give you medicine for the flux. You can use it yourself if you ail, or take it to whomever needs it and sent you here."

"You lie," the boy hissed.

I crossed myself like a good Christian and said, "As God is my witness." Thankfully Gaston did not roll his eyes.

The boy now appeared quite confused. "Why? Why would you do this?"

Gaston sighed. "Tell him I have taken an oath to God to harm none with my medical knowledge."

As he had expressed such sentiments to me before, I did not ask him about the *oath to God* part of the statement. I translated it for the boy.

The child now glared suspiciously at me.

"I serve him," I added, and indicated Gaston.

Our prisoner reverted to confusion, but at least this bout of it loosened his tongue. "If you lie, it will not matter."

"Why?" I asked kindly.

"She will die without the medicine if I cannot bring it. And if you give me a poison, she will die. And if you find her, she will die."

"Your mother?" I guessed, not liking his fatalistic reasoning, but not having a lever to dislodge it as of yet.

"No, my sister."

"All right, well, we will not follow you, so we will not find her. We will not give you a poison, but you will have to trust in God concerning that; and she might well die if you do not bring her something. So we will give you medicine, and you will sneak out of town the way you entered, and may God grant you speed in saving your sister."

With that, I motioned for Gaston to release him.

The boy sat where he was as Gaston went and fished around in drawers and cupboards, and mixed various substances in two separate bowls, which he then poured into two bags: one small, the other large. Then he had me instruct the boy that the small bag must be steeped in boiling water and drunk first; and that it would serve to clean away all the bad and evil humors in her bowels. And then the second, larger bag was to be steeped in truly large quantities of boiled water and taken every hour until the bag was empty. The boy seemed to understand my instructions, and I had him repeat them several times. Then we shooed him out the door.

"What did you give him?" I asked when we were sure the boy was gone. "The first concoction sounds much like Michaels' gypsy remedy."

"It was," he sighed. "The second was some of those tea leaves from the orient mixed with sugar. I thought she would not consume enough water without it being made medicinal in some fashion."

I chuckled. "You are a truly fine physician."

"And liar," he said with a troubled frown.

"My love, you lie for the good of them. I will never fault you for that."

We returned to our task of arranging vials and pots and listing and re-labeling them. Unlike the physician in Puerto Principe, this man's handwriting was quite neat: Gaston simply did not like the names given to many of the substances, preferring to use others with which he was more familiar.

We heard the latch of the back door again several hours later, as we were beginning to tire. We did as we had before, and found the boy again. He did not panic at the sight of us this time.

"My mother wishes for me to thank you," he said solemnly. "My father died of the flux, and she is very scared she will lose us, too."

"When did your father die?" I asked kindly.

"Many years ago, when I was a baby," he said. "We have all been well since, but then we went to hide, and my sisters are becoming ill."

"You are the youngest, then?" I asked.

"Si, but I am the only boy," he said proudly.

"Ah, how many sisters?"

"Four."

Knowing what Gaston would wish to know when I relayed the boy's words, I asked, "What are you drinking at the hiding place?"

"Water from the well." He wrinkled his nose. "But it is an old well. Why?"

I told Gaston what he had said, and my matelot told me what I already knew they should be told; but it was best if the boy thought I translated the physician's words and not the other way around.

"You must boil the water from the old well before drinking it," I said.

Gaston fetched more of the tea leaves and gave it to him.

"Put that in it: you can sweeten it with sugar or honey," I said.

"Will you be here if more is needed?" the boy asked.

I sighed. "No, we are living at a house..." I described the location and look of our current dwelling as best I could; and told him that he should lurk about outside until he saw one of us, to make sure it was the correct house before speaking to anyone; and that those living there with us would not harm him, either, but he should trust none of our fellow pirates. He seemed confused by this, but he agreed to abide by it before I shooed him back out the door.

After he was gone, we doused our lamp and slipped out the front door, and returned to our house. We were quiet as we went, but Gaston pulled me to sit with him on a cot in the parlor once we were safely home.

"I truly wish to practice medicine," he said.

"Oui," I said.

"Non, not... like here. I wish to have an office and a hospital, like Doucette had, and serve some town or village."

"Truly? You want to tend fat men with gout?"

He nodded thoughtfully. "I might be able to heal people with gout – if they would listen to me, which they might if I had an office and I wore fine clothes."

"All right," I said, though I was appalled at the thought of having to cater to people's expectations as much as I imagined such an existence would require.

"What do you find wrong with it?" he asked with concern.

"Town physicians are expected to be respectable, and have a wife and children – which you will have – and not have a matelot."

"Oui, I suppose it would be much as we would have to live in France," he said sadly. Then he nodded and took my hand. "Maybe I will have to become an unrespectable physician."

"But then they would not listen to you as you would want them to," I said. I shook my head. "I am sorry, my love, we will find some way to..."

His fingers were on my lips. "Oui. We will find some way. And you are more important."

I gently pulled his hand away and kissed the back of it. "We do face the same problem as Striker and Pete, do we not?"

"Non," he said quickly. "We talk. It makes ours smaller."

We talked no more of it, choosing instead to curl together on the cot and sleep. I was still troubled, though; and I dreamed of chasing him down the road, but he was always just out of reach.

We woke to light streaming through the front shutters and yelling from the back room. It was a girl's voice, or perhaps a child's, and it was all invocations to saints and the Mother Mary in Castilian. Gaston and I hurried in and found Farley trying in vain to quiet the small girl who knelt in prayer upon the floor.

"Child, child!" I called as I knelt before her. "Who are you?"

She opened her tear-filled eyes and peered at me for but a moment before gasping and looking about wildly until she spotted Gaston. "You are the green-eyed physician and the blue-eyed servant. I have found you! Miguel said to come here. He said to run here because they have found us and you might help us."

"Miguel? Your younger brother? You have a sister with the flux?" I asked quickly.

"Si, si."

"And one of the pirates has found your hiding place?"

"Si, si. I saw him following Miguel when he returned with the medicine. I was fetching water from the well, and it was dark, but Miguel came, and then I saw the white face in the trees. Then he was gone. I told Miguel, and he said he must stay because he is the man of the house, but he told me how to come here. He said to beg you." She held up her prayer-locked hands plaintively, her eyes pleading. "Please, please, señor. Please..."

"No need for that," I assured her. "We will do what we can. You will need to lead us to your family's hiding place."

"Si, si."

I turned and explained to Gaston and Farley, and now Pete and Alonso, and Cramer and Dudley, a trusted pair of matelots and musketeers from the *Queen* who had been sleeping in the house.

"TheyTake'EmToTheChurch," Pete said as if there were little to be done.

"I am more concerned with what will occur before they reach the church," I said. "It is a mother and three adolescent girls."

Alonso swore, and Pete grimaced. Gaston was gathering our weapons and his medical bag.

"ItCouldBeATrap," Pete said.

"Aye," I said. "That is why we will be careful." It was more bravado than I cared to admit. But he had not seen the boy earlier. Yet, perhaps we were being naïve. "Are the Spanish known for sending their daughters as bait?"

"Nay," Pete said and glared at me. "ButWhoeverFound'EmKnowsThe BoyTalkedTaYou."

I cursed. "So you are not worried about the Spanish, but Brethren bounty hunters."

"Aye," he snapped.

Gaston leaned against the door, obviously torn. The girl looked from one of us to the other, and proffered her clasped hands and more invocations to the saints that we should hurry.

"You should not go," I told Gaston in French. "I will go: they do not want me."

"They might not care," he said. "You die, I die."

I looked from him to the pleading girl.

Gaston opened the door and glared back at Pete. "You are correct. It probably is a trap. But I will not sit here if I can save... someone."

"But we are here to rob them, and..." Farley said with a frown.

"Aye, rob, not rape," I said, and hefted my musket. "Even Morgan has said he does not wish for that to happen. If they are brought directly to the church, then there is no problem."

"I will come with you," Alonso said.

"Us, too," the men from the *Queen* said.

Pete stood resolute with his arms crossed and disapproval on his face. We left him there with Farley. The five of us followed the little girl, whose name was Consuelo, out of town and along a small rutted road into the swamp for at least a league. Gaston, Cramer, and Dudley urged us to stop often while they checked about for signs of an ambush, and it was left to me to quiet and calm the girl at these intervals.

While sitting in the bushes waiting, she whispered to me that she had seen angels and devils coming to her family in a dream, and that according to Miguel and her mother, we were angels. Her family seemed to possess the fatalism and abiding trust in God of the truly faithful. I found it disturbing.

At last we reached their hiding place in the stone-walled cellar of a house that had burned on some long-overgrown plantation. We saw no one else, and the men checked about quite thoroughly. We heard nothing, either. There was a stillness to the air that raised the hair on my neck. It was judged that Gaston or I should not enter first, so Dudley and Cramer crept to the slanted door and opened it from the side before peering in, each with two pistols cocked and aimed. Cramer stood very still, but Dudley stepped back and dropped a pistol to place his hand over his mouth.

"Keep the girl away!" Dudley gasped when he had apparently controlled his urge to retch.

Alonso was in the doorway next, and he too turned away for a moment before squaring his shoulders and stepping inside with his pistols drawn. He returned a moment later.

"Whoever did this is gone," he said quietly in English.

"Did what?" I asked. The girl crouched beside me with big concerned eyes.

"They be dead, all dead," Cramer said from the doorway. "It ain't pretty."

Gaston ran to the door and collapsed to his knees with a hoarse cry.

I pulled the girl to Dudley by her wrist and crammed her hand into his, and then pushed him back the way I had come. Then I was in the doorway with Gaston.

They were indeed all dead. The boy, Miguel, had been shot in the doorway, his body left to lie where it fell. The mother had likewise been simply shot: her heavy body was crumpled in the corner. But Consuelo and Miguel's three sisters had been bound and raped before being repeatedly stabbed. Their bodies were lined up along the mattresses at the wall.

"Why would any o' ours do this?" Cramer asked. "What were they thinkin'?"

"To make us angry," I said.

I knelt beside Gaston and pulled his gaze from the carnage. His eyes were so vastly sad that they tore at my heart, but I saw no madness in them.

"Either the boy was simply followed, and it has nothing to do with us, and some of our company is capable of doing this for a night's amusement, or... Someone has done this to make us mad with anger so we will trip and fall," I said.

"I am not mad," Gaston said with an understanding nod. "I am... It beckons. I feel the urge to... set them to rest. But I will not."

I nodded with relief. I did not wish for him to rearrange these bodies to honor them, any more than I wished for him to go on a rampage to avenge them.

He pulled himself up and led me to little Consuelo, who was pleading with Dudley to tell her what was wrong even though he spoke no Castilian.

"I must know." Gaston looked to me. "Ask her if she can describe the man she saw in the trees."

I translated his question, and she nodded distractedly and asked, "Where is my mother?"

"She is gone," I said simply. "She is not here."

She regarded me as if she knew I lied, and glanced at the other men around us for confirmation of her belief.

"I told her her mother is gone, that she is no longer here," I told them in English. There were nods all around.

I turned back to her. "Now, we are going back to town and to the church, where the nuns will help you find your mother. But first, we need to know about the man you saw."

She described a man that could have been nearly any of us: a white face, a dark kerchief, big pale eyes, and a canvas tunic.

"If you saw him, would you recognize him?" I asked.

She nodded solemnly. I took her hand and started walking back the way we had come. The others followed. I supposed we should bury the dead, or perhaps burn the remains of the structure around them, but I felt a small glimmer of hope that perhaps those bodies would anger others into punishing the guilty party appropriately. Merely saying someone had raped and murdered three girls and shot two others was a trivial thing when they were torturing men in the town square; but showing what someone did here – that it was not for money, but rather for sport – might incite them in the name of human decency.

Then I wondered who had done it. She had not described Hastings, at least not unless he had removed his eye patch altogether. And then I wondered how someone had done it so quickly. I supposed I did not know how long we slept, after last seeing her brother and returning to the hospital. It might have taken the girl hours to find our house; or perhaps she waited until dawn before approaching it. Still, whoever had done this thing had done it quickly, or there had been several of them. But why bind them and shoot the mother and boy, if there had been several men about to manage prisoners? Nay, it had been one man, and he had worked with great speed to insure all had been raped and killed and he had departed, prior to our arrival. I tried to wonder at that, to consider other options; but unless the perpetrator knew the girl was going to us, there was no reason for him to hurry at all. Thus my first conclusion seemed correct: this had been done to anger us and us alone. He must have watched the boy send his sister to us. He must have seen the boy come and go from the physician's house. I felt very cold.

I shared my suppositions with the others. All agreed with my assessment. Gaston came and took my hand. I was pleased he appeared so calm when he met my gaze, as I was unsure of my footing. I felt someone had thrown blood before us to make the road slick.

And so we arrived in Maracaibo, me with a small dark-haired girl clutching one hand, my matelot clutching the other, and three sad men in our wake. I instructed Consuelo to look upon the men we passed as we entered the square, but then I realized that whoever had done it was likely asleep now: as it was now only mid-morning and they had not slept during the night.

And then she stopped and pointed at a man emerging from the courthouse. With her hair disheveled in a black cloud about her shoulders, her small face in an expression of sternness beyond her years, and her finger extended like an arrow, she looked like an angel of judgment as depicted in the windows of a cathedral.

I stopped with her and stared at the accused. I did not know him. He was a large and very pale man with slightly stooped shoulders and a moon of a face. He was standing next to Morgan, Bradley, and Norman. I began to lead her toward them, but she held back, suddenly afraid.

Gaston and the others had seen who she accused. My matelot was in motion before I could even shout. He reached the man, and in a flurry of movement, pounded him into the wall and down to the ground, all the while shouting curses in French. Then he was borne under by a mob of men attempting to restrain him. I howled and tried to reach him, but I too was restrained. Thankfully Morgan began some yelling of his own, and Gaston and I were carried inside the courthouse.

My matelot had ceased to struggle, and now stood stiff and livid with rage in the hands of those holding him. I met his gaze and found him angry, but not mad.

The moon-faced man, now very bloody, was howling that Gaston was a madman.

Morgan was casting about frantically.

"That bastard murdered the little girl's family," I roared. "Her mother and little brother were shot in cold blood, and her sisters were raped and stabbed more times than was necessary to kill them."

"I never!" the man yelled with horror.

Morgan yelled at the men holding me. "Release him!" Then he roared the same to those holding Gaston. Then his eyes were boring into mine. "What the Devil is going on? That man!" He pointed at the accused. "Came here this morning and accused you and your matelot of allowing Spaniards to escape and possibly even offering them succor."

It was not a good thing to be charged with, and it was also true. I lied. "We found the boy in the physician's house seeking medicine. We gave him some in the hope we could gain his trust and thus learn where his family was hidden and gain their gold for the common treasure. Sometimes sugar accomplishes more than torture," I growled.

"You let him go!" the accused countered. "You did not follow him."

"How would you know unless you were spying upon us?" I roared back.

He shut his mouth at that, and took a step back. "I were just about...

And I thought it funny there were a lamp lit in that house."

I was not convinced, and I could see Morgan did not appear to be, either.

"What did he tell you earlier?" I asked Morgan.

He made a disgruntled sound and said, "We did not ask. We thought we would address the particulars once we had a chance to gather all the parties."

"He followed the boy we gave the medicine to," I said. "The boy's sister saw him. The boy realized they had been found, and he thought for them to surrender to us, as we had been kind, and not to another; and so he sent his sister to lead us to them. When we arrived, we found the family dead: raped and murdered."

Hard eyes were upon the accused man now.

"I did not," he said with quite convincing fear. "I saw where he went. I did not know how many might be hidin' in there, so I ran back and told... I told... I didn't hurt no one." Then his fear made him wily. "How do we know your mad matelot not done it? He just attacked me. Everyone know he be mad. And what you say is what a madman would do. I'm an honest man." That part was not convincing.

Gaston growled, but he did not move. He stood with his arms tightly crossed and murder upon his face, but the hard glitter of his Horse at His worst was still absent from his eyes.

"There are a number of matters to be considered here," Morgan said.

"Only two," Bradley said with a glare at me. I noted with a chill along my spine that he had been standing next to Hastings. I had seen him conversing quietly with someone, but in the confusion I had not realized the other man to be his one-eyed quartermaster.

"There is nothing in the articles to address the killing of Spaniards," Bradley said. "Be they man, woman, or child. And though you discourage rape," he said to Morgan, "the dead cannot say as to whether or not it was willing."

"You bastard!" I spat.

Morgan waved me to silence.

"So according to the articles we all have agreed to, there are only two charges we need consider here," Bradley continued, as if he were the voice of reason in the name of necessity. "One, the hoarding of gold or valuables by any member of the Brethren. If you sought to gather this family's gold for your own use, it is punishable by the loss of ears and nose. And two, striking another buccaneer outside of a duel. That is punishable by flogging."

He said the last with regret, which was the only thing that stopped me from closing the distance between us and putting a dagger in his ribs.

"Not if he's mad, and all know the Ghoul to be mad," Morgan said tiredly.

"He does not look mad," Bradley said.

"He suffered a bout when he struck him and he has now recovered,"

I growled.

"Nay," Bradley said, and this time he sounded vindictive. "I have seen him suffer bouts. He is raving for days with no knowledge of who or where he is."

"He does look sane," Morgan said quietly, and then spoke louder for the men crowded in the doorway and along the walls. "I will ignore the charge of hoarding, as I question their accuser and his motivations. But I can't have my men striking one another, no matter the cause. There must be some discipline. Unless of course one of them is mad or drunk, or has some other excuse for losing the reason God grants all men."

I turned on my matelot. "Gaston, control yourself," I hissed with great urgency, and then I had my hands on his shoulders, my eyes boring into his. He appeared panicked, and then oddly bemused, as if he would laugh. I knew he realized what he must do, but I quickly saw he did not know how to simply become mad.

I pulled him close and whispered in his ear in French. "Think of those dead girls and how that damn man will never be punished. Think of your sister and mother suffering the same fate. Or Agnes, or Jamaica. Think of them tying you to a post and flogging you as your father did. Think of me having to watch them hurt you."

He let out a low groan and I was flung aside as he tore into the men around us. Thankfully, they had removed his weapons when first bearing him down. Still, I saw three men drop before over a dozen piled atop him.

I turned to Morgan, who had backed away, and spoke like one greatly concerned. "He is quite mad. He was just having a moment of calm, like an animal in a trap."

Morgan fought a smile and nodded curtly. "Then I see nothing here that must be punished within the articles. But your man is a danger to those around him, and I want him locked away until he calms. Put him on the *Queen*. In chains if you cannot control him."

"Aye, sir," I said.

I glanced at Bradley as I turned to the door. He was furious. Beyond him, Hastings was amused.

Some of the men present were from the *Queen*. They proffered rope quite helpfully. I prepared to have to make a great show of binding Gaston, but when I finally shouldered my way through the men who had hauled him outside, I found he was truly so enraged he did need to be restrained. Upon meeting my eyes, he calmed enough to allow me to bind him, though.

We were nearly to the wharf when Ash caught up to us. He was panting and frantic. "The house was attacked. Farley has been shot. Pete is hurt and unconscious."

"Striker?" I asked.

"He's fine," Ash assured us.

I pulled a knife and cut Gaston's bonds, and we ran for the house with a dozen men. I once again found myself blaming the Gods for madness in all its forms.

Eighty-One

Wherein We Are Ensnared

We found the house full of men from the *Queen*, including Alonso, Cramer, and Dudley, and the little girl, Consuelo. Farley was lying on the table speaking frantically with Cudro, who was attempting to staunch a wound in the physician's leg. Pete was lying on the floor with his head on his matelot's lap. Striker had a pistol resting on Pete's chest, a whole cache of loaded pieces arrayed before him on the floor, all within easy reach, and another tucked butt-first beneath his right arm, which he was reloading – quite deftly – with his left hand. I surmised he had been doing something other than merely lying about these last weeks: mainly, practicing doing necessary things left-handed.

Gaston went to Pete, and I went to the table to assist Cudro. It took some coaxing, but I was able to get Farley to lie down. Then I answered his panicked question: whether the blood was seeping or spurting from the wound. It was not spurting, but it was flowing well. I used his belt to constrict his leg above the wound, and turned to check on Gaston. He was examining a large, swollen gash on the back of Pete's skull.

I caught Striker's gaze. "What happened?"

"One of them must have caught Pete unawares and clubbed him good," he said with worry as he looked down at his matelot. Then his words were angry. "Then they stood about and argued on whether or not they needed to kill him, too; because one of them knew he would hunt them down like dogs if they let him live. Farley surprised them as I was getting out of bed, and they shot him and he fell back down the stairs. Then I shot them. There were two. I thank God I went to the door with four pistols, because I shot both of them twice once I saw Pete lying there."

He regarded me with accusation. "Where the Devil were you two?"

"That is a long story," I sighed. "The short of it is that Hastings has attempted to frame us and Gaston is supposed to be in chains on the *Queen* at this moment."

Striker swore. "Let us go there, and not because of that. I want a deck beneath me."

Gaston was looking at him. "His wound should be sewn, but he should wake."

"Remembering things?" Striker whispered, and chewed his lip.

My matelot nodded tightly. "Aye, it is swelling on the outside. It should not hurt his brain."

Then he stood to examine Farley's wound. The physician was still distraught, but he did not try to look as Gaston probed his leg. He winced and gritted his teeth and studied the ceiling. The wound was on the outside of the leg, up high, and I could see where the ball had passed through.

"Let us move to the ship," Gaston said. "This can be bandaged there as well."

After some discussion, we got Pete and Farley on two of the narrow cots, and six men carried each of them. Cudro, Alonso, and I swept through the house gathering things and instructing others as to what should be brought, such as the supplies of quinine and laudanum. I realized someone might threaten to cut off my nose for that; but I did not care, and felt we could mount a better battle over the matter from the *Queen's* decks.

When I went upstairs, I stumbled over the bodies of Striker's would-be assassins in the hall. I rolled them over and did not recognize either of them. I supposed one of us should go and tell Morgan. I thought perhaps it should be Cudro. I was not concerned about facing Morgan; but as I felt now, I thought it was best I avoid Bradley, as I would likely get myself flogged, or worse.

As we were readying to leave, Alonso called my name and pointed at the girl standing in the corner. There was nothing I could do for her that would not be better done by her own people, and I did not think ours could hurt her worse than they already had.

"Have we captured any nuns?" I asked Cudro as he hurried past.

He stopped and regarded me stupidly for a several moments. "Aye, and priests. You have need of one?"

I shook my head, and instructed Dudley and Cramer to take the girl to the church.

As we followed the wounded and supplies to the wharf, I told Cudro he should speak with Morgan.

He nodded. "Aye, as soon as I hear the whole of the story. We are getting our people safe first. From everyone."

He was surprised when I turned and embraced him.

The Bard was, of course, quite surprised to see us rowing out to him in an assortment of boats and canoes. Once we were aboard, Cudro sent most of our men back to shore with the extra boats. Then I sat on the quarterdeck steps and gulped wine, and told the tale of our night's and morning's adventures to everyone, while Gaston tended to Farley's and Pete's wounds.

"Who was it that accused you? The one the girl saw?" Cudro asked.

"I do not know his name," I said.

"He be Headley," one of our men who had been in the courtroom supplied. "Sails on the *Fortune*. And we seen him stalkin' about your house afore."

The wine dulled my need to ask them why they had failed to mention that before. Instead, I asked, "What of the assassins?"

Most had not seen the bodies and so could not identify them.

"We will find out," Cudro said.

"How did they take Pete?" the Bard asked.

"They hid and hit him on the back of the head," Gaston said with surety.

"Sometimes he does get hit," Striker said with loving amusement. "He's not invincible."

People guffawed and protested that.

Gaston finished bandaging Pete's head and came to join us. He had finished with Farley a while earlier, and the physician was resting comfortably in a haze of laudanum.

"And you don't think this Headley killed the girl's family?" the Bard asked.

"I think Hastings did," I said. "I think he was following us as well, and he followed Headley, and when Headley returned, he raped and murdered them and left them for us to find."

"Why?" the Bard asked.

"Because he could. Because he enjoys killing," I said. "Because he wished to anger us."

"Nay, why do you feel it was Hastings?" he protested. "I know he might have killed Michaels, but we don't even know that as a thing we could present in court. And now this. You are supposing a great deal."

"I just know," I said, knowing the wine made me sound stupid and stubborn. "He did it to anger us."

"So Cudro will tell Morgan I killed two assassins," Striker said. "And Gaston is mad and must remain aboard." He chuckled.

"If Will says I am," my matelot said with a small smile.

"I wish I could have seen that," Striker laughed.

"Aye," Gaston said wryly. "I have spent most of my life trying to control my madness, not lose myself to it."

Recalling those moments and what I said to him, I was overcome with the feeling that the wine would no longer hold the shakes at bay if I remained among them. Without any word of parting – as I did not trust myself to say a sensible thing – I retreated to our cabin and crawled into our nest. Gaston was on my heels, and his arms closed around me comfortingly as we lay nose to nose. I saw my fear and lingering anger mirrored in his eyes.

His right eye was swollen and dark where he had received a blow when they brought him down. I knew his body was covered in bruises and abrasions from his mistreatment. I touched the bruises I could see and cried.

He held me and spoke softly. "I was angry and scared that we were charged with hoarding; and I knew I would kill them or die trying before I would allow them to maim you. Not that I would not love you without a nose, but I cannot see you hurt. And I knew you would find some way to protect me, to take all the blame.

"I would have let them flog me, though. It would have been a cat, and nothing like what my father used. It probably wouldn't even draw blood over my scars. And I thought it should be the price I paid. I broke the law by striking him; I was not lost to madness when I did it. My Horse and I charged and ran him down as one. If I am to be sane, then I must accept the consequences of sanity, even if it would drive me mad."

He snorted with amusement. "But then, you were so magnificent in defending us, as you always are, and you asked… And you were correct: I could not bear the thought of you being forced to watch, because it would hurt you. All the rest I could hold the reins against, but not that."

I wiped my eyes. "I hate them all for threatening us with such… Here we are amongst such lawless men, and yet they have laws, and… Damn it! I have never crossed another lawless man. I would not. We kill one another. You do not do such a thing unless you plan to kill them first. That is a thing I understand. Men accusing other killers of things that have punishments less than death, as if we were some damn township is… wrong, in my thinking."

He smiled. "There must be some rule among thieves."

"I do not like living within the rules of civilized men, because they have never protected me – or anyone, but the wolves from justice. They are never civilized. It is another word for ordered thievery. These thieves are no different from any other. If a man does not pay his taxes in Christendom, he is publicly tortured in punishment. Here, as there, the pain stops when the silver crosses the palm.

"I am an outlaw in heart as well as fact. The only reason I do not kill all who cross me is because there are more of them who might take reprisal against me, or you, or… I felt helpless today, and I wanted justice for those poor people, and it was not going to come because they were worthless to the men judging us. And instead, we are threatened!

"I so want to kill them!" I hissed. "It is madness! It is all madness! I come again and again to the knowledge that we are sane, and all the world is mad."

He was smiling at me with great love. I took a long breath and tried to calm my racing thoughts.

He chuckled and rolled on his back to regard the ceiling with a happy smile. "I have the most precious treasure in the world, the thing all men wish for but do not understand, the secret to all that is holy and good; and I am hoarding it from my Brethren. I will share it with no one except those I love most."

"The light of truth and sanity beyond the cave?" I asked; pleased to see him so happy despite all that had occurred. It was truly a balm to my anger and frustration.

"Non." He turned back to me, his eyes full of love and challenge. "You."

A refutation rose to my lips; but his challenge was to hold it back: to suppress it; nay, to deny it in its entirety. And the jests. And the reasoning. The challenge was to stand there unflinching and raise no defense in the face of the staggering power of his adoration: to submit fully and completely to my fate, and allow it to wash over me and pull me under and have the faith that I would yet be able to breathe. It was very hard to do, and yet I did it for him.

His smile widened, and his lips covered mine, and I could not breathe between his mouth and the swelling of love in my chest; but my soul drank him in, in great lungfuls of delight.

The rest of the day passed in a fog of pleasure and contentment. I could not save the world, but I could please him in the attempt; and for these hours, I could please him more with my body and abiding love.

That night, we woke to the sound of Pete cursing, and peered down from our hammock to find Striker helping his matelot into the cabin and onto their mattress. Gaston climbed down and spoke to the Golden One at length, assessing whether or not he was damaged beyond the obvious. It quickly became apparent that the only thing broken beneath Pete's great thick skull was his sense of humor. He knew who and where he was, and remembered with great clarity how he had been attacked. He had heard something upstairs and gone to see if it were Striker, who he had thought was napping. Upon rounding the corner in the upper hallway, he had been struck from behind by someone who must have been hiding in one of the other rooms. He cursed his stupidity vehemently, and then cursed us roundly for abandoning them. And so I climbed down and told him of our morning. This did little to mollify him. Apparently we were all fools who had nearly thrown ourselves at our enemy's feet. Gaston at last dosed him with a small amount of laudanum, and we – including Striker – retreated from his wrath in hopes he would rest.

"He was happy for a moment to find me alive," Striker muttered once we were on deck.

"He is in great pain from that wound," Gaston assured him.

"And scared I might have died. I know," Striker sighed and smiled. "But he'll heal?"

Gaston nodded.

Striker appeared much relieved. "I thought it a good sign when he started cursing. He seemed to know exactly who he wanted to curse."

Chuckling, we went and joined the few men aboard: near the cook fire, where they all lounged about in the smoke to thwart the damn insects. They had a bottle, and we passed it and talked until Cudro and Ash arrived from shore. They told us Morgan had gathered all the men in town and announced he would not tolerate any of our company seeking a bounty on another. He would hang any man who even planned such a thing. We thought this good, if the attempts we had seen had been all the pawns – but bad, if the best had not attempted to strike, as now they would wait until we returned to Port Royal.

I, of course, thought Hastings was already in play; the others, save my matelot, were not so sure. Though I knew it was foolhardy to wish for the man to make an attempt on our lives, I wished for him to do so: to vindicate my hatred of him, and more importantly, to give me an opportunity to kill him.

A week passed. We fished, sparred, drank, cared for Farley, treated one of our men who was stabbed while on a sortie, and trysted a great deal. Pete recovered his good spirits and apologized for cursing us as he had. We fashioned crutches for Farley so he might hobble about. It was peaceful, and seemingly far removed from the activities in the town. Our only complaint was that the water smelled and appeared too foul for swimming. And the damn insects were certainly worse upon the water than they were on shore. On the second morning, I fetched all the netting from the house, and we tacked it to the inside of the cabin windows and draped it before the door.

My only other complaint was Alonso. As there were only a dozen of us aboard, it was difficult to ignore him when we sat about and talked. He seemed more cheerful, and was pleasant to Gaston and me; but I saw shadows in his eyes, and wondered what he was about.

Our idyllic days were short-lived, though. Just over a fortnight after our arrival at Maracaibo, Cudro sent a man to the ship to tell us that men were beginning to fever. Much discussion occurred as to which of our physicians should investigate. Farley was doing tolerably well hobbling about the ship on his crutches; but his leg still pained him, and clambering down to a boat, up the wharf, and then walking about town for hours would be onerous for him. So Gaston elected to go: with me, of course, and several trusted men.

Only one of the men yet reported ill was from the *Queen*, and Cudro had ordered him brought to the house we had used. Gaston examined him and concluded it was the malaria. He administered quinine and left the man with his matelot, and we went in search of the others who ailed and the surgeons charged with their care. We found two other fevering men: both had the malaria. Gaston dispensed some of the quinine to the surgeons and instructed them in its use. Most of the medical men sailing with us were good for little more than extracting bullets, setting bones, sewing gashes, and removing limbs. They knew nothing of medicine; but many of them had been with us at Porto Bello, and they knew well the epidemic we faced if men sickened here as they had there.

Then we went to Morgan. He seemed pleased to see us, and rose in greeting from the table he shared with several of the captains, including Norman, Bradley, and pleasantly, Cudro. Bradley would not look at us. Cudro saw the expressions upon our faces and nodded gravely.

"Men have begun to ail with the malaria," I said once we were seated with them.

There was swearing all about.

"Are you sure?" Bradley asked.

"That it is the malaria, or that they ail?" I retorted.

He looked away.

"What if we move on?" Morgan asked. "If it is beginning to afflict us now, what if we move on? We have been speaking of going south to the head of the lake; there is a town there named Gibraltar that the French also visited."

"Is it on a swamp too?" Gaston asked.

"Presumably," Morgan sighed. "But perhaps being different air..."

Gaston shook his head. "We do not know how it is caused. We only know, as the Spanish do, that being near a swamp for several weeks can bring it on; and the Indian medicine, quinine, will treat it. But we have a limited supply of quinine. More than we had in Porto Bello, but still not enough to treat more than a few dozen men."

"This Gibraltar might have more," I said. "And since we found it for sale at the apothecary's and the physician's, it is likely the wealthier citizens here had it on their plantations. Men who know what to look for should be dispatched, or all the medicines should be collected and be brought here and sorted." It was a thing we had discussed but not wished to suggest to Morgan until we were sure men would be afflicted with the disease.

Morgan was nodding. "Let us do that. Send a few men to all the plantations we've already visited, and have them look for medicines." He looked to me. "And you two should search through the things already collected from the houses. And you told me you already searched the town before..."

I nodded. "I do not want us wandering about the streets without escort – even with your edict – but we can continue searching here."

"Should we separate the ailing men?" Norman asked. "We didn't at Porto Bello, but damn near half our men were ill."

"It is not thought to be contagious like the plague," Gaston said. "And even with that, men do not always fall ill after being around the dying."

Norman looked to Morgan. "And moving on didn't help at Porto Bello. Most of my men began to ail after we sailed."

"Aye, aye," Morgan sighed. "Still, I think we are nearly done here. And Gibraltar might have more medicine. And gold." He shrugged. "Let us spend the remainder of this week collecting our men and medicines and any other booty, and move on to Gibraltar."

Everyone who had a say in the matter nodded. I felt I did not, so I said and did nothing.

Gaston was quiet as we returned to the ship.

"We stand a better chance of saving men here than we did last year," I said to cheer him.

He frowned. "Oui, because we are perceived as being more respectable: your jaw is not broken, and I am not wounded, and…" He sighed and regarded me with a tinge of guilt.

I grinned. "Oui, medical advice dispensed by madmen is deemed suspect."

He smiled sadly. "I do not wish to spend my life wearing a coat and collar in order to save lives. It is not fair."

I sighed and put an arm around his shoulder. "We will discover some path through that thicket."

"Oui," he said and adjusted his step to match mine.

The week passed with our picking through the booty collected from the Spanish, amidst which we found two bottles of quinine, and searching the remaining houses, which yielded another. In that time, two dozen more men fell ill. Thankfully, the ones being treated with quinine were already improving.

I often saw Hastings, and even the bastard, Headley, peering at us during these excursions, along with others. I ignored all but Hastings, as I always found him smiling at me when our gazes happened to meet. I knew we would fight; I just did not know how or when.

Finally we withdrew to the ships and sailed south a good thirty leagues to Gibraltar. The Spanish there had been alerted to our arrival; and we entered an empty town just as we had at Maracaibo. Once again, Morgan had our men claim and occupy the central square. And once again, our cabal was reluctant to go ashore and leave the relative comfort and safety of the *Queen*; but we did anyway, taking another house with large lower rooms to use as a hospital. This time Gaston and I managed to obtain a private bedroom, much to our delight.

Sadly, for many reasons, we were not given time to enjoy it. The number of fevering men had risen to over three dozen, and the ships were now sending them all to us. Once the ailing men were situated, Gaston and I set out with an escort from the *Queen* to locate the apothecary and any physicians' homes. This search yielded a goodly amount of quinine, most of it from the church. In the good Fathers' defense, they had apparently been dispensing it regularly in the infirmary they maintained for the poor, and not hoarding it for their own use.

Our search also yielded valuables other than medicines, and we were sure to make great show of delivering them to the pile of booty in the town square.

Once the primary targets were stripped of medicines and supplies, Gaston was needed at the hospital; and I decided to go in search of more useful items in the individual homes, with Dudley, Cramer, and to my annoyance, Alonso, as my assistants and bodyguards. Though he had acted very helpful and cheerful of late, it was obvious Alonso had no interest in, or talent for, tending feverish men. Caretaking was simply not within the purview of skills he possessed or ever intended to lay claim to. He was good at searching houses, though; and I doubted he would let anyone kill me.

By the third day of searching, not having seen any Spanish or others who might mean us harm lurking about, we decided to speed the process by separating into two teams. Of course, since Cramer and Dudley were matelots, that meant I was stuck with Alonso.

"Alone at last," he murmured in Castilian as we finished wandering through a house, looking for hiding Spaniards.

I snorted. "Take the upstairs; I will do the cook house and stores."

"We should talk," he said, and remained at the foot of the stairs. "I have been waiting to speak with you."

I swore and turned to growl, "Alonso…" I was going to say that we had nothing to say to one another; but perhaps he wished to apologize for being an arse or stubborn. That I would hear.

"Speak," I said with less rancor. "Say what you feel you need to say, and let us be done with it."

He studied me. I could not read him in the dim light of the room: my eyes were still adjusting from the harsh noontime light beyond the door. He was a mass of shadows.

"No," he said softly and sadly. "You are correct; there is nothing to be gained by words now." He turned away and walked up the stairs.

I sighed and went in search of the house's storeroom. I had just liberated a promising-looking chest from amongst a phalanx of jars when I was struck in the head from behind. The chest went flying, and I was thrown down upon sacks of grain, my vision reeling and my ears ringing.

There was a weight upon my back, and my arm was seized and twisted behind me before I could gather my thoughts and muscles to move. And then when I knew I must move at all costs, the ungainly and yielding bags beneath me prevented me getting my knees under me or twisting about. The grip on my arm tightened.

"Stop struggling, Uly," Alonso whispered in my ear. "You know you want this. I have seen what you want. I was a fool to be so gentle. You want to be taken. You have been waiting for me to take you back, have you not?"

Icy claws clutched my heart so that it stopped painfully for a moment, only to thud and thunder again such that I could hear nothing but the pounding of it in my ears. The words *you know you want this* twisted and tumbled through my mind, as if they fell down a deep and empty well, never to strike bottom and splash rage to the surface as they once had. I felt nothing, not even fear.

I did not feel helpless, either. Nor did the idea of what he wished to do as he fumbled with my breeches cause me lust as I had once feared. My Horse had no interest in submitting to him. Nor did my reeling vision and pinioned arm remind me of Shane, though I was now actually in the position in which he had often put me. I stood beyond all that.

Alonso was correct; I was correct. We were now so very far beyond what words could accomplish.

I twisted up and away, hard, and felt something snap in my arm. The pain cut through my aching and muzzy thoughts. I had a pistol in my left hand before I finished standing. I had thrown him off; but not far, as we had been next to the shelving. He knocked the gun away, grabbing my wrist and attempting to pound my arm to make me drop it. I did, and tried to kick him, but my breeches were about my knees and hindered anything I could do with my legs. I could move my right arm, but trying to make a fist made my vision reel and my stomach clench.

I dove away, backing farther into the narrow room, and kicked my breeches free. He was diving at me: his eyes were black and full of his Horse, and I felt a poor peasant before an armored knight on a destrier born in the bowels of Hades.

I hit him with a jar of fruit. It cracked open and covered the side of his head in sticky yellow. When that staggered him, I began to empty the shelves upon his head. He retreated, covering his head with his arms. I pulled my rapier and followed, tripping on bags of grain, broken glass, and candied fruit.

We emerged into the house's rear entryway, and he retreated further still into the dining hall, where there was room to maneuver beside a great table. He had his rapier and a dagger drawn. I knew I could clutch nothing with my right. I would have to block with the arm itself and see if I could take the dagger from him. I was already slipping on my blood and praising the Gods I could not feel the pain in my feet yet. One more wound would not kill me, but not receiving it might.

He closed, his eyes speculative: testing.

I parried confidently. I was better than he. I always had been.

He came again; this time the dagger was a flash to my right. I swung my bad arm, and felt the blade cut deep, but I did not manage to disarm him. He danced back, surprised at my attempt.

"Uly," he whispered with equal parts admonishment and wonder.

I smiled and feinted; he parried and found a chair kicked before him. I leapt atop the table and kicked the fruit bowl at him. As he dodged, I charged. He barely turned my blade in time, his right coming up in defense. He broke away and dove back.

And then there was another figure in the room, between us: a dark kerchief and ecru tunic. And then Alonso was falling back with a dagger in his chest. My former lover looked up at me with horror and surprise. I tore my gaze from him and found Hastings grinning up at me.

We stood still in a timeless moment. The lack of movement of battle was enough to allow my pain to catch me. I gasped and put all my strength into holding my shaking blade steady between me and Hastings, as my vision wavered and my stomach clenched.

Hastings smiled and stepped away, his hands wide. His words were quiet, barely audible over the pounding in my ears. "Thank you. I could not have arranged it better if I tried." He gave a moue. "And I did try." He grinned again. Then he was gone.

I sank to the table, even that slow motion unsteady and graceless, but I did not collapse. I was proud of that. I glanced toward Alonso. He was dead. I leaned to the edge of the table and retched.

Dudley and Cramer found me there, sometime later. They had probably been speaking, but until one of them waved a hand before my eyes, I did not see them.

"Help," I breathed.

"What 'appened?" Dudley asked. He appeared very worried.

"Alonso attacked me," I whispered.

"Why?"

"He sought to make me love him again."

"Ohhhh..." Cramer breathed. "Daft bastard."

"Where are your breeches?" Dudley asked.

I looked down and saw I was naked save my tunic. I pointed toward the storeroom.

"Gaston," I said. "Please find him."

"Aye, aye," Cramer said. "We'll take ya to 'im. But ya got glass in yur feet."

Dudley returned with my breeches and said, "I'll go fetch yur matelot."

They talked quietly for a moment about the wisdom of separating. I tried not to listen, as I did not wish to become frustrated if one of them would not do as I wished. Instead, I looked at my aching right foot and regretted it.

Thankfully, Dudley did go, and with one eye upon the door Cramer set about giving me water, assisting me with donning my breeches, pulling glass from my feet, and binding my wounds.

We were almost ready for me to attempt to stand when we heard the clatter of men entering. I looked up hopefully, expecting to see worried green eyes, and found Norman instead.

He looked at me with concern; then at Alonso; and then at the evidence of our battle. He came to me. "You are to come with us."

I nodded. I thought we would surely encounter Gaston on our way to the hospital, so I need not worry about anything other than walking on my hastily bound feet and not moving my arm, for which we had not yet fashioned a sling. As I did not feel I could bend it without fainting, I had not been in a hurry about the sling.

But Norman and his men led me to the town square; and when I protested, they closed in around me, which prompted Cramer to call them all fools.

"You killed a man," Norman said.

"Nay," I said. "Hastings did."

He regarded me as if I were mad. I began to feel very ill, and it was not from the pain.

We went to the courthouse; and as I had dreaded, Hastings was speaking with Morgan. They turned to me as I entered, and I could see Hastings fight a grin; but Morgan appeared appalled at my condition, and he regarded Hastings speculatively.

"I told you they fought," Hastings said with a shrug.

I shook my head and approached Morgan.

"What did he say happened?" I asked. My words seemed quiet even to me, but I felt too weak to make an attempt of projection. It was hard enough just to speak.

Morgan regarded me with concern. "Nay, what do you say happened?"

"Alonso attacked me. He… We were lovers long ago, in Florence. We came upon him in Porto Bello, and he came to sail on the *Virgin Queen* because… he held hope of gaining my love again. And… He decided he would take me back by force this day. He… attacked me. We fought. And then Hastings appeared and stabbed him."

It sounded insane, and I saw that judgment in Morgan's eyes. I nearly thought I should ask if it would be better if I said I had stabbed Alonso. It would be more believable.

"What has he said?" I asked again.

Morgan shrugged. "He says that he heard sounds of a fight, and came in and saw you fighting Alonso, and that you stabbed your lover."

"He was not my lover," I said. "Not… now."

Morgan leaned his head to the side and grimaced a little. "He says he has seen the two of you trysting."

I did not look at Hastings. I did not wish to see him grinning. I wondered what he thought to gain by this. Why claim Alonso and I were lovers? Was there some law against that in the articles I had forgotten? He was already claiming I killed a man. It was my word against his as to who attacked who.

"Why?" I asked Morgan.

He frowned at me. "Why what?"

"Why would he say that?"

His frown deepened. "Will, are you well?"

"Nay, my arm is broken and cut, my feet are bleeding, and I have been struck in the head."

Morgan nodded. "Sit down."

"Aye," I said. He had been swaying for a while now, and I realized it had actually been me. "I need to see Gaston."

"Of course," Morgan said as he led me to a chair.

I sat. "I did not kill Alonso. I was going to, but I did not."

"Well, imagine that, he is as mad as his matelot," Hastings said.

I turned to him. "What do you want?"

He looked away quickly. "Justice."

"That is shite," I said. I turned back to Morgan. "What is this about? Am I on trial?"

Morgan shook his head and spoke as if he were addressing an imbecile. "He has accused you of murdering a man. You have accused him of murdering the same man. It is your word against his. Matters of this nature are settled by duel. But you cannot duel."

Hastings snorted. "It's ironic. He's been trying to goad me into dueling him for weeks. But now he can't. How convenient. Perhaps your matelot will stand for you. That's if he believes your story and not mine."

I sucked breath into my lungs as the fog parted and I saw where he sailed.

"Are you daft?" I asked. "That is what this is about? You think you will win?"

Hastings smiled slyly at me before donning a mask of self-righteousness. "I will defend my honor. I am tired of you and your matelot making groundless accusations against me."

"I am tired of you breathing," I said.

There was a commotion outside, and Gaston entered with Pete, Striker, and Cudro. My matelot saw me and ran to my side. His eyes were frantic with worry. His hands began to explore my injuries.

I laid fingers on his lips and pulled his eyes to mine. "I will live. Hastings wishes to duel you," I whispered in French. "He thinks he will win. He is very devious. He is making accusations designed to anger you."

"Did he do this to you?" Gaston hissed, the Horse filling his eyes.

I frowned. "Non. Alonso. And he is dead. Be wary. Hastings thinks he will win," I cautioned again.

The Horse melded with the man, and I saw cunning and power such as I had rarely seen in my man's eyes. I smiled.

He grinned. "He wishes to die," he breathed.

"Kill him," I breathed. "I want to go home."

Gaston stood. All this while, Morgan had been explaining the conflicting charges and the need for a duel.

When he finished, Hastings asked Gaston, "So will you stand for your matelot?" He spat the word. "Even though he has been fucking some Spaniard behind your back?"

Gaston snorted. "I would defend my matelot's honor even if you claimed he had been fucking you behind my back. Name your terms."

Hastings' eye narrowed ever so slightly at that. He looked to Morgan. "I only ask to choose the weapon. I know this man's reputation. I feel choice of weapon is the only advantage I can gain."

Gaston shrugged. "Name it."

Hastings, despite his smooth mask, could not contain his smile of triumph. "Whips."

There was a hush and then murmuring about the room.

Gaston laughed unpleasantly. "That is your secret weapon? Good. Here. Now. To the death."

"With whips?" Morgan questioned. "To the death with whips?"

"It will be long and painful," Gaston growled.

Morgan backed away with narrowed eyes. "In the square, then." He led everyone outside.

Hastings frowned over his shoulder at Gaston as he went. I saw concern in his black eye, and it gladdened my heart. Then he slid his eye patch from one eye to the other as he stepped into the light. I feared some other trick.

"Be careful," I whispered to Gaston.

He leaned down and kissed me lightly, and I saw great regard in his beast-filled eyes. Then he stood and looked to Pete and Cudro.

"See to Will," he ordered, and walked out the door.

They did not bristle at his command. Instead they moved to help me stand.

"Will, what the Devil happened to you?" Striker asked. "Morgan said…"

I waved his words away. "Not now. Later… When I am drunk or drugged… or both," I gasped as I tried to put weight on my right foot to take a step.

Pete picked me up and carried me outside.

The men had cleared a large circle between the courthouse steps and the central fountain. Pete set me on the lowest step and ordered men aside until I could see.

Gaston and Hastings stood in the circle. Someone had already found them whips: great bull whips some fifteen feet in length. There was a murmur of incredulity all about the square as Gaston grasped his and inspected the length of it quickly before snaking it back to test its weight and suppleness with a sinuous roll of his arm and shoulder. I smiled: he had been wise to not tell anyone he had conquered his fear of whips. It would be Hastings' death.

Once both men were armed, Morgan verified that they knew the terms. This fight was to the death, with whips to be used as the only weapon.

When the order to begin was given, Hastings hesitated; Gaston waited. Then the eye-patched man moved. He was fast and strong, and the braid roared through the air at Gaston. My matelot did not flinch. He raised his left arm and took the blow so that the end of the whip wrapped around and around his forearm, drawing blood and raising a welt as it went. Then Hastings stood holding the end of a tether. Gaston deftly looped his whip so it was shorter, and snapped his opponent, so the tip wrapped around Hastings' back, shredding cloth as it went and biting deep to draw blood on the man's right breast. Gaston did it again and again, each blow sounding like a pistol crack, until Hastings released his hold on his whip with a curse and staggered away with blood lining and dotting his tunic. Gaston grinned and stirred the air with his left arm, until he had coiled Hastings' whip around it like a sheath and held the haft in his hand. Then he lazily slithered his whip back and forth across the cobblestones: striking like lightning on occasion, leaving welts on Hastings' legs and driving him back.

As the damn man passed me, I could see the fear and frustration in his eye. Gaston was death incarnate: cold and cruel.

Hastings decided he could take no more. He charged. Gaston threw up his leather-wrapped arm to ward off the blow, and men yelled "Knife!" all along that side of the circle. Gaston feinted and kicked his opponent's legs from under him: pouncing before Hastings finished falling, so that his weight drove the air from Hastings' lungs as they landed. Gaston pinned the knife-wielding hand with his knee, and coiled his own whip about his right hand and proceeded methodically, and with great force – such that it twisted his entire body with each blow – to strike Hastings in the face until there was no more face to strike and Gaston's hand dripped blood and flesh.

The crowd had at first cheered; but as the beating continued and the body grew still, they quieted, so that when Gaston stood and spat on the faceless corpse, the square was so silent I heard his spittle land.

I hoped the Gods were pleased with this day's amusement: though I was pleased with the outcome, I was not pleased with the cost.

Eighty-Two

Wherein We Must Escape

My matelot divested himself of the whips, picked me up, and carried me from the square to the hospital and then up the stairs to the bedroom we had claimed. He set me on the bed and knelt before me to press his forehead to my breastbone. Our friends crowded the doorway so it was filled with curious, worried, and expectant faces.

I did not wish to speak to them. I wished to curl with my matelot in the bed on which I sat and pretend the last hour had not occurred. But that would require laudanum, which I did not have at hand; and I did not wish to sully the bed with my filthy fruit- and blood-covered feet; and I knew I required stitches, and Gaston bandages; and I knew fetching those things was beyond my capability – or, seemingly, Gaston's. Thus, I must exchange the coin of human kindness and speak.

"There is nothing to be done now," I assured them quietly. "All those who need to be dead, are dead. Well... all those here. There are others elsewhere who must die, but we need not worry about them now. Now, we need a basin and bandages, and Gaston's medicine chest. Please."

Most of them seemed disinclined to move, their curiosity and concern instilling them with stubbornness.

But Pete nodded sagely. "We'llFetchThat." Then he bellowed such that Gaston twitched and clutched at the bed linen. "ClearOut! AllO'Ya! YouToo," he added quietly, and hooked an arm around Striker to drag him into the hall.

Cudro chuckled as he closed the door. It sounded as if annoyed cattle were being herded down the stairs, but we were at last alone and safe.

Gaston breathed a heavy sigh of relief, and the tension drained from his shoulders. He sat back, and without looking up to meet my gaze, began to consider my wounds. He touched my bandaged feet. "What?"

"Glass. Jars of candied fruit. I was throwing them. Then I had to run through the room. Cramer removed the glass we could find."

His fingers were on my arm, and he frowned at the crude splint. "How is it broken?"

"I know not. I cannot close my hand without pain, or bend my elbow. He had my arm twisted behind me and I... knew it would break, but I had to move."

He had found the bloody part of the bandaging on my forearm.

"He had a dagger," I continued. "I had to block with it, since the arm was damn useless for anything else."

He was running his fingers lightly over the rest of me.

"Nothing else except my head, I think." I said. "He hit me from behind when he attacked."

His fingers gingerly probed the swelling on the back of my skull. I winced, and he met my gaze, letting his Horse and even the physician fall away to reveal only him: and he was very worried.

"It was so like what Shane used to do," I said.

Gaston closed his eyes in pain.

"Non, non, listen," I breathed. "It did not end like it did with Shane."

He looked at me through tears and sighed with relief. "I do not want you ever hurt in that way again. Thinking about it is enough to drive me to madness. I have been holding it very far from my thoughts."

I smiled. "You need not fear. I will not be hurt in that way again. I will die first. I learned that today. It was one thing for me to overcome my fear and fight you as I did last year. But that was madness and... I did not lose myself to madness this time."

He smiled. "Neither did I."

"I know. I am so very proud."

There was a polite knock on the door; and at my word, Cudro entered with Pete. They had brought all I asked for – and a bottle of rum. They left with smiles that said they needed no thanks.

Gaston pulled the medicine chest to the bed, gave us each a small dose of laudanum, and began to clean, sew, and bind our wounds.

"Tell me what happened," he said as he unwrapped my arm and examined it.

I did not feel I could begin any tale when I felt pain was so very imminent. "Non, set it as you must, first. The thought of moving it makes me wish to retch."

He handed me a stick to bite upon while he manipulated my poor arm to determine exactly where it was injured.

"It will need to be wrapped and put in a sling," he said at last. "It is broken at the joints, not the long bones. But first I need to stitch this gash."

That, I felt I could talk through, but only because the drug was making my eyes heavy and the pain distant. So he began to work, and – after he had soaked the wound in rum, which stung such that I had to bite the stick a bit more – I told him of being alone with Alonso, and his cryptic words, and how I had gone to the storeroom.

"It was truly like Shane would do. He would catch me unawares, and hit me to stun me and knock me to my knees, and then he would pin me. Alonso even said the hated words. But... I felt nothing: no fear, no..." I sighed. "I think I have been afraid that I would succumb to the fear, or my Horse's lust, if I were put in that position again. I have worried that my Horse did not care who brought me to my knees. But it does care. My love of being taken *is* only for you. All I felt with Alonso was astonishment, and then the need to kill him – and even that was not a thing born of red-hot rage and madness. I knew I would die before I would let him, and therefore it was a duel to the death. And so we fought. Me with one arm, and my head aching, and no breeches, and my feet bleeding, and... Still, I knew I must win. And then Hastings was there, and he stabbed Alonso and made some comment about arranging things and ran off..."

I sighed. "Hastings must have been following me. He realized he could get to you through me. He told Morgan that Alonso and I had been trysting; and I wondered why, and then I realized he wished to anger you, just as he had wished to anger us with the death of that family. He was goading us, but he did not want to duel me. There was no bounty on my head. He did not think he knew my weaknesses so that he could win. I doubt he even wanted the money. Perhaps he saw it as a challenge."

Gaston shook his head thoughtfully as he bandaged my now-stitched arm. "He surrendered to his fear when I got him down," he said. "I have seen the eyes of many men fighting me for their lives. I was not a man to him in that moment before I began to strike him. I was the Devil."

He sighed. "I wish I could have beaten Alonso's face in, too."

"Oui," I said with sincere wistfulness. "That is my only regret over his death: that I did not strike the killing blow. I feel cheated."

"Let your arm rest at your side until we are done," he said as he began to unwrap my feet. "You were cheated." His face tightened with anger. "I want to kill anyone that thinks you will submit to them merely because you submit to me. It is an honor you give me. It is not a thing that any man can take."

"Non," I soothed. "It must be earned, and you alone have earned it." But that was not true. Shane had earned it once. But that was a shame I did not wish to contemplate at the moment. Someday, that too, would be resolved.

"I do not want others to know that we play as we do," Gaston said as he bathed my feet.

I nodded solemnly. I realized I did not want them to know, either. "Non, it will be a private thing. I would say I feel no shame in it, and I do not, but... non, others do not see it as we do."

He leaned forward and kissed my knee and looked up at me with loving eyes. "You should lie on your belly for me to stitch these wounds and examine your head."

I smiled, remembering the first time he had needed to stitch my feet, and my unease at lying on my belly and giving him my back. "I do not find alarm at that. I have traveled far."

He rose up on his knees until he could kiss my lips gently, and then he pressed his temple to mine. "We have traveled far. Do we still have far to go? Or is there a meadow that we will reach someday and the road need go no further? And we can frolic about the cart for the rest of our days."

I heard the hope and worry in his words. "I hope so," I breathed. "But I feel we have a ways farther yet to go."

He nodded, and sat back on his heels to regard me with sad amusement. "First we must go home. You are wounded, so we should be able to do that now."

I chuckled. "Is that what is required for us to end these damn voyages? If I had known that, I would stabbed myself weeks ago."

But as I lay on my belly and he worked on my feet, I thought of all the things waiting for us on Jamaica, and how very steep the road seemed there; and I wondered why we wished to return.

Later, after he finished examining the lump on my head, he bathed my naked body with a cloth. I drifted on the drug and luxuriated in the slow strokes.

"I want you," I whispered when he stopped.

He gave a quiet snort of amusement, and I turned my head and found him administering unguents to the whip marks on his forearm. None were so deep as to require stitching, and I thought it likely he would only have thin white lines for scars for a year or so. When he finished bandaging the cuts, he lay beside me.

"I took too much," he whispered. "I cannot rise even for you."

"Perhaps tomorrow, then," I said with amusement.

"Definitely tomorrow," he sighed happily and closed his eyes.

I woke to sunlight streaming through the shutters, and pain. As the window faced east, I thought it likely dawn. Gaston still slept beside me. I nudged him, and he woke with sleepy blinks. He dosed me to ease the pain of my body – no other part of me suffered – and we relieved our bladders and he dressed slowly to face the day. I knew I could not walk without pain for several days, and crutches were not an option with my arm as it was. So I resigned myself to being forced to lie about and do nothing. He went to fetch us food and water.

He returned with Striker, Pete, Cudro, Ash, and Farley, and I wondered if they had done anything but wait about at the foot of the stairs all damn night. So I ate bacon and drank coconut milk and told my tale, while they sat about the bed or in the room's two chairs and listened.

"Bloody Hell," Striker said as I finished. "We should have shot him in Porto Bello."

I snorted. "Nay, I should have slit his throat as he lay sleeping in Florence. But it is either the curse or blessing of man that we cannot see the future."

"I am sorry," Farley said, with guilt suffusing his face.

"For what?" I asked.

"I feel..." Farley sighed and considered his words while chewing his lip. "He became moody after he recovered from his head wound. I knew not whether it was because of the wound; or that... Well, he spoke of you a great deal. He spoke often of how you lived together in Florence. He seemed quite convinced you would return to him, or... could be made to return to him." He sighed and grimaced. "I knew he was not entirely as he had been before, thus my feeling a need to keep an eye on him; but I said nothing of all that because... As I said, I was unsure of the cause. His memory returned, and in all other ways he seemed free of any permanent damage from the wound; and so... I thought he might have been merely in love with you, and your assisting him in recovering gave him false hope.

"He never said he would do as he did, though," Farley added quickly. "Though... there was some discussion regarding people having preferences for..."

"It is not your fault," I said quickly. "Perhaps he was mad as a result of the wound, but... I think it was because he thought he loved me. To him, I ... was... the epitome of another time in his life, when he felt he was happier."

Gaston was regarding me with a knowing look.

I sighed and awarded him a sad smile, even as I spoke to Farley. "He loved me still, despite my not wishing it; and he was quite intent upon winning me back: I knew that. The injury must have impaired his reason as to what method might be effective in obtaining that end."

Farley nodded thoughtfully. "It is a sad thing. I would hope he would not have done as he did if his reason had not been so impaired. I still wish I had realized the extent of it. As I said, I felt something was wrong, but..." He sighed and shrugged.

"I do not blame you in the slightest," I assured him.

He nodded with relief.

"So was Hastings the last of the pawns?" Cudro asked in the silence that followed.

Pete shrugged. "NoWayTaKnow. ButOneSetFailedWithTryin'TaShoot Us. An'AnotherFailedAtDuelin'. An'Morgan'sGoneAnMadeARuleAboutIt. AnyLeft, TheyWon'tShowNowLestTheyBeStupid. An'TheStupidOnes WouldNa'O'WaitedThisLong."

"So we can return home and face them there," I said.

He nodded with a grimace. "Aye. BestWeCanDo." Then he frowned. "ItBeBestThatBastardHastingsDied'Ere IfYaBeRight'Bout'ImBein'TheOne WhoKilledThemWomen."

"Aye," I said, not wishing to think of the likes of Hastings being anywhere near our women. But that only made me worry about who might be near them while we were away. I could see my thought echoed in other eyes about the bed.

I sighed. "How much longer will we remain here?"

"Too long," Cudro rumbled with a tired sigh.

They left us, and Gaston began to gather his things to go and look in on the wounded.

"I do not blame the head wound," I said sadly.

He awarded me a grim smile. "Perhaps you should. Perhaps it unseated him upon his Horse enough that he no longer controlled the animal."

I could see that, and I sighed, "I do not wish to feel sorry for him."

Gaston came to kneel before me on the bed. His mien was curious and teasing. "Why should you? It was his Horse. It was still him: unless he was truly mad. But even you will admit – once forced to – that he always loved you, and that it was ever a thing of his Horse and his Man in concert."

I agreed with him, but his taking that side of the argument amused me. I chided, "Are you not the one ever concerned with your Horse's horrible thoughts?"

He frowned and cocked his head before grinning. "True, but... Pete and you are correct: it is what a man does, not what he thinks. As you have often made mention, I never acted on those horrible thoughts. We allow our Horses to play together."

I smiled. "Oui." And mine had proven with Alonso that it did not wish to run for the sake of running, or down paths alone without me. And I knew Gaston's loved me. We rode in harmony with our beasts, and were better men for it.

Gaston sighed and awarded me a bemused smile.

"So, oui, I should not berate myself."

He kissed my nose. "And you need not feel sorry for him."

I shook my head. "Non, I should. He... never listened to his Horse, or truth: of his heart or any other. He was always enamored of the shadows on the wall – the world of men and lies – and he lost me because of it, and... His Horse regretted that; and perhaps made more of it than it would have, if he had simply let it have its head when we were together. He was a fool."

"Pity him, then," Gaston said. "But do not grieve."

I shook my head. "Non, never that." I gazed upon him and was filled with wonder at how very far we had come these last years.

He cocked his head again, in apparent curiosity at my expression; and then quickly seized upon this new angle to kiss me deeply.

"I love you," I breathed when we parted.

"I know," he sighed happily.

With that, I pushed him away. "Go tend your patients."

He sighed and nuzzled me for a moment, our breath mingling, and then he climbed from the bed and finished gathering his things. He paused at the door and turned back to me, his face suffused with great regard. "Thank you."

I did not ask him what for, I merely nodded and said, "You are always welcome."

We remained in Gibraltar for over a month. The time passed pleasantly enough for me. My feet healed such that the stitches could be removed and I could walk upon them. My arm began to ache less, but Gaston warned me it would be another month before he would allow me to do much of anything with it. I began to teach Striker left-handed swordplay. Gaston and I trysted often, with great pleasure.

For others, the time passed in misery. We lost two-score men to the malaria; though, we did manage to save over a hundred lives before we ran out of quinine. I thanked the Gods daily that we were not afflicted, and Gaston wondered endlessly why we were not.

Those not ailing were sent out in large sorties for a week at a time; always returning with more men ill, more slaves, mules laden with treasure, and hundreds of prisoners. At the hospital, the days and nights were filled with moaning from the feverish and wounded, and distant screams from tortured men and women. Morgan himself led a foray in hopes of capturing the governor; but heavy rains and swollen rivers caused havoc with that and many of the other attempts to gain booty. One group was somewhat successful in capturing barges loaded with goods from Maracaibo, though.

Finally, in the last week of April, we loaded several Spanish barges with valuables, slaves and hostages – as Morgan planned to ransom them and the town – and sailed north to Maracaibo. We had left a small number of men there to hold the town; and we were happy to find them still alive and the place not overrun with vengeful Spaniards. However, we soon learned we would have preferred that to what actually awaited us.

There were three galleons in the passage to the sea, and the Spanish had rebuilt and manned the fortress they abandoned when we arrived. The smallest of their warships had more guns than our largest vessel, and the largest of them had more cannon than our entire fleet. They fired on the sloop we sent to investigate them; but they stayed stubbornly in the channel and were not so foolish as to come and chase us about so that we might have a slim chance of sailing past them. Of course, even if they had followed the ships we sent, the guns of the fort would have destroyed us as we tried to escape the lake.

We had given them nearly two months to summon aid of this nature and repair the fort: I knew not what else we should have expected. Yet, to a man – myself included – we could not have been more discouraged and frightened than if we had woken from a nightmare to a pistol in our faces.

When we learned of it, Gaston pulled me aside and said. "If we must, we will abandon the ship and go overland."

"All of us?" I asked.

He shook his head. "Just our friends. It will be hard enough with only a few mouths to feed."

"Oui," I agreed. "I cannot see dying here."

Morgan sent for me as soon as the investigating sloop returned. I was not surprised.

"What do you want to tell them?" I asked Morgan, as I joined him and the captains and quartermasters in the Maracaibo courthouse.

He led me to the office chamber in the back of the building where we had first spoken privately, and offered me a chair at the desk. There was a sheaf of paper, quill, and ink awaiting me.

"We are ransoming the town," he said as I sat.

I regarded him with something between curiosity and incredulity.

"I wish to keep them engaged in discussion until we decide what we will do," he sighed.

"That is probably best," I said sincerely, and then we discussed the amount of his demand. I wrote the missive, and he took it to someone to find a Spanish messenger for it. I doubted we would have a response for days.

Morgan returned to the office after dispatching the note, and handed me a bottle before I could leave.

I took a pull of rum. "Do you have a stratagem in mind, might I ask?"

"Not yet," he sighed. "Do you have any ideas?"

I shrugged. "I will ask Pete."

"Pete? Striker's Pete?" he asked.

"Aye. He is a genius at all things martial, and the best chess player I have ever seen."

"Truly? I thought him somewhat an imbecile." He shrugged. "The way he speaks."

I snorted. "It is a good thing he is not your enemy."

He snorted with amusement and then sighed distractedly. "I have been well educated, but not in things classical. You have. What would the great generals of antiquity have done? Alexander the Great? Achilles?"

"Achilles was a character in an epic poem. Alexander was a real man, though; but I do not think he fought naval battles. The Caesars, though... I will think on it, and see what Gaston and I can recall."

"Ah, aye, your matelot is a lord's son, too." He regarded the bottle he held speculatively, and I knew his expression had little to do with its contents. "And he is not at war with his father," he said absently.

"Nay, he is not," I said with curiosity.

He met my gaze and smiled slyly. "Let us see if we can survive this debacle, and then we should speak."

"I shall be very happy to keep that appointment," I said as I stood.

"You think I have something to say that you wish to hear?" he asked.

"Nay, it will require we both survive."

He laughed and waved me out the door.

Cudro and Ash joined me in returning to the *Queen*. More than half our men were ashore, enjoying Spanish wine as if it might be their last night alive – which it very well could be.

Once our cabal was gathered on the quarterdeck, I told them of Morgan's ransom demand and his request for any and all ideas or stratagems, including those gleaned from the antics of ancient generals.

"How's that going to help?" the Bard asked. "They didn't have cannon. Or sails."

He was possibly the most melancholy of us all. He was always the one to stay with the ship; and despite whatever might happen ashore, the ships were always able to escape. Being trapped and truly in danger was new to him.

"Nay," I said. "They had sails; they just used them very little. The principal means of moving the vessels about was rowing. They carried huge numbers of slaves, who rowed their ships, called galleys, about. At least the Romans and Egyptians did, during the time of Julius Caesar and the like. Before that, your fighting men would actually row the ships about; much like the Vikings. That is what is described in the *Iliad* and the *Odyssey*."

"So how did they attack one another?" Cudro asked. "Chase alongside and board?"

"Aye, that, and they rammed one another. The Romans had their ships fitted with great bronze prows so they could split another ship in two. And you had archers. And they often used flame arrows; or flaming ballista bolts; or even pots of burning oil or pitch flung with catapults mounted in the front or back of a ship."

"Fire ships," Gaston said.

"Aye, aye," I said. "And they would on occasion use a smaller vessel designed to burn, and sail it or set it adrift into the enemy vessels if they were in a tight formation."

Pete laughed, and I met his eyes, and we smiled as I came to understand what had been said of import. I looked about; the others were lost in thought, but Gaston was smiling, too.

"What?" Striker asked as he caught sight of our expressions.

"AFireShipLikeWillWereSayin'. TheyBeAllTightInThatChannel. OneGoesBurnin' TheRest'll'AveTaScatter. An'Iffn'TheOneBlowsLikeThe *Oxford*Did It'llMakeARightMessO'ThatChannelAnAnyShipCloseTo'Er."

The Bard was shaking his head. "Then how the Devil do we leave?"

Cudro was rumbling with amusement. "If they're fighting fires and sailing amuck with their sheets aflame, they won't be manning their cannon very well. We can sail in close with the sloops and board them. Then we can take on the fortress by land or by sea."

I grinned and exchanged a look of happiness with Gaston. I felt much better about our chances of survival now.

The next day, we told no one else, but we went about considering the small Spanish cargo ships at Maracaibo, assessing how much burning material could be packed onto one, and how it could be disguised to get it close enough to the Spanish without them realizing what it was.

The day after, a missive returned from the Spanish. I read it to Morgan privately in the office of the courthouse. We were dealing with one Don Alonzo del Campo y Espinosa, general aboard the galleon *Magdalena*. He was, of course, appalled at our audacity. He was angry with the cowards who had abandoned the fort and let us into the lake in the first place. And if we did not agree to his terms, he would keep us blockaded in the lake and send for smaller ships from Cartegena with which to ferry his marines ashore and hunt us down and kill us all. His terms were that we surrender graciously all treasure we had taken, including slaves and any other hostages or prisoners. In return for our abandoning our ill-gotten gains, he would allow us to leave the lake unmolested. I found that incredible, as did Morgan.

"We have a stratagem," I told Morgan after he stopped cursing the general's ancestry. I told him of the fire ship. To say he was delighted would be an understatement.

He called for all our men to assemble in the town square; and once they were there, he had me read the letter in English, and again in French for those few among us from Tortuga. Then he gave a stirring performance, asking if they would rather fight for their treasure or surrender it and have nothing to show for their hardship these past months. The decision was unanimous in favor of fighting. I would have hated him, had I not known he now had an alternative. As it was, I still thought him quite disingenuous, in the manner of leaders everywhere.

Then he had me tell them of the fire ship and explain how she should be outfitted and how she would function. There were cheers all around.

Within the hour, men led by Cudro and Pete were gathering the materials we would need and starting work on altering the commandeered Spanish vessel. Meanwhile, Morgan and I were writing another letter to the general as a distraction. Morgan offered to forego ransoming any prisoners or towns, and to surrendering half the slaves, in exchange for our free passage with the remaining treasure.

Of course, in a day and a half we received a response. The good general refused to accept our proposals, and if we did not surrender according to his original conditions within two days, he would destroy us by all means at his disposal. Thankfully, the fire ship was almost finished.

The small commandeered Spanish ship had been gutted, so she would burn and explode more quickly. Her hull had been packed with pitch and tar; and barrels of gunpowder – stolen from the Spanish fortress when we arrived – had been placed below what was left of her decking. Hollow logs were positioned along her sides to look like cannon; other logs were propped about with caps on their tops to look like men at a distance. She would be sailed by twelve men, who were to get her as near as possible to whichever of the warships they could manage;

grapple said ship; light the fuses, and dive overboard and swim away.

Pete stood proudly before her as Morgan and the captains came to inspect her. "I'llCommand'Er," Pete announced.

"What?" Striker roared.

"ICanSail'Er," Pete countered. He gestured at the captains, who were regarding the flimsy little firetrap with trepidation and slowly inching back as if someone might suggest they do it. "NoOneElseWantsTa. An'I 'Ave Na'DoneOneFunThingThisRaid. I'Aven'tEvenShotAMan. I'mGoin' TaBeARomanForADay!"

Striker swore and yelled, "She's not going to be sailed! We'll have to tow her there, if she doesn't sink before we can even get to the mouth of the lake, and then she'll only reach her target with luck, the current, and some rowing. The wind in her sheet will have little to do with any of it.

"And that's if the Spanish don't blow her out of the water before she gets close," he continued, "or their musketeers don't shoot every man on board before they can be grappled."

He regarded his resolute matelot; their gazes locked. Then Striker grinned, though his utterance was defiant. "I'm going with you!"

"You can't swim with one arm," Cudro said.

"Aye I can!" Striker snapped, and began shedding weapons as he walked toward the end of the wharf.

Gaston stepped in front of him. "Non. People piss in this water."

Striker eyed the water with concern and gave a nod of acknowledgment. "All right, we'll row farther out and I'll prove I can swim. It doesn't take two arms."

"I'll accept that you can swim," Morgan said. "You can always clutch a barrel or something and have your matelot pull you along if it came to it. So, you wish to command this fire ship?"

Striker had walked back to us. "Nay. Pete does. I'm going as crew."

Morgan nodded affably and turned to Pete. "Congratulations, then, Pete. You do us all a fine service. We'll surely not survive this endeavor with our treasure intact without this vessel. Can you find other volunteers?"

"Aye," Pete said with assurance, and turned to bellow at the men who had been working with him to ready the craft. "NeedTenWhoCan Swim!"

A few hands raised, some with alacrity; but many of the men appeared uncomfortable.

"I can't swim," one man said pathetically.

Beside me, Gaston raised his hand.

"You can't go," Cudro said. "You're our best physician."

"I am also one of our best swimmers and fighters; and if this does not work, you will not need my other skills," Gaston said calmly.

I raised my hand.

My matelot grimaced as he glanced at my recently broken arm, but he nodded.

Pete's smile was a lantern of happiness shining upon all about him.

"ThisIsGonnaBeFun!"

"Aye, it is," Morgan said sincerely, the light of adventure blazing in his eyes. "I wish I was going with you. As it is, we'll have to take some of them if all goes well. I'm leading the first boarding party."

The men cheered and pounded Pete heartily on the back. All now appeared to be brave and dangerous warriors, and not men tired of slogging about in swamps robbing people and dying of fevers, or madmen now expected to fight an enemy that vastly out-numbered and -gunned them.

Morgan had everyone gather in the town square again so he could explain our plan of attack. Then he had all swear an oath to stand by their fellow buccaneers until the last man.

Not knowing what would occur, we loaded the treasure, slaves and most prominent prisoners upon our ships and the barges, and sailed for the mouth of the lake on April twenty-ninth. We towed the fire ship for most of the distance, and we arrived late in the evening and anchored well out of the great ships' cannon range. I was thankful those of us who would crew her were not to remain on the fire ship for the night. She stank, and I was afraid she would somehow catch an errant spark.

There the galleons sat, the Brethren watching them, and them watching us, until dawn. I watched nothing but the light in my matelot's eyes as we stormed Heaven. I heard nothing but Pete and Striker doing the same. In the hour before dawn, we woke and prepared to slip down to the fire ship. Pete hesitated at the cabin door and turned around. He shed his weapons and clothing, taking up only a cutlass before preparing to leave again.

"What the devil are you doing?" Striker asked.

"Won'tBeTimeFerTheRest. An'ClothesCatchFlameFasterThanSkin."

"I'm partnered with a madman," Striker said as he shed his baldric and belt.

"Are not we all?" I asked, as Gaston and I shed our weapons and clothing while giggling like boys.

With a grin, Striker dropped his breeches as well; and we marched onto deck naked, to the amusement of the crew. The men who would go with us did the same; and thus twelve naked men scampered down the ropes with nothing but cutlasses – and matches carefully held in clay pots.

All ships, both Spanish and English, raised anchor at the first golden light along the horizon, and then everything was in motion.

Our little fire ship could sail to some degree, and though Pete commanded her, Striker was our master of sail; and it was a damn good thing he was with us, because it took all his knowledge of wind and current to keep us aimed at our target: the largest of the galleons, a ship of forty guns. She was every bit as big as the warship we had taken that summer two years ago. And, like that day as the *North Wind* closed on her stern and we prepared to board, I kept expecting the gun ports to open and the deadly mouths of cannon to emerge. That day they had not, but this day they finally did; but by then we were so close and moving so fast that they missed. The balls roared by overhead and geysered water in our wake.

We stayed low and tried to keep ourselves from being easy targets for their musketeers. But I could hear men arguing on deck about whether or not they should fire down upon us, if we were indeed a fire ship. The sensible officer won, and they began to send men down the ropes even as we attached our grapples. Gaston and another man were already lighting fuses, and we began to leap into the water like giant naked rats.

I did not see the explosion. My matelot had jumped atop me and dragged us far beneath the surface. My body was buffeted and my ears rang; and the murky water was suddenly illuminated with red light; and we swam deep and far until I was sure my lungs would burst. I was dizzy by the time we reached the surface.

Two of our men had become unconscious and been towed by their fellows; and Pete had an arm about Striker; but we were all alive as we turned to regard our handiwork. It was an amazing sight. The galleon's sails were all aflame, and fire raced along her hull in the lines of pitch, and smoke was beginning to pour from her gun ports. The Spanish could not save her, or even themselves. Screaming men dove into the water with their clothes afire. Others raced about the deck, setting even more things on fire when they fell.

We were still very close; but thankfully the great ship was being carried away from us by the current. However, that meant we were swimming against that current. Proud of ourselves, but knowing we were still in danger, we looked about; and spotting the *Queen*, we began to swim for her. She made the task considerably easier by sailing to meet us.

Once we were safely aboard, we were able to see the rest of our handiwork. The second ship had turned as rapidly as she could to avoid her flaming sister and reach the safety of the fort. She had promptly run aground on one of the sand bars. Before any of our ships could reach her, the crew had thrown themselves into boats, or ran and swam across the shallow bars to the safety of the fort: burning their own ship in their wake to keep us from taking her.

The third ship – the smallest of the three, with only twenty-four guns – had veered in the other direction. Norman and Morgan had gone after her on the *Lilly*, and even now we could see fighting on her deck. Another of our sloops was joining that fray.

Cudro decided we should try to pick up survivors from the burning vessels, but we soon found none of them wished to be rescued. They chose to swim to deeper water and drown rather than fall into our hands. We finally abandoned our efforts, and turned around to join the rest of the fleet and the captured galleon.

All were in high spirits. We had been amazingly successful for only three hours of battle. Now we had to take the fortress.

Morgan ordered most of our men ashore, and they attacked with vigor that soon turned to frustration. We had only muskets and grenadoes; the Spanish had cannon and walls too thick for our ships' artillery to penetrate, even if we had been willing to bring our vessels within range of their larger guns. And we could not bring the captured warship into position, because of her burning sister still in the channel. So our musketeers killed any Spaniard they could see upon the walls; but our attempts to storm those walls lost us over thirty men and gained us as many more wounded, as the Spanish met our every attack with firepots and grenadoes.

At dusk, we retreated to our ships and sat waiting. The great ship was now breaking up and sinking in the channel. Our ships noticed Spaniards trying to swim to her, though we did not know why; and we turned them back.

I saw none of this: I stayed at Gaston's side, helping with the wounded, until Morgan summoned me. I considered telling him to wait, but then thought better of it: I would be serving the common good in writing whatever message he most probably wished to send to the fortress.

When I reached the captured galleon, I was led to Morgan in the captain's cabin, a great and fine room filled with carved teak and linen. Morgan offered me a goblet of wine. There was another man at the table, in soot-smudged Spanish clothing. He looked fearful, but nodded politely in greeting. I accepted the glass and took a chair.

"I believe this man wishes to be cooperative," Morgan said. "I think his name is Juan."

"Are you known as Juan?" I asked in Castilian.

The man sighed with relief. "Si, si, señor; please do not hurt me, I am a foreigner. I am only with the Spanish as a pilot." He spoke with a Portugese accent.

I explained this to Morgan, who nodded at the man encouragingly. We plied him with wine, and Juan began to speak a great deal. He told us of the small fleet that had been sent here in response to our taking Porto Bello last year, and how the various ships had gotten separated and these three had been sent to this lake under Espinosa's command. It was apparent that, in a rather disorganized fashion, they had been waiting for us, but only arrived where we were by happenstance.

Upon their arrival, Espinosa had fired a cannon, to call for a pilot familiar with the entrance to the lake – and been greeted by men from the abandoned fort who told him we were here. The good general had admonished these men for cowardice in abandoning their posts; then he had gathered them and set them to rebuilding the fort. He had promised all his men whatever plunder they could take from us – which I found odd, in that it would be plunder we had just taken from his own people – and made them all swear an oath, in a ceremony as part of the Mass, to accept and give no quarter to the English.

Don Espinosa had been informed two days ago by an escaped slave that we were building a fire ship. The great general had scoffed at this notion, saying we English were too stupid to know what a fire ship was, much less equip one.

After we shared a good laugh over that bit of information, Juan imparted a thing that truly made our hearts glad. The large ship that had burned in the channel had been carrying a great deal of plate and forty thousand pieces of eight.

Morgan embraced the man and told him he was welcome to join our company, and would be given a full share as if he had always sailed with us. Juan was no fool: he accepted this offer quite gratefully.

The next morning, we left the *Mayflower* to guard the passage and retrieve what silver and gold she could from the remains of the sunken ship. The rest of us sailed back to Maracaibo. Once there, I composed yet another message to the good general telling him we were ransoming the town for thirty thousand pieces of eight and five hundred cattle. The response was much faster than the previous, and did not come from Don Espinosa. The Spanish who actually lived in this region eventually agreed to twenty thousand pieces of eight and five hundred cattle, in exchange for our releasing the prisoners and not burning the town. Espinosa had not been party to this agreement.

The next day, the Spanish arrived with the ransom and cattle, and our men worked feverishly to slaughter and salt the beef. Then we boarded our ships again and headed for the lake mouth with the prisoners. The Spanish who had delivered the ransom were quite incensed with that development; but Morgan was determined to keep the prisoners until we were clear of the fortress. The Spanish protested that they had no control of the fortress: Don Espinosa did, and he would not let us pass. So Morgan sent several of the prisoners to speak with the general, urging them to do all in their power to convince him to let us pass lest he begin to hang their fellows from the yardarms. The general sent them back chastised for being cowards and letting us get into the lake in the first place.

We were now faced with a dilemma. With the ransom, we had a great deal more treasure than we originally gathered. And the *Mayflower* had managed to raise fifteen thousand pieces of eight from the sunken ship, in addition to a number of lumps of melted silver and plate, some as large as thirty pounds. We also had a captured galleon. But we still could not leave the damn lake.

Morgan held a meeting of the captains and other people he deemed worthy of attending, which now thankfully included Striker, Pete, Gaston, and me. Though Morgan did have a new and cunning stratagem – much to the relief of many – it was decided it would still involve a great deal of risk, and we had best share the treasure out now, in case any of our ships were sunk in the attempt or lost on their ways to some other rendezvous.

When the meeting concluded, Morgan invited Gaston and me to stay.

"I think we shall survive," Morgan said, as he poured himself another goblet of wine and put his feet on the massive teak table that graced the captured galleon's main cabin.

"Ah," I said. "So you have a thing to tell me."

He nodded and motioned for us to sit. We did, and I poured wine for both of us. Gaston and Morgan studied one another across their goblets. This would be the first time since my new relationship with Morgan that Gaston was present.

Morgan's gaze shifted back to me. "I might be of some assistance."

"In what manner?" I asked.

"Modyford," he said with a grim smile. "I am on occasion privy to his business, though... He holds his cards like any sensible man. And, on occasion he accepts my counsel, because... there are things he wishes of me."

I was relieved he did not embellish his friendship with Modyford. It made what he said far more believable.

"What are you offering?" I asked with a wry smile. "And perhaps of more import, what do you wish to gain?"

He cocked his head with a subtle moue. "I want Panama. I need the French."

Gaston snorted.

I smiled. "After the fiasco with the *Cour Volant* this year, and the matter with Burroughs and that damn duel, and Puerte Principe being nearly worthless last year, surely you jest."

Morgan shrugged. "But they have now heard how Porto Bello made all who continued on with me rich last year, and... The *Cour Volant* was not my fault."

"Saying all that is true, why do you think we could produce them?" I asked.

"Peirrot and Savant like you," he said. "And you stand a better chance than anyone. You have the Devil's silver tongue."

"Aye, perhaps, but you realize that my way of convincing them will be to tell them you are a greedy and ambitious bastard, and the only reason they should go is that they can share in it."

Morgan smirked. "That is precisely why I should send you. Your honesty will win them over."

I glanced at my matelot, and found him smiling to himself and studying his wine goblet.

I shrugged. "All right; say we agree to do this thing. What can you truly offer us?"

He smiled. "As you have already guessed, Modyford is in the employ of your father. I don't know how long he has been corresponding with your father; possibly since before your arrival. But he expects to reap great benefit from the arrangement, when he eventually leaves Jamaica and returns to England."

I sighed. "And you?"

Morgan snorted, and spoke nonchalantly, without malice. "I am no one's man, though I allow Modyford to believe whatever is convenient for me. I have never corresponded with your father. However, his agent,

Washington, came to visit me when we returned from Porto Bello. He bore a note of introduction from Modyford instructing me to be forthcoming with the man. He asked me a great many questions about how buccaneers live. He was especially interested in the practice of matelotage. And then he asked me a number of questions about you. He wanted to know if I had reason to believe that you engaged in sodomy – and whether I would be willing to testify to that in court."

Lead formed in my belly, and I felt Gaston tense beside me. "And you told him?" I asked.

"That I did not know you that well," he chuckled, but quickly sobered. "And then I went and argued with Modyford. Obviously matelotage is the Way of the Coast. Good Lord, it keeps men from fighting over one another and the few whores we have. It's not a thing I wish to engage in, or have need of, but I care not what my men do. And, if that damn fool Modyford begins to charge and convict men of it, I know damn well the buccaneers will all go to Tortuga. I convinced him of that – that he could not even go after you at your father's behest, because it would cause rioting in the streets. Lynch and the other proper gentlemen on the council tend to forget that the buccaneers make up most of the militia. Damn fools."

I was stunned, and I downed my glass and filled another.

"This was months ago?" I asked.

He nodded sadly.

"We have been blind and stupid," I said, and drank more.

Morgan shrugged. "Nay. You're like a prize bull: it's often discussed if you should be shown at the fair, bred, or slaughtered – but not in front of you. Your man Theodore has been carefully handled lest he become aware of what was about."

"So I can trust no one of any consequence on Jamaica?" I asked.

"Will," he said with a trace of amusement, "I would not trust men of little consequence on Jamaica, if I were you. Even your own family."

"My uncle?"

He nodded. "He was at the governor's – in the next room – when you arrived with that declaration you wanted signed. He's a curious fellow. He seemed quite heartbroken that you're such a fool as to do such a thing, but then he worries at what your father will do to you in the end. Modyford will not bring charges against you here, yet. But he has talked of doing other things to force you to comply with your father's wishes – which I am confused by."

"I think my father likes to keep us all confused," I said. "He lies to everyone to suit his purposes. What other things? I have no idea what he wants of me; I only know I want nothing of him."

"I actually understand that," Morgan said, as if he found that confusing, too. He shrugged. "Well, there was that business with Vines' daughter. He gathered a great deal of evidence concerning your wife, in order to be able to discredit any child she might bear. And he has occasionally stirred up trouble with some of the other merchants about there being a business in town managed by a woman. And despite that magnificent emerald Striker gave him, he might very well move to seize your ship. He threatened it once, when I made some comment about whether or not Striker would sail with us. The only thing that I believe has stayed his hand before we sailed, and even after, is the revelation that your man here's father is a marquis. He's unsure of what to do concerning that, and is awaiting instruction from your father."

I buried my head in my hands. I would have demanded to know why he hadn't bothered to tell us any of this before, but that would have been foolishness: we had been on the precipice of truly being enemies before, and he had not cared if Striker and I were destroyed.

Gaston rubbed my shoulder. "What would you advise?" he asked Morgan.

"Honestly," Morgan said with a lengthy sigh. "Leave Jamaica. All of you: your sister; Theodore; everyone. Go to Tortuga." He shrugged. "And while you're there, get the French to sail with me against Panama."

I chuckled mirthlessly.

"I give you my word we will do what we can," Gaston said. "And now, if you will excuse us, we have much to discuss."

Morgan nodded solemnly.

Gaston and I were silent as we climbed down to a canoe and rowed toward the *Queen*; but then he stopped in the darkness between the vessels, and said, "We should not tell anyone yet. Not until we truly escape this place."

"Oui," I said with little emotion, as I felt nothing but cold. "As I do not wish to know any of it, I do not see where they should be troubled with it, when we have more immediate matters of concern."

And then the rage hit, tearing from me a wordless cry of pain and rage; and I doubled over in the canoe afraid the power of what I now felt would tear me in two.

Gaston pushed off my kerchief and rubbed my scalp. He could not hold me, as the canoe was too narrow to allow him to turn. So I moved so I could cling to his back.

We sat in the darkness, with him only rowing to keep us from flowing out of the lake with the current. We could have escaped, just us: the fortress never would have seen the small dark dot that we were. But then what would we do? Where would we go?

We had to take our chances with our friends. They had cast their lot with ours, and now we owed them. We must all escape together.

I finally calmed enough for us to row to the *Queen*.

"Composing more nasty notes to that bastard general?" Striker asked as we joined our cabal on the quarterdeck.

"Aye," I said. "There are things he needs to hear."

They were peering at us – or rather me – and I knew I was not so composed as I wished to seem.

"Don't fret," Striker said and handed me a bottle, of which he had already consumed quite a bit. "Morgan's plan'll work."

I choked on the wine. "It had best."

Gaston wrapped his arms around me, and we sat in silence. I tried to tell myself that, truly, most of our friends and family would find life little different if our home was Cayonne and not Port Royal. They would simply have to learn French.

But I would miss our little home at Negril.

And Gaston's name had not yet been cleared.

The next morning, the treasure – some two hundred and fifty thousand pieces of eight in ready money, and more in jewels and other valuables – was divided amongst our vessels, based upon how many men and other shares each ship had. Then we set about sharing it out on each ship. This took the better part of a day. Barring extra shares for various posts, each man came away with some one hundred and fifty pounds.

The next day, we put Morgan's ingenious plan for escaping the lake into effect. We began to dispatch our boats and canoes to shore filled with men, and appeared to land them out of sight of the fort; but we did not leave any men ashore. The men not rowing a boat lay flat in its bottom, as each craft returned to its vessel and pretended to load more men on the side of the ship opposite the fort. Meanwhile, more and more men hid in the holds on our ships, until the decks appeared empty. In this way we attempted to convince the general we were sending all our men ashore to attack him at night by land. It seemed to be working: we could see them repositioning many of their cannon to bear inland.

When night came, there was a full moon, and our fleet weighed anchor; and, leaving our sails furled, we drifted with the outgoing tide into the channel, until we were even with the fort. Then we raised sail and shot through the passage under the fort's guns, with the seaward wind at our backs. The Spanish did fire upon us, and several of our vessels were struck, but to no great damage; and we were soon all safely at sea.

Once beyond their guns, Morgan released the prisoners, and fired a salvo in salute from the captured warship. I imagined I could hear Don Espinosa grinding his teeth. I began to think of how I wanted to hear my father grind his; but, of course, all our pending misfortune on Jamaica was the result of my already having angered my sire such that he ground his teeth. I would just never get to hear it.

All the imprecations Espinosa surely heaped upon us were repaid by the Gods with a brutal storm that blew in from the northeast on our second day sailing home. It was in every way equal to the tempest that had destroyed the galleon and the *North Wind* two years before.

We furled our sails, tied off the rudder, lashed ourselves down, and prayed. Men filled the hold and cabin, but Gaston was afraid of being below deck, in case the ship was swamped or rolled. So we tied ourselves, some weapons, and a bag of food, water, medicine, and ammunition to the forward quarterdeck rail.

As the first hours wore on, I began to lose myself: the winds howled inside my mind as well as out. Everything I had ever done had been punished. The Gods hated me. God hated me. My father hated me. All because I could not be what they wished.

And then somewhere amidst it all, I felt my matelot fumbling with my breeches and a familiar pressure behind me. I turned my head and felt his cold lips upon my cheek. Even if he had tried to scream in my ear with his broken voice, I could not have heard him in the tempest; but I felt him, and he was soon warm inside me, and thus I was soon warm.

The winds did not howl in Heaven, and in the aftermath of that glow, it was easy to order my thoughts. The Gods did love us.

And to prove it to me and further earn my trust, the storm at last abated. It was not an immediate thing; nay, it took three days, but at last we sailed on calm seas. No one had died. The hull was leaking, but not so it could not be repaired.

I felt the sun shining in the aftermath as the beneficence of the Gods given earthly form; and I considered what we all must do next with faith and surety.

Epilogue

After such a storm, and sitting about in lake water for over two months, and not being careened since January, the *Virgin Queen's* hull was in sorry shape: she seeped everywhere, and we had to form a bucket line to bail her. The damn storm had blown us back toward the Spanish coast, and the Bard did not wish to risk sailing north across a goodly expanse of the open Northern Sea to reach Hispaniola. We had lost sight of the rest of our fleet; and until we returned to Port Royal, we could not even know who had survived. Thus we returned to Ruba, as it was a relatively safe haven, and found what beach we could to careen. Though we made fast work of it, it was still a week before we were underway again. We guessed we would arrive in Port Royal at the end of May.

Gaston and I held our tongues throughout, and waited until we were only two days from Port Royal before we gathered our cabal in the cabin. They were quiet after I finished relaying all Morgan had imparted to us. Gaston and I had discussed it, and we had found it likely that several of our friends might choose to disbelieve or mistrust this new information. I had questioned it myself in the days since we heard it, but always returned to whence I began: whether or not the specific threats Morgan spoke of were real, the danger surely was.

I saw some incredulity as I spoke to our friends; once I finished, they were thoughtful, but seemingly disinclined to meet my gaze.

"So... would we be welcome in Cayonne?" Dickey asked at last.

"Now that things are well with Gaston's father, and..." I sighed. He was correct to ask, and that too was a thing of which Gaston and I had oft whispered; though we had befriended Savant somewhat, and Peirrot liked us anyway, there were many others among the French buccaneers who might still harbor ill will over Doucette. And, of course, there was always the matter of Gaston's legal status looming before us – but perhaps we would receive good news on that front upon reaching Port Royal.

"I do not know," I sighed at last.

"There's always Petit Goave," Cudro said.

"I don't speak French, either way," the Bard said.

I sighed. "There is also the option that... Gaston and I, and Sarah, and thus Striker and Pete – essentially anyone my father would wish to harm – remove themselves from the ownership of the company and the ship."

Cudro shrugged and looked to his matelot. "We should discuss it, but I care not if I sail from a French port or an English one: I'm neither."

Ash shrugged and smiled at him. "If I cared about being a proper Englishman, I would return to my father on Barbados."

Cudro grinned. "Apparently it matters not to us. And... I would rather sail from a port your father can't buy the governor of."

"Well," I said with a smile. "It is either that, or cease your association with me."

"Too many people have seen us together," the Bard drawled, and then he grinned and shrugged. "I don't give a damn. The French ship cargo too." But he, too, looked to his matelot.

"I have already been exiled from England once," Dickey said. "I do not miss it. I can think of nothing of Port Royal I will miss, other than my share of the haberdashery."

"You all have land," I said.

The Bard snorted. "Will, they can take that too."

"Aye, of course." Then I felt compelled to ask. "And none of you question..."

The Bard and Cudro shook their heads.

"We've been talking of it for a while, now," the Bard said. "The ship is a likely target. They can claim it never cleared the Admiralty Court."

I nodded, and looked to Pete and Striker. They had been silent. Pete had spent much of the time watching his matelot, who was studying the floor.

"Sarah will be angry," I prompted.

Pete smiled but kept his eyes on Striker, who snorted.

"What of your women?" Striker asked.

"Vivian is more afraid of men like my father than I am," I said, "and Agnes will probably not care where she lives, as long as she is allowed the freedoms she desires."

Unless, of course, she had acquired a lover while we were away.

In echo of my thoughts, Striker said, "We don't know what has happened while we've been gone. It's been six bloody months. We shouldn't have left them."

Pete grimaced and looked away. "ItWereANecessaryRisk. KilledOff HastingsAn'SomeOthers, An'WillMadeFriendsWithMorgan."

Cudro and the Bard chuckled, but Striker was silent and still would not regard me.

"What do you wish to do?" I asked.

"Not have to learn French," he said tiredly. "But I don't see where we have much choice." He finally met my gaze. "It's like we spoke of with Theodore, that day before we left. I don't blame you. It's just not something I want."

"I know," I said with sorrow. "I am sorry."

And there I was, apologizing for my friends having the misfortune of knowing me again.

Pete yawned and stretched. "ThePityOfItIs, Killin'YurDamnFather Won'tMendItAll."

"It will make me feel better," I said.

Gaston smiled. "Amen."

End ~ Volume Three

Continued in

Wolves: Raised By Wolves, Volume Four

For more information, please visit
www.alienperspective.com

Bibliography

The following titles do not represent the entirety of the author's studies; but they were the ones she found the most useful, and the ones she recommends to anyone interested in doing their own reading about the buccaneers and this period of history. To that end, they are ranked in order of usefulness to her research.

Exquemelin, Alexander O., *The Buccaneers of America* (translated by Alexis Brown, 1969), Dover Publications, Inc., 2000. Original publication, Amsterdam, 1678.

Haring, C.H., *The Buccaneers of the West Indies in The XVII Century*, New York: E.P. Hutton, 1910.

Burney, James, *History of the Buccaneers of America*, London: Unit Library, Limited, 1902. First edition, London, 1816.

Burg, B.R., *Sodomy And The Perception of Evil: English Sea Rovers in The Seventeenth-Century Caribbean*, New York: New York University Press, 1983.

Pawson, Michael & David Buisserat, *Port Royal Jamaica*, Jamaica: The University of the West Indies Press, 1974.

Buisserat, David, *Historic Jamaica From The Air*, Jamaica: Ian Randle Publishers, 1996. First edition, 1969.

Marx, Robert F., *Pirate Port: The Story of the Sunken City of Port Royal*, New York: The World Publishing Company, 1967.

Briggs, Peter, *Buccaneer Harbor: The Fabulous History of Port Royal, Jamaica*, New York: Simon And Schuster, 1970.

Dunn, Richard S., *Sugar and Slaves: The Rise of the Planter Class in the English West Indies, 1624-1713*, New York: W.W.Norton & Company, Inc., 1972.

Apestegui, Cruz, *Pirates of the Caribbean: Buccaneers, Privateers, Freebooters and Filibusters 1493-1720*, London: Conway Maritime Press, 2002.

Marrin, Albert, *Terror of the Spanish Main: Sir Henry Morgan and His Buccaneers*, New York: Dutton Children's Books, 1999.

Pyle, Howard, *Howard Pyle's Book of Pirates*, New York: Harper & Row, Publishers, 1921.

Cordingly, David, *Under The Black Flag*, New York: Random House, 1995.

Kongstam, Angus, *The History of Pirates*, Canada: The Lyons Press, 1999.

About the Cover

The illustration used on the cover of this book is a detail of Howard Pyle's *Buccaneer of the Caribbean* (There are several alternate titles for this painting). The piece was painted in 1907, as part of a series of paintings and illustrations for <u>Howard Pyle's Book of Pirates</u>. It is not used here to represent any particular character in this series.

Howard Pyle is regarded by many as the father of American illustration. There are numerous books and web sites devoted to his work and legacy, so we will not waste words here saying what many others can tell you. Pyle seems to be one of the few illustrators who ever read Exquemelin or Burney (see bibliography). In his art and writing, he accurately depicts what is known of the buccaneers in terms of dress and tactics. He essentially represents buccaneers, circa 1630-1680, and not romanticized notions from later centuries about "pirates" from the Golden Age of Piracy, 1680-1720.

About the Author

W.A. Hoffman, aka Wynette A. Hoffman, really hates trying to condense her life or her reasons for writing what she does into a paragraph. She knows how arbitrary and subjective words and labels are; and she would rather not make a bad impression, or have her work misconstrued because someone interprets a word differently than she intended. Words and terms that Wynette would use to describe herself, such as artist, storyteller, novelist, filmmaker, geek, nerd, genius, gamer, collector, pansexual, transgendered, fetishist, married, militant agnostic, humanist, lapsed atheist, heretical neo-pagan, borderline sociopath, anarchist, iconoclast, situational ethicist, and Venus-ruled Pisces with a Leo ascendant and a Sun/Mars/Mercury conjunction in the eighth house, have different meanings to different people, and they have had different meanings or levels of import in Wynette's life over her forty plus years.

There has been one overriding constant in Wynette's life, though: she has always been an outsider looking in: an *alien perspective*, from her relationship to her birth sex to her manner of pursuing her career in writing and publishing. Sometimes this has resulted from a fluke of genetics and upbringing, and other times it represents the sum total of all the times she's been the outsider. Now she can't really figure out how to conform even if she wants to – which she doesn't.

Printed in the United States
113495LV00007BA/26/P